The House on '

The Tenafly Road Series Book One

By
Adrienne Morris

This is a work of fiction. Similarities to real people, places, or events are entirely co-incidental.

THE HOUSE ON TENAFLY ROAD

First edition. March 28, 2013.

Copyright © 2013 Adrienne Morris.

ISBN: 978-1481839532

Written by Adrienne Morris.

For my parents, children and Timothy

Chapter One

John Weldon's head throbbed as he focused on the strange man standing above him.

"Sergeant Weldon, one day soon you will be free of pain and medication," the doctor said as he gave his patient more morphine through a new British syringe in the bright, garland-trimmed soldiers' hospital in Washington on the first warm day of late spring. Weldon remembered little past the sun and fire of the Wilderness. The room smelled of coffee and dried blood. Flies buzzed at unreachable parts of his stiff body. Weldon's head boiled and his body resisted the lightest duty between doses, and when once he had begged one of the nurses, Penny Garner, for more morphine and caught a look in her eye—the same look he'd seen people give his mother, a drunken Delaware, so many times in his childhood—he never asked again.

The doctor lifted Weldon's bandages and shook his head. As he walked away he said to Penny, "Dear girl, I know that you have a soft spot for that one, but he has no hope." He put an arm around her as she cried. "Can't believe he's hung on this long. We can just keep him comfortable. It's a shame, I know."

Weldon stayed awake at night, worrying the doctors would send him to the dying room again or cut his medication, so he stole it when he could and even found three syringes, shoving them under his bedding. He remembered being whole and well and watching contemptuously the sorry lines of soldiers on sick call hoping for tiny doses of opium or brandy. Weldon had control.

The rush of warmth the doses provided took him deep inside himself where a tiny hum of satisfaction lived if only briefly. The loneliness and hunger, the black something he'd never escaped, disappeared.

A trim officer sauntered by and spoke with one of the medical staff. Weldon worried that his military career would be over if anyone caught him stealing, but no one understood his pain. He vowed to hold this weakness closer than any person could ever come, and he *would stop*—someday. The army was his home.

That night Penny caught Weldon holding his guts in and knocking things about the dispensary, and she brought him back to his bed. She wrapped a new bandage around his middle before helping him lower his swollen leg into the itchy trousers she found for him and laced a brand new pair of expensive boots, just his size, for him to slip into.

She kissed him before helping him to the door. He smiled, feeling a small, ridiculous thrill as he adjusted his old haversack filled with morphine and limped with the help of a cane into the fragrant, leaf-filtered moonlight of late June. Penny handed him five dollars in change.

"Good luck, sir," she whispered, her eyes shiny with tears, before disappearing behind the closed door.

Weldon's head still throbbed as he licked his rough, parched lips. He took cautious breaths of clean, moist air, stepping out tentatively in one direction and then the other. He'd felt this way once before—that last day in the Wilderness with Simon. No. Simon McCullough had deserted. Weldon pulled at the hair behind his ear. The moon sank away and a tender breeze chilled him as he stood in this spot for hours under an ancient tree like the ones his father had been crushed under in the Western Reserve of his youth. Weldon slid down and into a deep sleep beneath the tree until a gentle hand tapped his shoulder.

"Sergeant Weldon, by golly, it *is* you!" A ruddy-faced private stood above him.

Weldon pulled himself up on his elbows as the dried pus at his side cracked beneath his shirt. The morning sun hurt his eyes.

"I'm Private Patrick Hazelton, sir. Do you remember me?"

Weldon held his side with one hand and used other to grab the man's hand. The surprised private helped Weldon to his feet and readjusted his hat.

"Sir, you look a caution. Better head back in." Hazelton nodded toward the Washington hospital. He took Weldon by the arm, but Weldon stood still.

"Who are you?" Weldon asked.

"A few years back, sir, Lieutenant McCullough convinced you not to report me to my unit for leaving my camp to go looking for girls. You and the lieutenant saved me much grief with my company commander—that incompetent ass. He's been mustered out since, thank the Lord."

"Simon McCullough is a bastard," Weldon said from a faraway surface of himself. "He d-deserted and left me dead."

"No, sergeant, you and him were best friends," Hazelton said with hesitation. "I don't believe a word. McCullough's a captain now, I hear. After the Grand Parade he took leave but never deserted."

"Grand Parade?"

"The war's over ... sergeant, you need to go back inside. You're not yourself and you're shaking."

"No. I'm lost. They can't help me, you idiot!"

"Now, sergeant, I don't blame you for being sore. Times are tough. Washington's a rough place to wander with money hanging out your trousers. Where will you go?"

Weldon stood with the oak, paralyzed again. "I don't know."

Hazelton reached forward and grabbed Weldon's leather money pouch. "Someone will swipe this if you ain't careful."

"It's mostly empty," Weldon said, taking it back and opening it to drop in the loose change in his trouser pocket. A green wrinkled sheet of thick card caught his eye, and he pulled it out between his two long fingers. Hand-drawn timorous trees in black ink dressed the card's message from the only package he had ever received. That first Christmas of the war ... Christmas ... the most dismal time of year for a soldier without family. He found ways to avoid mail call, but one day someone shouted his name. When the call came again more impatiently he slunk up, with his sunken, dark eyes lowered and his crow-black hair shorn short since the summer of lice. The heavy, battered box had his name on it. His face burned. He cut the top with his knife and reached in to find soft mittens and socks—hand-knit and familiar in a way. They were like McCullough's, and for a horrible moment he thought there had been an embarrassing mistake. He fumbled to close the box but noticed a tiny, hand-drawn card with funny little trees around the edge. "A friend of Simon's is a friend of ours! Merry Christmas! Warm Regards—Scott, Sarah and Katherine McCullough."

Hazelton sidled up and read the card. On the back in the same small script was an address in Englewood, New Jersey, Simon McCullough had talked of endlessly—like someplace in a fairytale—as if the McCullough family expected Weldon to write. He had never done so, but had run his fingers over the little tree drawings many times.

"Sir, you need help, and if it ain't the hospital you're going to then I'm going to put you on the train."

"I don't know them ... I can't face Simon ... I ..."

"Any place is better than here, and Simon is your friend."

Weldon had done everything he could think of to repulse this invasion, this toppling of his defenses, but Simon McCullough charmed him. The whole world loved him—no Simon pretended to love the whole world—he even played with the darkie children.

He remembered squeezing into his first army boots at Carlisle Barracks and then going off to the war with a commander who convinced him to volunteer for a Jersey regiment on a lark. There he met Simon, and for a sparkling few years Weldon pretended at being someone else. But now fevers came on strong. He held the pus-filled flap of skin at his side tighter. How had he been so damned stupid? How had he ever let Simon McCullough in?—that piece of shit. What a terrible, stupid blunder. Weldon would bring it all to him. Just shove it in the lieutenant's face—all the suffering he caused. Weldon had always expected a life of aching and scratching and he could die doing it, but not before presenting it to the one person who duped him just long enough to give him hope.

Chapter Two

The walk up the hill from the ornate little train station in Englewood taxed his underused muscles. Weldon had slicked his hair at the Englewood Hotel, shaved, and cut himself. His homespun trousers and shirt embarrassed him, so he dressed in uniform. Wandering through the Irish neighborhood on Waldo Place, he took his time watching the work being done on what appeared to be a new church. A flock of sheep passed before him into a small field adjacent to a mature stand of trees. The shepherd passed with a smile at Weldon's Union blue.

"Do you know the McCullough family?" Weldon asked, cringing at the sound of his voice.

"Everyone does. Right up around that turn in the road. Tenafly Road. A big white house with green shutters."

Weldon wiped his face and caught his breath. He considered turning back, but a small woman passed him in a hurry. She whirled back with a smile. "Are you lost, young man? You look lost."

"The McCullough house, ma'am ... I ..."

"I'm a McCullough, and something tells me you've come to see my son, Simon," she said with a happy grin. "I'm just back from a flower trade with Mrs. Williams down the path. Took longer than expected and supper to begin soon enough. Come along, I'll get you a nice drink."

Weldon hesitated. He hated talking to strangers and hadn't figured on dealing with Simon's family, but Sarah McCullough did all the talking.

"You know when Englewood was still young the roads weren't the tidy affairs they are today. I used to pick daisies right out of the ravines in the middle of the road. Stray dogs and farmers on the way to market were the main travelers up here, but now there's the Wall Streeters in their fancy surreys off down Demarest Avenue to the train in a hurry."

They walked together up the shaded drive, stopping here and there as Sarah pulled a weed or pointed to a particularly lovely rose bloom. The simple yet solid house stood with an inviting swing on the front porch and flowering vines climbing a white picket fence that surrounded a colorful garden.

Sarah brought Weldon through the side kitchen door after nudging a small family of cats from the stairs and made him sit at the smooth wooden table while she prepared him a meal.

"Eat, Sergeant Weldon," she said. "It's not poison."

"Pardon me, ma'am," he said, savoring the potato stew and oatmeal bread topped with smooth, white butter.

"The captain will be home shortly. He's off racing with the horses and his sister. Their father doesn't like the horses used the way they do. The townsfolk complain they cause a ruckus, but the two children, I mean to say Simon and Katherine, drive me to drink sometimes with their arguments at the table. I need my peace sometimes too, so I send them out. Do you have strong opinions on the Freedmen's Bureau, sergeant?"

"No." Weldon listened to the cuckoo clock announce the hour. An old upholstered chair rested before an open hearth that the family didn't use for cooking. Meals were made on a brand new cook stove bigger than he had ever seen.

"That Simon likes to get his sister in a huff over politics and rights and such and she's far too emotional over it. It always ends in tears or blows, and to think they're grown adults. It's frightening to see how poorly they turned out. Those poor, emancipated souls need all the help they can get, but Simon likes to remind us he's the expert since tutoring the colored children in camp during the war."

It was Weldon who had tried his hand at tutoring with mixed results. The pupils, in nothing more than rags and discarded uniforms, came to love Simon's pranks and teasing and lost all interest in learning their letters.

He smiled for a moment remembering, falling again for even the memory of Simon's friendship, but then his thoughts turned to the present and his stomach churned as he half-listened to this plump woman, her braids wrapped around her head in a silver crown, talk of the new strawberry patch she planned for pin money. Was that all she had to worry about? But her food ... *it was good.*

Sarah glanced out the window and sighed.

"Ah, there they are now," Sarah said with a touch of consternation and pride as she patted her hands on the bleached apron around her middle. "The neighbors just hate how they tear into the road."

Weldon stood, using the solid table cluttered with unfamiliar cooking utensils, as his support. His eyes blurred as the dull pain at his side and in his leg begged him to stay seated. But he had come a long way for this moment ... if only this kitchen wasn't so cozy. His resolve softened. Before Weldon could recover his thoughts, Simon and his sister, Katherine, barreled in with six dainty toy spaniel dogs. The girl laughed while summarizing her victorious race before noticing the stranger at the table. With reddened cheeks she scooped up a noisy pup to quiet it.

"Oh, so many ridiculous dogs, you must think, Mr. Weldon," Sarah said, "but Katie didn't mind her father's words and let them breed, and of course her father refused to make her part with them. Simon, you didn't tell me you'd made any friends with manners during the war." Sarah flashed the sergeant a generous grin.

"Yes, Mother, indeed." Simon outstretched his hand stiffly. "Weldon, this is a surprise. It's good to see you ... recovered."

"N-no ..." Weldon stammered, scratching his scalp as Sarah and the girl stared. Simon withdrew his hand.

"Weldon. You're back from the dead almost. I'm so surprised ... happily so. It was tough in the end ..." Simon looked toward his women. "It was *very* tough for Weldon in the end."

Weldon said nothing.

"Mr. Weldon, my son is rude," Sarah said as she put her arm through his. "Please allow me to introduce my daughter, Katherine."

"S-Simon t-talked about you." Without the morphine Weldon stuttered more. Sarah's arm was warm and soft like yeast dough. The sound of a cat licking itself under the table seemed loud and vulgar. It distracted him. "Pardon, what was the girl's name again?"

The girl turned red and gazed longingly at the door.

"Her name is Katherine, poor boy. You look wore out. Now sit again and you'll stay for supper."

That evening Sarah seated the girl, wearing a powder-blue tea dress with navy trim, next to Weldon. "I don't understand why you didn't wear the flouncy dress I made you," Sarah complained in a whisper.

Katherine blushed but said nothing. She smelled of lilacs, and once she brushed against Weldon's sleeve with her poker-thin arm. He noticed the blond little hairs on it and a freckle just above her wrist.

Scott McCullough had just arrived home a few moments before and had not seemed pleased with having company. "So, Sergeant Weldon, are you going to tell us all about your brave feats during the war?"

Weldon answered the patriarch's war questions simply and personal questions vaguely. He tried to be polite, but his head ached every time he glanced at Simon. Simon was a captain now? It sickened him. His wool uniform scratched the back of his neck.

"Simon tells me you were in the Regular Army before the war," Scott said. "What interested you in the military?"

"I s-suppose, sir, it was the food and discipline," Weldon said as he carefully placed his fork on the fine china plate before him. His father's tales of the old dragoons and the British navy of his grandfather's day had offered a dream of escape as a young boy, while the strange, staggered stories his mother told of hunts and ceremonies and hunger frightened him, being too close and real. Army food wasn't good, but it came in steady allotments. Discipline put his life in order. Weldon found his place tucked between uniformed others. Every button and boot counted for something. His lack of eloquence and grace did not prevent him from being a part of something larger than himself.

"Do you hear that, Sarah? This boy is so unlike our Simon. Our boy's never known a rule he couldn't break."

"Must you tease?" Sarah asked, motioning for Weldon's plate to be refilled. Glancing down the table she caught her daughter, again, with a vacant look in her eyes, picking over her food. "Katherine, do you have anything to add to the conversation?"

"No, Mother."

"Then you may clear the plates," Sarah ordered. "Simon says we should hire one of the new colored women in town for help, but a woman should run an economical and efficient home on her own. We're strong enough for it. Don't you think, Mr. Weldon? What about your mother? I bet she's strong."

"I d-don't recall, I ... My m-mother died, but ..."

"Sergeant Weldon, I'm sorry," Sarah interrupted with pained expression. "Would you like a little more meat?"

Katherine stood over Weldon waiting. All eyes were upon him, and he couldn't take another bite. "I don't know ..."

Katherine slipped his plate away before he could answer.

As the men made themselves comfortable in Scott's library around an enormous stone fireplace, the tribe of dogs wandered in, sitting at Weldon's feet.

"Katie does love her nuisance pets," Scott said. "That one wants your lap, sergeant."

Weldon picked up the dog feeling ridiculous. His mind drifted as Scott poured the men a drink .... He sat at the edge of the bloody stream, picking at the sores on his scalp. It had started at the ear, his right ear, behind it—just pulling bits of hair, and it had been satisfying for a time. And then there were secondary spots and sometimes he'd pull at the finest threads and sometimes, most times, clumps and it felt like sin and he couldn't stop even with praying.

He would NOT cry, and he would not do another bad thing. This was it. This one last thing. His shaking fingers ran over the soft scar hidden at his collar from his father's last flogging. John had lost a contest at Sunday school—Scripture memory—and his father had bragged on him, but the prim, eagle-beaked young lady in charge had unnerved him, and he lost the first word in a fluttering, stammering blur of sounds.

These things were his—his hair, his skin—and he needed to keep track of them. He needed to hold onto this little bit of territory. Something, a tiny voice, caught his attention, and he turned toward the water, toward the bag of his pups. John thought he had beaten them dead, but the bag moved a little, and in a rush of small hope he cut the bag open and the creatures, all mutilated and bloody, tumbled into the muddy, slow-moving stream. But one—with small opened mouth—expressed the surprise, the sorrow of being expendable and unloved. John pulled it from the rest and saw it could not live and that it was broken and he twisted its neck till it snapped and tossed it with the others, but as soon as he did he imagined he could have saved that last one. John was a murderer—no. He had obeyed his mother, and it was for the best. The bitch that birthed them beneath the cabin was a starveling and soon would die too. He could blame his mother, but with all the big trees slain to make room for corn and whiskey, God would know what had happened, and John begged to be forgiven this one last thing.

"Weldon?" Simon pulled him back. "Are you all right?"

The door creaked and Katherine, with a drab knit shawl wrapped around her thin frame, tiptoed in along the volumes lining the walls floor-to-ceiling until she had stowed herself away in the window seat with its well-worn cushions.

The shelves bursting with toppling piles of books and journals around the room served as reminders of Weldon's limited education. He scanned the leather bindings with envy. Not once in the years of the war did he spot Simon with a book, except for the dirty one he had confiscated from a private. Katherine and her father were the readers. Weldon guessed it by the way the girl lovingly fingered her way through the onionskin pages of a Dickens novel.

"Have you read all these books, sir?" Weldon asked but regretted it.

Scott laughed tracing his fingers over the rim of his glass with a self-satisfied air. "These and more. A person is nothing without a mind for knowledge. I had high hopes for Simon and bought every book here for his education." He sighed.

Simon took a drink, his expressionless face aimed toward the fire.

"Well, when things turned sour, and we sent Simon off to military school ... our Katherine kept reading for enjoyment's sake, I suppose. She has a decent mind for a girl, but an education is wasted on women. And truth be told, Simon was no scholar."

Simon, with his light hair slicked back and his brawny shoulders pent up in fine summer linen, oozed a restlessness which annoyed his father and saddened Katherine, who knew that Englewood was too small for him now. Simon poured another drink in the stifling silence. Katherine mourned over something lost in him. She went to a shelf and took out the scrapbook she had made since his first going away to West Point and then the war. She ran her fingers over the tintypes of Simon at war and the yellowing newsprint which had brought the battles home to her. The boy who used to bring her into his world had never come back as a man.

Scott's eyes fell upon Katherine with an air of sad disappointment.

Simon noticed and broke into a story. "Father, you'd have been appalled at the antics of the soldiers away from home doing as they pleased. One officer even tended bar in a bawdy house in full uniform ... or so I hear." Simon winked at Weldon. "And some of the girls were pretty ... from a distance, anyway. Father, you know the Renners from English Neighborhood? Remember, Weldon, how we caught him out? It was a laugh. We were just walking through Murder Bay—for an evening stroll to round up the boys, Father, nothing more—and who do we come across after leaving a drinking establishment but Renner as tight as can be in an alley. How idiotic he looked with his trousers around his ankles and a Cyprian with her mouth around his ..."

"Simon! Enough of this story, I've got the idea."

"So we come along and surprise him, but he doesn't mind. Asks us if we'd like to join him since he's got another standing there waiting for her three dollars. Land sakes, they were ugly. So we declined, not because they were ugly, but because it was wrong, Father," Simon said pouring more Scotch into his glass. "Well, I say as a small joke, I ask him if he's been cured of the clap yet, and the girl at his waist stops bobbing her head and just bites down hard. He sobered up enough after that. Of course he never had the clap, but will have to explain to his girl back home about the scar."

Scott turned to Katherine. "Your brother has a talent for bringing up conversation unsuitable for mixed company."

"My apologies, Father," Simon said with a grin. In the firelight any hint of age vanished from his sunburned good looks.

The men watched the fire or pretended to. Weldon's eyes were on Katherine.

"Katherine," Scott said, disconcerted by the look on Weldon's face, "dear, please go to see if your mother needs help."

"Yes, Father."

The library door creaked as Katherine returned with a teetering tray. Setting it upon her parents' wedding table a cup tumbled. Weldon's quick hand saved it as the little dog yipped and jumped from his lap.

"For God's sake, Katherine, be more of a lady for once!" Scott moved the tray.

Katherine's small voice shook. "Sergeant Weldon, how do you prefer your coffee?"

Her mother entered with a flourish, carrying her gorgeous confections. "Now then boys, please help yourselves. Sergeant Weldon, please eat."

Scott looked at his wife with pride. "Mrs. M, sit and Katherine too. We need more enlightened conversation." His wife sat between the two soldiers. Katherine sat at her father's feet, staring into the glimmering embers.

"Father, let's offer our guest one of your better cigars," Simon said, standing up.

Scott waved him away. "Don't want you foraging through my things, son," he said, pulling the smokes from a drawer himself and nodding dismissively when Weldon thanked him.

"Father, Weldon here loved these cigars. Being the friendly sort, I took the young soldier under my wings during the war."

"Poor boy," Scott said.

"Ha-ha, Father. Weldon kept to himself—not originally from the Garden State and all. Lied to the army at Carlisle about his age to join the cavalry. Bookish too—you'd like that, I'd say, Father. He once told me how he'd stolen books from the old librarian at Carlisle because he loved the books so, right, Weldon? You should hear how he recites things from the Bible."

Sarah brightened. "Now that's a very nice thing. Will you show us?"

"I-I don't remember n-now ..."

"Oh, what a shame. Well, can you recite poetry?" she asked.

"M-my father taught me to read, ma'am, from the Bible only. It's the only book he cared for ... the only one we had."

Scott smoked his cigar. "I'm not much for the revival-preaching westerners."

"Father," Simon said, reaching behind him for another bottle of something on his father's lower shelf, "Weldon got it in his mind that I wanted his expert military advice—that I came by for a chat in camp each day to gain knowledge of regulations regarding the company sinks—thought the cigars a bribe of some sort, right, Weldon?"

"I don't recall ... I ..." Weldon stammered, having trouble reaching the ashtray from his seat.

"Father, on his small salary Weldon bought me the best cigars he could get hold of to repay me. Told me not to play at friendship ... a hard nut to crack, he was."

"Sounds like childishness to me," Sarah said. "Simon doesn't play at friendship. That wouldn't be Christian now would it, Mr. Weldon?"

"I w-was ..."

"He was rough around the edges, I'd say. Weldon wasn't shoved off to West Point like I was, but I sensed a good fellow beneath it all, and after I realized how much he loved your socks and preserves, Mother, I knew he couldn't be all bad. It took me a while to figure who was stealing them."

Weldon cringed.

"I knit my fingers raw trying to fill your requests for socks! My Simon—what a kind soul to care for the less fortunate. I can't tell you how much it pleases me to know that my strawberries were thoroughly enjoyed, Mr. Weldon." Sarah patted Weldon's knee.

"I never stole ... I ..."

"Come now, Weldon." Simon laughed. "No hard feelings."

"Land sakes, and if those aren't the very boots Mother sent for Simon two sizes too big like he asked," Katherine said.

"At the hospital, I had no idea ... they just appeared." Weldon itched all over.

"Katherine, apologize for being rude to our guest," Sarah said.

"Mr. Weldon, I meant no harm," Katherine whispered, sinking into her chair. She looked as small as Weldon felt.

"And so, sergeant, what will you do now that we're at peace?" Scott asked, wiping his spectacles.

"I'll g-go back to my regiment, sir."

"Really? So you enjoy the vagabond life of a soldier? Business of some sort or finance is of no interest to you?"

"Father," Simon said, draining the contents of his father's Scotch, "Weldon is an excellent soldier. So many times he got me out of a jam—remember that night of the big poker game, Weldon? Oh, he didn't care for cards, though he has the poker face. Anyway, I came away with big winnings—a young private's watch and a fair amount of his other truck. Weldon covered for me in his morning report. Could have gotten in a heap of trouble over it, but he's true. Very dependable. Our army would do well to have more like Weldon enlist. As it is, we officers will have it rough with the dregs that may now join."

"Yes, I've heard that many of the enlisted men are of the disreputable sort. Cover-ups don't impress me," Scott said. "The military has corrupted your values, son. All the stand-up men have gone home since the war."

"You wouldn't know a thing about it, Father. Weldon is of a better breed. He's loyal."

"I meant no offense to you, Mr. Weldon," Scott said. "I'm sure you've overcome many obstacles to make it this far. Speaking of breed where is your family from? Weldon is an English name is it not, but ..."

"Ohio, sir. The Western Reserve." Weldon scratched his arm.

"I believe there's a fair amount of Indians out in Ohio, Weldon?"

"Not so many as there once were, I suppose."

Scott took his time looking Weldon over. "Terrible what those Sioux did to those farmers up in Minnesota a few years back. Four hundred dead that first day and some nailed right to their doors—children too. Wasn't it half-breeds involved somehow?"

"I didn't keep track of the details, sir, while off f-f-fighting a war."

"I thought you might take an interest in such things. My wife thinks you look Italian or Indian."

"Father!" Simon complained.

"Mr. McCullough, I am part ..."

Simon grabbed his friend's arm. "No, Weldon, my father is being rude. Don't give him the satisfaction of answering his idiotic questions!"

"Pardon me, Sergeant Weldon, I only meant to make conversation. My son is far too confrontational since the war. I hear fighting can cause a man to become alcoholic and aggressive ..."

Sarah took up the coffee pot. "Sergeant Weldon, more?"

"No, thank you, Mrs. McCullough." Weldon wiped his face. "You have been far too generous. I th-think I shall leave before I overstay my w-welcome."

They all stood but Scott, who poked at the fire.

"Father!" Simon begged.

"Oh, yes, good night, Weldon."

After awkward maneuvering, the crowded room emptied. Simon led his guest out past Katherine.

"Good night, Miss Katherine," Weldon said, glancing at her.

She tapped his shoulder. "Sir, good night ... I wanted to say ..." She checked to see that the others were outside. "I wanted to say you're the nicest soldier yet Simon has brought home to marry me off to. You didn't talk about Gettysburg once or get drunk. The last one got so drunk he lost his new teeth in the lilac bushes and had to be hauled down to the station in a donkey cart after he made a mess on my father's library rug."

Katherine stepped backward, tucking her loose hair behind her ears and disappeared into the kitchen.

"Weldon, will I drive you into town?" Simon called from the porch.

The lanterns in the yard softened the faces of Simon's parents as they strolled off around back through Sarah's garden. The scent of a pleasant flower passed in the breeze and fireflies flitted around. Weldon waited.

"The Wilderness ... Sir, I ..."

"I don't want to talk about any of it. I'm just happy to see you, old friend."

Simon passed him another good cigar. Weldon took it.

"No need to pay me back now. You were a caution back then."

"I couldn't understand your generosity ... I still don't ..." This was not going according to plan. "Your sister ..."

"Poor thing," Simon shook his head.

"She thinks I've come to marry her."

Simon laughed but saw a look on Weldon's face. "Well, you can't."

"I don't want to!"

Weldon turned to go, but Simon jumped the stairs after him. "It's not me. It would be grand to have you as a brother ... but my father ... he hates half-breeds and everyone else not a McCullough. And Katie's so ..."

"Too good ... I understand. It's always the same with you ... You're an ass!" Weldon said.

"That's probably true, but I'm trying to protect you."

"It's your fault ..." Weldon began, summoning his anger as best he could.

"What? That you admire my sister? Katie's pretty in a way, isn't she? I have no control over that or you coming here, but my sister cannot get hurt."

"I d-don't think I want to marry your sister. Why did you never invite me here like you did the others?"

"Weldon, you were my best chum ... they moved you to Washington and said you had no chance. I sent the boots ... I hoped ... but I still had to fight and then I wanted to go home .... Is there anything else you want to say?" Simon folded his arms after a quick rub of his chin like a boy waiting for the lecture to be over. "I have an engagement at the Liberty Pole tonight ..."

"I need to tell you ..."

"For God sakes, what?"

"I don't know, I ...would it be all right if I come by again tomorrow?"

Simon stared at him while chewing his cigar.

"Forget it, I won't," Weldon said, hugging his side.

"Are you all right?" Simon asked with the same care and gravity Weldon had admired and distrusted through most of the war.

Weldon stood silent, his insides wanting to burst and his throat full of melancholy.

"Just come then," Simon said. "You always want a special invitation and make a fuss over everything ... that much hasn't changed. Good night."

Simon left Weldon without a ride. As he crossed the yard, a bat grazed his hat and disappeared in the dark. Tiny stone paths, hardly big enough for a man's stride but perfect for Sarah's, cut the orderly beds of fruit and flower. Peach tree leaves lit in the moonlight along the fence and statuesque delphiniums waved in the light breeze. Weldon pulled himself close, afraid to put something out of place. He glanced back one last time at the warmly lit house and saw the curtain in an upstairs window drop. The girl had been watching him.

Chapter Three

The next day came and went...and the next. Weldon stayed in his room at the new yet shabby Englewood Hotel only a short walk up Spring Lane to the Palisades along the Hudson. A big city bustled just across the water, but even this small town unnerved him. Weldon's ungainly step and homespun clothes set him apart. His uniform wouldn't mask his inferiority forever—not here in the newly built and wealthy little New Jersey town, where there were committees formed for every conceivable purpose—new lanterns and shade trees, churches and theaters and a library. Weldon imagined that if his father had lived he'd still be cutting and burning huge stumps from his property and listening to the wolves in the moon's eerie light. And John would probably be beside him, never having escaped into the light of day.

On the third day in the evening Weldon made up his mind to leave, but this town had something he needed. The pus at his side had come on strong again, yet he wasn't sure anymore if the pain was real or an excuse and who cared? He had done everything right and followed orders. Took care of his men and read the goddamned Bible but what for?

On the day it happened, on the day he fell, after the initial shock of the war actually hitting him, a peace quieted him as he stared up into the spring sky. It could have been a noble ending.

But nothing ended. The war had been the embarkation point for the prison ship he had no business being on. He had not momentarily lost his will. It had been seized from him the moment the assistant surgeon gave him his first dose of morphine on the field.

The druggist might still be open. Wrapping his side tightly, Weldon pulled his jacket close and walked out through the crowded lobby and into light rain. "Oh, a hop ..." he said to himself as he scanned the young crowd pushing its way into the hotel. He spotted Simon and Katherine McCullough. They had gotten the worst of the rain.

"I can't go in like this. My slippers are soaked and look at all the girls in those pretty, dry silks!" Katherine cried.

"It was a stupid choice to walk, Katie." Simon smiled at a girl.

"I want to go home."

"Mother will be huffed if I let you leave early again, and I want a dance ..."

Weldon hadn't meant to walk up. It just happened.

Katherine turned toward the sound of the evening train whistle. "Father's train's come in. Maybe I'll go and meet him. Oh, Mr. Weldon."

"You beat all, Weldon," Simon laughed. "We'd given you up for gone."

"Not for the first time …" Weldon said.

"Pardon me?"

"Nothing, sir. I see you're off to the dancing." Weldon glanced at Katherine.

"Come along, Weldon," Simon said with a hint of discomfort in his voice. "A man in uniform always gets a full night of country girls."

Katherine slipped through the crowd and into the gaslit hotel.

"Well, I must go to mind my sister. Will you come?"

Weldon followed. He always followed Simon McCullough. The scene was warm with music and candles. Weldon half listened to Simon impressing young farm boys about the war. Across the room under an enormous mirror stood two distinct groups, accentuated by the color and quality of their gowns. Katherine's frosted peach silk should have placed her squarely into the more elite of the two parties where the girls quietly gossiped and turned inward, but Weldon did not see her. The farm girls called attention to themselves. Their squeals of raucous laughter reminded Weldon of home.

"I have to go …" he muttered.

"Don't be a humbug, Weldon." Simon pulled him. "Oh, shit, here she comes. She's spotted us."

"Your sister?"

"No. Margaret Brown."

A tree trunk of a girl with a deliberate step and thick coarse hair, which Margaret never managed fully to tame, charged over. Her full lips parted, and her large teeth glistened. Margaret Brown always got noticed. She intimidated men. Her well-made clothes accentuated her broad shoulders. Some might mistake her for a farmer's daughter, but she never worked a day in her life.

"Simon! There you are," she said, pointing her finger into Simon's chest. "Well, while you enjoy yourself, I'm stuck with your sad little sister."

"Your best friend."

"Yes, Katherine is indeed, but not good company here. And no one will dance with her as wet and saggy as she is. A gentleman would have brought an umbrella—but you're no gent!"

"Margaret, you're very humorous." Simon looked past her.

"Captain McCullough, how could you break young Kitty Lamont's heart the other day at the picnic? It's scandalous!" Margaret boomed over the fiddle.

"Miss Brown, I didn't know that you were acquainted with her. Where do you get your information?"

"Simon, dear, I have a host of friends and acquaintances who tell all."

"What a claim to fame. I bet they wear their gossip like a badge of honor, but tell me, who are these friends of yours? I've yet to see them." Simon flicked his cigar.

Margaret turned her attention to John Weldon. "Now who is this *Private So and So?*"

"This is *Sergeant* Weldon, Margaret," Simon stated, pointing to the chevron on his jacket.

"Oh, so he's practically a real officer then? I thought the war department made everybody at least a captain. All I hear is *brevet* this and *brevet* that ... were you brevetted something at least, sir? But brevet is a phony promotion anyhow, is it not?"

"No." Weldon bristled.

"Oh, don't feel bad. Probably half the boys lie, and maybe you'll make something of yourself as a civilian," Margaret said. "Are you staying at the McCullough house?"

"Sergeant Weldon's got a room here at the hotel—didn't want to burden my mother," Simon said.

"It's such a sleepy little town, Mr. Weldon, you must be bored to tears here ... and the hotel must be mighty hard on a soldier's pay, or did you get into the army on a bounty? I've read there was quite a bit of money made that way."

"I've b-been a soldier for years! I never took a bounty!" Weldon shook now.

Simon grabbed his arm to steady him, but Weldon slipped loose and pulled his jacket straight.

"Margaret, you need to stop talking," Simon said. "Don't listen to her. She's ignorant." He nervously puffed his cigar. "There's Dottie Taylor," he said. "She's some pumpkins. Weldon, do me the favor of dancing with Katie. Just one dance ..."

Margaret and Weldon watched Simon go.

"Well? Are you going to dance with Katherine or not?" Margaret asked. "You understand I don't like soldiers at all. I don't care if they freed every darkie on the planet."

"There she is ... leaving ..."

"Come on then!" Margaret grabbed Weldon. "Katherine! Wait!"

Katherine wiped her teary eyes. Weldon's feet stuck in place now, but Margaret shoved him closer.

"M-miss, w-would you like a d-dance?"

"No!"

"That's fine," Weldon replied, stepping backward. "My leg aches, and I'll just go ..."

"I'm wet, and my hair and, oh, I hate these things with the girls ..." Katherine sobbed. "Mr. Weldon, will you please take me home?"

"No, I couldn't possibly, I agreed to a dance ..."

"You agreed? Were you paid? Then I'll pay you to take me home!"

"Miss, I didn't mean to upset you ... I d-don't know why I came. I'd love a dance with you—your brother suggested it—but I wanted to ..."

"I'm all wet ..."

"Oh, I don't mind. I have a headache ..."

Katherine laughed. Her mouth seemed too small for a full smile. Her eyes were soft, and she had an upturned nose with delicate freckles across the bridge.

Weldon took Katherine's hand in his and limped onto the floor. A German dance was called. "I don't know it. I should go ..."

"Will I show you the dance?" Katherine asked.

The fiddler broke his string, so the couples were at loose ends. Margaret came up as another full-figured girl introduced herself to Weldon. "Sir, I'm Louisa Van Brunt. What frolic this is! I never thought you'd find a partner, Katie—they'd all be afraid of what Simon might do to them."

Weldon jumped in. "Simon McCullough is a friend."

"Oh, that explains it. Trust Simon to find a way. He's been working at getting Katherine someone, anyone, but this town is so judgmental. It's a shame. Mr. Weldon, I admire your courage getting involved with the McCulloughs—they're always up to such mischief."

"Louisa Van Brunt, hold your tongue," Margaret huffed. "I see you're not engaged and you have no brothers to blame for scaring off the boys."

"For your information, I have a few boys interested in me, but I'm patient and considerate. I want them to know everything about me so there are no surprises later. Don't you agree that's a good plan, Katherine?"

Katherine stood perfectly still.

"Miss Van Brunt, the truth is a man can tell a person's character very quickly," Weldon said. "You don't need every detail of a person to get an impression of them. If they're cruel and ignorant, an expensive dress can't hide it."

Louisa took a step back and smiled. "Rustic wisdom—how very charming."

"Don't you dare talk down to Mr. Weldon!" Katherine cried.

"The mouse speaks! Are you madly in love like the Undercliff boy?"

"Louisa!" Margaret shouted.

Katherine pushed past them all for the lobby and into the street.

"Miss McCullough!" Weldon tried to keep up. "Wait!"

"I'm not madly in love!" Katherine cried.

Weldon was a little disappointed. "Miss, you shouldn't walk out in the rain on your own.... Thank you for defending me ..." He laughed. "If you wait I'll get an umbrella and walk you."

"No, everyone talks." Katherine cried again. "I'm sorry. I'm not always like this." Weldon smiled.

"I mean I'm always like this—wet or messy or awkward. And I'm so ... trapped. Everything ends here on the Palisades for me. I'm sorry ... you must think ..."

"I think you're pretty."

Katherine pulled her wet hair off her face and rolled her eyes, but she smiled a little. "My mother told me I looked just like a spinster."

Simon ran out. "Katherine, just like you to make a show of yourself! Let's go."

"Sir, the girls weren't very nice," Weldon said.

"Weldon, you don't understand the first thing about girls." Simon jerked Katherine's arm. "I never should have let you ... oh, never mind."

"Don't pull her like that." Weldon stood five inches taller than Simon. "I want to see your sister tomorrow."

"Who do you think you are? You have no right to lecture me."

"I'd like to see Miss Katherine."

"Well, I don't care a bit. It's my father."

"Tomorrow then ... if m-miss, if you approve."

Katherine nodded but set her sights on Simon. He worked his jaw as Weldon walked off.

"I'm sorry, Simon. I didn't mean to spoil your night," Katherine said.

"Really? You always find a way to make a show of yourself." Simon pulled a flask from his jacket. "I can't wait to leave here."

"Take me with you," Katherine begged.

Simon rolled his eyes and took a swig.

"I wish ... I wish you wouldn't drink so much," Katherine said, timidly trying to tuck her arm under his.

Simon resisted at first. "Damn, you're cold as ice. Here, take my coat."

"No, I couldn't. You're always too good to me at your own expense. I never wanted that." Her chin quivered.

"Now stop it. My helping you got me out of this town in the first place. I'm eternally grateful."

"Didn't you ever miss us, Simon? I missed you more than anything. I thought when you came home it would all go back to the way it was. Remember our resting place by the brook under that tree with all the moss? We could tell each other everything."

Simon gave Katherine a squeeze as they headed home. "You know why I didn't come home that Christmas when I could have? Well, I was sick. Gonorrhea."

"What's that?"

"You get it from bad women. I tried it on with a darkie—wanted to see if they were different. Weldon brought me to the soldiers' hospital. Lots of us got it—a southern conspiracy. But I'm cured."

"Does Sergeant Weldon have it?" Katherine asked, blushing.

"You like him, don't you?" Simon shook his head. "Weldon is religious or something. I don't know, but I doubt he's got anything. Never saw him with a girl. He's awkward, don't you think? Self-taught and all. Be nice to him."

"Why wouldn't I be?"

"Because Father will have none of it."

Katherine stood quietly for a moment. "So you're better now? Cured. Are they ...different? The darkie girls?"

"Katie," Simon laughed, "do you really want to know?"

"No, not really."

"Well, the doctor said it was because it was her monthlies that I got it. They used syringes of mercury to cure me. Really awful. I couldn't ride for a month—Weldon chuckled at that—and they said I shouldn't dance or eat asparagus." He laughed. "Where would I get asparagus in the army?"

"I just want you to be like you always were."

"Some of us have to grow up, sis," he said with a sigh and another sip of his flask. He winked at her and forced a grin. They walked the rest of the way in their own thoughts.

The clocks in the house struck three in the morning at nearly the same time in different tones and textures. The sky and low hanging moon cast an ancient glow over the room as Katherine's mind drifted in and out of consciousness. She rose from her bed to hear Simon whistling an old war song out of tune. From her window she could see Simon's rumpled figure, hands in pockets and stooped forward like an old used-up farmer. This sad glow and aged light brought Simon, her best friend, back to her—his rosy-cheeked and full-lipped calling out in the snow making teams with his mates. Organizing, always organizing them ...

The glare from the late afternoon sun in winter blinded her to the others. She was on Simon's team. The dull white landscape of noon had turned to fire with glowing trees and burning bushes, long shadows and the thick smell of wood burning.

Soon they would all go home. Her throat was raw when she swallowed the frosty air, but she didn't care about the cold. She raced through the tunnels and over the ruined forts they had been at work on for days and threw herself into a dugout cave of snow, out of the wind and hidden from the marauding snowball armies. The pale blue sky in the east soothed her as she stared up at it, mulling over a phenomenon she had learned about in school, "aurora borealis, aurora borealis," she repeated just above a whisper. The voices of Simon and his mates faded away, but the calling of a jay, blue in the highest tree, took her fancy.

A boy from Undercliff, a stranger, pounced on her then. The boy's breath was hot as he straddled her waist and crushed her elbows beneath his knees. Before she could scream, he shoved her mouth full of dirty snow. She spit it out, choking, but he smacked her hard and covered her mouth with his foul-smelling wool glove. Kicking, she only managed to lose her boot—her mother had bought them two sizes too large for economy. The boy was a nobody. She remembered his teeth were already rotten when he smiled.

"You think you're somethin' little miss—all fancy," he whispered in her face.

She kicked and tried to free her arms, but he weighed too much. He ripped at her coat—a smart sailor coat with brass buttons that flew like sparks into the snow—and then the boy with cracked lips shoved his hand beneath her wintry layers. He looked past her like a strange doctor, feeling around for something uncommon. "Boy, you're just a little thing—nothin' to get too excited over. Whatcha cryin' for? I ain't gonna hurt you unless you make me." He grabbed her face to kiss it.

She bit the boy's nose and he leveled a punch aimed at her face but got her ear instead. She never told anyone when the ringing stopped that she could no longer hear on that side.

The Undercliff boy wrestled her skirt up and threw himself between her legs. Now she could claw him, but it made no difference. She thought she could scream, but she couldn't hear herself. The fiery glare from the sun blinded her. She felt a jolt and waited for another blow, but the weight lifted from her. One of Simon's friends sat her up and wrapped his scarf around her while pulling her skirts back down. He shouted to someone and kneeled and spoke to her, but she couldn't hear him with the ringing. She would have laughed if she could, watching him struggle to get her stocking back on her blue foot, but she wanted her brother to stop it—what she now saw that he was doing. It scared her.

Simon had lost his hat somehow, and she remembered his red ears and his straw-colored hair tousled with sweat. Simon had the nobody by the throat and the boy bled. His body hung naked—he hadn't the chance to fasten his trousers back

on—and it shocked her, his motives. What the Undercliff boy had done to her became clear and awful and humiliating. The boy's nose and mouth bled and his skin
flapped under his eye and she wished that she had not let her mouth touch any part
of him. Simon had got hold of her boot with the big heavy heel. He wasn't speaking or shouting as his mates were, as they stood there in a casual semi-circle. Simon's
mouth was a grim line of rage, and he threw the Undercliff boy to the ground and
set upon him with blunt blows of the heel, kicking the boy's face in like a pumpkin being smashed. No one stopped him, although one friend did turn away. Simon
stood up, his nose dripping onto the lifeless form beneath him. He kicked snow over
the face and the others joined in. One by one they came to gather around Simon's
little sister, who remained in shock, sitting in the snow.

They bundled her up with their coats and hats and put her on their little bobsled. They were just boys who wanted to help. The men of the town visited the Mc-
Cullough home later. Both children refused to speak for days, but the story came
out through the others. The Village Protection Society formed soon afterward—Simon a sort of mascot.

Scott sent Simon off to a military prep school to study for West Point. For
Katherine there were no more carefree wanderings (they were from then on forbidden by Scott), no more school (the other girls whispered things she couldn't quite
hear and her grades were slipping), and no more dreams. The lines had been drawn.
The world had been cut in half like her hearing. Her mother examined her—there
were no signs of damage. There was just the one thing that crept into her mind: that
without Simon she was nobody.

Chapter Four

Simon shadowed his mother in the morning, teasing her and making her happy. "Mother, your coffee is not like the good stuff in the army. I'm afraid you've lost your touch without me here to guide you."

"You'll just have to stay to get me back in shape," she said, taking his cup. "That's enough or you'll swim away."

"No, I enjoy my morning time with you, Mother."

"Coffee keeps you from the barn," Scott said from beside the kitchen hearth, "and your small bit of chores. Maybe it's time you go back to the army."

"Don't you mind him," Sarah said. "This is your home."

Simon kissed his mother.

"Dear, you smell like a tavern," she said, shaking her head.

Simon shrugged. "Oh, Father, I'll have your ride ready in no time, and I'll clean up after I drive you to the station. It makes no difference. I've got all day."

"Does this cavalryman understand that horses like to be fed at regular intervals, Sarah?"

"That's why I switched to infantry," Simon replied, winking at Katherine.

"Stop it, Simon," she said.

"All right, Father, get your things, and I'll get the surrey ready."

"Katherine, bring me over the dishes, and when we're finished we'll air the rugs in the yard," Sarah said, pulling down the drained goat cheese she had hanging from hooks above the basin.

Katherine slid from the tall stool and stacked the white china dishes like a wedding cake before carrying them to the steaming water. They fell with a clatter. Rolling up the sleeves of her faded indigo work dress, she warmed her hands in the soapy water.

"What kind of wife will you be, always daydreaming, Katie? Get to work or we'll be in this kitchen all day," Sarah said.

Outside, the crickets sang in full concert, and the landscape swayed with overgrown foliage. Summer had passed its peak, and the autumn waited a slight tilt of the earth away. The birds in the yard sang a more satisfied tune now. Their offspring had grown, their nests emptied, and their hunger satiated. Mourning doves cooed, and the train whistle blew.

"Mother, what do you think of Sergeant Weldon?" Katherine asked.

Sarah raised her brows, brushing crumbs from the table. "Too quiet for my liking. Mr. Weldon is rather average I suppose."

Katherine's chest tightened. "So you don't think much of him for being a sergeant."

"No, being a sergeant is probably exactly what he should be, but you can do better. Today we should go into town. I need some fabric from Mr. Deuel's. And wear that bonnet we bought last week. It makes you look pretty."

Katherine hated the bonnet. She had no desire to spend the afternoon in town. Lately and especially today, life was disappointing and small. "I don't want to go."

"What was that, dear?" Sarah stopped cleaning. "Oh, you're annoyed aren't you? You asked for my opinion, and all I did was answer honestly. Where's the harm in that? I understand that you're feeling desperate, but you shouldn't. God has a plan." Sarah put her arm around Katherine's shoulders and led her back toward the dishes. "You know, I was talking to Reverend Booth the other day about donating some of my strawberries next spring for a young mothers' social. Isn't that a nice idea? I remember after you I was so bone tired. I would have loved time with other young ladies in my same position. Giving birth to you was a struggle."

"Yes, I know, Mother."

"The doctor said I should have no more children after Simon—that I should be content with three wonderful, jolly children, but God had other plans. You were a surprise, but thank God for you after your sisters died. Not that you said or did much for the first two years—nothing like Simon or the girls. I suppose we spoiled you and made you lazy. Simon talked and smiled—a real charmer. Ah well, everyone is different."

"Mother, did you have a point?"

"Why, yes, I did. Maybe God wants you for other work ... maybe volunteering in the church. Many a lonely girl has found a new lease on life working for others."

"I'll die if I stay here with you forever!" Katherine cried.

"What an awful thing to say." Sarah crossed her arms and frowned. "You have never expressed a single aspiration of your own in all of your nineteen years. The only thing I've ever seen you enthusiastic over is tea. *Tea*, of all things! We haven't pushed you since all that's happened. I've protected you against so many slurs. Now you ask my opinion about a man, and I become your worst company simply for answering honestly. You will need a special man to understand your circumstances, and I don't believe that someone from the backwoods of nowhere is that man!"

"I'm sorry."

Scott barreled into the kitchen, a big man made bigger by Sarah's cooking. His serious and deep blue eyes framed in gold spectacles gave him an owlish air. "For

God's sake, where is that son of yours? I've never seen the likes of such indolence. His attitude would never do in business!"

"Then it's lucky for both of you that he is not interested in business." Sarah kissed his chin just as the kitchen door swung open.

"I found someone on our front porch at this early hour," Simon said, dragging in his sergeant.

"Oh my, Simon! We're hardly dressed for visitors!" Sarah exclaimed, shooing Katherine out of the room. "Simon, take your friend outside for a while if you would."

"What about my ride to the station?" Scott asked.

"Shit! I forgot, Father. I'll get the surrey ready now. Weldon, come along with me and be of some use," he said, slapping his friend's back.

Scott threw up his hands. "What kind of men roam the yard at 8 o'clock in the morning?"

"Have a good day, dear," Sarah said.

Katherine pulled back the curtains in her room, her heart racing as Simon pulled out the horse and small carriage. Weldon held out his hand. Mr. McCullough looked him over before accepting his greeting with an annoyed toss of the head. "There's no room in this contraption for three, Simon. What will your friend do?"

"Oh, Weldon can take care of himself," Simon said, rolling his eyes for the benefit of his friend, who stood glumly with his hands in his pockets, looking over the garden. "Weldon, make yourself comfortable in the yard. I'll be back lickety split."

Weldon nodded and stepped back from the horse as it pulled away. His hands sweated. He had stayed away the Sunday but could not stand to be alone another day. A rabbit ran through the garden of ripe tomatoes and green pumpkins. A small tortoiseshell cat lay sunning itself on the side porch, where brooms and yard tools were hidden by trailing morning glories in blue and purple.

Weldon considered bolting. He didn't belong here, but after a quick glance toward the house he crouched down to run his fingers over the hilly pumpkin skins and the soft round tomatoes. Weldon pulled a furry leaf from the low-lying lamb's ears and slipped it into his pocket. Sunny black-eyed Susans burst out where they'd be most pleasing. The wild lilies stood at attention like well-disciplined followers of an inspired leader. Weldon marveled at the planning. His visit was unplanned, unannounced—that had been a blunder. The McCullough family might not like such surprises, and it was still so early in the day.

He hadn't slept, and the night had seemed forever. He had two or three days without the urges ... just enough time to meet this girl—he'd stop for her. Simon took forever in town. Maybe he met up with friends and forgot Weldon standing here.

"Sergeant Weldon, are you coming in?" Katherine called from the porch in a flaming red dress with bold black ribbons flapping in the breeze.

"I, I didn't want to intrude ... I didn't consider the time. It was foolish."

"Mother asks would you like breakfast," she said, leaning over the bannister.

"No, Miss McCullough, I won't trouble her."

Katherine's shoulders slumped, and she bit her lower lip. "It'll trouble her more if you don't eat what she's already set about making. Come in, please."

The young veteran ate everything Sarah set before him. Katherine blushed every time Weldon glanced her way.

"Tell me, Sergeant Weldon, what are your plans?" Sarah asked.

"For today?"

"No, young man, I mean for the next while."

"Not until December do I have to report back, ma'am," Weldon said, uncomfortably. "But you needn't feed me till then .... I mean—"

"It's wise not to make serious attachments then, don't you agree?" Sarah asked, taking his plate and refilling his cup.

Weldon cleared his throat.

Sarah shook her head but smiled and sat with them. "Dear Sergeant Weldon, this is probably the first time you are so attracted to a girl, and you might find it hard to imagine, but in time you'll see it's blinded your good sense."

Katherine opened her mouth to speak, but her mother continued more stridently. "You should not be so quick to express your feelings. Wait until you're sure. You might find many flaws in my daughter and have to suffer the embarrassment of taking back the nice things you've said."

"I haven't s-s-said anything nice yet. I mean, I intend to ... but your daughter seems ..." He glanced at Katherine and lost his sense of the conversation.

"Sergeant Weldon?" Sarah tried to bring him back. "*Mr. Weldon*!"

"Ma'am?"

"My husband has very strong opinions, and he won't approve of Katherine traipsing around the world with a man she hardly knows."

"I'll stay on your property then."

"We could sit on the porch," Katherine suggested.

"Katherine, you push me to my limits ... but I suppose a little while on the porch ..."

"Thank you, Mrs. McCullough," Weldon said, his face lighting up with the warmest smile Katherine had ever seen.

Katherine jumped up, took his hand, and led him to the porch. Weldon noticed her eyelashes as she pinned on her straw hat. Her hair fell loose and in no particular style. She directed him to the best chair and sat close beside him on a wicker ottoman. Weldon pulled a bag of chocolates from his pocket and offered it to her. She dipped her ungloved hand in the bag.

"Land sakes! They're a pool of mud!" Katherine said, grinning and licking her fingers.

"I'm awful sorry. I guess they've melted."

"Sergeant Weldon, it was sweet to bring me candy. Mother says I shouldn't have chocolates, so maybe I shouldn't."

He shrugged. She laughed and reached up to smudge his nose with her sticky hand.

He wiped it off with a smile, took her arm, and smeared it back on her.

"You're horrible!" Katherine laughed. "Now the bees will come for me and bite me to bits! You'll see."

Weldon pulled his sleeve and wiped her arm clean. Katherine took his hand in her lap and kept it there, and they both grew quiet again. Weldon pulled away at the sound of the carriage. Simon jumped out before them with a sly grin and a new gun. Another young man and two giggling girls from town sat waiting in the surrey. One girl waved at Katherine.

"How's this for hunting, Weldon?" Simon asked, as he trotted up to the porch. "Just bought it off Mr. Adriance, a farmer round the corner, for next to nothing—old fool."

"Nice, sir," Weldon said as he stood up shakily.

Simon took in his friend's appearance with mild concern.

"Won't you come for a ride with my friends? I'll introduce you to Anna—the one on the left. She's not all that bad as long as she doesn't show her teeth—they're a caution."

"No, sir. I'm not feeling myself today. I'd rather ..." He looked to Katherine.

Simon tipped his hat with a sigh. "You'll miss a good frolic. There's a haying party tonight, but have your way. See you, then."

Weldon gingerly sat back down, and the two watched as Simon jumped back into the surrey. The girls looked so elegant to Katherine. She played with the black velvet ribbons on the front of her dress. "I noticed, Mr. Weldon, that you've got a limp."

"Stiffness. I'm better though," Weldon said, rubbing his leg as if he didn't own it.

"Simon says things were hard for you."

"Your brother doesn't know the half of it," he said more bitingly than he meant. "Miss, m-may we change the subject?"

"Land sakes, I didn't mean to annoy you."

"No, you didn't. I'm sorry, I just ... well, the war's in the past right?"

Katherine brightened. "Everything is. Isn't that a comfort? We can always start fresh, don't you think? That's what I try."

Weldon smiled. "Maybe I'll try too."

A robin stirred in the tree above them. "I love robins" Katherine said after too much silence. "Things seem so mournful when they're not around."

"Bluebirds. My mother liked them more than anything."

Silence again.

"How do you like my dress, Mr. Weldon? Mother made me wear it."

Weldon eyed it quickly, shyly. "I don't much like it, miss ..." He tipped his hat off and ran his fingers through his thick hair. His face reddened, and he looked to the heavens.

Katherine stared at him.

"Miss, I only meant to say, well, you look better in something simple—like the other night. You don't need a whole lot of finery. You've pretty hair though."

"Oh," Katherine said, clasping her hands in her lap, trying to think of something impressive to say. "Mr. Weldon ... I'm afraid I'm not much good at entertaining men."

"That's a good thing, I think," Weldon quipped, but retreated.

Sarah sang in the kitchen.

"I've said something foolish, haven't I?" Katherine asked.

Her blush charmed him.

"I meant to say that if you're bored you don't have to stay."

"Do you want me to leave?" he asked.

"No ... but I'm quiet, backwards even, and now you're quiet."

"This quiet," Weldon confided, "it's all I've wanted. I'm enjoying myself."

"Really, Mr. Weldon? That's bully because I am too."

"Fine." Weldon smiled and leaned deeper into his chair. As he looked out over the manicured lawn dappled with sunlight and listened to the quiet sounds of chickens clucking in the next yard, his eyes grew heavy and he closed them for a moment. Weldon finally slept, but on someone's porch with a strange girl watching. Was it all day? The light was changed when he awoke. The girl was gone, and he had been covered with a sweet smelling blanket. This was a dream, wasn't it? But no, here came the girl again.

"Beg your pardon, miss. I didn't mean to fall ..."

"All veterans sleep when they get here."

"Oh."

Katherine seemed to like something about the way he looked as she stood over him. "I've chores in the barn."

"I'll come with you." He pulled himself up. The pain in his side came back, and his leg ached.

"Bully."

Katherine skipped ahead. Weldon worried for a second that she might be too young but remembered Simon saying she was past eighteen. Was she really not allowed candy?

When she turned and smiled again he forgot his thoughts.

"Oh, that Simon will land us both in trouble over the state of this place." Katherine ran in and gathered the tack and the grooming supplies from the floor. Weldon swept a little but not for long. The sweet scent of hay and Katherine's busy movements distracted him. He must behave like a gentleman.

Only the smallest wedge of light came through the window after Katherine shut the barn doors. "I'm not afraid of you, Mr. Weldon, even though we might kiss."

"You're an odd girl," he said when she got close. He tentatively pulled a strand of hair from her face. Her lips looked so soft. Moving his hands around her waist, he felt the bones of her corset through her dress.

Katherine slipped her hand beneath Weldon's checked shirt. "You're mighty thin, Sergeant Weldon," she whispered, finding a secret through his flannel undershirt—-a weakness, a wound that had not healed beneath its bandage—and the barn door opened.

"Land sakes!" cried Simon.

"Simon, please escort your friend out of my sight this instant!" Scott shouted.

"Sir ... s-sir, it's all my doing," Weldon stammered, trying to tuck his shirt.

"*Simon*!" Scott said through gritted teeth. "Get this stuttering fool out of my barn before I throttle him!"

Weldon tried to speak but Simon, knowing his father, dragged his friend away.

Katherine shook as she redid the hooks of her dress. She scooped up Weldon's hat and attempted to get past her father, but he pulled her by the arm, exposing the whites of her undergarments. Scott batted the hat from her hand and slapped her hard across the face. "Look at yourself, Katherine! You have shamed me more than I can bear! How could you let this happen? All I've ever worried about was protecting you, and you do this like a common prostitute! Do you think soldiers respected the women in Washington that your brother talks about?"

"Let me alone, Father! I'm old enough now to make my own decisions! You want me to stay here and do dishes and hold your shovel in the garden and wait for Simon's letters just like before, but I won't! This is my chance!"

"You're far dumber than I ever imagined if you believe a man who shows you so little respect would make a proper suitor! Sergeant Weldon is a mongrel. Doesn't even look a man in the eye."

"Father, you're too hard on Katie and Weldon," Simon said. "He's a good man down deep."

"I don't want to dig deep for my daughter," Scott explained coldly. "There's something not right about your friend, but you're always too drunk to see it."

"What the hell has this to do with my drinking? That's it, I'm done here," Simon said, walking off toward his favorite establishment, The Liberty Pole.

Katherine stood in silence with her chin out and her mouth tight.

Scott moved to touch her red cheek, but she pulled away and his anger revived. "Now get to your room," he said. "You've disappointed me beyond words."

Katherine ran in a blur of tears up into the house through the kitchen past her mother. "Katie! For heaven's sake!"

Before Sarah could go after her, Scott thrust open the door. "Sarah, I blame you!"

"Mercy, what are you on about, man?"

"My God, are you blind, deaf, and dumb to everything that goes on around you?" Scott threw up his hands and collapsed into his chair. "I just found your daughter and that sneaky bastard in the barn together!"

"Oh, Scott, is that all? Don't you take on enough of the world's problems? Of course there's going to be sparking between them—like there was between us."

"This was no little kissing. They were half undressed! Oh, the shame of it. I'll never be able to go into the barn without seeing an image of my daughter with her top undone."

"My dear husband, I'm sure that your barn will be fine. Now where is the Weldon boy? It's nearly supper."

"He's not a boy, but a man who doesn't respect our daughter. I sent him away. If he knows what's good for him he'll leave town by morning."

"Did you challenge him to a duel, dear? Poor Katie," Sarah said as she walked to the door.

"Poor Katie? Poor us! Saddled with two ne'er-do-well children. It's disappointing in the extreme."

"Now, Scott, my own Fuss and Feathers, calm down. You don't mean what you say."

Scott sighed and grabbed his newspaper, opening it with a flourish. "No one listens to me, but you'll see it will all end in tears."

***

Simon found his ruffled sergeant seated at The Liberty Pole tavern when he arrived. Weldon never drank during the war. "What the hell are you doing here? My father hasn't driven you drinking that quick, has he?"

"No, sir. I'm just tired of the hotel is all," Weldon replied, stirring his coffee.

"So, you're creating quite an impression with my father ... stealing his daughter to have your wicked way with her."

"Sir, if you don't mind, I don't see the humor in this. I always find a way to ruin things."

"Oh, please, Weldon! I've never heard you be so self-pitying. It's not you. You make me laugh. I get into trouble now and again, but so what? Try as you might to avoid it—it still comes, so you may as well please yourself. It's less work, and as long as it causes no real harm ..."

"But your selfish ways sometimes bring harm you never realize! Your father is right to be angry. I let my emotions get the best of me."

Simon gave him a skeptical look. "Your emotions? I doubt it was sentimental emotion that drove you to undress her."

Weldon smiled. "Your sister is very pretty."

"Please spare me the details. I'm just happily surprised that you and Katie are warm-blooded after all."

Chapter Five

Even the heavy lion's-head knocker on the front door intimidated Weldon. He watched Scott McCullough through the entranceway windows lighting the hallway lamp in his slippers and smoking jacket. The old man wore an ornate cap with gold tassels Sarah had made for him. The dogs caused an uproar at the sound of the knock. Sarah and Simon shooed them into the kitchen before Scott opened the door a crack.

"I made myself clear earlier tonight, Mr. Weldon. You are not welcome here."

Weldon pushed his way through as he spoke. "Mr. McCullough, I've come to apologize to you, sir."

"There's no need to apologize. The army is no training ground for manners."

"I d-disagree, sir. It is because I acted so common and not the gentleman I've been trained to be that I landed myself and your daughter, Miss Katherine, I mean, into trouble."

Scott cleared his throat. "Well, we can forget the whole affair, but I think it wise for you to put an end to this little romantic interlude. Katherine is not fit for the army."

"Miss McCullough seems a strong girl, even if smallish." Weldon looked past Scott for any sign of Katherine.

Scott eyed him as if he had said something insane. "I traveled with the Sanitary Commission during the war and witnessed the debauchery the soldiers got up to. Katherine behaved foolishly—or worse today. I don't want you imagining you've got a camp follower to use here and then desert. And she *will not* live in a hovel fit for a pack animal."

"Sir! I never ... I don't consider Miss Katherine in any low way at all! If you allow us to marry I will do anything to gain promotion. I would never bring her out unless I could keep her comfortable and safe." *What was he saying?*

"Are you asking for permission to marry my daughter after only a few days of knowing her?"

"Sir ... I ... well ... it's just that ... your daughter, I mean Miss Katherine ..."

"Son, I know who you are referring to."

"Yes, well, I think I could love her ... I mean, I know that I am—*in love*. At least what I imagined it to feel like—though I hardly imagined it at all ..." Weldon took a few steps back.

Scott said nothing. The kitchen door creaked. Scott shot his wife and son a menacing glance before the door closed again.

Simon and Sarah whispered and muffled their laughter.

"Mr. Weldon, I don't know about you. I don't even like you, but I have to consider Katherine." Scott called up the stairs, "Katherine, stop hiding up there and come down if you are decent."

Katherine came into the light in her paisley wrapper. Her hair hung in a long braid with a blue bow tied at the end. Weldon smiled at her tiny blue slippers peeking out on each step.

"Katherine, did you hear what Mr. Weldon has just said?" Scott asked.

"Father, I could never be happier than if you gave me permission to marry Mr. Weldon!"

"How did we raise such foolish children, Sarah?" Scott called.

Sarah pushed a small dog snout back as she squeezed through the door in a hurry.

"We've spoiled them, I'm afraid," she said with wide eyes and an excited grin.

"And how would this marriage work?" Scott said. The dogs were running riot in the kitchen. Simon kicked a few back and joined the group. "Mr. Weldon would be stationed where?"

Katherine looked to Weldon.

Simon stepped in. "Father, only commissioned officers bring along wives. Sergeants marry laundresses, but not Katie ..."

Sarah looked appalled.

"But, that's okay," Simon went on. "Weldon will make a fine lieutenant one day if I have anything to say about it. Father, Colonel Langellier likes me, and I'll have his ear. I wish I could bring Katie along with me, but how would that look for Katherine to attend affairs Weldon would be excluded from?"

"I intend to take Miss McCullough with me, Simon," Weldon said. "Someday *I* will take her. I'm going to work hard *myself*. I won't depend on you or anyone, sir."

"I didn't mean ..." Simon grew quiet.

Weldon shook. Not even his legs were steady and secure. He waited for a shipwreck, taking a deep breath.

The family stood in silent contemplation.

"And how would it be, Katie?" Sarah spoke up. "A marriage this week and a child the next?"

"I don't know ..."

"The girl knows nothing, Sarah! It's astonishing. And don't think I'll support you financially so that your soldier can gamble the money away."

"I don't gamble, sir."

"Father, I wish you'd stop talking of money. It's embarrassing and beneath you," Simon said.

"What I say about my money is my business. When and if you ever earn any, son, then you will have the same right," Scott lectured. He took a magnanimous breath and crossed his arms. "Well, truth is, Katherine has few options left to her now. She's put off most gentlemen who would take her. You've had your way with her. I dare say Katie has no wits to be left alone for five minutes. She hasn't a proper education. I don't know what will become of her, but I despair at the thought of supporting a bitter old spinster when I retire. I guess Mr. Weldon is the best she can do. No offense."

The color rose in Katherine's face.

"Father, why are you so cruel?" Simon asked.

"Cruelty? I'm simply stating facts. We mustn't all have our head in the sand."

"Why couldn't you let her head be in the clouds just this once?"

"You, of all people, Simon, who loves to defend your sister ... how do you not see that Katie is not fit for an army wife?"

"What is Katie fit for then?" Simon said. "Staying locked up here with you? Books are fine, but she has to experience life too, and you and Mother are young enough yet. You don't need her help."

Weldon inched away from the gaslight and into the shadows near the door. Simon grabbed his arm and continued speaking. "John Weldon comes off awkward and dull, but he's steady and smarter than you think. I've never seen him look at any girl the way he does Katie. They're sweet."

"How romantic," Scott said, softening. "It's what lands you in trouble with the girls. You're far too hopeful, but *maybe* I'm too judgmental. I only want Katie to be happy and well cared for by a fellow of high caliber." He gave Weldon a withering glance.

"Father, I wonder at you. I have my prejudices, but you ... I imagined you believed all that humbug you spouted before the war. What burns me is your contempt for Weldon, who fought your war."

"I hope you're not under any illusions about your intelligence. This has nothing to do with Weldon's mixed race—it has to do with his position. And if Katherine thinks it will be easy to live on thirteen dollars a month ..." Scott huffed. "And I have no room for Mr. Weldon in my business."

Simon shook his head. "You have nothing to fear on that account. Weldon is set on remaining in the military, like I am. Don't trouble yourself about our presence."

Sarah cried and grabbed Simon and Weldon by the arm. "Oh, pooh. You're welcome here always. You must visit *me* often! I couldn't bear the thought of not seeing my children!"

Scott sighed. "Mr. Weldon, I apologize for my son's behavior. He makes things awkward when he speaks."

Sarah glared at Scott, and he relented.

"I'm ashamed of my behavior also," Scott said. "But, this is such a big surprise, and a father has a right to want the best for his daughter. I hope my son is right about you."

Sarah rushed up. She kissed Weldon on the cheek which signaled to all but Weldon that the storm was over.

"Katherine," Sarah gushed, "I'll take care of the wedding arrangements—no rushing—we must have a dress made, and I'll cook and bake, but we don't want the weather too cold. October is best. That will allow you and Mr. Weldon to be husband and wife before he leaves."

Scott went in search of a nice bottle for a toast (on Sarah's suggestion).

"Sakes alive, Weldon," Simon said with a chuckle. "My father gave in so easily."

Weldon tried to smile.

They listened to Scott cursing in the root cellar over some mess not cleaned up, and Katherine and Simon rushed to settle him.

Weldon stood with his eyes to the ground.

"You're surprised and scared at your luck," Sarah observed.

"Yes, a bit, Mrs. McCullough."

Sarah took Weldon by the arm and led him to the kitchen. They sat by the fire, and Sarah poured tea. "It's not luck, dear. Katherine is a bright and good-hearted person, and she recognizes that you are just the same. You'll see. Love makes its own luck. It gives you the strength to make things happen in life—like tonight."

"I guess."

"And, Mr. Weldon, I'm sure you will try your best, but ... I worry you don't realize the responsibility you are taking on ... financially. Katherine is used to nice things. She doesn't realize what she will miss of the comforts of home when she no longer has them. And, this hurts me to say about my daughter, but Katie has been ill-used by a boy—you understand that you will not be her first."

"I have money saved. I can buy her things." Weldon's chest tightened.

"Mr. Weldon, I know a soldier's salary—remember I have a soldier in the family, and he is forever borrowing from us."

"Well, that's because Simon's wasteful and careless!"

"You see what I mean?" Sarah said, stirring her tea. "To you—coming from, well, less affluent circumstances—to you Simon's needs seem wasteful and foolish. Katherine will be the same."

"No, Simon is truly wasteful!"

"Please don't take this so emotionally. I just want my daughter—and you—to think a little about the realities of this marriage." Sarah handed Weldon a cup. "This is very quick indeed."

"I have thought—" Weldon spilled his tea a little. His eyes wandered around the cluttered kitchen, and for the first time he tried to put a price to everything he saw. The ornate oven, the upholstered wing chairs, so solid and substantial, by the great stone fireplace—how much did they cost? There were china dishes of blue and white drying on their rack and a handsome clock elaborately carved of wood. Even the large table covered with the day's baking no longer looked inviting, but expensive.

Katherine skipped into the room and on closer inspection Weldon noticed the fine fabric of her dress and shoes. For his entire life Weldon had lived in homes or shelters half the size of this kitchen. *He hadn't thought*. Katherine had no idea about army quarters even for officers. Everything—the crystal for the toast, the champagne—was an expense Weldon had never considered.

"I have to go," he announced.

They hadn't even made a toast.

"Weldon?" Simon said. "Are you well? Do you need to lie down?"

"No, I just ... I need to go."

Sarah crossed her arms, shaking her head.

Katherine walked him out. "Mr. Weldon, what's the matter?"

"Nothing."

"Will I see you tomorrow?"

"I don't know ... I have some errands. Maybe not tomorrow." He found himself unable to look at her. His eyes were on the road.

"Mr. Weldon, what's happened? Did my mother say something?"

"Don't depend on me, miss."

Weldon turned and walked back to his bleak hotel room lit by the smallest of gas lamps. Flies buzzed, attracted to the rotting flesh at his side wrapped from even his own view. The doctors told Weldon he was dead. How was he still here? He rummaged through his things. His side pained him; it had not stopped oozing the foul smelling pus. Sprinkling the tiny jar of powder—less than he was used to—over his unwrapped side, he groaned as relief came, a dream when he rubbed it into his wound.

Chapter Six

Breakfast came and went, but for Katherine there was no reason to leave the table.

"Where is Mr. Weldon this morning?" Sarah asked.

"Errands, Mother. He has errands today."

Sarah slapped her daughter's hand. "Stop picking at the food. You'll make yourself sick. Now give me that plate."

"Can't we have one day without rain in it?" Katherine complained.

Sarah came over and pulled on Katherine's hair. "Your hair is our barometer—when it's nice and smooth there will be sun, but with a kink like this I'm afraid there's no hope."

Katherine pinned her hair up in a high bun and tied on her apron.

"Dear, you shouldn't wear your hair up. You look like an old spinster," Sarah said, dumping coffee grinds into the bin for her garden.

Katherine stopped drying the dishes. "Isn't that what you want, Mother?"

"What are you on about now?"

"Mother, did you say anything to Mr. Weldon that may have ..."

"Now you're being foolish. If a man really cares, a mother's concerns won't stop him."

"So you *did* say something!"

"All I told him is that you both need to consider the realities of army life and if you will be able to adjust."

"Of course you made it seem that I wouldn't be able," Katherine cried. "I bet you told him about all that happened with Mickey Jones!"

"How dare you accuse me of bringing up the Undercliff boy?" Sarah shouted. "I would never even pronounce his name! What he did to you should never be spoken of!"

"You blame me, Mother! If it hadn't happened you'd still have Simon hanging off you like a child."

"Simon is different because of you. That I won't deny. He drinks and ... he's lost something in his eyes. I know you were too stupid to take care of yourself back then." Sarah sobbed, running to her daughter and cupping the birdlike face in her hands. "How can I blame you for that? It's how God made you! But, Katie, it's a mother's job to love even the least of her offspring, and I do love you and want what's best."

Katherine tore off her apron and threw it at the peg on the wall of the little oak shelved pantry. It fell to the floor. "I'm going out."

"But today is our sewing circle, dear."

"I've always hated the sewing circle. Go without me!" Katherine changed into her brown plaid day dress, coiled her hair in a low knot, and pinned on her porkpie hat.

Katherine made her way up the hill to her only friend, Margaret Brown.

Margaret opened the door.

"Maggie, will you come to town with me? I need new ribbon for my riding hat, or I might buy a bonnet."

Margaret pursed her lips and crossed her arms for a moment but relented. "Why, Katherine, I've never seen you wear a bonnet a day in your life. Don't you hate them?"

"Well, there's no point in trying to be attractive if I'm going to be an old maid forever."

"Now don't be morbid," Margaret said. "We'll marry you off somehow."

"Yesterday was the happiest day of my life!" Katherine cried.

Margaret ushered her inside. "What's happened?"

"Sergeant Weldon from the dance ... he asked to marry me."

Margaret gasped. "The scrawny one? Land sakes, no. Can he put two sentences together even? Your parents would never let you marry a Catholic anyway—he's Italian, isn't he?"

"No, he's some sort of half-Indian..."

Margaret laughed. "You're not serious. But ... your father said no? It's for the best, Katie. You knew him for, what—one day? You're so childish sometimes."

"Margaret, do you ever realize how unchristian you sound? Simon says Weldon is a good man."

"Simon's a good judge now? Do you know anything about his family? Your mother would have been mortified." Margaret draped a shawl around her shoulders and glanced at herself in the mirror. "Did I tell you I met a man at the dance too? A Doctor Graham Crenshaw. Not stunning but substantial." Margaret put her arm through Katherine's. "Oh, I can tell you don't want to hear a word about him. Well, all I can say as your only true friend is that you should let this soldier write you a few letters from whatever garrison he goes to, until he finds someone more suitable. But that's all. Those Catholics will take your children and turn them into priests and nuns. I heard that they have disgusting orgies—even just between women!"

"You've read too many novels, Maggie, and I told you he's not Catholic."

"I've read *The Last of the Mohicans* too. Your father was right to say no."

"But he didn't say no!" Katherine cried. "My mother told Mr. Weldon everything about me, and now he doesn't want me any longer."

"Oh, Katie, please don't cry. I didn't trust him a bit—something dark about him. Even with the rape you're better than he is. Oh, I shouldn't have said that, but it's true." Margaret wiped Katherine's tears. "You never seemed in a hurry to marry," she said, pushing Katherine to the door. "You have the right idea. Let's go shop for a nice, beautiful hat—no bonnets, young lady. You're not to give up!" She took Katherine's hand and marched her into town.

The newest and brightest storefront beckoned just off Palisades Avenue, Millie's Millinery. The two young ladies poked their heads in and their skirts followed.

"Good day, girls. What dreary weather we're having of late," said Millie, a fortyish lady just out of mourning for her husband who died of dysentery in the camps during the war. Millie's creations dripped with ribbons and birds and feathers and veils in riots of breathtaking color.

"My friend here is suffering from a broken heart, and we want something festive to cheer her," Margaret announced, suddenly overcome by the beauty of a yellow flower-bedecked bonnet with polka-dot ribbons. She tried it on. Katherine cringed.

"Oh, another broken heart? Not gotten at the dance too? A mouse of a girl was in on Monday upset over a young man back from the war who didn't pay her as much attention as she had hoped. The boy sounded a real rascal."

Margaret exchanged a knowing glance with Katherine.

Millie came over to Katherine and sat a small brown delicacy upon her head at an angle. "But broken hearts mend, they say, and it's true. I'm happier than I've ever been now although I went through a time after Sam. But he'd be happy to see me doing what I love and have always dreamed about."

Katherine found it depressing that a poor soldier in his grave could be so easily replaced by a store full of straw and ribbon but said nothing. Katherine took the brown hat. Millie wrapped it while Margaret complained it was too plain.

They lifted their skirts over the soggy but passable road to cross to the other side of Van Brunt and walked past the druggist's store. Katherine glanced inside through the large window. "Maggie!" she pulled her friend back. "He's in there! John Weldon!"

"So?" Margaret replied. "Let's go! Let him stay in the past ... come on now!" But she couldn't move Katherine fast enough, and Weldon soon joined them on the street, holding a small paper bag.

"Why, Miss McCullough!" Weldon tried to sound pleased.

"Mr. Weldon, are you sick? What's in the bag? Whiskey?" Margaret asked.

Weldon shoved the bag in his pocket.

Margaret rolled her eyes. "Katherine, let's go—I'm expecting a visitor this afternoon."

"Go ahead, Margaret. I'll catch up," Katherine said, gazing at Weldon.

Margaret protested.

Katherine gave her a vicious look. Margaret huffed, turned, and with long, hard strides that rattled the wooden planks beneath them, stormed up toward home. Weldon kept his eyes up the road long after Margaret had turned off it.

Katherine touched his arm with her index finger. "Mr. Weldon, are you sick?" she asked. "Maybe I can help you."

"Would you come for a walk with me, Miss McCullough?"

Weldon dragged Katherine up through the rough terrain of a still-undeveloped tract of the Palisades hill, her skirt catching on the thick undergrowth.

As the land leveled off, Katherine clutched her chest and pulled him to stop. She sat on an old stump trying to fasten her hair back up into a bun.

Weldon came over and took her hair in his hands. "I wish I could always see it like this."

Katherine giggled like a gullible child. This annoyed him.

He backed away and leaned against an oak with names carved all around it. "Miss, I've done an idiotic thing saying I'd m-marry you. I'd be a misery."

"Misery?" Katherine ran up and pulled him from the tree. "Stand up straight and talk to me. Did my mother tell you awful things?"

"No, no, Miss McCullough. I just see what you have here in Englewood. I can never give you anything like it."

"Mr. Weldon, you don't see a thing. You don't see how miserable and joyless my life is here. My parents hate me."

"No one could hate you ..." Weldon began. "What's in the box?"

Katherine sighed. "Yes, it's an expensive, ridiculous hat. For the rest of my life I can have tons of hats—but I would rather have you."

"You don't even know me, miss. This is no light thing for me. I want to do things right," he said, "but I'm a mess."

"Then we'll clean you up, sir. My heart is pounding this very minute for you. I can't sleep since the dance. Not a wink!" Katherine laughed, all nerves. "Besides, I *do* know you. You're the man that Simon picked for me, and he's always right about things."

Weldon would really stop. He'd stop for good. Pulling her behind the oak, he kissed her.

She wrapped her arms around him gently, mindful of his unspoken wound. He smelled of cigars and pine soap. He was warm, and as his hand touched her hair it sent a wave of sudden excitement through her and she pulled away.

"Miss, I'm sorry. I didn't mean to ..."

"No, what must you think of me?" Katherine smoothed her hair.

Weldon touched her thin face. "I think ... I think I'll be the luckiest man one day if you marry me. I want to do it soon before I mess it up."

The train whistle blew.

"Merciful heavens! My father! I'm to walk home with him!"

"Shall I fetch you a ride?" Weldon asked.

"No, I'll just run along," she said but lingered. "You'll come by tomorrow then?"

Weldon smiled but said nothing, surprised at the turn of the day. Katherine gave him a quick, light kiss on the cheek and skipped off. Weldon stood in the woods until all sight of Katherine vanished. He pulled the druggist's bottle from his pocket and threw it over the cliffs, then treated himself to a nice meal and went to bed a happy man.

Chapter Seven

From the kitchen window, Simon watched Katherine in the yard pounding the parlor rug. He noted the way her eyes flitted toward any sound that might herald Weldon's arrival and the way her shoulders slumped with each disappointment. It had been three days since anyone had seen Weldon, and Simon worried. When the mail arrived with a note from Washington, Simon slipped out the front door and headed for the hotel.

"Weldon, are you in there? It's me, Simon. I'm concerned about you." Simon turned the unlocked knob. "What on earth? It smells like death in here!"

"You've come," Weldon said from bed. "Lieutenant, don't let them bury me. I'm shot, sir."

"You're sick, Weldon. I'm captain now, remember? I received a disturbing letter from Washington today. Hazelton says you left the hospital prematurely." Simon tossed the letter onto Weldon's chest.

Weldon went cold and sat up. His hands fumbled over the paper. A Private Hazelton? He read further, but his head ached. His side stabbed him.

"Why would you put your life in jeopardy to come to Englewood?" Simon asked. "You seemed fine when you first arrived. I don't understand."

"I'm all right. It's just my side. It comes and goes. It's pretty bad this week, but I didn't think ..."

"Didn't think we'd worry?" Simon asked as he uncharacteristically picked up clothes from the floor. "You're going to be a part of the family soon. You can't keep secrets from us, especially not from Katie."

"Don't tell her, sir."

"Why not? There's no shame in it."

"No, I need to take care of this myself ..." Weldon began.

"What are you, a wild animal that goes off to lick its wounds in a thicket somewhere?" Simon interrupted. "Sakes alive, this place is a terrible mess. Your winter quarters were always in perfect order ..."

"I'll be better with some rest."

"Did you come here to make me feel bad?" Simon asked, tossing socks on to the pile of dirty laundry. "I did everything I could. I found you, remember? And brought you to the surgeon ... you would have died."

"Simon, you killed me," Weldon said. "I'm not the same anymore ... don't tell her. Your sister is my only hope ... I can't stop on my own."

"What are you on about?" Simon felt the sergeant's head. "My God! You're on fire!"

"I came to you, Lieutenant McCullough ..." Weldon mumbled.

"It's captain, remember?"

"To ask for help ..."

"I'm no doctor, Weldon. It was a stupid thing to do."

"But don't tell the girl."

Simon pulled the blanket before Weldon could prevent him and found the source of the sickening odor. The pus had saturated his flannel shirt and the bandage beneath it. Simon pulled away the layers to find the wound red and full.

Weldon tried to explain. "I didn't get the chance to dress it this morning is all."

"Holy Christ, we need a doctor for this!" Simon said.

"No! You left me to the doctors before," Weldon snapped.

"Don't be a fool!" Simon looked around for clean water. "There won't be a wedding if you're dead, and now Katie's set on it."

"I can't marry her with this ache, Simon. You don't understand ... it won't go no matter how I try to give it up. It keeps coming ..."

"If I know my sister she'll want to care for you, but first we need a doctor," Simon said. He ran out into the hallway but swayed at the top of the stairs, his stomach in knots.

"Sir, are you all right?" a man said as he passed.

Simon ran his hands over his face. "Yes, really, I'm fine. Just a bit dizzy for a second." He raced down the steps of the hotel and into the lobby. In the lounge he spotted a familiar face. "Crenshaw, Doctor Crenshaw is that you?" he asked the army surgeon from the dance. Crenshaw stood up and stepped forward to greet him. He had soft full features, a florid face, and the look of someone constantly taking mental notes. "Good to see you again, Captain McCullough."

"What luck to find you staying here ..."

"Well, I'm not really. I'm meeting an old acquaintance from the city who's thinking of buying a place here. We worked at the Central Park Hospital after ..."

"I'm glad you're here. You see, it's my friend Weldon. John Weldon. You remember the sergeant from the other night?" Simon said, rushing him to the stairs. "He's in an awful way. A war wound—it's inflamed. He's hidden it and shouldn't have left the hospital. I'm to blame. He won't tell my sister, and they're to be married soon if he doesn't die!"

"I'm afraid I'm no longer practicing," Crenshaw said, turning back toward the lounge. "I can't be of any help."

"But you must come!" Simon raised his voice. "You will not shirk your duty! I won't allow it!"

Guests murmured and raised eyebrows at the two.

The doctor relented uneasily.

They found Weldon in a fitful sleep. The doctor examined the wound with little enthusiasm and washed it. "These bandages should be changed regularly," Crenshaw said in annoyance.

"I know. It's all very strange," Simon said. "He's usually so fastidious about things ..."

The doctor put pressure on the raised skin, awakening his patient. He took a small knife from his jacket and cut at the abscess letting the pus drain more freely, mopping it up with a shirt from off the floor. Pressing until the skin flattened, he cleansed the wound again and sent Simon for clean bandages.

Crenshaw spoke softly. "Have you been medicating yourself, Sergeant Weldon?"

Weldon stared at him.

"Your friend told me about the letter he received. Before I quit medicine ... I worried that some of our long-term patients were having trouble giving up the laudanum and morphine they'd grown accustomed to."

"No. I ... sometimes ... take something for the pain in my side. What are you accusing me of?"

"Nothing, I'm wondering how you manage to get around and hide this—this horrible wound. There's nothing wrong with wanting relief from pain. It's just that if you're having trouble with it ..."

"I have no trouble but my side and nosy people conspiring against me. It's because of the likes of you that ... Who are you anyway, and where's the lieutenant?"

"You mean the captain? Don't you remember he left to get fresh bandages?"

"Yes, yes, of course," Weldon grumbled, frightened at his lapse in memory. Had he given anything away to Simon?

The doctor mopped his forehead and fumbled with a pocket watch.

"Antique?" Weldon asked.

"Excuse me?" Crenshaw turned back toward him. His straight hair fell over his left eye and he brushed it back. "Oh, the watch. Just sentimental."

"I saw a lot of them during the war," Weldon said. "Bet you had your pick in the field hospitals."

The doctor's face reddened. "How dare you insinuate I would steal from the dead and dying! This watch belonged to my brother who died at Gettysburg. I found him too late."

"You people are always too late."

The door opened, and Simon slipped in.

"Simon?"

"Yes, Weldon, don't worry. You'll soon be as good as new."

The doctor gave Simon a look and pulled him into the hallway. "Your friend needs complete rest. No stimulation whatsoever or he won't recover. There's been some sloughing of the tissue and an excessive amount of pus."

"But it's laudable pus, right? The good kind?"

"No, I'm afraid," Crenshaw said, with a strange mix of nerves and resentment, "but I did drain it and that may help. If the fever breaks he may be out of the woods, but I'm not confident. He has been far too active and has excited his body too much. He needs a hospital."

"Oh, he won't go ... it's impossible. But he seemed fine, I don't understand."

"I would send for your sister ... just in case."

"Will he die?"

"Nothing's certain in life, is it?"

"That's not comforting from a doctor," Simon said.

"I told you, I'm no doctor." Crenshaw turned away, wiping his hands. "And you shouldn't have asked me to come."

Simon sent for Katherine and Sarah came too, huffing and puffing behind her daughter who tore up to Weldon's room. Simon greeted them with the same grey face he had come home with after the war. "I'm sorry, Katie ..."

Katherine ran to the edge of the sergeant's bed. "Mr. Weldon, how could you?" she cried and took his hand in hers. "Why didn't you tell me?"

Sarah came to the bed too. "Mr. Weldon, we're taking you home."

"No, I won't go."

"You have no choice, young man. What kind of people would we be to let you suffer here on your own? Besides, you boys are babies who wouldn't know the first thing about taking care of yourselves. We need a healthy groom. The invitations have been sent." Sarah gave Simon a worried glance.

Katherine embraced Weldon with a tender kiss. She played with the damp curls at his neck. This man she hardly knew would one day take her away from here, and she would take care of him. "Don't you dare leave me, Mr. Weldon. Promise me," Katherine whispered.

Chapter Eight

Scott demanded an explanation that evening. "Why was I not met at the station? It was lashing rain yet no one cares!"

Katherine brought her father a cup of hot tea at the fireplace where he warmed away the chill. "I'll die of the influenza or tuberculosis and no one will even notice!"

Simon stood by sullenly smoking and gazing into the flames. Scott watched his daughter add honey to his cup drip by drip. "Katherine where's your mother?" A sudden look of panic swept over him. "Has your mother been hurt?! She wasn't climbing to clean the gutters? I told her to wait!"

The heavy step of Sarah on the stairs relieved him of worry. Sarah burst in, happy to be of service. "Oh, Scott, what a day ... why, you're all wet! Where's your umbrella?" She kissed him in a hurry. During the war Sarah had wanted to travel with the troops as a nurse, but there was Katherine still at home and her committee work, and Scott wouldn't allow it. "I'm sure the children have told to you ..."

"Told me what, for God's sake? They've been dumb as donkeys!"

"Now Scott, watch your language. It's Mr. Weldon ..."

"Is he gone?" Scott asked hopefully.

"Don't be silly. Where would he go in his state? Mr. Weldon has no family. You know that. He's here with us now. I knew you wouldn't mind." She kissed him again.

Scott turned to Simon and then Katherine. "Children, please explain what this madwoman is on about before I explode!"

Simon flicked his cigar into the fire. "Weldon is pretty bad. He could die."

Katherine cried and collapsed into her chair at the kitchen table.

Sarah wrapped a throw around Scott as she spoke, only mildly soothing him. "Simon, no one is going to die in this house. I'll see to that! The poor thing kept his suffering a secret, but Simon found Mr. Weldon out, and I'm determined to have him well before the wedding."

Scott huffed. "So now Katherine will marry an invalid! I see the whole picture clearly. The sergeant is too used up to stay in the military and wants a clean, warm place to live out his days!" Scott got up like a man on fire. "By thunder, I won't have it! We'll make him well to spite him—the lazy son-of-a ..."

"Scott!"

He took a swig of his tea and grimaced—it had gone cold. Scott splashed it into the fire nearly putting out the flames. "Sarah, I don't want the girl playing nurse to this soldier—it's scandalous. I put you in charge."

Sarah smiled.

"I've read recently—and you all laugh at my medical journals—of some such spray—an experiment by a man called Lister—that relieves external inflammation. I must go and see." He went off to his library.

In the meantime Katherine was allowed to bring the patient something to eat—a plain vanilla custard and beef tea on a tray.

"No touching the bandages, dear. I have them just so," Sarah called after her.

Weldon rested in Simon's bed. Simon would sleep on the smaller guest bed next to him. When Katherine pushed open the door, Weldon sat up in obvious discomfort. "Honestly miss, I shouldn't be here ..."

Katherine put the tray down and sat beside him. "You're wrong, sir."

"I don't feel myself."

"It's the fever, but my father insists that you get well and you will."

"The nurses—they tried but I never could ..."

Katherine patted his hand in an awkward, matronly way. "Sir, how was it that you got hurt?"

"Simon never told?" Weldon rolled his eyes.

Katherine shook her head. "Are you angry with me for asking?"

"No, miss. Well, my leg caught it—only a round ball, but then my side ... and a surgeon on the field gave me ... oh, people tire of war stories. I just want to be happy."

Katherine remembered the custard and spooned some out, but Weldon grumbled. "I can feed myself, miss."

"You have no right to be snippy with me, sir. I should be angry at you for leaving the hospital too soon."

Katherine took the rag by the side of the bed, upsetting the tray.

"By gosh, I'm sorry!" she cried as Simon walked in.

"Captain, your sister tires me out," Weldon said, flashing Katherine a grin.

"Katherine, the doctor said Weldon needed complete rest. Why aren't you more careful? You really are goddamned clumsy!" Simon picked up the bowl. "And look, the bandages are covered in custard!"

Katherine looked stricken. "It was an accident ..."

"I know," Simon said. "Nothing is ever your fault! Really, Katie, maybe you should go find something useful to do!"

She fled the room.

"Sir, you were too hard on her."

"Hey, Weldon, she's not your wife yet, and she may never be if you don't recover."

Simon grumbled while digging for a cigar. Weldon smiled at his resemblance to his father.

"What are you grinning about, Weldon? You know for somebody on the brink of death you're incredibly good humored."

"Give me a smoke will you, Lieutenant—I mean Captain."

Simon thought about it. "Oh, what the hell."

Weldon eased back on to his pillow. "Can you guess how many times I've had the last rites said over me this past year? I had to tell them to quit it. It was embarrassing to open my eyes every day and have the m-man go on again. They've been telling me I'm gonna die since the hospital in Fredericksburg—no even before that. But you know what? I feel better than ever right now. I don't care what happens. I'm glad I'm here with you and your family. It's much easier to imagine dying that way."

"Stop this morbid nonsense. You won't be let die if my father has anything to say about it."

John laughed, but looked peaked.

"Father's angry enough thinking you'll ruin his daughter's wedding. Besides, he's superstitious about living where someone's died. That's why we moved here after my older sisters passed. Maybe we can move you to the barn. He thinks that you and Katie have already upset the place with your sparking."

Weldon smiled at the thought. "It was worth all of your father's anger."

Sarah hung by the door for a moment then pushed on through. "It's obvious my children are overstimulating the patient. Now, Simon, pull the curtains shut, but open the windows—it's too stuffy with those cigars. I told you not to smoke in your room."

"But the sergeant wanted to, Mother," Simon said with a grin.

"What on earth happened to this dressing? Never mind. I've never met a neat man in my life," Sarah went on. "Simon, your father wants the surrey taken out so he can go visit the homeopath."

The banister creaked under Simon's weight as he slid down it and jumped the final few steps like he'd always done.

Sarah shook her head. "I bet you never behaved like that for your mother," she said lightly, but noticed his eyes change. "I'm sorry, Mr. Weldon. That was unthinking. May I ask how old you were when she died?"

"Fifteen."

"Was she sick for a long time?"

"S-She was always drunk ... that's how I found her. She'd taken turpentine." Weldon watched to see her reaction, but she fixed her attention on the bandage. "You won't tell Miss Katherine, will you, Mrs. McCullough?"

Sarah patted Weldon's hand. "It's your place to tell her things like that not mine. No one's family is perfect. Let no one convince you otherwise. You'll see, now that you're part of ours."

"You all seem near perfect to me," he said.

Sarah laughed. "You need rest, young man. Everything will be all right now."

He believed it, and for a while it was true.

Chapter Nine

And now Weldon was back at the morphine. A few weeks spent in riches had not cured the ache, though his side was on the mend. Milky white sheets and full feather pillows did not lull his thoughts to rest. He tried and pretended. He smiled and fattened up on food made more lovingly than anything he had known in his life. The subtle scent of cleanliness floated into his life—a temporary dream—yet all he could think of was getting back to his shabby existence at the hotel. Only Scott had been happy to see him leave the house on Tenafly Road. How had he been so stupid? Now Weldon knew the torture of stopping. He tried to control it, dilute it, and find substitutes, but nothing satisfied enough to keep him from suffering.

How could Katherine and this ache come on so strong at the same time? Weldon noticed Katherine worrying on his cleanest days, when he stammered and sweated. Every day teetered between telling her about the morphine and giving in to it, but still he hoped tomorrow he would stop—and tomorrow and tomorrow....

Days began the same with the ache and the talk; talk so tedious, so maddening: "I'm a morphine eater. I'll try to give it up today, but I'll fail. This is it ... one last time. I'll throw it away after this, but somewhere safe where no one will see. I'll save it till I leave, but I won't use it. Just a few more days ... when it runs out, then I'll stop. It's not that bad ... I should just tell her ... but other people, stronger people just stop. I can manage this. It's only a little each day anyway. It helps me ... I need it. I'll just enjoy it this one last day. My wedding day."

Weldon slicked his hair and nicked his chin shaving before settling on the bed with his medicine. For only brief periods now it made him better. It made him so well that a wedding waiting at the tiny chapel in town across from the ravine held no interest for him. But this was a temporary sway. A few minutes in and Weldon heard the bell—the heart-stirring nobility of a church bell in a sunny small town where life was in order and someone cared for him.

The familiar take-two-steps-at-a-time racket of Simon coming to greet him filled Weldon with a mix of dread and gratitude as he tucked his small new syringe kit in his breast pocket.

Simon burst in. "Land sakes, you look a caution, and only twenty minutes to post time."

"I-I ..."

"Of course you're nervous as a cock in a bag so I've brought spirits ..."

"S-sir, you know I n-never drink, I ..."

"Yes, I know, but you don't mind if I take the edge off do you?" Simon said, pouring his flask full of Scotch from a stolen bottle of his father's best. "Weldon, is everything all right?"

"No, I should have told you ... about what happened at the Wilderness ... after ...it's why I came up here."

"Oh, now's not the time. Katherine's waiting. The war's over."

"Not for me."

"Maybe we can have a stirring talk but not today. I won't be a part of ruining Katie's big time. Let her have one day, for God's sake, Weldon, and stop being so damned selfish."

The bell rang again.

"Captain, I'm sorry. I'm not right for her ... I ..."

"What the hell are you saying?" Simon rolled his eyes. He sighed and finished his drink, looking in the mirror at the pale mustache he was trying, and failing, to grow.

Weldon bristled with resentment. "*Captain*, thank you. I know you'd hoped for better for Katherine, but ..."

"Jesus Christ, do you ever give up?" Simon said. "You know as well as I do that I had reason to believe you might never want to see me again. I never thought of you for Katherine because you never expressed an interest. That's all."

"Your father would have preferred a man from town. I appreciate that you've done nothing to interfere or make things awkward between us because you are ... really my only ... friend." Weldon's words never matched his feelings. "And I'd hate to end our friendship even after what happened ... I guess ... it's in the past anyway." Why was he letting Simon off the hook? But now it wasn't just Simon. It was Katherine and Simon. Katherine would make things right and even things out. "I *will* work hard to prove myself, sir."

"Weldon, you're like a brother to me. I worry for Katie only because she's so inexperienced in everything, but you don't need to prove anything. Forget about my father. He's a fool, but he'll come around."

"Simon, you are a good friend ... I ..."

"Now don't get all soft on me, Weldon. You'll send me into panic."

"Here." Weldon pulled an ostentatious emerald ring from his pocket. "Will Katherine like it?"

Simon had no heart to tell Weldon otherwise. He remembered the ring from their foraging days in the army taken from the home of a woman who had more money than taste. "We'd better make a run for it—it's nearly ten thirty."

Simon stole nips from his flask, and Weldon chewed his cigar nervously as they took the short walk down Palisades Avenue to the chapel. Weldon spotted Scott's surrey hitched to his fine Morgan, Polly, at the side of the chapel and felt green for a moment, hesitating before the side entrance. Simon laughed. "There's still time to call the whole thing off and make my father a happy man."

"No." The groom took a deep breath. "I wouldn't want that. Let's go."

Reverend Booth greeted the pair as they entered the dimly lit, stone edifice. The place smelled of flowers and newly cured wood. It took a moment for their eyes to adjust. In the shadows stood Scott. The morning sun filtered in through the arch-shaped, frosted windows trimmed in pastel stained glass. Guests Weldon didn't recognize murmured in their pews as he glimpsed around the wood-paneled divider that separated the clergy from the congregation.

Scott came forward stiffly, shaking Weldon's hand and Simon's too. Simon swayed a little.

The organist played fugues incessantly, adding to the nervous agitation of the men. The side door entrance opened again. Sarah pulled her skirts in, looking rosy-cheeked and excited in her navy gown and matching bonnet. Sarah was still an attractive woman when she made the effort.

"Scott, come bring in your daughter!" Sarah turned to Weldon, squeezing his arm. "Mr. Weldon, Katherine looks lovely, and you're so handsome today! Good luck!"

Weldon laughed, grateful for Katherine's lively mother. She backed out dragging her husband behind her.

"For God's sake, Sarah, hold on—I'll meet you out front," Scott said, slightly slurring his words.

Sarah turned to Simon for reassurance. Simon nodded her on.

"Of course, Weldon has to wear his lowly sergeant outfit in front of the whole town," Scott grumbled as he pulled something from his vest pocket, and before Simon could interfere Scott handed Weldon a ring—it looked as old as the ring Weldon had shown him earlier, but it gleamed with garnet and diamonds.

"No, sir ..." Weldon began.

"Father, Weldon has a ring already picked and engraved," Simon added.

"Well, this ring has been passed down through my family ..."

"I've never seen it before," Simon said.

Scott shoved Simon aside. "I thought you might want to give my daughter something of value—sentimental value—I mean to say. You may take it and decide," he said gruffly and slipped out the door.

Weldon rolled the sparkling piece of jewelry in the palm of his hand.

"Father meant to be helpful," Simon said. "I assure you, although the timing is questionable, he meant to give you something of value to him. It's a peace offering. I assure you. Weldon, Katie will want your ring. Put this one away."

"I won't deprive Katherine of a family keepsake." John looked dangerous for a moment. "But I'll give her *my* ring today."

Simon breathed a sigh of relief as the music changed and the reverend summoned the two. Weldon hesitated, but Simon shoved him forward.

Mrs. McCullough and Reverend Booth had seated those in attendance on both sides of the chapel so as not to highlight John Weldon's lack of friends and family. Most of the McCullough relations lived in Philadelphia and Brooklyn, and Sarah's people were from Albany so the pews were filled with town people associated with the various civic institutions Sarah and Scott spent their time and money on.

Margaret stood as Katherine's maid of honor. After an early peace settlement when Sarah asserted her control over her daughter's wedding, Margaret and Sarah had become inseparable, both happiest when planning other people's lives. Katherine was shut out and overpowered by the two whirlwinds, but realized that although she didn't like some of their ideas she had more time to spend with John. Katherine stood in front of the chapel beside her new little carriage bedecked with dried hydrangeas and ribbons. Margaret adjusted Katherine's orange blossom headpiece with serious intent. Katherine wished that she could sleep through the ceremony and wake up married. Girls waved from across the street admiring Katherine's heavy dress. Her parents joined them, Scott looking gallant and sobered up from a miserable drinking binge the night before. He pulled a bracelet from his pocket now.

Sarah moaned. "Oh, now, Scott, where on earth did you get that little piece of extravagance? I know you too well. This is just so you don't give a proper gift to the couple."

Scott waved Sarah off and slipped the bracelet on his daughter's wrist. "Katherine, this is expensive. Don't lose it. You might need it someday."

Katherine understood the insult and could not thank him or look at him. Her father took her by the chin. "Katie, forgive me. My only wish is for your happiness." Scott wiped his eyes. "I will miss you terribly when he takes you from us."

Katherine melted. "Father, if you want me to be happy then accept that I love John."

"Yes, Mother reminds me it is only important that *you* love him," Scott said, glancing at Sarah who scolded him with her eyes. "What I mean is that we support your decision."

Katherine knew her father lied, but that it took a lot for him to do it. "Oh, Father, I love you!" She threw herself at him as she had always done and hugged him.

Sarah pulled Katherine from Scott. "Oh, now that elegant braid we worked on all morning is come undone. I don't know what to do with you."

Margaret called to them, and Scott moved toward the door of the chapel.

Hanging back, Katherine cried.

"Poor child," Sarah soothed, smoothing stray wisps of hair from her daughter's face, "are you afraid?"

Katherine could only shake her head before sobbing again.

"Oh, I do feel sorry for you. How unprepared you are! But this is supposed to be a happy day. Aren't you happy?"

"Mother, I'm so sorry I disappoint you!"

"You are no disappointment to me!"

Katherine grabbed Sarah's hands. "But Father ... he thinks I'm making a terrible mistake. He makes me afraid that he's right."

"Your father is being a bear, but you've stayed a little girl to us for so long and then suddenly you're married to a man we hardly know. It's unusual."

"But Mother, please tell me you do like him," Katherine begged.

"Yes, dear, I like the way he looks at you when you speak to him. He adores you. He can't believe his luck. Your father worries because Mr. Weldon is such a different sort of man to him. Father is settled." Sarah glanced at the chapel door. She pulled Katherine close and straightened her dress. "Now I want you to tell me the truth and I will be satisfied. Are you truly happy with this man?"

"Mother, you don't know. He's the world to me. I can't bear the thought of not having him."

"It's not because he is the first man to really love you ..."

"I have met other men, but they weren't John. I don't care if he's just a soldier or that he's quiet around Father. He thinks I'm—someone special. And he makes me laugh, and he loves me even though I'm not perfect."

Sarah hugged Katherine. "I know you're right, but I will always worry over my children. When you're a mother you'll see. John will make a fine husband for you. And you will be a wonderful wife and mother. I am proud of you, my little shadow!"

Simon walked up. "Katherine, I forgot to mention how beautiful you look today. When will you ever come inside? Weldon is shaking in his boots."

Katherine sniffled and kissed him.

"You know I want you to be happy with Weldon," Simon continued, "and that I'll help you however I can. Don't you?"

"Yes, Simon, I know it."

Chapter Ten

John Weldon stood in the presence of God after a long absence. The only thing his father had left for him was the Bible, but the Christian principles and faith he had climbed out of childhood with he spurned after the jostling ambulance unceremoniously dumped him addicted and neglected at the foot of the billowing tent hospital in Washington.

Weldon kept living, much to the annoyance of the doctors. They talked about keeping him comfortable, but where was the comfort in being treated as if you were a waste of bed space, already dead but still living? That nurse, the one who kept him out of the dying ward, had come too late. Weldon was too comfortable with the new syringe and the powders and the liquids.

All the stories his father had given him, all the faith and the prayers and the temptations avoided, had been for nothing. Weldon wished for one thing—one small dose to get him through the rough spots of his wedding day. Weldon's hunger bristled through every nerve. The smiling strangers accentuated how naive he had once been to place any hope in a great and benevolent higher power.

Sometimes Weldon thought because he had killed people, and at times in the heat of battle almost enjoyed it, God had seen fit to punish him. But Weldon did no more harm than the rest of his chums, like Simon, and they got on with their lives all right. Weldon hated the people sitting uncomfortably on their shiny wooden pews. The hard, straight benches pressed against their well-fed bodies were as uncomfortable as their long lives would get. Like Katherine's father, they had probably discussed and organized for abolition, never once risking their sainthoods in battle. In his youth he imagined he could win respect from the likes of these pillars of respectability, but he could not even respect himself now. Scott McCullough suspected what John Weldon knew—he was a liar and a fake.

But Katherine saw something in him that Weldon wanted to believe for himself. He was certain she had come along too late, but ... Weldon hoped that just this once he was wrong. It would have been more convenient to remain alone, but Katherine's gaze and her confidence in his strength gave him the willpower on some days to avoid the morphine. Katherine hung on his words; his opinions mattered to her. It was a brave thing for him to love her, to think this small, inexperienced girl would accept him. Weldon vowed to go through any penance, whatever suffering, to keep Katherine.

And now Katherine entered the church. The creamy outline of her dress peeked out just behind Margaret dressed in violet. The maid of honor's smile dazzled as

Margaret made her way up the aisle like she owned it, only briefly allowing the guests a look at the bride. John felt for Katherine. He understood her aversion to being the center of attention. Weldon's hunger faded as he caught sight of his girl and laughed with Simon when Margaret tripped. Katherine glided as best she could, with no hint of a smile on her serious face. When John met Katherine's eyes the congregation knew it—they both relaxed and grinned.

Katherine touched Weldon's fine dress uniform and whispered, "My father wasn't a brute, was he?"

Weldon lied, shaking his head. For the brief hour in the diminutive chapel all fear and self-doubt left him.

Reverend Booth addressed the congregation:

"On this mild and golden November morning we gather to celebrate the joining together in holy matrimony of Katherine Frances McCullough and John William Weldon. We have before us two young people full of hope and health. John, a hero of our recent war against the evils of slavery, will embark today on a life journey with skirmishes all its own. We are certain though that the same almighty hand that carried you off the battlefield unscathed will give you the courage and guidance to love and protect your wife and family.

"Miss Katherine McCullough, you have been a member of our congregation long before we had a chapel to celebrate in. How fitting to see you, always such a kind girl, marry here in this place before God and the people who have seen you grow into a woman ready for marriage. Your innocence will soon fade, and you will have your share of struggles, but it is God's hope and ours that you will be the strong, supportive, and kind helpmate that your husband will need."

There seemed to be a question in his delivery, and Katherine sought to answer it. "I don't mind about the struggles, Reverend. I will be supportive and kind and ..."

Weldon reached over with a smile. "Katherine ..."

The congregation and even Scott smiled and giggled at her unrehearsed speech. Katherine glanced back, mortified. Simon came to her side and whispered, "Katie, don't worry—that was nice." He kissed her cheek and went back to his place as the women sighed at his gallantry.

The wedding kiss that sealed John Weldon's fate came and went in a blur of nerves and cautious happiness. Katherine seemed as eager as he was to leave behind the judging eyes of the wedding attendees as they strode down the aisle and out into the churchyard.

Weldon helped Katherine into their buggy—a smart new runabout painted Union blue with the smallest bit of red trim. Katherine's parents lingered on the lawn with the guests. They did not crowd her as they usually did, and Katherine wondered if she'd ever miss their smothering love. She *would* miss Simon when he and Weldon left for the army, but here was Simon now. "Weldon, is she being kind and supportive enough—after all she did say ..."

"Simon, leave my girl alone," Weldon warned him with a grin.

Simon brushed his fingernails against the front of his jacket. "As best man it's my duty to see you well taken care of by your helpmate," he said with a wink before running off to help one of the elderly guests into his carriage. Everybody waved and cheered as Weldon snapped the reigns moving Hope, Scott's sturdy Morgan, out into the street.

"Will we take a detour, John?" Katherine suggested. They rode out toward the cliffs and past the ornate new homes eating up the hillside. Farther north, along Engle Street, the land spread out before them. The old orchards clung to their few flecks of color still. The autumn had been mild, but in the stray gusts here and there the wind hinted at the change of seasons.

Weldon noticed Katherine eyeing her ring.

"Do you like it much?" he asked tentatively.

"I love it. Did you choose it or did my mother?"

"No, I'm afraid I did it myself."

"Then I love it even more!" Katherine proclaimed as she leaned her head against his shoulder and then on second thought kissed him. Weldon grinned and squeezed her. He slowed Hope along a quiet stretch of farmland half bedded down for the winter.

The frosty cobalt sky stretched behind a large and boisterous flock of geese, late journeymen, flying overhead. In the distance, a stooped old farmer walked the lay of his land.

"I'd like that someday," Weldon said.

"A farm?" Katherine asked, a little surprised.

"Yes, well, something peaceful like that." Weldon turned to her. "We could have our own things. The two of us. And I'd buy you a horse—a fast one."

"You don't have to buy me things, John Weldon. I'd live anywhere..." Katherine assured him.

"Katherine, I promise you, as soon as possible I will send for you."

"Please, let's not talk about that today. These months have been a dream for me and I fear the sleepless nights when you're gone."

Weldon smiled at her theatrical language. "You'll be missed if we don't return soon," he said, snapping the reins more reluctantly now, knowing the best part of the day was over.

Chapter Eleven

"Here they are now!" someone from the garden party shouted. Bay and sorrel horses stretched their necks and feasted on hay from the barn. Well-shined carriages littered the drive, and complacent men with gold watch fobs draping over their prosperous midriffs sat and stood on the porch, drinking Scotch and puffing Scott's good cigars.

A patchwork of elegance and sophistication appeared around back in the fall garden. Women wore their garden hats and lace shawls hung at their elbows. Some made small vain attempts at helping Sarah, but even on this special day, with so much to do, Sarah declined the use of servants. Her guests enjoyed her peculiarities and wondered at her energy. Except for washing clothes and windows, she did all housework herself (sometimes with the reluctant help of her daughter). "I believe in keeping busy (what's that saying about the devil?)," she joked as she dashed off to refill pitchers of tea and lemonade and her famous strawberry shrub. Guests must entertain themselves at the McCullough home. Sarah only allowed herself to relax in other people's homes.

She greeted the newlyweds first. "Did you ride out into the country? Good. Some time to yourselves—but now you must make haste and join the party." Sarah helped Katherine down before Weldon could, dragging her toward the female guests in the backyard.

Weldon plodded to the porch of men oblivious to his arrival. Scott caught Weldon's eye and finished what he was saying about a bracelet that cost him as much as a sturdy house would. Simon appeared from nowhere, saving Weldon from ambush. "Congratulations, Weldon!" Simon said, his shirt untucked and his hair tousled.

Weldon envied Simon his ability to disregard the opinions of others. Drunk or sober Simon drew Weldon close. They sat on the kitchen porch, smoking and laughing, Simon with his bottle hidden behind a pot of rosemary. Sarah came with Weldon's sweet coffee. "I'm so proud of my two boys today," she mused, her cheeks flushed with wine and work.

Simon took a long slug from his bottle as if daring his mother to say something. She did not.

"Come join the girls for food," Sarah said and took them both by the arm to be fussed over. Weldon smiled, accepting congratulations, but kept his eye on Katherine, and as soon as Simon won the spotlight he went to her and gave her a kiss. "You look like a dress-up doll in that outfit."

Katherine made room for him on the bench beside her, but Margaret walked over, and Simon signaled Weldon to the food. Margaret shook her head after him. "Mr. Weldon is not one for sparkling conversation, but—oh well, everybody's different. Walk with me around the yard. You look a caution just sitting here moping on your wedding day."

"I wasn't moping, Margaret. I was relaxing!" Katherine stood up awkwardly in her heavy gown. One blossom from her headpiece drooped over her eye, so Katherine pulled the entire construction from her hair.

"You shouldn't have done that, Katie," Margaret said. "Your hair's a mess now."

Katherine laughed. "I don't much care, you humbug!"

Mrs. Wheeler, the church organist, came upon them. "Dear Katherine!"

"Mrs. Wheeler, you were wonderful today at the ceremony. Thank you," Katherine said.

"Good, good. My, it's hard to imagine you as an army wife. You *are* brave. My husband tells me they'll cut the officer staff mightily this year if the politicians have their way. Your father might support two unemployed soldiers then! He-he."

Margaret huffed. "Mrs. Wheeler, Weldon is not a proper officer yet anyhow, so the cuts won't affect him. How is your son doing at Princeton? We hear he bought his way out of fighting to study ... what was it again?"

Mrs. Wheeler turned grim. "Margaret Brown, you know my son is far too sickly to have ever survived a campaign in the military. Not all men are suited to such work. He's far too clever to waste his ..." She stopped and scanned the little crowd. "Oh, there's Mrs. Van Brunt. I must speak to her. Excuse me, girls."

"Please send our regards to your son, Mrs. Wheeler!" Margaret called, slipping her arm through Katherine's and bumping her hip. "Awful old hag, that one is!"

Cakes heavily laden with fruit from the garden and cream from the Vissers' Jersey cow were brought out. Simon jumped up on to a chair, swayed, but righted himself with a charming grin and proposed a toast as his father suffered along in consternation. He began like any good politician. "Dear fellow Englewood citizens!" A muted laugh arose from the guests. "We are gathered together to celebrate Katherine's marriage to John here. Weldon battled from the first to the last days of his service alongside me and bravely—with little fanfare, indeed not a promotion to speak of, though he deserved it more than me. His visit to Englewood was a surprise, but it's given me the chance to rekindle a friendship with the best man I know and to gain a brother."

The men huzzahed with true military flair, and the women wiped their eyes. Simon waved the noise away and continued. "So it's like watching my brother marry my sister. No, that's not what I meant ..."

The men guffawed.

Simon pulled out his flask, took a gulp, and continued. "My two best friends I watch here today, and although I'm happy for them it's mixed with envy and sadness. Katie and Weldon both belonged to me, and now they have each other—and they look so goddamned satisfied."

Sarah covered her mouth, afraid of what Simon might say next, but her guests were taken with Simon—he could say anything. "After all the despair and sickening loss of boys, most younger than any of us standing here today ... in this beautiful garden so full of life even in November ... it's good to look at these two and envy them a little the power they have in their union to give us hope again, to bring up new young ones who will remember the sacrifices made for the Union and who will help rebuild this great nation into something more perfect and more humane for us all."

Moved, the small party cheered after a breathless moment.

"Please, let us raise our glasses to John and Katherine Weldon, wishing them great happiness and good luck. *Love bears all things, believes all things, hopes all things, endures all things.*"

And so it was done.

Chapter Twelve

The afternoon turned a slate grey, and Katherine happily changed into her warm traveling dress. The little cabin the couple would spend their first night in together waited a few miles away in Peetzburg. It belonged to the family of a church member. Originally a tiny stone tavern for the sailors on the Hackensack River, the family had converted it into a quaint fishing cabin for a grandfather just recently dead. Sarah, with Simon in tow, had dressed the place up with lace-trimmed linens and Sarah's flowers the previous day. Hope would have to make do under a rickety lean-to at the edge of the water for the night.

Twilight filtered through the dark branches of the trees lining the banks, and somewhere in the distance the whistle of yet another train making its way through the farmlands of the county waltzed upon the wind. Katherine thought of Simon and his drinking. The barking of a crow added to her sudden gloom.

Weldon fumbled for the all-important key when they arrived. He threw the door open as if afraid of ghosts and stuck his head in adjusting his eyes to the dim light of the interior. They walked in together hand in hand. The familiar scents of home were here—the cinnamon from her mother's coffee bread and the dried roses from her spring garden near the barn. Katherine blinked away tears. It was foolish. In two days she would be back home again.

Weldon set to work on a quick fire, his back to her. Katherine wondered what he was thinking. When Weldon turned, his face was red. "I didn't expect this to feel so strange," he confessed, wiping his brow. "I suddenly have nothing to say to you."

Katherine giggled, but she worried and gazed at the sputtering flames.

Weldon sighed and sat down beside her. As he unhooked her blouse Katherine pulled away. "Oh, I can't let you! It makes my skin crawl. The thought of it! I'm so ugly!" she cried.

Weldon kissed her forehead. "I won't hurt you. I p-promise."

Katherine stood up, holding her blouse shut tightly. "There's a reason no one likes me in town. I couldn't tell you because I loved you right away. I was selfish and dishonest!" she cried.

"Miss, Simon told me your s-story."

"What do you mean?"

"Simon was drunk—during the war—in camp. Said he didn't look after you ... it was his fault. I know how that is ..."

"No! It wasn't Simon's fault! I was stupid. I strayed from him," Katherine cried. "He can't think it was his fault. I want to go home!"

"Home? No, we can't now ... miss, it's all right. Let Simon be." Weldon was tempted to argue with her, to blame Simon for not protecting her, but what would it gain him? "Miss, all that happened ... it was nobody's fault but the boy who did it. It wasn't your fault."

"But everyone thinks ..."

"No. I know you're a good, good girl," Weldon said with sweating palms. "I have not a single doubt about you and only want to make you happy."

"You'll stop if I don't like it?" she pleaded, her tiny feet tapping nervously against the wood flooring.

"I'll do whatever you want me to do."

"Will you love me even if I don't like it?"

Weldon scratched his head. "Maybe you'll like it."

"But ..." Her eyes shone.

"Miss Katherine, I'll love you no matter what, but maybe you *will* like it."

The room danced as the fire finally took hold. Weldon ran his fingers along Katherine's shoulders as she bashfully pulled his shirt open. She worried when her hands came close that she might be repulsed at the sight of Weldon's wound, but it wasn't nearly as horrible as she'd imagined. He relaxed as she kissed the puckered skin around his ribcage, and the rest came naturally to them both.

The night passed, and an orange sliver of dawn cast a blue, cold glow on the windowsill. The room, in chill silhouette, lay silent but for Katherine's breathing. Weldon slipped from the bed to shake the loneliness that came with morning. His wife awakened briefly as he sifted through their things looking for a cigar, but soon she drifted back asleep.

Weldon slipped on trousers and boots. He'd take just a little this time. It had been close to 23 hours, he figured. His head throbbed, and he felt sick.

The calls of the first birds grated. The soft linens and feather pillows were like crushed glass, sharp against his body. His fingertips burned holding his cigar. Weldon threw it into the cold hearth. He could touch nothing without it rubbing him the wrong way.

As Weldon opened the door, he glanced back at his new wife. Her long hair fell around her. He resolved to make this his last time, again.

Weldon admired his smaller, more discrete new syringe as he prepped himself for it. Hope whinnied as he pulled up behind the shelter and released a strong dose—after all, it was his last—into his bloodstream. The rush of relief and euphoria quickly mingled with regret and fear. How would he hide this? It had been a long time since Weldon had taken so much at one go.

As he put his things away, Katherine tiptoed up, her breath visible in the cold air. The slant and frost of the November sunshine lit the path back to the cabin behind her. She shivered in just her sheer gown. "Mr. Weldon, what are you doing?"

"Ch-checking th-the horse ... I ..."

"But, what's that? Why are you hiding out here?"

Weldon scratched his head and tried to smile through blue, thin lips. "Well, it was early ... I didn't want to wake you."

"Are you drunk?" Katherine cried. "You're different."

"No. It's only ... the doctors said it was all right for me to use sometimes for pain ..."

"You're in pain? Why didn't you tell me? Why is it a secret?" Katherine stepped closer.

Weldon's mind blurred. He panicked, mortified and angry. "If the army finds me sick, they'll kick me out!"

"No, that makes no sense," Katherine said, pulling at his hand. "We should talk to Simon and ..."

"*No*! You mustn't tell anyone! No one can find out! I won't do it anymore. I promise!" He kissed her hand.

Katherine stared at him. "What kind of medicine?"

"For the pain. But it's getting better all the time."

"My father says morphine and laudanum are addictive."

Weldon hated the scared look in her eyes. "I'd never do those sorts of things!" he lied. "No, this just numbs the pain. You trust me, don't you?"

"Yes, I think so," Katherine said with a little sigh. "I mean yes, I do. I'm your wife now, so please don't hide things from me."

Weldon kissed her and wrapped his arms around her shivering body. "Will you forgive me? It was foolish to hide such a trifling thing, and now with you here I won't need anything else."

***

The final hours of the day brought them out into the bracing cold again. Weldon and Katherine had planned a small fishing expedition on a fragile craft tied near Hope. Since arriving in Englewood, Weldon had put together a smattering of ill-fitted civilian clothes. Katherine smiled primly in her tartan plaid skirt with matching beret, watching him dress layer upon flimsy layer. Weldon worried what she was thinking and sighed.

"Do you still care for me?" he asked with an edge.

"Mr. Weldon, you are a silly," Katherine swallowed hard—as if she feared him and was putting on a brave front. "I was just admiring your rugged good looks."

Weldon brooded as they rowed out and pretended at enthusiasm for fish as their fingers and noses grew sore in the wind. The songbirds had moved elsewhere, but crows complained and squirrels sat gossiping at the edges of their nests.

After a few false starts at good humor, Katherine stared past Weldon, listening to the steady rowing of Weldon's oars.

"I've said something to offend you, haven't I? I've been trying to think what it could be," Katherine said with a sniffle, "and I haven't any idea."

"Katherine ... stop crying ..."

She covered her face with her perfect kid gloves.

Weldon pulled her hands in his. "Katherine, Kate, how could I be angry with you? I've never been with anyone like you. I'm very pleased with you."

"But you look so troubled, and I think you think I was spying on you this morning."

"Spying?" Weldon laughed.

Katherine looked at him, eyes still shining and not quite reassured.

"If you're worried what I was thinking, I'll tell you. I was thinking ... of ways I need to improve for you." Now he spoke the truth.

Katherine brightened. "But you need never change a thing!"

Weldon looked at his hands, and at the same time it came to both of them that the oars were lost. Behind them in the distance the pair bobbed up and down lazily. For a moment as they contemplated their situation they were silent, but soon the banks echoed with their laughter and the thrashing of hands to water as the two made their way to shore after much effort and splashing.

Chapter Thirteen

Katherine had never thought much about having children. She didn't dislike them, but at church when the new babies were fussed over, she stood aloof.

Why did it come as a surprise to her now? Katherine understood how everything worked. Her hands shook, and a queasy, all over sensation came as she sat up in the enormous bed Sarah had given as a wedding gift to the couple. It crowded the little yellow room, and Katherine needed a step stool to climb in and out. She sat for a while, with legs dangling, just looking around. John's small case had adopted the corner next to her bureau as its home, and his shaving mug and gun and loose pocket change littered her vanity table. And then there were his jackets and a belt and red suspenders Sarah had picked up in town and a pocket watch he never seemed to remember that she had bought him for their wedding. Weldon had an old Bible and a small leather notebook which he kept hidden though she'd found them poking around his things. He hardly ever snuck cigars in like Simon did, but Katherine still smelled them slightly in her curtains. Sometimes he used hair oil, and the scent lingered on the collar of his jacket. She thought it needed mending. Her mother suggested they make him a new warm one for Christmas.

Sarah had asked her the day before, while they sat in the kitchen over tea and pie, if she was feeling all right—that knowing, hopeful look. Katherine shied away, annoyed at her mother's sixth sense. Sarah came around to her side of the table and squeezed her before taking the dishes to the wash basin.

Now up in her room, Katherine counted back over and over to see if it was possible even though she knew it was. Her middle was sore, so she put on a wrapper instead of her corset and day dress. Katherine held her body like it might break, like somehow the news and the child might escape through an open window before she told anyone. A note in John's rigid script said he went to town with Simon.

Getting back into bed, Katherine listened to the rocker moaning on the porch, pushed by the winds from the north. Even in December, she liked the windows slightly ajar so she could hear the weather. The air was cool, almost cold, but the sounds of the yard, the same ones she had heard most of her life, comforted her. It had rained a torrential pour in the night. The smell of damp places drifted over her, and she fell back asleep, dreaming of armies of children dashing over her childhood gardens.

"Katie! Mother wants you in the kitchen," Simon yelled at the foot of the stairs.

Katherine glanced at the clock on the mantle. She had forgotten to wind it but could tell by the dull light slanting through her window that she had slept the day away. She slid out of bed and down the stairs to the kitchen. Sarah stood at the window. "Now look what your crazy Mr. Weldon has done."

Katherine didn't like to look but peeked out the window. Weldon led a mud soaked horse around to the barn. With one shy glance at her opinionated parents Katherine darted out the door.

Sarah shouted helplessly after her, "Katie, put shoes on before you catch your death!"

"John, what are you doing?" Katherine asked with a grin as she ran up beside him.

Weldon turned around disappointed. "Well, now you've done it, Kate. It was supposed to be a surprise."

"Oh, John, where did you get him?"

The filthy horse leaned into his new best friend and by the look of things it wasn't the first time. Weldon's jacket needed washing. "This is the second part of your wedding gift, but I wanted to clean him up before you saw him. Anyway he's a Morgan underneath all of this muck, and sweet too."

She gave him a hug and a long kiss. He gruffly turned back to leading the horse, fending off the Morgan's friendly but powerful nudges. Simon and Sarah watched from the window, and Weldon waved to them before leading the horse into the barn. Katherine skipped after him.

"What shall we name him?" Katherine asked. "How about Handsome like his owner?"

Weldon smiled. "You name him what you like, Kate. He's all yours." Then he hitched the horse up before brushing off loose dirt with his hands. Katherine found a curry comb, but Weldon noticed her feet. "Get back into the house this minute! You can't help clean your own gift! Now go, you foolish girl, before you catch cold."

Back in the house Scott contemplated aloud, stirring his coffee, "That Weldon should have saved his money. What does Katherine need with her own horse? The sergeant has no sense ... "

Katherine shivered as she entered. Scott started to repeat his words, but Simon interrupted. "Katie, it seems a sturdy horse. You know we've been on the search for days. Weldon was bent on getting you a gentle one for driving. He worries too much about you. I suggested a nice thoroughbred but ..."

Scott moaned, "Oh yes, a temperamental stallion, I bet. As senseless as Weldon may be, we have worse right here in front of us."

"What a nice thing to say on my final day," Simon began but caught the looks on the women's faces and didn't finish. "Anyway, a nice, old gentleman from the English Neighborhood couldn't care for his animals any longer, and they took a shine to Weldon. He could have had all nine of them for near nothing. But that's Weldon all over. Horses fall madly in love with him. I guess that explains Katherine's attraction."

"Simon, stop it," Sarah scolded." This son of ours will never grow up."

"Katherine, how do *you* like him? He's a beaut, don't you agree?" Simon asked, attempting to lift her fallen spirits. "Now you won't be as lonely for Weldon."

John and Simon were leaving tomorrow for a post out west. Katherine would have the baby alone. The horse was not a wedding gift but a going away present. Simon looked helplessly to Sarah, who shook her head.

Weldon came in, sizing up the situation. "Kate, what's the matter? Don't you like him?"

Katherine sobbed and Scott moaned. "There's far too much emotion in this house!" he declared and stalked off to his library.

Sarah intervened. "Mr. Weldon, it's not the horse. She'll miss you is all. Katherine, enough tears. Is this how you want to send off your husband so he can be all miserable and lonely? Mr. Weldon has done a fine thing for you and this is no repayment. Now go upstairs, get dressed, and go out for a while before supper. I've made lots of special things for our boys' last meal." Her voice quivered, and she left the room in a hurry.

Simon and Weldon waited in silence. Katherine got up. "Mother is right, I guess. Would you like a walk?"

Weldon nodded. They both dressed for town and as they rounded the corner on to Demarest Avenue it began to snow. A strong gust of wind ripped Katherine's hat from her head and into the road. John ran to retrieve it and came back grinning and brushing it off. "Kate, you should get yourself a nice warm bonnet."

"I hate bonnets! You know that. I won't ever wear one. It's a stupid suggestion." She wiped away a tear.

"I'm sorry, Kate. I didn't know bonnets were such a sore spot for you. Retrieve your own hats for all I care."

The snow and the wind picked up, so Katherine had to hold her hat for most of the way into the valley. Her ears pinched in the cold. A bonnet would be warmer.

The first jingle bells sounded down a snowy lane, but Katherine grumbled. "Why did you have to go and join the army anyway? And before Christmas?"

"Why ask questions you already know the answers to? I don't want to leave you, but it's too late to change things. Why can't you be happy for our time together right now? I thought you'd be happy with the horse."

"I'm happy with you, and you'll be gone maybe forever," Katherine cried.

"Forever? Don't be silly. I promise you ... I'll work so hard to make a place for you."

"I just want more time," Katherine said and thought of the little things she would miss about Weldon. His skin chafed under wool where the hairs at his neck met his collar on warm days. He loved the daily papers. Sometimes he quoted from the Bible, which impressed Sarah, and he liked strong and sweet coffee. He seemed to step through each minute as if he never experienced a normal day in his life before. "I'm sorry, John, for yelling at you. Thank you for getting my hat back."

Weldon laughed and kissed her while pulling her scarf tighter. Grinning still, he reached down into the snow as they crossed the park and threw it Katherine's way.

"You devil you!" she shouted, though her voice muffled in the heavy air. She bent to make a ball of her own and found herself sitting on the sidewalk.

"Kate!" Weldon helped her to her feet.

"I'm dizzy," she said. John cleared a bench of snow and made her sit.

"We need to get you home. Are you sick?"

Katherine laughed. "John, you're to blame."

"I told you not to come out with no shoes."

"John, I'm in the family way ... are you happy?"

He shook his hat free of snow and threw it back on, his face grim. "Happy? I'm not sure ... are you certain?"

Katherine's stomach turned and her face reddened. "I *am* certain of it and I hoped you might be happy!" She stood up and turned to leave him.

He came after her. "It's just that I didn't expect..."

"What did you imagine might happen if we stayed in that bed all day?"

"But the timing of it," he continued. "It's bad timing."

Katherine stopped a moment. "Don't you want us to have children?"

"I'm not sure, Kate."

She slapped his hand from her arm. "I'm glad to see you go then. Maybe you can decide what you're sure of when I'm not with you!"

Weldon blinked, trying to gather words. "Katherine! Wait ..."

She ran ahead up the hill with Weldon plodding behind. She slipped on the icy path, but when he tried to help her she turned on him. "I don't need your help! Stay away from me!"

Supper was spoiled because Katherine refused to come down from her room. Sarah served the men their food, looking lost and miserable every time Simon spoke a word. Soon enough, he stopped opening his mouth except to take a drink. Scott and Weldon were not to be depended upon for conversation, so it was the wind from the storm rattling the windows that did all the talking.

Weldon excused himself and went to the barn to check on Handsome, staying there much of the night. The storm subsided. He cleaned and reorganized everything, much to the amusement of Simon and Scott, who looked from the doorway on the kitchen porch as they smoked. "Weldon's unusual, Father."

"Yes, well I hope he remembers to turn the lantern out so there's no fire in my hay," Scott grumbled.

Simon shook his head and went to bed.

Weldon pulled the hair at the secret place behind his ear, stunned that everything was coming so easily—a wife, a child, and an extended family. He feared Katherine would die in childbirth, and he wouldn't be there. She seemed too small for children. He even considered asking her to find a doctor in the city to quietly end the pregnancy. He knew she wouldn't, and he couldn't really bear the thought himself.

Weldon regretted his behavior. He had never created anything from pleasure and didn't know how to feel about it. Right now Katherine was enough for him. He wouldn't make a good parent. His parents had taught him nothing, and he feared he had missed key elements, secrets he needed to succeed at it.

What could he offer the universe in gratitude for this new life of his? What could he offer Katherine and the child? A safe orderly life? He clung to the order he found in being a soldier and understood the military but was not sure where Katherine and a new baby fit in.

He worried he might not have any love for this child. She must think him idiotic. She only wanted him to be happy and was probably scared too. He cursed himself for being unreasonable and hurting her and couldn't wait to leave. He turned out the lantern and closed up the barn. The house was dark but for a small light in the parlor, where he spied Sarah packing the new stockings she had knitted for her son into his bag. Weldon slipped up the steps into Katherine's room and under the covers. "Kate ..." He knew she was awake, but she didn't answer him.

In the morning, Simon roused him from bed, eager for the road. "Weldon, what has my sister done to you—turning you into a lazy devil. Get up or I'll leave without you!"

Weldon turned to wake Katherine, but she'd slipped out already.

"Oh, Katie's up for hours with your horse. I guess you're the hero then with her," Simon said and left for breakfast.

Weldon gathered his things and brought them down into the hallway by the front door next to Simon's bag. He went to Katherine in the barn.

As he opened the door, Katherine whispered to Handsome, petting his sleek fur.

He went over and patted the horse affectionately. "Katherine, how are you this morning?"

"Fine. Why do you care?"

"Please. Don't be angry with me. It's my last minutes with you."

"Don't you think I know that? I wish you would leave already so I can stop feeling this way!" she cried. "You've made me the loneliest and saddest girl in the world ..."

"Katherine, about the baby ... I ..."

"You don't want it and neither do I. I don't want to talk about it anymore. Don't concern yourself!" She began sobbing. He tried to touch her, but she wouldn't allow it. "I never imagined you'd be so mean."

"I behaved like a fool. I don't know why it surprised me so much. I'm sorry."

"John Weldon, sometimes apologies are too late. Whenever I think of this child I will remember your first reaction to it. You've ruined it!" Katherine pressed her face into the horse's fur. She wanted to give him a chance to make things right, but her pride stood in the way. "Some men would have reacted quite differently—better ..."

Weldon looked as if she'd punched him. "Well, maybe you should find a different man to raise the child—how about your father? He can surely turn it into a spoiled, unforgiving wretch like you! Shit!" He pushed open the barn door and slammed it hard behind him, causing the horses to jump.

Katherine heard Simon calling to Weldon and Weldon saying something in return. Soon Simon came to the barn. "Land sakes, Katie, you've got him madder than a hornet."

Katherine said nothing, brushing Handsome roughly.

"Come on then. At least you should pay some attention to me before I go. We're leaving now."

She came around with tears on her dirty cheeks and embraced him. "Simon, I'll miss you so much. I'll die here without you."

"Don't be morbid. You'll see us soon. I promise. But won't you say goodbye to Weldon then?" Simon asked.

"No, I couldn't. I'll fall apart completely seeing you two go. I just can't do it."

"Katie, you're making a mistake letting him leave this way." He waited for her to come to her senses, but she didn't. "Okay, suit yourself, but you'll be sorry."

The coach came to take them away. Weldon stared out the window after climbing in, waiting for Katherine to come running out, but she didn't and he cursed her and himself. Weldon made up his mind to stay away for good. Finally this ridiculous dream was over and he could get on with his life.

Simon went through his bag, afraid that he had forgotten something. "Hey, what's this?" he asked with a smile. "Just like my mother to cheer me up."

Weldon assumed it was the stockings, but Simon pulled out a small wrapped package. He opened it and found a plain bound book with pictures from the wedding. "My God, was I tight that day!" Simon laughed as he flipped through the book. Weldon looked out the window, feigning disinterest.

"Weldon, check your bag. My mother was knitting you something."

Weldon smiled when he saw the thick mittens and scarf. "You have some mother," he said.

Simon smiled with pride. He shoved the book back into his things and lit his cigar just as Weldon felt in his own bag what he knew now to be a book of pictures of his own.

Simon watched as Englewood went away from him. He missed it already but was glad to have a destination and a purpose again. Weldon lingered on the pages and pictures of Katherine. It was stupid to have left in anger. He wasn't angry anymore. Katherine McCullough was still his wife. These pictures were of their day. It wasn't a dream or a fading photograph. Weldon ran his thumb over the sober picture of just the two of them, her small hand resting on his shoulder. He turned to Simon. "Captain, we're gonna have a baby ... Kate and I." He smiled and then laughed.

"You joke!" Simon brightened. "So soon? Well that beats all. A little Weldon! That is splendid news."

"Yes, it is."

Chapter Fourteen

Tenafly Road

Englewood, N.J.

May 27, 1866

My Dearest John,

We received your letter and Simon's from the 28th January only today after a long and miserable winter of waiting with hearts in mouth. Even though we knew the army would send word if you had been at the Fetterman Massacre, my mother and I could not help but worry night and day. Everyone back east railed against the Sioux for what they had done to the poor soldiers on that hill. Are the stories about mutilations exaggerated? Was Fetterman such a fool to allow so many men to be slaughtered? To think of you and Simon among such savagery!

We tried to find your location on an old map Father has, but we are disappointed with your description of the place. The Missouri is a big river, John. Please send more information in your next letter, which I hope will be much longer and more personal—I promise I will not share it with anyone if you are so afraid of letting people know how sweet you are! It was kind of you not to mention Simon's run-in with the Indians and his superiors, but Simon wrote all about it as if it were a funny anecdote for Mother who nearly collapsed at the idea of Simon out hunting with Indians lurking. He deserved the trouble he got, but I am so grateful to you for seeing he wasn't scalped. Sometimes I can't believe I've married such a brave man, but then our little baby kicks and I am filled with happiness that you are certainly real.

Father says Simon was hunting because those western outposts are not supplied with enough food. Please make sure you eat. I wonder if all wives with soldiers for husbands worry as much as I do. Please become an officer soon! I want so much to take care of you like a real wife.

I do not know if you received any of my letters, so I will chance repeating myself. I cannot tell you how my conscience suffered over my behavior toward you on that last day before you left. I miss you and do want this baby. I hope you will write more regularly now that we are friends again. Even your handwriting delights me.

Mother and I have been getting along miserably since you left. I want peace, but rarely get it. I am too pale or too rosy or the baby hasn't moved enough, etc. I was very ill in the beginning I will admit, but feel strong and healthy now. Also my mother, who insists on keeping me like a prisoner, went off into town and came back with the most hideous fabric to sew a loose dress for me (your baby has changed my shape dramatically, John Weldon!). I said it was ugly. Mother said, "Go, Katherine, and pick something you like with all of your money. I was trying to save you trouble, but you know what's best!"

The garden is just blooming now with the pale pink tulips you helped us plant in the fall, so you see you brighten my day even when you are so far away.

Speaking of big bellies, Handsome has fattened to the point of non-recognition. I suspect that along with my spoiling him, Father does too. He cannot help admiring a fine horse. Handsome likes to pull our buggy, but feels put upon when he is asked to drive out under the big carriage's weight. Mr. Adriance, a farmer, thinks he will one day convince me to sell Handsome to him!

I am so lonesome for you. Father says it will be years before I see you again. Is there not any way for me to come to you and soon? It is a bitter pill to have my Father so smug over my situation.

My dearest, I promise I will not let you go again away from me when we are angry. I have learned my lesson. Please write more frequently and at greater length. I am interested in everything you do.

Your loving wife,

Katherine Weldon

P.S. If the baby is a boy my parents would like for us to consider the name Hiram Frances in honor of an ancient uncle! If you are against such a name you should come home right away and establish a defense against it!

***

Fort Sully, Dakota

August 1866

Dear Little Wife,

I hope you will listen to your mother. I do not mean to scold you, but I must insist that you relieve me of worries about your condition.

All is sad and lonely here. We are stationed at a horrible post and I am miserable without you. The men have not been paid and are slipping away in the night—a dangerous thing for them, but also for us they leave behind. I think we shall be fine though. I want to see you, but I'm afraid this is no place to visit. Only one lady is here, and she is a tough old bird.

Yesterday our company of 69 men registered 38 for active duty. Three men were missing, and the rest struck down by something in the meat they got from a 'friendly' Indian. They were warned against such trade, but there are always stupid men.

That is my news.

Yours,

Sergeant John Weldon

***

John Weldon and the soldiers of the West had to shout most days to be heard in conversation over the relentless wind blowing through the forlorn barracks, so they rarely bothered unless inside their flimsy shelters. The troops were supposed to be fortifying the place, but most claimed illness and the lieutenant colonel in charge suffered from incapacitating sickness every time he came back from down river where Soldier's Delight poured freely at the nearest settlement.

Weldon hated loose ends. He stopped to stuff his pipe with dried and stale tobacco leaves he'd bought on the way out. Simon teased him about being swindled since they ran out of Simon's cigars a while back. Weldon ducked between two sheds to light up.

"Sergeant Weldon!" called the young Irish wife of a sergeant Weldon disliked and outranked.

Too heartsick to do the simple chore of laundry himself, Weldon paid the laundress a small fee to do it for him.

"Sergeant Weldon, will ye ever slow yourself. I'm near out of breath chasin' ya down."

Weldon never much spoke to the woman from Sudsville, as the men called her tiny spot of earth, and was unnerved by her attention. "Yes, Mrs. Lyons, how may I help you?" he asked, glancing around.

Tall and striking with enormous black eyes and hair curling down to her waist, held in check by a long strip of wool knotted at her neck, Oonagh Lyons exuded a forwardness that intrigued and repulsed Weldon. "Sir, it's I who may help you. I'm just after findin' this in your coat," she said, but before Oonagh even spoke the words, Weldon guessed what she was fishing from her apron pocket.

Weldon grabbed the syringe from her, trying to put words together.

"Now don't go gettin' all rattled on me, Sergeant Weldon. I'm no rat, but you're as fit as a fiddle so I'm thinkin' you do it for pleasure. I've seen it before. You're a veteran—I'd wager that's how it started."

Weldon stood in silence as the sand whistled and spun around them.

"Sir, if you don't mind, I'm wonderin' how you keep supplied. I won't let on to nobody if it's secret, that you can be sure." Oonagh looked him over and clicked her tongue. "It's a real shame ain't it, sir. In yer prime bein' a slave to a needle."

Weldon spoke with feeble words, "I'm no slave ... I was wounded."

She waved him away. "Go on, sir, I don't much care what your excuses are. I'm sure you'd rather no one knew, but seein' as I do, all I ask is that you're a little light on my husband."

"Your husband?"

"Yes, and I may be able to get you a higher quality medicine."

"That is unnecessary, Mrs. Lyons." Weldon's voice shook with anger and humiliation.

"Well, sergeant, I'll be seein' you, I suspect," she said with a devilish smile.

"I think not," Weldon tried to say with dignity.

"To pick up your duds?" She laughed.

"Yes, I see, okay then," he stammered as he stalked off for his quarters.

Having no real work until evening, Weldon paced, fingering the small syringe in the pocket of the jacket Sarah had made for him with Katherine's help. He could not spend the day with morphine, worrying about Katherine, a baby, the washerwoman, or her husband.

Weldon needed to work.

"Weldon, have you seen a ghost?" Simon asked when Weldon rushed into headquarters.

"I'm reporting for duty, sir," he said, trying to appear sharp.

"No, you're not, sergeant." Simon shook his head, laughing, but concern traced his face. "Sit down. You look ready to collapse ... is it your side again?"

Weldon pulled up a chair and came close to confessing his vain attempts at giving up the medication.

Simon stretched. He had just given up the idea of facial hair and rubbed his hand along his clean-shaven chin. "It must be awful rough on you, having to leave my sister the way you did, but I'm certain it will all work its way out. In the meantime you should use this extra day to lie about." He looked steadily at Weldon. "Is there something else? Are you sure your side ..."

"Can you get it through your head I'm fine?! I just need to keep busy! I can't keep thinking and thinking of this child!"

Simon didn't take these little outbursts to heart. "Okay, if you insist on badgering me for work and keep in this rotten humor, the only thing for me to do is comply or fight you, which I'm too queasy to do. Me and the boys had a big night. Paulsen is down again with delirium tremens, so if you want to you can help me with the morning reports and some ordinance papers. Finish the maps you began on the way out. The lieutenant colonel is impressed with what we did so far."

Weldon nodded. "I'll begin right away." He took the maps and tried to focus on the smudged pencil marks.

Simon took a brief nap with legs outstretched over the top of his paperwork until the post came after dark.

"Land sakes, if you two ain't the popularist men along the Missoura! A letter for each of you. Good news I hope," the soldier said and excused himself after touching his cap.

Weldon ripped open the letter and read it out loud:

Englewood, New Jersey

July 15, 1866

Dear John,

Congratulations! Your baby has made his arrival—a beautiful boy with a full head of hair like yours, but with the McCullough spunk. He decided to come over a month too soon. Both mother and child are weak, but Doctor Currie and the midwife are cautiously optimistic about their survival.

Simon stood over Weldon's shoulder reading along. Weldon paused as the two came to their own conclusions about the less than comforting lines. The letter continued:

Katherine was despondent without you here, Sergeant Weldon, which may have contributed to her weakened state, but then Sarah had hardships in delivering all of our children, and I was with her every day.

John leaned back stung by Scott's words. Simon took the letter and read the rest of it.

Katherine asks that I send you her love and tell you that she will write when she is stronger. The poor thing felt guilty about you leaving her! We hope you are having some sort of success out there.

Scott McCullough

"Well," Simon said, "it's unfortunate that my father was the one to write but ... we should celebrate."

Weldon shook his head miserably. "I wonder what Katherine named him."

"Of course it will be *William* as you both decided—Katherine wouldn't leave your wishes out," Simon assured him but realized how difficult this marriage would continue to be with his sister so far away. It might be months before Weldon could be certain of his first son's name. Weldon would not attend a christening or probably a Christmas. A few of the officers here hadn't gone home in over five years. As much as Simon enjoyed a good celebration, he understood his friend's lack of enthusiasm.

"Weldon, listen. Katherine is alive. Your biggest fear is lifted."

"But they are only cautiously optimistic," Weldon said, flipping the note in hopes of more information.

Simon sighed. "Remember who wrote the letter. My father knows how to get under your skin, and he's a bastard for doing it now, but you must not let him succeed. You were there as long as you could be. Katherine knows that."

"Yes, I know, but I wish ... " Weldon looked out to the dark parade ground.

"John Weldon, stop this. You have just received wonderful news. Celebrate when you can in life."

"Why is it in life whenever something good happens it's so surrounded by shit?"

"Father says that everything evens out in life. I don't like that theory, but nothing's ever perfect. You have to choose what to focus on."

"Yes, it's all in the attitude, right? I've tried different attitudes, and they didn't work any better."

"I can only take just so much self-pity, sergeant. Where's the man I knew in the war! You lie anyway. Once you stopped being so standoffish and superior during the war the men grew fond of you. It *was* all attitude."

"Maybe you have something there," Weldon said with a faint smile. "I don't know. I think it was just luck to meet the right people."

"Yes, but ... anyway, will we tell the boys your news?" Simon suggested. "Give them an excuse to be cheerful for the night."

***

July 28, 1866

Dear John,

Finally I am allowed to write! Having a child is tiring, yet having a mother who interferes is more so. I see the little man hardly at all and only yesterday left my bed. I feel like a wretch and look like one too! But I should not give you reason to tire of me! Maybe you will find a place for us? I do not care where it is.

William is a comfort because he looks so like you—his eyes are quite dark so far. I only wish you could hold him once when he is so small, but I must be patient or so Mother says.

Simon is a regular gossip and sent Mother a letter saying you were in an awful state and not caring for yourself. I have a mother to care for me, but you are alone. You must hide nothing from Simon. If you are unwell you must confide in him. Please promise me you will stay strong and avoid as much trouble as you can.

I have not fully recovered from the shock of Fort Kearney and how close you and Simon were to being stationed there! I read in the papers how foolish the officers were, but how the poor brave soldiers followed orders. Sometimes I must admit that like my father I wish you and my brother had picked more comfortable careers back here, but I am weaker than the both of you and put my wants and needs before that of my country.

I cannot understand that sort of devotion to an idea when I am concerned about your welfare. I wish the country could just take care of itself for all the respect the army is given nowadays—are not these the same brave men our government sent into battle year after year of the war? It amazes me how quickly people forget. I do wonder why I must bear separation from you for the protection of a few settlers out in the distant west. It was their decision to pull up their roots and travel on an adventure. I have read that the settlers are a rough sort who start trouble with the Indians and expect the soldiers to do the mopping up. I know the railroads must go through and I will be happy to use them to see you, but oh well, I am too tired to sort the world's problems. I just miss you. Someday soon we can pore over the papers together like old times and discuss government policies and peace commissions.

William will be christened as we planned, and I will be praying for you, my love.

Yours truly,

Katherine

***

Captain Simon McCullough

April 1867

Dear Katherine,

My regards to you and your little boy! Mother wrote and said he was the image of me—lucky fellow. I hope he is stronger now. It is maddening to receive the letters you send all at once and so late.

It must be nearly mid-spring in Englewood now but here it is winter and winter and winter. The men tell me that May brings a change, and I am certainly ready for it. We are put here to defend this place and not one square foot outside of it. It makes the men irritable. Last evening we tried a dance with just the men. It was very pathetic and interest dwindled halfway through. Spring must come soon or we will lose the entire fort to madness or desertion. The constant threat of pay cuts does not help! Some of us have spent our entire adult lives in the service and feel quite bitter when we read of the treatment of veterans. Please send no more Eastern newspapers!

A few weeks back Lieutenant Colonel Langellier sent me, Weldon and Lieutenant Frazier to find two men who had run off and put themselves and the rest of us in grave danger.

Most of the men who leave go to a small settlement downriver, sell off their government-issue stuff, and have a frolic. Lieutenant Frazier suggested we disguise ourselves as civilians. The seedy lot of townsfolk don't much trust soldiers. This job seemed a perfectly delightful form of detached duty that could, if played right, lengthen into weeks or months. Langellier told us to leave no stone unturned and go as far as it took to find these men.

Taking five days rations and some money, we floated a tiny boat under the cover of darkness in the most repugnant civilian clothes we could round up and were off. Before long we rowed to the shore of the fleshpot town. We gave ourselves fictional names for the fun of it—I was to be Vladimir and Weldon christened himself O'Shaunessy. Our first stop was a shabby hut of a place called the Gypsy Rover. Weldon (O'Shaunessy) and Lieutenant Frazier, who called himself Joe, enjoyed saying and doing things quite unlike themselves, while I tried to keep some semblance of order (do not laugh) as we interviewed the few shadowy creatures of the establishment.

A glorious old wench of a woman took an interest in us. She wore more bangles and doodads than the vainest peacock of an officer in the army. Frazier asked her, "Were you originally from St. Louis?" It was just a guess by the accent.

"Why yes!" she replied.

Then Weldon saw his chance. "Then you must remember Vlad here!" he said pointing to me.

The whore looked at me and the most convincing act of recognition swept over her."Yes, I do remember him well now! He used to visit me awful frequent."

Frazier nodded approvingly at Weldon's little joke and sipped his drink. Weldon continued the interview quite seriously, only a glimmer in his eye hinting at the fun he was having watching me squirm at the idea of bedding such a used-up old whore. I do have my standards!

I must now tell you the real reason for writing. Weldon has me worried. Though he is mostly himself in the field, he suffers great bouts of melancholia when he is in camp and is skittish and more irritable than ever. If he is to be promoted, he will need to shape up soon. Please do write and encourage him as I am at a loss.

I am looking to be transferred elsewhere without Weldon. There is too much between us and I'm afraid my making excuses for him to our superiors is having an ill effect on both of our careers. It's hard for me to watch him so low. Before the Wilderness, Weldon was a different soldier, and he blames me for all that went wrong though he does not say it. I do not know what more I could have done.

There is a chance at promotion for your husband if he will only take it. One of our lieutenants may be court-martialed for over strenuous use of the doctor's medicinal spirits and insubordination upon being caught.

This is where I shall end for now. I have plans to slip out and find some fun myself. I do stay away from the horizontal refreshment—I have learned my lesson with the Cyprians.

Please write me soon and Weldon, too.

Regards,

Captain Simon McCullough

Chapter Fifteen

Sarah handed Scott a buttered biscuit as they sat for supper one late fall evening. "It's time the baby was weaned," she said.

"That's all fine and good, Sarah," Scott replied, "but Katie has no talent for cooking. I remember the last time she tried—the lime trifle—I don't think I need to say another word."

Sarah smiled. "Yes, it was a mistake to let her make dessert, but Katie was only ten. Of course I'll take care of the baby's diet once he's weaned. Katie's too weak anyhow," she said, making a plate for Katherine.

"For God's sake, Sarah, the girl won't eat all that!" Scott complained as Sarah heaped potatoes and gravy. Scott hated when his wife set her mind on slimming him down and grumbled as he finished his meager helping of roast beef.

A knock came at the door and then another and Scott cursed. "Visitors at this hour? I'll give them a piece of my mind!"

Off he went to the front door but was too late as the visitor raced to the kitchen porch and knocked more urgently. Sarah gasped and ran to the door with a grin. "Mr. Weldon! However did you get here?"

"Upstairs?" Weldon asked breathlessly, running past Sarah and into Scott. Without a word Weldon rushed the stairs to Katherine's room and burst in, the door banging the wall as he entered.

"Mr. Weldon!" Katherine cried, outstretching her arms as Weldon came to embrace her. "How did you know I need you now more than ever? I was so lonesome and your letters are awful—they're so short! I was scared that you didn't care any longer." She searched his face for hope. "Have you come to fetch me?"

"No, of course not!" Weldon said, pulling back to look at her. "You're in no condition! I—I just couldn't wait to see you! But you're alive and that's all that matters." Weldon kissed her again and again. "Don't cry! I came all this way, and I'm so happy."

Katherine pulled a handkerchief from her sleeve.

Weldon noticed her thin fingers and the tiny veins so close to the surface of her pale face as Katherine wiped her eyes. "Oh, I have something for you." He pulled open his overstuffed bag. "Kate, you'll think I'm odd ..."

Katherine laughed.

Weldon scratched his head. "I wanted to bring you something nice. At the first shop on my trip things were either too expensive or not right so I bought some candy ...and then again at the second stop and ..." He dumped a mountain of assorted sweets onto the bed. "Kate, I'm too poor and know so little about you or what you'd like—but ..."

"My dear silly soldier," Katherine said, pulling him close for a kiss, "you knew all along what I'd like most and so you came home to me. The candy is wonderful too. I shall hide it and savor one piece each day! Mother says it's no good for me to eat sugar, but I've such a craving for it!"

Weldon sat watching Katherine sift through the sweets for the perfect one. She grinned, held a ribbon candy to the light, and ate it as if it were the greatest delicacy in the world.

"I'm being transferred to Arizona—Simon too, though he told me not to tell your parents he's gone off on leave to Washington with our lieutenant colonel." Weldon watched for reaction. "All of us are sent to Arizona, so they let me go on extended leave."

"*Arizona*?! But how will I ever get there?" Katherine cried. "I've heard Arizona territory is the most godforsaken place to be sent as a soldier. And what about writing? I hardly get a letter now!"

"I'm ashamed of my letters, Katherine. And sometimes I pretend you don't really exist—just to get through."

"I don't exist?" Katherine cried, her lips pale and trembling.

"Oh, no, Kate, it came out different than I meant," he said, uneasy in the face of her emotions. "I'll have just about two months here, and we could try to be happy like a real husband and wife."

The little child in the elaborately carved crib whimpered. John looked to Katherine.

"Mr. Weldon, leave Willy be," Katherine said. "Mother will come soon for him and clean him up, but go look—he's gotten awful cute."

"You let him cry for your mother?" he asked as he went to meet his child for the first time. He towered over the crib as he lay his hat on the table beside it. "He's tiny, isn't he?"

"Father says it's my milk! It's no good, and William won't take to Father's strange potions. At least you've come before my pathetic mothering kills him!" Katherine cried again.

"I won't break him, will I?" Weldon asked as he undid the child's blankets. He maneuvered awkwardly, but the child stayed quiet and interested in this new man. After a moment William struggled to get down and Weldon helped him teeter on the carpet.

"My word! What is going on?" Sarah exclaimed upon entering the room. "John Weldon, you'll break the poor child's back that way, and he'll be deformed for life!" She slammed down Katherine's tray on the bed stand with an exasperated groan. "Give Willy over to me before I suffer nervous palpitations!"

Weldon scooped William up defiantly.

"Katherine has no way with babies, Mr. Weldon, and no sense letting you unwrap the child when he's wet—he'll catch a chill and die before he has time to recover from his broken spine," Sarah ranted prying William loose from his father. "Poor little lad, come with me now and we'll clean you all up and dress you—oh, don't cry—they didn't think is all!"

Weldon watched Sarah abscond with William to his nursery. "Kate, what's going on?"

Katherine pulled on the two long braids she wore. "Oh, Mr. Weldon, I'm so ashamed—it looks like I'm an awful mother after all. I hoped maybe I'd finally be good at something, but I'm clumsy and I don't ever seem to hold the child right at feeding and ... and one time I let the baby grab hold of a pin. What if he had swallowed it?" She sobbed.

"Kate, I've never met such a girl for crying," Weldon said and sat beside her. "But that's okay. Your mother, I'm sure, is trying to care for you both the way she thinks best, but you have to stand up to her. William is yours. Shouldn't he be walking by now?"

Sarah came back. "Well, here we are! Mr. Weldon, it's time for feeding. You'll have to wait outside," Sarah ordered with a cheerful smile. "There's food in the kitchen and you can have a chat with Mr. McCullough."

"Mrs. McCullough, pardon me, but I'll stay here with Katherine and the son I've only just met."

"Mr. Weldon, I care for you and I understand your position," Sarah explained firmly, "but you must understand that there is nothing I—I mean children hate more than a change in their routine. Now, you might not have noticed that this little boy of yours is far too small and sickly—that's because our Katie failed to heed her father's advice during her confinement. She didn't eat enough, and she was always running the stairs. That's why the baby came early. Katherine is still weak, and now you're upsetting Willy's meal." Sarah waited. "Go right ahead then and see if they're ever ready to join you in the West."

Weldon turned to Katherine hiding her candy beneath her blankets.

"John, it won't take long," Katherine assured him.

Weldon didn't want to make trouble for his wife, yet he wasn't fully convinced by Sarah's lecture. "All right then," he began with some hesitation. "I'll go take a look at Handsome."

Sarah and Katherine exchanged pained expressions.

"What? What's happened to our horse, Kate?" he asked.

"Well, nothing really ... it's just he's been loaned out," Katherine said.

"Loaned out? I used the last of my savings!" Weldon said, failing to hide his temper. "Have you sold the buggy too?"

"I didn't want to do it!" Katherine cried again throwing up her hands.

"It was for pin money, John," Sarah explained. "Mr. Adriance has been after the horse for a while, and he offered to keep Handsome exercised and trained to the carriage until Katie was up to driving again. A girl should be allowed a few nice things from the shops."

"Mr. Weldon," Katherine cried, "I promise—it was things for the baby I wanted and a Christmas gift for you."

Sarah pulled Weldon aside. "Katie didn't want to keep asking her father for funds."

"Kate! I send you my money—don't you receive it?" Weldon said, brushing Sarah aside.

"Well, it's not all that much," Sarah said.

"Mother! Stop it!" Katherine cried. "Mr. Weldon, I try to save it for when we make a home together."

"You silly girl," Weldon said. "I don't scrimp and save so you can live like a pauper here. It's not much I send, but it's enough to get by isn't it?"

"I don't need a thing," Katherine assured him but said it as if she were somehow betraying her mother. "I just wanted things for the baby and for you."

"Before I leave I'm getting Handsome back," Weldon stated. "He belongs to you and you should ride out for air and sun—you and William both. The women out west—the Indians especially—they recover much faster."

"Katherine is no half-breed!" Sarah said. "It's bad enough little Willy looks too dark. Oh dear, I shouldn't have said that, Mr. Weldon, but I worry for you all! Some people have strong prejudices."

Weldon tried to speak, but when nothing coherent came to mind he went to retrieve the horse. Upon return he found Scott in the barn. "Mr. McCullough," Weldon said through clenched teeth.

"Oh, so you've brought back Handsome, I see," Scott said by way of greeting. "I told the girls you wouldn't approve, but it's a foolish idea to bring him back. Katie has enough to care for—she's bedridden for God's sake."

"Kate needs to learn to care for herself and the child. Having the horse will cheer her up and get her out for exercise."

"Whatever you think best, *Doctor Weldon*, but who'll pay for the horse's feed?"

"The horse will. Looks like he's a good stallion. Kate was unaware of the profit Mr. Adriance stood to gain on new foals in spring. Anyway, Handsome will still help Adriance on market days and be fed on his hay for the rest of the winter. Kate will get a percentage of any money that comes from the foals. Then he'll be castrated. So that's all settled, sir. You might have thought to advise your daughter."

"You're proof of how well she follows my advice," Scott quipped, but thinking better of it softened his tone a little. "You do surprise me, Weldon. I never would have expected you to make the trip back to see my daughter. It seems hardly worth it."

"Seeing for myself that Katherine is well is worth it to me, sir."

Scott took Handsome. He led him to a clean stall and filled a bucket of feed ignoring the horse's excited affection and gruffly pushing Handsome's nose away.

"Thank you, sir," Weldon said.

"It's for the girl, I do it."

"Me too."

Scott groaned, but laughed. "Come on, let Sarah feed you—you're still thin as a rake. The blasted army always takes such good care of its own."

Chapter Sixteen

A harvest moon hung in the laced bay window. On nights like these Weldon did not sleep for fear of missing one second of the peaceful breathing of Katherine and William. The stately trees with the last of their leaves blown by a gentle wind cast shadows over the yellow wallpaper, and the occasional sound of strong and healthy horses pulling prosperous businessmen home seemed part of a comforting fantasy. The ache was there too, but Weldon had stayed clean since leaving the West and determined to remain so for Katherine. At first light he slipped from beneath the downy blankets and lavender-scented sheets and picked up his sleeping son. Despite his dark skin, William was handsome. The baby opened his eyes, and in a hoarse whisper Weldon sang him a song from the past:

All quiet along the Potomac to-night!
Where the soldiers lie peacefully dreaming;
And their tents in the rays of the clear autumn moon,
And the light of their camp-fires are gleaming.

Katherine tapped Weldon's shoulder, startling him. "Oh, Kate, isn't William handsome for a baby?"

"Just like his father," Katherine said, as she took William up in her arms. "I have to nurse him now."

"D-do you mind if I stay?"

Katherine blushed but patted the window seat beside her.

He kissed her ear. "I have something in my pocket I hope you'll like."

"I'd like anything you give me."

He fished in his jacket pocket hanging on a hook by the door. "I've been carrying these forever. I don't know why. They're not very nice, I guess, but they're ...they were my mother's from my father ... and expensive in their day ... from England."

"Oh, Mr. Weldon! They're so different and with some polishing they'll be beautiful!" Katherine said when Weldon showed her the little ear-bobs. She handed the baby to him and put the earrings on. "I will never take these off ... ever!"

"You like them?" he asked with a skeptical smile.

The baby finished nursing and was put back to bed to be changed by Sarah.

"Kate, would you like to do something before your mother comes up?"

Katherine pulled Weldon into her warm world where it seemed there was never anything to be afraid of.

Afterward Weldon ran his fingers over Katherine's small nose and lips, studying her.

Who is this whose glance is like
the dawn?
She is beautiful and bright,
As dazzling as the sun or
The moon ...
Weldon kissed her and continued,
... I am trembling: you
Have made
Me eager for love
As a chariot driver is for battle.

"Oh, Mr. Weldon, you *do* remember verse! It's lovely." Katherine sighed.

"Only sometimes. A useless talent."

"I never could get myself to pay much attention at church," Katherine confessed. "Your parents must have been proud."

"No. They never were."

"I'm sure you lie, Mr. Weldon," she teased, brushing the hair from his eyes. "Tell me more about them. It seems so odd for you to know everything about my family yet I don't know a stitch about yours."

He got up and fumbled around for his pipe. He could hear Sarah padding around in the kitchen downstairs. "There's nothing special to say about them. And I already told you they were dead, so what's the point?"

"Well, I just wanted to hear more about the young you out on the frontier. It sounds so adventurous and romantic."

"You really don't understand much about anything, do you, Kate?"

Katherine's lively eyes dimmed at the unexpected remark, and she retreated to bed.

"K-Kate, I didn't mean it the way it came out," he said, though he had meant it. "It's just my parents were different than yours. The last time I prayed it was in hopes that my mother would die, and soon after she did." He shrugged and tried to make light of it. "So that's all there is to it."

"Those scars on your wrists and feet—they're not from the war, are they?"

"I took a pig from the family living on my father's land right before Thanksgiving ... what *used* to be my father's land. My mother traded it for drink. I stole the pig, so I deserved it."

Katherine kissed his wrist. "Did you return the pig?"

He scratched his head. "It was the family's winter meat, all fattened up. I tried my hand at butchering and smoking it in the woods. They knew it was me. I remember the father was not so big, but his rifle was and it convinced me to fess up. It was a real loss."

"But it belonged to the other family," Katherine reasoned. "Maybe your mother should have gotten a piglet in spring. They're not too expensive then."

"Katherine, my mother never took care of things except to humiliate me. She sold off everything my father ever had. When she found out about the pig—she took my hands to the fire. The pig owners were shocked and vowed to send a lady missionary traveling west for the first time to come get me. She came up behind and scared me one day when I was chopping wood. By then my wrists were thick with infection. There were flies everywhere—all over my skin—and she took me down to the stream and scraped the rot off me and promised to take me away. She had a real optimistic look, and I half wanted to go." He remembered how he'd hung around the missionary's waist, pleading to go. "But my mother lied and told her I started fires and that's how I got burnt so many times. The missionary had soft green eyes, that lady did, but she didn't want me to hurt her *real* children. I saw her a few years later. I guess God wanted her where she was, and she told me she'd thought of me often and prayed." He laughed and stuffed his pipe. "'Praise God,' she said, 'you seem to have come out all right.' And I guess I did." He fingered the hair behind his ear.

"How could anyone want to hurt you?" Katherine asked, kneeling on the bed with its expensive blankets and pillows. "How come you didn't run away?"

"I know you think I came from nothing, but that land was my father's!" Weldon said. "He came from England and served with the dragoons. He *was* something. I know it." Weldon cursed under his breath. "You think I was a coward, don't you?"

"You were a child. I don't know how you managed. It's heartbreaking." She made him sit and leaned her head on his shoulder.

It bothered him.

"I never lived outside that gloomy cabin, and I thought all boys had it the same ... the day my mother died was the best day of my life because I had to leave those woods." Weldon hated Katherine's sympathy. "I'm glad for everything, really. I l-learned how to take care of m-myself with no one's help."

"Well, I've made up my mind to do everything I can to take care of you from now on," Katherine said in her most grown-up way.

Chapter Seventeen

"Mr. Weldon, don't be so silly," Katherine said. "It's our money to share—you sent it home, and I saved what I could. Go into town and buy yourself some new things and maybe a gift for Willy."

For the past month Weldon had avoided walking in town alone. The druggist was there. "Won't you come along?"

Katherine said she was tired and looked at him with such trust. Weldon went with the best of intentions to buy new union suits and a gift for William, but his mind raced on a track all its own. After the underwear, his feet dragged behind the conversation in his head. Weldon brushed against people as he tried to convince his body to move toward a shop with general items and toys. He tried to make his feet go toward a window decked with lovely things for his wife, but the bell clattered behind him as he closed the door on that part of his world and trudged grimly up to the polished counter. *I'll just get a bit of something ... just in case. I won't use it. Anyway I know I can stop ... I did these last weeks.* The conversation in his head never changed.

"May I help you, son?" a prim looking beanpole of a man with a booming voice asked.

Weldon nearly jumped from his skin.

"Sorry to startle you. May I *help* you?" the man repeated impatiently. His wife had just sent over his midday meal and it was getting cold on the counter.

"I'm in the army." Weldon glanced around at the tall shelves of plenty. "I'm bringing things back for the boys and ... well, um, some medical things for medical purposes."

"Are you an army surgeon?"

Weldon pulled the hair behind his ear. Why hadn't Kate come with him today? The druggist stood in his crisp white apron, clicking his pencil on the rich oak countertop.

"My apologies, it's j-just that w-we will be far out in Arizona, and I thought ..."

The druggist leaned forward like the straight hand of a clock and beckoned Weldon closer. Not a soul was in the store. "There's nothing to be ashamed of, boy. You served your country well I'd say and still at it," he whispered. "My son, he fought with the 2nd New Jersey Infantry. Shot right through the eye. Lucky not to have lost the whole pumpkin, but his head gives him an awful lot of pain sometimes. The other eye is throwin' in the fiddle now too. It's natural, the doctors say ... call it some kind of sympathy for a good eye to go out with the bad one like a matched team of horses. It's natural for you to want pain relief. What did they give you?"

Weldon hesitated. He knew that he could have whatever he wanted ... Katherine or the morphine, but the morphine was right there for the asking. "Morphine, laudanum ... but I'll take anything like it," he blurted out. Weldon clenched his teeth shut, but the words had already bolted and the clock's hands had turned to deliver him in a timely fashion back to where he started.

"How much will the 'boys' need out there?" the druggist asked.

Taking out his money, Katherine's money, the change from the underwear, he placed it on the smooth wood. The druggist brought Weldon his cure-all in pill and liquid form ... in case the necessity arose.

Once on course there was no turning back to the house on Tenafly Road. Like the stops on a train that were not his—his new familial bonds tugged, but not enough to change from his chosen destination. Next time Weldon would choose a different stop, but that was next time.

Almost willing pain back into his leg and side for the excuse Weldon needed, he tramped for miles out over the hills of prosperity and comfort, where supper bells tinkled and lamps awakened to the coming night and on up north of Englewood where only the foundations of dreams had yet been built. Stone breastworks, the beginnings of country palaces, lurked beneath last summer's overgrowth and the fallen leaves of autumn, victims of life's economy, of growth and recession.

Up to the edge of the world he stood where the living earth gave way to the stone beneath it. The Palisades afforded Weldon a view of the world; he was but one small speck in this huge country. What difference would it make if he disappeared from it for just a while? He hung his legs out over the edge. He had thrown away his syringe and would have to find another, so he took the pills and waited for escape. Rain began to fall and settle over him like a blanket of memories. He lay back on the sturdy edge of the world and dreamt of cornfields—the green corn he stole in childhood and later in the army. The late summer cicadas, dropping like flies after their final symphonies rose and fell. Weldon dreamt of hunger again in the cabin of his youth while surrounded by fields of plenty—his father's fields, his fields. The spring of '64—May and blossoms on the trees and no retreats with Grant and fighting even harder and finally the whole thing over for him on the ground like thousands of others—a different kind of symphony—men like flipped-over insects, moving limbs getting them nowhere—intensely alive to their dying but with no lovely final chorus.

Weldon hadn't moaned or screamed. He listened and waited. Waited for God. At first he detected no angels on the battlefield. He stayed still and that feeling he had been hoping for came and almost took him over—peace and comfort—but he had been saved and brought back to his life with just one more problem to take care of. It was too much and unfair.

Now in the pelting rain he was still ravenous. The God he had watched for had never come. There were promises, but it was the drug that delivered.

Chapter Eighteen

Weldon awoke on an unfinished floor before a frigid hearth of one of the unfinished houses on the hill. The rain had turned to snow in the night, and Weldon shielded his eyes from the unforgiving glare. His joints ached where he wasn't numb. He sat up and lit a damp, cheap cigar as he tried to remember where he was. For a few moments he was back in the war, but his civilian clothes and the sodden paper bag that carried his underwear jolted him back to the present. He climbed out the space where a window would one day be and relieved himself in the glistening wonderland. With his bag tucked under his arm, he shoved his icy fingers into his empty pockets and headed for the train station.

Weldon couldn't go back home to Tenafly Road. It wasn't his home anyway. Why did Katherine give him all that money? She was too naive. He needed to be with someone different ... no that wasn't true. He was thirsty for Katherine, but he had to jump in the McCullough well to get her. He trotted now to the just-arrived train, wishing he had the courage to put himself under it. The station looked merry and festive in the newly fallen snow. Christmas would arrive here but not in Arizona.

Someone grabbed his shoulder, turned him like a whirligig, and punched him in the jaw, sending him to the ground. Weldon scuttled to his feet in shock.

"John Weldon, you bastard, what in God's name are you doing here?" shouted Scott, grabbing Weldon's collar. "Do you dare desert my daughter, you wretch? Is this the treatment Katie deserves?"

"This is no concern of yours, Mr. McCullough," Weldon said, a sudden rage taking hold. "It's between your daughter and me."

"Not my concern? This marriage is the disaster I imagined. I'm sorry to have allowed it."

"I would have done it with or without your damned blessing."

The older man's face turned purple, and his body shook. More violence was one smart comment away. "I will do everything in my power to see that my *two* grandchildren are protected from your corrupting influences!" Scott said, glaring at Weldon who stood blank faced. "Yes, Weldon, for the love of Christ, you'd have to be blind not to notice the signs that Katherine will have another child of yours!"

Weldon turned away from Scott without looking back, running, slipping and sliding in the melting snow as it soaked through his shoes. His lungs swelled and burned in the cold and exertion. The crazy idea of leaving without a trace melted away as he ran up the hill to the only place, the only people he had ever warmed up to.

The flood of heat from the kitchen was more than he bargained for as he stood in the open doorway. William, half-dressed after a bath, crawled over to greet him as Sarah struggled to her feet after him. "Close the door! The chill will be the death of the child."

Weldon closed the door and reached for William too late. Sarah scooped him up and took him to the fire where a knit blue sweater and cap awaited.

"Mrs. McCullough, I ..."

"No, John, explain to your wife," Sarah said with a severe look. "To think that this is Katie's town, and you out gallivanting after her reputation is already sullied!"

"I-I haven't done ... I did nothing to bring on suspicion. I mean, I did nothing at all!"

Weldon raced the stairs to Katherine's room. She sat waiting for him in bed beneath the new winter quilts Sarah had made. Katherine's face was drawn and grey as it had been yesterday and maybe the day before. Weldon went awkwardly to her, playing with his hair.

"Stop it!" Katherine ordered. "That habit of yours is so maddening! And you're filthy. Stay off the bed—everything was changed this morning."

Weldon stopped not far from the door, fingering his bag. "Kate, why didn't you tell me about the baby?"

"It was to be a surprise. Last night—that's why I sent you off." Her voice trembled as she turned the ring on her finger. "I wanted to announce it to you and Father. So Mother and I made a nice meal."

Weldon cringed, knowing how hard Sarah was on Katherine in her kitchen.

"But you never came home."

"Katherine."

"Where is my money?"

"What?"

"My money or a gift for Willy or something!"

Weldon threw the bag of union suits on the bed.

"This is it? You're going to the desert, and this is what you buy? Where is the *rest* of *my money*?"

"I lost the money," he answered defiantly, sorry all the same as he watched Katherine take it in.

"You lost my money—for Christmas? For heaven's sake, where were you?"

"I needed time to myself," he mumbled.

"I know when you lie!" Katherine cried. "Just go. It hurts to have you here anymore."

"But Katherine, I love you," he said, stepping closer.

"I don't believe you." She clutched the bed sheet in her hands. "If you loved me you wouldn't leave me here for months without a word. You wouldn't humiliate me like you did last night. Were you drinking?" Katherine asked almost hopefully.

Weldon shook his head.

"Well then I can't imagine what you're up to." She waited for a response "Am I not enough for you?"

"Katherine, you're everything to me. It's madness for you to think I could want anything more after the weeks we've had! I was alone last night. I promise you that." He looked away. "I was thinking."

"About what? Not about me or Willy—you didn't even get him a gift."

"I always think about you!" he lied again. "I was just miserable about having to leave soon."

Katherine fell back on to her pillows and turned from him in tears.

The clatter of silverware against the table and William's strong-lunged blabbering filled the house as Weldon reentered the kitchen. Sarah refused to acknowledge her son-in-law as she tried to convince Willy to eat some gruel—an invention of Scott's designed to improve the child's immunity. "Come, young man, eat for Grammy."

Weldon slipped into the chair across from Sarah, who bristled at his presence. He listened to the clock and the baby, hoping Sarah would say something.

"John Weldon, I'm exceptionally disappointed in you."

Weldon looked forward to taking something later—when this was over.

"I care for you almost like a son," Sarah said, "but if you hurt my Katie I will always come down on her side."

William howled. Weldon took up the spoon, patted the child's head, and offered more of the cereal to his son, who reluctantly complied. John gave him a big smile. "Now you try, Willy," Weldon said, giving the toddler his spoon. This was new to the boy who had not yet been allowed such a task.

"Mr. Weldon, you must realize that I'm your one ally in this house, but how am I to defend your actions last night? You must understand how hard it is for Scott—and me—to see our daughter plan something special only to be humiliated by your absence."

"Oh, Mrs. McCullough, I thought when I met Katherine all my bad habits and behaviors would fall away, but every time I have some success they come back even stronger. I despair at ever changing. I'm getting worse!"

"Habits can be changed with the help of God. It's much harder to change someone's heart after you've broken it," Sarah counseled, watching William follow every movement John made. The boy pulled the tipsy spoon to his mouth and ate. "You know we live in a modern time. Couldn't you write more or send a telegram?"

Weldon stared blankly.

"Poor boy, is it that you don't know how?"

Weldon flushed and replied, "Of course I can write! N-no, it's just finding good words."

"John, maybe you married too young. Most boys need a little time to be out and go wild, but ..."

"No, that's not what I want at all! I was alone last night. I wasn't drinking, I ..."

"It makes no difference what you were up to. It makes no difference if I think you married too young. You are married now and two children will soon depend upon you." Sarah watched Weldon wipe his son's face and kiss it. "Weldon, you make a good father. Did you want a family?"

"More than anything."

"Listen to me then. You're doing a poor job keeping one. Maybe you were never taught the right ways, but that's no excuse. There are people here to help you, and you're smart enough to remember what caused you to suffer as a child. You don't want your wife and children to suffer in the same way."

"Mrs. McCullough, if Katherine knew everything about me ..."

"If you ever want security in marriage you must be honest. You can't pretend. Have you an interest in other women?"

"No. Katherine's perfect."

Mrs. McCullough rested her hands on her hips. "No one is perfect. But Katherine is devoted to you and has faith in you. That's a special thing, but if you don't trust her, she will begin to distrust you."

"You're right," he admitted, "but I've apologized so many times. I almost wish Kate would do something wrong just once!"

Sarah laughed and patted his face. "Now go clean up and start fresh. You're a good boy, but you must behave like one."

Impulsively Weldon pulled Sarah into a bear hug and gave her a peck on the cheek.

"Mrs. McCullough, if God exists he works through you! Thank you." He picked up William and left the room, still dirty but with a clean clarity of purpose. He knocked on the bedroom door and barreled in. "Kate, please let me speak with you."

Disobeying orders, he sat on the new bedding with Willy. Katherine pulled herself up wearily. William clung to his father.

"Katherine, I should have come home last night. There's no defense," he said. "But I'll make it up to you. I'll come get you before the baby arrives."

"It breaks my heart," Katherine began, "but I misjudged you. Somehow the man I married left and joined the army never to return. I'd be afraid to go with you anywhere. I'm tired of being forgotten," she cried, but choked it back. "I'm worn out and now I have another baby to worry about."

"Katherine! Please don't say anymore! Let me talk now. I'm a mess. I know that, but I try not to be. I don't care for myself anymore. I only want to be good for you. Your mother says nobody's perfect. But she can't convince me you're not. Without you I would have given up long ago. You're my only hope. You had faith in me once. I want to win that back. Please just give me one more chance to prove myself."

"I forgive you," Katherine said with no confidence. "I just don't understand how yesterday you were so clean and fit. I lose my footing somehow when you're around."

Chapter Nineteen

Baltimore

December 1868

Dear Katherine and William,

Merry Christmas!

I never said that to anyone before. I hate myself. Do you still love me? How can you? I am afraid of you. If I lose you I will die. You are the only person to ever make me feel I exist, but I have lied to you and cannot bear to deceive you any longer. I was given morphine by the surgeons but I cannot explain to you why I continue with it. It no longer helps me, and I have tried to stop so many times, but it is stronger than me. I thought my love for you would make it go away, but it has not. I am ashamed of my weakness. If only you can still love me. Your faith in me breaks my heart. I do not want to disappoint you. I will stop this for you and William ...

Galveston, Texas ... Decided not to send a letter until I had more to tell you, little girl. I miss you. There was a small storm when we started out and made for much seasickness. No the sickness is in me. When I come to get you you'll be much delighted by the waters of the south. If you come. If I come back. During the long dull days we watch porpoises dash through the waves and we fly fish. The evenings are the prettiest when the water glows with what looks like underwater fireflies. I don't care about fireflies. I want to. I want to feel something just out of reach. I never catch a thing. Stay below in the dark. Baltimore, Galveston, San Francisco—no place compares to Englewood, New Jersey, and I would give the duds off my back and the tobacco in my pocket—the only things I own!—to be back trying to win you over. My sweet beautiful girl, I will not let another Christmas pass with us apart and I will make you proud.

Enclosed is a gift I picked up for you in a little shop. I hope you like it. Also a little something for Willy.

Your loving husband,

John Weldon

Weldon hesitated. He considered signing the letter, but in a burst he shoved it in his old haversack. He wrapped the lavender brooch with a tiny lady on horseback in paper. Thievery had come back to him easily in San Francisco—a piece of jewelry slipped into a pocket was simply done. He tied the package closed and carefully uncorked the small medicinal vial of liquid beside him. The pills were gone, and the liquid was nicer. He had "found" a new syringe. The newer ones were better, smaller, and discreet. He gave himself a dose and drifted along to Arizona.

***

Captain S. McCullough

May 1869

Dear John,

Thank you first off for responding so quickly to my correspondence (note sarcasm). I am beginning to feel I am the only member of the family who cares to know what the rest are doing! A few lines now and then, Weldon, would be nice. I hear occasionally only from Mother who for some reason thinks I care more about the new Catholic church in Englewood than I do about our family. By the way, thank you for mentioning the new baby on the way—very kind of you.

Maybe you would like to know how I am enjoying my visit to Washington. How two months have turned into eight, I'll never know. My parents will be annoyed, when I tell them, but I've asked Langellier to have me sent back in the field—Mrs. Langellier is doing quite poorly after a stroke so I think the old man will resign, but for now it's a leave of absence only—looks like my ride with him is done, though it is now my responsibility that his nieces get back to the regiment to be with their father. God help me. I'll be in Arizona soon, but it holds no appeal—I hope to be transferred to the Platte or even the Pacific. I know you have said your experience in the Pacific before the war was dismal, but I would rather any weather than heat year round.

Anyone who says Washington is a bully place to be and dreams of a staff job should reconsider. You couldn't pay me enough to get mixed up in this recon-

struction business. I am sorry to say I have gotten a whole new opinion about women mixing with soldiers. They all marry for rank which is fair enough, I guess, but they bicker and bring all sorts of tempers out in the men. I've gotten more enjoyment watching mules fight than watching the jackasses at these socials trample each other for the chance to make some impression on a superior—while men in the field must hope for an old soldier to tumble over. I will admit that I did some trampling myself one night for the chance to shake General Sherman's hand. He was quite impressive as you would expect.

The real point of my letter: A few weeks back, and you are lucky that this occurred early in the night, the colonel and I—along with his annoying temperance nieces who are the bane of my existence—came across a staff clerk. We were chatting about the war and then the Indians and the shambles of Arizona. The leadership not the best etc. I mentioned you and he laughed in recognition of your name.

"Well," he says, "man alive, it seems from this Weldon's papers, he's a one man army. My cousin is a quartermaster out there. About the only thing working at Fort ———— is your Weldon. Came out of the blue these last months, according to my cousin, full of grim determination. Whipped his small group into shape. Seems he's the only one they trust on detached duty to come back."

He went on about you bringing in some bandits and Indians too. All small affairs, he said, but impressive just the same. He mentioned you have even made the men take better care of their animals! Is there anything you have not attempted, Weldon?

Colonel Langellier wonders what has changed you, but I tell him this is the old Weldon from the war.

Anyway, the short of this story is that you were to be recommended for promotion, but there was the problem of your being married. I am sure you know the rules and regulations better than me. I asked was there any way around this rule to which he replied that there were always ways and that it mattered little to him if the papers were "incorrectly" filled out. We shook hands, and that was that.

On the street today, I happened upon him again, and he said it was all a done deal and the papers would be sent shortly and that you were to prepare yourself for the examination in Washington in September!

This letter is a race against those papers as I wanted to be the one to give you the news. I will not tell a soul. Good luck!

Regards,

Simon McCullough

Chapter Twenty

Scott and Sarah hid the secret telegram from Katherine at Weldon's request. Soon Weldon would come to take the last of Sarah's children away. But still Scott and Sarah hoped that somehow *their* William would be left behind. Katherine hadn't said no, and the boy hardly knew his father. Sarah made a point of alerting Katherine to how fragile William's health was and how stability was the best thing for a child, but Katherine was too busy caring for her new baby girl to listen much to her mother's hints. Scott said not a word about Weldon. The new lieutenant had the upper hand. William was Weldon's son no matter how little he deserved such a fine lad.

An air of mourning hung around the place, but Katherine hardly noticed. Elizabeth Sarah Weldon had arrived on time and healthy but with a definite preference for Katherine over anyone else. Sarah was hurt the first few times Eliza bawled in her arms. Katherine was glad.

One morning Katherine found Sarah in Scott's arms in the kitchen.

"Mother, what's happened?"

Scott explained. "Your mother's burnt the breakfast."

Sarah laughed with tears still rolling over her full cheeks and slapped Scott. "You'll be late for the train, old man."

William sat on the floor with the little wooden toys Scott had made for him. They were rough and unimaginative but carved with care, and William enjoyed them thoroughly. He jumped up and ran after his grandfather to walk with him to the gate as he did each morning.

Sarah looked after William wiping a tear away. "Katherine, I've loved taking care of Willy."

"Yes, Mother," Katherine said, bouncing Eliza.

"Not like that, Katie—you'll shake her to death!"

"Mother, please!"

"Oh, poor Katie! I didn't prepare you well for adulthood, did I? Would you like to cook with me today?"

Katherine laughed. "I know you hate me in your kitchen and besides, I'm tired." She kissed Sarah and took Eliza with her back up to bed. The cool air breezed through the window. A slow clip-clop of someone's horse on the freshly paved road faded into the distance. Eliza sighed and fell asleep, and Katherine set her down in the cradle before falling into a deep soft sleep herself.

She heard a voice. It couldn't be John because he would have sent word. She jumped from bed and raced down the stairs with her heart in her mouth. "Please let it be true!" she whispered over and over again. Weldon had kept to his word this past year and written her often. It had been a struggle at first, but the words flowed by the third letter.

Katherine peeked into the dining room. Weldon in full dress uniform had his back to her. As soon as his promotion had become official he boarded the train north to make good on his promise. His hair was short and neat. Sarah stopped mid-sentence, and John turned to Katherine. She stood still a moment, stunned at how handsome and well he looked. He beamed at her, a proud second lieutenant.

"Here's your officer come to get you," Sarah cried.

William gazed up at Weldon from behind Sarah's full skirt.

"John!" Katherine threw herself in to Weldon's arms. "You brute! Not telling me a thing! Oh, but it doesn't matter! You're here!"

"I wanted to surprise you," he said, delighted by Katherine's response. For once he had carried something through. "Thank you, Kate, for waiting."

Katherine laughed up at him. "I would have waited forever."

Sarah pushed William. "Go to Papa."

Willy shuffled over with head down.

"Son, I've brought candy if you'll show me your sister," John bargained.

"Okay," the boy replied, all business, and marched the stairs with Weldon and a giggling Katherine behind him.

Sarah hid in the kitchen, trying to regain her composure.

The baby was awake and complaining. "John, I'm afraid Eliza cries a lot when I don't hold her," Katherine warned.

"Oh well, she'll just have to get used to me holding her, won't she?" He pulled Eliza up before him. They stared at each other. "Look at those blue eyes! Just the same as yours. My, she's got some head of hair too!" He cradled Eliza and sat on their bed. "See, she likes me!"

Katherine remembered how afraid they had both been of Willy at first. She held William's hand and marveled at her husband. John looked older and stronger—maybe it was his hair. Katherine panicked—he had done better without her.

Weldon read her mind. "Little girl, come sit up by me."

She eagerly complied. William hung back.

"Don't you want your candy, son?" John grinned, pulling it from his pocket.

William held out his hand, and Weldon dragged him up onto the enormous bed. Katherine sat next to her husband with hands folded. John had become a lieutenant and had adventures with interesting and exotic people. What had she to show for herself? John took her chin and kissed her forehead. "Kate, I can't believe I'm here with you."

"It must seem so boring after ..." she began.

"There's nothing boring about you, or our little family. The last time I was here ..."

"Let's not talk about that," she said.

"No, I have to," he replied. "No one ever held me to account, but you did, and I'm so glad to have married a girl who ... who made me work hard and succeed."

"Simon says you were always hard-working."

"That was before ... you remember I promised to take you with me, but Arizona, Kate, it's hot and I'm being sent to Camp Grant. Are you still sure you'd like to come?"

"John Weldon! You will not be let leave here without me!"

"And the children," Weldon added.

"Of course ... Eliza is still nursing."

"I don't care what nonsense your parents filled you with. I don't care how attached they are to William. He's my son, our son. And he is coming with us!"

"But Willy loves them best," she said.

He pulled her close to him. "Kate, you'll be a fine mother to William once you're left alone. He's coming. That is my final decision."

Katherine was surprised by his spunk.

"William, would you like to come be a soldier with me?" he asked.

The boy did not hesitate. There might be more candy in it for him. "Yes, please."

"John, how did you ever get so much more handsome?" Katherine asked, suddenly aware of the shoddy cover-up she wore.

"Clean living, I guess. You know, in all my travels I didn't see one girl near as pretty as you. But I am disappointed I didn't see you before now." Weldon rubbed his hand over his wife's middle. "You never sent a picture!"

She blushed and kissed him. "Finally, Mr. Weldon, I will be near you forever."

Weldon ran his hand through his short hair. Some things never changed, and she was glad. "Things can't get any better than this."

"My dear sweet husband, it can only get better now that we're all together."

The kitchen door downstairs banged and soon a gruff call came for William. Scott was home. Willy bounded from the bed and slid down the hallway banister. "Grandpa, it's Papa home and come to fetch us!"

Katherine knew the news would not be greeted with any hint of enthusiasm. She made to leave before William could say anything more to upset her parents, but John pulled her back. "Come here a minute, Kate. I won't go downstairs without a proper kiss from you! I've waited a year!"

Katherine poked his sides. "I'm afraid I won't be able to stop at just a kiss, Lieutenant Weldon, if we start."

Sarah knocked at the door. "Katherine, your father would like to speak to you both."

Katherine heard the broken-hearted crack in her mother's voice and opened the door just as Sarah made her descent. Turning to face Katherine Sarah said, "How dare you send a small boy to tell us the awful news! It's cruel and cowardly, and your father is crushed!"

"But Mrs. McCullough, I told you I was coming," Weldon began, but Sarah waved him off and ran down the stairs overcome with emotion. John looked to Katherine, and they reluctantly made their way into the kitchen.

Scott had William on his knee by the hearth. Scott's demeanor provoked Weldon. "William, come here, son."

"No," William replied, sinking further back into his grandfather's arms.

"You see, Mr. Weldon, a lieutenancy does not impress everyone. You haven't been a real father to this boy. William doesn't even know you. And to think how pathetic it is to send the boy do your bidding when he doesn't understand what it all means!" Scott was clearly happy in his small triumph.

Weldon stood tall. "I appreciate everything you've done for my family, sir, but it was always my intention to come back and take them when I could."

"Except when you were thinking of deserting them last year at the station," Scott said.

"John?" Katherine stared at him.

"I'll explain later," he said, shaken at how easy it was for someone like Scott to cut him down to size.

"And Katherine will swallow whatever fairy tale you feed her," Scott said. "You stand so smugly before me as if you've defeated me, but you'll see when Katherine fails you as a wife."

"Pardon me, Mr. McCullough, but it is you who has decided this is a war. I won't listen to you belittle my wife. Anyone can learn to cook."

"Is that all Katie is to you?" Sarah asked, offended at his low regard for the fine art of cooking.

"No, Mrs. McCullough, I only mean Katherine will do well at anything she sets her mind to, including cooking." Weldon couldn't figure how the argument had turned to food.

Scott guided the talk back to more important issues. He neatened William's hair and took the bag of candy from him. "This is no good for little boys with weak constitutions. Weldon, your pretty and multitalented wife has shown little interest in her son since you've been away—don't be fooled. Katie practically promised my wife that William would stay with us at least until you were settled."

John turned to Katherine for explanation, but all his wife could do was cry.

"I don't care what my foolish wife promised you, and I'm sure it was through manipulation that you secured the promise. I'm taking them all. They're mine."

Katherine spoke. "John, forgive me. I didn't say yes or no. Maybe I let them believe. William doesn't seem to like me much ... not the way he does them, and we can have more children."

"Katherine, stop it this instant! Don't you see what they've done? They've undermined your confidence! How could you give up William this easily?" John took William and shoved the candy into his hands. "I'm sorry you both will be lonely for William, but he is coming to Arizona, and he will learn to have normal tender feelings for his parents. We will leave in the morning."

Sarah gasped. "Tomorrow morning?"

"Yes," John said with finality. "Under the circumstances I think it best I get a room in town for the night."

"Don't be silly," Sarah said, trying to be polite.

"Mrs. McCullough, you'll want time with the boy and Kate in private. I can't stay here another minute and listen to any of this!"

Katherine followed him to the door and out on to the porch. She tugged at him feeling unequal and childish. "I beg you, Mr. Weldon. Forgive me!"

"Katherine, stop it."

"I never told them they could *have* Willy. They just took over, and they were so much better at ..."

"You don't have to explain. I'm smart enough to see what's happened. I'm just disappointed you didn't fight harder for William."

"I didn't want to hurt their feelings, and I was afraid I would do something wrong."

"What about my feelings? Did you really think I would leave my firstborn son with them? You're his mother! They've turned the child against us both."

"I'm pathetic and useless!" Katherine sobbed.

Weldon smiled. "That's what they want you to think. I won't allow it to continue," he said, bringing her under his arm. "You need time to grow up away from them. Willy will just have to get used to us, that's all."

Katherine wiped her face. "I'm having a hard time getting used to you! I feel like a tiny weakling next to my new lieutenant."

"I see now that I left you here too long on your own," he said. "The West will make you strong."

"But I've disappointed you now. I'm so sorry about Willy."

Weldon laughed and kissed Katherine. "You know, my little girl, it's a relief. Finally you are not so perfect after all. I was tired of making all the mistakes. At least I never almost gave our son away!"

Katherine stared at him. This was not the man she married, and tomorrow Lieutenant Weldon would take her away.

Chapter Twenty-One

The first giddy days of travel away from the narrow streets and views of Englewood had long since passed and with it Katherine's optimistic hope of starting over and being heroic. Along the cliffs and hills, Apache smoke signals, ascending like snakes charmed by the musical clatter of the army mules, reminded Katherine she was no longer safe. She sat unnerved, brain-rattled, and hungry, holding Eliza tightly in her tired arms.

The head driver had been found stupefied with drink and now slept beside her, snoring in the hot covered wagon. William, stripped to the waist against Katherine's orders, climbed over the supplies precariously, just out of reach of his mother. The drunk driver was oblivious to the tumbling boxes, pans, and blankets as they moved over rough terrain. The air was still and bright. Katherine pulled her wilting bonnet over her aching head. The baby needed to be changed and her bag was somewhere nearby, but the deadening heat kept Katherine glued to her seat. With one hand she unscrewed her canteen and sipped from it delicately. The train stopped once again, and she sighed.

"Kate, are you all right in there?" John asked, popping his head through the closed canvas.

"I'm roasted!"

"Well, I know, but it's worse out here, I can tell you." Weldon's eyes were dark with worry. "Poor Kate, I know this ain't what you expected. I'm sorry. M-maybe I shouldn't have let you come."

"We'll be fine. You'll see." Katherine managed a false smile.

Mountains peaked with billowing pine. Dry alkali desert and canyons glowed in harsh, terrible beauty. Katherine longed for something familiar and as the journey progressed Katherine thought more of the terrain they had covered and how difficult and dangerous it would be to turn back now. She grew lonesome and tried not to think about Father and Mother and how long the mail would take to get where they were going, but she could not share her feelings without hurting her husband.

Eliza was fussy in the heat, and Katherine fretted at the thought of big red heathens, naked and violent, overtaking the army wagon train. Squeezing Eliza tighter, she begged Willy to come back and sit beside her. Caked in dust, he finally fell victim to the heat and settled between two bags to sleep.

The light changed, and the wagons lurched to a stop. The fierce language of the teamsters, impossible to translate, rose like a wave from the front to the back of the line. They would camp here for the night next to a small stream the soldiers complained was sour-tasting. Katherine crawled to the back of the wagon and looked out. All was pink and soft as the sun dipped from the sky. A copse of cottonwoods stood in a rosy display of green finery, and as the pack animals and the army settled, the birds sang bedtime stories.

A private helped Katherine from the wagon and walked off, too exhausted and perplexed at his lot in life to conform to the civilities of small talk.

John came up on a thin, worn-out horse and hopped down to her, looking red and puffed from the sun. "Kate, it looks like they're right about this place. It's awful. I'm burnt to a cinder."

Katherine turned him around and pulled at his collar. "Mr. Weldon, your neck is fried! Where's your neck tie?"

"Well, at least we can rest under the trees if we're quick about it," he said. "There's a wind picking up for once. Maybe it won't be so hot tonight."

Katherine laughed.

"What?"

"We are traveling to the end of the world together. It's so ridiculous with the children and the dust and the drunken Mr. Hornsby. I never expected to be this far from home."

"Katherine, I know it ain't—*it's not* fair to ask you to stay, but I had no idea that it would be this rugged and so ..."

"No, no, John, you don't understand me. I'm laughing because you have so bewitched me I'd follow you into Hell and this is very much like it! But you're here at the end of each day, and as scared as I am I'm happy too."

Weldon shoved his hands in his trouser pockets and rocked on his boots, looking around again with a grin. "This is Hell, Kate, but you're bully." He kissed her nose and grabbed her bag and their tenting supplies from the wagon. "Let's get comfortable before it gets too dark."

Beneath the trees they found a small patch of soft, cool grass where Katherine could clean the baby and set the soiled things to dry after laundering them in the muddy stream. The horses and the mules down the line drank enthusiastically, but the soldiers grumbled. New recruits cursed their decision not to slip from the army before the desert. Now they must stay on or die alone by thirst or Indians.

"Shall we start a fire and make supper?" Weldon asked, running to do one thing and another.

"I want to feed the baby and go to sleep," Katherine said.

A look of impatience swept over Weldon's face at her refusal to help with the meal. He took a deep breath. "When I'm done with the tent, Willy and I will make supper while you have a nap. We'll wake you when it's ready."

She watched her husband struggle with the tent and Willy getting in the way, but she could not make her body move until the tent was up. She crawled inside with Eliza. Weldon had thrown down a blanket, but the grass beneath was cooler so Katherine rolled it up as a pillow and to the lullaby of the sleepy birds and the clinking tools of men preparing camp dinners she fell asleep.

She dreamt of wind and stray hairs racing over her face, and she grabbed at them and pulled them behind her ears, but it was no use. The baby whimpered and squirmed at her elbow. In the twilight John and Willy were listening to an old teamster talk of the Apache who murdered a Mexican two months earlier on this trail, and Katherine realized that she wasn't dreaming. Insects scurried over her, and she batted them off in silent panic. The ants ran over the baby's eyes and under her clothes. "*John*!"

Weldon opened the fly and grabbed Eliza, pulling the large ants from her face and hair and brushing the rest to the ground as Katherine frantically stripped down to her stockings and boots. John shooed Willy away, and the teamster asked what the trouble was.

"Ants."

"Oh, I coulda' told you to watch for 'em under these darned trees. Probably set camp on a mound of 'em."

"Yes, thanks for that, Hornsby," Weldon said. He turned to Katherine shaking out her chemise and flicked an ant from her shoulder.

Katherine sent him a vicious look when he smiled. "I'm glad you find this amusing, John Weldon, but I don't."

"You stripped so fast I hardly had time to enjoy it."

"You find ants crawling all over my body attractive?"

Weldon thought a moment and laughed. "No, of course not. It's disgusting, and I'm glad it's over." He laughed again. "Kate, you do beat all."

Katherine went back to examining her clothes in the dimming light.

Supper was burnt once again, but they ate ravenously. Every so often John reached over to pick a stray but imaginary bug from Katherine's hair and chuckled. She pretended to be annoyed.

"Is it getting cold or is it just my sun burn?" Weldon asked, pouring himself the last cup of coffee.

Katherine pulled their blankets, shaken of bugs, over the sleeping children and sat beside John as he sang:

I love the merry, merry sunshine, it makes the heart so gay,
To hear the sweet birds singing on their summer holiday.
With their wildwood notes of duty, from the hawthorn bush and tree,
Oh, the sunshine is all beauty—oh the merry, merry sun for me!

Katherine smiled at his terrible voice. Hornsby the teamster stumbled up again. "No more bugs in the unmentionables, ma'am? Appears we're gonna get a norther—hope you brought yer flannels."

They woke to the whistle of the wind curling up under the canvas where a stake had loosened. Their breath steamed before them. Weldon jumped into his clothes, started a tiny fire, which the wind conspired to put out, and went in search of more blankets and stray coats. Over a breakfast of hard bread and cool coffee, Katherine and William grumbled about the cold as much as they had done about the heat the previous morning but were silenced when John presented them with wrinkled uniform jackets. Someone even lent the boy a moth-eaten wool cap to pull over his ears. Katherine wondered which of the men had last worn it. But still they shivered. Wrapped in all they could find including the canvas tent, Katherine, William, and Eliza settled into the wagon once more. John rode off in the lightest of jackets to start the day. Katherine did not know then that he had sold off the coat she and Sarah had made for him.

Finally Camp Grant came into sight. A small, faraway and quiet band played a welcome. Distorted by the wind, it sounded hollow and sad. William jumped before Katherine could stop him and ran along the column of men, glorying in the display of flags and guidons. The horses trotted now, and even the ornery mules brightened as they led their wagons over the parade ground. Katherine in the wagon could see only the barren wilderness lit by the morning sun behind her until the wagon slowed to a stop. She climbed out with Eliza in tow. Having imagined the fort to be an oasis in the desert, she stood for a moment catching her breath.

The military men of the post said a few words that she could not hear. The ceremony reminded her of the blustery funerals she had been dragged to as a child. When the officers fell silent, the wind kicked up and the ranks broke. Some soldiers had a stoic grace, but most looked disappointed that their lives had come to this. They lingered with their hands in their armpits or pockets, bracing against the cold wind fingering through their scant duds.

On one side of the parade ground stood what at first appeared to be stables, but the eager animals were led elsewhere. The adobe and wood structures acted as officers' quarters. The small dark windows looked out on the newcomers forbiddingly. Across the grounds an even more ungainly mass of ramshackle structures sat waiting to be beautified by the ranks.

The commissary and hospital shacks lay at the far end of the parade ground, and now Katherine saw the beasts of burden being led to the stables and corral behind them. Stray dogs yapped and skittered around the new family until John kicked them off. Debris tumbled like circus dancers across the barren expanse. Even the flag flew pale.

The men who came up to greet the newcomers were in various states of undress and had a decidedly low look, as if the desert wind had knocked the polish from them, carrying away buttons, hair scissors, and even the will to bathe, but one was friendly. "Will ye look at that—two youngins fer the camp. Well, they sure is fine, ma'am, and the boys'll have some frolic with 'em, I reckon. Woo wee, if it ain't the plumb coldest day out here. Rest easy, ma'am. We'll get ya the coziest bunk, so we will. Lieutenant, sir, ya may as well know you'll have to bump the Lyons tribe and they're an ornery lot, but rules is rules and you just about outrank them. Sergeant Lyons got lucky so far cause this place was undermanned. They shoulda' moved right off, but no one had the balls ta tell the missus till today. We thought you'd be here soon enough, and I guess we was pretty right about it. Jus' follow me, jus' here ..."

Weldon swallowed hard as they stepped onto the "porch" of a place that looked more like an outhouse than a home. He had hoped his request to have Oonagh Lyons and her hapless husband transferred went through.

The cheerful private knocked like a bull at the door. "Hey there, missus!"

The door opened a crack. Two stone-eyed girls peered out first but were shoved aside by the woman with a cynical grin John had grown so dependent on before he straightened himself out this year. She folded her arms and turned to the young man. "Yeah, private?"

"Mrs. Lyons, pack up yer gear, I'm sorry ta say."

Oonagh glared at Katherine. "And you're what all the fuss is over?"

Katherine turned to John. "A fuss?"

Oonagh laughed.

"M-Mrs. Lyons was with the r-regiment at F-Fort ..." John explained, but his voice trailed off.

The cry of a baby within unsettled Katherine. "I can't steal her home! I can't do it!"

"Mrs. Weldon, it's the army's way. Ya cain't change it, and Lieutenant Weldon has rank he earned," the private said. "One fine mornin' when yer set jus the way ya like it, you might be put out too, so don't be too upset takin' what's rightfully yers."

The wind slapped the branches of the ramada porch, and Eliza howled. Katherine handed the baby to Weldon, who had no better luck with her and gave her back.

Oonagh Lyons looked on wryly. "Ain't you a tiny thing, Mrs. Weldon? Good luck to ya."

William clung to Katherine's skirt, his nose dripping, his body shivering. Eliza swung her arms and scratched at her mother.

Oonagh pushed through them to fetch a makeshift wheelbarrow. The private offered to help.

Katherine said to John, "Won't you help her too?"

He hesitated but took a step forward.

Oonagh scowled at them. "Sure, I can do it meself!"

Even in fine eastern clothes Katherine could not compete with Oonagh's wild beauty. Oonagh threw a few pots and pans, a quilt and some candles into the barrow. The children followed barefoot, dragging a carpetbag with them. They looked hunched and rickety, and John worried about rations for his own family. He grabbed the bag from the girls, but Oonagh spoke to her children. "You take it yerselves, we don't want none of their help."

Reluctantly the children took the bag from the equally reluctant Weldon. "That's mean of you, Oonagh—I mean Mrs. Lyons. The bag's too damned heavy for Theresa and Maeve."

"Enjoy yer new home, lieutenant. It's a palace! Just mind yer own children. I'll take care of mine how I see fit."

John turned to Katherine and shrugged though he wanted to pummel Oonagh. He would not let his children starve out here. "Where's Sergeant Lyons, private?"

"Course he's off in the guardhouse or in Tucson—the paymaster's just been on a flyin' visit after mus' be six months. Surprised there's as many here as is, but I guess some is still getting over the fever that's been round." The private entered the quarters. "Darn shame they mussed the paint job us soldiers did on the place jus a few months ago. Never shoulda' let them dirty micks in here when there weren't no officer. They ain't fit fer luxuries, I reckon."

Katherine stepped timidly over the threshold, the wild flames from a half broken cook stove changing the private's features grimly. A crooked bunk with legs crippled and gnawed at looked fit for nightmares. A table made of old boxes and covered with what appeared to be the grease and soot from a hundred horrible meals lay toppled on the lone chair. The walls had cave paintings of the most inelegant sort. Splashes of color that could only come from spilled slop buckets and bedpans decorated the once-whitewashed corners of their abode.

The private threw more fuel on the fire, setting the stovepipe into a frenzy of smoky coughs and spits. "Oh, they've gone and cracked the pipe," he said as Katherine and John looked on despairingly.

Eliza still cried and now coughed from the black smoke. Katherine bounced her nervously. John brought in the rest of their things and the private went off.

Sitting on the edge of the bed frame, Katherine yelped as it gave way beneath her. William laughed as she sat crying on the dirt floor with Eliza screaming now. Weldon rolled his eyes. He pulled his wife up and held her in his arms. "Oh, Kate, don't cry!" he begged. "I'll fix it up somehow. I can make us a better bed, but don't cry—it only makes things worse."

"I can't help it. I keep thinking about our things. I can't imagine how I'll make this place homey without them. And what about our clothes and dishes, John? We have nothing."

"That's not true—we have a frying pan. And look, one lone teacup from your set."

Just then a large centipede scurried over Katherine's bag. John brushed it off as calmly as he could.

"What was that, John?"

He shook his head and plunged into work. He dragged the dirty linen and hay mattress outside. As Weldon did, a blizzard of assorted insects and other small creatures fled from their home in a frenzied stampede. Katherine ran from the room in panic only to be met on the porch by three squaws with broad, flat faces half-hidden beneath musky-scented black bangs. With one hand Katherine grabbed Willy, who was mesmerized by the women, and in the other arm she held Eliza. She tried to back into their quarters, but Weldon wouldn't let her. "Kate, be calm," he said gently as he put his arm around her.

"They're like trolls with rodent eyes ... and the one ... what's happened to her nose?" Katherine whispered.

"Apache men hack the noses from wives they think betray them," he said matter-of-factly.

Even in the cold too much of their bodies hung out. They spoke in an aggressive tongue as they poked the crying baby with their thick-skinned, misshapen fingers. Katherine clung even tighter to Eliza.

"Katherine, they only want to see Eliza."

"Child—cry baby," one of the women said. Her sun-baked skin crinkled like wastepaper, and she spoke to the others and back to Weldon and Katherine again. "Cry-baby weak—no good."

"She's not weak!" Katherine said.

The woman mumbled, and her friend nodded in agreement. "Cry-baby no good," she said again and wrung her hands around an imaginary child's neck. "Too much trouble—won't live long—get rid."

"Get out of here!" Weldon shouted and waved his gun. "Stay away from us."

The women pulled their blankets around themselves and walked off. The butchered one laughed and looked back at them. Katherine watched them go in silence and went back inside with Weldon at her heels.

"Oh, John! We have to escape! I'll never survive!"

"Where would we go? Those women—they're harmless. They were just trying to scare us."

"It worked! I won't be able to leave this bug-infested place at all. And what will I do when you're not here? Oh, John, I'm afraid I've made a big mistake following you. I love you, but …"

"Katherine, my pet, don't give up so easily! I know you're scared and miss your comforts, but I also know you're a brave little thing deep down."

Katherine searched his face, unsure if he believed what he was saying.

There was a knock at the door. Weldon sat Katherine on the only chair and opened the door in dread but was relieved to find a statuesque woman, trim and neatly dressed, smiling coquettishly at him. She touched his arm with her bleached glove and spoke with an Eastern, educated accent. "Good day, Mr. Weldon. The boys tell me you've lost your things on the trip out. Is Mrs. Weldon in?"

"Oh, yeah, yes," Weldon answered and allowed the lady to pass him.

Her back was long and straight against the rough angles of the room. "I'm Julia James, the colonel's wife. Mr. Weldon, my husband was sent good reports about you from Colonel Langellier. Your brother-in-law was to be stationed here with you, but he was too good for us, I suppose. Always one for a party and quite the favorite with the Langellier girls and that's dangerous. It's best that Captain McCullough gets away from temptation, and it's ever so nice that Simon has connections. It's how you were promoted, or so I've heard. The army being such a small world. We end up knowing everything." Julia smiled, holding out her hand and gazing at Katherine. "Pleased to meet you."

Katherine spoke shakily over the baby. "I'm Katherine ... Weldon." Again she cried. John took the children and went outside. "My mother packed so many pretty things and a lovely tea set and books for John ... all lost!"

Mrs. James patted Katherine's back smelling of rose perfume. "Oh, you're overwhelmed aren't you? We all were when we got here. It's so different. But you'll get used to it. The ladies will send over clean things, and once you're settled we'll make you a nice meal and discuss what you need to have on hand from the commissary. Sometimes we even go into Tucson for a day of shopping. We're all in this together. Just remember that." Julia brushed the hair from Katherine's face. With her large green eyes and full mouth turned up slightly, the colonel's wife got intimately close. "I'm in charge here, Katherine Weldon."

Katherine couldn't meet her eyes.

Julia smiled again. "So you can depend upon me."

Chapter Twenty-Two

The weak, unskilled warble of the bugler at Camp Grant annoyed most soldiers awake, but Katherine loved the first staccato notes of morning. John had gotten in a "dog robber" for his wife—a soldier hired to help her. At first Katherine resented the idea, but her attempts at cooking and keeping the fire hot were such failures she relented.

"I'm paying Higgins to teach you, little girl. So I don't want to find you hiding in your sketchbooks. Here he is now."

"Mornin' lieutenant," the boy said, looking no older than fifteen with a gap-toothed grin and ruddy complexion. Even in a uniform he looked roughed up and motherless.

Weldon lingered a moment. "Higgins, you won't touch my wife ..."

Private Higgins' face went red. "Ain't never hardly talked to a lady, sir."

"Leave the door open, Kate," Weldon said and left.

Katherine nodded obediently after him, not sure why she felt angry and upset now.

Higgins pulled a chair close to the cold stove and clenched his pipe between his teeth. "Bastard, hypocrite, your husband is."

"You'll get in trouble if you say that again, young man," Katherine said shakily.

"I'm no younger'n you, I bet, miss."

"I'm Mrs. Weldon, please, and right now I'm not sure why you'd come to upset me and make me feel foolish."

"Foolish to marry the likes of ..."

"My husband is in charge of you! And he's a good man."

"You met Oonagh?" Higgins asked with a mean chuckle.

"Yes, I wish we hadn't bumped her out. Is she a friend of yours?"

"Nope. The laundress ain't *my* friend," the private said.

"Mr. Higgins, why do you hate me so soon? I just want to be a good wife and make a fire for once," she said, pulling the corner of her sooty apron to wipe her face. Stiffly she began on her own to place kindling in the stove. The boy huffed as Katherine failed yet again at a lasting flame. Eliza cried from the box acting as crib by the table.

"I guess I had better nurse my little girl, sir," Katherine said, picking up Eliza. "Mr. Higgins, please leave."

Higgins looked around the messy, dark little hovel and sighed. "I reckon it ain't right, how I behaved just now, ma'am. You didn't do nothin' to me. I just don't like it when folks can't trust me. I never hurt a fly, and yer husband shouldna' said anything, but you can't help it, can you?" The boy clasped his hands as Katherine stared in all innocence. "Besides, everything about the lieutenant is rumors. Can you forgive me this once?"

"Please speak up. I'm afraid I can hardly hear you," she said. "I was hoping when you first walked up that I might make a friend."

Higgins frowned as if the last thing in the world he needed was a friend, but he went to the baby in her arms. "Hmm, it's cute ain't it?" He ran his dark hand over Eliza's face, and the baby took his fingers in her mouth. Katherine pulled away.

"My dirty fingers is the least of your worries. This child has teeth and is hungrier than the devil for souls." Higgins pulled stale bread from his pocket.

"Oh, no. My father says solids are too much for her system."

"You must love your papa to listen to such stuff a nonsense. The child's hungry, that's plain." Higgins handed Eliza the bread and after a brief second of investigation the child devoured it.

As the private made his way to the cold stove the next morning, he asked, "Did you remember to put the beans out to soak overnight, ma'am?"

"Oops! I must have forgotten!"

Higgins pulled his sweat-stained kepi off and wiped his greased hair back over his boney scalp. His teeth were badly out of place, but his smile was nice. "You must have forgotten? You know you have, young girl! Now don't be a baby today."

Katherine jumped up from her chair.

"Oh, watch the apron! Oh, you shoulda hemmed it!" Higgins muttered as she tripped. "My you're a caution, girl, but we'll get you fixed up."

Katherine smiled weakly at his optimism. "I'm sorry, but I don't think I can do this. And having you stand here and just stare doesn't help."

"Listen, I see the problem here, and we're gonna solve it once for all. You got yerself in a flutter over this housework stuff. If a caveman could build a fire, don't you think you can? Here's how it's done, ma'am, but I'm only startin' it then you call me from the porch when it's ready for them biscuits you started. I'll show you a shortcut with the beans if yer good and tell you about the colonel and his wife."

"No, but the lieutenant wants you to mind me at the stove, especially after what happened last night."

"Oh, it could a happened to anyone. The fire was just a little out of control ... and that's better'n no fire at all. I'll be right outside if you try to burn the house down again. Yer better without an audience." Higgins patted her on the back. "I got confidence in you."

Even so early in the day the room was an oven. Katherine watched the small flame glow and fed it carefully and less enthusiastically than she had done last night. Grabbing the coffee pot she ran to the door and splashed the remains over the side of the porch.

"Coulda kept that coffee for your garden," Higgins pointed out with his heels up on a box. "But it's yer life."

Katherine huffed but said nothing and rushed back to her fire. "Mr. Higgins!"

"Good work, girl. Now set the coffee to boil and get out the beans."

Katherine and Higgins greased the Dutch oven with pork and filled it with the biscuits before giving the beans a shortcut to cook for supper. John came and went for his coffee and the two cooks sat for a chat.

"Looks like you'll be invited to supper at the colonel's one day soon," Higgins said.

Since the first acts of kindness shown by the officers' wives, they had kept their distance, and Katherine worried that she had already offended them.

"Really? How do you know?"

"I ain't no gossip, but their cook loves to talk—broken English, but I get the gist."

"I don't know how I feel about the news," Katherine said, pulling her hair back into its tight bun. "I can't make out if Mrs. James is nice or not."

"The colonel's wife is popular with the boys, as pretty as she is, and she's smart as a whip. There's a story—can't say for sure it's true—but on a visit to one of the mountain tribes, a chief was so taken by Julia James and her fine needlework he asked if the colonel would swap her. 'Course James was tickled by the offer and declined quick enough. The chief took it all right I guess, or we wouldn't know. You mightn't want to see their quarters though. Yer the sort who'll get demoralized with yer own place after seein' all she's done—a fine housewife and she can recite poems and verse like Shakespeare."

"All right, I've got the idea of her now," Katherine said irritably, smoothing her wrinkled and soiled skirt.

"Well, I best be off, young lady. You mind the biscuits and stir the beans every so often, and you'll have a fine meal for Lieutenant Weldon tonight."

The day had gotten off to a good start. Katherine wiped the table, washed up Willy, and sent him out in the small yard John had set up for the boy under an old piece of canvas for shade. With the bed made and the room swept, she took the dirty water and splashed it over her future garden plot. As hot as it was in the tiny house it was nicer than in the full sun, and she enjoyed being around John's things. Weldon's extra boots and the shirts she had promised to mend were waiting by the bed. Grabbing the shirts and her sewing kit in one hand and Eliza in the other, she braved the sun's heat and joined Willy beneath the canvas porch, hitching the cradleboard a soldier had given her to a peg on the wall where Eliza could see her. William stacked pebbles. His eyes were copper, but they rarely met hers. Most days the boy kept to himself until John came in.

A gourd filled with cool water hung in the shade. She dipped her hand and splashed her fingers at Willy. He kept at his work. She did it again, and he laughed. She stood up and took the gourd in her hands. "Willy, come here."

William sighed but obeyed, and she dumped the water over his head. The boy screamed and laughed and jumped at her, soaking Katherine's thin white dress just as the colonel's wife turned the corner in a starched linen walking suit with a matching parasol. Julia James stepped back. "Well, that's one way to waste a poor soldier's water, Mrs. Weldon. For shame!"

"That serves as Willy's bath for the week, Mrs. James!" Katherine said. "Would you like to join us?"

Julia laughed, but unpleasantly. "No, of course I will not join you, and I suggest you send for more suitable swim gear if you're that sort. I see clear through your bodice!"

Katherine draped one of John's shirts around her.

"Mrs. Weldon, I'm certain your mother raised you better. The Mexican girls are enough for the boys here without one of our own traipsing around indecently!"

"Mrs. James, I'm sorry to offend you, but I thought I was alone, and the soldiers can hardly see me on their rounds unless they make an effort."

Julia shrugged and sighed. "I suppose you're right. You know best for yourself." She kept her eyes on Katherine until Katherine squirmed. "Yes, the reason I'm here is to invite you for a supper tonight with Lieutenant Weldon. Of course you'll be cleaned up by then."

"Tonight?" Katherine thought of her meal all prepared. "I don't know."

"The colonel tells me Mr. Weldon jumped at the idea of a meal out. I know how boring it can be to eat the same army fare night after night," Julia said. "And we hear the trouble you have at cooking."

"I suppose if Mr. Weldon jumped at the idea I'll bring the biscuits I've prepared." Katherine's heart leapt and she ran inside and pulled the burned, black rocks from the oven.

"Oh, well, don't bother bringing them tonight then," Julia said, "but do come by at seven."

Chapter Twenty-Three

When Katherine said goodbye to her parents in Englewood, she imagined they would come visit her one day and be impressed with her, but that flight of fancy dimmed on the arduous journey out. Father would never make such a trip. The final remnants of such hope disappeared upon seeing her quarters.

She realized the moment she set foot in the colonel's quarters that Private Higgins was right. Julia James had expertly turned a rugged few rooms into a peaceful and well-appointed home. After a few envious moments, Katherine noticed that the settee covered in elegant blue chintz with pillows to match had been constructed with just a few army boxes. The curtains over the lone window hung from ceiling to floor making the ceiling feel not so oppressively low. The only true piece of proper furniture was a small cabinet darkened with age. "What a beautiful piece," she whispered.

"Why thank you, Mrs. Weldon. It's from my home state and dates from before the Revolution."

"What state, may I ask? The cabinet reminds me of home in New Jersey." "Oh my! I'm from Trenton. Well, isn't that a nice bit of luck? I hope we can become the best of friends," Julia said, pulling her close.

"I'm overwhelmed by your room. It's so prettily done up, Mrs. James. It reminds me of a playhouse for a child. Private Higgins warned me, but it's beyond my expectations."

"I hope you won't spend much time gossiping with that boy. Higgins is an awful liar and a sneak. I see you've hired him on for help, but how would you know how foolish that was unless you made it your business to ask one of us beforehand?" Julia shifted her gaze toward her husband speaking with John. "I find it telling that you call my home a room. I'll give you a little advice. You're used to high living back east, but I don't appreciate your uppity tone, especially since you're married to a lowly second lieutenant."

"Pardon me, Mrs. James." Katherine's voice shook. "I meant no insult. Your home is lovely, and I only hope one day to have something half as nice."

"Poor girl, you're a pathetic little creature," Mrs. James said as she poured Katherine a liqueur and waited for her to take a timid sip. "I pride myself on judging people, especially army wives, justly and fairly, and I'll say that the likes of you never last. All your sniveling and shyness. It won't do." Julia sighed and then with an odd smile pulled Katherine to the table to join the men.

"So, Lieutenant Weldon, how does it feel to be stationed at the most desolate post in all of North America?" the colonel asked as they sat down to a supper of roast bird, tinned oysters, and white potatoes.

"I guess it's too hard to tell yet, sir, but the heat is more than I bargained for." Weldon stared at Katherine until she put down her drink with a blush.

Colonel James, with heavy brow and full mustache, towered even over Weldon and filled the room with his movement and vitality. "Yes, the infernal heat. After the war I expected a nice little post somewhere pleasant. Even helping out with the coloreds would be better than this. Julia says it right—this is more a punishment than a promotion, and no matter what we do for them, it's never enough for the citizenry of these parts. Thankless work, I tell you. I long for the day of transfer. You see the caliber of men here. I've given them up completely."

"Sir, I think all men can be whipped into shape somehow."

The colonel eyed Weldon. "Well then, maybe you're the one to do it. Would you like an old-fashioned army toddy?"

"Water will do, sir. Thank you."

"Oh, a temperance man!" Julia said, laughing. "My, you two get better and better—an animal rescuer and a clean-living man—you're saints. You'll have your work cut out for you!"

"Mrs. James is appalled by the debauchery that goes on here," the colonel said with what sounded like sarcasm. "It's a man's world, as they say, and you can't blame a man for his natural urges. The officers are curbed by their families."

"Oh, really?" Julia mumbled, but Katherine caught it.

The colonel poured a drink for himself and a smaller bit for Julia, who threw it back when she thought no one was looking.

"I had expected to see more Indians out here," Weldon ventured, clearing his throat.

"Well, that, young man, is the problem. We can't find *them*, but *they* find the settlers and do real damage. Hundreds of head of livestock stolen in the surrounding parts and sold to the Mexicans—not to mention the human loss. Grant's Peace Policy is the last thing the people of Arizona want, and I can't say I blame them. Funny though, if between the Mexicans and our troops we exterminated the Apache, the citizenry would be in a real bind—most money they make is in supplying our troops. In fact the Mexicans do a fair Comanchero business with the tribes, buying and selling stolen goods. The army just don't have the manpower to cover the hundreds of miles necessary to protect all the people who clamor for it. So I say damn it all to hell and try to get by dealing with them all as little as possible and making merry on my own terms."

Katherine and John glanced at each other.

"We spent time at Fort Riley before being ordered here," Julia said. "Now there was a social spot—so many young officers and graceful girls, dances, and theatricals. We try to bring some of that to life here, but the cultured type I so enjoy are far and few." She sighed with nostalgia.

"I told Mrs. James to invite the Mexican girls. They're by far the most fetching of women. No race can beat them—the ones with Cortez blood, of course."

"As I told you, colonel, when you rustle up enough handsome officers I'll allow the Mexican girls—with Mr. Weldon, you're off to a good start!"

Weldon fumbled with his fork.

"Mrs. Weldon, my wife tells me you're quite a climber. Where did you learn that skill?" the colonel asked.

"Oh," Katherine blushed, "it's not a skill—I just got caught up in the excitement."

"Ah, that's a nice feeling—being caught up in the passion at hand," Colonel James said.

Katherine hesitated, glancing uncomfortably at Weldon. "The poor girl, she was sweet and knocked at my door. I'd never seen someone so upset over a little bird before, but it seems the family loves it so."

"The laundresses are an odd lot—where the men pick them up I'll never know, but they can't be trusted," warned Julia on her third sizable drink now.

"They're not that bad when they're young," the colonel added, raising his brow, "So go on, Mrs. Weldon ..."

"Well, the bird escaped from its cage, and Suzy's children were devastated—it's their only thing from home, and the men had teased the children by saying they'd have a shooting contest if they found it. But there it was on our roof—on the stovepipe of all places—luckily I still couldn't start a fire to save myself. There were no men about, so I had no choice. Susanna is far too heavy for climbing, and there was the bird ... so I climbed up and caught it."

"That was adventurous of you, Mrs. Weldon," Julia said, "but you would do well by your husband not to associate with the laundresses."

"Now, Julia, you're too all consumed with rank and class. This is a free country. You must not assume everyone cares to be promoted or given agreeable assignments," said the colonel, finishing up the last of his meal and leaning back luxuriously in his chair.

"My father and mother have taught me to be helpful to all sorts when I can," Katherine said.

"Don't upset yourself now," Julia said. "I'm sure they meant well, but I imagine even they would be embarrassed to see you climb ridgepoles doing the bidding of a common woman. That's what privates are for, dear. How fair would it be to Lieutenant Weldon if you broke your little neck, and he had to care for you instead of the other way around?"

The colonel added in a fatherly tone, "This may be a lonely outpost, but there must still be standards of civilization or we're no better than the Indians."

"I'm sorry I managed to bring on the downfall of civilization so quickly!" Katherine said.

"Dear, don't be silly. We're here to teach you the ins and outs of this camp. We like things done a certain way, and you'll see it's for the best. I suggest too that you hire one of the quieter privates or a Mexican old lady to help you. Get rid of Higgins and don't hire a laundress—they're awful forward and would be all over the likes of your husband." Julia cast a sly smile across the table. "Mrs. Lyons says you were a good customer of hers before, Mr. Weldon."

Katherine turned to her husband. Weldon sat red-faced, unable to look up from his plate. Eliza cried from her box on the floor.

"I don't know how people manage children—they're so bothersome, and I couldn't bear it!" exclaimed Julia, her tiny white hands covering her ears.

"I consider it an honor to help in carrying on my husband's name. I'm sorry for women who are unable to do so." Katherine picked up Eliza.

"Excuse us, Colonel James, sir, and Mrs. James," John said. "The meal was nice, but we should take the children home. W-we don't want for them to spoil your evening."

As they made for the door, carrying their children, the colonel whispered to Weldon, "I hear childbirth loosens a woman up. I like a good tight squeeze."

"Sir, I'm sorry to say I find your words disgusting and offensive."

"So you don't drink or joke ... you'll be a real fine addition here."

John and Katherine stalked off together, unsettled and quiet. After putting the children to bed, they collapsed into their own.

"You climbed the roof?"

"I had to. The poor thing would have perished, and it's a short roof. I didn't expect to be lectured on it."

"You're my little card!" Weldon laughed uncomfortably. "So we're stuck with a rough man and his pretty wife. Maybe you should be more careful with the laundresses."

"You think Julia's pretty?"

"Well, yes, she is but ... not like you."

"Not like me? What am I if I'm something other than pretty?"

"You're beautiful and perfect, Kate." Weldon squeezed her. "And that's all."

"Why would you say she's pretty? I already dislike her intensely!"

"They're awful—the both of them, and I'd say they don't care for us much either. We're off to a great start," John stated, kicking off his boots. "It's so blasted hot in here. Won't you even consider sleeping outside under the ramada?"

"I'll not have strange people staring at me while I sleep! But maybe you want to show yourself off to the pretty one!"

"You're being foolish."

"I heard what that disgusting man said to you."

"Katherine, he's a man we should avoid. Mrs. James is pretty, but you're the only girl I've ever wanted."

"Why, because you think you could do no better?"

"Of course I can do no better," John assured her.

"Julia makes her place so homey. I could never ..."

"Julia James is selfish and mean—that's clear. For all of her nice looks, it's her meanness that shines through. You're smart and kind and the only one who knows me and still likes me."

Katherine laughed. "Yes, I still like you." She messed his hair, but then something else pricked her nerves. "John, what about Oonagh Lyons?"

"Jesus Christ! What about her?"

"Why are you overreacting?" Katherine asked. "Why did you lie about doing your own laundry in the past?"

"It wasn't a lie!" He turned on his back and stared at the low ceiling. "I was tired of doing it so I paid her sometimes ... to wash my shirts. So now you've caught me out—are you happy?"

"John Weldon, there's something wrong that you won't say, because you don't trust me. It's Oonagh, isn't it? Do you like *her*?"

"No! She's an awful bitch! I ... I love you and sometimes ... it's almost unbearable how much." Weldon threw the light blanket off and got up. "How many times can I ask you to forgive me? I'm sorry about the clothes. I don't want you to leave. I shouldn't have lied."

"Leave? Over shirts? John, you must be mad! I don't care a fig who did your laundry." She pulled him back to bed. "If Oonagh made your life easier ..."

"Let's not talk about her anymore. She's not worth the time. Now you'll do the laundry." He kissed her, but it felt forced. "And I'll depend on you alone. I want to make you proud."

"I'm already proud," she said. "You are the only man here who carries himself like a true soldier."

"Katherine, how did I get so lucky to catch you?"

"There's no luck, my mother says, just grace," she said, tucking herself beneath his arm.

Chapter Twenty-Four

The baby and the bugler often woke the family at the same time. Katherine struggled with her new early hours, but once awake feeding Eliza and watching John stumble around getting ready, she hummed. How had she let herself miss so many early mornings in life? Out here in the desert it was the only time of the day that hinted at cool. John, with freshly washed face, pulled her to the porch. A few enlisted men had moved their cots to the outdoors to catch the slightest of breezes, and now they walked like the dead rising up after a long battle in purgatory, stretching and yawning in their undergarments and pulling their beds inside again.

"Will you look at that, Kate," John said, pointing to the iridescent glow of a flock of skittish hummingbirds feasting on the cactus fruit the men left alone. The tiny birds darted to and fro before dashing off. "It makes me think maybe ... God might really exist when a day starts this way. It's so perfect—the little details of it all—that could only come from someone who loved to make things." Weldon sighed and kissed Eliza's small grasping hand. "I have little hope the rest of the day will be as inspirational. The men almost mutiny at the suggestion of discipline."

"Poor John. You'll win them over, I know it!"

"Yesterday only eight men showed up for fatigue, and they were the same who grumbled through stable duty—rightly so—why should they do the work of twenty men? I bet they'll be suddenly sick today, and what can I do? The surgeon will agree that they're too ill, if he's out of bed before noon." Weldon spotted two men making their way onto the grounds. He chuckled. "Two men. What a day we'll have. Kate, you'll make us coffee, won't you?"

She kissed him and went inside to try the fire once again.

"Morning, men," Weldon greeted his charges on parade.

"Sir."

"Before stable duty, we'll take a walk around the place to see what the men are up to."

The three strolled toward the barracks, John with pencil and notebook in hand. Men lay still sleeping off their nights in the lanes between their shelters unaware of the new lieutenant and his men helpfully giving names to figures. Weldon kicked one dumb enough to pass out on his intended path until he awoke in befuddled resentment. The lanes smelled of urine and strong spirits.

"I'll prefer charges against you if you aren't on parade in ten minutes," Weldon said. "Take this as your final warning."

The soldiers drank but made none of the boisterous noise the drunken soldiers used to make during the war. Instead they drank aimlessly, miserably, out of boredom and loneliness for kinfolk, reminding Weldon of his childhood. Drill and work took only a few hours off the day. The boys were Weldon without the war, but he refused to let them drag him back into the life he lived before the army set him straight. The soldiers straggled unsteadily into line over the next ten minutes as Weldon fumed. "You, private, yes, you! Fall out!" he yelled. The man fell out, stumbling to his knees while the others snickered. "Casey, take him to the guardhouse at once."

Casey, one of the sober two, tried pulling him to his feet but gave up. "Sir, this man has fever."

"Sleeping in his own piss might have made him sick. Billings, you and Casey bring him to the guardhouse—I don't care what he's got right now. We'll send the surgeon to him at sick call."

The men in line exchanged contemptuous glances and stood with arms folded or leaning on one leg and then the other as if waiting to go off somewhere in a hurry. Their captain had disappeared on extended sick leave.

"Men—if I can still rightly call you that—you'll be expected to fall in fifteen minutes after reveille each morning. It's the tradition of the army, and we'll not break with tradition. If it suits you to drink each and every night that's none of my concern, but you'll be here on time or sent to the guardhouse or to the sinks to clean them properly. There will be no human wastage near the sleeping quarters. I'm embarrassed to have to remind you, we're stuck in one of the unhealthiest places I've ever served, but we can improve it with a few simple rules. Finally, if you own any of the pets—the dogs that roam the place—and I find them where they aren't supposed be making a mess of things, you'll have extended police duty picking up shit—human and otherwise—and your animal will be shot or sent to live with the Apache who may like dog meat for all I know."

"And you seem to think you know a lot," someone said.

"I don't tolerate insubordination. Step forward who ever said that."

A gaunt, messy private with crooked teeth and tousled auburn hair pushed through the front line with hands in his pockets. "Why don't you take that stick from your ass, lieutenant?"

"You little ass-wipe." Weldon threw the man to the ground and carved his heel into the man's chest. "I could kill you right now, and no one would care, but I'll give you a chance to make things right."

"I'll desert first!"

Weldon put his weight into his shoe. "Try it, and I'll personally hunt you down and shoot you in short order. Or you can volunteer for sink duty …"

"I will not!"

"As you please. Casey and Billings, when they come back, will see to it that you don't move from the platform you'll be placed on for the day … in the sun. If you make an effort to escape they'll shoot you as a deserter. My guards will be in the shade and will be relieved of fatigue for a week as reward for consistently showing up on time and in good order." The lieutenant turned to the other men now. "It's your choice, men, the way you want to be treated."

The men rolled their eyes.

"Truth is, you all joined the army for some reason. This place is desolate, but you have to serve your time, and work will make it faster. If we can get ourselves from bed we can do the work against the Apaches that needs to be done. I for one would rather go on a scout than build another useless outbuilding. The settlers will have no respect for us till we put a force against the Indians. We must do it or go mad waiting here day after day."

Chapter Twenty-Five

"Weldon!" called the colonel, who rarely made it up before noon.

"Yes, sir?"

James cleared his throat and spit, smelling as usual of the previous night's whiskey as he entered headquarters. "I've noticed that you're fond of putting things in order ... always working on this or that report about what I don't know."

"You might like to read them sometime, sir."

James laughed. "Why would I want to do that? From my shady ramada I can see full well that, aside from the occasional intoxicated savage wandering in and cursing the government or the dogs humping each other on parade, nothing much is happening here. You entertain me with your harsh style of discipline though. Nearly drowning Lyons for drunkenness was such excitement we hardly ever have. My lovely wife takes bets on when an all-out mutiny will occur. Mrs. James is quite taken with you, Weldon, but I warn you—you may look, but you can't touch."

"I have no wish to be anywhere near Mrs. James, sir. As usual you've found a new way to disgust me." Weldon dipped his pen and made as if to get back to work.

"Be careful, Weldon, I'm still your superior. I tolerate you because you foolishly take your assignments seriously. As you know, my hands are tied when it comes to real promotions—it's the system."

"I know, sir. Is that all?"

"Don't be so quick to dismiss me, lieutenant. I may be of some help to you."

Weldon glanced up, shook his head, and went back to his paperwork.

"Really, you might want to curb your suspicious nature. It's off-putting." James fingered through the pile of papers on Weldon's desk. "Now, we've come upon a problem with Beckenbauer. Although he's tried his darnedest to run the commissary and the quartermaster departments here, he's failed. On our last scout before you arrived, he went plumb loco in the heat and is near an imbecile now. Mind you, he was always a little off. Men would find him fondling himself at strange and inappropriate times, like when the Jesuits came for a visit. Anyway, it makes one sick to think that he ever handled food and such."

"What will become of him, sir?"

"Oh, I'll bring him up on charges and get rid of him, but that's no concern of yours. This place is disease ridden, and a person has to be strong here to survive. I bet you could do with some extras for the little ones and Mrs. Weldon. General Stoneman has designated this location as a feeding station for the friendly Apaches—what a laugh—but we need someone to manage the books. There may be some financial incentives too."

"A raise in pay, sir?"

"Well, I'm not sure of the details, but I need an answer soon. I want the books in order before anyone comes snooping around."

"May I ask why you expect snoops?"

The colonel huffed impatiently and his nose, enlarged from sun and drink, took on a purple glow. "If you must know every detail, I will tell you. I pitied Beckenbauer for far too long, and I suspect he may have made a right mess of the books. We can ill afford such incompetence when the supplies for the Indians arrive. I can order you to do it, but you'll be better served if you accept my offer."

"I'll discuss it with Mrs. Weldon and ..."

"My Weldon, I see you must jump through hoops to get that twat. Maybe that's why you are so hard on your men."

"Sir, I'll do my best to carry out your orders, but I wonder, sir, if you've given any thought to a scout."

"Frankly, lieutenant, I never give much thought to scouts—I just jump in come what may when the mood strikes. And most of the men here don't enjoy marching out and camping."

"The better men have expressed an interest and are tired of the papers saying we're not doing our job."

"Oh, so you've convinced the men to work, have you? I'm sure they're just avoiding being horsewhipped by you. I told you having the local papers for the men to read would be a bad idea. We don't answer to the Tucson papers."

"Well, who do we answer to, sir?"

"The people of the United States, and most of them don't want us to do a damned thing. That suits me fine—you'll find that most men agree with me."

"If we aren't going to do our job then there's no point in drilling the men."

"My point exactly," James said, tapping the reports again.

"Some soldiers want to do their duty, sir."

"Don't you dare, Lieutenant Weldon," the colonel said, looking hurt. "I served my time in Mexico and during the war. You're nothing but a small-time martinet with lots of big ideas you couldn't possibly carry out. I asked about you and correspond with my friends in Washington. Seems you got quite a lot of men to go follow you in the Wilderness. I hear most ain't around to tell about it, and you were rash and lacking in judgment. Don't go insinuating I don't know my job."

Weldon's heart pounded. "S-sir, if you allow me to organize a scout for the men wanting to go, I'll be able to write a report to the papers showing we're trying to protect the citizens. It would look good for you, sir."

The colonel mulled over the idea and clapped his hands together. "Yes, Weldon, you may do it. You're a pain in my arse, but you've hit upon something. It may keep the higher-ups off my back if you write something favorable. But you had better not take my best euchre players."

"There's no worry about that, and I'll invite along the newsman."

"*A newsman*? Well, that changes everything then. I shall come along too."

Weldon kicked himself all the way back to his quarters that evening and sat sullenly through another less-than-ample meal.

Chapter Twenty-Six

John avoided the quartermaster's baffled look when the books were turned over and he was escorted to the guardhouse. Weldon did not have time to reflect upon the orderly stores or the precision displayed in the books. He worried night and day over supplies for the scout, the route they would take, or the lack of one altogether. Where would they find water? He poured over old and incomplete maps. Weldon figured the horses would show wear after a day or two of mountain climbing, but the colonel insisted they go out as proper cavalry, not lowly foot soldiers. The colonel suggested he knew a way to keep the horses healthy—a nice ride into Tucson for cards and women.

James liked the lowlands. Weldon felt they might have more luck finding hidden rancheros in among the cliffs and ridges of the Mogollon Rim. On the desert plains the soldiers could be spotted, evaded, and made easy targets unless they got used to climbing and marching on the ridges as the Indians did. The colonel, not wanting another strategy lesson over lunch, suggested they compromise and do a bit of both as long as supplies held out and men were willing.

Weldon argued with a sergeant over the arrangement of the train as an army ambulance raced up to the guards on duty, stopping the men from their work. The driver wore a slouched white hat covering most of his face, but Weldon recognized the man's style as Simon's. The guards pointed to Weldon, and Simon raced his worn-out horse to within inches of Weldon and the flustered sergeant standing beside him.

"I've come!" Simon announced. "Sergeant, help the ladies in back, please. They'll be staying with the colonel." He smiled at Weldon with bleached white teeth and hair.

Once the girls walked off, Weldon jumped up and shook Simon's hand. Simon's confidence and verve awed him.

"Some dump this is, Weldon." Simon laughed. "Can you believe I'm stationed in Texas? I thought I'd be here with you at least a little while. The army must want me out. And where's my sister?"

"I-I'm glad to see you, sir."

Simon slapped his back. "Since when do we stand on formalities? I hear Colonel James is a real prick."

"Yes."

"Frugal with words, as usual. I'm only here a few days so tell me all the news."

"I've already made a mess here, sir, I mean, Captain. I'm off on a scout tomorrow and ..."

"Bully for you! From what I hear, it's about time. The atmosphere in Tucson is tense to say the least. So, where's my sis? And the little ones?"

"It's just that James is a drunk too, and the men ..."

"Weldon, you'll be fine as always." Simon spotted the run-down corral. "Listen, I have papers to deliver to headquarters. Will you take care of this? I'll meet you at your place."

"S-sir, but ..."

Simon jumped down and ran off. Before Weldon made it home, Simon and the two young girls he was delivering to Texas knocked at Katherine's door. Katherine's hair was in rag curlers for the dance tonight, and her one clean dress had been burnt that morning. Higgins refused to do laundry, and John forbid her to send it to Oonagh Lyons. She had nothing decent to wear in her small yard, so she washed in the dirty and dark little room. William stomped in the mud and sand, and Katherine in an overheated temper scolded him before noticing the knocking. William ran to open the door, and Eliza bawled.

Simon lowered his head and bounded in with a shout. "Your favorite brother, Katherine!" Simon stopped when he saw the state of her, but it was too late.

The horrified young ladies followed right behind him.

"Oh, Katie, put something on, for heaven's sake. You've got company!" Eliza pulled Katherine's wrap open to be fed and Simon covered his eyes. "Land sakes, this is grim."

Katherine dropped the little girl in her cradleboard and fell upon Simon in a heap of tears. "It's not always this bad, Simon," she lied. "Oh, I can't manage a thing!"

Simon embraced his sister. "There, there, Katie. Girls, put on some water for tea."

"But the fire's out," Katherine sobbed. "Mr. Higgins will be cross about it too, but it's so hot!"

"Katie, sit down." Simon looked for a chair not covered with clothes. "Willy, shove off, little man, and let your mother rest. Is Weldon himself, sis?"

"Whatever do you mean? Of course he is."

"He usually can't stand a mess. I just wonder sometimes ..."

"I'm a complete failure!" she said. "No one likes me, and I make such a bad wife. Don't blame John. He's busy."

Weldon stepped into the crowd just then. Eliza was still crying. "What the hell?" Simon gave Weldon a troubled look.

"K-Katherine, I-I w-would have helped!" John said, with exasperation in his voice.

"Weldon, you remember Varina and Emily Watson," Simon said. "Katherine, these are Colonel Langellier's nieces. You get to know each other while Weldon and I take a small stroll over the parade."

"No, Simon, don't leave yet," Katherine begged.

"Don't fret. I'm not going very far until tomorrow."

After the men and Willy left, Katherine stripped out of her soiled robe and in just her drawers and chemise she bounded past the shocked guests for a tattered dress hanging from a peg. No one said a word for a long moment. One girl poured herself cold tea leftover from a pot and cradled it in her lap. The other girl held the pot and stared at Katherine. "Where's her corset?" one whispered to the other.

Katherine didn't apologize. The stockings she wore smelled of mud too, but modesty prevented her from changing them in these cramped quarters with two sets of repulsed eyes upon her. Their civilized tea was brought to ruin by this filthy girl. The cuckoo clock broke the silence as did the faint call of the sentry, "Eleven o'clock—all's well!"

Neither girl managed a word, but one smiled in sickly fashion, avoiding eye contact. They had matching snowy complexions and cream-colored hair pulled back into tight buns, but only one passed for attractive.

"Pleased to meet you both." Katherine's chin trembled.

They nodded as if their neck muscles might snap. It was painful to watch them sip tea. Their skin looked so like wax that Katherine imagined it melting in the Arizona sun. "So, was your trip a torment for you?"

"Oh, no, Mrs. Weldon," Varina explained. "We're active in the temperance movement. Our mother worked in the Christian Commission during the war. One day we plan to work among the Indians. Isn't that so, Emily?"

Emily nodded. "Sister says the men here will give us good practice with savages."

Varina spoke with an affected private school accent. "The Lord is calling us to fight against sins of the flesh. Intoxication in the army leads many of these undeveloped men to ruination. Gambling, fighting, and even rude treatment of women stem from the ease with which liquor is attained."

Emily leaned forward earnestly. She had tiny blue drop earrings on that matched her large, wide eyes. Katherine envied her. "We plan to help our father with the troops in Texas."

Varina sipped her tea. "The enlisted man's pay should be held from him until he leaves the service."

"To protect him," Emily added.

"Yes. Most of the boys know little about finance. A cut in their monthly spending is just the thing to train them in the practice of economy."

"Pardon me, Miss Varina and Miss Emily, but as the wife of a veteran and former enlisted man who always goes without, you had better find a more humane way to keep the less disciplined men from earthly pleasures."

"Sinful pleasures," Varina corrected.

"She is such a gosling, sister," Emily giggled. When she smiled Emily looked soft, sweet and not as erect as Varina.

"A gosling?" Katherine asked.

The girls laughed.

"That just means you're inexperienced in the army," Emily explained. "We held temperance meetings every Thursday evening when we were last west with Lieutenant Weldon and Captain McCullough. Katherine, if I may call you by your Christian name, I feel we'll be friends."

"I'd prefer to be called Mrs. Weldon, please."

They all waited for someone to speak.

Katherine realized they were expecting something from her. "I'm glad you both have a constructive hobby, and thank you for telling me about it, but I don't involve myself in causes." She tried to rise from her stool, but Emily took her by the arm.

"You might try to convince your brother, Captain McCullough."

Katherine laughed. "Simon would never ... I hope you do not insinuate that the captain ..."

"No, of course not," said Varina. "It's just that the men are fond of him and enjoy his company. If Captain McCullough gave up the spirits the others might follow."

"No. Accept my apologies. I appreciate your opinions, but I don't intend to force them on my brother. Simon has a right to live his life the way he sees fit."

"Even if it hurts others, Mrs. Weldon?" Emily asked, noticeably ruffled.

"Who has Simon hurt?"

"He hurts the men under him who don't have the sophistication to get themselves out of situations the captain leads them into. You cannot expect boys of eighteen to give up game playing if their captain is often seen at the games."

Katherine pulled away from Emily and brushed her sleeve. "People make their own decisions in this country. No one forces someone to get drunk or gamble away his wages. If they can't afford it they shouldn't join the fun."

"Drunkenness is fun?" Varina asked.

"No!" Katherine shook her head. "It's common among men to seek entertainment after long monotonous work at a thankless job."

"Rewards are gotten in heaven, Mrs. Weldon," Varina said.

"All men shouldn't be punished because a few of them can't handle themselves and act foolishly," Katherine said, giving Eliza a crust of bread.

"Has the paymaster come in yet?" Varina asked.

"No."

The girls exchanged grins. "Well, that explains it then. You'll be surprised how the boys change. Some sneak out never to return, some get lost in Indian country. One was killed right in sight of the fort, but there weren't enough soldiers inside to save him. They used to steal little boats and find liquor wherever they could."

"I suppose it makes more sense to provide the men with a small bit of drink inside the fort," Katherine thought aloud.

"Wait till you witness it. Oh, how they change. Even the lieutenant came to a few of our meetings after a spree. He was *quite* changed."

"Sister, hold your tongue," Varina said.

"Forgive me, Mrs. Weldon. That was so rude of me."

"How dare you condescend to me and tell me lies about my husband so you can succeed at your little Christian project! You're just the type I've always hated. You're gossips and busybodies, pretending to be concerned about the men. I'll tell my brother about this, and he'll laugh at you both. And if my husband made the mistake of trusting the likes of you I'll make sure it doesn't ever happen again!"

"Please accept our apologies."

"I don't care for your easy apologies. I'll never forgive you speaking about John that way!" Katherine shouted before scooping up Eliza and vanishing behind the curtain to the bed.

Katherine heard the girls whispering. Pulling the threadbare curtain back Varina offered, "Please, you must forgive us. Sometimes our faith causes us to be overbearing. Please pray that the Lord will give us more guidance."

"I hope we can still be friends while we're here, Mrs. Weldon," Emily added in a more genuine tone.

Katherine refused Emily's outstretched hand.

Chapter Twenty-Seven

Weldon drew ten days' rations, and Colonel James tucked extra medicinal spirits aboard a wagon for safekeeping. Each man received a small dose to keep on his person "in case of emergency." The men would be half-lit before even starting. Simon watched on in sympathy until James ordered him in to have drinks with the newsman.

By seven that evening, Simon and the newsman were drunk with the colonel and Mrs. James. All commissioned and noncommissioned officers and their wives had been invited to an evening's entertainment under the colonel's large ramada. James had sent for Mexican musicians who wanted to come on the scout to kill Indians in retribution for theft and murder across the border. The colonel said he'd consider it over whiskey and song.

Katherine uncoiled the rags from her hair and pulled the curls back into an elegant comb, perfuming the long ringlets with dabs of Sarah's lavender water. Hearing from John that Simon was already drunk spoiled her mood. Why did John always point out Simon's faults?

Weldon smiled with his feet up on a box. "Kate, ain't you overdoing it a little?"

"No, I'm not! This is our last night together for a while, and I want to send you off right."

"Mrs. James will be huffed. You're giving her stiff competition."

Katherine changed the subject. "You do what's right for the men, I know, but sometimes I think you could be softer on them. They try their best."

"You don't understand the first thing about soldiering, so don't give stupid advice."

"So now I'm stupid? Well, you're mean to the men, and they'll hate you in the end. Even someone as slow-witted as me can see that!"

"I'm sorry. I didn't mean it. It just hurts when you criticize me, especially the night before my first real work since coming here. I am tough on the boys. I was them when I first went to Carlisle years ago. They're so used to slovenly behavior. I want to help them be their best. I hoped this expedition might teach them self-discipline, but I fear it will become a hot and merry picnic with James along."

"Well, I suppose you know best about most things," she replied as she undid her dress.

"What are you doing?"

"You go without me and discuss all the ways to motivate men. You aren't so talented with women."

"I can't go alone. I don't want to."

"I'm too unqualified to speak with soldiers." Katherine took her ear-bobs out. "Simon will make a fool of himself, and the girls will be proven right about you both." "Both?"

"I suppose all your talk of the quiet life in the army was a lie. The Langellier girls said you slipped up sometimes after payday. I didn't believe them, really."

"They're liars! I *never* got drunk—*ever*!" Weldon looked to hit something, but seeing her horrified expression, he shoved his hands in his pockets. "Kate, I ..."

"I don't care what those girls say!" she said, but something in her eyes scared him. "The way you quote the Bible—you would never be so irresponsible."

"Forget about God and the Bible! In this world you can't expect God to solve your problems and throw manna from heaven to support your family. I can't afford to slip up because I have to take care of *you*!" He ran his hand over his face. "I don't want to talk about this now! Why do you attack me?"

"Oh, John, I'm sorry I've made you angry. Please forgive me." She hooked her dress again.

He waved her off. "It's too late now. I'm going myself."

"Please don't," she begged, confused and angry. "You brute! Give my regards to Mrs. James! I'm sure she's smart enough for you!"

"I've had enough of this!" he said, slamming the door behind him. As he kicked the sandy path, a bundle of nerves over tomorrow and upset about tonight, he spotted Simon in the distance on the parade ground with Emily Watson. Emily hit Simon before running off.

"Captain!" Weldon called.

"Weldon," Simon slurred as he staggered up. "Off to the party? I've had enough of that blackguard James and his wife. Texas doesn't seem half bad."

"What was the matter with the girl just now?"

"She thinks she owns me because I kissed her once," Simon said with drunken bravado. "Didn't we fight a war to end human property?"

"I thought *you* fought to save the union?" Weldon quipped.

"Don't tell my parents that!" Simon pulled out two cigars and passed one to his friend. "Where's Katie?"

"She's huffed at me again."

"Listen, Weldon." Simon stumbled just a little. "For your own good, I hope you're staying away from that laundress."

"Simon, I ..."

"No, of course there's nothing between you, but if I ever found out you and that Lyons girl ..."

"I assure you, I would never dishonor your sister. I have more respect for women than you do!"

"I don't appreciate your tone. I don't understand it, especially when I've tried my best with you."

"Have you?"

"Have I what? What are you trying to say?" Simon poked his finger aggressively against Weldon's chest.

"Nothing, *captain*."

"If this is about the war again ..."

"No, of course not," Weldon replied, taking a long drag from the cigar. "Why should I care about your desertion?"

"*What was that*?" Simon jumped to attention. "You think I deserted that day? That's a lie!"

"Your unsoldierly behavior affected us all. You were no help ... that day."

"How dare you! And coming from a man who got half our men killed! And your behavior since the war has been erratic enough to prevent promotion, you un-grateful bastard, but I recommended you anyway. I go through a lot of troubles to come visit you and my sister, and you insult me! I wish I had known your true feel-ings all along."

"You enjoy stepping in and playing the hero, Simon. You only recommended me because of Katherine and your guilt."

"What I did during the war—at war's end—I appreciate the sacrifices you made for me."

"We sacrificed more than promotions covering for you."

"The war is long since over. We shouldn't live in the past. We're both the lucky ones—fully functioning. Why attack each other?"

Weldon laughed.

"Look, old friend, I made mistakes, but who didn't?" Simon asked. "I've done nothing to purposely undercut you, and since you've become a family member I've tried to help you along for your sake and Katie's."

Weldon sighed, putting the half-used cigar out on his boot heel. "Captain, things have been hard with me, and Katherine is ... well, she tries, but this isn't what she's used to and ..."

"Give her a chance. Katie's stronger than she knows. Maybe it's good she'll be left to herself for a little while, and it's good I'll be away from you, Weldon. The past is done, and I hope one day we can be real friends again, but for now we need to make our own way."

"Yes, sir, but sometimes ... I miss the old times, the early times in camp and such."

Simon slapped Weldon's back gruffly. "Me too, old fellow. Me too."

Chapter Twenty-Eight

Katherine looked at herself in the glass and cried. The curls had been a waste. John was at a party without her.

Soon Private Higgins came to babysit. "Ma'am, your first James shindig, and you're looking mighty pretty if you don't mind me saying so," he commented breezily, entering the room as if he owned it. "Lieutenant Weldon tells me you're getting to be a fair cook and housewife. I knew you could do it. Darn proud of you, he is. The only time the boys can get the lieutenant to act half human is when they ask him about you and the young ones. Ah, but he's all right and the boys are awful proud of their improvements and such." Higgins dusted the bookcase with his sleeve. "They're all in excitement over the scout. So where's the lieutenant and the captain? I foraged this nice sausage on the last work detail into town. Thought I'd cook them tonight for you all. Always liked your brother, ma'am."

"They've gone to the party."

"Are you sick?" Higgins asked. "It's Willy, is he sick?"

"No, no, private. We've had a quarrel, and now Mr. Weldon is gone without me."

The private checked on the stove and shook his head either over the state of the stove or at Katherine's situation. "Well, if you don't mind me saying so, that was a foolish thing to do on your part. What if the lieutenant is killed in a freakish accident (I mean, the colonel is going along so anything is likely), or what if they get ambushed by the Apaches? It's a bad way to end things, ma'am. And then there's Julia James all liquored up and frisky. You can hear her laughing all the way to Tucson, I reckon. I bet she's wearing a nice dress too—from home. Ma'am, we all need a night of fun sometimes, and you haven't a thing to worry about here with me and the babies. Remember, I helped raise my momma's ten after Papa keeled over and died. Besides I bet those officers would like you if you let them, and you'd make things smoother for Lieutenant Weldon."

Katherine watched him slide the sausages into the fryer and begin his work. Willy pushed a chair next to the soldier and sat, watching the meat get warm and savory-smelling with a big grin.

"There'll be talk if you don't go."

Katherine stood for a minute longer, grabbed a bright Mexican sash to tie around her expanding waist and left nervously, thanking the private.

Bright paper lanterns lit a path to the James' quarters in the dark. The musicians played colorful, heated melodies about beautiful señoritas and passion and death. Katherine did not understand a single word. The notes were hypnotic and frightening as Katherine stepped forward, afraid of losing her courage if she lingered. Making her way up the path, "Cook," the James' Mexican house lady, greeted her. "Buenas noches, Señora."

Katherine nodded and peered in. A few shadowy figures sat at the table, but the real party appeared to be around back with the band. Cook handed her a strong drink, and Katherine sipped it for courage before walking on.

A year's worth of army candles burned all around a makeshift dance floor. More of the exotic lanterns Julia had sent for from a Chinese railway man in San Francisco hung along the fence line of the yard.

The colonel had gotten his allotment of youthful Mexican señoritas. They were variations of the same theme—large, full-mouthed girls in brightly woven skirts, laughing and dancing with the colonel joyously. The three bachelor officers pointed to their favorites.

For over four months Katherine had tried but failed to gain the friendship of the other officers' wives. A round and sour wife sat with Varina and a demoralized-looking Emily. Her expression suddenly changed when Julia waved to her. The officer's wife laughed and said something as her jowls shook, but as soon as Julia turned so did her face.

John stood at the edge of the festivities until Julia pulled at him to dance. Weldon laughed with bright eyes, but his body was stiff and stubborn. As Katherine watched, he made one fatal step forward, and Katherine was crushed.

Julia's dress was indeed sent from back east with a gorgeous bustle and narrow skirt in pale blue that glowed in the lantern light. Her hair hung in curls like Katherine's but more simply adorned with a single jeweled clip. The dress was enough. It accentuated Julia's full bosom and her slender waist. Katherine fingered her rough Mexican garb and made to leave, but John passed her in dancing and their eyes met.

"Excuse me, Mrs. James, but ..."

"No, Mr. Weldon, you mustn't be rude to the colonel's wife. Yours will understand." Julia pulled him along until the music ended. The colonel and his girls had disappeared and so too had Katherine. Julia held Weldon's hand as he strode off. "I'll help you find her ... to explain."

"There's nothing to explain, Mrs. James. I danced with you to save you embarrassment in front of your guests. That's all. It's my wife I want. I have no feelings for you."

"Dear Mr. Weldon, it was sweet of you to consider my feelings on the dance floor, and I appreciate your honesty, but keep in mind that when I'm happy so too is Dixon James."

"Well, I hope you find happiness somehow," he said and walked around front into the smoky quarters. Before entering, he knew Katherine would not be inside alone with strangers. Only the colonel was familiar to him. A few Mexicans and old mountain men lounged on Mrs. James' nice furniture. Weldon recognized the familiar opium pipes from his time in San Francisco and couldn't move.

"Ah, Lieutenant Temperance has arrived," joked the colonel.

Julia lightly touched Weldon's waist as she brushed by him and sat next to the colonel. She held the pipe in her mouth for a moment and turned to Weldon.

"Take a seat, Weldon," the colonel suggested.

But Julia caught the longing in Weldon's expression. "Oh, so you've done this before. Come on in, silly boy. It's written all over you—you want it."

"No," was all Weldon could muster as he escaped into the open air shaken.

In the distance he saw Katherine's white dress and ran to her, calling her name. She had pulled the cheap decoration from her hair and it littered the ground. A snake slithered behind some brush at the sound of Weldon's boots. Katherine didn't hear her husband until he was right upon her near the commissary building. He pounced on her, and Katherine screamed. He put his mouth to hers violently, and they slipped to the ground. "Katherine! I'm so sorry! Please promise you will never leave me to myself again. Promise you will never leave me."

"John, don't dance with other girls, and I won't leave."

Weldon looked at her oddly, desperately, but laughed and rested his head in her arms like a child. It was not the way Katherine had imagined their last night together.

Chapter Twenty-Nine

The stifling air of the desert kept Weldon from sleep. The sound of Katherine's easy breathing annoyed him. For a second, he had considered smoking the opium and spent most of the night fretting over that second. Katherine turned to face him, but he couldn't look at her—he might tell her if he did.

He dreamt of burning forests until Katherine brought him coffee and nudged him awake.

"I don't think I can do this. I don't feel well."

He ran his fingers through the wet sticky hair at his stiff neck. His eyes were puffed and sore from the previous day's sun.

"You'll do a wonderful job. Private Higgins assured me that the men are happy with you. They know they can depend upon you."

"But I hate the colonel," he said, sitting up and taking the coffee.

"Well, haven't you always? What makes today different from the others?"

"Last night makes things different, Kate."

"We knew he was no angel, and if Julia doesn't mind the women I guess it's none of our concern."

"No, it's not that ... James worries me, and he's a bad influence on the m-men. And promise me you'll stay away from that wife of his. Julia's corrupt and dangerous."

Katherine took a sip of her coffee. It was too strong. "Did something happen last night?"

"Yes, I saw things," he said, watching her reaction. "Opium, I think it was, and they were smoking."

"Merciful heavens! The colonel? And Mrs. James too? That's disgusting in the extreme. I expected low behavior, but that beats all! I think it's addicting too, and, well, Chinese people do that, don't they? They have no morals whatever to sink so low down. Did you say anything to them?"

"No. Just promise me you'll avoid Julia."

"Don't worry, John." Katherine kissed his forehead. "I promise to avoid all bad influences and continue my cooking studies for when you return. Please be careful. Do you have extra stockings packed?" Her voice suddenly trembled.

Weldon stretched into his clothes and shook his boots free of vermin before pulling them on. "Sometime I'll take us into Tucson for a likeness of our little family. I'd like to carry it when I'm away."

"John, I wish I was a boy so I could come with you. What if something happens?"

"I've got to go and check on things, but I'll be back before reveille."

He strode past the officers' quiet quarters in the half-dawn. The three Mexican musicians lay in front of the James place under a lean-to of their own blankets and clothes. The door hung open to the James' quarters like a toothless yawn, dark and silent inside. Weldon quickened his pace and rounded the corner to the commissary to find the colonel urinating against the quartermaster's shed. The lieutenant turned away in disgust—the smell of that wall had been appalling even after the men had cleaned the sinks and begun to use them.

James saw his man. "Hey, Weldon, all set? My God, it must be almost morning, and here we both are still awake. Some frolic though. The horizontal refreshment was of the highest caliber. The wife is like a corpse in bed. I've got blue balls most of the time. Thank Christ for the Mexicans, I tell you. If your wife ever dries up I can get you a girl any time for next to nothing." He laughed. "I'll be sore in a nice way for days."

"Sir, it's nearly time for the boys to be up for our trip."

"Oh, Weldon, I won't be up for hours. I'll be happy if we're out by noon."

"But, sir, noon is the worst time. I planned to be at least four hours on the trail by then. The horses won't march well in the midday heat!"

"Don't start your shit with me at this hour. Do what you want, but I'm not going until my wagon is prepared. I can sleep in there while you scan the horizon for Indians." James put his finger to one nostril blowing phlegm out the other and staggered back around to his quarters.

"Please, never let me get like that!" Weldon whispered to himself as he opened the commissary. The place had been in perfect order the previous evening but had been ransacked for the last of the medicinal spirits. Weldon cursed and half-heartedly stacked a few boxes. "This will have to wait." Most of the supplies had already been loaded into the wagons for the mules to pull. He hoped that the men he had put in charge were sober this morning as reveille sounded.

Closing the place up, he walked home. William ran out to greet him, fell and tried again more carefully. Weldon laughed and scooped him up. The child smelled of Katherine's perfume. The boy's hair was copper in the sun, and Weldon was glad he looked so white. Katherine stood under the ramada with a smudged gingham apron wrapped around her and last night's curls drooping and pulled back with ribbon.

"You look too young to be a wife and mother," John said.

She pulled him in and kissed him. From her apron pocket she took out a small package wrapped in paper decorated with her delicate drawings of desert flowers. "Open it."

It was a handmade journal sewn with Katherine's irregular stitching over scraps of fabric traded with Suzy.

"Why did you go and do that? I didn't think to get you anything."

"Mr. Weldon, when will you realize that love isn't about even trades every time? I wasn't expecting anything in return except your happiness."

"You make me happy," John said, tipping his hat back and grinning. "I'll carry this where ever I go."

"Well, I'd like you to write everything down so you don't forget to tell us all the interesting things you do and see."

"Of course, Kate," he replied, pinching her chin.

"And when you come back from roll call I'll give you a nice breakfast of sausages from Private Higgins."

"I don't feel much like eating," he started, but realized how proud Katherine was of her fire. "I'll probably be starved when I come back."

**

Two hours after Weldon's scheduled departure, the colonel stumbled into his wagon, and the scouting party of thirty-five men, fairly sober and cheerful, stood ready to leave. The women stood under Julia's ramada as she sat in her chair fanning herself. Katherine did not join them. She peered out from her own shady spot with Eliza in her arms and William at her feet.

Simon came up now looking sick and overheated. "Weldon has gotten everything in fine order, sis. Guess you're proud as anything."

"I'm frightened, Simon," she confessed, placing her hand against her brother's smooth face. "I'm worried about you too. Won't you ever consider not drinking so much?"

"Leave me be, Katie. I hardly drink at all in comparison to other men."

"Which other men?"

He shook his head and laughed. "I know you mean well, but I'm not in the mood for a lecture. There's no need to fuss. Besides, what does it matter anyhow? After a good bit of fighting during the war, this is my reward? I'm sent to a post in the middle of nowhere. I didn't struggle through engineering courses at the Point to end up in this wretched desert. So who cares what I do? As long as I get my small bit of work done, all's well with the world." Simon put on a bright face. "At least I got to see you for a short while, anyway. Why don't you write me more?"

"I've been awful horrible to you," Katherine cried. "I will write more. I promise. I don't want you to go. I miss you already."

He grabbed her around the shoulders. "You're a bully girl, so you are." And off he went.

Chapter Thirty

Weldon spoke to the teamsters and didn't look back. He hoped the opium was a rare excess for James and was relieved to find the Mexican musicians had not been permitted to come. He patted his pockets to make sure he had Katherine's gift and ordered the men to march out.

The sun baked the men till their limbs felt like clay. Dust took flight under wagon and hoof. They would have to march four hours in search of a tiny stream as they headed for the mountains. James, in full and heavy uniform, boiled in a semiconscious dream state from the inside of his wagon, oblivious to plans as they moved from the soft ground of the low desert into the hills of the ridge.

The mules kicked at every chance but showed no sign of wear as they stomped into noontime. Not a wild animal stirred, not a person made himself seen, but Weldon knew there were signs everywhere they could not read. Colonel James had been adamantly opposed to taking an Apache scout. They could not be trusted, he said, and Weldon half agreed. Indian fires slid smoke up in the mountain air, but they were too far away to mean much to the soldiers.

Sergeant Simpson trotted up. "Sir, shall we wake the colonel?"

"For God's sake, no!" Weldon answered. "We'll push on for another hour if we can. On the old map I found, it showed a small mountain stream or spring. We can rest there until the air cools and then go on another few hours."

The sergeant pulled his broad-brimmed hat another inch lower and seemed inclined to speak.

"Yes, sergeant?"

"Well, sir, you'll have a hard time going much further once we find this stream. The ranks are grumbling already."

"Sergeant, according to the maps, the stream is exposed and not a decent place to settle. The boys should be convinced of it when they see the place—and the colonel too."

"The colonel won't be too impressed with where you've taken us so far, Lieutenant Weldon, sir."

Weldon rubbed his forehead. "Sergeant Simpson, leave the colonel to me. It's not your worry."

"Sir, pardon, but it is my worry. I like you, and the colonel can be awful spiteful with folks he don't like. I don't think he likes you much."

Weldon laughed. "You've got a good eye. The colonel gave me his permission to go into the mountains at some point and so here we are. There ain't no Indians dumb enough to stand around with their plunder on the main trail to Tucson. We're here to find the men who harass the settlers. Our trip will be a failure if we don't find some."

The party slogged on, and Weldon's horse began to move more tenderly. John jumped off and led it for a while. The complaining of the men to the rear grew more strident. Weldon pretended not to hear. What he did hear now was the pulse of water over rock. He made a silent apology to his mount, jumped back on and trotted ahead to find the source of the happy noise. It was far beyond his expectations. Lush green grass grew in small tidy patches, tempting the horse so tired of dry feed. He yanked the animal's head around and pushed the horse back to the others with his spurs. He need not say a thing. The spirit of the horse told the story, and the others followed at a quick trot. The men and animals jockeyed for position at the stream until Weldon pointed out to the men that cleaner refreshment could be had upstream from the horses.

The colonel descended from his ambulance, scratching himself. "Where's the bane of my existence—that son of a bitch Weldon?"

The men hung in groups, shirtless, wet and refreshed waiting for their lunches. Weldon, enjoying this small success, went to check on the teamsters and their mules.

"Sir, I'll bet we nab us some Apache right soon," ventured one of the men with great optimism as he pulled off his boot to empty it of sand.

Weldon smiled.

"For Christ's sake, Weldon, where've you taken us?" shouted the colonel smoking a cigar and soaking his feet in the stream down a little from the others.

"Sir, this is where we'll find some Indians, with luck."

"I don't give a fuck about Indians, and you're about as lucky as a fly in a frog pond. Where is that damned reporter? There you are. Strike what I said about the Indians from your notes."

The reporter nodded reluctantly.

"Sir," Weldon said, "you should calm down. We're only stopped for water. There's a place on the old map more suitable for camp."

"You mean to tell me this godawful ride isn't up yet?"

"S-Sir, this is what we discussed all week."

"But I had no intention of actually carrying it off—strike that too, young man! I'm beginning to regret bringing that newsman along, Weldon—he's like a spy. Can't even take a dump without him snooping around."

The young newsman glanced at Weldon, shrugged, and continued his notes.

"Colonel, we must press on. This is an exposed location, sir."

James pulled himself up out of the water, his ankles swollen and his belly hanging over his trousers. "Great God, I think I know that, but you shouldn't have brought us here then."

Weldon's head pounded in the heat. "Colonel, have some coffee, and I'll set about feeding the men their lunches."

The colonel made a strange face and sat down on a boulder to rub his feet. "What were the men to take along besides hardtack?"

"Well, the meat of course, sir. It's not the best but ..."

The colonel shook his head.

"Colonel James?"

"I sure do hope you don't mean the stuff stored in my ambulance."

"Sir?"

James looked to the newsman as he jerked his boots on and stood up. "Well, I wasn't myself this morning. The Mexicans were vexed when I told them you didn't like for them to come along so I gave them the cases of meat. I figured you'd have given the men their own food."

"But we were to be out at least a fortnight. How could each man carry all that he needed? Shit! So we have nothing for the men then?"

"Well, it's a darn good thing we are so close to home," James said. "You should go tell the men now."

"We're four hours from home. I won't tell the men."

The newsman scribbled every word.

"I don't know who you think you are, but you will do as I say and we will go back tonight."

"Sir, we can't go back tonight. The path was tough enough in daylight—it's too dangerous. The camp I propose is only an hour's march from here."

"Jesus Christ! I said *no*! Do you understand English? I've put up with your insolence long enough. We won't go a step further today unless it's in the direction of Camp Grant."

"Colonel James, may I speak to you in private?"

The colonel stared with small eyes and a tight mouth considering the man before him. "You're so naive, Weldon. It amuses me. You can say all you want in front of *your* newsman, but he knows that I'm in charge here, and he'll write only what I see fit to have him write or he'll never be invited back when the top brass come through looking to make peace."

The writer turned away from Weldon.

"Well then, colonel, you may place me under arrest now, but as far as I know I'm the only one who paid enough attention on the way up to get us back and you can tell the men that they'll backtrack, break down their good mounts, and go hungry for no reason other than you're a lazy piece of shit."

The colonel shifted in his boots and ran his hand over his large skull. "Hmmm, that won't do. The only thing to do is compromise. We'll stay as we are for the night. Post a guard and such and then tomorrow put it to a vote."

"Vote, sir? Since when is the army a democracy?"

"I don't want a political debate right now, you shit-ass," James said. "I've got a steaming head, and I know just the thing to do about it. You run along and straighten things out with the men."

Weldon stormed off. He was out of his league. The blame would fall squarely on his shoulders, and he would be hated by soldier and citizen alike.

"Excuse me, sir," Sergeant Simpson called, trotting up. "The men have found a large school of fish in a pool up a ways and want permission to catch them."

"Of course, sergeant!" Weldon replied in relief. "And tell the men to make themselves comfortable for the night. We'll post guards shortly."

The sergeant gave him a knowing glance and walked off.

Now and again a ripple of purple smoke climbed up over the mountain peaks, and as the sun set lower the blue sky and the rough land changed to gold. One private set the record catching seven large fish. As they lounged around full of food and burnt from the sun, most counted the day a success. They had gotten out of camp, gone fishing, and had grassy beds as comfortable as any in the West. The stream sang out, and the night came on with a welcome chill and the usual dazzling sunset.

Only a few worried about the Indians. More began to steal sips from their bottles.

The men sent Weldon, who sat mulling over the day on his own, a steaming heap of fish and fried hardtack to go with his coffee.

"Cheer up, sir. We know you're tryin' yer best. The colonel told us you forgot the meat, but you found us much better grub at this stream."

"The fish were just luck."

"Divine providence, sir."

"Anyway, I didn't forget the meat. Never mind, Carson. Thank you for the meal."

"Well, it's from the lot of us that's still sober, sir."

Weldon gulped the food down and then set about putting out the men's fires.

The men, with some reluctance, followed orders. A few suddenly felt less than secure as the light faded. The horses worried too, making skittish movements on the line. Weldon would stay with the guard.

Sergeant Simpson and Private Flynn had become Weldon's most dependable men and made up part of his line. He could just see the whites of Simpson's eyes and the faint shine of his carbine as he left him. Ten others who seemed sober enough took up watch.

Weldon would check position to position all night and check on camp too, where a fire roared. He ran up. "Colonel James, sir, we have to conceal ourselves for the night!"

"Weldon, if they have the balls to come upon us then I want to see the look of them before I plug them with my Spencer. Say, where is my gun anyway?"

Weldon dumped water over the inferno, and James made to get up but lost balance. "You're one of them, ain't you? You're gonna spring a trap on us! Boys, it's Weldon here we need to be afraid of, bringing us out this way without even a pinch to eat!"

The men humored the colonel, and the newsman strained to get it all down.

"Sir, the guard is posted, but your party will bring the Indians to us if the noise keeps up," Weldon explained testily.

"Go find someone else's ass to crawl up," the colonel snickered while his men flaunted their drinking.

Walking back to the line of guard, Weldon glanced over his shoulder to see a new flame set for the colonel. Laughter echoed through the canyon. Weldon cursed and took out his journal, but from where he was it was too dark and he had nothing to say.

The men made merry in camp and the guards complained at missing the fun. Some slipped off only to return intoxicated and cut up against the rocks. A few remained steadfast and were asked to move along the ridge—ripe targets silhouetted against the firelight. For a second Weldon closed his eyes. When he woke all was quiet, but shadows moved past him in the darkness. He scurried to his feet and took aim at the one he could see and missed but struck the Apache on the second shot from his repeater. The guard now knew of the danger but not before suffering two hits and allowing the intruders to pass them unmolested.

Men around the still-simmering fire awoke groggily but rolled behind boulders or wagon wheels once realizing what was happening and shot out at all movement, nearly killing a few of their own men.

Soon the horses and mules stampeded, set free by a nimble-fingered Apache. One horse in panic lost its footing and fell into a ravine, but the rest were led off at speed by the raiders who would sell them to the Mexicans. Some men never lifted their heads, so drunk they were, while others slipped off to safety. The colonel was nowhere to be found, and two of his finest euchre players were gone too.

Weldon and a few others made a dash down through the passages of stone left over time but were not limber enough to follow the Indians, who seemed to disappear into the canyons through magic doors.

"I think I'm clairvoyant, if I didn't feel this was bound to happen," Weldon moaned, making his way back up the side of the mountain wall with the others following.

Some men showed concern for their safety and their egos. They had been bested by five or six savages with only one taken down by the lieutenant they loved to hate. They blamed the sentries; they blamed the brass; they blamed each other and hid their empty bottles. Weldon had the sergeant call them into line. As rumpled and dazed as the soldiers were, for a change they all fell in but for the two euchre players.

"Men, I told you before setting out I believed we'd see action, but not this way! Most of you know the plan I favored for yesterday. It was ignored. Instead you enjoyed yourselves. Our rations are gone, our animals are run off, and we're exposed." Weldon glanced around at the faces in the shadows. "The colonel and his friends are nowhere to be found. I assume they're skulking around somewhere. I didn't see them taken off by Indians. Have any of you seen them since earlier tonight?"

The men kicked the ground or looked at the stars before a private spoke. "Sir, seem to recall them wanderin' off last night. Didn't see them after that, but I was pretty tight, I'm sorry to say, sir."

"I respect your honesty, Private Helmer. Of course, all of you will be brought up on charges if things don't change."

"Well, sir, we got through all the whiskey last night so I reckon we ain't got no choice anyhow."

"Sergeant, send out two parties to look around for the colonel," Weldon ordered. "Let's hope they left on their own and weren't taken."

It looked as if the idea that the colonel had been captured or killed had never occurred to them. Weldon said a silent prayer for his sanity and went to consider his next move with the reporter close behind.

"Lieutenant Weldon, sorry to leave you out yesterday, but the colonel has friends who may help me get me a job at one of the big papers back east."

Two excited men called out. "Lieutenant Weldon, sir, we found the colonel's things! They must have been ambushed!"

Daylight broke now. The men gathered again, some having gone off to fish but straggling back. Weldon wanted to horsewhip them all but would have to wait. "I don't get the impression you realize the serious nature of our problems now."

"We never shoulda' come up here—like the colonel said."

"Shut your trap, Taylor—if it weren't fer yous drinkin' we woulda' been okay."

"Everyone shut the hell up!" Weldon snapped. "It doesn't matter now. We're in a trap. If we stay here we'll have food and water, but we can't stay here forever. The Apache could come again with more men and wipe us out. We can't leave the colonel, as much as I'd love to. Some of you will stay and make this a safer camp. Use the wagons as barricades. All the Indians in this area probably know we're here, so expect the worst." He turned to Simpson now. "Sergeant, you'll take a party to circle to the south and the east. I'll take my men further northwest. Our goal is to be back by nightfall. Tomorrow we'll turn back for Camp Grant—another long march and without animals. If the colonel isn't found we'll bring further dishonor to ourselves. Remember that! Fall out and good luck to us all."

The men packed their pockets full of ammunition and hardtack. Canteens and empty bottles were rinsed and filled at the stream—clear without the horses. They pulled their hats over their faces, wet their bandanas one last time and tied them to cover their bare necks and faces.

"Land sakes, we're in the infantry again," grumbled one man as they started down a rocky slope full of shadows and drop-offs.

"If'n we find the colonel drunk in a ditch, I'll kill the blamed devil!"

Weldon led the pack. The nerves of yesterday disappeared. If they didn't make it back, Katherine would be alone at Fort Grant. He could not go back without some honor. They must find Dixon James.

The slopes gave way to a vast and torrid plain that rippled under a blanket of heat. The men felt the weather through the soles of their shoes and walked as if over a pan at the fire. Their stomachs soon grumbled, yet when they pulled hardtack from their pockets the men spit it out, their mouths too dry to swallow. Still they dragged on, watching the angle of the sun and watching, too, for signs of Apaches hiding in the hills. Paranoia set in. Spanish bayonet grew all around, but the men did not know how to eat it. Every shadow seemed to stalk them. Their guns got too hot to hold, but they held them anyway. What if they were lost? The men had put their faith in a quiet, harsh man they had known for only a few months.

And then the drinkers began to fall out, to stumble and complain. They had emptied their canteens. Their heads were steam engines going like forty and their limbs shook. Weldon pushed them since there was no shade to rest. The temperance men refused to share their water. The lieutenant sympathized with them, but they needed these men so he ordered drinks shared and shared his own.

"It's no use going any further," Weldon said. "We have no idea where there might be water or Indians. We have to turn back. It's our only choice."

"Lieutenant Weldon, I can't go another minute in this heat. My brain is fried, sir."

In an hour the sun would fall behind the mountains, but the Indians might pounce on them as they groped their way back. Weldon saw in the eyes of the motley lot that they would not move. "We have to start up again in the next hour the latest," he said, looking back on the stark terrain they must retrace now. "Strip down to your under things. That'll help."

"Lieutenant," one joked, "I didn't think you cared."

Weldon smiled. The hour felt like three.

"We look a right foolish bunch in our whites. Well, some of us have whites, Jones," a private mocked his comrade.

"You're such a caution, you are," Jones answered, wrapping his belt around his dirty underwear.

They moved like burnt slugs. Now Weldon felt his legs give, felt he could not think clearly. The men bumped each other when one stopped. A few wished to be shot by Indians so they might rest, but the Indians let them alone.

"Sir, I heard somewhere to cut yerself," Jones said. "The blood will get us through if we're lucky—but not too much—you might grow to like it."

The dazed men stared at him, but then one by one cut themselves with Weldon's knife—fingertips first but as time wore on they took to their arms looking for a better supply.

The sun hid at last. Their limbs were anchors on a sinking ship when they reached the rough mountains, but they heaved themselves one shaky stretch at a time. With sliced-up hands and knees, bloody arms, and burnt skin they stumbled into camp long after midnight. On this night there were sober sentries to greet them. A small fire hidden beneath rocks warmed fish for them, but the men made for the water and fell dead asleep soon after satisfying their thirst.

Sergeant Simpson had not made it back. There was nothing to do but wait, so Weldon wrapped his hands, drank some water, and faded to sleep.

***

"For God's sake, Weldon, wake up!"

Weldon leaned up on his elbows, aching all over. The moon lit the man above him. "Colonel?"

"What the hell happened here, and where are the animals, you luckless bastard?" James roared. "And where are your clothes?"

"Where were *you*, Colonel James? Did the sergeant find you?"

"No, Weldon, he did not. We made our own way back. Thank you very much."

"You really are a piece of shit! The party spent the entire day looking for you and nearly killing ourselves doing it. Simpson isn't back yet?"

"Well, I wasn't looking for him. Simpson is probably lost in these goddamned mountains like we were."

"Lost? He could be dead for all you care."

"Course I care. That's why I was against this brainchild of yours from the start. Weldon, you're not the type to have much success in life. This disaster should break you of that dream once and for all."

Weldon lunged, but the colonel got the better of him, punching him down with a blow to the eye and a kick to the ribs.

"Lieutenant Weldon, never presume to take charge of *my* men again," James shouted. "You come from nothing, and you are nothing. If it wasn't that I feel sorry for your wife and little ones I'd have you thrown out of the army!" He walked off.

Private Jones with a bad case of sun poisoning came to Weldon's side. "Lieutenant, you done yer best. He's drunk again, that cunt! He probably saved the best spirits for himself."

Weldon held his head. "You heard what the colonel said. I'm no longer in charge so why don't you go get drunk with him now if you can."

"Well, sir, the way I see it is you're gonna get us home whether he likes it or don't. He ain't fit to lead a pig to slop. And the sergeant's still out. Rather go lookin' for him than James any day."

"Thanks, Jones. Suppose we could sneak out after the colonel retreats to his wagon," Weldon whispered, looking around. "See if you can gather a few men quietly. Tell them to bring water."

"Yes, sir!"

Five men came up and piled their accoutrements onto a wagon. They shoved bottles and cartridges into their pockets and belts and were off. Once away from camp, they complained about the colonel and the state of their feet, but Weldon silenced them. The moon reflected off their guns. The soldiers jumped but held their fire every time an animal crossed their path. Finally, they thought they heard something human, something familiar. They listened with fingers on their triggers, and there it was again—just a wavering note—the sound of Benton's harmonica! Weldon bounded down into the canyon with brush scratching his face and arms. The others followed more cautiously with one man left to watch the trail.

"Lieutenant!" Simpson whispered. "We're here!"

After meeting some Indians, Simpson and Benton had taken cover in a ravine. Weldon and Jones scurried down to meet them.

"Where are the others, sergeant?" Jones asked.

"They're gone," Simpson stated breathlessly. An arrow burrowed in his side.

Benton spoke. "Maloney panicked and ran. We followed him, but he was already caught and mutilated, sir—godawful. We were outnumbered. Maloney put us in a tight spot, and they got the sergeant. The men scattered after seeing what those sons of bitches did to Maloney. Castration, sir."

"How long ago was this?" asked Weldon.

"The Indians tore off about an hour ago, sir, but it seemed like there might be a camp off in that direction. We found some everyday things scattered about."

"This is the safest place for you, Simpson. We'll come back soon with the rest of the men. Private Benton, do your best to keep him comfortable till we can get him the surgeon. The rest of you come along."

Weldon scaled the rocks again, loose soil falling everywhere. The men followed as he went off toward the supposed Indian camp. They made quiet time and chanced upon the faintest light from the smallest fire in a ravine. Weldon signaled for his men to crawl on their knees, and finally their bellies, as they inched over to the boulders that concealed their progress. The small camp had a few shelters. Two braves sat at the fire. At Weldon's signal the soldiers fired into camp startling, but missing the two. Weldon slid, walked and tumbled after them, shot again and caught one. Another went down, but the rest escaped into the darkness. The soldiers tore the shelters and ransacked them for whatever they thought worth taking. A mother and child huddled inside one, too panicked to move. Weldon grabbed the woman and tied her hands after passing the child to another soldier.

"Shall we take the heads of the braves to show the citizens?" asked a private.

"No, let's get the hell out of here," Weldon replied, taking the woman by her arm as the sun rose. "We have prisoners and injured men to worry about."

Sending two more men to stay with the sergeant, Weldon led the rest of the party back to camp just as the men there finished their morning coffee.

The colonel and the reporter shielded their eyes from the morning glare as the men came in. A shirtless James stood sipping coffee, his suspenders hanging around his legs, but the reporter trotted up for news. Weldon brushed by him. The others were happy to give their accounts of the events so far.

"Weldon, again you defied me!" James yelled, scratching the peeling sunburn on his chest.

"Sir, the sergeant is hurt but safe for now," Weldon said with the Indian woman in tow. "I suggest we start back as soon as possible for Camp Grant."

"Weldon, make the preparations. I'll see to the prisoner," James said, spilling his coffee at Weldon's feet and handing him the cup before pulling up his trousers. Weldon threw the tin on the ground and went to get the men from the stream.

The Apache woman screamed when the colonel cut her clothes from her. "Take a good look at that quim, boys." James laughed, inviting the boys to poke her with their guns. No one did. The colonel took her by the hair and dragged her to his wagon. A few of James' cronies cheered. The newsman had stopped writing and watched with his arms folded and his face dumb as stone.

"What the hell's going on?" cried Weldon running up. "Where's the child?"

The writer reported, "Nits make lice, as they say."

James cursed from the wagon. Weldon and a few others jumped on back but it was too late. The girl fell out before them.

"That filthy bitch bit me!" the colonel announced, jumping down. He grabbed his pistol. The men pulled at James, but he was not to be deterred. The woman tried to run but James caught up with her and knocked the butt of his gun against her skull with a heavy thud.

No one laughed now. One man vomited as the woman lay oozing blood and brain.

"Private Darlington, get rid of this mess. Pick a friend to help you," the colonel ordered. At that moment the poor private had no friends. He tapped Jones on the shoulder and received a savage look.

"By jinks, these Indians have soft skulls," James said. "I hardly hit her." He glanced at his audience and once at the lifeless woman, small and soft. "Weldon, get us out of here. I'm tired of this scouting business," the colonel said with a touch of emotion. "You got us into this mess, now you get us out!"

James ordered a large fire set to the wagons and anything else that could not be taken along. Darlington and Jones wrapped the woman in a blanket and rolled her over a steep hill until she hit rock. The ground was too tough to dig and there wasn't time.

Chapter Thirty-One

Katherine took a long breath and thumbed through a book on European history. She moved to the door and opened it to the night. The few men left behind to guard the camp were supposed to take turns at watch, but it looked as if most were asleep with their beds dragged out under the stars. Leaning on the frame of the doorway, she gazed past the barracks and searched the barely detectable desert horizon, lonesome not just for John but for the world. Living here was like being abandoned. Everyone she knew had their own lives. Father and Mother, Simon, and now John. Her children would grow up and desert her just as she and Simon had done their parents. Any remnants of the close ties were loosened by the irregular mail in Arizona.

Simon used to tell her in his letters home during the war that they could see the same stars in the sky even with state lines and mountains and streams between them. Before the war and before the Undercliff boy and before Simon had been sent away, the two had imagined on humid nights under tall elms that they would tramp the world together gathering stars. Instead they caught fireflies, killing them in sealed jars by mistake. Katherine's one foolish winter daydream had sealed Simon's fate and taken all of their summer nights away forever.

A hollow, useless wind blew over the parade ground, a tease. A dog yelped in one of the quarters begging for supper scraps. Someone's door hung loose on its hinges and tapped open and shut in the small melancholy gusts. Why had she come all this way? Her thoughts turned morbid, and she imagined a funeral after a quick illness. No one would know what dress to put her in or who to send word to if John were away.

And now she had children. What would come next for her? And what if something happened to John? She would have no one for the rest of her life; no one else would ever do. A coyote mourned the passing of another day and Katherine wondered if John thought of her or if he enjoyed their time apart. "Please God, let me die first! I couldn't stand to lose him!"

Katherine splashed her face with water and lay down on the bed, knowing she would not sleep, but closed her eyes and remembered the rain—large drops of summer rain in Englewood sliding over broad leaves outside her bedroom window and the sweet smell that came up from her mother's gardens of lilacs and roses. The porch swing was so cool during an afternoon thunderstorm, and she used to watch the steam rise from the earth, feeling refreshed and alive. Often her mother suggested a stroll then through the bright evening. There was no place to walk out here.

There was no safety past the barracks and nothing to see. Besides, she could not leave the children alone. When John was here she could bear it, but now only three days since he'd left, she worried. How would she feel after ten days? How would she feel to be stationed out here for good?

Sitting up again, she decided to finish a letter to her parents. She picked up her pen and sighed.

Suddenly the camp came alive with shouts and running to the sound of the returning party. Suzy pounded the door. "Mrs. Weldon, come quick!"

The brawn of the colonel and his colorful movements were recognizable even in the dark as he rode by. Suzy spotted two men carrying a stretcher and ran to it. Katherine pushed past the broken-down horse the colonel sat on like a victorious general.

Straggling behind the others were the men who had gone with John in search of James. And there was John, with his eye purple and swollen shut. The sun had done its damage too, and the brush he had pushed past left its jagged marks on his face. Katherine ran up, afraid to touch him. He looked so tender and sore, but Weldon had no such reservations and pulled her close.

"John, what's happened?"

He said nothing as she led him home, holding him the entire time. "Lie down, you poor thing!"

"Oh, Kate," he choked, once inside. "I'm such a failure!"

She put him to bed. "I don't believe it, John Weldon, not for a second! You're a good man. I know you did your best." She worried that maybe he did blunder in the mountains, but it didn't matter. He was with her now and she would help him.

"Kate, I missed you."

"I couldn't have stood two weeks without you," she said. "Do you really love me the best?"

"Kate, what do you think?"

He struggled with his shirt.

"Let me help you." She gasped at his condition. "What happened to your arms?"

"I'm all right," he said but refused to show his middle.

"No you're not." She tugged gently at his shirt. "The Apache are less than human to do this to you!"

"It wasn't the Indians." His old wound was inflamed again. "Katherine, I'm a loser in life. I don't know why you stay. The colonel bested me. He stripped the journey of all dignity. James bought off the newsman somehow—and brought the Indians to us—and he did awful things, terrible things, and I couldn't stop him! I tried to stop him, Kate, I did, but he duped me at every turn. He can have his way with me in the papers and in the army. I don't know how things will go now."

"John, we're together, and you're alive. That's all that matters."

Someone knocked at the door. Weldon opened it to find Jones in a lather.

"Sir, the colonel wants you this instant."

"What for?"

"The deserters, Fielding and Sparks, have come in, sir. Seems James wants them taken care of tonight."

"Well, what does he need me for? Land sakes, will this ever end?" Weldon pulled on a jacket and gave Katherine a sorry look as he left.

"That damned James!" Jones said. "Riding in on the only horse and keeping us working till all hours. Cook has made him a fancy meal, I can tell you that. Where does he get all he does, the son of a bitch? Well, I'll tell you, sir, if that wasn't the worst scout I've ever been on."

"Thanks for stating the obvious, Jones. But you're right. It couldn't have been worse."

"Oh, I'd have to disagree with you there, sir," Jones said. "It would've been a heck of a lot worse if you weren't there."

"But you forget we wouldn't have been there if it wasn't for me, and you wouldn't still be at work this night."

"'Course, you're right in a way, but we're soldiers, ain't we after all? It ain't much of a life out here without real work to do. Digging ditches can only distract a man for so long before he up and wants to quit it all and shove off—or at least get drunk."

Weldon lit his pipe and smiled. "I've never met such a bunch as this for drinking, and I've been around a while. They find pleasure in nothing else. Even on a Saturday there's no races or sport or even gambling. I'm surprised."

"The colonel cheated at the races and never paid his debts so we lost interest. James likes to keep us down and miserable, sir."

The colonel's quarters were well lit with candles. Weldon braced himself and knocked at the door. Julia opened it and let them in. "My, boys, you both look played out after your little march in the mountains. Colonel, what's happened to Mr. Weldon's good looks? I do hope this scouting is out of your system now, lieutenant. Your little wife can hardly care for herself and those children on her own. Poor Mrs. Weldon was completely demoralized when I visited her, and there was no end to the children's bawling. It's not fair to expect us to care for your wife when we have our own concerns—I did try to help her in my little way. I promised to keep it secret from you. The poor thing was so ashamed of herself." Julia smiled as Weldon's cheeks burned.

"Colonel James, what is it you need from me, sir?"

Cook poured a fragrant Mexican sauce over the colonel's meal as Weldon and Jones looked on.

The colonel took a mouthful, wiped his mustache, and spoke. "So we had two deserters in the mountains."

"Sir, they didn't desert," Jones said. "They came back here."

"Did I address you, private?"

"No, sir."

"Colonel James," Weldon said, clearing his throat first, "I agree with Jones. Fielding and Spark are good and sober men, sir. From what I saw and heard, the men got separated and probably figured they were the only survivors."

"You don't surprise me anymore, Weldon. I don't see how you've made it this far without someone taking you out and shooting you for your own good. All along you've been ridiculously hard on the men for the tiniest infractions, and now you want to go easy on the cowards who left us for dead?"

"Do you mean while you were off fishing and playing cards, sir? You put all the men in danger. For many it was their first time out. I understand you don't like me, sir, but to jeopardize every man to make a fool of me ..."

The colonel laughed and choked on his meat. "Dear Weldon, I don't have to work to make a fool of you—you have that covered. You were responsible for the trip. I told you that from the start, and you'll be held accountable for all that happened. But I'm tired of squabbling with you. I want all the men brought out tonight."

"Sir? But it's already lights out an hour ago."

"I want an example made of the cowards tonight. Shave their heads and brand their faces. Have them drummed from camp."

Jones and Weldon balked.

"Weldon, I'll have you cashiered if you disobey me. There's enough witnesses to your insubordination over the past few days."

Julia stood behind her husband with a smug glow on her face.

After pained salutes to their superior, Weldon and Jones walked out. Jones ordered the men to gather on the parade grounds.

The tip of the colonel's cigar glowed from his ramada as the men appeared. Katherine watched with growing apprehension from the small window of their quarters. A few men built a small fire, and Katherine could see John's deformed face in the light like something from a nightmare. Two figures stumbled up, their hands tied behind their backs. John's knife glistened, and Katherine turned away as John shaved the hair and eyebrow on Fielding's left side. Spark would not stay still when his turn came. He pleaded with John who grabbed him by the arm and said something to him which calmed him a little. John watched as a beleaguered private heated a branding iron at the fire.

When John saw Katherine—the outline of her under their ramada—he threw down the hot iron.

"*Sir*!" Fielding shouted, "Oh, thank God!"

Spark stood soberly as the colonel strode up.

"*Weldon*!" James shouted.

"Colonel, I won't do it," Weldon said. "They s-s-should be allowed a trial or at least a v-v-vote from the men."

"You son-of-a-bitch! I've had it with you. I'm placing you under arrest!" The colonel turned to Jones. "Bring your friend to the guardhouse!"

"No sir, I will not!"

"You little Welsh pissant! How dare you defy me! Howell and Coutret, take these rascals to the guardhouse and have them bucked and gagged indefinitely."

The colonel reheated the brand and burned the coward's C into the deserters' cheeks. He ordered the fife and drum to play the "Rogues March," and the two disappeared into the night. Katherine, leaving the children to themselves, ran after John.

"Kate, please go home!"

She grabbed Coutret's arm. "What will you do to him?"

The soldier pulled from her, angry and embarrassed by her display. "You heard the colonel—we're to buck and gag 'im."

"*Katherine*, go home!" John yelled.

She stood still for a moment, but obeyed and turned away.

Bound and gagged, Weldon had time to think. His jaw ached and his sore side throbbed under the pressure of his knees bound against his middle. He never wanted to see Katherine again. His mother used to tie him sometimes when he stole things in the Western Reserve, and now it was the same again. Yet in a strange way he felt relieved. He could fight no more, he needn't worry. Just as in childhood, he was powerless, and just as in childhood he let his mind wander to cope. When he was young he dreamed of his father's games and his readings from Scripture. No verses came now. As his limbs and back ached for movement, morphine was what he thought of most.

James carried a great steaming cup of coffee when he arrived next morning. "Enjoying yourselves, Weldon? Jones?" he asked before turning to the soldier on guard. "Release Jones."

The private was untied but needed help getting back to the barracks.

"Well, these have been trying times for us all, Weldon, and it's clear you've brought it all upon us. I could set up a court-martial proceeding and see you stripped of rank or thrown out altogether. Because I have a weak spot for women and children, I think a demotion would bring less embarrassment to your family. Of course your wife should go back east and soon. At the least I intend to make quite an example of you. I don't want any other knuckleheads following your lead. You've upset the delicate balance of this shithole. You'll be under guard until I can get up a party of men to give you a fair trial, but because I'm humane I'll allow you a day—this day—to square things with your little family. They can leave with the teamsters bringing the supplies for the Indians. Mrs. Weldon never fit in anyway, Weldon. It's for the best. I'll have Hayes release you when he comes back." The colonel lit his cigar and strolled out into the light.

John stumbled to his quarters with the help of two soldiers. They brought him to the unmade bed and left. He turned his face to the wall and said nothing.

"John, did they hurt you anymore?" Katherine said scurrying to his side. "You're home now, and I can take care of you."

"Leave me alone," he mumbled, refusing to face her.

"Are you angry with me?" Her voice quivered.

"*No*, Kate! I'm *not* angry with you. Not everything is about you! Can't you just leave me be for once? You're always hanging off me. I wish you were more independent!"

The words stabbed her. She rose from the bed ashamed of her neediness and pretended to check the bread dough she'd been watching rise before tiptoeing out into the heat. The sun burned away her essence. She was just a generic anybody—an army wife. She couldn't storm off, she couldn't yell and have the whole fort hear so she went back inside.

The children cried. Katherine changed her daughter and nearly threw her into the bed with her husband. "They're yours too, John Weldon. You take care of them!"

Weldon sat up and pulled Eliza into his arms. "I never want to be alone," he said. "You're not alone ..."

"Are you blind, deaf, and dumb? I disobeyed the colonel and took the men out and got all of our animals taken."

"Please, I'm not as dumb as everybody thinks," she said, not trusting her words, yet angry that Weldon suddenly perceived her weaknesses so keenly.

"You have to leave here with the teamsters when they deliver the Indian rations."

"No, I won't." This wasn't bravery or stubbornness but a deep fear that without John Weldon, Katherine could not survive.

"You have no choice," John said flatly. "James will try to suspend my pay and he'll put you out of our quarters."

"I can send for things from home, and we'll live in a tent," Katherine replied, standing near the bed, afraid another step closer would bring more pain.

"Katherine," Weldon sighed, "you've tried hard, but I want you to leave."

"Julia James was right! You're tired of me!"

Weldon jumped from the bed and grabbed her. "You're so stupid, Katherine! Can't you see you're the only thing that holds any charm for me in life? I'm so tired of you doubting it!"

She looked up at him. "But the dance floor that night ... I don't know ..."

"I don't want you to leave me," he shouted, and the baby on the bed whimpered. "I don't think I can be without you anymore, but the colonel and his wife will make it impossible for you to stay."

"What will we do?"

"Katherine, I'm so close to losing everything. I ..."

"Don't say it. You'll only scare me more."

"But I can't keep this to myself any longer," he began to tell her. He couldn't look at her. "When I'm alone ... I'm no good ... I'm afraid I'll disgrace you."

"You could never, John. I know you enough now. You can't convince me of your bad ways."

Chapter Thirty-Two

By chance the mail came in early and with it the local paper from town. Just as reveille played there was a pounding at the door. John jumped from bed fully dressed.

"Lieutenant Weldon! Look at this!" Jones said. Katherine came up behind them. "Morning, Mrs. Weldon. Land sakes, lieutenant, it came out fast, didn't it?"

Weldon scanned the story from the newsman, running his fingers through his hair. "The ineptitude and corruption of Colonel Dixon James became apparent .... The lieutenant and his men behaved admirably, even heroically ... saving their fallen comrade and putting the savage Apaches on the run .... The prisoners were mishandled by the colonel .... The writer suggests the true heroes should be put in charge of military operations in our victimized territory ..."

"It's bully, sir, don't you think?"

Weldon said nothing for a long while and then passed the paper to Katherine.

"I thought you'd be happy, sir. I don't gather you are," Jones said.

"Don't let any of the men see this," Weldon warned, glancing across the empty land.

"But why, sir?"

"The colonel will have our heads for this."

"*Weldon*!!" came a thunderous shout. Jones backed away to face the colonel as he trotted over to them. "You sneaky, lying son-of-a-bitch!" James roared, waving a copy of the paper in Weldon's face. "You think you've won? You're a goddamned, ill-bred, halfwit. I have friends, Weldon, who will vouch for my word against this trash!"

"But sir, we were all there," said Jones.

James clobbered him.

Weldon did not miss his chance to get the better of the colonel this time. His fist hit James' jaw with such force that Weldon figured he'd broken his hand. The colonel didn't fall, but staggered back, cradling the side of his face. It was light now, and the men had gathered on the parade ground in silence not wanting to spoil the show. Katherine stood, gaping in the doorway.

The colonel lunged forward, but missed his mark and spit blood. "You son of a bitch!"

Weldon grabbed him, but before he could get off another punch the colonel dragged Weldon to the ground, kicking and throwing fists. Katherine stepped between them, timidly tugging at the colonel. James turned and clutched her by the neck throwing her against the wall. Weldon dragged a lantern from atop a nearby crate and smashed it over the colonel's head, shattering the glass and slashing the colonel's face and neck. "You piece of shit! *Never* touch my wife, you miserable bastard! I'll kill you!"

While James pulled shards of glass from his bloody face, John took a knife from his belt and went for the colonel's throat, but the colonel flipped him with a horrible grunt.

"Men, take this rascal to the guardhouse!"

No one stepped forward.

"Sentiment may cause some of you to side with this little family here. But I can assure you that army regulations do not. This man has tried to kill a superior." James stood with blood dripping down his chin. "And it's my right to put down insurrection—mutiny. The crime is punishable by death, boys. So I suggest that someone step forward to bring this outsider, this scoundrel, to the guardhouse."

Five men stepped up and as James stumbled to his feet they all took out their revolvers and aimed them at the colonel. "You must be bloody joking, fellows. I'm not the enemy," James chuckled uncomfortably. "Recognize your folly."

Jones stepped forward. "We know you stand to make a pretty penny when the Indian rations arrive. We know that you've cheated us, and General Stoneman don't much like you neither. But we'll stay shut up if you let Lieutenant Weldon be."

John tried to sit up, but James pushed him down.

The colonel took out a rag and wiped his face. He picked one last shard from his forehead. "That sounds like a deal I can live with, Jones, you snake-in-the-grass. I underestimated you. You caught me with my trousers down, but it won't happen again."

***

Camp Grant

February 1871

Dear Mr. and Mrs. McCullough,

I am writing to inform you of the sad news that while Katherine is out of all danger, the new baby did not survive into his second week. I write this in hope of preventing any gifts from being sent for the new child that might come just as Katherine truly recovers. She misses her mother at times like this I think—and her father too.

I was with her the entire time and have never been so proud of Katherine. She was very brave. The baby was named Simon John Weldon, but his color was not right from the start.

William and Eliza are big and strong. I will take good care of their mother so please try not to worry.

Sincerely,

John Weldon

***

Camp Grant, Arizona

May 27, 1871

Dear Father and Mother,

Mail service here is still so awful so I do not know how long it will be until you get this letter. I have begun so many in the past, but I get so despondent when I think of how long it takes for them to reach Englewood. Did you receive my last letters? I have not had a letter from you in months. I hope that you have not forgotten about us out here.

There has been a lot of excitement of late in our area. I have learned that the newspapers often change their stories to suit their purposes, and I do not want you worrying about things which might be reported inaccurately.

You may know that General Stoneman has set up our camp as a sort of feeding station for the peaceful Apaches. The hope had been that the Indians would not raid and kill if they were given all that they needed by the government until they learned to support themselves through farming and other useful endeavors. Colonel James has put John in charge of the commissary stores and Indian rations. The Indians like their presents. But no one here believes that all who come in have completely given up their raids. Some Apaches try very hard to be good, but raiding is the way of life here and the raiders are proud of their traditions. On the other hand the Papago Indians, the Mexicans and the Americans are not so happy with it, especially if a family member is used or killed!

I will tell you both my version of the Camp Grant Massacre, as it is being called. Probably the papers in the east will have carried the story, but how am I to know out here in the desert?

Many Indians started to settle close by Camp Grant in the Aravaipa Canyon down by the San Pedro River. Some, mostly women, even expressed an interest in farming. The men of Camp Grant and some of us women tried to help them get started. The Apaches make a drink called tizwin, and when it is ready after a long fermenting process they have celebrations. There seem to be a lot of these celebrations! Sometimes they would all be too sick to work. On other days we all worked chirkily together, coaxing the soil with our makeshift shovels and hoes. And then there were the days when the men of the tribe would be ominously absent, and usually before long we would receive complaints about a raid against the Papagos, who are trying so hard to survive, or against some Mexican rancher who had just restocked his little place with sheep to replace the ones taken on a previous raid!

And so over a series of months, with the Apaches showing no signs of quitting their ancient, brutal ways and with the government seen to be rewarding the Apaches with gifts and army protection in the canyon, there began to be real rumblings from the settlers, especially around Tucson. The papers were growing more strident in their calls for something more drastic to be done to the Apaches. Some editors suggested getting rid of the Regular Army altogether and forming a citizen one instead. Finally, under the leadership of a Tucson lawyer, that's just what they did.

It was still early morning when a badly injured Apache girl crawled into camp. John said later that he had not really wanted me along, having a sense of what we would find, but it was beyond even his worst fears. The sight we came upon in the canyon was nightmarish in the extreme and gruesome beyond words.

The citizen army had fallen upon the camp before dawn looking for raiders, but as fate would have it, the Apache men were indeed out raiding. I suppose this angered the undisciplined mob of about 150 men. Women and their children were beaten and killed. I knew them all and recognized some as my friends, but to see children the size of my own butchered and flung like rag dolls to their deaths was disturbing beyond words! This is the Indian style of warfare and we have now sunk to it!

Some children, about thirty of them, I am told, were sold off into the Mexican slave trade. I shudder still when I think of the feeling of evil that pervaded the canyon that day.

The citizens of Tucson for the most part celebrated the act. Most of the killers were Papagos, which may explain the brutality of the massacre, and the rest were Mexicans who like to play both sides of the border and have been profiting as much as suffering for their involvement with the Apache raiders for as long as anyone can remember. There were six whites involved.

I think of all the violent events over the years, from the Sioux Uprising to the Fetterman Massacre and the Sand Creek Massacre and the list goes on. All sides seem hopelessly driven to more and more violence. It's all a muddle and maybe it is where education and missionary work should come in. I wonder about religion sometimes. The Mexicans are Catholic and most settlers profess to be Christians, and even the Indians must have some moral code—but I guess the Bible is right that no real peace will come until the Lord visits the earth again. We have tried so hard to help out here and I had such hope for the Apaches if only they had stopped their raids.

Most likely all the people involved in the massacre will go free. Not a citizen would think of convicting them.

Now a little about us. John is overworked, but enjoying the respect he deserves. William is forever fighting off catarrh, but is cheerful and becoming a happy nuisance. He gets around so easily and quietly gets up to all sorts of mischief. Eliza is sturdy and grows at an alarming rate. She is by far the most vocal child I have ever seen and happiest when her father has her on his lap. Cooking is still a trial for me.

I hope and pray that you are both well. Also please send news of Simon. I miss his letters so full of fun. I know that he has been on the move to Texas, but it has been such a while since I have heard anything that it worries me. I wish that John and Simon were still stationed together, but foolish Simon always has to go his own way! If you write to him send him my love and scold him so he will start up his letters again. I cannot remember a time since be-

fore West Point that I did not have a stack of his antics to read about until now!

Give Handsome a nice pet for me, Father!

Yours affectionately,

Katherine Weldon

Chapter Thirty-Three

"Lieutenant are you at home?" Jones called.

Weldon shook his head and muttered to Katherine, "Where else would I be at this hour?" and to Jones, "Come in, private. What is it now?"

Jones popped his head in, aware that he was interrupting their meal. "Sir, Sergeant Simpson's fever has broke."

"Merciful heavens!" Katherine exclaimed, standing. "That's jolly news!"

"Yes it is, ma'am. Lieutenant, he asks for you," Jones continued, delighting in being the bearer of good news for a change.

"Well, let's go then!" Weldon said.

Katherine lifted Eliza on to her back.

"For God's sake, Kate," John scolded, "How will you ever be yourself again if you keep straining yourself? Let me take Elly. Let Willy walk."

She hated being treated like an invalid, especially in front of the soldiers, and was embarrassed at how haggard she looked.

John took her hand and smiled, and she forgot her annoyance.

"I'll take Willy to play by the horses, sir. If you don't mind," Jones offered.

Katherine waited in the stuffy but neat main room as Suzy led John with Eliza on his hip to the sergeant. John took off his hat and nodded to Suzy in his usual reticent way with women before sitting on a chair beside the convalescent with Eliza bouncing on his knee. "You've been an awful worry to us, sergeant."

"My apologies, sir, but I was dying," Simpson joked.

Weldon patted the man's good shoulder. "Fair enough, but when will you come back to work with us? I need my best sergeant, you know."

Simpson shook his head.

"Simpson, please, take all the time you need," Weldon assured him. "I only wanted to tell you you're missed."

"Sir, is there a way—I mean to say—my wife has suffered here, and the doctor says we can stay in San Francisco for a while." He coughed in obvious great pain—not out of the woods yet.

"Of course, but you should wait till you're stronger."

Simpson's eyes shined, reminding Weldon of men he'd seen at the hospital during the war, and he shuddered.

"No! I want to bring Suzy away for a while to a nice place. Jones tells me we may be bumped from here with General Crook sending in new men."

John rolled his eyes, "That Jones can always be depended upon for news. I'll do my best to get you the safest trip back to California if you promise to come back to us healthy. Kate will miss Mrs. Simpson, I suspect, so you put me in a bind."

Katherine came over. "Don't you listen to the lieutenant! I'm happy that you'll be in a real home together for a while—just family. It will do a world of good for you all."

The colonel and Mrs. James strode in. The bedroom became small now. Suzy shooed the children outside. Colonel James took a direct path to the bed, nearly knocking Katherine into the whatnot in the corner.

"Simpson, great to see you lucid again, although it was always a rare thing with you, my boy. Lost your good arm for card playing too. Shame it is, but I hear they make damned good body parts now."

Simpson coughed again. Suzy pushed past the colonel and sat at the edge of the bed, rubbing her husband's chest to calm him while looking up at James bitterly.

James cleared his throat, "Simpson, now that you'll be well soon we should discuss your quarters."

Weldon flashed him a look, "Sir, not now."

"The girl will need some notice to pack up their things, and he won't be much help, poor devil."

Suzy burst into tears. Katherine grabbed her hand and brought her outside. "That old scoundrel! Don't worry, John will sort things out."

"I just want to be away from here for good with my husband. I don't want him to find a good arm and stay in the army. The colonel is right. Daniel was a mess before your husband took him under his wing. I'll always be so grateful to you both, but in a way I never want to see any of you again if it has to be here."

"I know, Suzy. I understand," Katherine said, jealous of her friend's opportunity to leave.

Julia strolled out with a perfumed hanky at her nose. "The smell of sickness is so disgusting. Weldon's men will scrub the place down once you're out of here. Suzy, don't worry yourself about cleaning up." Julia took note of the effect the words had on the woman before her. "Oh, dear, I'm sorry, that was rude of me. It's good to see your husband with color again. I do miss his funny ways when he used to play bluff with the colonel."

Suzy boiled. "How dare you come here now, Mrs. James, to remind me of your wretchedness! My husband chose me in the end!"

Julia took out her fan, the feathers wilting in the heat, and with mock humor fluttered it Suzy's way. "Now don't get hot and bothered. You and your husband were too dimwitted to understand harmless flirtation."

"If you hadn't plied him with drink he ..."

"If that's what you need to believe, Suzy, that's fine," Julia said. "As you say, he's yours now—armless and all. Of course you have no worries. He will realize how lucky he is that anyone would want him. The surgeon made an awful mess of the stump."

"Mrs. James, do you have a Christian bone in your body?" Katherine cried. "I'm forever stunned by your hateful ways. I never knew a person so beautiful could be so ugly underneath."

Julia made as if she hadn't noticed Katherine. "Oh you, little miss perfect. So it's the opposite for you, I suppose. You haven't managed to lose that thickness around the middle yet that men find so unappealing—a shame really, but Weldon is such a pitiful character he couldn't handle a better woman."

"Get off my porch, Mrs. James, before I physically force the issue," warned Suzy.

Julia laughed.

The colonel stooped through the low door with John behind him. "Well, it's nice to see the girls together, ain't it, Weldon?" James observed. "Suzy, Weldon has suggested an extended leave of absence for your husband—tells me the doc has a place for you all—but I'll be honest with you girl, I don't like the look of Simpson one bit. There's something still in his system, I think."

Suzy cried and ran inside.

Weldon grabbed Katherine by the arm and walked off in exasperation. "They are the most disgusting couple. I've never seen the likes of their meanness toward others!"

"Is Simpson still sick, do you think?"

"I can't rightly say. Simpson's convinced he won't last the year but won't say why he feels it. I think he's just weak and melancholy over the arm. California will do him good. But Kate, I wanted to ask you about our little savings. I know you want to go visit home someday, but ..."

"Yes, John, you're right. We should give it to them."

"Good," Weldon said, squeezing her around the waist.

Katherine pushed him away.

"What's wrong? I didn't hurt you, did I?"

"*No*! I'm not a china doll! I'm just so ugly!" She began sobbing.

"Land sakes! Where did this come from?" he asked, looking back at Julia. "Katie, what did she say to you now?"

Katherine tried to calm down, so mad at herself for listening to Julia. "Look what the baby has done to me, and he goes and dies anyway!"

"Oh, Katie, it's all right."

"No, it's not! Suzy will leave and you will succeed at work and I'll grow fat and old!"

"Kate! You're not fat," Weldon assured her as they walked into their quarters. "So you're a little soft around the middle ..."

She stared at him. "How is that any different?"

"Well, the truth is, I like you when you're not so skinny. You feel nice to me, and I think you're even prettier, but you do look so tired."

"I'm like a prisoner here. I know you're trying to protect me, but I need to work a little. I feel so useless and down-spirited."

He thought about it. "You're right. I'm suffocating you. I'll try to stop, but I have something that might cheer you. What if I get you a horse of your own?"

"And how will you do that? We have no money."

"Well, the colonel has been stealing from the Indians. James is using a fixed scale, and I've been keeping track of it. He would want me to keep quiet about it."

She stared. "John Weldon, what has become of you to even think of doing such a thing? Look what this place has done to you! You would consider *blackmail*?"

He hesitated, "Why should he profit while we all live like Spartans?"

"You're not serious? I couldn't be more disappointed in you."

"I can't help it! I want to make the colonel pay for the humiliation he put me through!"

"That's no excuse for joining in his corruption!"

"I just want to give you something nice," he continued.

"John, I want you to promise that you will *never* even consider anything like this again. I want you to promise to stay the same man I married—honest and good!"

Weldon squirmed at the description. "I only wish I could give you things."

"John, I don't need my own horse. I don't need anything but you, even when I'm fat and ugly."

"Come here! You are the loveliest girl in the world. I love your soft little belly, and I love how you keep me from doing things I shouldn't. Do you see what a mess I'd be without you?"

And so within the week the Simpsons packed and loaded their things onto a teamster car that would take them to the Colorado River and onward by steamer to

San Diego and finally San Francisco. Katherine worried now at the state of Simpson, for while he maintained a cheerful and pleasant attitude there was a desperate look in his eyes.

She baked cakes to give them, but they were a failure and never rose.

"Oh, Mrs. Weldon, you've done enough," Suzy said, hugging her friend for the last time and coughing deeply. Katherine stood back. "Suzy, are you unwell?"

"Oh, it's just catarrh. None of us have been able to shake it. It's all the worry, I reckon, but we'll be better away from here."

Katherine smiled grimly, feeling guilty for not wanting to stand too close.

Weldon discreetly gave the last of their money to Simpson as the wagon lurched forward. John jumped down, and they watched until the Simpsons were out of sight.

The doctor had overslept, but hurried out now. "I've missed them then?" he asked, flustered.

"I'm afraid so, doctor," Katherine answered knowing John would not.

"Well, it's a shame. The whole lot of them probably got it," he mumbled to himself.

Weldon turned to him now. "Doctor Milroy, what are you saying?"

"The consumption, of course. You might have heard the cough."

"What?"

"Simpson used to spend a lot of time consorting with the Apaches when their tizwin was ready. A lot of them got the sickness. I suspect that's how he picked it up, and I heard the cough on the wife, but she wouldn't believe it—you know, with all them children to consider. Funny how life is, Weldon. You went through a lot of trouble to save a man who likely already had a death sentence."

Chapter Thirty-Four

John traveled to Tucson for supplies. Katherine decided to go fishing at the river. The soft, early evening sun made staying in camp unbearable. She tied a dog to a rope for company and walked out with the two children, one on her back and the other helping with the fishing supplies as best he could. A few soldiers by the sick house watched the stuck-on-herself lady pass by with her nose in the air.

"That Weldon got himself an independent one."

"No, she's a scared little thing. She probably don't have much food," another guessed as he shivered with the ague.

Katherine relaxed once out of earshot and sang with her children:

The sunny, sunny hours of childhood,
How soon, how soon they pass away,
Like flowers, like flowers in the wildwood,
That once bloomed fresh and gay;
But the perfume of the flowers,
And the freshness of the heart,
Live but a few brief hours,
And then for age depart.

The songs missed John's voice, and the dog broke free and ran back to camp. The Apache women refused to eat fish from this water. They thought it had been hexed and filled with poison for their people, but Katherine and the soldiers found the fish tasty and escaped from camp any time they could to catch them.

Willy was the first, after a day in the sun, to fade, snoring on the blanket Katherine had laid out for them. Leaned up against a boulder, Eliza in her cradleboard (Sarah would be horrified if she knew the girl still spent so much time in it) sang out her nonsense songs. The stream bubbled along dark and cool. Katherine kicked off her moccasins and dipped her feet into the water. A large bird's shadow passed overhead, an eagle or a hawk—Katherine couldn't tell in the glare of the bright evening sky. The stars and the moon glistened. Clouds rode by like purple feathers. Mountains and sky and the murmuring of the water conspired to set Katherine at ease. She glanced around. Eliza looked past her, eyes half-closed to the world. Katherine unbraided her hair and slipped out of her dress. She glided into the water. It caressed her, caved in on her, and blanketed her in peace. Why had she never done this before? Every night from now on, she determined. Her arms were so brown now. She let her hands float over her body, over her belly and hips. Lying back, she wet her hair and made a wish on a star. She ran her hands up her thighs and thought of John.

Fish nibbled at Katherine's toes, and she smiled with eyes closed at the strange and beautiful world she lived in. The fish pulled her hair. Katherine blinked open her eyes, and in silent panic pulled away from the Apache warrior squatting down beside her but he still had her hair. Then a shout rang out, and the Apache splashed and fled away from her. A horse galloped in and John jumped down. He aimed his gun at the Apache as he raced away. Pulling Katherine up from the water, he grabbed his dirty blanket and wrapped her in it, the ends weighed down in the stream.

Weldon dragged Katherine to the shore, and the horse followed. Katherine's teeth chattered as she grabbed her dress and pulled it over her head in a daze.

"Kate! There are Apaches all around! Why would you leave camp alone at night?" He put Eliza on his back and tried to shake Katherine out of her stupor. "They could have taken you all! What the devil were you thinking?"

She looked at him. "I was dreaming about you. I was foolish and bored. Forgive me!"

"Oh, Kate!" he began and pulled her close. He'd found opium after a court-martial hearing in Tucson with the colonel. James could not leave Tucson without one last big night out so let his men do as they wished. Weldon traded the pocket watch Simpson had given him as a gift to get what he wanted.

"I know this life isn't for you," he said, pulling the hair behind his ear. "What would your mother say if she knew what just happened?"

Katherine reached up and caressed his face. "Mother would say I married the bravest, most honorable man."

"Please, Katherine, stop it. Don't say those things about me. I was not so brave and honorable in Tucson. We shouldn't stay here any longer. It's dangerous." He helped his wife and Willy onto the horse, then jumped on too with Eliza and rode back.

Camp Grant looked so different and alive with all new men bustling about. "Kate, General Crook has arrived."

She realized how she must look in her frayed Mexican dress and muddy wet hair. Weldon spotted one of the men who had earlier admitted to him that he let her go off fishing and jumped from the horse. "You little piece of shit. You never should have let my wife go unescorted anywhere off camp. Do you understand?"

"Yes, sir. My apologies, sir."

John took off his hat and ran his fingers through his hair. "Okay, well then—go see if there's anything the sergeant needs you to do."

"Yes, sir," the soldier answered and passed by Katherine. "I'm dreadful sorry, ma'am."

She smiled at him. Now John was shaking hands shyly with a dashing, dark-haired soldier. He had Irish looks and a full mustache. The man glanced over at her and William and grinned. He made a wry comment to her husband—she could tell by his animated expression. John brought him over. "Pleased to meet you, Mrs. Weldon. I'm Lieutenant Bourke. Your husband tells me you've had some trouble tonight while fishing."

She blushed.

"Oh, that's all right. At least you married a good soldier with impeccable timing. But tell me, do you usually get so wet when you fish?" Bourke laughed.

She laughed nervously.

"Lieutenant Weldon says you both like to fish."

"Well, sir, there isn't much else to do," Katherine said.

"Yes, of course," Bourke said, but he looked curious and happy to be there. "The general loves to fish and hunt so you must tell us the best places."

Suddenly the very man Bourke spoke of stood before them, looking nothing like a soldier of rank. Unlike Colonel James, who even at his worst usually wore enough army-issue gear to convince even the novice spectator of his importance, General Crook looked much more like a careworn mountain man with frizzled and graying hair and an eccentrically parted beard. His grey, frosty eyes reminded Katherine of a rat's.

"And who are you?" Crook asked with a mirthless smile.

"She is Mrs. Weldon, sir," Lieutenant Bourke answered. "Lieutenant Weldon's wife."

The general tipped his hat and turned to John. "Weldon, you look familiar. Why is that?"

John stammered and Katherine held her breath feeling his nerves. "In the P-Pacific, sir, before the war, sir."

General Crook looked John over and laughed. "Now I remember! You're from the Western Reserve."

"Yes, sir."

"And you were far too young to be in the service."

John smiled. "Not far too young."

"Do you still hunt, lieutenant?"

"Well, sir, it's forbidden by the colonel."

Bourke looked at Crook incredulously.

Crook said, "We'll see that's changed." He glanced up at Katherine. "And how are you liking your stay in the desert, young lady?"

She tried to speak, but all the while the idea that the Indian might have killed her and the children, that it was unsafe here, took hold and she burst into tears. The three men fell over each other helping her from the horse. Bourke took William, who tried pulling his mustache. Crook got flustered and asked gruffly, "What's wrong with her?"

"There was an Indian down at the river, sir," Weldon began.

Bourke finished the story telling of John's rescue.

"There, there Mrs. Weldon. You're safe now. I let my men use their guns, and we'll crush these Indians yet." And to Weldon he added, "I give these girls credit. This is no place for a lady. Mrs. Crook visits on occasion, but they are short stays to be sure." He patted Katherine's back uncomfortably. "Mrs. Weldon, the next time you fish wait for us, will you?" he said, turning to go.

Bourke set Willy down, tipped his hat, and walked off with Crook.

"I don't know but the rugged little camp wives are the most interesting," Crook said with a grin. "Off fishing on her own at this place!"

Katherine buried her face in John's arms. "I'm so sorry!"

"Kate, just promise me you won't do anything like that again," Weldon said, pulling hair from her face. "If I wasn't so darned scared for you down at the river, I could have admired you longer. I imagine that Indian felt lucky to be in your lap."

"John Weldon!"

"I might have to take you fishing more often if you promise to take your clothes off every time," Weldon teased, trying to make himself feel better over what might have happened if he had not come in time. He kissed her head. "You smell like the river."

She pushed him away. He grabbed her back. "Oh, come on, Kate, I'd hate to think what I look and smell like."

She giggled. "I love the look and smell of you. I want to hear everything that went on in Tucson."

"No, I want to leave it alone. It's done now. I just want to make you proud again."

"I never stopped being proud," she assured him.

He accepted her words but knew that she expected success from men. That was what she was used to, how she had been raised. His heart sank when he thought of his behavior in Tucson. The watch had been special to Simpson.

Chapter Thirty-Five

Katherine hummed a tune as she swept their quarters with a new sense of optimism in the morning. John was home, back to work and her hero. She had stayed up the night before, luxuriating in his body heat and reliving how he had saved her. As she pulled the loose dirt with her broom, someone tapped her shoulder and she jumped as did Lieutenant Bourke.

"Sorry, ma'am. I didn't mean to frighten you. I assumed you heard me. Is the lieutenant here?"

"No, he's doing the books."

"The books?" Bourke asked strangely. "We were told ... well ... that he was not to be trusted with the books."

She hesitated. "What do you mean?"

"We were told ... well, never mind."

"Please lieutenant, tell me," she pressed.

"So there was no problem with the books?" Bourke asked.

She gasped. "Oh! How dare the colonel! He's an awful man! John has tried, really he has, but the colonel is a drunkard, and he steals from the Indians and the men. There are always unexplained shortages, but John does his best. You must believe me! The colonel nearly had him cashiered!"

"Cashiered?" Bourke asked in surprise.

"But the men stopped it and ..."

"Mrs. Weldon, you should mind what you say."

Katherine looked at him in panic.

"General Crook is a good judge of character. Your husband is probably safe, but you don't want to involve yourself in such a mess that is bound to happen. You needn't worry, Mrs. Weldon. I shouldn't have troubled you."

Bourke tipped his hat and was gone. She walked out to watch him go. There was such an optimistic air about him. She hoped it signaled a change for Camp Grant. One of the things she missed most about the East was the pride the people had in themselves, the way they spoke and dressed, the way they took care of their surroundings. Out here John had to threaten the men to get them, on occasion, to clean themselves. Maybe it was the desert or the class of men or just Colonel James and his negative influence. She hoped Crook saw the colonel for what he was.

One day had changed the camp completely. There were so many new faces and mules! The animals brayed and kicked up dust—so much so that William, who loved their rebellious tendencies and peculiar antics, wheezed and coughed, but he could not be convinced to stay indoors and she couldn't blame him. They both craved color. Men walked by tipping their hats, and Katherine caught snippets of their conversations.

"Crook won't keep us here too long, I'd say. This camp should be shut up. Heard him say there's been a lot of the shakes here."

Katherine worried about the intermittent fevers too, but knew quite a few of the "shakes" cases were more alcoholic in nature and smiled.

A few soldiers raced in and out of the barracks lanes after a runaway mule. An older couple, a captain and his lady, strode up clasped at the elbows and stopped before the Weldon quarters. Both stood tall and handsome. The lady's wispy silver hair suited her.

"Good morning, young lady. Lovely children," the captain said while tipping his hat in a most graceful manner.

Katherine liked them already. "Thank you."

They smiled but seemed hesitant to leave.

"Oh! How rude of me. Won't you both come out of the sun?" Katherine was proud of her little porch now, with columbine and forget-me-not growing in the shady spots. She had made pillows for the rustic old chairs too. "Oh, bully," she exclaimed as they joined her under the ramada, "and I've just made lemonade from the last of the lemons John brought back from his recent trip into town. It may be too sweet. I get carried away with the sugar!"

She ran into the kitchen checking for smudges on the tin cups, grabbed a plate of singed gingersnaps and carried them to the door. That she had baked something however burnt just this morning made her inordinately proud. While she pulled the lemonade from the cooling container on the wall, she imagined the lady to be just like Sarah—the fine chats they might have!

William had climbed on to the man's knee and listened gravely to the man's talk of the stormy sea they came in on and the Modoc Indians he had left to come to this dry and dusty land. The lady ran her fingers through the shiny black curls on Eliza's head.

Katherine poured drinks, and they sat in silence, watching the day drift by and the children eat the gingersnaps. "This is silly. I've forgotten to mention my name. It's Katherine Weldon."

"Yes, we know, dear. We imagined you differently," the wife said.

Katherine waited.

"I'm Captain Masters, and this is my wife Mrs. Mary Masters. We are Julia's parents."

Katherine stared at them. They looked exceedingly uncomfortable now and stood up. The captain spoke, "Mrs. Weldon, you know how it goes in the military, seniority gets choice of quarters. If you'd please have your things moved sometime today."

"Today?" Katherine asked, the color leaving her face. "But ..." She looked into their faces and saw the set expression she had seen so many times on their daughter's face. They would have their way. Katherine took the tins from them still half full, spilled them on the dirt and scooped up the gingersnaps. Inside she threw it all on the table. Mrs. Masters followed her in.

"Now, dear, don't cry. It's happened to us all. You can't expect an old soldier like my husband to rough it any more than he has to."

"Yes, I understand, but with my children ... we just got things set up nicely."

"Well, you should have considered the children before bringing them out here, I'm afraid. I didn't bring my little ones out in the field with the captain till they were at least seven, and still I lost two to the cholera. But the young ones always know best, I suppose. I don't mean to be hard, but these are the lessons we all learn as army wives. So by sometime this afternoon you'll be packed up? Julia says there's a nice little vacant room closer to the stables."

Katherine glared at her.

"Of course you don't think this has anything to do with the trouble you've given my daughter and her husband," Mrs. Masters said. "I let her sort out her own problems. She did suggest that you might benefit from some guidance in the etiquette of camp life, so if you need anything ..."

Katherine could not tell if the woman before her was speaking with sarcasm or concern. "You should leave so I can pack," she said as her ears burned.

"Yes. I understand. And don't worry about cleaning things. We'll have someone come in and do it properly—maybe that cook woman of Julia's."

Katherine turned away from her guest and pulled things from the few shelves she had. Photographs of her parents and a picture of Simon from the war, the clock that John had picked up from somewhere with a broken cuckoo, and a few tarnished spoons for tea she had always meant to polish. Katherine refused to answer when the Masters said their goodbyes.

William tumbled in with a piece of penny candy the old man had given him on the sly. He grinned and danced, enjoying the fine flavor. Katherine pulled it from his mouth with her finger and licked the treat herself before giving it back. She sat and miserably ate the gingersnaps, throwing the blackened edges into the fire. The heat of it annoyed her, and she ran off with the children to find John at the commissary.

New men stood all around who looked as though they hadn't seen a woman in ages. She brushed by them as some leered and others smiled, but she kept her eyes averted as her face burned. Pushing the door open without a glance, she shoved Willy forward and said, "John, we've been bumped!"

John, Crook, and Bourke looked up from the papers strewn over the desktop. "Oh, beg your pardon. I'm sorry to interrupt," she said, looking guiltily at John.

"Come in, Mrs. Weldon. What's the trouble?" Crook asked.

"It's nothing really," she lied trying unsuccessfully to corral William, who wanted to climb. Lieutenant Bourke took the boy under his arms and placed him before Katherine with a slight grin. She smiled back. "Thank you. I'll just be going now."

Bourke stood with his hands on his hips surveying the children. He looked back at her. "Did you say you were bumped?"

"Yes, I wasn't sure what to do."

"Lieutenant Weldon, help your wife," Crook said. "We can finish up from here."

"Yes, sir," John replied, flashing Katherine a jubilant look. He took her by the arm and brought her into the harsh light of day past the men who turned their eyes away this time when she passed. "Kate! Who cares where we sleep tonight!"

"John?"

"I shouldn't say a word. I might ruin it, but we won't have any more trouble where James is concerned."

"How's that?"

"There was so much going on last night I didn't have time to tell you. James came in drunk, not expecting Crook's men just yet."

She clapped merrily, imagining the impression James must have made. Luckily John had been able to get only a small supply of opium for himself and was clear-headed by the time he had come back to camp. "Yes, so James was wallpapered before Crook and his men and disrespectful too. He refused to take orders from a lieutenant colonel. James insisted that he outranked Crook until it was pointed out by Crook that President Grant had authorized the takeover himself. Anyway, they already heard bad things about James. They know about the failed scouts and the bad blood between him and the citizens of Tucson. I showed them the books and all the discrepancies from before I took over and told them how I knew the colonel was selling off Indian supplies, but they already had their suspicions. I think they trusted me."

"Well, of course they would!" she assured him. "So what will happen to the colonel then?"

"I want him humiliated just as I was! I hope they will put him under guard and bring charges against him, but Crook is determined to get rid of him. Thank God the colonel was stupid enough to think if he paid me off I would stay quiet. He thought I would take the fall, but I was smarter than that. I kept two sets of books. It's a wonder he never suspected, but I guess he was too lazy to care."

"You took payoffs?"

"Yes, but not for keeps. I hid everything as proof."

"But what if no one had believed you? That was foolish! How would I ever explain to my family that you were merely pretending to be a thief?"

He scratched his chin. He needed a shave. "Oh, I don't know, Kate, but anyway Crook believed me and that's all that matters. I gave him the funds to do with as he liked, and he told me to let the men take their turns at hunting. Crook's happy with the way I drilled the men this morning and wants me to help his men to get everything ready for real scouting." John paced and waved his arms with great animation. "Crook has a keen interest in mules—proper use of them, he says, can keep us out in the field longer and better supplied. I don't know, but his attitude makes me feel like a soldier again!" He gave her a rough kiss on the cheek.

Longer out in the field ... she didn't like the sound of it, but she was happy that a real soldier had finally come who appreciated her husband. She squeezed his arm.

"Things will turn for us now, Kate. I can feel it," he said as they made their way to their quarters. Out under their ramada, things were already being stacked by a few soldiers.

John ran up. "You ... Private Cummings, what's the idea?"

The freckled soldier turned his way and saluted. "Sir!"

Mrs. Masters came and stood in her new doorway. "What's the trouble?"

"Mrs. Masters, I told you I would have our things packed this afternoon!" Katherine said.

"Yes, and that's fine, but I need to make room for my things. What difference is it if you pack from here or inside? I thought you might be happy for the help." Mrs. Masters turned to John. "And you must be Mr. Weldon. Julia has mentioned you in letters. Mrs. Weldon, if you ever need help making do on an army diet I'd gladly advise you. Sakes alive, your man is thin as they come! How will the two of you have the strength to move your things?"

Katherine spotted the last little teacup from her mother's set—the only one to make the trip out west successfully—shoved under a blanket and chipped.

John was not going to let his day be ruined by Mrs. Masters and Julia picking through Katherine's things. The two women gazed on in disappointment once they realized that they could not goad the Weldons into battle. John whistled as he loaded their things into a wheelbarrow and pushed them off. Katherine followed his lead and as they left she shouted back, "Good luck with the stove!"

Katherine and John laughed walking side by side, and she too felt she could sleep anywhere now.

Their optimism was tested when they beheld what appeared to be their new home. At best one could say it was unfinished. Three walls stood, but no fourth. Scrub plants grew everywhere inside and out—no columbine or forget-me-nots here.

John put their things down with a groan not a whistle and looked to Katherine. With the teacup dangling from her fingers she surveyed the walls, found a peg, and hung the cup. She gave John a weak smile and began pulling the weeds from the soil floor. They cut her fingers, so she pulled an old apron from their pile of things and wrapped her hands to tug and clear the annoying plants from their home. John put Eliza against a shaded wall, and William amused himself with their small collection of tin plates and cups, making a racket.

Katherine and John stretched canvas over to make a roof, and John promised to get a stove from somewhere. For now they would rely on an open camp fire, no worse really than the unpredictable stove. They went back for the rest of their things and spoke not a word to the two ladies who were tearing the Weldon place to pieces.

She swallowed her pride as she saw her private possessions put out on display. She scooped up her favorite chemise and corset and wrapped them in a skirt, adding them to the already toppling supplies in the wheelbarrow. John smiled at her modesty and the careful way she protected the unmentionables he loved to see her in.

By day's end they had a cozy set up in their new camp with a small fire, coffee, and each other. The added privacy of a calico sheet as their fourth wall, made it more cheerful than their old place, darkened by the heavy ramada. The heat at midday would be unbearable, and they would have to construct some shade, but for now things were perfect.

"Ho! Are you in, Weldon? And family?"

Crook and Bourke came in for an unexpected visit. They stepped over the fire's dying to embers as Katherine fumbled for her wrap and John buttoned his blouse. Bourke looked on amused. Crook didn't notice the couple's embarrassment.

"Good evening, sir!" John said.

"May we join you?" Crook asked, taking a seat.

"They really must have it in for you, Weldon. This is even more primitive than anything I've encountered, except in the field. You must have truly ingratiated yourself to the James fellow." Bourke flashed a teasing smile then glanced Katherine's way. "Don't worry ma'am, we'll get the boys to come help you fix the place up."

Katherine blushed. John took note.

"Weldon, I wouldn't get too settled here. I'm none too happy with this camp's location. It's unhealthy. Too many men end up on the sick roll."

Weldon quietly accepted the man's words but gave away his doubt.

Crook smiled. "Do you think these men are not sick?"

"It depends on what you call sick, sir. Delirium tremens is the main symptom of illness here."

"I see. Well, even so, there's a high rate of fever and ague reported in these parts even among civilians. We need to erect a new camp with a few healthy rooms for our men and the nice ladies they bring along. This place won't do." Crook turned to Katherine. "So you were a laundress during the war, Mrs. Weldon?"

She laughed, thinking that if he saw her less-than-perfect work in that area he would have his answer, but John took offense. "No sir, she was not! Why would you think it?"

Crook raised his brow, surprised at the heated answer coming from the lieutenant. He still had trouble squaring Weldon with the shy and awkward pup he knew from before the war. "Lieutenant Weldon, I meant no offense. This is what we were told by Mrs. James."

Katherine laughed again. "Sir, she hates us more than even the colonel does. Men are so easily fooled by beautiful women."

Bourke chuckled. "Have you had that experience, ma'am?"

She stammered, "Would anyone like coffee?"

Weldon watched in annoyance. John Bourke, a quick-witted, articulate, and relaxed veteran of the war—decorated too and a graduate of West Point—unnerved him. Over the course of the morning spent with Crook (also a West Pointer) and Bourke, he could not help feeling at a great disadvantage. He had no amusing anecdotes to share about courses of study or cadet camaraderie. Crook seemed more inclined to irreverence about his student days and enjoyed sticking it to the more erudite Bourke, who had a weakness for peppering his talk with quotes from the great thinkers he had picked over in the Jesuit Academy he attended in his comfortable youth.

Crook changed the subject to something which interested him more. "I should like to get things more organized at once, and I need a few men at each camp I can trust to carry out my orders efficiently. I'd be interested in your version of the last scout you had with the colonel. I've seen the papers in Tucson and see the leadership here, or the lack thereof. Lieutenant Bourke will stay behind here, but I want you to help getting the men into battle-ready discipline. Bourke is to help you with rounding up as many friendlies to work as scouts. Here are your orders until I return. Technically Captain Masters is in charge, but he's in poor health. He is related to James but is first and foremost a trusted and experienced Indian fighter. Rely on him for any questions you might need answered. He's not one for political games. You can trust him. James will be put under guard for drunkenness until I have everything I need to make a good case for his removal. I will send word and be back here soon enough to get our campaign under way."

Chapter Thirty-Six

Preparations were made for a thirty-day scout through territory rarely visited by white men. Crook, a true outdoorsman, had made careful study of as much of the terrain as possible. Katherine and William spent many a day in awe as the Navajo, Apache, Opatas, and Pueblo men who volunteered to scout for the U.S. Army came in wearing a stunning array of unusual regalia. The scouts ranged from forbidding men of dignity and purpose to the lowest groveling schemer bent on receiving whatever could be had at army expense.

Crook's mission on this scout was to have the men get acquainted and trained for serious campaigning this winter. The days of boredom and aimlessness were over for the men, and real work and danger awaited. Katherine found some comfort in Crook's quiet but true affection for the men. Unlike James, he would do his best to keep them out of harm's way. But Crook, in seeking peace with the Apaches, would have to bring his men through war.

Crook spent every moment of the day since his return sponging up knowledge from the Indian scouts. Occasionally even Katherine helped with interpretation as she had a natural patience for it. Bourke joked with her in French, and she couldn't help but be complimented by it. Under the benevolent leadership of Crook, Weldon brought about in the men an esprit de corps quite impressive to them all.

Katherine overheard a conversation between a lowly private and Crook. The private wondered about the blame and where it should fall in the starting of these Indian wars.

"Well, private, it makes little sense philosophizing over hundreds of years of ingrained habits and hatreds. It's not our mission to decide the score between the red men, the Mexicans, and the whites. Our mission is to bring all groups into peace. Tucson citizens cannot be let to slaughter women and children no matter how provoked. The same is true of the Apaches, who had their way for centuries slaughtering and robbing from Indians and Mexicans and are at it still. I'm confident that a proper show of force is the only thing that will convince them now that they must embrace a new way of living under the rule of law."

"But, sir, they seem to like their way of life just fine," the private said.

"With prodding and fair treatment the Apache people can be convinced, as some of them already have been, that farming and other forms of modern occupation will bring them great benefits—the most important being peace. Soon enough there will be no game to hunt, and the Mexicans and Americans will not stand for their plundering any longer. The massacres will come on a grander scale if the army doesn't bring in the stubborn ones who fail to see the future. Just like children you care for—sometimes only a sound thrashing convinces them of their need to grow up and settle down."

Every evening John came in exhausted and fell contentedly to sleep as soon as supper was cleared. For now Katherine would have to be satisfied with watching him from a distance as he fought with mules one day and drilled the men the next.

Lieutenant Bourke strolled up one afternoon in heat that registered 110 degrees and presented Katherine with a small bouquet of canyon flowers, slightly wilted, which he had gathered on his daily trek in search of unusual flora. "De magnifiques fleurs pour une tres belle dame."

She smiled. "Oh, my mother would love these! I'll press some for her."

"Mrs. Weldon, you should enjoy them yourself."

She put the bunch to her nose, but it was devoid of smell.

"What a strange thing to have such beauty but to possess no enchanting scent," Bourke mused. "You always smell so lovely. Is it lavender?"

Katherine's face burned. "Are you looking for Lieutenant Weldon?"

"No, I just enjoy visiting with you. You remind me of friends back east, and I sympathize with you."

"Well, there's no need for that. I am not as pathetic as I may appear," she said.

"Oh no, you take me up wrong," Bourke said with a laugh. "The other women here are of the most uninteresting type. It's no wonder their men are so eager to be away. But it's a sad thing to see a lady with such charm and intelligence have so little choice in friends."

"I have *no* friends here any longer, Mr. Bourke."

Bourke smiled. He opened his pocket watch and snapped it shut again. "You can consider me a friend. How will you pass the time when the lieutenant is away?"

Katherine's stoic front collapsed. "I'll think of nothing but Lieutenant Weldon's safety, I'm afraid. He is the only reason I stay here—and my best company. You must promise to take good care of him."

"John Weldon can take good care of himself," he said chuckling.

"Yes, but as a favor to me ... you might make sure ... as a friend," Katherine said, forgetting herself and taking his hand imploringly.

He squeezed her hand before withdrawing his. "Would you like to swap some books before we go? You have very nice volumes."

"I'd love that! Take what you like. I've read everything twice over and so has John."

"Lieutenant Weldon surprises me with the odd assortment of things he's studied. The self-made man holds far greater interest for me than the scholar who is led by the nose to study what the world deems important—although I do enjoy putting a puffed-up fool in his place with a useless though impressive bit of obscure knowledge."

That seemed a mean-spirited remark, and while she mulled it over and he grabbed a few books, a dusty and annoyed John tramped up, unhappy to see Bourke beneath their half-finished ramada. Katherine still held the desert blooms and swung them behind her back.

"Weldon, I'm just after borrowing one of Mrs. Weldon's books for the journey."

"They're *my* books, sent to me from Mrs. Weldon's father." Weldon gave Katherine an odd glance before regaining his composure. "I suppose you may borrow one if you like."

"Oh, I see," Bourke replied uncomfortably. "Yes, well, thank you, old fellow. I will come by to drop a few things off for Mrs. Weldon to read while we're off traveling."

Weldon nodded then turned to Katherine. "When you have a minute come by the stables, will you?"

"Oh, of course. I'll be just a second," she said.

Both men cordially took leave.

Katherine put on her hat and left Eliza asleep in her cradleboard hanging from a peg on the wall. Dashing to the corral with Willy at her side, she spotted John speaking to a corporal about a mule. She waited for John to notice her hanging on the fence. He did and ran up, his dark eyes as handsome as ever.

"John, when will you come home tonight?" she asked.

"I don't know. Why?"

"I don't want you to leave wondering anything about Bourke. I never should have taken the flowers."

"What flowers?" Weldon's eyes betrayed his jealousy. He pulled his hat lower and sighed. "I didn't see the flowers, but why shouldn't you take gifts when given in all innocence, right?"

She kissed his hand and said, "My dear John, how could I ever care for anyone but you."

"Yes, we're married and all," he said with a false grin.

She heard in his voice the now-familiar distance that came between them when she inadvertently hurt him, but as fast as it came it was gone.

"I'm so glad you're here. I had wanted to surprise you with a horse," he said, warming to his subject. "Don't worry. I came by it honestly. She's lame and old, but with a little pampering she'll be as good as new. She's no Handsome, but ... well, I have no time now. We'll come down after supper."

A few of John's men waited for guidance and wrestled in the dust as their friends goaded them on. Katherine laughed but felt off balance and not as excited about the gift as she imagined she should. "I'm going to make you something nice for our final supper," she said.

"Final?" he asked as a joke, but it fell flat between them. "I'm sure it'll be real nice."

William remained quietly at her side as usual. She worried about his limited words, but John insisted the boy just took after his father. William didn't seem to lack intelligence and often climbed upon his father's lap and ran his fingers along the lines of print as John read aloud. But without a voice, William was hard to know. On their walk back, though, he talked more than usual, speaking of horses and now Papa. She kissed his hot little head as they rounded the corner, only to find Lieutenant Bourke and Mrs. Masters at her door. William squirmed for release and ran to the soldier. Julia's mother held a smiling Eliza.

"Land sakes, what's going on?" Katherine cried, grabbing hold of the baby.

"Mrs. Weldon, you're lucky I was strolling along. I heard the little girl bawling as if someone were killing her!"

"Eliza was asleep when I left her not five minutes ago," Katherine said.

Bourke chatted with Willy.

"Well, it's irresponsible to leave a child alone in this wild place," Mrs. Masters lectured.

"She was in her cradle as safe as can be."

The old lady shook her head in disappointment. "I've heard of Indians running off with babies and eating them for dinner."

Bourke perked up at this with a guffaw.

"Oh, you men in the army always make light of the threats out here. And what about big cats?" Mrs. Masters asked, putting her hand to Eliza's head. "She's feverish, probably malaria. Is it wise to keep the child crammed in that Indian contraption? Bad for the limbs, I'd say."

"Oh, I am so tired of everyone's advice and opinions! Mrs. Masters, my children are fine. You have driven me from my home, but that doesn't give you the right to invade my new one! We will have trouble if you continue to meddle in my affairs!"

Mrs. Masters crossed her arms in affront. "I was trying to help you despite all you and your husband have done to my daughter. We were foolish to ever push our Julia to marry Dixon James, and he deserves what he gets, but don't judge me or my daughter by the actions of my son-in-law. I only try to be useful."

"I judge each person as an individual, Mrs. Masters," Katherine said, bouncing Eliza on her hip until the little girl cried. "I'd like for you to leave and save your advice. You have done no great job of child rearing if Julia is your best work!"

"You are an awful girl! I can see now the reason for my daughter disliking you." Katherine held her tongue as Mrs. Masters stormed off.

"My, Mrs. Weldon," Bourke said. "You told her, didn't you?"

Katherine could not tell if he was impressed or disgusted by her behavior, and it troubled her that she cared to know.

"So, here are the books I promised," he said.

"Oh! These are lovely—and magazines too!" Katherine said. "You are so kind, but I'm sure I'll feel ten times worse about my wardrobe after reading *Godey's*!"

"It's not the clothes that make a woman of beauty," he said, tipping his hat.

Her face flushed as it often did when he spoke.

"Oh and this," he added, handing her a ragged old journal. "It appears to be the lieutenant's. I found it in the commissary store behind some boxes. He must have dropped it. I'll admit that I read a few pages, looking for the name of its owner. Lieutenant Weldon has a nice writing style."

She took the book suspiciously. She remembered long ago in Englewood his notebooks but had never seen him write in them.

"I should be going. Make sure to mind your children," Bourke joked and sauntered off.

"Thank you, Mr. Bourke, for the books!" she called and waved a farewell.

Nursing a hot and fussy Eliza, she thumbed through the journal but tossed it aside, not sure if she should read it—knowing that she shouldn't. Finally, Eliza settled down on their bed. She lounged next to her and grabbed the journal with a deep sigh before opening it. The writing was tiny, like a secret. She flipped through to the beginning. It predated their time together. It was older than time—the war, Carlisle Barracks, a bounty of withheld information. Maybe she should hide it and look it over a little at a time. What did she want to read first? She flipped and flipped—the month when they met, the day ... and she found it. Her heart raced.

Visited Captain McCullough. I intended to talk to him about all that has happened since the Wilderness, but he was off with his sister racing horses and I hated them for their perfect little world where even the flowers matched. The girl seemed stuck on her-

self for someone so small and boyish, but then she wore a blue dress for supper and she smelled so nice. After the meal I couldn't help stare at her, but I don't think she noticed, she was rudely reading the whole time like she was bored with us all. Simon is just the same—spoiled and fun and I can't decide to forgive him or not. The father was rude, but the mother was generous and warm. Simon has asked me to spend the day tomorrow and maybe I shall to see the girl ...

Had races at McCullough's. Blundered about as usual—horses still a problem for me—even after those years in the cavalry! I ended up in the family garden like a fool. Ruined the mother's kale. Simon McCullough takes everything in stride. I must leave in the morning or I'll tell all and I wouldn't want Katherine McCullough to think any less of me than she must. She wore a lovely outfit this morning. I hoped that she had worn it for my benefit, but I doubt it. That door, that brief hope I had of having a normal happy life died at the Wilderness. But there is something about that girl. Coming to New Jersey has made me see how much I will miss in life. How much I always miss. Katherine McCullough will think nothing more of me, but I will never forget almost dancing with her.

Weldon's boots scuffed the floor on the other side of the curtain now, and Katherine slapped the book shut.

"What have you got there?" he asked as he came around to see her.

She stayed on the bed. "Oh, nothing."

"Come on, what are you up to?"

"Did you really think I was stuck on myself when you first met me?" She couldn't help giggling.

He sat down beside her, tugging at his boot. "Why do you ask?"

"No reason. Do you think I didn't see you staring at me that first night in my father's library?" She purred and tickled his chin.

He wasn't smiling now. "Why do you ask? I don't understand. It was so long ago."

"It's funny you didn't notice how nervous you made me. I was hiding behind my book listening to every word you said." She pulled the journal out from behind her and placed it on his lap with a grin. "I'm sorry I read it without your permission, but it's lovely to go back to those days."

"You read it all?" he cried.

She sat up. "John, I'm sorry. I shouldn't have, but Mr. Bourke said the writing was impressive. I couldn't help myself."

"Bourke saw it? He read it?" he asked, panicking. "I'm found out!"

"He said it was good! He only read enough to find your name somewhere."

"Katherine, now you can see I'm ruined! How can you take it so lightly?"

"What are you talking about? So now the world will see our romance?"

"I can't believe you read it!"

"Only about us and the way you felt on our first meeting—you are such a surprise—how could you deprive me of reading it? It made me happy."

"It was private! And now Bourke knows!" Weldon paced, pulling his hair. "How did he seem?"

She laughed at her husband's discomfort. "He seemed impressed by your style and nothing more. He just wanted to return it to its rightful owner."

John took the journal and threw it into the fire before Katherine could stop him. He clutched his hair in both hands as she looked on in shock. Gently she pried his hands loose and took them in hers. "My darling, what was in that journal that you're so afraid of?"

He looked at her searchingly. "You only read about our meeting?"

"You're scaring me. Please be honest with me. Did you have doubts about us?"

"Yes," he answered miserably, knowing that she would never guess the truth if she hadn't read it, and he would not have the courage to present it.

"Still?" she asked.

"Yes ... sometimes. You'll find things you won't like about me."

"I already have, John. You snore and you don't clean up after breakfast, and you don't trust me enough, but I will always love you."

He moaned and felt he might be sick. He wanted to tell her how naive she was, how blind and foolish ... and it angered him. He resented her for having so little to worry about, but ... he loved her still. It was that unquestioning devotion, that blind faith. "Katherine, I am saved by you. My foolish thoughts and actions from before ... I'm glad to be rid of them."

She pulled him close. "You spend so much time worrying over the past that it clouds our future. I wonder what it is—it must be worse than I can imagine—that causes you to suffer. You say it has nothing to do with us, but then why won't you tell me? What have you done?"

Her calmness surprised him. Now was the time to tell. Her eyes were set on him. She was determined to hear anything, to accept anything. He would tell her, and she would understand.

"During the war I let down my company. I tried to be someone I wasn't. I even stole from your brother."

"Yes, strawberry preserves."

He continued impatiently. He must tell her everything ... "Yes, I did it more than once too. And I used to steal more than that from Simon, and he knew all along, but then he called me on it. Thieves are hated in the army."

The idea of anyone taking advantage of Simon annoyed her. "Yes, thieves are the lowest of the low," she blurted and regretted it. He flashed her a look like a door closing, got up, and went for a smoke.

She followed him. If Simon forgave him then she should. "I'm sorry, John. I asked you to be honest and then I made it difficult."

"That's all there is to the story," he said, but he remembered it like yesterday.

It was winter camp. Simon was on the outs with Captain O'Malley for flirting with the captain's fiancée and for bleeding the captain dry at cards. Simon had also upstaged him in all the real fighting they had done so far and would probably be promoted soon. So Simon fell in with the noncommissioned officers—anyone would have him. He never lacked for invitations. Reluctantly Weldon agreed to let him stay in the small but warm shelter he had built for himself.

"This place sure looks like a crazy beaver's dam to me, Weldon, but it's warm. Not very cozy though with that sour look on your face, but at least I'll have peace when I want it. It's big enough for a game of Bluff with the fellows. What do you think?" Simon threw out a teasing grin. "All right, no poker, but how about a few shelves? And we should name the place—for fun."

Weldon looked up from his book. "I'd rather we remained anonymous, lieutenant."

"Of course you would, but it's too late for that. Your architectural style has already been noted by the boys."

Weldon went back to his reading, but stealthily eyed Simon's larder. Mostly Simon gave things away, but found that his mother's preserves got him a fair bit of bargaining power so he requested a lot and sold a lot. The profits disappeared in town among friends and acquaintances when they ran the picket and went on a spree, but Weldon also noticed delicate things sent off to one of his girls, he figured.

"No, this is for my sister, Weldon. Do you think I'd be stupid enough to leave some little flower pining for me at home? My family would be under all sorts of pressure to keep me on the straight and narrow. Why put extra strain on the home-folks?"

It annoyed Weldon to be in this man's company. Simon always had the right thing to say and the luck to do as he pleased and get away with it. But Weldon couldn't help being curious. "So what's she like—your sister?"

"Oh, Katie's sweet as they come, poor thing." Simon looked at him and said no more. "I'll be back with some wood for the new sign for our door."

What had possessed Weldon to do it that first time? It was such a foolish thing. Weldon wasn't hungry, and he needed no money. He took a jar of strawberry preserves, ate the contents, and hid the empty jar. Not quite satisfied, he lifted the lid of Simon's ridiculously childish bank and grabbed a few notes.

Simon hadn't noticed it the first few times, but then one night Weldon watched as he counted and recounted his stash. He threw himself on his bunk and whistled a bit. "The men in the officers' mess say I'm nuts to be sharing a place with you, Weldon, but I tell them it suits me fine—you'll be an officer soon anyway, I imagine. You know I'm about to make a good trade of the preserves for some excellent contraband tobacco."

"That's nice," Weldon replied, writing in his journal.

"You never do write letters, Weldon."

"I know."

"Well, did you have a terrible falling out with your family?"

"They're dead, lieutenant."

Simon shifted awkwardly.

"All of them?"

"Yes."

"At the same time?" Simon pressed.

"No, my father was crushed felling trees, and my mother died in her own vomit."

"By golly, that's rough."

"I'm sure you wouldn't know."

Simon shook his head. "You have such a pleasant way about you."

Weldon laughed despite himself.

Simon sat up and offered him a cigar, and they smoked in contented silence.

"You know, Weldon, it wouldn't take a genius to figure out you've been lifting my strawberries."

Weldon said nothing—just stared at the ceiling.

"I've been wondering about why you might do it for a while now. You've just cleared it up for me. You shouldn't try to deny it—your mattress is full of those jars my mother uses. I think you're younger than you say—about my age—and you ran off and joined the cavalry and since your father died you didn't have much so ..."

"You win the prize," Weldon said.

"The thing that makes it interesting is why you steal from me when you know I'd share freely with you," Simon said, flicking his ash on the floor.

"So you'll run me out of camp then, I bet."

Simon wasn't finished pondering. "You follow every rule in the book then you steal from a friend."

"What will you do then?"

"Is this a test? Well, I'll tell you I won't be getting you kicked out over preserves."

"Why not?"

"I guess I've had a good Christian upbringing and enough of my own sins to forgive your strawberry habit. You're always at the Bible—ever read that old standby, the Ten Commandments?"

Weldon sat up and grabbed his kepi, pulling on the buttons.

"You almost seem disappointed, Weldon. Did you suddenly want to leave the army?"

"No, it's not that. I'm ashamed is all and sorry. Truth is I've been trying hard to hate you, but I can't now, can I?"

"Others have told me if they concentrate on my dashing good looks and the luck I have with the girls they can keep up a healthy resentment," Simon joked. "But listen, I don't get played the fool more than once, Weldon. Don't let me find you at my stuff again. Ask and you shall receive. You know you are such a thorn in my side, but for some reason you're like family—life's strange that way. But stealing strawberries ... some might think you're touched in the head."

Weldon smiled. He would never take anything again.

"Here," Simon said, "shove this in your pack and come with me for a trade. You owe me."

Simon had been right. He did do enough of his own mischief to forgive John his peculiarities, but Katherine was perfect, and stealing preserves and a few dollars was nothing like what Weldon hid now. Not enough time had passed since his last slip to give Weldon any confidence in his mastery over the morphine. Wearily he wondered if he'd ever be able to stop wrestling this thing nudging him toward imminent disgrace. Weldon fantasized about languorous days with Katherine on a shady porch in a small comfortable town with petunia beds and a nice flag hung. He fantasized that one day he would be the man he was in the army before the morphine, that one day he could just relax.

He didn't want to leave Katherine now, not even to go on this scout. As his chance to prove himself approached, he was skittish and doubtful. He worried about Katherine and Bourke. It was foolish since he could not prevent what might happen. Bourke could offer Katherine a fuller life if he failed.

Watching her in her faded work dress with her hair pulled back into a tight knot at her neck tending the fire, he despised her surroundings. Life was so hard out here—nothing like her family would have expected. She never spoke of her parents visiting—it was too far, but it would also be too humiliating. Things wouldn't change much either. He would never have the money or the marketable skills that Scott had, or Simon's connections. He wasn't meant to have a family, to have children. Willy and Eliza were young now, but they would need to have a proper education and with it decent clothing and enough to eat. How would that happen?

All the excitement he had had for this scout, this army life, flew away across the boundless desert. Bourke had found his writing. Why had he saved his history in a stupid, pointless journal? It was all so miserable and humiliating.

Katherine watched from the corner of her eye as he played with his unlit pipe. She left him to his own thoughts, not as patient or as certain now that he would one day tell her everything about himself as she once was.

She made their last meal with little enthusiasm. Weldon cleaned his carbine and stacked his things by the door, lit a few candles, and tried to avoid getting in her way. The burnt journal troubled her. When he threw it into the fire she understood at once how little he trusted her.

Eliza was still warm when she woke and would not nurse. As the home got dark, a veil of hopelessness settled over Katherine, and by the time she set the steaming, bland army rations before her husband in his blue checked army-issue shirt (one of only two that he owned), tears hung on her lashes. Katherine had joined the army, left her home, and lost every material possession for this man who hid things from her. She had deluded herself, imagining they were the closest of friends.

"Kate, what a nice meal," he said in obvious discomfort.

She poked at the meat but couldn't bring herself to eat it. No spice could make up for the fact that it was second-rate. She wiped her eyes. "John, I'm so hurt by your secrets."

He pushed away his plate and took her hands in his. "Kate, I love you."

"But that's not enough for me. I thought I knew you, but that journal made it clear that I don't, and you are my only friend in the world! I feel like you're fooling me somehow, and now you'll be gone for who knows how long. I'll be here imagining the worst about the past and the future. Why can't things be like they were at my mother's kitchen table? Or were you hiding from me then too?"

"No, I never meant to fool you. I've tried to tell you everything. The journal was a self-pitying list of my weaknesses. Why would I want you to see that?"

"I want to know everything about you. If something bothers you then I want to know."

"Some things a man has to fix on his own. Just by being here with me, just by picking me to marry, you've changed me. I have done nothing purposely to hurt you, and I've tried to be honest. You're the only person in the world I trust, but sometimes I need to work things out on my own. My journal was full of thoughts that would embarrass me. As much as I love you, I don't want you to read me at my worst."

"But that means you never let your guard down with me! I need you to trust me because I trust you. Now is the time, John, to tell me everything—when I am ready to accept anything."

He didn't believe her. He had seen the way she looked down upon the men with no self-control. It would be asking too much of her to accept that she had married an uneducated soldier with little hope of promotion, destined to move from one desolate post to another, who also loved morphine. Weldon compared Simon's drinking to what happened to him when he smoked opium or shot morphine. How could he explain that when he was doing it he loved it more than he loved her and the children? It sickened him to be so weak. "Please trust that I will always love you, and that I tell you everything about me I can. Let the embarrassments of my past stay in the past."

"There have been no women?" she asked.

And now he lied to satisfy her, to keep her from the real truth. "Before I met you there was one ..."

She was hurt yet relieved—an affair with a woman was normal, something she could live with. "Why didn't you tell me?"

He tripped over his words. "I was ashamed. It was with a ... well ... a colored girl."

She pulled her hands away from his. She knew he was lying to her. It was Simon's story he was stealing.

He kept his eyes averted. "It was only once," he stammered, making things worse.

"I forgive you for that," she lied icily, "but if there is something else and I find out, I will never forgive you."

"I will never lie to you again," he said, lost at sea now. He had never lied to her outright before, and what a stupid lie he came up with! Things would never be quite the same between them, yet he'd escaped once more and vowed—no more lies and no more medication!

"Papa! Papa. Horses!" Willy said over his mess of a meal.

John stared at him, and the child spoke again about horses and stars, soldiers, and Mama.

"Willy started really talking today. I wanted to surprise you," Katherine said, stacking their dishes.

He hated the distance she put between them and grabbed her before she could clear the table. "I might never see you again, Kate. You must believe me—I love you more than life itself. I always have since the beginning till now and forever. I lied to protect you from me. I wasn't a good man when you met me, but I've tried to become one for you. That is my only goal." He clung to her.

The sudden reality that this could be their last night scared her more than his weird lie. Whatever was in that journal was gone. All that she had with him was in this room, and that would have to be enough.

The family walked to the stables with only Willy talking for a change. Eliza leaned listlessly upon John's chest as he carried her. They came to the stall John had reserved for the broken-down gift horse. Its back sloped and the poor creature was tender-footed on its left side, but it had soulful, melancholy eyes and a white star on the bridge of its nose. It brightened as they fussed over it. It was just like John to save it from certain death, and John knew that she loved the dark horses. William talked and talked and made them laugh with all the words he had stored up until now. She could see behind John's laughter that he was missing the children already, and she kissed him. He smiled in his disarming way and pulled her over to him.

"I found the side saddle for you too, so you can show up the awful bitches here."

"John Weldon, mind your mouth!"

She laughed as the cloud lifted for now.

Chapter Thirty-Seven

On a searing hot July morning, the men left along the post road for what would be a shakedown mission separating true soldiers and scouts from the rest. Katherine watched until the last pack mule sifted through the sand out of sight. All of John's things were gone, the place was empty, and Eliza was ill.

Fort Apache

Dearest Katherine,

I am at Fort Apache and afraid you will hardly recognize me when I return. There is no call for general upkeep when there are only other men to impress.

I am glad you found out about the journal now because I see I was holding on to an old way of dealing with trouble in my life. Kate, if you knew how little companionship I have had over my life you might understand why I kept my thoughts in a book.

Now let me tell you about this trip so far. While most of our march has been hot and grueling, we have been fortunate to find lovely places to rest our weary heads in the evenings. The scenery changes quickly as we climb into the higher elevations of this region. Today we marched through strange coniferous forests where the dry air prevents the growth of underbrush and the horses and men walk over soft roads seemingly made just for them. Just a touch of sun filtered down over our heads, and the only sound came from the men's happy conversation and the bells clanging their soft music on the mules. It was like a dream until an Indian or two tried to take a shot at us from somewhere in the forest. No one was hurt but the Indian after we found him.

Around a corner and suddenly a homesick soldier is treated to a blanket of the most vibrant flowers stretching across a wide valley of sorts. I do not know the names the way Bourke and Crook do, but I enjoy them just the same.

At times as we slog through the desert the temperature reaches 115 degrees. Some men have given out with sunstroke and dehydration. Barnes, the poor fellow, has lost his reasoning completely. It is a sad thing to see a future officer so full of promise be wasted that way, but it can happen out here if one does not take proper rest and water.

Of the scouts employed, only the Apaches are worth their price. Strange to say, but they are the most intent on taking their own down. The others have no real interest in any work. The Apaches are amazingly equipped for this type of mission. They know all the signs of Indian presence of which we have seen little.

Crook seems happy with me. I often spend time at his fire in the evenings listening to the other officers jostling for his attention. Bourke keeps us entertained with his stories and quips, and I wonder at the confidence he has in himself and how much he loves the sound of his own voice. I see Bourke's worth though and understand why Crook has chosen him to be at his side. The other day I shot a bear up in the mountains and the officers' mess was a merry place to be that night. Crook will keep the trophy skin. I suppose our little home would look ridiculous covered in bear.

We have also discovered strange mountain tracts of lush grass which our animals could not get enough of. Mexicans and settlers will be able to raise livestock without the threat of roving Indians.

I meant to say to you that little Elly seemed warm before I left. I hope you have worked your miracles with her and that she is healthy again. It is nice to feel useful, but I look forward to being home with you.

Your loving husband,

Lieutenant John Weldon

Katherine folded and unfolded the letter so many times, looking over his tiny words traced across both sides of the smudged and wrinkled paper, but found no hidden messages or assurances. At night she dreamt of Englewood or being in John's arms, but a child would whine or the bugle would blow and reality crashed in.

After five worrying days Eliza's fever broke, and she nursed again, but not as enthusiastically. It was time for real camp food. Katherine at once felt liberated from the feedings yet saddened. Elly no longer depended upon her completely.

The little girl, now two, ran about with limbs long and lean and, unlike William, her hair remained curly and the color of rich coffee. Katherine had relied too long on the cradleboard, the doctor said. The girl needed exercise to build up her lungs and legs. Since the men had gone, the three of them spent their days with their horse "Northy," so named for the star they spent their evenings looking to in hopes that someone they knew was doing the same. Before long, but after much grooming and pampering, the old mare adopted its new family, whinnying at their approach and gently avoiding tramping on Elly who always found her way to the horse's tail. Willy sat with soldierly bearing on the horse's back, trotting and cantering, and only under great protest was made to come down for meals. He had the McCullough blood, Katherine proudly noted. Since her illness, Eliza tired quickly and was often left sleeping in the stables hidden by hay bales from any stray Indian who might want a small child.

Dust rose up one day. All work and all play stopped as everyone strained to get a first look at Vincent Colyer's presidential peace commission. Mrs. Masters edged up to Katherine with her strong, graceful arms folded and burnt from the sun. Katherine stood rigidly trying to ignore her.

"Well, Mrs. Weldon, that president of ours has sent a government do-gooder. I've heard Colyer is highly regarded and looks impressive, but between you and me anything less than all-out war on the Apaches will be seen by the Indians as weakness. We need a proper war too—no Tucson renegades! Only after a sound whipping will the Indians be ready for talks."

"Spoken like a true army wife," Katherine said in a tone dripping with condescension. She had high hopes for the Secretary of the Board of Indian Commissioners, having read about him in an old San Francisco newspaper Lieutenant Bourke had left her.

"Don't be so high and mighty with me, young lady. I have experience. Negotiations and handshakes are meaningless unless your enemy respects your firepower." Mrs. Masters was mildly ruffled, but Katherine refused to look at her. "How is the little girl now?"

Katherine stared at her in a most unpleasant way. "Eliza's fine, thank you."

Mrs. Masters pulled her bonnet tighter and flattened the wrinkles in her skirt. "The captain's doing poorly and won't see another winter, I suppose."

"Oh, Mrs. Masters, I am truly sorry to hear it." Katherine couldn't help but like the old gentleman, who in the weeks leading up to the scout had taken a shine to John. She often watched John stride up to the captain with a smile as he sat under wraps on his little porch. It was clear that John felt comfortable with the old man, and she was grateful for that. "Why do you stay here? Isn't there someplace more comfortable for him to go?"

"The army is Captain Masters' home, and when he got the chance to spend the last few months near his daughter ... well, you understand I'm sure. It hasn't been as nice as we had hoped though. But the bugles and the lazy men's conversations as they go about their duties—these things comfort him. The captain has lasted longer than most. We've been lucky. From before the war with Mexico till now he's been in the thick of things. There's not much glory in this though, is there? Skirmishes here and there. The end's a foregone conclusion. Progress doesn't wait for the slow and the stubborn to catch up."

"But we can help the Indians make the transition, can't we?" Katherine asked. "I've seen a few take to modern life with enthusiasm."

Mrs. Masters smiled ruefully. "It's a funny world—the darkie wants to be civilized and we have fools lynching them for it, and the red man doesn't want to be civilized and we try to force him to it."

"But some of them do want it, and it's for their own good," Katherine said, intimidated by Mrs. Masters' years of experience.

"Who's to say it's for their own good?" Mrs. Masters replied. "To be sure it's good for the whole country and anyone who admires our form of government, but these Indians are used to doing just as they please. The rule of law means nothing to them."

"But the Bible says ..." began Katherine, thinking of her mother.

"Yes, of course. Expose them to Scripture and the Lord, but they'll always miss the colorful life—their quaint notions of the world—like some of us miss childhood. It's the next generation—the children we might change. A child likes the sound of drums beating and his own silly utterances. You must be educated over time to appreciate Mozart's operas."

Katherine only knew that, given the choice between a dusty life in the open or a cool kitchen with things put by and money in her pocket, she would pick a real eastern home if it weren't for John.

"And Mrs. Weldon, I don't know how you ever cooked a thing on that blasted stove."

Katherine laughed, happy the stove was no friend to Mrs. Masters.

"You are a different girl when you smile," the older woman said. "I'm sorry we got off to such a bad start. Maybe it's the old army wife in me, but I hate to see a girl—one of ours—all alone and kept to herself."

"I'm fine. The arrangement suits me fine."

"Well, I'm impressed by your strength and independence. When I was your age my husband was away off in the army drinking himself nearly to death. It was a sad and lonely time when I finally gathered the courage to take my little ones to meet their daddy. The captain was so wild—nearly wrecked his career. But that's what women are for, to support their boys till they become men. I'm still trying to figure out if that ever really happens. The poor captain is a baby once again I'm afraid. Oh, but he did—still does—have some fine manly traits."

"I don't think my husband needs to mature," Katherine said, annoyed at the simplified role of women Mrs. Masters presented.

"Hmmm—he seems serious about himself," Mrs. Masters said, "like he's still trying to prove something."

"Men are not just big children, and we are not their mothers," Katherine said. "They bear the brunt of war and the responsibilities of providing for their families and holding jobs. I wouldn't want to have their position in life one bit! Marriage is a partnership. We each have our place. Women hold no claim to superiority or maturity."

Mrs. Masters laughed at Katherine's sudden spunk. "I agree that marriage is a partnership, but it is far from an equal one. Men do as they please, and we still love them, but turn the tables and watch what happens! I didn't mean to say we are all mothers to our husbands, but as a nurse during the war I sat in those disease-ridden hospitals with dying men who begged not for their sweethearts or fathers but for their mothers. The ones far gone with fever insisted that I was their mother, and it comforted them to think it. Once I made the blunder of correcting a young man—it broke my heart to see the disappointment on him.

"I was always a hard woman till then—felt I had to be to survive living with my husband. I fought him on every little thing, foolishly thinking I could control him. But it never worked. Then the Lord granted me a chance to have peace. The captain was put down with a bullet in the calf—almost lost his leg. I had come to prove I was just as tough and as immune to suffering as I imagined him to be, but really I was keeping my eye on him. My callous urge to outdo him brought me to nurse in the rooms with the lost causes. They changed my heart, and I gained a real sympathy for those lonely souls at death's door. My captain was laid up in the same hospital, but we weren't talking. No one would have guessed we even knew each other, and I passed him every day, spitefully asking after all but him.

"One night—it was late and gloomy—I sat with a bloodless boy from Ohio in my arms, humming a little song my mother used to sing to us when the wolves were at the door in the big woods. The captain slipped in. I didn't hear him and went about tucking the boy—I'm sorry, a man really, nearly thirty—tucking him in with comforting words that only come at times like that in the wee hours. I heard sniffling and turned to see the captain on crutches, grey in the dimly lit doorway." Mrs. Masters laughed, but didn't seem to find the story funny. "And the captain said—whispered it—this was when we were thirty years married, mind you, with two children already in their graves—and he said, 'I don't understand. Will I have to be near dead before you show me that kindness or is it just that you don't care for me a wink?'"

Mrs. Masters turned to Katherine with tears coursing the delicate wrinkles that spread from her pale eyes. "*A wink*—I'll always remember how he said that—it melted my heart. I don't know why, but from then on it felt like making up for lost time. I always loved him, but I never understood what he wanted from me, and he never would tell. The captain insists that night never happened, but everything changed after that."

"That is a lovely story," Katherine said. "My first impression of the two of you was that you were perfectly suited ... the way you walked together."

Mrs. Masters' face lit. "Thank you for noticing. Yes, we've walked our lives together and made plenty of mistakes, like pushing Julie to marry Dixon. We were impatient for her to find what we had, yet we raised her too wild. Dixon in those days was charming right after the war, but I guess the drink has ruined him. It was a low blow for him to be sent to this godforsaken place. You are lucky to have a man immune to the boredom and hopelessness of this western army. The captain has grown fond of your husband. Seems like as mature as your lieutenant is, he's looking real hard for a father, and my captain's the one for that. Julie should have had a man like Lieutenant Weldon."

"Maybe so, but he is mine, and I intend to keep him."

"Of course." Mrs. Masters laughed.

Katherine turned to go back to her chores. The peacemakers had gone by the stables.

Mrs. Masters pulled Katherine's sleeve. "I must prepare the captain for visitors. Could I trouble you for a favor, Mrs. Weldon? Would you come to help me with the stove? We are the ranking family with the colonel locked up. Colyer will come to us. Please bring the little ones. The captain loves children and has a way with them."

Katherine agreed reluctantly and followed the captain's wife to her old home, surprised at how little had been done with it. From the corner the captain called out. Mrs. Masters whispered, "Some days are better than others. He forgets and is embarrassed by it. Captain, we've got visitors from the peace commission coming."

"Peace?" he asked.

Katherine turned her attention to the stove and had it off to a good start in record time. She pretended to take longer so as to give the captain his privacy as his wife helped him to button up.

"This is the poor girl we had to displace," the captain said as Katherine came over.

Her bitterness melted away. "Oh, don't worry. Our new place is just fine."

The captain patted her hand with a kind, glossy-eyed gaze, and she felt she would do anything for him.

By the time Colyer arrived, Katherine and the Masterses had several cups of strong tea and laughter over the children, who entertained the captain.

Katherine didn't ask about Julia, and Mrs. Masters didn't tell, but it was odd that the mother and daughter spent so little time together. After Colyer's arrival, Katherine was asked each day for tea, and on days when the captain was strong enough he walked with Willy to the stables and watched the boy ride.

On one such day Mrs. Masters had just set out her china when the captain called, and William galloped up on Northy. Katherine ran out under the ramada and shouted, "William Weldon! You little ruffian! Stop racing this instant!" She jumped right in front of the horse who stopped on a nickel.

"I didn't mean to race her, but Papa's coming!" William said.

The captain chuckled as he caught up out of breath.

"Captain Masters, please don't tire yourself with Willy!" She took his arm.

Captain Masters saw her glance past him. "Go on, Katie. I know where you want to be. I can manage."

She smiled and brought the old man to his ramada, and Mrs. Masters set him in his chair.

William tied Northy to the post out front of their quarters like an expert and ran up next to his mother and Eliza, who walked at her side with a coltish gait. The men came by in good spirits and tipped their hats to the little family. Katherine smiled, searching for John.

The three of them stood and gaped at the man with ragged-kneed trousers and a gun over his shoulder walking toward them. Weldon's beard was thick and his face dark with sun and dust. Katherine tried to move forward, but the children wouldn't budge. They refused to believe this man was their father. Katherine saw Weldon's mildly hurt look flash out at her. "Oh, John, come here!" she cried and held out her arms.

After they had embraced for a long while, she broke free and pulled at his beard. They made their way back to their quarters not saying a word. The children followed warily. She boiled water for coffee and sat with Willy and Eliza as John cleaned him-self up but did not shave. She was disappointed and ill at ease as the children hid be-hind her. John was bashful, and when he tried to touch Willy the child pulled away.

"Willy! Don't be frightened. It's Papa," Katherine said trying to reassure him.

"I ain't skeered," William announced.

John flashed his wife an amused grin.

"John, it's the beard. You don't look yourself."

"So you don't like it, then?" he asked, rubbing it hard.

"I'm afraid not. We want the old Lieutenant Weldon, please."

Eliza and Katherine watched as he came out from under the facial hair after many dangerous strokes of the razor. The little girl gaped at the transformative process. Katherine laughed at the funny tan line left on John's face but was much relieved. She kissed him and pulled her chair next to his when he sat for his coffee. Willy still wasn't impressed, and she got up to drag him over.

"No, Kate, he'll come when he's ready," John said, trying to hide his disappoint-ment.

The homemade chime hanging from the rafters of their ramada sounded. Katherine poured more coffee into John's cup, and John spoke since no one else would. "Eliza has grown."

"Has she?"

"Yes, what a difference a month makes. It's like you're all afraid I'll bite." Weldon wondered if Katherine still upset over the journal, but then she sat on his lap and ran her hand through his hair.

"I'm not afraid of getting bitten. It might be nice." She gave him a saucy grin. "But all of my trivial news can wait. I just want to enjoy you sitting here with us."

"Well, do you think you might talk soon?" John asked. "You're all making me nervous. Did you get my letter?"

She pulled it from her apron pocket. "I've read it to pieces."

Eliza came up now and pulled on John's sleeve. She opened her mouth to show a new tooth, and Weldon took happy interest in it. Willy stayed by the bed with his hands on his lap.

"William come here," John said. "Look in my haversack. There are things in there you might like."

With hidden enthusiasm the boy brought the bag to the table and dumped its contents.

"A small geological study for you, Willy. That's a fossil of an old fish. Imagine that ... in the desert ... and some Indian things, feathers and arrows and, well, Willy, you see what you like."

"Can I keep it all?" Willy asked.

John grabbed him in a bear hug and laughed at his new talking son. "Only if you stop being so huffed at me."

"Okay."

They talked for hours at the table, exchanging news. Crook and Bourke were up in Prescott by now. If the Indians did not come in by February 15 there would be a winter campaign. Katherine and the children talked about Northy and Colyer in that order. She was not impressed in the end with Colyer's unfettered optimism and faith when it came to peace with the Apaches and noted how the few warriors who did meet with Colyer were polite and respectful to his face but sneering when his back was turned. The fort was now becoming crowded with Indians and while some were friendly and the women sometimes shared their exotic culinary skills with Katherine others were surly and waiting for a chance to take advantage. As soon as the Secretary of the Board of Indian Commissioners and his long title were out of sight and heading back toward civilization, the reports of more atrocities directed at the small villages and ranches that dotted lower Arizona came in.

The rest of the year flew by filled with hunting parties on the lookout for small scurrying game, dances organized by the captain's wife and cooler days watching Willy on the horse. While this part of Arizona could rarely promise a white Christmas, it blessed its occupants with a chill in the evenings that made blankets comfortable again and the mornings a pleasure sipping coffee in the crisp blue air.

For Christmas they traveled to Tucson with some other officers and men. They ate at the one real restaurant in town run by an older señora and her beaten-down husband, and they attended Christmas Eve mass with the Catholics in a Mexican church. Julia James came along, escorted by a sympathetic soldier, but was not herself and spent much time in her little room overlooking the central square.

The raids continued everywhere, and the heat of the spicy food was mixed with the peppery talk of angry citizens. Vincent Colyer's peace negotiations were roundly cursed, as was Grant's peace policy in general. When it was realized that the little traveling party was made up of soldiers, they became targets of insult. "On vacation are you? From what? The government pays you to see the sights and polish your guns instead of using them!"

February came and went, and once again a new peace delegation was sent for one more round of talks. Some in Washington considered progress made if some

Indians came on to the new reservations, but the marauding continued. The army collectively threw up its hands and tried to endure the empty months as best they could until Crook could be unleashed.

Colonel James awaited news of his court-martial, but no news came. Military law stated a soldier could not be held under guard for more than a month at a time without a small break, and on those breaks James, with nothing to lose, would gather up a small coterie of soldiers and scouts and get blind drunk. Lately, Mrs. Masters seemed more irritable and upset with her daughter and complained about Julia's lack of apparent concern for her father. Captain Masters had survived the winter but was bedridden now. The doctor whispered to Katherine that it was cancer that pained him. But even as the captain suffered he was kind and gentle and begged for the children's visits. She could not deny him.

One morning Mrs. Masters met her at the door before she even knocked. The wind blew the bright day's heat away. Mrs. Masters closed the door behind her and clutched Katherine's hand, dragging her to the James place. The children raced along, their shouts lost in the gusts of dry desert air.

Mrs. Masters knocked at her daughter's door. The curtains were drawn shut, but they flapped in the wind. No movement, no sound came from within and Mrs. Masters called, "Julia, are you up?"

Katherine pushed the door open not standing on ceremony. The table was littered with a mass of bottles and pipes. The crumpled-up form of Julia moaned from the bed in the dark corner. Mrs. Masters ran to her and pulled her up, her silken hair a mess of knots over her face. The smell of stale liquor was sickening.

"Jules! You're drunk!" Mrs. Masters cried. "That's not good for the baby!"

"Mama, for God's sake there is *no baby*! I lied to shut you up! There can never be one no matter how you wish and pray. Just leave me alone! And why is she here? Just to taunt me? Little Katie is the daughter you always wanted!"

"Julia!" Mrs. Masters tried to calm her. Pulling her hair from her face, she gasped. Julia's face was crushed on the left side.

"My poor child, what's happened?"

"It was Dixon," Julia cried. "But he didn't mean it. I said cruel things to him!"

Katherine sent the children outside and set a fire in the beautiful stove. "Mrs. Masters, should I get the doctor?" she asked.

"*No!*" Julia commanded. "Of course you'd like everyone to know, you pathetic bitch!"

Mrs. Masters pushed her daughter back onto her pillow, smoothing her hair away. "How long has Dixon been hurting you?"

"Forever!" Julia sobbed, "but I always bring it on myself!"

"My poor girl, but why would you never tell us?" Mrs. Masters cried.

"I don't know! I just want to be with you and Father now!"

Katherine brought over a bowl and rags. Julia grabbed them. "I don't want you touching me, little miss perfect!"

"*Julia*! Stop it! Katherine has been such a comfort to your father in his final hours."

"Mama?"

"Julie, I came to tell you he was gone. Early this morning. I told you to come last night when I saw you. You don't remember?"

Julia buried her head in the blanket and sobbed.

Katherine backed out of the room and grabbed the children outside. John had slept in on a rare day off and was just up smoking contentedly under the ramada, reading an old *Englewood Times* sent from back east, when Katherine arrived. "The captain is dead," she announced.

"It's about time, I guess. The poor old fellow suffered so much. It doesn't seem fair." John sighed and stood up. "I guess I'll go see what Mrs. Masters needs."

"You won't find her at home. There's more to it than that. The colonel was drunk and beat Julia badly ... and she's drunk too! She doesn't want anyone to know."

"That bastard!" Weldon cried. "He has to go!"

"Julia brought this on herself. She didn't even go to visit with her father last night. Drunkenness is especially disgusting in a woman."

"Well, that's pretty heartless, Katherine," he said, flopping his shoddy hat onto his head. "I feel sorry for her."

"*Sorry*? How?" she asked. "Poor Captain Masters! I can tell you that Mrs. Masters was fit to kill Julia until she saw the shape her daughter was in. Her father meant that little to her?"

"You're being too harsh," he said. "Some people can't help themselves."

Katherine folded her arms. "Then they deserve what they get!"

"Maybe the beating by Dixon James had something to do with her not coming," John said.

"Why do you make excuses for her? It's her own fault she married a drunkard."

"What would you have her do?"

"I never would have picked such a soft man. But if I did, I would never forgive him for the humiliation. I wouldn't start drinking myself! That makes no sense at all, and of course I would leave him." Katherine felt herself glorying in Julia's suffering.

"You're a cruel woman," Weldon said and left her there.

Katherine should be allowed a few minutes of enjoyment at Julia's expense, she tried to convince herself, but she grew more miserable by the second. She stood and sighed. Pinning on her apron and securing her hat, she braved the sandy winds again with the children complaining all the way. William had been promised a ride. Eliza fretted, having missed her nap and begged to be held. A mangy dog came sniffing along, and she kicked it away. The door was open at the Masters place, two soldiers outside chatting quietly. "Is she in?" Katherine asked. They nodded somberly.

The old lady sat by her husband, waiting for the coffin to be brought. "I used to complain so much about the heat he gave off. The captain always ran hot, but it's surprising how quick they go cold. Feel his hand and see."

"No, Mrs. Masters, I couldn't ... is there anything you need?"

"I need to be alone with him. Your husband has already been here and gone."

Katherine walked out knowing John went to Julia's. Her heart beat with anger, but when she knocked it was Julia, looking every bit as gruesome as before, who answered. "Come in," she said.

Katherine complied. The children did not and raced each other around the house screaming.

"Can you make them stop?" Julia asked.

"No, I can't, but I can help you clean things up if you let me," Katherine offered, looking around the room she had once been so impressed with. How quickly things had fallen into disrepair. And the bottles with their sour and stale odor were still everywhere—the pipes she had noticed earlier were gone.

"Katherine Weldon, you must be delighted seeing me like this, but I don't care anymore. This is my life, I'm sick of hiding it. Poor Dixon, he tried his best with me."

"You married a brute," Katherine said, hardened with self-righteousness.

Julia laughed, holding her face, which would never be the same. "I've always been so good at making people see things my way. It's a sickness." She spilled a dirty-looking drink onto the floor and refilled the glass with something potent from a flask she hid by the stove. Katherine attempted to stop her.

"Do you think you can save me, you stupid little fool?" Julia asked and emptied her glass. Katherine tried to go, but Julia pulled her back. "You and your husband sicken me, but you already know that. You're like my parents—meant to be. Dixon was a good man when I met him. My parents loved him. He wanted to be a teacher, of all things, after the war, but I had my heart set on marrying a military man so he stayed in. My father," Julia cried, "he was a lovely man, but he used to let me drink with him sometimes on the sly. It was our secret. But when he stopped drinking, well, I never could. I never wanted to. I ran off with a boy from the 2nd New Jersey—a bounty jumper—he was the handsomest man I'd ever seen," Julia said bitterly. "I would marry him and show my parents how well I could do on my own. Such a stupid cliche story. Dixon was away being brave and all of that. We were engaged, but I went with the other boy. Afterward, my mother took me to a midwife, and she scraped and flushed me out so hard. I'd never be able to feel anything but pain. Dixon loved me and didn't even realize that half of the time I was drunk. The midwife said the pain would go, but it didn't. Dixon assumed I must be shy those first few nights of our marriage, and he sort of liked that. But one night when I had gotten us tight—he wasn't much for drink back then—he looked at me. I showed him what that midwife had done and at first he didn't know what to think—he had saved himself for marriage! But then I just told him in my drunken misery—just laid it out plain that I had been poked by another soldier and there could be no children, no pleasure between us."

"You shouldn't be telling me this," Katherine said, shaken.

"But you listen. I don't like you, but you really listen," Julia said as she poured another drink and ran her fingers over the rim of the glass. "Have you ever taken a drink, Katherine Weldon?"

"Yes."

"Why can you control it and I can't? I used to try to stop, and Dixon would allow himself to hope. We avoided people. Dixon gave up his staff job, but I would always slip and in time I dragged Dixon with me. I know the colonel would have stopped long ago if it wasn't for me, but for some reason, somehow he still loves me in a way. Or maybe I've become his habit along with all the other habits I've led him to." She held her face shakily. "I told him he looked old and called him a drunk and a failure one too many times, and he hit me with everything in him and ran off. All while my father lay dying."

As discreetly as possible at this small camp, John organized a search for the colonel. James must be put to justice. After scouring the buildings for sign of him, John trudged down to the stables with sand blowing in his eyes. There the colonel sat picking horse shit from his boots. He looked up at the sound of Weldon's footfall. "The hero of Camp Grant has arrived," James said with a bitter laugh. A broad scratch crossed the pale skin of his forehead.

"Come along, colonel. Back to the guardhouse for you."

"It seems we take turns there, Weldon. Has the captain died yet?"

"Yes, he has," answered the lieutenant, surprised at the cool manner of the colonel. "As if you care."

"I have often told you not to make judgments on people you know so little about. You seem to like to pretend that you are a simple and supremely pure man. I know you were more than tempted to take that money I gave you. I saw it in your eyes. If you had had more time with it you would have given in."

"You know no such thing, James."

"Oh! It's James is it? Until I am tried and cashiered I still outrank you," the colonel said looking Weldon over. "You have entertained me for months with this show you put on for the world—that you're better than the rest of us. Your story starts out so heart-wrenching in writing. One would almost pull for you if not for the hypocrite you have become. You write well about the war. Those passages in your little diary were so clear and crisp—but you lost me with all the self-pity. Poor Katherine doesn't seem to know a thing. But she will one day, and she will hate you most for deceiving her—take my word for it."

Weldon shook with anger and shock but could say nothing.

"Don't you look surprised, Lieutenant Weldon! For Christ's sake, you didn't even change the location of the journal. It was better than Dickens—everyday getting a new update on your trials and tribulations. I don't think you got the depth of my character just right, and probably your foxy little wife is too romanticized, but overall it deserves a medal of some sort. Oh, and by the way I saw you at that quaint little spot in Tucson three sheets to the wind—a real slip for you. Sad ..."

Weldon threw a punch and got one in return. The colonel threw his full weight at Weldon, sending them both to the dirt. Weldon was faster and got on top of the colonel to finish the match, but the colonel was not through. "I have a deal for you, Weldon. I won't say a word to your wife about your journal."

"She wouldn't believe you," Weldon said breathlessly.

"Do you want to take that chance?"

Weldon stared at him.

"I don't mind taking a back seat to you. I have no interest in the Indians anymore, but I'd prefer to leave here honorably for my wife's sake. You should lose the commissary book that so perfectly shows my corruption—say it's been stolen or whatever you like, and I won't say a word about your little problem to your wife."

***

Camp Grant, Arizona

March 21, 1872

Dear Mother,

I'm afraid even with the money you have sent us it is still impossible for us to come home for a visit any time soon. John will not leave here if there is the slightest chance of meeting with the enemy in battle. I am a prisoner here. The shocking news of the surveying team at Wickenberg being massacred with the tragic loss of Frederick Loring has everyone on edge. I've been told Loring was a bright new star in the literary world, but you would know better than me. Out here no one is sure whether the Indians worked alone or with bandits, but some of the Indians bragged about the disgusting act after a drinking spree paid for in American dollars.

O. O. Howard, will be here soon to try his luck with the Apache. The army is stalled and restless, growing impatient with the Washington crowd who come on flying visits to negotiate empty promises with the Indians.

John does not want me talking—in his mind flirting—with any of the men here. I resent it. There are no women here at all now that Captain Masters is dead, except for Julia who keeps to herself. Her face still is not right.

Lieutenant Bourke has asked me to help him discover the secrets of the Apache tongue. He asked me to listen to the women who visit and try to write their words down as best I can.

I am almost fluent in Spanish now. There is so little to do here so all the men have taken up learning the language as a challenge. John has no ear or interest in it, but Lieutenant Bourke does.

John is under the mistaken notion that I want for more leisure time, but it is not that which makes me irritable. It is normal for a man to spend most of his time working, but there is something else. John seems to avoid me, to be angry with me. He used to ask me about my day, but I think he has become bored with my stories. Lieutenant Bourke's little assignments give me something to do, but I dare not tell John about them. I have nightmares in which I will wake to find John gone, and when I do really wake and try to hold him he brushes me away.

I would love to come home, but I am still so in love with my husband and so afraid I am losing him. I do not know what to do.

Yours affectionately,

Katherine Weldon

***

Tenafly Road

Englewood, N.J.

Dearest Katie,

Your father and I are fine. Thank you for asking. Here is some advice from someone who loves you most. Bring an end to this "work" you do for Lieutenant Bourke if you care about your marriage as you say you do, no matter how innocently you may have entered into it. That you are keeping it a secret is telling. You are having nightmares because you are feeling guilty. I do not believe that Bourke has just scholarship on his mind. As you say there are few women around and you are pretty. You might think that John suspects nothing and maybe he is working too hard, but you need to discuss this with him. Guessing and wondering in marriage are not useful ways of dealing with doubts.

Father and I love you and pray for you all. I hope the little things I sent for the children will fit. Will you ever have a likeness of our little granddaughter made up and sent to us?

May God bless you~

Sarah McCullough

Katherine gathered her notes for Bourke and brought them to his quarters, slipping them beneath his sword left carelessly upon a rustic chair under the ramada. She turned to leave but Bourke heard her and came out to greet her. "Mrs. Weldon, I'm surprised. What are you doing here?"

"I can't help you anymore, lieutenant."

"Is it Lieutenant Weldon?" he asked as if he already knew. "Do as you like, Mrs. Weldon. It's sad, though, that you are talented at something and forced to quit it."

"Lieutenant Bourke, I'm sorry I disappoint you."

She tramped away and waited that evening for John to come home long after the other soldiers slept quietly across in the barracks. "John, you're so late!" she whispered, setting aside her darning.

"Yes, I wanted to check on a few things." He bristled at his wife's annoying new habit of following him around the tiny quarters.

"Sit down now for supper," she pleaded. "I thought you would have come in for lunch today."

He waved her away. "No, I'm tired. I couldn't eat."

"Please sit with me. It's important."

He glanced her way irritably and sat heavily in his chair.

"Why are you so angry with me?" she asked.

"I'm not."

"Well, since the captain's death ..."

"I have lots of work ..."

"I know I disappointed you with the uncharitable things I said about Julia and the colonel." Katherine felt as if this sin had somehow been tremendously awful and repugnant to him.

"What? Oh, you were right," he muttered. "They deserve no sympathy. They are the scum of the earth."

"John, I must ask your forgiveness, but I'm afraid you're upset with me already. I love you," she said, her heart pounding. "Lieutenant Bourke asked me to take notes on the Apache for his studies and I did, but I realized it was wrong to do it and while my intention was to relieve my boredom only, it might be seen differently by you so I stopped."

"How *dare* ..." Weldon began, but checked his emotions. "Kate, it's all right if you want to spend time with Bourke. Maybe you need to do that ..."

She cried out, "You don't love me anymore!"

"No! That's not it. I just can't keep you happy."

"You haven't even tried! Why do you sneak into bed now? Are you repulsed by me?"

"No ..."

"It's been a month!"

He turned away scratching at his arm—a new habit of his. "Katherine, the evidence against James is gone. Stolen."

"How?"

"And medical supplies too. This may be the end of my career when I tell Crook." He spoke as if in a dream.

"But it's not your fault ..."

"It *is* my fault! I'm in charge, and I let it happen!" he shouted, taking out a cigar but returning it to his pocket.

William stirred. "Papa?"

"Go back to sleep, for God's sake!" Weldon shot back.

"You've been working yourself to the bone," Katherine said nervously. "It's too much, John—for all of us. You look terrible. You don't eat. Even your hair ... it's thinning. You're making yourself sick. With all this work you do, Crook won't blame you."

"But I haven't got lots of work done. I can't concentrate ..."

"You must rest," she urged, pulling him toward the bed. He wouldn't look at her and resisted every step. Before he could stop her, she had her hands beneath his shirt, tugging it from his trousers and she saw it—the old battle scar, a festering, open wound again. "My Lord, take this off right now!" she cried. "What's happened to you? Why would you hide this? We must get the doctor!"

"No, it will get better. It will ..."

He had taken a small dose in powder form—just enough to relax him after burning the James evidence. Promising himself that he'd never depend on a needle again, he cut his inflamed wound a little, just deep enough to rub the powder in—but the relief had been minimal, only serving to aggravate the wound. That had been weeks ago, but the senile old surgeon made things too easy and the hunger grew as it always did. The alarm he felt when he lifted his shirt and saw the ulcerated wound was tempered only by the next dose by syringe or tablets.

"My dear John, what will I ever do with you?"

"You should leave me," he said through cracked lips.

"Don't even think it!" she said with comforting firmness. "I'm not much of a nurse, but I won't allow you out of my sight until you're healed. You can't fight me on this." She poured clean water into a basin and pulled a rag from the drying line over the stove. "Are you crying?" she asked, sitting beside him. "John, don't worry. Everything will be all right. I promise ..."

John looked so desperate. Katherine thought about the dying rooms in the hospitals Mrs. Masters had talked about. She thought about how John had cared for her when they lost the baby and how he had saved her from the Indian. Now it was her turn. She soaked and dressed his wound and tucked him into bed, staying with him until he was almost asleep.

"Kate, don't leave me alone."

"Never."

***

Every strand of hair, every pore, the tips of every nerve surged delightfully, smoothly like a gentle wave, like a dream, like a great celebration—for a short pocket of time. How long did high tide last or a sunset or the joy of looking at your child for the first time? First came the quick surge of energy when it felt like everything could be, must be done now, this minute. But then came the doubts and suspicions. Someone knew. Everybody knew. And that's when hiding in the commissary or the doctor's office while the old man slept soundly seemed like a good idea. Finally, the deepening melancholia and exhaustion that did not allow for sleep settled in. The horrible dreams came too and then more pain.

Now every hair, every pore, the tips of every nerve felt on fire. Thousands upon thousands of needles—as a punishment for ever using the one. His limbs were stones that strained every aching joint and he wished they would just fall off.

Katherine brought in the doctor. A strange desert fever—best to keep him away from the other men—he pronounced and left. The scratching that had begun lately continued and his arms bled. Katherine prayed, but felt certain he would die. If he lived they must leave this place. She'd had enough of soldiering, and then one night he came back. She had fallen asleep next to him, but woke instantly at his touch. "John!" she said and turned to him.

"Katherine, how many times will you save me?"

Chapter Thirty-Eight

General Howard with his one arm, his Bible, and his reputation sullied over affairs at the Freedmen's Bureau came to try his Christian charity with the Indians as he had done with the former slaves. Howard arrived during John's withdrawal. Bourke came to ask about the "stolen" papers. Katherine told him what she believed to be true, and James gained freedom. Howard was acquainted with the James and the Masters families from back east. Crook, with obvious disgust greeted his superior and James.

"Crook, how nice to see you again. God bless you and your works," Howard said, extending his good arm.

Crook saluted the general and shook hands with James. "Welcome to Arizona, General Howard," he said politely but with reticence.

"Get settled and we'll talk later," Howard suggested. "James here has invited me to a small prayer meeting for peace—and supper. He tells me he has a great cook."

"Crook, you are welcome to join our service, although I'm afraid Cook wouldn't have made enough for supper," James added.

"No, thank you. I have things to go over with the men," Crook replied and stalked off to Weldon's place, ready to have him for supper, but as he turned the corner and saw the state of the lieutenant wrapped in an Indian blanket he thought better of reprimanding him now. Weldon made to rise upon seeing his superior, but Crook motioned him down. "No, at ease, Weldon. I can see you are ill."

"I'm almost better, sir."

"How is it that James is loose again?"

"It's my fault, sir," Weldon began, faltering. "The records are gone ... stolen ... and I'm b-behind in my work."

"Calm down. You need to rest and not worry. I should have taken the records with me .... What does the doctor say?"

"A fever—of some sort, but I'm better."

"You know that James sent me a letter accusing you of dipping into the hospital morphine, but I put him in his place. That man will resort to any lies." Crook checked for his reaction, but Weldon didn't flinch.

"Sir, I'm afraid that I did little of what you asked."

Katherine came out with a cool molasses drink for Crook.

"Thank you, ma'am. Are you taking good care of the lieutenant here?"

"I'm trying," she answered, fearing Crook's reaction over the missing book and the unfinished work. "I thought I might lose him, sir ..." She covered her face and ran inside.

Crook shook his head. "I hate to see you and Mrs. Weldon suffer under men like James. General Howard is a pompous ass, between you and me, parading the grounds with a drunkard and a wife beater. But he gives us a little extra time. I need you to get well, lieutenant. Howard will fail at making peace, and then we will be allowed to fight."

"Yes, sir."

Crook smiled and patted Weldon's shoulder stiffly.

Chapter Thirty-Nine

Dearest Kate,

I write this with an unsteady hand, just recovered from an illness not brought on by the desert but by me. If I had courage I would tell you I cut myself, that I couldn't stop the feeling that stalks me still when I am alone and quiet.

You are right to think a man who is a slave to any substance is pathetic. The things I have done to keep this from you are shameful.

Did I really tell you I went with a colored girl? My lies are ridiculous and cruel. You have been the only interest of my life. This morning I watched you pour coffee with your free hand on your hip and your wedding ring on your tiny finger. There was a smudge from the fire on your chin, and you were talking about something—the children maybe—but I didn't hear a thing. I was smiling watching you not even notice the coffee missing the cup, and I was so grateful, I am so grateful to have my feelings back; the feelings that a man has for his wife when she is beautiful and half-dressed and her hair is lit by the sun coming through the hole in the canvas roof. The physical feelings leave when the morphine takes over, and I am humiliated and ashamed.

And so I have made up my mind. No more waiting for the right time to tell you. I will never tell. I will never tell that it began during the war; that Simon saved and cursed me at the same time; that I may never be free of it. I must lie because I can't afford to lose you. My world is black and dead without you. I will never forget how you prayed over me each night …

Weldon had taken to carrying a haversack full of paper, even scraps, and when the temptations struck he wrote. His journal was gone, and he would never be so foolish to leave anything where it could be found, but he could never give up his scribbled thoughts. This worked for now. And each day he felt stronger and more hopeful again. He went back to work, but followed Crook's and Katherine's orders to go home when the bugle called the day over.

Katherine took pride in John's recovery. In desperation she quizzed the Apache women. How did they stay healthy in this place? Katherine set about learning their foods, tried them on her family, and wrote it all down for herself … not Bourke. John dropped by during the day. She fed him and checked his side, all the while hinting at the things they would do later. John left for the afternoon happily frustrated.

Camp Grant, Arizona

Dear Father and Mother,

I hope you are both in good spirits and health. The fog that hung over me has lifted, but not before much worry and trouble. John was dreadfully ill, but after a week or more of insecurity and suffering he recovered and is now heartier and hungrier than ever. I have finally learned to cook from the Indians and Mexicans! Their food is much more suited to this climate, and we are strengthened by it.

John comes home early now and plays with the children, and I wish our nights could last forever.

Colonel James and his wife still haunt the place, but they have no power and keep to themselves.

General Crook has big plans for John. It is amusing to watch them together. Crook is as quiet as John, but somehow they communicate well enough. I worry though, because beneath the unassuming image Crook has made for himself there is a man of stone. His eyes are still frightening no matter how friendly he tries to be. John will do anything to impress this man, and I worry when they are out in the field John will put himself in danger and take silly risks. But when John is happy so am I. Mrs. Masters told me once that I needed to find my own way, my own entertainment and not depend on John as much as I do, but for now I love nothing better that seeing my family grow fat and healthy on my cooking. Mother, when did I become so like you?

I do play each day with our mare and that is enough time on my own. I finally feel at home here. Somehow I found something in myself while caring for John, and our life has never been happier.

I know you both want to hear firsthand about General Howard. He is pious. Most of us were disappointed with Colyer's pathetic performance and had no higher hopes for Howard. I instantly had reason to dislike Howard, as he freed Colonel James! They paraded together as if the best of friends. Poor John watched from under a heap of blankets on our ramada.

Howard did his best to gain popularity with the officers, and he succeeded with the most corrupt ones loyal to James. John was at home when Howard came to meet him. The general suggested that those officers loyal to him might be rewarded with plumb staff appointments in Washington. I was excited by this, hoping that we could be nearer to you one day soon, but John shook his head and said he had met the general's type before and that nothing would come of his promises. John has put his lot with Crook, and he will see where he takes him.

General Howard had invited the Tucson citizenry to the big Indian meeting, and they crowded in to see the famous general. Crook and Howard set out blankets beneath a stand of cottonwoods near the river. What a difference there was between the two former West Point men! General Howard was grand and glittering like a statue of gold, while Crook blended with his dull desert gear into the surroundings. The Indians were impressed with Howard and his dramatic ways, so much so that he inadvertently terrified them when he dropped to his knees in a ridiculous way to open the ceremony with a prayer. All the fantastically dressed and armed warriors ran off and hid behind buildings and trees. I clung to John, who had his weapon concealed beneath the blanket he still wore in the desert heat. James was called in, as he had been friendly with some of the Indians, and they trusted him!

General Howard started with the Christ-like admonition that if the Apache did not behave he would exterminate them. For all of his bluster not a single warrior looked won over.

Eskimmi-yan or "Skimmy," an Apache leader, said that Howard was like the man who was so pure the gods kept him on an island to protect the man from human frailty. Skimmy and his friends are suspected of having been involved in the death of a citizen just outside of Camp Grant, but he avoided answering any questions about the affair. Howard succeeded only in keeping the Indians under the illusion that they were in charge and in keeping the citizens in states of apoplectic rage.

Skimmy listened to Howard's entreaties, but announced that he would not agree to anything until the children kidnapped after the Camp Grant mas-

sacre were returned to him. Howard had induced some of these adoptive parents to bring their children to the meeting. It was amazing to see the change in the children. A few carried the scars of the massacre, but most looked healthy, neat, and civilized. It became clear that the children after a year with their new families were loath to go back among the Apaches.

The children pitched and screamed and clung to their new parents. The general seemed perplexed and irritated by the commotion. One little girl dressed in starched whites fought hardest and refused to go with the wild men who stood before her. Every woman in the crowd cried at the sight.

John pushed through the crowd shouting that only brutes would send children back to lives of squalor and degradation.

Lieutenant Bourke took John in hand before Howard could find where the damning words were coming from, and the crowd did their part to shield him with their own shouts and hisses. In the end the general compromised. Howard had the children put under the care of a Catholic woman in town where they could be visited like animals in a zoo by both parties until someone of higher authority in Washington could settle the dispute.

Skimmy placed a stone in the general's hand and said that their friendship would last until the stone melted. Crook and Howard went off together. John and Bourke smoked under the shade of our ramada. We were all upset about the children. John and Bourke argued about the status of the children, and Bourke even insulted John by suggesting he was a half-breed.

Once Bourke was out of earshot John grumbled but I told him I didn't care if he was descended from slugs.

Write soon!

Affectionately,

Katherine Weldon

The children grew and changed and became real people to Katherine while John prepared for war. Even Howard admitted force would be needed to get the Indians settled on their new reservations. Katherine spent her evenings contentedly pulling the hems down on Willy's trouser legs and letting her husband's trousers out. John had never looked so full and fit. The weight suited him, and it was all her doing. John brought in an old stove one day more forlorn looking than their last, but it worked well, and she gloried in being able to bake muffins and breads. She tried not to think about him going away.

No one knew how long the campaign would last. Crook said it would be till they smashed the Indians all to pieces, but since Katherine had never yet seen that done she could have no idea how long she'd be without John. Colyer and Howard had established new reservations, and over 5,000 Indians had come in. In the fall of 1872 Howard had managed to make peace with the Chiricahua leader, Cochise, who ten years earlier had been wrongfully accused of kidnapping and ever since had been on a destructive and ruthless campaign against the settlers.

But still there was no lasting peace. In the past year the Apache and Yavapai had murdered at least forty people, raided countless ranches, and stolen nearly five hundred head of livestock. The citizens were finished with talk. Something must be done and Crook meant to do it.

The orders came in.

"Kate, it's finally come, I guess. We'll leave here on the fifteenth of November with Captain Brown."

"For how long?"

"Till it's over, I'd say ..."

"Well, how long do you think?"

Weldon scratched his head. "Months, the winter ... till we win," he said, glancing her way. "Don't worry. The time will race by, I bet." He tried to convince himself that he could be without her for that long. "The scouts will play a major role, but we knew that. It looks like we will try to force them to leave their winter camps in the lower elevations and make them choose between the snowy mountains and food. If we can get them into the Tonto Basin we can concentrate our forces and go in for the kill."

"I hate this talk," she complained.

"This is what I do, Kate. Someone's got to."

Katherine wiped Eliza's face. "All over a piece of awful, rough land. It seems so foolish."

"Kate, it's not for me to ask why. What would be the point? This land has been a war zone for hundreds of years. If we can bring peace, then that's good enough for me."

"But it's the Indians' land," she began.

"Which Indians? All of this land is theirs no matter how far they wander and how little they improve it? It's the law of nature that you can only own what you can defend. We intend to see what they can do."

"That's brutal."

"That's life. There's no point in feeling bad about it. Who's to say these Indians didn't kill off a weaker tribe that came before them? And look how they treat the Papagos. The Apaches don't give a lick about them, and in the end they want what conquest can get for them—this lonesome piece of desert and stolen goods. That's why we need to set borders and ground rules with them. They're too stupid to do it on their own. Once they learn to respect property lines, we can have some rest from them."

Katherine mulled over his words and asked, "Well, what would God have us do?"

John gave her an amused look. "Howard likes to speak for Jesus, and he seems pretty sure we should fight," he replied. "Are you suggesting the citizens should turn the other cheek, or we should all just learn to love one another and share? I don't know. I think Jesus was just a delusional man."

"John, you shouldn't say such things! It's horrible! When did you develop this attitude?"

"I've tried everything it says to do in the Bible and nothing worked for me. I was never rewarded with even one day of peace. Since I've put my faith in other things—like you—my life has been much better."

"We need to get you to church right away. I can't be a substitute for God! That's blasphemous and too much of a burden placed on me! I will always fail you somehow, but God never will!"

"I don't understand why this upsets you so much. You've never taken much interest in religious matters."

"I guess I imagined you had enough faith and enthusiasm for both of us with all of your quoting the Bible and such," she said.

"The Bible has fine language, I still like the sound of it, but it's all humbug."

She sat at the table, wiping her eyes. "I don't know why it bothers me, but it does. I guess I would like to think you feel our lives together were blessed or meant to be, and that there's a purpose."

"It's chance and luck—no purpose at all really. The Bible doesn't tell me who to be with or what work I should do. It tells me to have nice thoughts and turn the other cheek, and in doing so I've gotten beaten and starved and tricked. I've prayed and forgiven others and never received anything for it. I had to decide. Did I believe in a

God who refused to help me—who must hate me—or believe that there was no real God and that it was up to me to defend and feed and care for myself? Although I haven't always been so good at it, I was a hell of a lot better at taking care of myself than God."

She shook her head. "I don't even know what to say to that. I feel you're wrong, but I have no words to express why. You never mentioned any of this before." She looked into his eyes. "What will we tell our children?"

"You may tell them any fairy tale you like, and I will say nothing. Maybe they should know the stuff for academic reasons anyway."

She walked out into the sunlight, squinting her eyes. John followed. "Kate, what are you thinking?"

"Somehow it hurts me that you believe in so little. You must think it silly that the children and I pray for you when you are away."

"No," John replied, running his hand over her head and down to the small of her back. "It's nice that you think of me."

Katherine sobbed. "But now you've taken the power, the magic from it."

"But how? If it comforts you ..."

"No! I want my prayers to protect you!" Katherine cried. "Now I feel you're somehow blocking them!"

Weldon laughed. "That's silly, Kate. I don't think prayers get blocked."

"But you don't believe in their power so they're lost on you."

"Anything happens in life. There's no clear plan."

"You're wrong! You are not meant to know the plan! But that doesn't mean one doesn't exist for you. God planned for you to meet me. That I know."

Weldon looked amused. "How?"

"When Simon used to write during the war, yours was the only name that came up with any regularity—like God was paving the way for you in my mind."

Weldon patted her face. "Simon and I were friends ...of course ..."

"No John, you can't convince me to take the magic from our meeting. Simon brought home different acquaintances and friends from the war with names like Burt Sloane and Sandy Metcalfe, and even their names ruined them. They were all dull."

John smiled, remembering the men he had fought alongside of during the war. It still annoyed him that Simon brought them home for his sister and not him.

She put her arms around his waist and looked up to him. "And when you appeared in our kitchen that day, when I heard your name—John Weldon—it wasn't music exactly or bells, but there was no dull ring to it. There was clarity, and by the time you left me at the dance—by that time your name was music I couldn't keep out of my head."

He didn't let her finish, he couldn't. He kissed her and dragged her inside, and whether it was God or luck or the stars they were together and it was good.

Chapter Forty

As November 15th approached, new men arrived, and the place came alive with plans and the laughter of soldiers whiling the days away before their departure into the unexplored heart of Indian country. More men and more horses meant evening races when the day's work ended. Katherine looked on enthusiastically but declined all attempts by the men to get her involved. Soldiers and animals camped everywhere. It surprised her that the army had hidden so many men on the desert and could call them in so quickly. Major Brown took over the command at Camp Grant.

Two companies of the 5th Cavalry and a detachment of thirty scouts made up the party that would climb over the Mescal, Pinal, Superstition, and Matitzal ranges to Camp McDowell to receive further orders. John would go with them.

The children took little interest in John's preparations for departure, but Katherine hovered. "Are you certain you can't take your other coat? You may wish for it in the mountains, and I don't want to think of you catching your death."

"Kate, I'll be just fine. This is all we can bring."

She looked him over. "Can't you at least sneak a little extra food?"

He smiled, enjoying her concern. "You know you've gotten me fattened up for this journey well enough. You're a good girl."

She patted his belly with a smile. "You will try to write ... and if you get hurt you'll take care of yourself?" she asked, already lonesome.

"I won't get hurt."

"Well, take this extra chocolate in case you get tired of coffee ..." She produced a small bag of his favorite treat with trembling hands.

Weldon tickled under her chin, but couldn't speak. He sighed and knelt in front of the children, whispering goodbye and to do as their mother asked. They were used to his comings and goings each day and saw no difference in his leaving today.

"Kate, I left gifts hidden out back for Christmas. If I don't come home ... I mean if I don't come home before Christmas ..." Weldon saw the look on her face. "Don't look that way. There's thirty days' rations. December fifteenth maybe or a little after we could be back."

He picked up his bag and walked out. A ceremonial send-off for the troops had been planned, but she promised him she would not attend. She gazed out the window and listened to the military band play their rousing march as the men trotted off, followed by the long procession of mule-led wagon trains. The soldiers left behind to mind the garrison followed the parade wistfully with their eyes and turned as the final white-capped ships of the desert fell out of sight. She drank the last of the coffee and began her normal cleaning routine. She pulled the quilt from the bed to air it out under the ramada, fighting the urge to sleep the day away, but an envelope fell to the floor, and she opened it.

Dearest Kate,

This is the hardest day of my life. I write this while you are still sleeping. It is the hardest day because I must make my way without you. In the past when we were apart I missed you because I loved you and there is still that, but it is more now. It has taken me such a long time to realize that I am not alone in the world any longer. I never thought you would stay with me this long, but now I begin to believe I can rely on you. It frightens me that I might crave and enjoy your attention too much, but it feels so nice.

This trip is special because in the past I worked to prove my worth to myself, but this time I will do everything for you. I want to make you proud. I want you to be with someone special.

You have rescued me from countless demons and I intend to spend the rest of my life working to give you all you deserve. One day we'll transfer to one of the pretty little towns back east and live a comfortable life together. I will miss you every minute of the day.

Your devoted husband,

John Weldon

The men rode out along the river where sagebrush and mesquite grew in profusion, until they crossed the Gila where the terrain turned broken and rough. Cholla cactus, manzanita, scrub oak, and Spanish bayonet fought their way up between the broken granite and pudding stones until the men climbed to the higher elevations of the Pinal range. Glistening pine and juniper greeted the men, whose senses had been so dulled by the bleak desert below, but with this new color came bracing winds and snow-covered terrain. Sometimes the snow rose hip deep and uncomfortable. Weldon wished he had gone against orders like some of the others, who now wrapped themselves snugly in their heaviest coats. But despite the chills, Weldon enjoyed the bright, crisp mountain air and scenery.

The first day's march was done, and the shivering men were ordered to search for firewood. Without a dry place to sit and no warm food to speak of, the camp fell into a lonely human silence. The creaking trees in the shrill wind and the occasional thud of snow falling from heavy branches as the sun cast its dull late afternoon shadows made for a miserable scene.

The officers rubbing their arms and stomping their feet congregated around a snow-cleared pit as if indeed there were a fire. Weldon stood with them, imagining that if he left they would all suddenly become animated with talk of similar exploits and education. It was foolish. No one wanted to speak in the cold and misery.

"If I can find some cedar it might burn," he stammered, his voice sounding hollow in the cold.

The men grumbled, but Lieutenant Almy perked up. "Weldon, I'll give you a hand if you don't mind."

He did mind but nodded for his comrade to come along. They slogged through the snow with saturated trousers, still finding it more agreeable than standing in camp. Almy talked easily about trifling things—a certain scout's odd habits, a letter from home—and he didn't require much input from Weldon. Suddenly Weldon stopped him and pointed off to movement in the distance behind a thick stand of pine. Weldon raised his carbine and put the animal in sight. It went down with the first shot. Almy and Weldon ran to investigate their prize—an old, fat buck with an abscess on its leg that had slowed it.

"What a shot, Weldon! Bully for you!"

Weldon laughed giddily. He looked up at the sky—only a small bit of daylight left. "If we find no cedar then this kill is a waste."

"Oh, we'll find cedar even if I have to search all night!" Almy exclaimed prophetically, and in twenty minutes the good dry wood appeared. They loaded it onto a makeshift sled, along with the buck on top, then the two men dragged their supper home with rope tied around their middles.

The officers had hardly changed position when Almy shouted, "Mess call!"

"By Jove!" Bourke cried as he raced up with the others. They all did their bit to get the meal prepared. Coffee brewed as the appetizer of choice. Poor privates skirted the officers' mess, dreamily taking in the scent of the animal. The officers presented Crook with the first and choicest meat.

"No, let Almy and Weldon get their fill. This is what I expect of a Western Reserve boy, Weldon—making your own luck."

Weldon smiled and passed the plate to Almy, who let it go no further. Not one to stand on ceremony, he shoveled the entire piece, juice running over his half-grown beard, into his mouth with a groan of pleasure.

The quiet party once warmed up and fed grew lively again. A few favorite sergeants picked what was left from the bones of the buck and were given room to brew coffee before the fire went out. Bourke told yet another story about pretty señoritas bathing in a canyon stream. The officers politely listened, but the night belonged to Weldon.

Almy wanted details about his scouting misadventures. "What about James? Is he as bad as they say?"

"I don't know …" he hedged.

"Oh come now, Weldon," Bourke pushed him. He liked Weldon even though the feeling obviously wasn't mutual. "The whole story was printed in the *Army Gazette*. It was easy enough to read between the lines and see the colonel's ineptitude."

"The *Army Gazette*?" Weldon asked.

"I suppose they picked up the story from a local paper," Bourke said.

Captain Taylor spoke. "No, I remember it. They printed a section of the official report and a firsthand narrative by a sergeant, I think."

A sergeant making coffee interrupted, "Permission to speak, sir. It was Sergeant Simpson. The man Lieutenant Weldon saved in the canyon."

"Oh, yes, that was it," the captain said.

Almy hadn't any details, "Do tell, Weldon."

Weldon poked the fire. "It was a disaster …"

Crook groaned. "My God, Weldon, you are your own worst enemy." He glanced around at his officers, animated by the fire, and said playfully, "Remind me never to let this one relay stories to the press."

The newsman brought along laughed.

Captain Taylor added, "There's no need to worry about Weldon running off at the mouth!"

The men chuckled.

Crook sat beside Weldon and patted his shoulder. "Modesty is a good thing to a point. Boys, I remember this man as a young private. Like a beanpole he was. Weighed less than his gun I bet, but could he shoot and fish! Weldon was generous to a fault though. We used to laugh at first, wondering how he stayed so thin after all the food he brought in, but we discovered the other privates taking advantage of him. I had to order him to eat first and share second. We didn't want to lose our best shot to starvation."

The men smiled, remembering the hard lessons of being a new soldier and wanting to gain acceptance, but Weldon's face burned.

"Well, I heard it was his reckless charge at the Wilderness that rallied his part of the field," Major Brown said.

Almy spoke up again, "Yes, some say he didn't get the recognition he deserved that day—his superior got the credit and a promotion to captain. But I want to know more about the scout with James. There are rumors that he raped and killed a squaw in front of the men. Is it true? The other accounts of it hinted ..."

"Other accounts?" Weldon asked.

The men laughed.

Bourke joked, "Weldon has little time to follow the reports of bravery and such. We've all seen the little romance he has with Mrs. Weldon. It makes the most confirmed bachelor jealous. That girl adores you. How did you manage that?"

The officers drank deeply from their cold cups, most having noticed Bourke's affection for Mrs. Weldon.

Almy pushed on. "I heard you got a few kills on your own and rallied the men against James."

"No! I would never rally against a superior!" Weldon said shaken by the attention.

Crook smiled and stirred the embers.

"Colonel James was missing," Weldon explained. "We needed to find him, and then the sergeant and his men ... we stumbled into the Indian camp and found a few of the men who had attacked our camp."

"And you cut their heads off. Bully for you."

"I did no such thing. It was suggested, but I ordered against it. I was made aware that my orders were not followed later when one night I tripped over a heavy bag behind my quarters."

The men chuckled at the idea of Weldon kicking an Indian head around the yard. They got up to bring their blankets and ponchos to the fire's edge to sleep.

Weldon and Crook sat staring into the orange embers of the dying fire. "Weldon, it's about time to start thinking of promotion. I will certainly recommend it if all continues to go well. How would you like a captaincy?"

"But sir, I'm only a second lieutenant."

Crook laughed shaking his head. "The only thing you lack is self-confidence, but we'll work on that."

***

The scouts under Archie MacIntosh, a half-breed trusted above all others by Crook, were kept a day's march in front of the column but were in constant communication with it.

Early on, an officer made a point of introducing Weldon to MacIntosh. It annoyed John that people assumed he might have a special wish to meet others who shared the cruel fate of being half-Indian. Archie, a slovenly man, was just the sort Weldon would rather avoid.

"You know, lieutenant," Archie said, rolling a cigarette, "it's the hardest thing in the world to get these Apaches to hold back once they catch scent of their prey. You would expect them to have loyalty to their own ... not like us, who can pick and choose. But it's real trouble to make them wait for the soldiers to come up. I bet you and I are just the same—tamed by our better halves. I've Scotch blood and you?" He seemed to sense Weldon's disdain.

"English, I'm half English," Weldon answered testily. He had no interest in any similarities between himself and the scout. MacIntosh was a raving alcoholic. Admittedly he was also a brilliant scout and outdoorsman. Crook put up with his extreme binging. So far it hadn't affected his work, and the men enjoyed watching what small bit of nuisance he would make of himself. MacIntosh played out the predictable behavior Weldon imagined all whites expected of half-breeds. If a proper soldier attempted the same behavior it would not be accepted.

One night while checking on the guards posted around camp, Weldon came upon MacIntosh in the woods, half-naked and raving. His first thought was to leave the scout in the dark, but his presence had not escaped the drunkard. "Hey you, Weldon, come help me, you son of a bitch!"

Weldon hung back, still deciding.

"God damn it, you piece-of-shit rascal! I'm trapped under this fallen tree."

There was no tree. Weldon approached skittishly. He held his hand out to the delirious scout. The smell of urine and whiskey sickened him.

"I don't want your hand, Johnnie, you stupid kid. I'm trapped. Can't you see?"

Weldon looked again in the darkness. There was no tree.

Archie laughed and made to kick him. "Do you speak or are you dumb too?"

Weldon could make out the whites of Archie's eyes, wild with drink. The belligerence brought Weldon home to childhood. Only one person had ever called him Johnnie when she was drunk. He remembered what to do. He moved the nonexistent tree, ignored Archie's tumbling list of insults as best he could, and dragged the man to his feet. Weldon took the blows the man threw at him and led him back to camp.

Late the following day, skirting the camp so as not to alert Crook he was not where he should be, a contrite MacIntosh found Weldon repairing his boot. "My apologies, friend."

Weldon threw his boot at the scout. "Don't ever come near me again or I'll kill you. We are nothing alike, you and I. I spent far too much of my life caring for the likes of you, and I'm finished with it. Let the men who find you such an amusement keep you alive!"

Bourke walked over. "Any trouble fellows?"

"No," Weldon grunted.

MacIntosh reached down and grabbed Weldon's boot. "Just tell Crook I was here to tell him there's nothing new to report." He laughed at Weldon with dark, troubled eyes and tossed the boot back to the lieutenant. Bourke shrugged and moved on.

Camp MacDowell

December

Dear Katherine,

I am here at Camp McDowell for Christmas. I'm sorry to have told you we would be home by now. I hope you are having a nicer time than me and that you enjoyed your presents.

Today we were joined by Company G of the 5th Cavalry. This adds about forty enlisted men to our party and Captain Burns. If not an actual reason for celebration, the infusion of new men was at least a diversion from the nostalgia we all feel spending a holiday away from our families and friends. Everyone pooled their rations for a feast, which in the end was pretty pathetic. Half the men were drunk all day and the volunteer cooks were among them. There was a strange taste to the stew they made, but we ate it since there was nothing else but hardtack and canned peaches. You would have enjoyed the races although maybe not the idea of gambling on Christmas. We set off tomorrow in search of Delchay and his bunch of Apache hostiles. A scout who spent his youth with the band remembers a cave where they may be wintering. The scouts say "poco tiempo," soon we will find them. Not soon enough for me. All of us have made moccasins for quiet climbing into the Indian strongholds. Some of us have made nicer ones than others. I'm afraid I am no good with needle and leather.

You might think I prefer being out with the men, but really it is no frolic. Most of this trip has been dull and hard. We are told not to shoot when we are out in the field, so we often go on only the scantest meals. It is hard to imagine that I once enjoyed army rations, but you have spoiled me, you naughty girl! Captain Burns has adopted an Indian boy of five or six who can kill quail with stones, but even this is not enough to satisfy every officer's hunger.

I hope that we do inflict damage soon. I've never been more homesick in my life—homesick for Camp Grant?!

My warmest regards and love,

John Weldon

"The major wants all officers," Almy called to Weldon, who sat reading a three-month-old St. Louis paper.

The officers gathered on the banks of the stream cutting through the Cottonwood Creek canyon.

"Men, I've just been speaking with Nantaje," the major began, referring to one of the Apache scouts, "who says he can take us to the cave in the canyon on Salt River where he believes the Indians are. Only the strongest of our party should go. He says that the terrain is brutal and treacherous. Pack animals are out of the question as well as horses, of course. We will need to set up protection for those who must stay behind. I want breastworks constructed from our supplies and *aparejos*. Extend a picket line and tie the horses and mules. All of your men should set about preparing the weapons. Have them each take twenty extra cartridges on top of the normal supply. Weldon and Almy, see to it that the men get their rations and water. The scouts are cooking up the sick mule for themselves."

After readying their guns and drawing their shares of bacon, bread, and cartridges, the men drank one last cup of hot coffee before heading into the cold, clear night. Nantaje would move only when a certain star appeared in the big sky, so the men, anxious to warm up in the frigid air, stood around with their eyes up and their hands in pockets or armpits. By eight o'clock the party struck out, grateful for the opportunity to walk themselves into warmth. Their muscles loosened and their minds cleared as they exerted themselves on the rough-ridged terrain. If the sun rose before they could reach their destination, their silhouettes would get them slaughtered. A whispered command to lie down until the rear guard came up frustrated the progress of the limbered team, but no one groused. Even coughs were hidden in blankets.

Weldon appreciated the need for scouts but did not fully trust them and half expected to be led into a trap. While he lay there in waiting, he thought of Bourke and his growing respect and interest in the Indian way of life. It always seemed to Weldon that those who had everything often wanted to preserve or were inordinately impressed by people more primitive than themselves. Bourke agreed that Indian children would have to be civilized, but Weldon got the sense that Bourke wished for the Indians to stay just the same, at least until he was done being entertained by them and writing about them. Weldon saw soldiering and this growing love affair with the Apache ways as diametrically opposed. He would not get caught in the past. Life must go forward. The past crippled those who clung to it as he so often had—but no more.

The fires of Indians appeared as faint pink lights ahead. Archie MacIntosh arrived from the front. Almy and Weldon crawled to hear his intelligence report to the major. "Seems some Pima and white settlements were raided. We found a bunch of ponies, all foot-sore and hungry in a little nook. We also found what looked to be the remains of a small camp, but the Indians escaped. Maybe they were aware of us, sir."

The news spread along through the mass of men shivering on the ground wrapped in their blankets.

"They could be surrounding us right now!" Almy whispered nervously.

"These Indians are scoundrels," groaned Weldon who checked his ammunition again.

A form came crouching toward them. It was Lieutenant Ross. "Weldon, the major has ordered his best shots into the canyon. Come on then."

Weldon followed the scout Nantaje and about fifteen other men down the slippery earth as the light of first dawn traced the edges of the horizon. One slip on the jagged path and a man would be cut and dead at the bottom of a great drop. They descended, careful but quick, keeping their curses tightly between their lips.

Once down they followed a narrow path strewn with boulders. They kept low as they rounded a massive canyon wall. The precipice was hundreds of feet high. Within it at about three hundred feet was a cave, its opening obscured by the natural rock ramparts. At once they spotted a small party of men seemingly celebrating a night's raid. Their women tended the fire and things were festive with singing and ritualistic dancing before the quivering firelight which perfectly illuminated the warriors. The Apaches were protected from all angles and may have had some luck against the advance party if they had not been dancing and singing.

Without saying a word the soldiers readied their weapons waiting for the whispered order, "Ready, aim, FIRE!" and they shot. The great volley sounded and bounced against the walls of stone. Weldon aimed and aimed again trying to kill anyone who moved.

The Apaches in panic ran to the shelter of their cave, shooting arrows that landed haphazardly among the soldiers just as Major Brown brought up the rest of the command, ordering everyone to hide themselves among the boulders as they crawled and scurried to close in on both flanks of the cave. A foolish Apache fighter climbed to the crest of the canyon, laughing and taunting the men below. The backlit man made himself the perfect target for the soldiers, and they shot him full of holes, all claiming the hit as their own.

Arrows and bullets rained upon the soldiers who waited for further orders. Through an interpreter Major Brown ordered the cave dwellers to surrender and suffer no harm. Jeers and threats along with a flurry of arrows punctured the air.

"They say your soldiers crouching like rabbits will be meals for the vultures before the day is through," said the interpreter.

"Tell them to let their women and children come forward. Tell them they will be treated gently."

The interpreter sighed knowing that the Indians would never trust the soldiers and would never give up. He called to them anyway with only more shrieks of rage and threats as an answer. The women reloaded their men's weapons. The soldiers below could see their thin arms.

For a few minutes both sides weighed the situation. From where the soldiers hid to the entrance of the cave was a wall smooth as glass. A frontal assault would lose half the men as they reached the top. The Apache sent endless streams of arrows arcing over the soldiers in the front line hoping that an unsuspecting teamster or rear guard might be surprised.

Sharpshooters with their carbines aimed and ready set up in hospitable shelters to annoy any Indian who might show himself from behind the cave ramparts. The men formed in two lines. The second line was to show patience. Weldon called to the men near him, "Shoot as much as you like and aim for the interior ceiling of the cave. That should take out a bunch!"

The sound of ricocheting bullets bouncing with deadly randomness inside the cave was deafening. Arrows whirred all around as squaws handed their men the reloaded weapons. During the short intermissions, the eerie sound of women wailing over the dead echoed in the cavity. The soldiers' aim grew steadier, their shots taking their toll on the occupants of the cave. Cartridges lay strewn across every rock while the men shot and reloaded.

All at once the Apache grew tired of the cave.

"They're going to charge!" someone shouted.

The Apaches, a blur of furious bravado, rushed down a jagged slope toward the soldiers. Weldon leapt forward with the others. He heard someone yell, maybe it was Bourke. The crowd swarming over them meant to divert the soldiers' attention from the escape path of the Apaches who looked to be trying to surround their right flank.

An arrow nicked Weldon's ear. He could feel the tickle of blood coursing down his neck and beneath his flannel collar as he moved to stop the advance on the flank. A large and handsome warrior jumped in his path and aimed his army issue gun before Weldon could react, but the gun misfired. The Indian looked stupefied. He glanced at his bow almost apologetically before Weldon shot him.

A cool sharp sensation and then no sensation at all took Weldon's arm. He dropped his gun and bent to pick it up just as a private he'd reprimanded for his recklessness earlier bludgeoned the Apache responsible for piercing Weldon. Weldon scrambled up annoyed to find that the lance had rendered his right arm useless.

An Apache penetrated the line and jumped triumphantly upon a large boulder. He was surprised to meet the 40 carbines aimed at him in the rear. Ten men could claim a part in the kill.

Weldon stumbled behind a rock. The private wrapped his limp arm and glanced over the rocks to see how things were sorting themselves out. Quiet reigned for a strange minute.

"By golly, sir, there's a boy!"

Weldon pulled himself up to see. The men stopped to watch breathlessly as a boy no more than five years old wandered out into the fray. "They should have surrendered the children, those bastards," Weldon said, getting to his feet with the intention of rescuing the child, but his men pulled him back as arrows and shot crowded the air.

"What the hell are you doing?" one shouted. "You don't even have your gun! Look!"

They turned to watch Nantaje run the gauntlet toward the child, who'd been knocked off his feet by a ricochet bullet to the head. He was alive but stunned as the scout carried him down. The soldiers cheered as the wails from the women in the cave reached fever pitch.

No more Indians bounded over the ramparts. The battle stalled. The soldiers would have to storm the cave. Major Brown had sent Captain Burns and Company G along a different path under the assumption that maybe the Apache raiders had split off in another direction. Burns had marched his men on a fruitless all-night search, finally circling back to camp. His men were alerted to the fight by the roar of the carbines. Racing up and leaning over the canyon, Burns understood that the forces below could not train their bullets to the back of the cave, where the rest of the living huddled. As the men watched from below in the kind of amusement that could only be felt in the surreal heat of battle, Captain Burns' men, using their comrades' suspenders, were lowered with carbines loaded over the edge of the canyon on their bellies. They delivered surprise and death to those below. Some men cheered like happy children while others silently watched the scene play out. As a finale, the men from above pushed boulders down on to the hapless combatants and their families with crushing precision. The Indians had no haven. The men from below fired up again as the boulder assault gained momentum. Men gleefully forced the rocks from their ancient seats, sending them crashing in a bewildering cacophony.

Major Brown ordered the soldiers to cease fire and signaled for the company overhead to hold back their boulders. The noon sun shone overhead as the soldiers charged up over the parapets to the carnage within. Weldon had exchanged his carbine for Almy's sidearm and made his way into the cave from the path, unable to clamber over the jagged rock with the frontal assault of men because of his useless arm. He stood over the dying men who might in desperation make one last move on a soldier's life. Blood from his wound dripped from the tips of his fingers and onto the cracked skull of a small girl, so he moved. "They never protect their own," he mumbled.

No one celebrated as they shifted rocks off the dead men, women, and children so recently alive and vital. A medicine man who had impressed the soldiers with his fortitude and bravery lay smashed beyond repair, and for him they were truly sorry. Children with innocence and fear still full on their open-eyed faces had shattered skulls and crushed chests.

Apache scouts sifted through the enemies' things, eating from the plentiful stores of jerky and mescal. The soldiers' prejudice kept most of them from joining in the feast.

Bourke came alongside of Weldon. "Sad really."

Weldon glanced at him. "What? What's sad?"

"All of this, the children."

Weldon laughed. "You're not serious, I hope."

Bourke looked shocked. "Come now, Weldon. We've won here. Show some humanity."

"Don't tell me how to be. You are far too sentimental for your own good about these savages."

"But the children ..."

"Children who would have fought right beside the adults in time," Weldon said.

"You have no hope for them?" Bourke asked.

Weldon looked around, noticing the blood on the walls and dripping from his throbbing arm. "I don't know. I just don't care what happens to them."

"But they had no choice in all of this."

Weldon glared at him. "Very few of us are given real choices in life."

Almy interrupted. "Major Brown fears an attack from another band. The squaws say they are nearby. We have to round up the prisoners and try to help the injured quickly. Decide which of them can survive a march. Weldon! Your arm—I'd hate to see the looks of it under that wrap. How does it feel?"

"Fine," Weldon lied, sweating in pain.

"This blasted army doesn't think enough of us here in Arizona to send proper medical help!" Almy unwrapped Weldon's arm. "Well, it's deep anyway."

"Just tighten the bandage, Almy," Weldon ordered irritably. "Please."

***

Dear Mrs. Weldon,

We are far up in the mountains now—the Sierra Ancha and the Matitzal present quite a lot of challenges for our merry little group. This is my last sheet of paper and it is devoted to you.

Although we have had our successes, the campaign is far from over and is made more difficult with the outbreak of an epizootic among the horses and mules.

The other day some poor settlers just over from Wales or England were taken down by Apache raiders outside of Wickenburg. We arrived just too late, but saw the men tied to cacti and riddled with arrows. One had broken free and fallen. He must have rolled in agony because the ends of the arrows were broken off on the sand. Their horses and cattle were killed or taken over the Bradshaw Mountains into the Tonto basin and up to the Apache stronghold on Turret Butte.

We pursued them and scaled the mountains on our bellies so as to make no noise. We surprised them so thoroughly at midnight that many a young Apache jumped to his death in trying to escape us. We are demoralizing them, but do not know when the end might come.

Lieutenant Weldon sits beside me unable to write because of his arm, but sends you his warm regards.

From your friend and well-wisher,

Lieutenant John Bourke

Chapter Forty-One

Katherine watched as the soldier on mail duty, a slight, blond teenager, trotted on his pony into camp. It had been over three months since John's last letter. If she was not so afraid of leaving Arizona on her own, she would have been in Englewood by now. Instead she filled her days with mindless chores and small lessons for Willy but had time enough to worry. What had happened to John's arm? Why no more word? Surely he must realize her concern.

This postman had been lucky. Despite the natives and the terrain he had remained on duty for over a year—quite an accomplishment. He liked his job. It kept him from garrison duty, but he did not like to see Mrs. Weldon each time he arrived, standing in the sun with her hands shielding her eyes and waiting for letters that did not come. Most times the men cheered the arrival of the post. Mrs. Weldon dampened his spirits. The postman pulled his faded blue bandana from his face and chatted from his high perch to a private who had run up to ask if there was any word from his mail-order bride-to-be—there was. The happy soldier would be out of the service in a month and planned to get land to farm with his small savings. Others came out and shared news. The postman had a lot of it for a change. He donated magazines and papers to the soldiers' collection and tied his horse outside the commissary away from the other horses.

Katherine watered her small garden with Eliza's bath water. The postman walked up. "Mrs. Weldon, good day to you," he said, pulling his hat from his head.

She nodded, wondering why he went out of his way to greet her. The postman always seemed aggravated when she asked him to check his bags one more time for a letter.

"Mrs. Weldon, I have good news. Peace has been made with the Apaches."

"Are you certain?" She clasped her hands.

"Yes," he replied. "I was at Camp Verde when everyone came in. Cha-lipin was there and said they would fight no more."

"Oh, what wonderful news!"

He laughed, happy to give her pleasure. "Yes, it was a spectacular scene. The poor chief said they had never been afraid of the Americans alone, but now that their own people were against them it was too much. The Apaches found no rest all winter with the scouts tracking them and the soldiers following and cleaning out their winter food and shelter. They have agreed to try the settled life and already under Lieutenant Schuyler they were beginning an irrigation ditch."

Katherine hesitated, taking up her broom with white knuckles. "Did you see ...?"

"Yes, Lieutenant Weldon was there ..."

"Did you ask him if he had any letters?"

"Mrs. Weldon, do you think I'd be so cruel seeing you month after month waiting and not seek him out?"

She laughed. "So you have something for me then? Please give it over!"

"No, you misunderstand. I spoke with him, but there is no letter. Lieutenant Weldon told me to tell you he'd be home soon."

The postman hated seeing her crestfallen expression.

"The lieutenant said nothing else?"

"No, I'm afraid not, ma'am, but he was with the other officers."

"Doing what, that he couldn't write a small note?" she cried.

The postman stepped back, shaking his head and kicking himself for having said anything. "Well, ma'am, there were citizens giving them a banquet, I think."

"You think?" She asked angrily and with suspicion. "I'm sure you know. And who was in attendance? Were there women?"

He put his hands up afraid she might push or hit him. "Well yes, but ... Lieutenant Weldon ..." He stopped, flustered. His words were making matters worse. The banquet had seemed innocent enough to him, but any description of it would serve only to hurt this lonesome military wife.

"Thank you for your news!" she said, putting an end to the man's painful handling of the information. She turned away and with no further words slammed her door shut.

The next day Weldon arrived home. He shaved this time. It felt odd yet appropriate to knock on the door after six months away. A wreath of chili peppers hung from it, and the forget-me-not borders were in full bloom under the shade of the ramada. Eastern papers sent from Scott and Sarah sat neatly stacked beneath a bleached animal skull. Two small pairs of moccasins lay beside a fishing pole and a homemade popgun abandoned next to the door.

John listened first to the voices within. They had their own little world without him. He wanted to be let back into it. He knocked. A chair moved, and Eliza opened the door with big eyes. Before Weldon could say a word, Eliza lifted her arms to him and cried, "Papa!"

He patted her head. "No, Elly, I can't pick you up."

The perceived rebuff did not go over well, and Eliza marched off in tears. John stepped in and grinned while pulling his hat from his head. "Kate!"

William and Katherine remained seated and refused to look at him. Weldon kicked his things to the corner and sat opposite them. "Now what's wrong?" he asked impatiently.

She pounded her fist on the table, rattling the dishes and the children. "*Now what*? Is that all you can say? As if we have asked too much of you?"

"No, I didn't mean it that way. I just expected you'd be happy to see me."

"Are you happy to see us?" she asked.

"Kate, of course!"

"How could you leave us here for six months with no word?"

"Five and a half months—I did write to you."

"One letter at Christmas!"

"Didn't you get Bourke's letter explaining ..."

"You mean *letters*? Yes, I did. So good of you to send your regards."

"Bourke sent you more than one letter? I don't understand why."

"Maybe he realized how lonely I was while you were enjoying your banquets!"

"I thought you'd be proud of me, Kate."

"I'm happy for you. The men and women of Arizona love you now. You didn't need to convince me that you're a good soldier, but I hoped you were a good husband!"

"Well, I've tried my best!" he said indignantly.

"Your best is pathetic! If an acquaintance manages three letters and you can only write *one*, what does that say?"

Weldon stood, kicking the chair out of his way. "Maybe if you bothered to look at me you'd see it's been impossible for me to write you a personal letter. Since Christmas my arm is destroyed. I have no use of it and would rather it be taken off it pains me so! I refuse to let Bourke or any of the others know my relationship to you. It's private! But of course you think the worst of me!"

William leapt from his chair, six months taller and with long hair bleached from the sun. "Papa, please don't leave us! We were so scared for you and Mother too, and she killed a big cat that tried to eat us, and Northy up and died, and Elly was sick!"

John crouched down, and Willy wrapped his arms around his father's neck. Elly stood behind John with her hand on his shoulder. John looked to Katherine, who stood above him. Still clutching Willy with his good arm, he rose to face her. "Kate, I'm so sorry. I got carried away, and I did think that it would all end sooner. I didn't want to ask for any help. I was afraid they'd send me home before the mission was completed. I should have thought more about your feelings."

"You should have. We missed you," she cried, wiping her eyes and nose on her apron.

"I did miss you too! But for the first time I've been successful at something on my own."

"And I'm proud and happy for you, but what about us? I don't think I can stand this army life any longer—being shut away for months while you go on your adventures. During the war I could stand Simon being away only because I knew the war must end, and he wrote! But now I see that this is how the rest of our lives will be, and it's torture!"

Weldon's face whitened. "Then maybe you should go home, Katherine. I can't promise you anything better than this."

"But wouldn't you at least consider another line of work?" she begged.

He stiffened. "No, I can't and I won't. I'm good at this—really good after all of these years. I can't start from the bottom again. I won't do it. I thought you supported me!"

"I do support you! You know that. But what about me? Who supports me when you're gone?"

"Well, you have to support yourself a little I'm afraid."

"How dare you be so arrogant with me? If this is your new successful attitude then I'm greatly disappointed!"

"Kate, I am not being arrogant! But you knew when you married me who I was. I don't understand why now, when things are finally going well, you behave like this."

She threw up her hands. "Because you forgot me, John! I waited and waited for even one scribbled line, one sign that you were thinking of me, of us!"

"Katherine! Look here!" He pulled clumsily at his haversack with his good hand. Papers fell onto the floor, and she picked them up. She laughed and cried as she read the indecipherable letters or at least attempts in smudged ink and pencil—forty or fifty of them.

"I would never trust another man with my feelings for you, Katherine Weldon, so I waited to tell you myself."

Katherine smothered him with kisses before sitting him down to undress his arm. While the lance left only a small scar on the skin, his arm was misshapen now. John asked hopefully for her opinion. "It doesn't look so bad," she assured him with a weak smile he didn't believe. "And now that you're home you can be more careful with it. You'll see, it will be fine."

Willy came back over but didn't get too close. The weird shape of the arm troubled him. "Papa, did you bring us anything?"

John laughed. "Nope."

"That's okay, Papa," the boy said timidly, patting Weldon's shoulder. John pulled him close with his good arm, and Willy smiled a toothless grin.

"Sakes alive, all your teeth gone at once?"

Willy gave his mother a worried look, but she smiled at him so he explained. "There was a boy who come through with his uncle, and he wanted to see the horses, and he set to teasin' the naughty old Indian pony, and I made him stop and got kicked just the same—stupid horse!"

"Katherine," John complained, "I told you he's too young for the horses by himself..."

"Well, those teeth needed to come out anyway, and William learned his lesson, I think, not to let strange boys at the horses." Katherine was matter-of-fact about it. The incident happened months ago.

"William, I know I can't stop you," John said, "but I do wish you'd give up the riding."

"John, you're being too silly. Willy is already an excellent rider. It was just an accident," Katherine said and kissed John again. "Children, we'll make Papa a nice meal while he cleans himself up." She turned to him. "Will you need help?"

"I'm fine—and hungry," he said with a smile, but his arm was on fire.

William skipped to the wash basin. I'll help you, Papa! Guess what? Mother can make real good biscuits now and muffins with currants. We like them now, don't we, Mother?"

Eliza spoke. "And she made a cake once, and it rose up real big with fancy sugar too!"

"And Elly ate it all up on us when we was sleepin' and it's not fair she didn't get in trouble," Willy complained.

John distracted his son with a tickle and turned back to Katherine. He came up behind her and grabbed her in a gentle neck hold. "I'm darn proud of the way you've done things, Kate, and the way the children are." He kissed her neck.

She pushed him to get washed, noticing how thin he was again, and set to putting a big meal together. The children fought over how a story should be told, and John laughed while intercepting their playful punches. Katherine tried to stick to the task at hand but couldn't keep her eyes off her husband. "Children, mind your father's arm now!"

John looked in their little mirror giving himself the once over. "Kate, I do believe I've got silver sprouting in my hair."

"I didn't think you were so vain," she said.

He turned to her. His smile had grown and spread to his eyes and body since Crook came to Arizona, as if the work had finally relaxed that something he used to hold so tightly. Even with a bad arm he looked happier than she had ever seen him. "Oh, no, sweetheart, I'd be glad to have a few grey hairs. I look forward to our old days together—it'll be nice. Do you mind cutting this hair for me sometime? It's annoying me."

She embraced him and put her hand through his wet mop. "Any time you want, my dear. But what will you do for me in return?"

Weldon raised his brow. "Anything you like."

"You know exactly what I like, John Weldon."

"I'm happy to oblige. We can save the haircut for tomorrow."

"Mommy, what's that smell?" Elly asked, tugging on Katherine's sleeve.

"Oh darn! It's the beans! They'll be burnt to a cinder!" Katherine cried. She ran to the stove and found them a blackened mush.

"Who cares about the beans? Don't worry," John assured her, though achingly hungry.

"I care! You look wasted!"

He pulled her over and sat her on his lap. "Come here, pet. How did you ever get so beautiful?"

"But I'm the worst cook!"

"Now you know that's a lie, and you feed me in so many other ways!"

"But, John, putting aside silly romance, you are skin and bones. I worry about you all the time, but my worrying does nothing to improve my abilities."

He laughed. "But I like our silly romance and aside from our wonderfully silly children it's all I care about. If you died tomorrow do you think I'd talk about your biscuit-making skills?"

"Thank you, Mr. Weldon, for killing me off!"

"You're welcome," he said, giving her a playful smack. "Come on, I'm sure there's something we can throw together for supper. How's the garden doing?"

Katherine and the children looked at each other in dismay.

"It didn't seem to want to grow up, Papa," Eliza said and walked out the door.

Weldon shook his head at how old the girl acted.

"Papa, our lettuce by the door in the pot ain't too bad," William pointed out.

Katherine perked up having forgotten this one small success. "Oh yes, and the nasturtium that Mother sent has some flowers too."

"A salad sounds fine, and your biscuits smell like heaven," said John.

"The biscuits!" Katherine pulled the Dutch oven from the fire and danced—they were full and brown and not burnt a bit.

Evening came and a scant breeze rolled its way through the ramadas, and the little chime the children made of an old pot and a few spoons sang a faraway song as the family ate their meal of salad, the last can of oysters from San Francisco, and the biscuits outdoors.

"What's this about killing a cat?"

"Oh, it was exciting and mighty scary, Papa!" Willy exclaimed. "We was sleepin' and a noise woke Mother and me too and a big old cat was just about to pounce and Mother banged him on the head and kilt him! His eyeballs almost popped out!"

"Willy! Must you?" Katherine scolded him. "I haven't been able to sleep a wink since that night, John!"

"Well, I bet Crook will enjoy that story!"

"He's not here to stay, I hope—he intimidates me," Katherine said.

"Well, he's not so bad." Weldon smiled, thinking of his promised promotion.

A coyote howled and then another, and the family grew quiet to listen and take in the purple sky. John stretched his legs in front of him one over the other and pulled the hair behind his ear. Katherine batted his hand with a grin and took hold of it. "What's worrying you, dear?"

"Oh, nothing. I forgot to tell you ... but it's something foolish."

"What is it?"

"A young newsman was out with us, and we got to talking about the war. He was too young to have fought himself but was so full of curiosity about the little things—the small details of camp life back then. Anyway ... I don't know what made me say it. It's a stupid idea, I guess, but he seemed to like it ... that maybe I could write ... just a small article for the paper—his paper—about day to day life in camp. I don't know exactly what."

"You're gonna be a writer, Papa?" William asked.

"No, maybe just one little article for the paper," Weldon said with a grin.

"You beat all, John Weldon! You'd make a fine writer." Katherine kissed his hand.

"I don't know ... do you really think so?"

"I'm sure you can! It's exciting to think of your name in the papers as a writer!"

Weldon pulled his hand from hers and stretched his arm around her shoulders. "For a lark anyway, that's all," he mused, running his fingers over her arm. "Maybe I'll write about the different shelters we had. No, maybe the food. Oh and, Kate, I hope you don't mind, but I told him I'd send pictures—I thought you might draw them out."

"What do you mean?" she asked. "I can't draw."

"I like your little sketches, and I could describe things, and you could draw them like you always do anyway." He struggled to reach for her sketchbook lying on the table, but Willy raced to get it for him and put it on his lap. Suddenly they all realized how difficult it would be for John to do anything, let alone write with the damaged arm. Weldon tried to ignore their worried looks. "See, just like this. Your horses are fine and the soldiers too, but we'd have to make sure the details of the men were right—not like the way we are out here. It'll be a fun project!"

"I don't know. I think your writing should stand alone."

"No, I won't do it if you don't do your part—that's how I imagined it. I don't like standing alone anyway—not when I have you."

"Don't smile like that. You're such a charmer—when did that happen, I'd like to know?"

He winked at her and had William light his pipe for him. Eliza had fallen asleep right in her chair beneath the stars. A horse whinnied in the corral, and the moon rose, softening the tiny desert flowers that bordered their porch floor. Willy hung around his father's neck, asking him about this and that man, the scouts and the stars, and John played with his son's hands answering every single question until his even, solid voice made the boy slow and dreamy. William stumbled to the cot he liked to sleep on under the ramada and fell asleep.

The soft purr of the children's breathing drifted out to the desert, and the parents went inside. "My, Kate, look at the bed," John said.

The patchwork pillow shams and the calico duvet cover she made, even with their flaws, brightened the place.

She helped him out of his loose blouse. "Hmm, my arm makes things difficult."

"Don't worry. If we set our minds to it, we can make things work all right," she said as she undid her corset and slid from her underthings.

Weldon still had one good hand and knew where she liked it best. "Don't turn down the lamp, Kate. I want to see you."

She helped him into bed and got on top of him. She had never lost the belly after the last child, and it bothered her, but John didn't mind. "I'm old, grey and crippled, and you still keep looking better and better—now that's unfair," he joked.

"You are obviously losing your eyesight, Mr. Weldon," she said, laughing.

Weldon moved his hand over her curves. "And you know, if they print our article and use the pictures I'll get paid, and I'll buy you something real nice." He heaved a happy sigh.

"Won't we both be getting paid if I do the pictures?" she asked, a little annoyed.

He gently pushed her off of him so he could take off his boots. She tried to help, but he waved her away. "Well, yes, of course. I hadn't thought of it, but it's all the same anyway." He tickled her ribcage.

"It's not all the same because you'll spend the money without asking."

He threw off his boot. "Are you saying you don't trust me with our money?" he said with a sly smile. "Why can't you let me dream that I can buy you nice things without spoiling it?"

"That's not fair."

"Nothing's fair, my dear."

"No, it's not fair that you get to decide and buy me some impractical thing while I can buy you nothing at all."

"Land sakes, you know how to wreck a good time."

"John Weldon, don't be all sulky now. I feel funny taking gifts when you go with nothing."

"I have lots of things. All I want." He was still smiling.

"You need new boots."

"These ones are lucky."

She climbed back on top of him and kissed his neck hard. "Did you see any pretty girls at the banquets?"

"None as pretty as you," he said, tugging her hair playfully. "Are you sure you want no fine gifts from me?"

"What are you talking about?"

He grinned.

"What?"

"Crook has given us Christmas, Kate. I'm taking you home for next Christmas."

Chapter Forty-Two

Simon appeared first, a bit weather-beaten and fuller around the waist. Simon wouldn't say, but Sarah guessed there must be a woman in his life these days—she hoped. Sarah could depend on Simon for letters and was an expert at reading between lines. Since they were not sure when Katherine would arrive, Sarah and Scott made dubious excuses for not leaving the house, sending Simon on all sorts of tedious errands. Simon reluctantly complied, being just as eager for the little family's arrival.

Simon showed some impatience with Sarah when she sent him off to ask Edna Price down the road for the recipe she had promised to give Sarah for cranberry jelly. He muttered a few choice words as he exited the kitchen and buttoned his coat against the cold, looking up at the sky for signs of snow. A hired car made its way up Demarest and into the drive. Simon trotted alongside like a young boy until the horses hung their heads and came to a stop. Weldon's long leg dangled out as the door opened. As he climbed down his eyes lit at the sight of Simon.

"Weldon! So glad to see you!" Simon said, grinning at how solid and well his friend had become even with his arm in a sling.

"And you, captain," Weldon answered with a shy smile. He turned as William jumped from the coach wildly but righted himself like a cat. William stood before his uncle in silent awe. Simon grabbed him and set him upon his shoulders. "You remember me? I'm your favorite uncle."

"You're my only uncle," William said.

Simon shook him in mock annoyance. "Smart as a steel trap this one is. Now let's see the sis."

Weldon reached back. "Come now, Eliza, someone wants to see you."

A small, white face appeared with round blue eyes and full rosy cheeks in a navy bonnet and coat. John lifted Eliza in his good arm and looked toward Simon proudly. A rush of gratitude for his friend swept over Weldon, with a small bit of guilt for the resentment he sometimes harbored toward him. "It's so good to see you again," he said solemnly.

Simon gave him a wink and turned his attention to Eliza. "She's gorgeous—they both are. You look happy, Weldon," Simon observed with some jealousy.

Katherine came around behind the carriage and put her hands over her brother's eyes.

"Weldon, did you bring me home a lovely Mexican?" Simon asked.

Katherine slapped his head, and he turned to greet her. Her youthful looks had gone. "Katie, my God, you're so lovely and well. I'm completely overcome. The two of you are the picture of happiness."

Katherine and John smiled.

"You look tired, Simon," she said, pulling at his collar. "And what is that rash on your neck?"

Simon pushed her off mildly embarrassed. "It's nothing to worry yourself about, Katie. Now let's go surprise the old people!" He grabbed Willy's hand. The bags were left in the drive for later.

Scott and Sarah debated plans to demolish a lovely meadow in the center of Englewood to make way for new traffic, unaware that their guests had arrived. Simon interrupted them with a smug expression.

"Well, where is the recipe?" Sarah asked, still agitated with Scott.

Before Simon could announce the family, the smaller members announced themselves with their talk. Sarah jumped from her chair past Simon, who pulled himself out of the way just in time with a chuckle. Scott followed at a more dignified pace.

"Mother!" Katherine cried and embraced her. The children eyed the scene with suspicion, and John hung back with a stiff smile plastered on his face. Scott stretched past his daughter and awkwardly shook Weldon's left hand. Katherine interrupted when she took her father in her arms and kissed him.

Sarah pulled the grandchildren to her, quickly kissed John and set to taking the children out of their coats. "Oh my, Scott, look at the curls on Eliza!" she cried, pulling at the girl's sable locks.

Scott smiled, his arms folded over his chest.

"And little Willy! You're not a baby anymore!" Sarah said.

"Of course I'm not!" William answered darkly.

The grandparents took his attitude in stride and dragged the two children into the kitchen for cakes and cambric tea. Katherine and John followed, hand in hand. John loved this kitchen and tried not to compare it to his own. Simon stood at the kitchen window pouring a drink from his flask. Katherine eyed him with her old grin.

"What's that look for, Katie?" he asked after taking a long sip from his glass.

"You seem different," she said.

"We've all gotten older, I'd say," he said, "but Arizona and its privations have done the two of you no harm—except for your arm, Weldon. It seems someone is feeding you well for a change, though. Hired a dog-robber with your promotion?"

"No, we're done with that. Katherine has the job of taking care of my appetite now. She is becoming an excellent cook," Weldon said warmly.

Sarah perked up unable to imagine her daughter in the kitchen.

Katherine blushed. "Oh, John exaggerates! For a long while it was John who did the best cooking!"

"Weldon, a cook? I find that hard to believe!" Simon laughed. "I remember you eating raw pork belly to avoid cooking. I imagined the two of you raising your children on hardtack and coffee."

William interrupted, "I like hardtack!"

The adults laughed.

"Kate just doesn't have confidence in her ability," John explained, swinging her hand.

"Well, we all have our talents, I suppose," Sarah said. "Our Katie was never one for homemaking."

John began to speak in Katherine's defense, but Katherine cut him short with a sharp squeeze of his hand. Sarah brought pies—a vinegar and a custard—from the pantry and large powdery shortbread cookies for the children. Eliza ran to the table and grabbed a cookie for each hand, licking both before William pulled her away. Sarah motioned to him that it was all right. "I made them for you two. There's plenty. Go ahead."

William took one of the beautiful delicacies and stood by his father.

"You all look so full of vim and vigor! Oh but, Katie, you're not protecting your face from the sun. It will be leather when you're my age and then what will John do? Really it looks common to be so swarthy." Sarah was leaving no room for uncomfortable silences.

Scott cleared his throat, "Simon, we invited your Uncle Phillip and his wife to Christmas dinner—very successful on Wall Street."

"So you've said, Father. I'm interested to see them after all these years. I'd say Weldon and I will have quite a lot in common with the old financier."

Weldon, distracted by Eliza, glanced over at the sound of his name. "Simon?"

"Oh, nothing, Weldon. My father is just speaking of finance. Something you and I know little about."

Scott's furrowed brow proclaimed his annoyance at Simon for bringing Weldon into the conversation. "Son, if you ever settle down and start a family, a spot at the paper or with one of my associates in the city could be arranged. This wandering, vagabond life of a soldier is showing its wear on you. Haven't you had enough of it yet?"

"No, in fact, I haven't," Simon answered, pouring a sizable drink from his sizable flask to spite his father, who looked on in disgust.

"The supplying of liquor by white men to the Indians has led not only to the degradation of the Indians but also to the suppliers," Scott offered as food for thought.

"Come now, let's not get into this again. It's not my problem if white men sell firewater. If my drinking were a problem I would have only myself to blame. Luckily for me I own nothing of great value to sign over when I'm drunk." Simon's voice was more biting than they were used to.

"I hope you say these things just to shock me," Scott said, motioning to Sarah for more tea.

"I find it shocking how easy it is for you to dole out sympathy for the Indians in the west while you live on land once populated by illiterate, naked, and free natives," Simon said.

"It's not possible for me to take responsibility for the actions of our government and the people before I was born," Scott said.

"Well, that's convenient then. Personally, I don't much care for the full bloods I've met. From the beginning of time, those with better weapons and stronger cultures have had their way, and that's how it should be. We enjoy modern conveniences and great new inventions not to mention beautifully printed books, Father, because we have intelligent progressive thinkers and men of action. Even the Indians want our modern conveniences. Just like anyone else, they taste the future and they like the parts that make them stronger."

"So are you saying that since their cultures are inferior, it's reason enough to exterminate them?"

"First of all, I didn't say exterminate. Assimilation is quite a different thing. Isn't assimilation the very thing you espouse and support for the freedmen? After hearing what the Sioux did in Minnesota and then to Fetterman and his men—gouging out their eyes and chopping off body parts (and they do this to their Indian enemies too), I think they're barbarians. The ones that won't change should be shot."

"So you have fallen under General Sherman's spell? The only good Indian is a dead one?"

"I can't speak for the general, but I assume Sherman said that in anger. He's a soldier's general, and it's his men who carry out the work Easterners decide upon—and soldiers who get killed for it. I have little sympathy for Indians who sell out their own people, rape, pillage, and murder."

"And when you kill it's noble?" Scott asked scornfully.

"Father, you considered it noble when I killed to save the Union."

"It's not noble to kill women and children in their camps for the winter," Scott declared.

"Indians kill when they please, and their innocent women hide them and live off their plunder. There's no such thing as a neutral Indian—either they come in to the reservations and admit their defeat or they're at war."

"What is this war? I have no need to be a part of robbing from the Indians," Scott said with an air of superiority.

"Father, you are such a humanitarian when the humans are far from you. The Indians live a primitive life. I will admit that some of their ways hold great charm and beauty just as I might find a drawing done by Willy or Eliza charming, but I would not compare them to a Michelangelo or a Delacroix."

Katherine and Sarah smiled at Simon's references.

Simon continued. "The Indians can't keep their primitive lifestyles. Enough of them see that already and embrace our modern life—especially our guns. Anyway, the sheer number of settlers will wipe out their old ways."

"Well, immigration should be stopped. We have enough people," Scott said.

John joined in, "I think, Mr. McCullough, that it's easy for you to s-s-say. You have a comfortable spot here in Englewood with all the right connections. Not everyone in the world is so lucky. Besides, you talk about finance and don't seem to realize the money to be made as a country with the West opened up."

"I've worked hard, Mr. Weldon, for all I have," Scott said testily. "That land out there is being opened for miners and railroad moguls and you know it."

"There are plenty of families taking those trains out west," Simon said, "and making nice little lives for themselves that they could never make anywhere else. They work as hard as you with the threat of bad weather and Indians to boot." Simon searched the kitchen for a bottle to share with the rest of the family. "And with our tiny army we couldn't stop them all if we wanted to."

"Well, is it right to send soldiers in to take land from peaceful people?" Scott asked.

"Soldiers don't take the land from anyone. We're asked to protect both the Indians and the white settlers, and both sides are rarely satisfied with our efforts. The government's vacillating policies and half-hearted attempts at peace with only vague notions of the true situation in the West do the most damage. It doesn't take settlers long to overstep boundaries and to pour into what seems to most of them unpopulated land. And it doesn't take the Indians—the agency Indians—long to assist their warrior friends, and when violence breaks out the soldiers get the job of sorting things out." Simon poured his father some whiskey.

"I don't reckon all Indians are peace-loving people either," Weldon added.

Simon laughed. "Weldon, always the master of the understatement. The Sioux and the Cheyenne have terrorized their Indian brethren for ages. Life is for the strongest. You conquer, you make the rules. Even now the tribes plot against each other. Our form of government and its reliance on clear rules of law could bring peace to these tribes if they chose it, but they won't—not all of them. What annoys me are the friends of the noble savage who insist on giving guns to *friendly* Indians for hunting purposes—hunting soldiers is more like it. I wonder what the philanthropists drink at their meetings in New York and Philadelphia. Didn't Indians hunt quite well for themselves before American weapons came along?"

"Son, the colored men and the Indians deserve something more dignified than your contempt."

"Treating them like eternal victims keeps them nothing more than people worthy of contempt," Simon countered.

Scott turned to his son-in-law, "Weldon, may I ask your take on the Indian problem? My son seems to lean toward complete extermination of the race."

Simon frowned. "That is not what I said or meant."

Scott dismissed Simon and looked to Weldon, who squirmed under Scott's gaze.

"Well, I agree with the captain that coddling grown men—Indian, colored, or otherwise—is wrong. People should be judged on their merit alone. The Indians don't consider themselves a single or united race—which is a good thing for the army. It's gonna be tough to civilize them quickly, but it can be done. The young warriors are the most trying. But there are some Apaches who are ready for peace."

Simon guffawed. "Do you really believe that?"

Weldon continued, "General Crook is doing a good job convincing the Apaches to try. He's not easy on them, but he's fair. Some of the old chiefs and their young men make our lives difficult because they don't respect rules and order. They continue to come into the agencies, and then when the weather suits them or they're tired of rations, out again they go to annoy the settlers. They don't care that they bring danger and retaliation to their people."

"What about the settlers? Aren't they mostly responsible for the Indians' anger?" Scott asked.

"Well, it's not all settlers, not even most," Weldon explained. "There are fortune seekers, but you must realize that in the southwest people of all colors live lawlessly.

They've all had a hand in the troubles. But Crook is working to improve the Indians' lot."

"Crook seems an interesting character from what I've read in the papers," Scott said.

"He rubs a lot of people the wrong way in the army." Simon shook his head.

"The general whipped our department into shape and now may do the same for the Indians," John said. "They've planted acres of crops. It would be a shame if the government moves to consolidate the agencies. As I see it, the challenge is to convince the young bucks that warfare is not the only way to gain stature in the world."

Scott chuckled. "This must be an interesting notion for you, my friend."

John bristled. Katherine squeezed his hand. "Why do you say that, Mr. McCullough?"

"Oh, well, it was a joke. They must wonder if farming is such a manly pursuit, why are you not at it? The Indians must find it curious seeing one of their own in a lieutenant's uniform aiming to improve his station in life."

Katherine pulled at John attempting to distract him.

"Mr. McCullough, sir, if any of them ever confused me as one of their own I'd quickly set them right. As I've already said, if you were listening, each group regards itself as a distinct nation, but even within those groups individuals make their own decisions and alliances. In fact Crook gets most of his scouts from the tribes he sets out to bring in. They have no trouble siding with whoever seems to be winning at the moment. I, on the other hand, have always considered myself first an American, and I'm uncertain of why you feel it your constant duty to strike blows at my soundness or right to do as others do—such as your son."

"Oh, let me make myself plain," Scott said. "I'm not at all happy with Simon's choice in career. It's beneath him. I'm sure you, like most people, consider it an honor to serve in our military. Simon is cut of better stuff—or so I thought. I just wondered how you squared being an Indian with killing them."

"I am a soldier first. I respect the history and the discipline of a soldier's life. My father's family has always served in the military—the U.S. and the British before that. I don't see myself as an Indian or a savage because I never lived that way—neither did my father. I am a citizen of the United States. I had little choice in careers, but I have always taken my work seriously. While it's of course untrue that people are born equal, I do believe that everyone is entitled to better themselves in this country if they choose. That is what I have chosen, and I am proud of everything I've accomplished without the help of a prosperous family. How do I feel about killing Indians? Those who are stupid enough to take up arms when it's clear they are defeated

by the military and the force of population must be put in their place for the common good, and if they have any sense they will do as many have already done—mix
with and become Americans. The peace we fight for will benefit everyone who takes
advantage of it." Weldon took a deep breath and continued. "You people in the East
hatch up utopian plans and overly sentimental notions about Indians. They're not
all going to thank you for your concern. It's the Easterners who promise the Indians things that will never get through congressional appropriations, and when the
Indians get angry it's the settlers who pay, and we're sent in. For you it's just another
interesting topic over drinks, it's a game of chess." Weldon colored with embarrassment at the attention he had brought to himself. He caught Katherine staring up at
him and was surprised to see a look of pride on her face.

"Well done, Weldon," Scott said. "That's the most I've ever heard from you at
one time, and you make some sense, although you're too easy on your soldiers and
a fair bit too rough on us Easterners. We may not be among the Indians, but we are
benefited by a cool distance for perspective. Very nice."

Weldon felt like a schoolboy praised by his master. It was condescending, but he
could not help enjoy being taken seriously.

Sarah allowed herself to breathe again. Even the children stood at attention, understanding by their father's tone that they should stay quiet and let him finish.

"Men, shall we go for a smoke?" Scott suggested.

Simon moved first. John gave Katherine a conflicted look but followed the men.
Katherine giggled. Whenever she was not holding John's hand it was in his pocket
or hair. John was awkward but she loved that about him. Eliza reached for another
cookie, but Katherine slapped her hand with a smile, "Grammy will spoil you!"

"Oh, Katie, let the skinny little thing eat her fill!" Sarah gave her granddaughter
another cookie and kissed her. "My goodness, dear, that gave me an all-over feeling!
I feared they might come to blows and ruin Christmas—our first together in I don't
know how long!" Sarah burst into tears, hugging the children. Eliza squirmed, fear-
ful of this big crying woman.

Katherine embraced her mother. "Mother, how I wish you could live nearby! I
miss you so!"

"Arizona is just too far," Sarah sniffed. "You deprive a grandmother her little
joys. Ah, but they're here now, and there's no use in blubbering. I'm just glad you're
here safe and sound. I never imagined I'd have a child in the army, but now the army
has taken my whole family. It's been hard to read the papers. I thought I'd be done
with that after the war."

"Mother, I'm very safe. It helps to be surrounded by armed men, I suppose." Katherine laughed.

Sarah looked at her as if she'd gone mad. "But the children—the heat and the rowdy men—I worry for them."

Katherine felt brave and proud of her adventures now. In Arizona there were so many reckless and freewheeling people. Her steps were tiny next to theirs, but she imagined her dramas would seem quite exotic to the people of Englewood. Although she'd spent many hours in the desert dreaming of Englewood, now that she was here she was glad it was only for a visit. It would be too easy for her to fall into her old stilted existence. "William and Eliza are everybody's pets. They're spoiled even by the Apache women. William rides and has a grand time."

"But soon you will have to consider their education," Sarah said with a worried look.

"I can teach William the basics, and maybe in a few years John will be stationed where there are schools."

Sarah wiped the table. "Well, that's certainly a free and easy way of looking at things. From your letters you seem busy learning to cook and entertain. I don't know how my ways didn't rub off on you. So you really think you can teach too?"

"Mother, I don't spend the entire day entertaining!" Katherine replied defensively.

"I can see you spend little time at sewing," Sarah said. "That skirt needs a proper hem."

"Is there something wrong?" Katherine asked, smoothing a stray hair from her warm face. "I've been home for only a few hours, and you've hardly said a kind word to me."

"Katherine McCullough, that is not true. I said you looked well."

"I know it upsets you that we're so far away, but, Mother, I am so happy. I don't mind if my skirts are hemmed properly. There are so many strange and interesting people every day, and the children are always up to something that needs my attention. I get to spend my evenings with John when he's not on duty. Strange as it may seem, I prefer our little quarters to a big house. So much that is unnecessary falls away, and I can enjoy my life."

"Well, I'm glad all the things you had in this house growing up are of no importance," Sarah said, growing emotional. "Work and a comfortable place to live may not be as glamorous, but when your children make their way in the world do you want them to be at a social disadvantage?"

Katherine turned to her children. Willy was leafing through Scott's papers while Eliza annoyed him—unlacing his boots. "The children will do just fine. They are well-behaved and respectful. You imagine us living in a tent with a bunch of rough privates who would teach William all sorts of despicable habits, but there are polite gentlemen, and although I don't much care for the wives, they're not all as uncouth as you'd imagine."

Sarah sat back, arms folded. "My, the two of you have really changed. So sure of yourselves. It's wonderful, but pride goes before the fall. Children need a stable home."

"Our home is stable!" Katherine said.

"What about religion, how are you doing with that? Are you attending services at least?"

"Mother, you show absolutely no faith in my ability to care for a family. Of course we go to services," Katherine lied, "and John and Willy read from the scriptures every evening."

Sarah raised her brows. "Well, I knew John was a good boy."

"We are not children!" Katherine said, unable to control her temper, "and I don't know why you want to hurt me now when I was so looking forward to seeing you!"

"Katherine, you will always be my child, and I worry that this traveling life is not good for a family."

"If we are happy and healthy then it's a good life. The children can see their father any time they wish, and the post is a great big extended family for them."

"To take our place! I guess anyone will do!" Sarah cried, rising from the table and bringing the pies back to the pantry.

Katherine fully understood now how hard Sarah was taking their separation. "Mother, you should come visit!"

Sarah came back out of the pantry, drying her eyes with the corner of her apron. "Indian territory? I wouldn't have the nerve. I'm too old for it."

"But you always said you wanted to travel west," Katherine reminded her.

"Yes, but I meant maybe Pennsylvania."

"Mother, it's so beautiful at times and the plants—they would interest you, and you could show everyone how to cook properly." Katherine laughed. "We do miss you dreadfully—especially me. No one can take your place, but I am over the moon with John. His promotion and the children have changed him. I love him more now than ever. There is no end to his kindness toward me. It's impossible to describe, but I'm so proud of him."

Sarah wiped a tear away and handed Eliza yet another cookie. "Katie, I'm happy for you, but I will confess I feel useless without you and Simon here. I know I should take my own advice and join in at church activities again, but my heart's not in it."

Katherine had never seen her mother at loose ends, and it upset her.

"The truth is I'm a little jealous of you—just starting out. It's silly, I know, and I shouldn't be hard on you. Forgive me."

Sarah's mortality surfaced in her daughter's consciousness for the first time. Never again would she share in every little detail of Katherine's life. It seemed so unfair to be forced to choose between the old and the new, the past and the present. Katherine came around the table and embraced her mother from behind. "Of course I forgive you. You don't know how much I appreciate all of your letters and packages. They make me feel so close to you. I promise to write more!"

Sarah patted Katherine's hand hanging around her neck knowing that Katherine would continue to write only sporadically. The boys came in the room soon enough.

"Let's go for a ride, Katherine," Simon suggested, "and let the old folks get to know the little ones."

Katherine glanced out at the late afternoon in no mood to brave the cold, but she did not want to disappoint her brother. A sudden melancholia dampened her spirits. The guilt she felt for not writing to her parents and Simon was part of it, but the sense that their times together would be from now on limited and tinged with sadness and goodbyes nearly brought her to tears. John stood over her sweetly and Katherine smiled though her heart ached. Weldon gave her a little punch on the chin and off they went as the church bells rang the hour.

***

The Panic of '73 hit overzealous speculators hard, and many of the houses begun in the Palisades woods had been abandoned. John, Katherine, and Simon, with red noses and numb fingers, passed the foundation John had found himself in a few years back, but Simon joked as they reminisced about old times, making it easy to endure the cold and John's secret, humiliating memory.

As they trotted out of the Palisades Forest toward home Katherine was relieved that no one suggested racing this evening. It seemed for once the three were content to be equals. As they approached the village, acquaintances and friends greeted Simon and as an afterthought Katherine and her husband.

"So, Simon, it's nice to see you haven't lost your charm as well as your looks," Weldon teased as they passed Stagg's Saloon. Revelers sang and shouted within.

Simon grimaced. "Now you've hurt my feelings, Weldon."

"Any one of the girls in town would be lucky to have you," Katherine said, defending her brother like old times.

"Thank you, little sister. You're too kind." He laughed.

Palisades Avenue bustled with carolers and those on their way to visit friends.

"Simon, let's turn off here," Katherine suggested. "I don't like passing the old church site. It depresses me."

"You're too sentimental, Katie," Simon said, but turned as she wished. "You can't stop progress. At least they didn't just demolish the place."

"Well, they may as well have. Moving our wedding chapel to the Brookside Cemetery seems a bad omen."

"Please, there's no such thing as bad omens," Simon assured her and turned to John. "Weldon, what do you think?"

Weldon was thinking he was happy enough just to let the two of them talk. "I wish they would have kept the little place where it was, I guess," he answered. "I'm not sure about omens."

"I can't win with the two of you. It's always been that way since day one. It seems like only a short time ago ..." Simon pondered nostalgically.

"And now who's getting sentimental?" Katherine pointed out with a smile.

As the horses drew near home they quickened their pace, and the three riders quieted into their own thoughts. James Street glowed with the brilliantly decorated and illuminated windows of its comfortable homes. The tiny lanes were crowded with carriages of every fine make, and the air hummed with the voices of families over piano and violin singing their favorite yuletide tunes. Every night in Englewood one could hear music, exceptional and mediocre, being performed in parlors or with Mr. Kursteiner's choral club in the newly built athenaeum. Volunteer choirs had sprung up overnight, and some young men had taken to serenading the fashionable girls on the hill.

Katherine spied through the windows of a large house a party with luxurious gowns and draperies in the finest fabrics and styles. Back east even her mother had more panache.

"Katie, you are so nosy. Stop staring," Simon scolded. "You see, Weldon, they're all alike—easily distracted by luxury."

"That's unfair, Simon," Katherine shot back. "Especially coming from you, who is so easily distracted by so many things!"

John smiled approvingly. "Englewood is the merriest place in the world, I think. Where else can you be delivered to your house on the notes of a song?"

"It's not much different than being drummed out of the army," Simon joked.

"Yes, it's just like it except for the lashes and the abuse and the off time drumming," John said, laughing.

"Which reminds me of the elections when I was here last," Simon said. "It was quite a better time than I expected. It was a perfect day for voting. The air was crisp, birds chirping overhead—real festive. So I was in high spirits—going to vote for Grant—but that was before I found out he was such an Indian lover. You could pop into any shop and someone would plunk down the best applejack and try to convince you to vote their way. That stuff is lethal on an empty stomach, but enjoyable till you're sick. I took about five minutes to vote and eight hours to get home. The action at the Liberty Pole was thrilling where the votes were being called.

"There were remnants of a military band from out of the woodwork—I was wallpapered before I got there, and they sounded pretty good. The 'Fighting Chaplain' Reverend Dwight was there—you remember him don't you, Katherine? And members of the 22nd NJ. Colonel Jardine—a stumper—was there too."

"Simon!" Katherine cried. "You are so cold!"

"Listen, Kate, you'll like this story. So we were all partaking of the applejack and the band too—the music getting decidedly worse until the drummer collapsed and had to be dragged off. His friends played him 'The Rogue's March' and threw him around back. Well, a bottled up Wall-Streeter waiting in line to call out his vote for Seymour decides to have his say. He says, 'I'm tired of seeing drunken old soldiers—that's why I'm not voting for one.'

"Well that didn't go over too well with the boys from the 22nd or Stumpy, who by the looks of it was having trouble getting used to his new leg. Like magic or applejack, he threw away his crutches and hopped into the crowd with the lifeless leg trailing behind him. Land sakes, that boy could fight. He mauled the Wall-Streeter good. There was no need for a single other veteran to get involved. The poor Seymour supporter was unprepared and hit the pavement hard—knocked out completely. The soldiers dragged him out back to lie beside the drummer."

Katherine stared at her brother. "Now why on earth would I enjoy this story?"

"Well, Mother told me you visited the stump hospital in the city with Father and had a rough time of it there."

Katherine blushed. John gave her a surprised look.

"I thought you'd like to hear a story of a stump who made a difference—still active in society and all that."

Katherine shook her head. "How can you be so heartless? The men I saw … one of them could have been you."

John spoke up, "No, Kate, it would never have happened to him."

Simon gave Weldon a quick look and halted Hope. "What is that supposed to mean?"

Simon's tone and the look on his face surprised Katherine. A child was pounding out "We Three Kings" in the house to their left

"Simon, I only meant that you're the lucky sort," Weldon answered lightly, but Katherine noticed resentment in his eyes. He let out a forced laugh and then continued. "Kate, you should have seen him all through the war. McCullough could lead us into the thick of things—right out in front—and he'd suffer nary a scratch. Everyone who served with him noticed it."

"Well, that's not quite accurate, Weldon, I ..."

"It's perfectly accurate, captain," John insisted. "I can't tell you how many times your brother forded a river or lit a cigar or anything in one spot. The moment he moved, the sorry soul standing next to him would be done in."

"My God, Weldon, you're making me out to be invincible or a curse upon others—which is it?" Simon asked hotly.

"I don't know what it all means. I just think it's interesting. I didn't mean anything by it."

Simon gave Weldon a long hard look and decided to drop it. "Let's go home. Mother will be annoyed if we miss supper."

As always, Simon was tough on his mount and cracked his crop against Hope's backside, sending her off at a gallop. The other horses naturally followed. The party came barreling up the drive, kicking frozen gravel against the house as they made for the barn.

"That's some way to end a nice ride, Simon," Katherine said. "Now the animals will be overheated in the cold."

"Just throw blankets on them—they'll live," Simon snapped.

"Simon! Is something the matter?" she asked as she tied up her stirrups and took the saddle off of Handsome.

"No, I'm fine," he said, but his face was stiff with anger.

Katherine glanced at Weldon, who looked smug and satisfied. "John!" she whispered.

"Captain, I really didn't mean to anger you," Weldon said unconvincingly while lifting the bridle over his mount's ears.

"I'm not in the least bit angry, Weldon, but it is Christmas. Maybe we should leave the war stories alone."

"I agree," said Weldon, who set to grooming his horse. The work continued in icy silence, the horses steaming off their ride. Simon, never much of a groom, finished first and without a word stalked out of the barn. Katherine saw his cigar end lit on the porch.

John worked on his horse's mane.

"What was that all for?" Katherine asked.

Weldon shrugged. "Whatever it is, he'll get over it. He always does." He took Handsome from her and brought him to his stall after filling his manger with hay. Looking over into the next stall, he saw that Hope's was still empty. "Just like Simon to forget to feed Hope."

"John Weldon! Stop it!" Katherine said. "You two have been friends forever now. Is this how you are to each other?"

Weldon finished loading the stalls with hay and covered the animals with their blankets. Slapping the dust from his hands he leaned against the wooden pillar supporting the hayloft. Flecks of hay stood in his hair like rays of sunlight. Katherine tried not to smile.

"Kate, come on, don't be huffed with me. Simon and I are fine," Weldon said. He made to grab her frozen nose, but she shooed him away. Weldon took her around the waist. "I bet you'd love one of those fancy dresses we saw in the windows we passed tonight."

Pulling the hay from his hair, Katherine shook her head and said, "They'd be completely impractical in Arizona. But ... the hair on those girls ... that's what I miss most. Those pretty hairstyles."

Weldon kissed her.

Chapter Forty-Three

Christmas Day broke bright and frosty on the window in Katherine's old yellow room, but she was warm next to John and more comfortable now that the children had tiptoed downstairs to see their grandmother. Katherine's mantle clock still kept time ticking its soft monotonous tune. Sarah must have wound it for them. The scent of lavender on the sheets reminded Katherine of childhood Christmases, when mounds of candy magically appeared at her bedside along with a brand new book trimmed in gold.

Sarah cooking ham for breakfast awakened Katherine's appetite. Maybe she should go down and help her mother, but it was so nice to just listen and live within her memories for a while. She would stay in bed until she was summoned—why break with tradition? The wind blew the tree outside her window, and she remembered nightmares of small vexed elves knocking at her window and trying to enter her room. The high little voices of her children happily chatting with their grandmother made her smile. Her father was probably reading by the fire.

Katherine was back asleep when William raced in and jumped on the bed. "Mother! Papa! Here are treats for you both! Santa has come, and Mother, there's all sorts of things by the tree!" William tugged at John. "Papa, is Santa rich?"

John pulled the blankets back over his head and grumbled. Katherine said, "Now William, take a sweater and wait for us with Grammy."

"Grammy wants us for breakfast. You have to hurry. We've been waiting for you forever."

Katherine kissed William and sent him off. Looking through her old things still hanging in an armoire, she found a simple day dress of red and gold plaid. The fabric, soft with wear, had lost most of its elegance, but it felt like home. "John, will you ever wake up?"

He turned down the blankets only slightly.

"John, what's the matter? Is your arm sore?" She sat beside him.

"I think I'll sleep this day through, Kate. Do you mind?"

Katherine laughed. "You amuse me, John Weldon. Today will be lovely. Aren't you hungry?"

"No," John answered, sitting up and scratching his head. "I feel strange. This is the first Christmas I've spent with your family. I feel I'm imposing somehow."

"You, my love, are a strange man. How many times have I told you that?" She gently undid the bandage John still wore since the operation on his arm. It was healing well. "My family celebrates just as any other. They won't make you do anything unusual."

"I know I'm being foolish, but ..."

"You are. So get up and meet me in the kitchen," she said as she made her way out the door. "Do you need my help with your clothes?"

"I told you I can dress myself ... it just might take a while." He grinned knowing she would think he was being slow on purpose.

"You scamp, now hurry up!" she said before racing down the stairs. She cringed as she took a peek at the mounds of gifts on and around the tree and slid the doors shut before entering the kitchen.

"Momma," Eliza called. Katherine laughed at the children covered in flour, making Sarah's muffins just like Simon and she had done years ago. She went to her father snoozing by the fire and kissed his forehead. "Merry Christmas, Father."

Scott woke and straightened himself out. "Katie, come sit with me. It's so good to have you home again and the children ... they make your mother so happy," he whispered. "They are fine looking, the pair of them. I must admit looking forward to showing them off at services today."

"I'd say we'll have quite a bit of washing to do before we take them anywhere," Katherine said with a grin.

Simon, arriving next, wore a cotton undershirt and last night's trousers. "Well, my son, you look wrecked. I can see that not much has changed with you, and I was under the impression you had a woman caring for you out west. I don't see how any girl would put up with you."

"Mother," Simon moaned, pouring himself some cold coffee, "why do you start such vicious rumors? I've got a mind to stop writing to you."

Sarah smiled but thought her son might not be teasing. "Now, don't drink that. It's been waiting for you for ages. Wait till I make some fresh." She dragged him to the table where he could mind the children while she got things ready.

"And what are you two up to, making such a mess? Is that what they teach you in the army?" Simon quizzed the children. "I'm not sure I feel safe eating that stuff. I don't know where Willy's hands have been." The children giggled.

"Were you at Stagg's last night, Simon?" Scott asked.

"You went out? I thought you were off to sleep early last night," Katherine added.

"Why am I under such scrutiny? Can't I just take my coffee in peace?" Simon sighed in disgust. "If you must know I find it hard to sleep here, especially since I'm surrounded by Mother's sewing—those mannequins are spooky at night."

"Simon, we couldn't keep your room a museum—it's been years since you've needed it."

"I know. I don't care really," Simon said, sprinkling flour over the children, who screamed and retaliated as their father arrived in his best civilian duds. Simon turned from the table at the sound of Weldon and chuckled. "You look like some cracker ready to plow his field, Weldon!"

Sarah and Katherine suppressed their laughter, but Simon, Scott, and the children laughed heartily. John took it well and made his way over beside Sarah, who filled a cup for him.

"Now, Simon, there's no need to make a joke of your friend," Scott said. "I doubt he's ever spent Christmas in the East before. Checks and trousers are fine on the frontier, but we'll soon fix that."

"Oh, John, there's the cream and sugar on the table," Sarah said, redirecting the conversation.

"Mother, I was here first and Weldon gets coffee!" Simon complained.

Willy laughed.

"Simon, don't be a baby. You'll get your coffee," Sarah scolded.

"Watch yourselves with Grandma. She's a tough one," Simon half-whispered to the children, who didn't believe a word of it.

Christmas breakfast was always enormous. Sarah said stuffed children behaved better in church. Thick slabs of ham with apple butter, bowls of bubble and squeak, sweetbreads and rye toast for Scott began the meal. Sarah's strawberry preserves made an appearance, and she brought out apple tarts for the children and John, who could not resist. The cooled, fresh milk was the best the travelers had drunk in years.

With the last of the tarts devoured, the children begged to go to the parlor to see their gifts. William and Eliza impatiently submitted to being washed and sent out with Simon to feed the horses. Scott and John went for an uncomfortable smoke in the library while Sarah and Katherine cleared the table.

When Simon and the children returned, drinks were brought into the parlor—a sparkling cherry jumble for the children and Scott's special Christmas toddy for the adults, served in the McCullough wedding crystal. Sarah slipped John eggnog—plain.

"Let's have a toast to a fine holiday spent with our most beloved family. We are thankful for their safe arrival and all of our continued good health. God bless us all," Scott said and drank.

Katherine handed a gift to her parents. "I hope they haven't broken."

Sarah opened a box of brightly colored and elaborate glass tree ornaments. "My Katherine, these are very showy. I've never seen the likes of them."

"We bought them in St. Louis, Mother. They're German. Do you like them?"

"From a German peddler, did you say?" Sarah asked.

Katherine breathed deeply, trying to hide her disappointment. "No, Mother, they are not from a peddler, but from a real shop! And we went to a lot of trouble so they wouldn't all be cracked."

"Well, of course you did. And look, only one is broken. What a shame—I mean about the one. Thank you both so much," Sarah said, placing the box down on the floor beside her.

Weldon's stomach churned. No present from the West could compete against Scott and Sarah's extravagance. It was unbearable. Katherine and John had spent all of their savings to come back, but it was not enough.

"Sarah, the children have waited long enough to play with their things," Scott said while pouring another drink for himself and Simon.

Under a quilt, Sarah and Scott had hidden the children's gifts, and now as Sarah unveiled them Eliza screamed and nearly trampled the German Christmas ornaments in getting to the fully furnished dollhouse. Littered around it were dolls' clothes and a new doll peeking out from beneath them, all made by Sarah the previous summer in the evenings after gardening had worn her out.

William stood back, stunned and shy. Scott pushed him forward. "Go ahead boy, there's nothing to be afraid of."

The boy reached tentatively first for the wooden rifle, but spotted the wooden logs and blocks before finally setting his attention on a large and intricately made ark too perfect for a child. William pointed to it in awe. "Is this for me?"

"Of course it is, Willy," Scott said with pride.

It amazed Katherine how appreciative William was of beauty. Eliza shoved her nice things behind her in search of more treasure, but William sat and spent time with each animal pair, petting them and wondering at their detail.

"Do you like them, Willy?" Sarah asked, already happy and sure of his answer.

"Grammy, I love them. I think Santa must have thought I was quite especially good this year," William started, but seemed perplexed. "But ... I wasn't really that good."

The adults laughed.

"Willy, you were especially good this year—don't think otherwise," John said.

"Katherine, I'll send all the gifts out," Sarah said. "Keep your fingers crossed they'll make it this time. There are books and clothes too, but I doubt they'll want to see them just now."

Weldon felt as if he sat in the audience, front row center, of a glittering Christmas theatrical. Not even in his boyhood had he believed such extravagant generosity existed or that he would ever be witness to it. Weldon wished they had brought along something more substantial. They should have done a better job of saving, but how? Weldon looked over at Simon sitting glumly in an armchair by the fire and was sorry for giving him a rough time of it yesterday. He considered everything he had. What did Simon have? Katherine edged closer to him and whispered, "Please John, I know what you're thinking. Stop it and just enjoy the day."

A sudden wave of gratitude for Katherine and the children nearly overcame him.

"Scott, give John and Katie their things," Sarah urged. Scott took hold of a shapeless pile of fabric and handed it to them.

"Outfits for Christmas services," Sarah explained with a pained expression, hoping they would appreciate her sewing efforts.

Katherine spoke first. "Mother this is so absolutely wonderful ... and in the newest style! I love it!"

"Your father picked the fabric—I dragged him," Sarah said while smiling at Scott.

The purple gown of silk had a modern bustle and a straight skirt. The top had ornate gold buttons and a sash that crossed diagonally from shoulder to waist in the same majestic purple.

"I hope it fits," Katherine cried.

"That's what corsets are for, dear," Sarah said.

"Mother!" Katherine blushed.

John Weldon didn't say a word which was not unusual, but it vexed Katherine, who knew how difficult a thing it was to make a man's suit. He sat running his hand over the seams, checking the stitching underneath—each stitch was so regular and lovingly placed. Katherine could take the awkward silence no more. "*John?*"

Weldon looked to Sarah. "I just don't know what to say." He thought of the men he had envied during the war, the men abused as dandies, who wore handmade uniforms. Their families would not think of sending their loved ones off in factory-made, government-issue uniforms.

"Well, I hope you *do* like it," Sarah said.

"Mrs. McCullough, I just don't think there is anything nicer you could have done for me. I've never received such a gift as this. I'm delighted with it!"

Sarah put her hand to her chest. "Well, my goodness, you nearly scared me to death, but I should be used to your ways by now, John Weldon. Merry Christmas then."

"Simon," Scott groused, "are you still with us? You've been as quiet as a mouse."

"I'm just tired."

"Here, son, a gift from your mother and me," Scott said as he tossed the silver cigar case with elaborate engraving to his son.

"Oh, a cigar case—how personal."

"Simon, you are impossible," Sarah cried. "You seem to have everything you need."

"I'm sorry, Mother. But you put some effort into other people's gifts."

"We gave them what they needed," Sarah said. "It was a terrible tragedy for Katherine to lose every nice thing we saved for her over the years on the way to Arizona."

"You're right, Mother. I apologize," Simon said only to avoid a scene.

Scott stared aggressively at his son. "Simon, perk up for the children's sake."

Simon rolled his eyes and looked toward the children, who were deeply engaged with their own imaginary worlds.

It was almost time for services now and all the gifts had been given.

"Come along, Eliza and Willy, so I can dress you," Katherine said. They moaned, but followed their mother. Sarah headed for the kitchen. Weldon awkwardly followed. Simon and Scott went to the library.

"Mrs. McCullough ..." John began.

"Yes dear." Sarah smiled at his schoolboy shyness.

"Well ... thank you again, Mrs. McCullough. No one except your daughter has ever treated me so well."

"Dear Mr. Weldon, you have come a long way. Katherine tells me you make her happy."

He looked away with a sheepish grin. "I would do anything for her. Anyway, I have something for you and Mr. McCullough too."

"But why didn't you give it to us in the parlor?"

"Oh no, they're not really Christmas gifts, exactly. They're just small things," he said. He took from his pocket a brown packet neatly folded and tied with string and gave it to Sarah. "It's just seeds. I've been collecting them for a while wherever I go ... for your garden, to see what happens. I know some might not grow."

Sarah sniffled, cried, and then grabbed his good arm. "You do beat all, John Weldon. To know that you have been thinking of your old mother-in-law during your travels! Now that is truly a thoughtful gift. I might just save these seeds someplace special to look at when I'm blue and missing you. What a lovely sentiment."

Weldon grinned and impetuously hugged Sarah. "I've sorely missed you, Mrs. McCullough."

"Now stop it, John. You need to let me get hold of myself."

John pulled a larger, flat package from his bags that had been left in the kitchen the night before. "This is for Mr. McCullough. I'll leave it on his chair. And thank you for everything."

"Thank you, John Weldon," Sarah answered, misty-eyed.

Chapter Forty-Four

No matter the weather, cold or stormy, the McCullough family walked to Christmas Day services. Scott's favorite horse went mysteriously lame one year before Christmas (after Simon raced it). Scott yelled and made empty threats, but after realizing the benefits of a good walk after Sarah's breakfast feast, Scott determined to make the brisk march a tradition. Most Englewood residents lived within easy walking distance of their houses of worship. Seeing friends out in the chilly air, crimson-cheeked and festively attired, added to the spirit of the day. The family bundled up, comfortably full, and went into the valley and up the hill where the new First Presbyterian building stood. It lacked the finishing touches but was gaily decorated for the season in pine boughs brought from the forest.

The sunshine made it seem more like an early March day than one in December. John struggled with a sleepy Eliza in his one strong arm. Eliza would not hold on so Katherine took her. William skipped alongside his uncle, whose spirits could never stay low for long.

"Look, William, over there!" Simon said. As soon as the boy looked, Simon knocked the cap from his head. William got the joke quickly but remained at Simon's side to have his cap knocked off again and again. William threw gentle punches his uncle's way, and Simon pretended at pain and laughed. Each time the cap was thrown off with more gusto. William feigned exasperation but scooped it up and trotted back over to Simon, keeping the game going.

"Simon, the child will catch a chill. Can't you behave?" Sarah called up to them.

He waved her off and continued to torment his happy nephew.

The angelic voices of Mr. Kursteiner's choral ensemble greeted them as they entered the church. Shoulder to shoulder in their pew, the family was warm and cozy. Eliza snoozed up against her father. It was difficult for all of them to stay awake. Katherine entertained herself poking Simon every time his eyes closed. Willy sat between Scott and Sarah looking handsome in his new blouse, navy trousers, and bright suspenders. The vaulted ceilings and the booming tones of the minister kept him in quiet awe. Absently Willy ran his small hands over his grandfather's. Katherine detected a faint look of pride in Scott's eyes.

After the service as they filed out, the Crenshaw family greeted the McCullough party.

"Mr. And Mrs. McCullough, merry Christmas to you both—and Simon! My, you *are* lucky to have your whole family home—and such a scary year out west.

Katherine, you must be delighted to have your children home safe and sound," Margaret said, embracing Katherine.

Katherine attempted to speak but was thwarted.

"And Mr. Weldon, how nice to see you. Are you enjoying your little battles against the Indians?" Margaret asked.

Graham Crenshaw gave his wife a pained look and spoke before Weldon could. "We were so pleased when we heard you received a promotion and were able to bring your family with you—that must be very nice."

Margaret smiled and spoke up again, "What an honor for someone with no academic training—but I suppose hunting for villages to surprise requires little in the way of education."

John dismissed Margaret's talk, looking impatiently up the road. Simon and Scott engaged Graham Crenshaw in small talk. Weldon joined them reluctantly. He set Eliza down, but she protested. A passing worry that Eliza was not acting herself troubled him.

"Weldon, your children are quite handsome," Crenshaw said. He wore a large fur hat and a fur-trimmed frock coat that just covered the expanse of his waist, presenting a stark contrast to the soldiers just off government rations.

"Where are your children?" Scott asked.

"Well, I'm rather embarrassed to say they are too badly behaved to be trusted at Christmas services. They put up such a fuss at the mere mention of getting dressed that we left them with their grandmother. They are spoiled by one and all, myself included." Crenshaw looked down at William, who hid behind his grandfather. "I guess the military has instilled some discipline in your little man, Lieutenant Weldon," he joked.

"Nonsense, Willy is just naturally good," said Scott, patting his grandson's back.

"I don't know, Father. Weldon can be a real task master with his men ..." Simon said.

"And your daughter, what a beauty," Crenshaw continued. "A bit tired though—holidays are tough on the little ones—too much excitement."

Against his better judgment John said, "I don't know, but I think she feels hot."

Crenshaw pulled off his glove. "May I?" he asked as he felt the lethargic child. "Hmm, I'd have to agree with you, lieutenant. How has she been lately?"

"Fine, just fine. I only noticed in church."

Crenshaw discerned that Weldon was the type of parent to panic and jump to all sorts of conclusions. "Well, there's no need to worry. She's probably just overtired from excitement," Graham assured John, but not convincingly. His medical instincts getting the best of him. "What about coughing or anything else you may have noticed?"

"No, nothing," Weldon replied too aggressively, his distrust of doctors coming to the fore. He looked over at the women. "Katherine, we should go."

Katherine jumped at his abrupt manner. "John, what's the matter?" she asked as she came to his side.

"Elly should be indoors in this cold," he said, angry at himself for taking Eliza out in the first place. "She's burning up." He shoved the little girl under Katherine's nose.

Crenshaw cut in, "Eliza doesn't seem to be burning up exactly, but she is warm. I think you would know best as her mother."

"I know quite well myself," John answered starting off before the others could react.

Katherine looked to Graham, "My apologies, Mr. Crenshaw. You know the lieutenant can be a little hot-headed."

"Yes," Graham said, unable to hide his concern, "but if you notice a cough or the fever gets any worse, the girl should be seen."

"Of course, Doctor Crenshaw," she assured him, fully confident all would be well. "Merry Christmas again to you both."

The families said their goodbyes, and Margaret promised to call in before they went back west. By the time Katherine and the others made it through the front door, John had put Eliza to bed and sat worrying by her side. Katherine and Sarah both went in to have a look. Eliza slept peacefully.

"John, dear, she'll be fine," Sarah said. "Katherine was just the same as a child. Whenever there was any excitement she would get sick—Simon too."

John nodded, smoothing Eliza's curls.

"I must get things set for our guests," Sarah whispered. "I'll leave you two alone." Letting down all pretenses once Sarah left the room, John ran his fingers through his hair. "Crenshaw looked like he saw something he didn't like."

"When it comes to doctors you allow your imagination to run wild. Let Eliza get some rest. It's the best thing for her," Katherine said and grabbed his hand. "Come downstairs. You can't fix Eliza by sitting here," she said, aware that although John would never wish sickness on his daughter, he might not be above using it as an excuse to avoid uncomfortable social situations. "I want my aunt and uncle to see the handsome man I married."

He gave her a dubious look but tucked Eliza in and followed Katherine down-stairs just as the guests arrived. She ran to the door to let them in, and Simon braved the cold to get hay and shelter for their horses.

"Uncle Phillip and Aunt Marcy, so nice to see you again," Katherine said with enthusiasm.

John stood still on the stairs taking the measure of them like a wary animal from the wilds stumbling upon civilization. Phillip's white hair and full eyebrows stretched like swan's wings to the sides of his angular face, and his eyes were dark and large like an eagle's. Dressed impeccably in a plum suit and beaver-trimmed coat, he made the Englewood McCullough family appear like poor country cousins.

When introduced to Weldon, Phillip shook his hand heartily. "Great to finally meet you, son. Scott tells me all his news over lunch at Delmonico's."

Phillip's deep voice betrayed his love for cigars and the Scotch whiskey he drank (and carried in with a red ribbon wrapped around it). In his youth he may have looked like Simon, but unlike Simon Phillip spent little time outdoors and had the sallow complexion of an invalid, which he was not.

Phillip's wife Marcy claimed to be an invalid with little success. Marcy was Phil's second wife. His first had died, leaving him with five ne'er-do-well children who were sent off to relatives in Brooklyn and Trenton. Mrs. Marcy McCullough had taken to luxury like a fish to water after leading an unhappy existence married to a young and penniless distant relation of a moderately wealthy Philadelphia family. Against her parents' wishes, the man had whisked Marcy with her small dowry up to New York City. The young man's dash and appeal faded as the money was lost on unsound investments during the war. Marcy could not go home to admit that her husband had now taken up with camp followers as a sutler selling shabby pies to the troops.

On a rainy day during the Peninsula campaign Marcy watched her husband cheat a skinny young soldier over a stale old pie like he had done so many times be-fore. As Marcy shivered alongside him listening to him explain to the boy that, once bought, there would be no exchanges and that the buyer should beware, Marcy felt she could kill him but never got the chance.

An old regular army sergeant took up the boy's case. "Look at this poor wretch of a boy, and you won't do nothin' but cheat him of a meal. You give 'im a proper cake. Go on now," the regular said.

"I can run my own business. If this here boy is old enough to take up a gun then he's sure as heck old enough to care for his own troubles over pie," the sutler said in a smug tone, turning away behind the counter sodden with rain, muddy fingerprints, and half-decomposed delicacies that only the hungriest men would have considered eating.

The old regular grabbed a couple of pies and threw them at Marcy's husband, and the young soldier with a long wet nose laughed and threw his too. Grabbing his pistol, Marcy's husband knocked his wife out of the way as he pushed past her on the mucky floor. The young soldier lunged at the sutler, trying in vain to ground the gun, but instead it went off sending a bullet through the sutler's thigh. The men tried to stop the bleeding, but he died, leaving Marcy destitute and aimless.

Marcy wasn't bright, but she was helpful and soon volunteered to nurse, following the troops to Antietam, where she was discovered by her future husband, Phillip McCullough. He was making a tour of the area with some business associates who were interested in selling the military useless and inappropriate objects. Although Phillip had no interest in things military or medical he accompanied his associates when given the tour of Sharpsburg and the grim battlefield. Phillip decided upon entering the makeshift field hospital that he would rescue the stunning redhead from a life of labor and that he would have no part in making direct profit from the war.

Phillip's instincts about both had been correct. His associates were soon brought up on charges for selling pretty but malfunctioning pistols to soldiers, and Marcy rewarded him with gratitude and laughter. Marcy never disagreed with Phillip. Her family was of a higher breed than he could have ever hoped for and eagerly took him into their fold—opening many Philadelphia-based business opportunities—and Marcy was sterile. Phillip had had enough of children. Sad experience had taught him that mothers were distracted and dull lovers. In their almost ten years together, Marcy had enjoyed the good life, and it showed. Clusters of jewels bedecked Marcy's fingers and stretched around her fleshy wrists. Some hinted that her weight (and the manner in which she continued to display it) was rather uncouth. Phillip figured as much, but he didn't care. Phillip had never imagined how thoroughly he could enjoy a woman's company. Marcy had no tiny waist, but she flattered Phillip with her attention and the way she enthusiastically took him to bed.

Beneath one arm Marcy carried a bag holding a sorry-looking, yappy dog. Sarah let out a low moan. Simon slipped back in as they all entered the parlor. William tiptoed out into the kitchen to flip through his new picture book.

When Aunt Marcy bumped past Weldon to take an armchair she struggled to squeeze into, Simon needed all of his self-control not to laugh at John's embarrassed expression. Simon enjoyed watching people of different sorts forced into cramped spaces. There was always a chance for ruffled feathers and fun. Weldon uncomfortably took a seat beside Uncle Phillip. Scott poured strong drinks for the men and Aunt Marcy while Katherine and Sarah carried in great bowls of nuts and dried fruit, cheese, and fancy breads.

Though starved, Weldon could not bring himself to reach over others for finger food. Simon whispered to him that he had better take some food while he could. The hungry hordes were stripping the land of value. Weldon smiled but was off-put and intimidated by the feeding frenzy. Luckily the residents of Tenafly Road had eaten their large breakfast. The dog was set free and fixated on Katherine's new outfit. She almost crushed him under foot twice as he dashed about yapping for scraps.

The visitors settled down and back into their seats with sighs and contented grins. Both guests had the annoying habit of patting their bellies in conversation, but as they spoke everyone relaxed.

"We almost failed to make it here today," Uncle Phillip began. "Poor Marcy had one of her bouts."

Marcy nodded dramatically, taking her fan to relieve herself of the sudden feverishness she imagined she felt.

"What sort of bout?" Simon asked gamely.

"Oh, the worst sort, let me see, there's the fainting spells brought on by the miasmas that often lurk in lowlands, which reminds me, dear—Phil told me this area can get mighty malarial. Is that true?"

"The swamps have been drained, Marcy," Sarah said.

"Oh, and then there's the fevers I get from dust. Simon, be a dear and open a window—you don't mind, Sarah, do you? I wouldn't want to ruin everyone's Christmas by having a spell, but don't worry anyhow. It's just life. We all suffer so we can enjoy the little things the creator sends our way, and isn't that what Christmas is all about?" Marcy looked around and, receiving no response, continued. "I'm able to digest only the blandest of foods. I'm sure, Sarah, your food will be fine—I don't remember it being too flavored, although I hope you don't mind if I pass on the glazed carrots. Too much cinnamon for my system."

"Maybe you're dressed too tightly," Sarah commented.

"Oh, no, that's not it at all," Marcy said with the faintest hint of annoyance. "The doctors tell me it's just that my system is delicate."

Simon looked deeply into his drink after noting John's bemused expression.

Uncle Phillip decided it was time to change the subject. Only Phillip knew how nervous Marcy was beneath her mindless ramblings. Her hypochondria was a small price to pay for the happiness she gave him. "Well, it's been a trying year, Scott, has it not? I assume Englewood speculators have been hard hit by the panic. I must say it's a nice little place here. I've been lucky in my conservative investments, so I've hardly felt a pinch."

Scott nodded but said nothing. Phil sized up Weldon. "Lieutenant, you've got a handsome son. Will we see your daughter?"

"Thank you, Mr. McCullough, but our little Eliza is not well. Maybe tomorrow."

"I understand, and please call me Phillip. We've heard so much about you, off fighting Apaches. From all I've read, Crook is doing an excellent job. I bet you have quite a few tales to tell, young man. And taking good care of my niece, I see. The two of you and the children will come visit us in New York one day soon I hope."

"Thank you again, Mr. McCullough," Weldon replied, squirming under Scott's glare.

"I'm afraid that for all Weldon's efforts, Phil, little long-term peace has been won," Scott said.

"Hmm, that may be so," Phil said. "Grant's peace policy has been a dismal failure from what I can tell. I may be wrong, as I have no military experience."

"You are right, Uncle Phil, most definitely," Simon said. "My stay at Fort Sill in '71 can prove that."

"Fort Sill?" Phil asked in surprise. "Your parents have been remiss. I thought you were still in Washington."

Sarah knew her son was sensitive. "Scott, I'm sure you must have told Phil about Simon!"

"Of course," Scott answered.

"So were you there for the Satanta mess?" Phil asked.

"I'm afraid you've lost me boys. Who or what is Satanta?" Marcy asked, sneaking cheese to her dog.

"He's a Kiowa, Aunt Marcy," Simon explained.

"Oh, I've heard they are the most warlike! And you fought them?" Marcy asked, sitting up excitedly in her chair.

"No, not exactly—not then. I just happened to be at Fort Sill when Satanta was arrested. General Sherman came close to being killed out there."

"I've always thought General Sherman an attractive man in pictures. Why was he out there?" Marcy asked, brushing the front of her dress free of crumbs.

"Sherman figured the Texas citizens were exaggerating the crimes the Indians were committing and wanted to see for himself," Simon said. "When news came in later that night at Fort Richardson that a war party of Kiowa had ambushed some teamsters of Captain Warren's train and killed and mutilated most of them, Sherman finally grasped their savagery. Poor Sam Elliot was found burnt to a crisp after being tied beneath his wagon and set on fire."

"It was stupid to have pacifist Quakers as Indian agents," Weldon added.

Phillip shifted in his seat. "I was under the impression the Christian agents were yielding results, and that there was less corruption at the agencies now."

"Indian policy east and west still seems corrupt enough," Simon said.

"There are no perfect people here on Earth I think," Marcy said sadly.

"The Indian agent at Fort Sill was a good man, as far as Quakers go," Simon continued. "Lowrie Tatum—but the Indians there were the surliest I've seen so far."

"What have you got against Quakers?" Aunt Marcy asked. "They seem such sincere, quaint people."

"They *speak* for the rights of others but don't fight once the battle is begun," Weldon said, remembering his dealings with two Friends during the war.

Simon nodded in agreement. "Yes, and history has shown that evil ideas and the men who carry them out don't just go away by praying. Tatum learned that in the end, and good for him."

"What happened to this Mr. Tatum?" Marcy asked.

Simon poured himself some of the whiskey his uncle brought and leaned against the bookcase behind him. "Tatum was your typical pacifist. He tried to treat the Indians like men and thought that kindness and respect would convince the Indians of peace. *Let Us Have Peace* as Grant would say. Anyway, if Jesus Christ couldn't win over his enemies, there was no way Tatum was going to. The agency at Fort Sill fed and armed the least peaceful elements of the tribes, and the citizens got angry. Out the Indians would go to plunder and murder and in they would slip to feed their bellies and reload their weapons right under the nose of Colonel Grierson—a good cavalryman during the war, as you all know, but far too gentle and naive for the job."

Weldon interrupted, "Some say Grierson's behavior was treasonous."

Simon shook his head. "No, I think he really trusted the Indians. He's very high-minded. The Indians call his colored troops the buffalo soldiers."

"How interesting," Marcy marveled.

"Grierson is just unfit to fight Indians. He admires them far too much to conquer them properly, and they *will* be conquered peacefully or by force—it's just a matter of time."

"Tell us more about what happened with Satanta," Phillip urged.

"Well, I was on detached duty with Lieutenant Colonel Langellier at Fort Sill. I'm stationed at Fort Richardson—Mother, Father, you might want to take note of that. How I ended up in Texas of all places is still a cruel mystery, but that's neither here nor there. Usually the Indians take a winter vacation from their raiding, but Grierson and Tatum threatened to withhold rations until hostages and stolen property were returned. The savages didn't like that and were out in full force all winter."

Scott bristled, mortified at his son's language and attitude in mixed company. "Simon, is there a point to this wandering talk? You're boring our guests, I'm sure."

"Oh, no, Simon, do go on!" Marcy pleaded.

Simon shrugged and continued. "So by February or March, Tatum was thinking he should call on the soldiers to help discipline the wayward Indians. Trouble is that it's hard as heck to tell the good from the bad, and as much as eastern civilians like to think all soldiers are bloodthirsty bastards most want to do what's right."

"Need I remind you of Sand Creek?" Scott asked. "How can you defend such inhumanity?"

"I don't. Chivington and his volunteers acted like animals. Remember they were not with the army, Father. When soldiers commit outrages they should be punished under the law. Indians have no such laws to punish their own. Anyway, poor Tatum the Quaker had only a few employees left with him by April. Most fled for their lives. I spoke with him briefly after Satanka and Satanta were arrested. Tatum admitted that he told Grierson it would be a bloody spring and summer, hinting that he wanted more troops, but Grierson still hoped when the annuities arrived things would settle down. They did not." Simon took a sip of his drink. "Fort Sill was well kept. It was clean. I guess Grierson did a good job with that."

Phillip took time to ponder aloud. "So here was a case of a soldier and a Quaker following Grant's peace policy and made to look utterly foolish."

"Yes, most certainly. Colonel Mackenzie the same year whipped Fort Richardson and the 4th Cavalry into top form. Grierson was much more lax with his men. But then they were colored and couldn't be expected to rise up to the standards of the other men."

Scott interrupted, "Son, your prejudice is appalling. Colored troops from what I've read have served our country valiantly."

"From what I've actually seen in real life, Father, they are indeed brave and willing to put up with great hardship, but they're as dumb as the chair you sit in. I don't say it's their fault or that in time they can't be improved."

"You talk of them as if they are livestock," Scott said.

"Well they were bred to be useful *physically* and before that they were butchering each other on the Dark Continent—how many freed slaves want to go back to Liberia? And remember, it was the darkies back there that sold their fellow Africans into slavery. What I find so amusing is how your friends ran President Johnson out of office for taking a conservative approach to enfranchisement for the Negro down south."

"Conservative?" Uncle Phil interrupted, "Johnson tried to run roughshod over Congress and offered no protection to the freedmen! I would have thought a soldier would appreciate Congress' attempt to put into place the ideals you were fighting for!"

Simon sighed and stretched leisurely. "Although I always held slavery to be an abomination, I fought only for the Union. The South had its way in this country for years, and when they took to sending border ruffians into the western territories to rig elections for slavery, that was too much. But if I knew we would follow this ridiculous policy of turning illiterate slaves into the new ruling class of the south, I may have taken French leave and gone to live in Canada!"

Phillip looked to Weldon who kept his own counsel. "Weldon, do you share my nephew's beliefs?"

John hesitated. "Well, I was in the army a while before the war, and I just tried to do my work. I had an idea that slavery was a threat to free labor, I guess .... I will say I was surprised at how quickly the contraband tried right away to improve themselves. They seemed to want to become good citizens."

"Oh, Weldon, wanting something and being prepared to work for it are two different things," Simon said, slurring his words. "You of all people should realize that! I mean, the only formal education you received was in the army—do you realize what a disadvantage that is for you in terms of promotion?"

Weldon could hardly bring himself to reply. "I feel the disadvantage more keenly than you can imagine, I'm afraid."

"It's fair to say," Simon continued, "that it will take a few more generations for your Indian blood to wash away, and though you pass well your background has held you back. But we should give the illiterate hordes in the south half the country to play with this minute. It's entirely unfair to people like Weldon. You couldn't pay me enough to live in the black south. The day New Jersey elects a black senator, Father, is the day I will accept your self-righteousness."

Katherine wanted to pummel Simon but worried that any attempt to defend John would make things more uncomfortable for him. An uneasy silence settled as everyone watched Simon pour yet another drink.

"Where were we?" he asked.

"You were educating us on the need to disenfranchise Negroes," Scott said sarcastically. Although Scott had no love for Weldon, he could not understand Simon's need to humiliate him.

"As usual I am misquoted," Simon said, feigning boredom. "I believe one day that educated Negroes should vote ..."

"What about educated women?" Sarah asked, hoping to steer the conversation away from Negroes and Indians.

"Oh, for God's sake, Mother, let's save that for another day," Simon moaned. "Blacks should be given their own schools to get them up to speed with the whites before they worry about voting. You don't seem to realize that we just finished a war, and our southern friends are still licking their wounds. There's no more slavery. The South is a burnt shell where women and children walk in rags begging for food. We should let things settle for a while. If all the New England fanatics push too hard there will be another war and a lot more innocent darkie blood spilled in the process. Mark my words, when you see little colored children going to school with your grandchildren you'll change your tune, Father."

"Interesting that you should bring that up, son. Englewood will vote on that question. I for one will proudly vote for a free public school for ALL who wish to attend," Scott announced smugly.

"Would you have sent us there?" Simon asked.

Scott saw where his son was going but answered honestly anyway. "Of course not, but that is because I have earned, through hard work, enough money to give my children the best. Although if what you say about colored people is true then academically you would have fit in nicely."

"*Scott!*" Sarah hissed.

Phillip shook his head. "Simon, I agree with your father. Your talk is unchristian. Maybe you are right that adult former slaves will struggle, but their children should be given the same opportunities as any other child. If the vote is not preserved now, then when?"

"Until recently, Uncle Phil, all white men were not given the privilege of voting ..."

Phil ignored Simon. "There will be violence no matter when the vote is put in place. I'm one of the few people who does not want to shrink the military at this crucial time. We must not forget that the South brought on this war and lost it. To hand them back their old society would be to dishonor all the soldiers who voted overwhelmingly for Lincoln in 1864. We will send missionaries, money, and soldiers if necessary to build a morally just South. The more they fight against it the more their culture and economy will suffer."

"Yes, Uncle Phil, I will try to keep in mind how morally superior we are," Simon said with sarcasm.

"I'm sorry, boys, but what do colored people have to do with the Indians? I'd like to hear the rest of your Satanta story," Marcy said, afraid the conversation was getting too personal and dangerous.

"Is it time for the meal?" Scott asked Sarah with an exasperated look.

"Soon Scott," Sarah answered, wishing the meal was already over.

"Well, Aunt Marcy, to cut to the chase ..." Simon continued.

Scott rolled his eyes.

"Ration day came and the usual Indians dropped by to chat with Tatum. Before he could even question them, Satanta and some other warriors bragged about their part in the killings of the teamsters. The agent sent word to Sherman, who called for a meeting with them in front of Grierson's quarters. Langellier and I watched from across the way. Satanta came in first on a beautiful horse but ruined his noble impression as he ran to escape when Sherman questioned him about the teamsters. Satanka came next, announcing he would rather die fighting than go to prison. As he pulled a gun from under his blanket, a squad of Grierson's soldiers threw open the shutters to Grierson's quarters with their guns loaded and aimed. Suddenly Satanka wasn't so sure he would rather die. It was a pitiful sight to see him beg for his life.

"Lone Wolf and his men arrived last. He dismounted his pony and threw off his blanket revealing a small arsenal—two carbines, bows, and a quiver. His friends were well-armed with modern weapons—Colts, Spencers, you name it. General Sherman is as cool and brave as they come. I guess the Indians were expecting to intimidate him, but the general just kept repeating that the men guilty of the teamster killings would have to stand trial. Lone Wolf kept a carbine for himself, handed the other weapons around, and threatened to shoot Grierson and Sherman at close range. Grierson gave a signal and four companies of soldiers at a trot surrounded the Indians. Lone Wolf in desperation aimed his gun at Sherman and would have killed him if it wasn't for Grierson, who lunged at the crazed Indian, knocking him to the ground. A translator and the threat of being slaughtered by a bunch of dark-skinned soldiers finally convinced the Indians that fighting was no use. Those Indians were lucky they were treated so fairly. Most were set free to continue on their merry way. Only Satanta and Satanka were put under guard."

"You must not be too happy that Satanka is now freed after such a short prison term then," Phil said.

"You can bet as we sit here that he is already planning new moves against the settlers."

"My word, Katherine, how can you bear raising your family in the army?" Aunt Marcy asked. "Aren't you frightened for your children?"

"Sometimes I do worry, but I never want to be away from John, no matter the danger," Katherine said with a blush.

Simon moaned. "I think I shall be sick, Katherine."

"Leave the girl alone, Simon. It's a nice thing to see a wife so devoted to her husband. You're a lucky man, Lieutenant Weldon," Phillip said. He liked the quieter of the two soldiers.

"Indeed, I am, sir," Weldon responded.

Uncle Phillip held his glass out to Simon, who poured more drinks all around. Katherine noticed the aggression in Simon's eyes. It did not bode well for dinner.

"Katherine, dear, will you help me in the kitchen?" Sarah asked as she rose from her seat.

"Still no kitchen help, Sarah? Maybe one day," Marcy noted.

"I've told you before that cooking is a great love of mine," Sarah said flatly.

"Yes, but day in and day out—your life must become quite tedious. I feel for you. I would offer my assistance, but ..."

"No, that's all right. I'd hate for the dust in my kitchen to bring on a fainting spell and land you in the fire," Sarah said, taking up a few empty bowls.

"You're right. I'll just have to content myself with the company of men," Marcy said, sleepily spreading herself out in the armchair with her hands clasped around her middle.

"Weldon, will you come for a smoke?" Simon asked. John did not hesitate.

In the kitchen mother and daughter pinned on their aprons and laughed quietly.

"If Aunt Marcy eats one more chestnut she'll burst!" Katherine whispered. "She'd snuff out the fire if she fell into it."

"Now, Katie, it's Christmas. There's no reason to make jokes about her size," Sarah scolded, but laughed. "It's her dreadful personality that merits abuse. Your uncle is a dear, but she is insufferable!"

Katherine stirred the boiling potatoes on the stove. "Simon is a runaway train, Mother. I hope he makes it through the meal."

Sarah stood beside her daughter scattering flour over a pan of butter to start her gravy. "Something tells me Simon has not been happy for a while now. Land sakes, I wish we would have put more effort into his gift, but we were at a loss. Seems real sorry for himself though—even in his letters."

"What has Simon written to you?" Katherine asked, feeling guilty for not noticing anything unusual in his letters.

"Well, there's a girl or there *was* a girl," Sarah said, "only hinted at mind you—and I think Simon may be feeling under-appreciated in the army."

Katherine chuckled. "Funny, I never got the impression Simon was all that serious about his work."

"Well, that's nonsense dear. He suffers a lack of confidence in himself."

Katherine stared at her mother. "Are we talking about the same Simon? He is the most confident person I know."

"You mistake gregariousness for confidence" Sarah said. "He's always depended too much on other people liking him. His confidence was lost in the war somehow."

"Land sakes, Mother, you have a peculiar way of seeing things."

"Maybe so, but Simon has been my son an awful long time now. I know him well enough. Maybe the boyish enthusiasm he held onto for so long has given way to adult realism, but I miss the old Simon," Sarah confessed.

"Mother, you can't judge everything on occasional letters ..."

"You mean twice-weekly letters, dear."

"All right then. But still letters leave a lot out. Simon is the same silly person I've always known him to be," Katherine said with less confidence. She noticed on this visit the changes her mother alluded to but did not want to admit them. There was no time to discover their root; soon enough they would all be back in the West.

Katherine slipped upstairs to check on Eliza and found John and Willy already at her bedside. "She feels cooler, Kate," John said hopefully, "but will you check her?"

Katherine kissed her temple. Eliza smiled, but was faded and shiny-eyed.

"Momma," she mumbled.

"Yes, sweetie, go back to sleep, and you'll be better in the morning."

"But my doll ..."

"Don't worry. We'll bring her up, okay?" Katherine whispered. She turned to John. "She still feels a little warm to me, but I don't think there's anything to worry about."

John pulled the blankets up under his daughter's pointed chin and wiped the curls from her face.

"Mr. Weldon, you are quite dashing in your new suit," Katherine said, kissing him. She adjusted his shirt over his bandaged arm. "Why are you not wearing the sling, darling?"

"It's too showy—I'm embarrassed by it, though it hurts a bit ..."

"You are a foolish man to be so shy. Of course, it hurts," Katherine said and kissed him again, more passionately. "Look, she's back asleep. Dinner is waiting."

Reluctantly Weldon followed her down the stairs and into the dining room. The sideboard groaned under the weight of the mince pies, the roast goose with potato stuffing, the sweetbread pie with chestnuts gathered on a drive along the Palisades, the blanched beans with cream, the glazed carrots and pickled cow cumbers, not to mention the clam and oyster soup, breadsticks, and salted pecans. After the prayers and toasts they all slid into their crowded places at the table.

"The countryside really works to build an appetite," Marcy said. "This is all so homey and rustic. A pass-around meal. It's sweet. I mean it, Sarah, although your food will be almost frozen by the time you get to sit and join us."

Sarah passed a full plate to Scott who passed it down the table.

"Don't worry yourself," Sarah said. "Just pass your plate."

"Oh, yes. By the by, what do you put in your potatoes, dear?" Marcy asked.

Sarah sighed. "A touch of rosemary, milk, and butter."

"Oh, no, that won't do. I had better not chance it. Is there garlic with the beans—yes, I thought I smelt it. No, rosemary and garlic give me catarrh and heartburn. Hmm, what's in the pies?"

Sarah gave her guest a hostile stare. "Meat and raisins ... just normal mincemeat, Marcy. That's all."

"No salt?"

"A pinch."

"Well, I suppose that's fine. I'll have some of that—a bit more if you would ..."

"That's quite a load," Simon said as he sat beside his aunt after staggering in. "Maybe you should go a little lighter on the pies."

"Young man, you should go a little lighter on the drink," Marcy replied, spreading a tiny napkin over her expansive skirt.

Uncle Phillip glared at Simon but quickly turned his attention to his brother. "So, Scott, how's the new business?"

"New business?" Simon interrupted.

Scott moved the decanter of whiskey away from his son. "It's fascinating."

"Scott, dear, what business are you up to?" Marcy asked.

"It's a small thing at present, but interesting all the same. A friend's son returned from the war pretty badly hurt—a leg gone—sad, really sad. He is a fine looking boy. The leg took some time to heal and was very tender to the touch. I took Katherine a few years back to the hospital in New York—when Weldon left her here. We both found it disturbing, but I got to thinking about prosthetics."

"I've read there's a shortage in the South," Phillip said.

"Right, and I followed the case of my friend's son and found that when the time came to be fitted out, the leg was rather uncomfortable for him, and although he had been enthusiastically looking forward to using it, he abandoned it because of the pain. It occurred to me that if I could ease the pain of our veterans ..."

"And make a damned good bit of money," Simon slurred.

"Watch your language, son," Scott warned, sending Sarah a look of disgust.

"Simon, dear, I need your help in the kitchen," Sarah said. Simon rose from the table with a moan and followed his mother.

"Well, it sounds like a nice thing to do, as I know you have always had such an interest in things medical," Phil said. "Is it worth your investment though? How will you sell enough?"

Scott passed a plate as he spoke. "We hope to convince the state governments to buy from us, and with science there are always advances and room for improvements in comfort and mobility. More natural replacements, we hope, would continue to be sold. Remember, most veterans are still young and will be interested for a long time in new products to make their lives easier. If we make enough profit, Katherine and I—and Simon if I can ever catch the boy sober—will be able to set up nice little education funds for the grandchildren."

Weldon turned to Katherine. "You're invested in your father's business?"

"Katherine, didn't you tell your husband?" Scott stammered.

"No, not yet, Father," Katherine said, suffocating under the stares of the men at the table.

"Excuse me, Mr. McCullough, but I am repulsed at making money off the suffering of others," John said.

Scott glared at him. "I will politely point out that this is between my daughter and me. Katherine chose to get involved. And, by the way, a soldier does earn a living off the suffering of others."

Weldon rose from his chair, but Phillip grabbed him. "Don't be foolish, boy. A soldier's pay needs to be supplemented somehow. You have your children to consider. Would you deny a grandfather the joy of doing something useful for his grandchildren?"

"Respectfully, sir, I must disagree with you," Weldon said. "This has little to do with my children. It's just another attempt to undermine my place in the family."

"If that's how you feel then maybe you shouldn't be in my family!" Scott shouted.

"Oh, here comes a spell!" Marcy whispered.

John and Scott glowered at each other.

Sarah re-entered without Simon, who had been sent to his room. "Everyone calm down! Merciful heavens!" she cried. "We have company and everyone at home and this is how you behave—embarrassing Uncle Phil and Aunt Marcy with our personal business!"

Phil turned to his upset hostess. "Sarah, it's all right—at least your children are bright enough to trust with investments."

"Well, that's good of you to say, Phil, but this is absolutely uncalled for. John Weldon, sit down. You are a member of this family and so you will remain. The two of you must stop behaving like bulls. I don't know why Katherine didn't tell you, John, but now in front of company is not the time to discuss your hurt feelings. And Scott, you would do well to censor yourself once in a while—on Christmas!"

"You're right, Sarah," he replied, taking the top from the decanter, but on second thought sealing it again and pushing it away. "I take the blame, Katie. If I had known your investment was a secret I would not have brought it up. My apologies to you, Katie—and to Weldon ... I mean John."

Katherine nodded with a weak smile and prayed, clinging to her napkin, that John would be gracious.

"There is no need to apologize, Mr. McCullough," Weldon said. "I overreacted, and you didn't realize Katherine was keeping secrets from me."

Katherine accepted John's remark in silence—this was no time to plead her case. William rubbed up against her picking food from her plate. "William Weldon, behave like a gentleman and take your place at the table," Katherine said.

"If Willy isn't the clingiest boy to his momma," Marcy said as she wiped her brow. "I'd nip that in the bud. You wouldn't want him to turn out a sissified man, being so pretty and all."

Sarah spoke for her daughter. "Marcy, I know you mean well, but as a mother myself I can tell you that a boy learns a lot about being a good man by spending time with his mother. Simon was the same."

Marcy shifted in her chair and smirked. "And will Simon be marrying any time soon? I'd love to be invited to his wedding."

"Sarah, is it time for desert yet?" Scott asked with urgency.

Sarah bit her lip and silently counted down from five. "Scott, dear, why don't you take the men into the library for a smoke while we clear the table and make things ready?"

Phillip was glad for the distraction. While he loved Marcy, he realized her eccentricities rubbed people the wrong way. Scott and Phillip would continue their lunches in the city, but holiday meetings were not the best idea.

"If you don't mind, Sarah, I need a little fresh, cool air. I'll be on the front porch." Marcy heaved herself up out of her chair, the napkin falling to the floor with pie crust crumbs.

Exasperated, Sarah pushed the stray hairs from her face. "Yes, you do that—*please* go outside."

Katherine and Sarah watched Marcy throw her cape on and exit onto the porch.

"Some marriages are a mystery, Katherine," Sarah said, bending to retrieve the napkin. She pushed the chairs in as she went around the table and stacked the china, thinking ahead to the enormous washing up job. "We should have kept things small. That's what I told your father, but he was so excited to show you all off."

"Father must be thrilled with us now," Katherine said as she scraped the dishes of food.

Sarah laughed in resignation. "Things never go as planned. We should be grateful to have averted the battles between our men so far."

"But Simon was so ..." Katherine began.

"Oh, your brother is harmless. He only hurts himself in the end. He'll feel right foolish tomorrow you can bet, and Father will not let him hear the end of it."

"Neither will I. Simon had no right to say what he did to John," Katherine said and blew on a low-burning candle, sending wax across the linen tablecloth.

"That's what candle snuffs are for," Sarah grumbled.

Katherine picked at the cooled splashes of wax.

"Well, I suppose you'll be apologizing tonight to your husband," Sarah said.

Gingerly carrying her mother's dishes stacked high in front of her, Katherine followed Sarah into the kitchen, where they found William fast asleep in his grandfather's armchair like a remiss sentry with his gun across his lap.

"Oh, Katie, Willy is the most gorgeous child. I never would have guessed he'd turn so blonde," Sarah purred and kissed him while setting the rifle on the floor. Grabbing an old quilt, Sarah tucked William in and moved the chair slightly away from the fire before feeding it a little from the wood box.

Katherine could almost touch and smell her youth as she pinned on her old apron of soft flannel. It occurred to her that she had spent little time with her children this Christmas, and as much as she loved being around family she would welcome the opportunity to be just the four of them again.

Sarah turned to her and smiled. "You coming back here has been the best thing for me, dear. Although it's bittersweet. When I'm puttering around this place alone at night sometimes, I feel such a sense of loss—and guilt too for squandering the time I could have spent with you and your brother when you were young."

"Mother, please don't cry. You spent all of your time with us!"

"But at times I resented it greatly and daydreamed and only pretended to listen to your little stories," Sarah sobbed.

Katherine put her arms around her mother. "You were wonderful. We noticed no resentment, but Mother, I sometimes feel that same way too. I think it might be normal, don't you?"

Sarah shook her head and sniffled. "You'll see when they're gone, your little ones. You'll wonder if you could have loved them a little more or stopped yourself from saying something they might always carry with them."

"Mother, you have allowed yourself too much time to think. Simon and I are fine."

"I'm not so sure. Sometimes I'm saddened by how amenable you both are to everyone. Maybe it's that you never had to fight for anything. I love you both dearly, but you both are so soft and compliant. I'm not sure what I could have done, but it upsets me just the same."

"Now you're being silly. We take care of ourselves."

"I hope that's true," Sarah continued, looking tired. "But you seem to have no dreams for yourselves, or if you do nurse hidden ambitions you're too timid to allow yourselves to admit them."

Katherine had not considered how many weeks of preparation her mother had put into this meal and the treats for the children and the sewing. "I am so lucky to have you, Mother. You may have faults, but they are invisible to me now. You worry too much. I am so happy." Inside, Katherine felt stung by Sarah's observations because, deep down, she had no ambitions for herself.

Weldon walked in wearing his army greatcoat.

"Oh, John, what a dear, feeding the animals are you?" Sarah asked.

"Yes, I'm so used to it being done on time, it unnerves me when they're kept waiting," he said.

"That's so good of you," Sarah continued. "Katie, you may go with him if you'd like. I can handle things here."

Katherine flashed her mother a vicious look but took her work coat from the peg it had waited on for years and followed her husband to the barn.

Weldon lit a lantern and then another and hung them on their nails. The barn was warm and cozy unlike John's cool attitude toward Katherine. They walked past the row of horses' backsides in their stalls. Handsome whinnied, awaiting his evening meal and Hope kicked at the door behind her. Uttering not a word, John climbed into the hayloft and threw a bale of hay which bounced, deceptively light, over the stairs. Two barn cats scuttled by trying to avoid the unwelcome footfall of a man they didn't recognize. The place smelled sweetly of hay and horse. Scott prided himself on a clean and orderly home for his Morgans, and they rewarded him with long years of service and calm steady demeanors.

John looked up at Katherine as he pulled the string from the hay. "Are you helping or are you just going to stand there?"

She should have changed into her old dress but had vainly kept the purple gown on, not imagining she would end the day doing barn work. As best as she could, Katherine picked up some hay and carried it at arm's length to Hope's stall, awkwardly tossing it over the lower side wall.

John shook his head. "Forget it, *Katie,* you should go back to your family."

"Stop it. You are my family. I'm sorry I didn't tell you about the investment."

"Are there other things you've kept from me?"

"No. I was just afraid to tell you."

"What have I ever done to make you afraid? You've humiliated me! Do you have so little faith in me that you must secretly make deals with your father for money?"

"No, that's not it at all," Katherine said. "It was right after you lost our money. I was angry and afraid. You behaved so strangely. When Father and I visited the hospital and saw the suffering, I truly wanted to do something. Father convinced me that providing good prosthetic limbs was more helpful and practical than volunteer work would be. I was easily swayed because I was too afraid to travel back and forth into the city on my own. I knew you wouldn't like that I was involved with my father."

"How does it make me look that you need to supplement our income? Things have improved since my promotion, and I thought you were happy with me," John said, absently sweeping away stray bits of hay.

"I am completely happy with you now, but things were different then, and once I was in it, it would have hurt my father if I withdrew. Plus my father has always had the intention of paying for our children's schooling."

"Isn't that something I should have known about?" John stormed. "What if I didn't want your father taking care of us?"

"How can you turn a blessing into a curse like that, John Weldon? This is what families do for each other. I should have told you, but everything changed once you took me to Arizona, and I didn't much worry about the soldiers back east anymore."

"I know I didn't give you much choice back then, but I'd like to think that I can take care of you, and you can be honest with me. Your father's reasons and your own for taking on this project are quite different, but I won't ask you to stop." He took her chin. "You know you're a great help to soldiers—one in particular."

She laughed. "You haven't needed my help one little bit. I wish you had. There's nothing I can do to repay you for the way you've changed my life."

He gave her an odd look she could not decipher. "Kate, you are far greater medicine than you'll ever know."

Chapter Forty-Five

The first snow of the season announced itself by the silence it brought and the cool light that edged its way beneath the window shade. Eliza sat perched at the end of the bed humming to her doll, cool and alert. "Is Christmas still here?" she asked, with eyes full of hope.

"I'm afraid not, pumpkin," Katherine whispered, "but Grammy is awake downstairs."

Eliza slid from the bed and toddled off to the kitchen where Sarah prepared breakfast. William begged to play in the snowy garden. "After a warm breakfast, Willy," Sarah said, but Scott got up from his chair with a grin and took the boy to find boots in the closet. Sarah laughed at her husband and hugged him. "You're so soft, old man."

Katherine slipped from her room in a moth-eaten shawl and across the hall into Simon's. The sight of him sleeping, surrounded by headless mannequins, made her laugh.

"What time is it?" he asked. He edged up but moaned and returned to his pillows. "I've got a crushing headache."

She sat on the edge of the bed and poured him some water. "Of course you do."

"God, how much of that awful whiskey did I drink, I wonder?" Simon shielded his eyes from the sun, squinting at her. "You must be here for a reason at this early hour. What on earth did I say?"

"I almost feel cruel reminding you."

"Then don't, will you?" he grumbled, forcing sips of water.

"You'll have to face everyone today anyway, so I may as well tell you the worst of it," she said. "You were quite outspoken about the Negroes and sounded just like an unreconstructed rebel."

"Oh, no—and in front of Phil and his horror of a wife too. Father must be livid. You know I only meant that if the Negroes are given things too quickly they'll be slaughtered. Even Grant couldn't keep his son from abusing that poor cadet at West Point in the North. No one up here understands the mentality of the people down there."

"Tell it to the judge," she said. "And you were insulting to Aunt Marcy."

"Well, she is a cow though, isn't she?"

They both laughed. Simon cursed the curtains as he pulled them shut. Katherine grew serious again. "You were cruel to John too—it's nearly unforgivable."

Simon tried to remember the previous day's events but drew a blank on Weldon.

"You embarrassed him with your uncalled-for reference to his lack of a formal education."

"Shit, Kate, I do remember ... but I didn't mean anything by it," he said unconvincingly.

"What's happened between the two of you? I've watched both of you trade veiled and not so veiled insults for the past few days. It's disappointing."

"Life is disappointing," he moaned.

"Since when? You've always been such an optimist .... Who is this girl Mother keeps hinting at?"

"I'm finding Mother to be an untrustworthy confidante. There is no girl." He reached for a cigar and lit it.

Katherine shook her head. "Mother will be annoyed—look at you, an absolute mess!"

He gave her a menacing stare. "Fine, take away my last happiness!" he said, throwing his cigar into the glass of water.

"Cigars are your only happiness? That is pathetic."

"Yes, so it is—I *am* pathetic," he said in resignation.

She took his hand, but he pulled it away.

"Please tell me why you're so changed. What's happened?" She feared the melancholia he had suffered after the war had returned. He had the same lost look. "Please, Simon ..."

"It's nothing, really. Life has just lost its charm for me," he said. "And I'm sorry I hurt John in any way—he doesn't deserve it from me. It's just ... well, things happened during the war, as I'm sure you know."

"Like what?" she asked in all innocence. Simon stared at his sister, comprehending from her expression that Weldon did not talk about those times with her.

"Oh, nothing. It's just hard to see you all so happy and perfect and not be jealous. I suppose I took it out on Weldon."

"I find this so surprising, especially after what you said about John being at such a disadvantage in life as a half-breed and illiterate."

Simon cringed. "Did I say that? What a way with words. After so many years together during the war I couldn't possibly think Weldon an illiterate. He was the only one of us who foraged for books. We called Weldon the headmaster."

"Well, you destroyed yesterday for Mother and Father. No one could get a word in edgewise," she said, pouring on the agony.

"Enough please!" he begged. "I fully comprehend what a jackass I was. I'll make my round of apologies. Will John accept, do you think?"

She was not ready to let him off just yet. "I really couldn't say."

"Please, Katie—say you accept my apology. You are my only ally in the world."

"Who said I was still your ally?" she asked. "John is my first concern now."

She saw by the look on his face that there had been no need to make the distinction.

"Of course John comes first, but I hope you can find it in your heart to keep me in your thoughts."

She laughed at this dramatic expression from him but saw that it pained him. "Simon, you're scaring me. I love you. You are always forgiven by me—that you can depend upon. But you are hardly guilty of any great offense. John cares for you too. He was angrier at me last night for something that came up at the table."

He looked at her as if he had not been listening to her at all. "I've done something terrible, sis. I've ruined a girl," he confessed on the verge of tears. Not since the day Simon's favorite pony died years ago had Katherine seen this much emotion in her brother.

She tried to make light of it. "Only one?"

He remained silent.

"I'm sorry, but why is this so different from what you've told me before? I never imagined you were more careful after the war."

He laughed without humor. "I'm glad to hear I instill such confidence in people."

"Well, you must tell me why this is such a sad story. I'm sure you can get out of it." She was smugly pleased that his conscience was awakening even as she worried for him.

"Get out of it? I *am* out of it, but not by my will," he said, staring at the half-dressed, lifeless forms around him. "I ruin everyone I care for."

"You didn't ruin me, Simon."

"Well, I guess you were lucky then ... and you've taken Weldon," he said wistfully. "It's just that I'm lonely I guess ... for the old times. It's childish, but I feel you've taken my only friend."

"I don't understand why you worked so hard to transfer then."

"I don't know. It's too hard to explain exactly. Sometimes I think he has every reason to hate me. And sometimes I don't like him much either. I don't know why ..."

Katherine sat with her hands clasped in her lap. "I'm afraid you're making little sense. Maybe you're just tired."

"For God's sake, why do women always assign what they don't understand to some physical state of being or ailment? I know what I know even if I can't state it as clearly as you need me to. I guess the simplest explanation is that sometimes I resent Weldon for getting on with his life so well and without me. Of course he deserves all of his success, but I feel sorry for myself. I used to think that in ways I was superior to him because he was such a stiff, and I got along with everyone. So stupid ... what did it matter about popularity? I had a good friend, and I took advantage ... he gave awful good advice too." Simon shook his head with a sad smile. "You didn't know him then, Katie, but he could be a right pain in his quiet way—always trying too hard to be perfect. I liked him right off because it was fun taking him down a few pegs. I guess he liked that someone took any notice at all, though he complained. The funny thing is that I thought I carried him along through the war, but he was the one who kept me on the straight and narrow ... and I nearly ruined him."

"How?"

"I can't talk about it, Kate, but it all worked out in the end, I guess."

She did not want to know how close her husband had come to ruination. "Well, I'm sure you'll get over this problem, just like you always do."

"You've been too long with him." He sighed, lighting another cigar in defiance of his mother's wishes. "I guess I'll get by, but you know, I'm finally learning that things *do* catch up with you."

"You know my feelings about low women—they make their own beds."

"No, you've got it all wrong about this girl. I don't know how it happened. It crept up on me somehow, but I care for her and convinced her to do things."

"Well, if she knew you at all then ..."

He rubbed his hands over his eyes in frustration. "She did know me—she does know me—too well now."

"Will she get rid of it?" Katherine asked quietly.

"Get rid of what? She's not going to have a baby! Now maybe she never will." Simon looked into his sister's puzzled eyes. "It seems I'm not really cured. Remember what I told you about Washington—and the hospital? It seems there might be no cure," he said, his eyes full of repressed emotion as he puffed his cigar.

She shook her head. "There must be a way to ..."

"No. There's not and I've passed it on to her, I think, because she won't speak to me. I wanted to marry her. I told her so—if she'd have me—but that was before and now she won't come near me."

"How could you be so foolish? I always thought so much of you! You can be so good. Why have you chosen to be so wicked?!" Katherine cried, afraid for her broth-

er's health and angry at his maddening lack of judgment. "You are such a disappointment! I can't bear it!"

"Get out! I hoped I could depend on you to help me. I trusted you would forgive my mistakes! I've never been as clever as you or as disciplined ..."

"Stop using Father's labels as an excuse for taking the easy way out!" she said in
lofty condescension. "It's beneath you! You're stupid to ruin yourself this way, but it's
not for lack of cleverness. You just do as you like!" She ran for the door. In the hallway she choked back tears. There was no cure! Nothing could be done. She could
not face Simon knowing he might die such an ignoble death! She couldn't help him
out of the mess he'd created for himself.

Leaning against the banister, not sure where she wanted to go, she heard John
stumble out of the tall bed and went in to help him dress.

"Eliza, is she well this morning?" he asked hopefully.

Katherine nodded but said nothing as she moved his arm into his soft homespun sleeve and buttoned it at the wrists and collar before heading out. She opened
her door at the same time Simon did. He looked more bleary-eyed than before.
"Katherine, do me the favor of never telling what I have so foolishly confided in
you."

"I have always kept my word on that, Simon. I will continue to do so."

He gave her a look that chilled her to the bone.

John came out after them, breezily unaware of the exchange. "Will you come
out for a smoke, captain? There is much I want to remind you of," he said, chuckling,
"just like old times."

Simon smiled weakly. "I'll come if you promise not to say a word. I've already
been filled in by my heavy-handed sister."

John frowned at her. He seemingly would forgive her brother all transgressions.
What a strange friendship they had, but then men were different. The men passed
through the kitchen, bundled up in silence—the house was deserted—and went out
under the half snowed-in porch to shiver and smoke. Simon reached into his jacket
for his flask and took a swig.

Weldon watched him and then turned to the garden. "That nasty little willow
tree you planted sure looks nice all covered in snow."

Simon grinned at his friend, wondering how he kept track of such trivial things
as plants. "You are an odd one, Weldon."

John smiled archly but said nothing.

"About yesterday ..." Simon began, rubbing his hands for warmth.

"Water under the bridge. I know what you were trying to say," Weldon assured him.

"I'm glad one of us does," Simon said, kicking snow from the porch.

Weldon cleared his throat. "Maybe you should go easy on the drinking today, captain."

Simon turned on him defensively but thought better of it. He took his flask and emptied it into the snow. "One thing I have grown too fond of since the war."

Weldon looked on in great sympathy. He still spent most mornings fighting off the urge to start up his habit again. "It's not like you to drink first thing—yesterday was a bit bad, but I've seen you worse."

"That's very consoling. Thanks."

"I do my best."

Simon laughed. "You know, not having you around has been a big loss for me."

"I'm around."

"Well, it's not the same, is it?"

John puffed on his cigar. "Thank God."

"I never would have admitted it then, but without your help I would have made even more a mess of things than I did during the war."

"We all make errors in judgment—you really weren't as bad as you're making out."

"I don't know."

"My God, Simon, are you developing a conscience?"

"Too little too late, I'm afraid."

Simon's willow shook its feathery plumage onto the perfectly shoveled garden paths that in summer were hot to the touch. The birdbaths were cakes on beautiful stands and decorated in delicate sparrows' prints. Simon and John could hear Marcy and Phil happily chatting in the kitchen, banging about like campers on their first adventure and not sure of what went where. John and Simon braced themselves against a sharp wind and relit their cigars.

"Have you tried the Mexican cigarettes with the tobacco rolled in cornhusks?" Weldon asked.

"Nope," Simon answered, "and I don't intend to."

Weldon chuckled. "They're like the stuff you make as a boy—awful really."

Only now did they notice Sarah and Eliza in the conservatory planting John's seeds and watering the hothouse flowers. From the street, sleigh bells in the distance told of someone's fast trot through the morning. A woolly child, wrapped to his eyes in red and gold striped scarves and dragging a bobsled, called out to his father and waved as well as he could beneath the layers of clothing. Scott trudged after the boy with a smile, a red face and an open coat—as usual overheating.

"Father, you look the image of a polar explorer," Simon said with forced cheer, hoping his father would let yesterday alone.

Scott nodded severely and directed his talk to his son-in-law. "Well, Weldon, you must have a very forgiving nature to be standing here with my son."

Weldon chose to ignore the words, glancing at Simon and then responding, "It's quite a chilly day for a walk, Mr. McCullough. How are the roads?"

"Perfect for a nice sleigh ride with one of the horses. You and Katie should take Handsome for some exercise."

Simon understood that John would be the beneficiary of Scott's goodwill for only as long as it suited him to make Simon suffer.

"Thank you, sir," John replied, also aware of Scott's intentions. "Willy, go in and warm up."

"I'm not cold yet. May I go see Grammy in the glass house?"

"Go ahead, son," Scott said, shaking his head. "Katherine and you are doing a fine job with those children ... even if they can't carry on the McCullough name. Looks like they may be the only grandchildren I'll ever have."

"I think I'll go see to it that my children don't overwhelm Mrs. McCullough," Weldon said, more interested in the new specimens Sarah had collected since they worked together years before than seeing Simon abused.

Simon watched his last hope for rescue join the happy group enclosed in glass. "All right, Father, before you say a word I want to apologize, and I intend to do the same with Uncle Phil and Aunt Marcy."

"Save your apologies," Scott whispered, wanting to shield his guests in the kitchen. "Apologies have become too easy for you and meaningless to us. You've always said and done as you pleased, but it is time for me to tell you how people really see you."

"You've been telling me all my life. One more laundry list of my many faults will make no difference."

Scott laughed at his son contemptuously. "You will listen for your own good."

"I don't think, Father, that you've ever done anything solely for my own good. Everything has been to suit you."

"You speak like a child, and now you will listen. Your behavior yesterday proved that your mother and I failed at our many attempts to bring you up as a decent member of society. Your drunkenness and lack of respect for people—even your so-called friend Weldon—disgust me."

"Father, don't talk about Weldon as if you give a lick about him," Simon sneered.

"It doesn't matter if I hate him or am saddened by the little mixed breeds—I know how to behave civilly."

"You make me sick, Father."

"The feeling is mutual, I'm afraid. All the wasted money on schools and tutors thrown away on soldiering, and now I must admit that your attitudes about people less fortunate, whom you are paid to protect, make you unfit even for that. Being a captain of men is even too good for you. You are a drunkard and an embarrassment to this family—even more than your sister and her tribe of Indians."

"For all the good you've done for the world out there—on the Sanitary Commission, the Abolition Committee, your stump work—you really don't give a damn about your own family. I may be nothing in your eyes—and maybe mine too—but I'm honest about why I do things and who I care about. I drink because I enjoy it. I'm a soldier because I want to back up my words with action."

"I'm glad things are so simple for you, son, but I don't buy a word of it. You drink because you are alone, and you stay in the military because you have nothing else to offer the world but good aim. You wondered why your uncle was surprised at where you were stationed. I was too ashamed to tell him the army thought so little of you that they stationed you as far away from civilization as they could."

Simon stammered, "But ... you know I asked to be transferred back west!"

"And what does that say about you?" Scott shouted. "You had people pulling for you in Washington, but you run away from success! I've made my peace with Katherine's ridiculous marriage, but you are *my* son—you carry on my name!"

"I'm leaving today, Father," Simon said.

"*Good*!"

Simon turned and went inside. He didn't hang up his coat, just took a deep breath as he prepared to face his aunt and uncle. Grimly he dragged himself forward, fully feeling the effects of last night's drinking.

"Ah, Simon," Phillip began with a tolerant smile. "How are you, nephew?"

Aunt Marcy sipped tea from her saucer and eyed Simon with the smallest of grins.

"I behaved miserably to you both yesterday. I apologize for anything I said that offended you," Simon said.

"Sit and drink some tea, dear," Marcy coaxed. "You were more amusing than not. Phil and I have had our times when we've taken things to extremes."

"No, I really couldn't, Aunt Marcy. Thank you for your kind words. I'm afraid my father sees things differently. I'll be preparing to go this afternoon. It was nice seeing you both again."

Simon knocked at his sister's door.

"Come in."

Simon opened the door and stood just within the room, uncomfortable in his own skin. Katherine's heart went out to him. He looked so miserable, but she could not hide her disappointment in him and felt repulsed by his disease.

"I came to say goodbye, Katherine."

She continued brushing her hair.

"Please don't stay angry with me forever," he pleaded.

"I hope it all works out for you, Simon. Maybe now you've learned a lesson," she said, her nose in the air.

Simon waited a moment, hoping she would break down and ask him to stay, but she was in no mood to have her husband insulted again or to watch Simon drink. He walked out and packed his few things, including his new cigar case and the trinkets John and Katherine had brought for him.

Sarah was at the bottom of the stairs with the children when he made his way down.

"Land sakes, Simon, where are you off to?" she asked.

He wanted to tell her everything, but dared not. "Mother, I'll write you as soon as I can," he said simply.

"You're not due to leave us for another fortnight," she cried. "Don't be so hasty. Your father and sister will be disappointed if you go!"

He laughed. "You have no idea what you're talking about." He kissed her, shook hands with a disappointed Willy, and patted Eliza's curly head of hair, unable to say more without betraying his feelings.

"Oh, Simon!" Sarah sobbed as he closed the door behind him. "Scott! Come here at once!"

Along with Scott came Phil and Marcy, alarmed at her tone.

"How dare you send him off!" Sarah wailed. Eliza and William joined their grandmother in emotion.

"Sarah, it was his idea ... and it's for the best," Scott reasoned weakly. "He has to grow up some time."

"Oh, dear Scott, I hope you didn't send him away on our account," Marcy worried. "The boy seemed quite contrite this morning. He did no real harm."

Scott shook his head. "Just like him to work on people's sympathies."

"You are the most cynical man I've ever met, Scott McCullough!" Sarah cried. "Of course he works on people's sympathies! People with hearts not made of stone are perceptive enough to notice when their relations are under the strain of something."

Scott's voice boomed. "You, Sarah, are responsible for all of his deficiencies—making excuses for him always. I want you to know that when he falls into complete ruin, you will pick up the pieces. I wash my hands of it all."

Phillip and Marcy stepped forward. "Now is as good a time as any to say our goodbyes," Phil said with obvious embarrassment.

"I'm sorry to you both," Sarah sobbed and ran upstairs to her room. The children bolted too but were caught on the landing by their mother, who had been listening at her bedroom door.

Coming out of the barn, Weldon spotted Simon plodding away. "Captain, where are you off to?" he asked as he caught up.

"To the station, Weldon. You don't need to follow like a lapdog," Simon said bitterly.

Following Simon's orders habitually, Weldon stopped, but asked, "What's happened?"

"Ask my sister."

He watched Simon march down into the valley alone. He disappeared behind the station as a southbound Hoboken train pulled in. Weldon turned for home. Back in the drive, he met Phil and Scott making the carriage ready for sudden departure. Phil half-trotted on his old legs up to Weldon with his hand out. "Best of luck, young man. Nice to have met you."

"And you, sir," Weldon replied, surprised at the mass exodus.

Marcy pushed out the side door, her bonnet's ribbons flapping in the gusting air and her dog howling in the cold. "What a day for a drive," she said brightly with a touch of sarcasm. With some effort, she was hoisted up into the carriage. Marcy waved farewell to Weldon. Scott received a kiss. The women had said their goodbyes indoors.

Scott and Weldon stood watching the relatives drive off under less-than-ideal conditions.

"It's a shame the way some things turn out, sir," Weldon observed uncomfortably.

"Especially with one's offspring," Scott commented, his tone intended to remind his son-in-law that Simon was not the only child to bring him disappointment.

The men walked back into the house silently and sought out their women.

Chapter Forty-Six

Katherine lounged with the children in the parlor, looking prim in her gold out-of-date dress from the war. The skirt was too long without its hoop and covered Katherine's feet like a blanket. Weldon came in and sat beside her. The holiday spirit of the place left with Simon, and the heavy letdown of another year approaching its end settled in with the clutter of the presents and the trays not yet cleared of yesterday's edibles.

"Simon is gone," Katherine said.

"I know. What did I miss?" John asked.

"You didn't miss a thing," she said. "You were witness to his behavior yesterday."

"That's it? That's why he left?"

She took a stale cookie from a tray. "I'm glad he's gone. I'm so tired of defending him and putting up with his embarrassing behavior. His drunkenness sickens me. He has no control. I never knew how weak-willed he was."

John shook his head. "You're too hard on him."

She tossed the cookie back on the tray. "Why must you defend him always when he can be so cruel to you?"

Weldon caught sight of an ancient daguerreotype of Simon as a child on the side table. The picture captured a childish eagerness to please that saddened him. "There are worse things than having too much to drink on a holiday."

Katherine huffed in disbelief. "How can you condone what he does? You never drink yourself, and you hate your mother for drinking, but Simon ..."

"I know ..." Weldon began haltingly, finding it a difficult subject to discuss. "Your brother would do the same for me ... he means well."

"Having good intentions is different from being good. I have no sympathy for my brother. He's always been thoughtless and undisciplined. Father said it many times, but I see now myself. I'm no longer blinded by stupid sisterly devotion! He's ruined himself."

Eliza pulled a Christmas ornament from the tree. Weldon retrieved her with a stern look, sitting her beside Katherine. "How has he ever hurt you?"

"My brother was disrespectful to you, and he continues to treat women badly," she replied.

John chuckled. "Simon has always treated women quite well."

"I'm glad you find it amusing. Simon takes advantage of women with no remorse at all," she said with her chin held high.

"I've never been his keeper ... but close enough," John said with an endearing blush. "It's an odd thing to discuss with one's wife, but Simon's girls always played along of their own free will."

Katherine felt certain by Weldon's levity that Simon had not informed him of the latest bit of news. "It doesn't matter anyway. He will never have a family now—he doesn't deserve one. Why does he always expect other people to clean up his messes?"

"Stop it! Your words do you a great disservice, and they're inaccurate. Simon has made mistakes, and maybe you have been called upon to help him, but you forget he's gone out of his way to help us—again and again. How often do you write him?"

Katherine huffed.

"How often does he write us? Once or twice a month—at least. He makes up for his sins as far as I'm concerned." Weldon suddenly realized how far he had come in forgiving Simon himself.

Katherine gazed up looking like royalty in gold as the sun caught her eyes and animated her features. "I'm sorry if you don't like my words, but I can't help feeling them, especially when I compare Simon to you."

Weldon's heart sank.

"You are temperate, brave, and dependable," she said. "Simon is the opposite!"

"He's incredibly brave!" John said. "You don't know the half of what your brother is, and if you knew anything about me ..."

She turned on him. "So now I don't know you? I've lived with you for four years in Arizona. By now I would have noticed cracks in your carefully constructed façade, don't you think? You are superior to Simon in every way. Only your modesty prevents you from seeing it."

He took in her trusting expression. "This conversation disgusts me, Kate. Simon and I do not compete for affection or anything else. I wonder though ... if I ever stumbled and ... started drinking ..."

She laughed. "But you wouldn't—you're too strong and good for that, Mr. Weldon."

"But if I did something like that, I wonder if you would judge me so harshly."

She pulled him down beside her. "We will never find out, my dear," she said. "You would never bring such disgrace into our lives."

This strange faith Katherine had in him—he was extremely grateful for it but in constant fear of destroying it. Weldon wondered how he had passed through her filter in those first shaky years of their marriage and concluded it was the shame of a quick divorce that had saved him.

Sarah wandered in, her chin quivering, her apron inside out, and a sodden handkerchief hanging from her sleeve. Determined to present a brave face, she gathered the trays—all her work a waste, she thought, and cried again.

"Mother, why don't you sit and have some tea," Katherine suggested, in no mood herself to clean but uncomfortable watching her mother do it alone and crying.

Weldon stood to leave. "Pardon me."

Sarah stopped him. "Do stay, John. It will be so soon when you're all gone again. You may as well know I'm devastated by today's events—but I'll recover."

"Mother, Simon behaved dreadfully yesterday and on many other occasions. We do him no favors allowing him to trample others for his own selfish pleasures."

"What pleasure do you speak of? He spoke rashly yesterday and was insensitive to you, John, although I hope you see how much we think of you—you're not wanting in intellect."

He smiled at Sarah's directness.

She continued, "But Simon took pleasure in nothing, so I have no idea what you mean."

"Forgive me, Mother," Katherine said, "but you were always too easy on him and now he suffers for it."

Sarah was taken aback. "How much you remind me of your Father this minute!"

Weldon interrupted, "Kate, you should be more respectful!"

"Simon has destroyed other people's lives with his reckless behavior," Katherine said with the aplomb of a lawyer sure of his case. The knowledge of this one good girl Simon had disgraced caused all the others alluded to over the years to come to life in her mind.

Weldon could stand no more. "Katherine! Please be quiet! Mrs. McCullough, I've had the honor of serving under your son and your effect on him is clear. Simon is lucky to have you as his mother."

Scott stood unnoticed in the doorway. "Hear, hear, Weldon," he said with mocking applause. "But you must understand for all your sickly sweet sentiment, my wife will never adopt you as her long, lost son. Sarah has a lost son already in Simon."

Mortified, Sarah raced from the room in tears.

"Father, how can you twist things and turn them so ugly?" Katherine cried.

Weldon stood tall with eyes flashing. Scott backed off, unsure if this western ruffian would strike him.

"As you have never served in the military, sir, I wouldn't expect you to understand that it's a point of honor to defend one's own and to never leave them behind in times of trouble—even when they disappoint you as men will do," Weldon said.

"Simon deserves better treatment than you give him, and I'll always risk your sarcasm to defend him—as family should, sir. We shall leave if you care to make us go, but as someone who has spent most of my life without a family, I think you should show some gratitude for all you've been given and don't waste what little time may be left to you!"

Scott's eyes bulged. Katherine and the children sat breathlessly watching the standoff. After an uneasy moment Scott stormed out of the parlor and into his bedroom, slamming the door behind him. Weldon turned to his family, surprised at himself, and laughed. Katherine made room on the sofa, shooing the children aside. When Weldon sat beside her she threw her arms around his neck.

"Well, I don't know if Father will hate you for good now, Mr. Weldon, but I've never enjoyed watching such a scolding as the one you just gave him!" Katherine kissed him and the children jumped in, merrily dangling off their father's back. "I love you, John Weldon! And you're right about Simon. I was too hard on him—I will write and tell him how sorry I am today!"

Weldon stretched out satisfied with himself and the people around him like a lion in his lair and fell asleep with Kate leaning against him and his children playing at his feet.

Chapter Forty-Seven

Chatter from children and the adults trying to quiet them on the porch outside the parlor windows stirred Katherine from her sleep. Scott's heavy footfall passed in the hall, and the door opened to the Crenshaw family—at least a few of its members. Margaret's strong-lunged voice and the more subtle tones of Graham's gentle words were just outside the parlor door now.

"John, wake up," Katherine whispered poking him. "We have visitors."

The great oak doors slid open, revealing the sleepy family to the bright and bedecked one just arrived. Margaret dazzled in a scarlet bonnet trimmed in pom-poms and black lace, a cerulean blue skirt in the old style with silk underskirts, and heaps of red velvet like icing on a cake draped on top. Everyone else faded in her company.

Graham and Margaret had been productive. Twin boys arrived soon after William's birth. A second set of twin girls came a year later, and by the looks of it Margaret was pregnant again. The boys, Fred and Buck, had come for the visit and were making their presence felt, pulling at each other, yelping and flailing their arms far too close to Sarah's fragile collections on display in the hall. Scott intervened as the heavier of the two boys dared to climb the banister and soon after jumped from it, tumbling into the basket full of umbrellas and fine parasols. William and Eliza watched, startled and delighted by the pair.

"Graham, will you please do something about the boys?" Margaret asked, as the twins took up umbrellas as weapons.

Buck and Fred burst into the library then and roughly thumbed through a pile of Simon's boyhood books set out for William.

Scott interrupted their explorations. "This room is off limits—it's for the grown and the privileged. If you behave you may be allowed entrance to view my things."

Fred and Buck wore fussy, blue suits, but no amount of fancy coverings could hide their spoiled and rowdy demeanors.

William stepped up with hands in pockets for a talk. He rocked on his feet as he spoke. "My grandpa has a gun from the French Indian War."

The boys looked at him contemptuously. Fred, the heavier one, replied, "So? What of it? Our daddy has lots of collections and more than just an old gun. He has a real howitzer cannon the Rebs used in the yard."

"Really?" William asked, impressed more with the boys than the howitzer. He pondered a minute and said, "Well, my papa is in the cavalry and has a carbine and he uses it and fights real Indians too, and was an infantryman before that ... so there."

"So there," Eliza repeated in support of her brother. William shoved her aside, but she stood her ground.

"Mr. McCullough, please send the boys outdoors, will you? And where is your wife? I've got sweets my mother sent over," Margaret said.

"Boys, go in the yard, but the barn's off limits—Willy, you make sure of it," Scott warned, not much trusting the velvet-attired duo.

The boys rushed out and Eliza too, after William helped put her coat on haphazardly. Katherine lifted her heavy skirt so as not to trip and stepped forward to greet the guests, glancing back with pained expression at an aloof John fussing with his hair.

A slight, smartly attired young man accompanied Graham and Margaret.

"Gerald, my word, it's been ages," exclaimed Katherine.

"My little brother is just up from the South trying to change the world," Margaret gushed over the runt of the litter. He was only about 5'3" in his heeled shoes but had the same fleshy cheeks and strong brow as all of Margaret's brothers. Unlike his sister and because he was the youngest of many siblings, Gerald rarely spoke unless spoken to and always waited his turn. The other men towered over him.

After a few handshakes and Christmas greetings, the room grew quiet until Scott reemerged from the kitchen with glasses and a nice bottle of spirits. "I'm sure you could all do with a warming drink."

"Oh, we'd love it." Margaret spoke for her men as usual. She turned to Katherine. "I told you I wouldn't let you escape town without a visit from your old friends."

They laughed uncomfortably.

"Father, please, I'll take a small bit too," Katherine said, remembering the unpleasant times this grouping of people had shared in the past.

Scott avoided Weldon, and Sarah soon made her appearance, noticeably subdued. Katherine beckoned Sarah to sit with her and took her hand. John set the fire ablaze. Its reflection softened the signs of another year gone by on everyone's faces. Katherine and Sarah each privately wondered where Simon spent this holiday night alone. Katherine imagined him blind drunk and sick in a wayside tavern.

Margaret expostulated on the trivial events of the day, no one really listening. Weldon wondered at Graham Crenshaw's choice in women as he watched the man daydream through his wife's endless pronouncements.

"... and I still feel it such a shame to lose Mr. Bollet and his charming wife over the ravine issue. Who ever heard of such a thing? To leave your friends and home over a few trees cut and a road expanded. I was one of the few people glad to see the ax men come and work that day. Driving that part of Palisades Avenue was treacherous with my spirited group and the untamed team Graham has got for me—you'd think he was conspiring to have me killed."

Weldon laughed.

Graham gazed steadily at his wife and explained, "If you weren't so strong with the whip you might manage the horses better." He turned to the others with a good-natured grin. "Margaret pleaded for the enormous Friesians, speckled and all, which we saw at the horse show in Hackensack. They eat us out of house and home. You can see for yourself how utterly ridiculous they are, and now she complains they are too much to manage!"

Katherine smiled. Graham Crenshaw was far too soft for his mate.

Sarah spoke. "That little ravine had the most beautiful old chestnut trees. When the children were young I would meet with friends there, and we would read together and watch the children fill their baskets with nuts."

"Yes, that's all well and good, Mrs. McCullough, but in the middle of the main thoroughfare in town? The Village Improvement Society has planted so many trees I don't see what all the fuss and bother is over the ravine."

"I see that sentiment is lost on the young," Sarah said, obviously annoyed.

"What's done is done," Scott interjected. "Sarah, saving that ravine would not have made your children young again."

Sarah's eyes welled with tears. "I didn't say it would. Did I?"

Katherine threw back her drink. Weldon wished to float away, but the visit continued.

"So, Gerald," Scott began, "I hear you will join the Village Protection Society now that you are back from your travels. I suspect you will find Englewood's woes a fair bit easier to handle than those of Mississippi."

"I don't know about that," Margaret interrupted. "There's been quite a few robberies here, and the economy since the panic shall only make things worse, I fear. I've noticed a hungrier look on the new faces rolling into town."

Sarah clucked her tongue, running low on patience. "Do we live in the same town, dear?"

Margaret spoke as if she were visiting Sarah in an old folks' home. "Sarah, dear, it's been a while since you've involved yourself in civic projects. I suspect your wanderings have not brought you into the less affluent sections of town, but it's becoming quite scary. Graham worries for me ... but I feel it my duty to help anyone in need."

"I worry for my horses only," Graham quipped to a delighted Weldon.

Scott again spoke to Gerald. "But for a rare burglary, it's quiet here—except for all the amateur musicians practicing at their windows in spring."

"Well, there was that bit of excitement when that man Kingsland broke out of Sing Sing," Sarah said.

Scott grew impatient with the women. "Men, would you care to join me for a smoke in the library?"

Graham and Gerald agreed so Weldon followed. Scott slid the doors shut and passed around the superb cigars he had intended to share with Phillip and Simon. "So tell us about the South; how is it from a Republican standpoint," Scott asked Gerald, who sat across from him enjoying his smoke and drink.

Gerald laughed. "The Republican party is dead in Mississippi. If Republicans concede anything to the white supremacist they're looked upon as being weak and the rebels have their way, yet the moment the party fights for more radical steps to protect the freedmen's rights, it's vilified and the members of the party are made to fear for their own lives." He blew smoke at the ceiling. "I naively thought I could make a difference, but even the freedmen have bizarre and complex relationships still with their old masters. It is a closed book between them. Unless you're a Yankee soldier you're not much liked or feared by any of the white low-downers."

"Is the poverty as widespread as the papers make it out to be?" Scott asked.

"Worse, I'd guess. Things are tough for everyone. The freedmen don't have a clue how to feed themselves. They're used to abuse, but they're also used to handouts and so a lot of them wait for the government to feed them. Same with the low-down whites. The plantations often took on the poor in their districts as charity cases and fed them. With a lot of the plantations in a state of chaos or abandoned, there's no surplus to go around. It's a mess with blame everywhere. And the Negroes are getting the worst of it. Whole towns are accused of murdering colored folk for this or that unproven reason, and when the law comes in the people scatter and not a soul betrays the criminals. It's a terrible mess."

"The government has passed some good amendments, but ..." Scott started.

"But if laws cannot be enforced locally then what use are they? The strain of racial hatred in Mississippi is of a far more virulent type than even the worst Jersey Democrat," the young man proposed. "All the giddy optimism of the carpetbaggers, the coloreds, and the Republicans has skedaddled."

"My son feared as much," Scott said.

"I'm sorry for your loss, sir," Gerald offered in misunderstanding.

"Oh, no, he's very much alive—in the cavalry." Scott laughed, embarrassed.

Graham asked, "Where is the captain today? I was under the impression he would be here a while longer."

Scott grew red in the face. Weldon looked on smugly enjoying Scott squirm.

"Simon was called back earlier than expected," Scott grumbled. "But back to you, Gerald. So you were saying that the Republicans are intimidated down there by the white liners?"

"If you'd prefer to call murder intimidation then yes, the Republicans are intimidated," Gerald replied. "Of course I've heard from friends elsewhere in the South quite different stories where the changes have happened with much less upheaval, but Grant does not do as much as he should. Although the country doesn't want it, the soldiers should be sent there in force. The old rebels have had a few years to rest and recoup, and in my opinion are threatening open rebellion again."

Graham cleared his throat and spoke with a force unusual for him. "Gerald, most of us in the North who are old enough to have witnessed the devastating effects of war want no more of it. A great many are tired of the race question. Every fall it's the same down there. They'll have to sort things out amongst themselves this time. I lost two brothers and many friends. We've passed the amendments—let the courts resolve the problems locally."

Gerald replied hotly, "I beg your pardon, Graham, but those dead soldiers you speak of will have fought for nothing if Grant does not send down men to enforce the laws of the land! Tenderness has led these men to the conclusion they are in control again. Arkansas intends to rewrite its constitution in defiance of the one they agreed to on reentering the union. This is bleeding Kansas all over again, the South doing as it pleases at the expense of our national character and the freedmen."

Weldon flicked his cigar. "I think Grant fears seeming a military dictator—there's little love for the soldier these days."

"Or maybe like me Grant is sick of seeing soldiers killed and maimed," Crenshaw offered.

"Grant the butcher didn't mind sending thousands to be slaughtered when it was his career he was fighting for during the war," Scott noted. "I never wanted him on the Republican ticket—but I'd say I was about the only one."

"Well, Grant did end the war," Weldon stated.

"Yes, but he doesn't have the same will to protect what he's won," Gerald said. "It's an outrage. To be honest, the South is a different world. It's not just black and white—it's black and mulatto half brothers and sisters to plantation families and then there's the low-downers—so many complex relationships. Without the old system there's a void. Most people are undereducated and not used to working for wages or paying wages. It's a confusing and demoralizing place for a Northerner like me to be. I feared if I stayed I would end my life a bitter old man."

"Strong words for someone so young," Scott said benevolently. "I hope you will regain some faith in human nature here in Englewood."

"Sometimes I think Grant has the right idea about shipping them all off to Santo Domingo," Gerald said. "The freedmen would be left alone, and those who stayed would have more bargaining power in negotiating for pay from the ex-masters who haven't run off to Brazil."

"You are still somewhat naive about people if you believe Grant has noble intentions for Santo Domingo!" Scott scoffed.

Graham let out a disgusted sigh, tired of the endless political debating that followed him throughout the holidays with Gerald. Weldon felt the same. Nothing ever went as planned. There were always new problems just when progress was hailed, and always there were corruptible men. It was depressing and boring.

Gerald could not read the two men's minds. "What is especially sad though is that so many in the North who fought for equality and free labor will never get to know the many bright and articulate colored men who are being most intimidated. I don't understand the lack of interest."

Scott colored in momentary shame at his own fickle mind. Since the war he had grown less interested in the more complex problems of the South—an open Pandora's box. In the patriotic and optimistic exhilaration of the first postwar days when soldiers were heroes, not Indian killers, and politicians spoke of the rights of men and not just those of their constituents—in those brief days of optimism Scott was a radical Republican.

Then Simon came home shattered and full of depressing news, of illiterate and destitute ex-slaves, of lands given and taken away, of a powerless Freedmen's Bureau, and of unrepentant southern secessionists. Issues in black and white Scott could get behind, but his interest waned in the grey areas—he had a business to run in a shaky market. There were no clear answers, no perfect heroes, and no sublime victims. Reality set in and Scott turned away. He wanted the South to pay for its sins, but with their economy and society destroyed it would be tough. It disturbed Scott to imagine more young Americans dying to bring the South in line. Once again compromises were hard to come by, and things after the war seemed just as unstable as before. The rest of the country was already looking west.

Even in this library so stuffed with books smelling of mildew, journals worn thin by endless perusals, and more furniture than was necessary, Weldon found a spot far from the other men, standing at the window as if ready at any moment to escape. The men talked on about the failures so far with Reconstruction, the various mythologies being written by players in the late war, and the trouble with England over their complicity in blockade running.

Weldon had read as much and experienced more (with the possible exception of Graham Crenshaw) of the war and its intricacies than Scott and Gerald combined. While this prepared him to educate them on the finer points of the war, his social discomfort—his lack of formal education—kept him from sharing his knowledge. Let them think they had their stories right—what did it matter?

A persistent thumping in the yard distracted Weldon from the conversation. Pulling the curtain from the window at his side, he saw the barn door swaying gently open and shut in the wind. "They're in the barn. Pardon me," he said as he abruptly left the room.

Only Scott heard what Weldon said and rose to follow. Just as Scott came into the yard, he spotted Eliza happily pulling a sled through the darkness around the back of the house and scooped her up still intending to give the boys a great talking to. "Elly, does your mother have no sense at all leaving you so long in the cold and dark?" Scott complained, kissing her wet face.

"Grumpy," Eliza said, sweetly mispronouncing his title.

Eliza was a lovely little thing, Scott thought. Maybe she would come back east to school. Scott pulled open the barn door to find a mess—a loose horse and William in anguish on the floor. Weldon shoved Handsome out of the way and knelt at his son's side. Willy clutched his arm, telling a jumbled story between yelps of pain. Before Weldon could say a word, Scott shouted, "William! What did I tell you about the barn? I knew it! You couldn't be trusted!"

Weldon flashed Scott an aggressive look and turned to his son. "What happened here? Calm down. Where are the boys?"

Buck and Fred peered over the edge of the hay loft. Scott noticed them first and ordered them to come down at once. "What in God's name happened to my grandson? You ruffians!"

Fred shoved Buck to the ladder and followed. Fred spoke first with no signs of remorse. "Willy fell. It's his own fault for forcing us up here when he wasn't allowed."

"We only did what he asked—he was showing off that plain old horse," Buck added, feeding off the confidence Fred displayed.

"They're lying!" Willy cried out. "They pushed me out of the loft when I tried to make them leave!"

Graham Crenshaw stood fuming at the door. He grabbed Handsome, who had been easing himself out the door for escape, and brought the horse to his stall. "Buck and Fred go to your mother at once!" he shouted. Everyone turned in surprise and watched the two boys go. At a safe distance they continued defending themselves. "Willy told us we had to go to the barn!" "What were we to do?"

John noticed Graham's labored breathing and the grey hairs at his temples and found again a small bit of sympathy for the man as he knelt down heavily to examine William, but commented, "Sorry, Crenshaw, no chance for an amputation here."

Graham gave him a mild look, but William grew more frightened. "Papa, don't let him take my arm!"

"William, squeeze my finger. There. No need to take the arm. Don't you worry," Graham assured him as he felt along William's arm. "We need to find where you've hurt it so we can set it straight. Okay?"

William nodded.

"Let's bring Willy into the house, and I'll be able to get a better look," the ex-doctor proposed.

Weldon curbed his desire to do the exact opposite and helped William to his feet, trying with great difficulty to keep the boy from bolting like a colt.

Graham stepped in, putting his big body before the door in front of Willy. "Listen to me. I know it hurts, but you can't fix it—only I can right now so you have to trust me."

Weldon rolled his eyes, but saw that William listened intently.

"I've done this many, many times during the war."

"You were a soldier?" William asked, sniffling.

"No," Graham said, uncomfortably aware of Weldon's contempt for his previous profession. "I was a surgeon and a pretty good one, so will you trust me?"

William stared in grim silence.

"Look at me, William. Do you think I'd be able to run very far?"

William did not want to hurt his feelings.

"Of course not," Graham said. "So you think I'd offer to help if I didn't know what I was doing? Your papa would come catch me if I did something wrong!"

William smiled, a glimmer of hope in his gold-flecked eyes. Somewhat calmed, he walked to the house leaning heavily on his father. Katherine stood in the snow, her hands up over her mouth in panic. She ran forward. "Oh, Willy!" she whispered, coming close and kissing his head as he passed mournfully.

Sarah peered from the window while Margaret and Gerald scolded the boys in the parlor.

With Eliza still in his arms, Scott ranted, "You girls should have been watching the children. I'm appalled!" He huffed and gave the girl to Katherine with a look of disappointment etched on his face. "The little thing could have wandered off!"

"Scott, settle down now," Sarah warned and tried to make herself useful. "Doctor, what shall I do?"

"Mrs. McCullough, we need to make a splint for the present. Do you have a couple of rulers or wooden spoons, some fabric, and a scissor? I'm afraid you'll have to say goodbye to this shirt, William, unless you'd like to pull it off."

"*No!*" William cried.

"Have you any more of that whiskey or maybe some brandy for the pain, Mr. McCullough?" Graham asked.

"No, that won't be necessary," Weldon interrupted.

"Pardon me?" Graham turned in confusion.

Weldon reddened and stammered, "I-I don't want him taking anything for the pain."

Katherine and the others stared.

Sarah waved Weldon off. "Don't be silly, John. The poor child suffers."

"I know, but ..." Weldon scratched his neck, unable to look at the others.

Scott grabbed the whiskey from the table and poured a glass. "It's heartless to make him suffer. Willy's just a boy."

Willy whimpered in the midst of it all. Sarah ran to get supplies. Graham held the boy's arm as he spoke. "Listen, Weldon, I have nothing else to give him, and when I set the bone it will hurt," he said and turned to Willy. "I'm sorry, but it will hurt a little more, then it will begin to feel much better."

The boy did not like the sound of it and squirmed to get free again.

"Weldon, I know you're a temperance man, but this is different. You realize that. I can get Willy some proper painkiller tomorrow."

"No! It's not right to give those things to a child!" Weldon said. "Willy's my son! I'll make the decisions for him."

Katherine grabbed the glass from her father and put it to Willy's lips quicker than John could prevent it without an embarrassing display of force. "John, don't be such a brute—he's a small boy, not one of your men!" Her disdain cut him to the quick.

He bowed his head in humiliated defeat. The doctor began his work, gingerly cutting the sleeve away from William's swollen arm. Graham glanced up at Weldon more than once. The painkiller ... Graham began to understand Weldon's behavior as apparently not even his wife did. "Once we set the arm your son will be in a lot less pain. That small bit of whiskey, Weldon, won't do him any harm. He'll be fine."

"Don't speak to me as if I am a child, Crenshaw!"

"You're most certainly behaving like one," Scott said just under his breath.

Katherine glared at him.

"It's late. I'll make a temporary splint for Willy and set something up more solidly in the morning, or you can go see Doctor Banks," Graham suggested.

William relaxed under the effects of the whiskey and the calm hands of the doctor. He rested his head against his father who stroked his hair. Katherine stood by with Eliza back in her arms, still dressed for the elements. Setting her on a chair, Katherine untied Eliza's wet bonnet. She opened her daughter's coat to find her pinafore drenched with perspiration.

William cried out as the doctor sought to make things right with his arm, and that's when it began—the coughing. Graham turned to the sound of it.

"You left the girl too long out in the snow, Katherine," Scott scolded, fed up with the poor parenting all of these young people were displaying.

Katherine said nothing, trying to hide from the others this disturbing new symptom—the sweats. She carried Eliza to the door, but not quickly enough.

"Good heavens!" Sarah gasped, "Eliza's soaked through!"

And then the coughing began again—not terrible coughs just dry and raspy—she had had them before—change-of-weather coughs, the doctor out west had said.

Graham wrapped William's arm and patted his head then reluctantly turned his attention to the florid-cheeked little girl, wilting in her mother's arms. He had seen this before—the fever and the cough, the malaise. During the war they learned to turn this type away—unfit for battle. Graham sighed and reluctantly asked, "Katherine, has she lost any weight?"

Weldon jumped in. "I think we'd notice, Crenshaw!"

"I never doubted it, Weldon," Graham said but remained focused on Katherine.

Katherine spoke in panic, feeling she was somehow betraying her husband. "Eliza's always been a small girl ... but ... yes, I have noticed just a little ... only a little ... she seems less sturdy."

Graham took Eliza's hand tenderly. "How are you, little one?"

The little girl looked up to her mother for the answer.

Graham turned to Weldon. "You told me only the other day that she was not coughing."

"How dare you! Are you accusing me of lying?" Weldon began and took Eliza from his wife. The will to fight left him when he saw Katherine's wet shirtwaist and felt his daughter against him.

All were silent. They knew well enough the symptoms of consumption.

"Please, Weldon, let me examine her," Graham urged.

"No, your children have hurt my son tonight—could have killed him. I don't want you near my daughter. She just has an occasional cough."

"A change-of-weather cough," Katherine put in for her husband.

"Yes, and she always recovers," Weldon said shakily.

Graham's fears were only elevated knowing it was a recurring cough, but parents in denial could not be helped until they were ready. In resignation he offered only simple advice. "Give her plenty of liquids and see someone tomorrow for your son's arm. Weldon, you're a good father and you'll do the right thing in the end."

"I don't need your approval, Crenshaw. I wish you would take your sons and go home now."

"Weldon, you should mind your tongue," Scott said. "The doctor has been a help to you."

"If Crenshaw hadn't come then none of this would be happening!"

Katherine took Weldon's arm, but he pulled from her and stalked out of the room with Eliza. William whimpered in pain, but all eyes looked to the doctor for hope, for new answers.

"I don't dare make a prognosis—I am out of practice." Graham took Katherine's hand. "I always had a tendency to fear the worst."

Katherine's voice left her and ripping her hand free, she ran for the door after her husband, tripping on her skirt as she climbed the stairs.

Scott wrapped William in a warm blanket and brought him to his chair. They sat together, Scott rubbing William's back as the boy nuzzled in close, happy for his grandfather's attention.

Sarah spoke in hushed tones to the doctor. "You know what's wrong with Eliza, don't you?" she asked visibly stricken.

"I know what I think it is, but it could be so much less serious than that. I hope I'm wrong," Graham answered, knowing that he rarely was. At the medical college he had prided himself on expert diagnosis, but in the field and now knowing the correct answer no longer brought on smug satisfaction. Graham called to Margaret, his voice breaking. He didn't know the Weldon family all too well, but he liked Katherine's quiet, sweet personality right away. John Weldon was another matter, but in the end he felt for him, for whatever else Weldon might be he was a loving father, and that always swayed Graham's opinion of a man. "Maggie, gather up your things and have Gerald ready the horses."

Margaret stood at the kitchen door a minute and apologized to William, who stared out in pain and exhaustion with glassy eyes. Sarah led Margaret away. "It's all right, Maggie, boys will boys."

Margaret looked at Sarah's pained expression, wondering what she had missed. She called back to her husband, "Graham, we will meet you outside then? Good night, Mr. and Mrs. McCullough. I'm so sorry again about Willy."

Sarah nodded, unable to speak, and led her out the door. Graham spoke to William. "You are a brave little man. Soon you'll be in shipshape again. Take care of your little sister, won't you?"

William smiled weakly. What beautiful children, the doctor thought. "Good night, all." He looked to Scott. "Please try to convince Katherine and John to have the girl seen—as hard as that would be for them." Graham put on his hat and pulled his blanket of a coat around his expansive waist.

"You're like Santa," William said.

Graham patted William's head again and sighed before letting himself out the kitchen door.

Sarah and Scott listened to the plodding steps of the Friesians as they faded along with the sleigh bells down Demarest Avenue toward home.

Scott ranted as quietly as his emotions would allow. "I knew living out among the uncivilized savages would bring hell to pay."

Sarah flashed an outraged look Scott's way as she cleared the table of flannel scraps. "Does it matter that you're right? Katie will be devastated by this! And poor John Weldon loves that little girl so!"

"Well, Weldon should have taken better care of her then!" Scott determined. He always needed a cause or culprit.

"Scott, that's awful to say and in front of Willy!"

"My papa always cares for us!" William cried.

Sarah came to the boy's side. "We know, little fellow. It's just that Grandfather worries and says silly things he doesn't mean."

Chapter Forty-Eight

Eliza shivered in her pantaloons as Katherine entered the room. Weldon cursed and sifted through their clothes piled haphazardly on chairs and dressers.

"John, she's freezing!" Katherine said, pulling a blanket around Eliza.

"If you didn't keep things in such a state I'd have found something to put Eliza in," Weldon grumbled.

Katherine found a flannel nightshirt from beneath one of John's shirts and slipped it over Eliza's dampened curls.

"Why did you have to tell Crenshaw Eliza's lost weight?" Weldon asked. "I wish we'd never come back. Everything was perfect in the desert."

"John, Eliza was out in the cold and maybe not have fully recovered from whatever she had the other day. That's all it is—I'm sure of it."

Weldon slumped down in Katherine's childhood reading chair stained with jam and tea and shoved the stockings and underclothing covering the arms on to the floor. "But if Crenshaw's right ... what if Eliza goes and then Willy and you as well? That's how it happens sometimes."

She tucked her drowsy daughter under the soft flannel sheets and went to John, putting her arms around his waist. As gently as he could, he freed himself from her.

"What kind of heartless God would do this to Eliza? The army is no place for a child—the filth and Indians! I knew bad things would happen if I married you!"

"John Weldon, how can you say such hurtful things?" Katherine cried. "I love you!"

"So what! How will that help Eliza? I was a fool to think being with you would change things. If only I'd stayed alone ..." Weldon sighed at his wife in tears. "I've gotten so used to you ... and the children. I thought I could relax a little, but it's all been a rotten trick! I've tried so hard for nothing!"

She grabbed his hands and held them tightly. "Listen to me. You can't give up. We can't give up! You're a fighter and strong. We depend on you!"

"Stop it! You put too much pressure on me and depend on me too much. I hate it." He tore his hands away. "I never wanted to be a father. I knew it wouldn't turn out right!"

"John, have faith."

"Faith is cruel—it's false hope. Eliza is going to die. I can feel it!"

"Enough! I won't hear any more of this!" she yelled, holding her hands to her ears.

Weldon slapped her hands down. "You don't like to hear anything, Katherine, unless it's perfect and good! You don't listen to life! You hum over the bad parts and can't do that this time. Now you will know what it means to lose and suffer!"

"You say it as if you're glad!"

"Kate, I can't stay here anymore. I feel like a failure in this house and want to leave. Stay or come as you like."

"Stay or come?" she cried. "Of course I'll go with you!"

"If that's what you want," he said dismissively.

"What do *you* want?"

He pulled the hair behind his ear. "I don't know. I can't think right now ... I wonder, could you leave me alone?"

"Certainly!" she said and ran from the room. Outside the door, she sank to the carpet, the rich gold she wore stained with tears and perspiration. Sarah found her and led her back to the kitchen, where Willy slept peacefully in his grandfather's arms. Scott looked mildly at Katherine but said nothing. The kettle whistled on the stove like a train carrying lonely passengers to a distant town. No real sickness had ever come to the house on Tenafly Road.

"How could Elly have gotten so ill, Katie?" Scott asked gruffly.

"I don't know! I don't know! And what does it matter?"

"We'll get the best doctors for her."

"No, Father. John says we'll leave in the morning. I'm sorry."

"You must be joking! Another long trip for your children is a terrible idea. Weldon is wrong to do this. You must stand up to him."

Katherine shook her head as Sarah pulled her into a chair and sat nearby with Scott.

"Katie, you must do what's right for the children," Sarah said. "You can't take them away just yet. You'll want company and help."

"No, Mother. I want John. He's my comfort. He makes me feel useful and strong, like you never did!" Katherine cried. "You undermine me, make me feel weak and pointless and an embarrassment to you since I was a child!"

"You're upset—you don't really think that," Sarah said.

"You've always hidden me away—but John found me anyway, and you hate that!" A dam broke inside Katherine.

"We've tried to protect you!"

"Ever since you were a child you've made foolish, stupid decisions!" Scott shouted. "You wander off on your own and get hurt every time! I've tried to be hopeful, but you embarrass yourself and your family just like Simon! I always thought you possessed more intelligence than him, but you make maddeningly ridiculous choices!"

"You pulled me from school!" Katherine sobbed. "I never got to see if I was intelligent!"

"People talked. Those horrible girls snickered at you after the Undercliff boy. I wanted to kill them like Simon killed the boy ... but instead I took you from school, and you were glad of it at the time."

"It wasn't my fault, Father!"

"Nothing ever is. You go wandering about in your dream world—off on the river or into the woods or out to the desert—and expect everyone around you to take care of things when something goes wrong."

"This is no time to discuss old news," Sarah said, motioning for them to be quiet as William stirred.

Katherine shook with rage as she walked to the door. "Father, I'll leave tomorrow with John."

"That's right, it's what I expect from you now—hitch your star to a man who can never give you what you need."

"You will always be the first of such men then," she replied and raced up the stairs again.

The oil light had dimmed, but the moon was full and cold, staring at her through the window. She held her emotions in her throat—her corset stabbing her sides as her chest heaved. Weldon pretended to sleep next to his now much cooler daughter. Blue-tinted air sat upon the countryside, with its apple trees groaning under a heavy burden of snow. The icy reflection lent an unearthly glow to Eliza's face. Katherine shuddered. She slipped into her nightclothes more suited for Arizona than an unheated room in the northeast. Katherine remembered the tiny tintypes Sarah kept of her first two daughters taken after their deaths. They only looked asleep. Katherine turned away from Eliza unable to choke back her tears. Weldon felt the rhythmic movement of the bed and listened. Her muffled cries were like needles to his brain. He had an urge to smother her and hated himself for it.

Chapter Forty-Nine

The light from the window was pink like a warm garden in the late afternoon sun, but it was cold in the yard. Weldon could see his breath even in this cozy room. His head throbbed and a familiar ache descended upon him. He got out of bed and dressed. Eliza was cool and quiet. Katherine looked soft and warm but worried even in her sleep. This would be the perfect time to escape—with this picture in his head, everyone quietly asleep. Maybe he could fool himself if he left and imagined them always this way.

How had this lark of a marriage trapped him? Katherine made him believe his life had changed for good, but his luck had ruined hers. Now Weldon felt soft and dependent like he had been as a child. Katherine had raised the stakes in Weldon's life.

This little family would now trip him up and desert him. He had always imagined something he did would end it all, but this illness just happened. He had worked hard at being exemplary, at being perfect, and for a while had succeeded. Everything *was* perfect, but now it was not.

Life was savage—Weldon's mother had always insisted he remember that. It had been years since he heard her voice in his head. After one last look at Katherine sleeping, he went to the old armoire filled with memories of his early marriage. A loose board just behind one of the heavy legs hid an old syringe and opium pills. A flood of memories, not quite happy but pleasant enough in ways, came to him—his mind playing tricks. Weldon had to get out of this house, clear his head, go for a walk. He skipped stairs and tip-toed out the door with the remains of a bottle of whiskey.

The snow beneath his boots crunched like stale crackers. He remembered hardtack and weevils floating in his mucket when he threw the infested crackers in his coffee for breakfast during the war. Weldon considered the flukiness of death and how he hadn't really cared too much about the men during the war. They saddened him like characters in the trashy novels passed around camp. When he finished a novel or buried a man in his company it was done. And back to cleaning his gun or complaining about some beat who wouldn't take part in burial detail.

He tramped past St. Cecilia's church and almost went in, but flashed a despairing look toward the heavens. This God he had prayed to beat him again. He was still the speck of a boy he had always been, carried along on life's winds like the volunteer seed that grows in barnyard manure.

A doe surprised him in the road. It stopped to sniff the air, liked it none too much, and dashed into the newly raised lots on Waldo Place where the Irish lived.

If Simon were here he could settle John with a smoke and a tale—but they were no longer young soldiers, and Eliza's health could not be joked away. Simon had deserted again.

Weldon pulled the tattered old Christmas card from his pocketbook and ran his fingers over Katherine's small neat writing then put it away.

The Palisades Woods were farther away than Weldon remembered. The barns at the back of the new sturdy homes loomed larger than the quarters at Camp Grant. He slipped on the icy cobblestone road before cutting through a yard, and there it stood—the foundation. As the sun warmed him, he wondered had he changed just enough ... he took a deep breath. Setting Scott's bottle on the stone wall and tossing the old syringe away, he pulled his pipe from his jacket, stuffed it with tobacco, and lit up.

Chapter Fifty

Camp Grant moved to a drier location, and the Weldon family settled into their new, clean and cheerful home. Eliza once back in the desert seemed to recover, but her illness was always there at the back of her parents' throats, a lump, this waiting, this bundle of nerves as they watched for signs to disprove Crenshaw's diagnosis. Englewood, so far away now, had been a nightmare, not real. The desert was real with the four of them together.

Eliza's cough hid, and her spunky attitude remained. Such a strong character could not be so sick, Weldon tried to convince himself, but he could not ignore her thin face, and when she fought with Willy or played with the soldiers it was not with as much enthusiasm.

Katherine held her tongue. She held her tongue when John made elaborate plans for Eliza's future, obsessing over her education. Eliza would go to a good school back east when John was transferred somewhere decent. They'd visit Eliza at the weekend and someday see her be a teacher or a nurse and then marry a nice man. Eliza said it would be a soldier like her papa. Katherine could hardly stand listening as over and over each day her husband and daughter lived a life that could never happen.

"Papa, what shall I be?" Willy asked.

"You're lucky. You can be anything you like."

The answer was inadequate and disappointing to his son, but Weldon imagined he had a lifetime to make it up to him.

And then the coughing hit hard.

Weldon was away for a fortnight. Fever and the night sweats came first, but by morning a cough delivered just the smallest amount of crimson blood.

William ran for the new surgeon, who made the diagnosis before seeing the girl. Doctor Dudley had already studied Eliza's wilting appearance. William's nervous details of the coughing and the fever confirmed his suspicions—bad news on such a lovely day. Before walking over to the bright new home the men had built for Mrs. Weldon, Dudley listened to William's chest, worried for the barefooted boy who always came around so full of news. William's chest was clear—that was something. Dudley tucked his stethoscope and some cough remedy into his bag and walked out across the new parade ground.

Katherine pulled herself together as best she could, wearing a pink and gold calico wrap brought from Englewood and smoothing her hair neatly into a low knot at her neck. The doctor knocked and followed William in. Dudley always loved visits here. Katherine decorated simply, careful with her husband's pay, but with a humble and soothing elegance. Blue gingham curtains waved slightly in a scant desert breeze and the children's collections were displayed on a shelf near the door. William had picked desert weeds for his mother's table, but they drooped over the jar used as vase. Katherine's delicate unpolished drawings for a project her husband was attempting lay scattered about.

He was still young, this Doctor Dudley and when he first arrived Katherine sought him out. In those early weeks, as Dudley settled in, he noticed Mrs. Weldon's bashful ways as she chased the children past his office and compared her favorably against the Boston upstart girls who were carving their way into the medical profession. Katherine was a real girl with a girl's manners. The old surgeon had retired, but the children didn't believe it and often ended up on the new doctor's porch. Dudley remembered the first time he and Katherine spoke.

"Good morning, Mrs. Weldon."

"Excuse us, Doctor Dudley," Katherine replied with a guarded smile, pulling William and Eliza along. "One day they may finally realize their old friend is gone."

"Maybe they can find it in their hearts to make a new friend," he'd said. "Back in Boston I had plenty of young folks around, and now it's just me. You children can come by anytime, although I'm probably a poor substitute for the old doctor."

His attention made the children shy and restless. They ran off kicking dust across the grounds. Katherine watched them go. The scene had played out the same way so many times before in the last two weeks. The lieutenant's wife seemed to want to ask him something but never did.

He had a girl back home who said she might wait for him but would not come into the army life. The woman before him, after months so long separated from home, with only her threadbare work dress on, made him more than the disinterested medical professional he knew he should be. It was still so early in the day and the sun was low. He shouldn't look, but it was impossible not to notice through the thin fabric lit by the sun that she was not wearing her underthings. It was scandalous, yet he sensed an innocence in her of the sun's effects on her appearance when she ran to get her children. She pulled on the lumps of her braid absently and turned to him. Her eyes were the exact pale blue of her dress.

"Mrs. Weldon ... is there something ..." he asked breathlessly.

She sighed as if pained to ask. "Doctor Dudley, it's Lieutenant Weldon."

"Yes?"

"I'm worried about his arm."

It was silly, but he was momentarily disappointed that she had brought Weldon into the picture. "Have the lieutenant come by this evening."

"Oh, no, doctor. My husband doesn't trust doctors."

"Well, I can't force a grown man to see me if he doesn't want to," he said, impatient with military stoicism.

"If it suits you, maybe you could come for supper and just visit for a while. Once he knows you he'll like you."

"How do you know my true nature won't have the opposite effect on him?"

Katherine didn't give the faintest hint of a smile. "Sir, you don't put on airs or act superior. He'll like that, and I'm desperate."

He warmed to the idea of a nice meal. "Any time you say, Mrs. Weldon, but don't go to any trouble."

"Tonight?"

"Oh. Well, yes I suppose that's fine ... full evening attire?"

She laughed. "Yes, something you'd wear to a wedding, sir. Thank you so much. Come at seven if that's all right."

He arrived on time only a few minutes after John, who was none too happy to greet him at the door. Weldon intimidated him. On this night, given strict orders to behave, Weldon did not cover his annoyance at having to share his home and his supper with the doctor—a complete stranger. Katherine whispered to the children while serving the men fresh bread and jam sent from Sarah. This brought a small bit of happiness to Weldon's face. "Mrs. Weldon's mother makes the best jam and preserves, and Kate makes the best bread."

The children with dirty little hands crawled on to Weldon's lap to steal his crust. Eliza brushed against his arm. He noted the pained expression on the lieutenant's face.

"I've always envied families with good mothers," he said.

Weldon glanced at the doctor, but went back to feeding Eliza.

He was suddenly comfortable—the jam maybe. "Yes, in the orphanage jam of this caliber was a rarity, and look at the handwritten labels too, mercy," he said shaking his head at the homeyness of everything.

"So you have no parents?" Weldon asked.

"Yes and no. They might still exist somewhere, but from what I remember of them, their habits and customs where not of the sort to recommend them as fit parents. They visited on a few occasions, but, well, things work out for the best. Someone finally convinced them to give me up."

Katherine sat. "Oh my, that's a sad story."

"No, not really. I used to think they gave up on me as a child, but the nuns who took me in were patient—I was wicked—and while they were too busy keeping us boys in order to make nice jams, they showed me how to take care of myself with God's help."

Weldon chuckled, gruff but interested. "God?"

"Yes, I believe God helped me through many scrapes."

"But you went to Harvard. How?" Weldon asked.

"I was destined to be a doctor, so why not go to the best school? People entered my life when I least expected it. I like to think they were messengers. I had some choice of course—to be either a thief or a doctor. Medicine won out on chance meetings. Right after the war I robbed a young lady—such an easy mark—all alone at twilight. I didn't hurt her. I never was one for violence, but I intimidated her enough, I guess. She handed over her bag, seeming not to care a bit for it. Maybe she was just happy that I was polite. She hurried off, and I went through her things. It was an impressive stash of money she had, and I was content until I came upon a note from the mother of a dead soldier killed off by disease to the girl asking her to deliver the boy's savings to the soldiers' hospital. Well, of course I knew where that was and began the walk there buying a drink and a sandwich along the way which went down bitterly. You can guess what happened next. When I met the veterans—some not much older than me—and saw how they made the most of their lives at the hospital I volunteered as a steward. A physician took notice of me and kept me on the straight and narrow. He was friends with the right people, and off to Harvard I went. God was in that for certain."

Katherine cupped her chin in her hands. "What a story. I agree with you—I've felt the hand of God. I've told Lieutenant Weldon over and over again that our meeting wasn't by chance. When I saw him it was as if I had known him forever."

"Kate, don't bring that up now," Weldon pleaded, but the doctor caught the tender look the lieutenant gave his wife.

"Excuse me for saying so, but what a nice family you have. You must feel blessed."

"I feel lucky, is all. God has never ... well, I don't like to discuss religion," John replied.

"Fair enough, lieutenant. How about medicine?"

"I wouldn't know much about that ..."

"Yes, Mrs. Weldon has told me," he said. "Do you mind if I examine your arm? I won't tell a soul."

Weldon soured, his brief friendliness pulled behind his usual reserve. "No, I wish Mrs. Weldon hadn't said anything." He shot his wife an angry look.

"Lieutenant, it may be too late to do anything for you, but what if we can ease some of the pain?"

"I won't take any medication." Weldon stood up as if to escape, but where could he go? For a second his expression exposed a hope ...

"Well, that's fine. I wasn't considering medication yet. I'll just examine it, and it will be between you and me. I won't do anything to make it worse for you."

Weldon relented after a long silence. They moved over behind the curtain that hid the bunks. He gingerly helped with Weldon's sleeve while Katherine got supper.

"It's not too bad, is it, doctor?" The veins on Weldon's forehead were visible under a slight sheen of sweat.

"Hmm. Well, it is actually. The muscle's torn from the bone looks like. No wonder it still pains you. Everything is where it shouldn't be."

"So, I guess there's nothing to be done," Weldon said, pulling away from the doctor's grasp.

"Oh, I'm sorry. I know this hurts." He pressed on. "I think I can mend it ... at least it won't be so sore and it will look a lot better. Lieutenant, your arm looks like a half-stuffed sausage."

Weldon agreed and laughed a little. "Some days I want to cut it off myself."

"I have no intention of cutting anything off. I may be able to make an incision and properly set what's left of the muscles in place. I don't expect that you will ever recover full motion, but the pain should go. A little morphine will ..."

"No, none of that. I can stand the pain. It can't be any worse than now."

Some men were like that and so the doctor consented. No morphine, just a little chloroform.

Today was a different day with no fixes. Katherine stood at the foot of Eliza's bed when he arrived. The pretended cheer since Christmas for her husband's sake had disappeared. Katherine's eyes were swollen and her chin quivered when she spoke, but she smelled of roses. "Dr. Dudley, I knew it all along. You don't have to tell me, but what can I do to help her?"

"Eliza, how are you today?"

"Plumb rotten," Eliza griped.

Dudley smiled at her downturned mouth.

She continued. "I didn't have a wink of sleep even. It's awful rough."

"Let me listen, darling," Dudley said, putting his stethoscope to her chest for ceremony only. "I'm sorry, Mrs. Weldon ..." He silently cursed himself for giving way to emotion as he wiped a tear away.

"Do I have to keep in bed a while? 'Cause I don't mind if it's only one day," Eliza said.

The doctor couldn't answer the girl and turned to Katherine. "Here's some cough medication. Use it sparingly. I don't like to give it to children but in the worst cases."

"So Eliza's one of the worst?"

Her plaintive tone stabbed the doctor through.

"No, no. But some little ones become addicted to the stuff. Please, Mrs. Weldon, some people recover and Eliza is ... strong. I wish there was more I could do, but we'll say our prayers, won't we?"

"Are you saying that only a miracle will cure her?"

"All cures are acts of God, so I suppose we see miracles all the time."

"How will I ever break the news to John?" she asked, doe-eyed.

Dudley touched her shoulder tentatively. "Mrs. Weldon, would you like me to tell the lieutenant when he comes back?"

"No, Doctor Dudley, you are too kind, but he'll only accept it from me."

Chapter Fifty-One

When Graham Crenshaw's words came into Weldon's mind, he cursed and dismissed them. This method of denial worked until now, as he went into the stables after another fruitless search for thieving Indians.

"Lieutenant Weldon, it's sad news about your daughter, sir."

"What do you mean?"

"Eliza, sir ... sakes alive!" the hapless corporal said, his curry comb in midair. "You don't know yet?"

Weldon pushed past the corporal, leaving him to care for his horse's tack and raced to his quarters, cradling his sore arm in his good.

For a moment everything was ordinary. Willy ran up and took John's hand as he climbed the stairs of their solid porch. Pots clanged from within, and Katherine spoke quietly to Eliza. Weldon opened the door looking for signs. Eliza looked a little tired but smiled just the same, and Katherine ran to Weldon and embraced him like always ... but she would not let go. Weldon spotted the medicine and the basket with stained washing. He pulled Katherine off him to read her face.

"I didn't want to cry, John," she explained breathlessly. "I wanted to be strong, but the news is bad and true and you must believe it this time. Eliza is sick as Graham Crenshaw feared."

"No ... She's the picture of health since we got back. You're alone too much and imagine things."

"Oh, please, John, don't do this. Dudley has seen Eliza and says it's consumption."

"What does he know?"

"You must face it. I need you to face it with me."

"*No*! You're all the sick ones!" he shouted. "You like to find things to worry about!"

"That's enough," she ordered. "I want Elly to be healthy, but she isn't!"

He shook his head and pulled Eliza up in his arm. "Eliza, you're fine aren't you, my love?"

"No, Papa, I'm terrible sick," she told him. "Every soldier has come by with treats and things, but nothing cheers me when my mouth bleeds. I bet I'll get better for you, Papa Oh, and they say special prayers for me too."

"Why does everyone know our business?" he asked aggressively. "Is this some misguided attempt at getting attention, Katherine? I wasn't gone so long that you couldn't have waited."

She crumpled into a chair to cry.

"Crying won't help a thing! And what's this?" he asked, his voice upsetting William and Eliza as he picked up the bottle and scanned its ingredients. "And you poison Eliza now? Where did you get this?"

Willy answered with a tremulous voice. "Doctor Dudley, sir, he gave it to Mother ..."

"Goddamn you, Katherine!" Weldon cried and left with the bottle to confront Dudley, who sat relaxing on his porch with an old medical journal.

"Dudley, I trusted you!"

The doctor sat up straight. "Sir?"

"I let you into my home, and now you fill Katherine with worry—and you feed my child this!"

The doctor didn't move. The man towering over him raved like a lunatic, so he waited for it to pass.

"And now Katherine has the whole place believing your lies!"

"Lieutenant, I know this is hard for you ..." Dudley tried to get up, but Weldon stood too close.

"You don't know nothing! You have no children!"

"Mrs. Weldon didn't tell anyone about Eliza. It was me. It was my fault. I felt she needed to have the support of the garrison. The garrison prayed for her and your daughter too."

"How dare you decide what my wife needs! That's my place not yours," Weldon shouted, but fell into the chair beside the doctor's, "and the men were here for her ... I wasn't."

"All of them together couldn't hold a match to you in Mrs. Weldon's eyes. You know that."

"I yelled at her and was cruel ... but I can't lose Eliza."

"Mrs. Weldon is just as hurt as you are. She didn't want to believe it until the first real attack. It was terrible for her."

Weldon thought of the blood in the basket and Katherine's tired face. "Dudley, why would you give her this medicine? I won't allow it."

"I don't think you would rather Eliza suffer. The coughs get quite upsetting and uncomfortable in this stage."

"What stage? Can't she be cured at all now? There's been hardly any symptoms," he lied to himself.

"She may have seemed well, but the disease works on the inside too quietly doing its damage, I'm afraid, and your daughter is so young."

"Eliza's going to die?"

"I believe she will. I'm terribly, terribly sorry lieutenant."

Chapter Fifty-Two

"Mother says I can't go in," William said when Weldon brushed past the boy into the house.

Katherine looked up, but it was Eliza he saw struggling through an attack.

"She's like a weathervane now, reacting to any upset," Katherine said simply.

"I'm sorry I ..."

"I really don't care for your apologies at the moment," she said. "Where is Eliza's medicine?"

"I ..." he stumbled. "I don't want Elly taking it in case she gets better, I ..."

"God help us! John, go get the bottle! It's the only thing that quiets the cough! Can't you see how she suffers? You may be cruel to me, but I won't allow it for her!"

"How did it get so bad?" he asked in an apologetic tone.

"Who cares? I made it worse. Is that what you want to hear?" Katherine cried. "While you are away I poison her! Now go get the medicine!"

"Kate ..."

"Oh, I can't listen to you right now!" she said, pushing him toward Eliza's bed. "Here, you're so good at everything. You care for her. Work your magic!"

Numbly Weldon put his arm around Eliza, and Katherine bolted from the room to retrieve the medicine. The little girl tried to smile. Weldon reached for a cool rag in the washbasin next to the bed, but his fingers could not come together to wring the water from it. He didn't want to move his good arm supporting Eliza. Frustrated and upset, he wiped her brow, but the rag dripped water everywhere. Eliza pushed it away. "Willy!" Weldon called. "William, come here!"

And then the blood escaped. Eliza tried to swallow. She didn't want to see it but felt it come up in her mouth and gagged.

"Oh, damn," Weldon mumbled. "Willy!"

Finally, William returned to his father, having gone halfway with Katherine before being sent back. He ran in at his father's call.

"Where the hell were you?" Weldon cried, blood all over his useless hand. "I can't do this!"

William stood still.

"Willy, stop staring and help me, goddamn it!"

The boy took the rag and threw it into the basket. William grabbed a clean one and wet it first, trying to wash his father's hand.

"No! Not me, the child! Wipe her face!"

"Eliza, it's okay. Don't be afraid ..." William said. The boy was so calm and spoke the words so soothingly.

Eliza took William's hand and breathed easier. The children shamed Weldon.

"William, how did you turn out so good?"

"Mother," William said. He resented his father's comings and goings and the way Weldon spoke to them now.

The metal chime rung on the porch as Katherine brushed by in haste, knocking over William's fishing supplies. "William, go put away your things for once!" she scolded. "Why in heaven's name is Elly all wet?"

"It was me, my fault ..." Weldon said.

Katherine ignored him. Finding the special spoon, she brought the medicine over.

"Please, Kate, Elly seems better now," Weldon begged. "Please don't give it to her."

"So you've cured her then? Look at her, John. Really look. She's wasted. This gives her some peace."

"I know that, but I'm afraid if Elly recovers she'll be addicted ..."

"John, she won't recover ... *ever*. I don't want to think of it, but we must prepare ourselves. God has given us this time to really appreciate her."

"I didn't need her to die to appreciate her!" he shouted. "If that's what God does then I want no part of Him."

"But, John, when the men prayed I could feel it."

"Wishful thinking," he grumbled. "Those men would forget you in a second."

"I don't care. It helped me when *you* weren't here."

"So I guess any man will do then."

She slapped him. "Eliza is dying and you think only about hurting me."

"I'm dying?" Eliza asked.

"Maybe if you had kept her away from Suzy's children ..." John started.

"How do you know it wasn't some stray Indian you have us living with?"

"Suzy was common ..."

"And what do you think *you* are?" Katherine said, shaking.

John moved away from Eliza. "Nothing. I'm nothing and what were you to marry me? Ill-used ..."

"What?" Katherine gasped.

"You probably let that Undercliff boy have you!"

"I was twelve! I didn't ..."

"Yes, you flirt with all the men—and you say I'm common!" He watched her confidence melt, and it satisfied something in him.

"Get out!" Katherine cried, pushing him uselessly.

"I wish I could stay away forever!"

Camp Grant, Arizona

August 1874

Dear Margaret,

Eliza is truly ill with consumption as Graham said. I was in some foolish way angry with him for noticing the truth at Christmas. And now all is black misery here. If only I had raised my children in dear old Englewood instead of this uncivilized desert!

The other day Eliza was well enough to play outside with William on the porch. William has been a near saint to put up with Eliza's strong will. John was cleaning his gun at the table, and the day was pleasant enough until Eliza let out a piercing scream. We raced out the door to find William pounding his sister with his fists. Eliza had smashed William's collection of artifacts to pieces. John grabbed Willy by the collar and threw the boy against the wall. To see a grown and powerful man stand over a small child like that disgusted me, and I said as much, but was ignored. John had never been violent before, and Eliza became frightened and upset which brought on an attack. The blood and the suffering are awful now, but I am almost immune to it!

"You little bastard! Look what you've done! Do you want Eliza to die? Pick up all this garbage and get the hell out of my sight or I will kick the shit out of you," John said to his own child!

I am sorry to use such language in a letter, but I need someone to know the torture I am under.

William ran off, but I was too busy with Eliza to take any notice. I went to get the prescribed medicine and poured a strong dose to spite John and fed it to Eliza quickly before he could stop me. John tore the bottle from my hand with such force I thought he might break my wrist and flung it to the wall, sending glass everywhere. I used language I never thought would escape my mouth. I said, "Shall we get in a medicine man? Is that what you prescribe? Are you so backward and stupid not to see she needs the medicine?" and he slapped me and ordered me to clean up the mess while he took Eliza inside. John has never ordered me to do anything before and I resented it greatly, but I cleaned it all up anyway like the pathetic groveling creature I have become. The more I try to please him the more he hates me. What can I do? I try sometimes to stop loving him, but it is impossible. I love him desperately.

Your friend,

Katherine Weldon

Chapter Fifty-Three

The garrison was down to skeletal staff. A company or two would come soon to take over for many of the men who were now leaving. Some had served their enlistment time and were ready for home. Others were reassigned to other locales. But Weldon stayed on and so did Katherine.

On occasion he gave her reason to hope, smiling at something she said to William or taking her to bed in the evening and being almost himself again, but by morning the fleeting intimacy was gone.

Sometimes she guiltily wished for Eliza to die. Maybe then he could love her again.

The new men arrived one morning while John dressed and Katherine made coffee, but the soldiers were of little interest to them until the door shook with a heavy knock. Weldon cursed before pulling it open. "Simon!"

"Where's Katherine?" Simon demanded, pushing past his old friend. At once upon seeing her, Simon burst into tears. "Oh, Katie, I was so worried for you!"

"Simon! I can't believe you're here!" she cried, running into his arms. "I'm so sorry for the way I treated you at Christmas!"

"Are you all right? I've come to take you home. I can get you as far as San Francisco or St. Louis. I'm transferred up to the Department of Platte."

"I'm not going anywhere," she said in surprise.

"I won't allow you to stay, I'm afraid," he said. "Mother sent word about Weldon and his treatment of you!"

"I'm fine!" she assured him, glancing at Weldon.

"Did you hit Katie, you bastard?" Simon asked.

"Yes."

"Only once," she explained. "I said awful things I didn't mean."

"I don't give a damn what you said. Nobody hits my sister and lives to tell ..."

Weldon sat down. "Fine, Simon, kill me then."

Simon looked to Katherine.

"Oh, no, Simon, it's a big misunderstanding. We are both so broken up over Eliza," she sobbed. "We can't seem to find ways not to hurt each other."

"I did slap her," Weldon mumbled. "It was horrible. I was stupid. I didn't want to believe the truth. You have every right to take her, but I really wish you wouldn't ..."

Katherine broke free from Simon and fell into Weldon's arms. "Oh, John, that's all I needed to know, that you want me to stay!"

He embraced her.

Simon watched as they behaved in the affectionate way he had always seen. Only then did he notice William sitting in the farthest corner from the fire, lacing his boots as if Simon had never appeared. "Willy!" Simon beckoned, but William would not come so Simon went to him. "Young William the Conqueror, it hasn't been that long that you don't remember your uncle?"

"I'm not a dullard. Of course I remember."

"Well, then come out with me for a short walk—a tour."

"Okay."

Simon did his best to liven up the boy with candy and tales of his exploits and escapades in Texas and succeeded fairly well. They sat against the stable wall as the sun like a blanket covered them. "So, Willy, how are you doing in all of this? It must be hard with Eliza so sick."

William's gold eyes went dark, and he played with his laces.

"Is Mother safe, Willy?"

He shrugged. "May I have more candy, please?"

Simon went into his pocket and pulled the brown bag out, handing it to the boy. "That's all my pay gone on those sweets."

"Really?" William asked and handed them back.

"No, I'm just teasing. Anyway, I bought them especially for you."

"Not for Eliza too?"

"Nope, just for you. A boy shouldn't have to share everything."

"Can I come live with you, Uncle Simon?"

"No, I'm afraid not, although you and I would have a bully time." Simon gave him a glance and a wink. "Your mother and father would be upset about it."

"No, I don't think they'd notice."

Simon put his arm around the boy. "They would notice. They need you now more than ever. Be patient. Right now they're sad over Eliza, but they care for you."

"I hate them," William cried, covering his face with his hat.

"It's okay. Go on and cry. I won't tell. But don't hate your parents—it's not right."

When the two returned, the place stood neat and orderly. Beds were made and the smell of chili and bread baking filled the house. Simon was proud of Katherine and all she had done with the place. She led Eliza to a chair on the porch. The thin girl was a strange color, though her cheeks and eyes were bright. Eliza's curls were long now, and she looked older, much older since Christmas. Simon attempted to chat with her, but she just smiled and looked past him, deep in her own dreams.

Katherine laughed and chirped on about how happy she was to see him, but he pulled her down to sit with him. "Katie, please, I don't want to be waited on. You're too nervous. It worries me."

She was distracted and uncomfortable but did what Simon asked.

"Are you really safe with Weldon, Kate?"

"Yes, perfectly!" she began, but the happy facade fell. "You're the only person who knows John like I do. I don't know how to help him ..."

"What about you? Why do girls always think they can help a man who doesn't help himself? And Weldon's not helping you is he? Eliza hasn't much time, has she? I can't leave you here thinking he isn't helping you through this."

"He's angry at me over the medication. He thinks I've stolen Eliza from him because she's like a ghost. But if I don't give it to her she coughs and begs and begs for it and I can't deny her. He says I'm wrong to give up and worries Eliza's too dependent on the medicine. It's ridiculous! I can't stand to hear him talk about her future anymore!" She sobbed and wiped her face on the sleeve of her threadbare dress.

Simon took her in his arms. "Oh, Katie, I don't know why this has to happen to you."

She rested her head on his chest. "I am evil though, Simon. Look at her. I give Eliza larger doses when I'm fagged out so she'll sleep a little. I can't take it anymore!"

"You need to be with Mother and Father. This is no place for children—or you."

"No, I may be a fool, but I love John and I can't leave. I'd rather die than be apart from him."

"You don't realize how strange you sound. He's a man, not a god. You need a break and maybe he does too—from this awful desert!"

She stood up as if he had not said a word and went inside to check on the food.

Simon walked to the commissary and then toward the horses, spotting Weldon treating a private roughly over some misdeed. The private shoved off by the time Simon reached his friend. "Have time for a smoke, Weldon? My father has sent me the best."

"I have time, captain. How long will you stay?"

Simon looked him over. "I'm using my time off to see that you and Katie are holding up then I'm off to the north finally. I'll never step foot on sand again, I hope."

They pulled two half barrels into the shade, turned them over and sat. "Weldon, my sister has placed her future in your hands."

"Stupid girl."

"You had better rethink your response," Simon said. "It's insulting and low even for you."

"Even for me, captain?"

"Yes. Low. What makes you low, Weldon, is you really make people pay for caring about you. Everything about you is guilt and envy. Katie gives you everything, and you insult her and make her feel guilty for your suffering."

"I don't want her to feel guilty," Weldon lied. "I don't want her to feel anything."

"That's bunk! I know you. You manipulate people. That's the way you get what you need. Everyone is to feel sorry for you, but I never let you away with it! You still tried it at Christmas about the Wilderness, and I'm tired of it!"

"You're a captain because of me," Weldon said. "How dare you twist things! I trusted you and saved your ass so many times! You used me—made a big show of befriending the outcast so I could cover for all your games!"

"How sick are you?" Simon asked in disgust. "You make yourself the outcast! You think my friendship for you during the war was put on? You exaggerate your usefulness to me. Anyone would have covered for my fun. I foolishly was under the impression you came to enjoy it all. Your personality is prickly enough, but you were until this conversation my dearest friend. You're full of poison!"

"You're responsible for it more than you know!"

"And what does that mean?"

"I have to fight everyday against what happened in the Wilderness!" Weldon shouted.

"My God! That was so long ago!" Simon said, watching a soldier walk past. "You have a wife and family now."

"One you never wanted me to have!"

"What on earth?"

"You never wanted me with Kate!"

"You're right," Simon admitted, "and look at how you hurt her! Katherine's losing Eliza too. Eliza will die. That's all there is to it. People die. You should know that! It's no one's fault."

"Yes, people die—it's no big thing to you, but Eliza's my daughter," Weldon choked. "I want you to leave! Take Katherine if she wants to go."

Simon burst back into the house red-faced. "Katherine, pack your things. Weldon has turned you into a groveling idiot, and I won't allow for it to go on any longer!"

She glared at him, still kneading the bread dough in front of her but now with more force. "Simon McCullough, if I'm a groveling idiot then that's what I choose to be! I'll wait for as long as it takes for the real John to come back to me."

"I don't think I've met the real *John* then," Simon huffed, wiping his neck with a wet rag.

"You're angry with him, I know, but don't be on account of me. I never should have confided in Margaret. John and I are meant to be together."

"You've always had your head in the clouds about him. Just because you think something doesn't make it so. He was never meant for you. Here you are sweltering in this awful section of the world away from Mother and Father. You have no friends. You have one set of old books and an abusive and selfish husband. You should have done better for yourself!"

"I'm sorry that my life disappoints you. I guess I should be perfect like you. You flit between one diseased woman to another and feel sorry only because it spoils your chance for more excitement or whatever you like to call it. You think I should throw John away because that's what you would do if a woman made things uncomfortable for you!"

"Yes, we all make mistakes. I've made my fair share, but today it's you who's mistaken. I've always cared deeply for you and Weldon. Why else would I be here? I was wrong to call you a groveling idiot. You're far worse. You and John are both unforgiving and uncaring. How can you bring up my illness to hurt me? I've lost my two best friends in the world this afternoon! When my time of trouble came, where were you? You smugly lectured me, never thinking how I suffered to hear your judgment. Do you think you helped me in any way? You don't know what it's like to be completely alone. We've all taken care of you, but what does it matter? When I came to you—the only person I trusted, did you care that I thought my only chance at happiness was destroyed?" Simon turned to leave the hot house.

She ran to him, throwing her arms around him. "Oh, Simon! Forgive me! I never should have judged you the way I did! I was smug and horrible to you. I really don't care a bit about your illness or how you got it. I love you more than life itself! I've been so ungrateful and I didn't think!"

"Let's stop this," Simon said. He closed his eyes and sighed. "Let's start over. You know I love you too and that won't change. Whatever happens between you and Weldon ... I just want what's best for you ... and him."

She kissed his cheek. "Oh, I wish you could stay here forever with us!"

He wiped her tears, and for a moment his old rakish look was back. "I have my own fish to fry, I'm afraid."

She smiled and held him a little longer.

John walked in, scratching his head. "Captain, no matter how I fight it, you always seem to be right about things. You and Kate both. I'm grateful that you've put up with me this long. Don't leave because of our talk. I have plenty of work at the commissary."

"I'm sure if you wanted to you could get the day off and find us a carriage to go for a drive. I'm leaving in the morning. I've already arranged it."

"Tomorrow already?" Katherine asked.

"Yes, I want to get back to ... well, I just have to go. This visit is way out of my way."

"We understand," Weldon assured him. John looked toward Eliza, who was listening and growing excited at the thought of a ride out. "Well, I guess we can go out as long as she's up to it."

"Bully, Papa. I feel fine. Really fine," Eliza whispered. Her arms were like sapling branches. John covered her quickly. After a few excited remarks, her strength was near gone, and she leaned her tired head against her father as they buttoned her oversized jacket.

Simon turned away and pretended cheer for the family's sake.

Chapter Fifty-Four

The wind blew all night through the fine desert grasses. The occasional ring of the chime on the porch reminded Katherine of the nights in their shelter at old Camp Grant. They used to dream of bigger quarters, but now there was too much space between them, and although John had been pleasant all day to her, he slept up against the wall as if he could not put enough distance between them. She got up and went to the kitchen in the dark. The air was heavy as she lit a lamp and perched herself on a stool. From the other rooms came the regular breathing of Willy and John mingled with Eliza's troubled breaths. She swallowed hard.

Simon lay curled on the sofa by the stove, his blonde hair neatly cropped as it always was, but his round face and boyish serenity had vanished. How could she have let herself say such cruel things to him? Who knew when they would see each other again? She had only vague notions about disreputable diseases, and for the first time she really worried for him. Her heart ached at how alone he must be with this illness. No one would love him now.

She wiped her eyes. The cuckoo struck three. If she went back to sleep, Simon would be gone too quickly, so she stayed awake reliving their lovely ride and how Simon and John joked, stiffly at first, and how the children clung to the men, so eager to be a part of their fun. She soaked it up, hoping the memories would buoy her spirits after Simon was gone.

She served a big breakfast as Simon pulled on his boots at dawn.

"Shit!" he groused, tugging at his leg like a lunatic. Out came a scorpion. "Goddamned desert! Good riddance to it all. My blasted toe!"

Weldon lit his pipe, smirking at Simon's misfortune, and the children hid their giggles. Simon glared at them. "So you think it's funny, do you, to see your poor uncle attacked?"

William lost his smile fast. "Sorry, Uncle Simon."

Eliza piped in, "Why are you sorry, Willy? Why, you've gotten awful bit up by those creatures, and you don't bawl and complain. I thought you were a brave soldier, Uncle Simon—a captain too!"

"Eliza Weldon!" Katherine scolded.

"Land sakes, you've raised two of the toughest sons of guns! Come here, you little ruffian!"

Simon grabbed and tickled Eliza until William stepped up nervously, eyeing his father. "No uncle, you had better stop."

"Mercy, I'm awful thick!" Simon said, but Eliza was full of life and kissed him through her giggles. "Uncle, may I sit on your lap today when we take you out, please?"

"Of course, my sweet. I've never been able to resist a pretty smile."

If any of them hoped today's journey would be as pleasant as the previous day's ride out they were to be greatly disappointed. The same bugs blew by, the same birds sang, and the desert was aglow with a carpet of flowers as John pointed out a spot in among the canyons he had always wanted to show Kate but had never gotten around to. Old Indian dwellings stood in eerie disrepair, but Simon was eager to get on with his journey. "Some old history enthusiast would love all this stuff," he said, "but I have no interest in the past."

Katherine took his remarks personally but hid her tears. "I wish we could all be together again for good."

He gave her a wistful look. "Maybe someday, Katie."

She had a feeling that he rushed to be away from them.

"Simon, please write ..."

"Maybe you should too."

"I hear it gets mighty cold in the Dakotas, captain, but you're certain to see some fighting," John said.

"I'd be happy to have either. One stormy day and I'd be pleased as punch. The end will come for the Indians soon, I'd say, with the buffalo gone and all. I bet Crook will be sent there next and you too."

John nodded and Katherine shuddered at the idea of cold, but if Simon was there it might not be so bad.

The family saw Simon off at a run-down ranch that looked the way they all felt. His ride would come soon. Simon gently handed Eliza, half asleep, over to her mother and kissed them both. Katherine's eyes were full and her chest heaved. She clung to Simon for a while but finally let him go. "Be safe, big brother! I miss you already, but I'm so glad you came."

Simon smiled and turned to William. "Watch the post, young man. I'll be on the lookout for things a boy might like." Simon hugged William roughly and smacked him lightly on the face. William turned away head down and shoulders slumped before climbing back into the wagon with his mother and sister.

"Weldon," Simon began and extended his hand.

Weldon laughed, his arm hanging limp.

"Boy, old fellow you're a mess. I'm sorry," Simon said and patted his friend's good arm. "Bear up, now. You've done such a bully job so far. We'll be praying for you."

John laughed again. "Okay, captain."

The creaking of the wheels and the moans of the hot team covered the silence of the passengers and the driver as they made their way back to camp. It was that awful part of the day just after three, when it seemed nothing good could come and it was almost better that evening arrive so one would have an excuse to crawl into bed and forget about it all. William stared out across the land squinting. Eliza slept beside him.

"I'm glad Simon's off to where he wants to go," John said. "I almost wish he hadn't come at all."

"Why? I wish he was here all the time," Katherine said.

"No, I just mean—well, I'll miss him more now than if he hadn't come."

"Me too," she said, "but you can't live life avoiding the good things because you'll miss them sometimes."

Weldon said nothing.

"John, please stop the horses ..."

"What for?"

"I'm sick!"

He leaned back in his seat and stopped the team but not quite quick enough. Katherine pulled herself over the edge of the wagon and vomited. He held the reins in his one hand always refusing to let her drive. "That damn army meat is no good! I told you that."

Katherine pulled a handkerchief from her reticule and wiped herself clean. Taking a deep breath she tried to smile. "I'm feeling much better now."

"It's not the meat is it?"

"No, I don't think so ... another baby ..."

Weldon slapped the reins hard over the horses' backsides, and the carriage sprang forward with a jolt. "Well, if this isn't the worst timing!"

"That's what you always say, as if I'm to blame! For once you could pretend having a child wasn't a curse!"

"Very nice, Katherine. In front of the boy!"

"Now you worry about William?"

"Are you saying I don't care about the children?"

"You care about Eliza ..."

"So you're angry that I care about our dying daughter?"

"No, John! It's just not my fault there'll be another baby."

"I didn't say it's your fault," he grumbled, his dark eyes narrow with anger. "It's my own! We should've stopped that nonsense long ago."

"I'd rather shrivel up and die than stop it!"

"Then you're stupid. We can hardly care for what we have. One is dying and look at the boy!" He turned to his son. "And where are your shoes?"

Willy cried as he always did when his parents fought.

"What do his shoes have to do with anything?"

"It's the point—we can't even get him shoes!"

"My shoes are at home, Papa!"

"Stop calling him 'boy.' He has a name."

Weldon shook his head. "We can try to get rid of it. I can send you to San Francisco. There are doctors... I'd never ask Dudley ..."

"*Why*? Would you actually be ashamed?"

"I'm being practical," he said, his mouth set grimly. "I don't want any more children."

She stared at him, her eyes shining, looking bluer than ever against the low sky behind her. "You don't want a wife anymore do you? Those doctors are dangerous."

He hesitated.

She gasped and punched him. "You have to think about it?"

He stopped the horses and grabbed her arm. "No, no, Kate," he said with tenderness and frustration. "But childbirth ... it's dangerous too for you. I can't lose anymore. You don't understand. I am so close to giving this all up! I can't handle the misery of this life we have."

"You think our life together is miserable?"

"*Yes*!" he shouted.

"You think our marriage was a mistake?" she said just above a whisper.

"Maybe ... look at all we managed to accomplish together—*nothing*! We live in a tiny house with two starving children. One is dying. The other's miserable!"

"I'm not miserable, Papa," William sobbed, "and I'm not hungry ..."

Weldon waved him off. "So as a team we make more children to bring into this terrible world."

"That's how you see us—just a short list of imperfections?" Katherine shivered through her words in shock.

"Yes," he said. "Yes."

Chapter Fifty-Five

Weldon could scribble his thoughts quickly now with his left hand:

As usual cruel and unkind to Katherine. With child again. I can't take caring for even one more person. This is worse than childhood. I'd gladly relive that 20 times than go through this! This is too beautiful and precious. When did life become so damn precious? When I met Kate. I almost hate her for the way she makes me feel when she is undressed and she doesn't even know it. I don't want to love anymore. I want something I can't have to make them just leave me be for a while. I wish she would leave—go to Englewood. The first thing I'd do is go to Oonagh ... Shouldn't think about it. I have to stay strong for Elly. It won't be long now, but I need to get away before I slip up—a scout maybe—just a few days. Something to take my time and energy. I don't mean it, Kate. The words I say. I love you too much it's wrong maybe. I don't know.

Crook came in from his headquarters at Prescott and was pleased with the progress at New Camp Grant. Since the Indian surrenders, he had less to do, and it wore on him. Soldiering had become gardening and laboring with the Indians and at less than civilian wages. Desertions were once again on the rise. He caught Weldon on the way to the quartermaster stores. Weldon saluted.

Crook spoke. "How is little Eliza?"

Weldon shrugged, unable to speak about her after a trying night.

"Yes, well, you may want to take some time for your family," Crook suggested.

"No, sir, I would prefer not to."

"Whatever suits you, Weldon," he said mildly as he glanced around. "Things here are progressing nicely. Mrs. Weldon must be happy with her new home. If our men keep up this pace all the officers' quarters will be done in a few months. You've got a real talent for organization."

"Thank you, sir," Weldon said, not caring one bit.

"I suppose you wouldn't want to travel with me and a few of the men to visit some of the other posts," he said, checking himself. "Oh, not with your little girl the way she is."

"Sir, I could be ready this evening."

"No, I shouldn't have mentioned it. Sad news about Almy, isn't it?" he said changing the subject.

"Please, sir, I would really like to come."

"But Mrs. Weldon ..." Crook said, surveying him.

"She won't mind. I'm certain."

Crook looked uncomfortable with the idea but wanted the lieutenant along. "All right. We'll leave in the morning, then. I've been having a real hullabaloo with the men of Tucson and Washington over moving the Indians to San Carlos Agency. Just when the tribe is settled! Of course it will be the army that looks like monsters to the *Friends of Indians* back east when we're sent to move them. I'll be happy enough to be assigned elsewhere."

"Elsewhere, sir?"

"All signs point to the events unfolding in the Black Hills. Custer and his survey are bound to ruffle the Indians' feathers—that power-hungry little fancy man. He wants a run for president—ha!" He grunted.

"My brother-in-law is already on his way up there."

"I don't know much about Captain McCullough—he was an aide to Colonel Langellier?"

"Yes."

Crook moved off. "See you first thing then, Weldon."

***

Weldon groomed his horse and polished his tack. He saw to it that all was how it should be at the commissary. He visited with his sergeants, drilled in the afternoon, and found more work overseeing men at the irrigation ditch before trudging home. William and his fishing pole were gone. Weldon remembered he had promised his son they would go today, just the two of them to the river. The curtains were drawn against the late, soft afternoon sun and all was perfect stillness. He heard some men finishing up a plaintive song by the horses and that was all.

He missed the smell of cooking in the kitchen. The rooms were cooler without the fire. Eliza lay on the sofa propped up with pillows, her eyes slightly open and glassy. John thought for a moment the end had come and rushed to her but hesitated before touching her arm. She moved and sighed, then closed her eyes.

Behind a curtain Katherine had decorated their private space with blue flowers, half-wilted and tumbling out of their small waterless jars on the thick windowsill next to Katherine's pocket watch and sketchbook. She lay sleeping in her under things, curled like a cat with her long braid hanging down over the side of their bed. Her skin was the color of copper, and the loose hair around her face was almost white from the sun. John picked up the book of drawings. He hadn't taken any interest in them of late. There were plenty of sketches of his things: his boots, a coat over a chair, even the slouch hat she hated. They were lonely drawings. No funny dapper soldiers or parading cavalry horses. No children or dogs. Just empty things ... his things. He dropped her pen, and the small noise woke her. She turned on her back and watched him dreamily, looking soft and warm and beautiful.

"There's no supper. You'll have to get it yourself for once," she said as the sleep wore off.

"Okay. What shall I make?"

She sat up and grabbed her ginger water, sipping it carefully. "Suit yourself."

"How ... how are you feeling?"

"Are you here to ask stupid questions or to torture me in some other way?" she asked, lying back again with a sick moan.

"Fine, lie in bed all day. I'll make something for Willy and me. Where is he?"

"He's with Dudley and Bourke," she replied, turning toward the wall. "They thought I might need a rest and Willy was lonely. *They* like to spend time with him."

"Some of us have to work," he said, turning back to the kitchen.

"Some of us prefer work to caring for our loved ones. Or should I say dependents—there's no sign of love here!"

He stewed, stoking the tiny fire, but said nothing as he tried to chop a soft, slimy onion. It slipped through his weak fingers. He threw the whole thing into a spattering, greasy skillet with some pork. Dragging the heavy Dutch oven to the heat, he stirred the burnt beans from breakfast. The clumsy noise woke Eliza, who had become so accustomed to her disease that when she coughed she dutifully cleaned herself, displaying no panic whatsoever.

Katherine came out and sat beside her daughter, brushing Eliza's hair and curling it around her fingers. She whispered to her and made the little girl laugh. Eliza pulled at her mother's braid, undid it, and stood on a stool, taking her turn at brushing Katherine's hair. John tried not to look as he sat eating his repulsive meal. It hurt him to see them so close, and it hurt him to see Katherine just starting to show, looking full and ripe. She was too beautiful. "Would you please put on proper clothes while I'm eating?"

"Seeing me ruins your appetite now?" Katherine ran from the room and jumped back into bed.

"Every day crying! Will you ever stop?" he complained, throwing down his fork and pushing his food away.

Eliza was still standing on the stool holding the brush. "You're not nice," she said to him with her arms folded. He pulled her down from the stool and went to his wife.

"Kate, I didn't mean it that way," he said, sitting at the edge of the bed and running his hands through his hair. "You're the loveliest creature I've ever seen. It's so hard for me to stay angry with you when you look the way you do."

"But why do you want to stay huffed at me? What have I done? I don't understand."

He slid his fingers over her hip, withdrawing quickly. "I don't know. I can't explain it, but ... I can't stay here with you right now," he said.

"What do you mean?"

"I'm going with Crook to help him at the other forts. He needs me."

"You must be joking. He would never make you go." She stared at him, and when he averted his eyes she knew. "You volunteered? You volunteered to leave me?"

"It's for the best. Before we hate each other."

"Hate?" she cried.

"I want this next promotion for us—it's more money for the children."

"What will Eliza need money for?" she asked. "The army will provide the coffin!"

"You see! I can't take the way you talk anymore!"

"You disappoint me, John. How you turn on your own. Wasn't it you who said the Apache disgusted you when they turned scout against each other so easily? Maybe you're more Indian than you like to think!"

He swung his hand at her but missed.

"Go ahead. Try again!" she cried miserably. "I want you to. Maybe I can begin to feel the hatred for you that you feel for me!"

"It's for the best I go. For a while ..." He grabbed his coat and walked out as William and the doctor came back. Dudley said something that tickled the boy, and he laughed until he saw his father.

"Dudley."

"Yes, sir?" Dudley's face dropped at the dark look of Weldon.

"Thank you for taking my boy out."

"Oh, it's my pleasure," he said, messing William's hair as the boy stood stiffly glowering at his father.

"I need a favor. I'll be going off with Crook tomorrow ..."

"For how long?" Dudley looked first at Willy then back at Weldon with concern. "What about Eliza?"

"It can't be helped. I have to go."

"Surely, Crook ..."

"Doctor! Listen. Please look out for them while I'm gone. You'll do it, won't you?" Weldon fumbled for his pipe.

"Of course, but ..." Dudley helped Weldon light his smoke.

"Katherine is stronger than she appears," Weldon said, more interested in his pipe. "She'll handle everything."

"Is that fair to her?"

"I asked if you would help. I didn't ask for advice. A Harvard man should know the difference."

Although Dudley had spent so much time with the Weldon family, he realized now that he never cracked the lieutenant. All along he had imagined he knew them. He knew Katherine and the children, but not Weldon. Dudley was bitterly disappointed in himself for putting too much faith in this little family. They were what he might like to have one day, and now they had fallen short of his expectations.

Since Eliza's illness, he had been invited over less and less, but he understood that. The family needed time alone. But the doctor began keeping track of how many late nights Weldon spent working in the commissary or elsewhere at the fort. He felt pathetic in a way for watching, but it was impossible not to notice from his porch.

It saddened him at first, but then it aggravated him as he saw Katherine on occasion looking pale. He had a horrible feeling as he looked at Weldon now that she would one day be deserted for good. Before the illness, when Dudley sat and sang songs with them in the evenings under the big cloudless sky, he imagined he would like to be a husband and a father just like the lieutenant, but he knew now that what he really wanted was a wife like Katherine.

Weldon stared at Frederick Dudley so deep in thought and grew impatient. "Doctor Dudley, are you listening?"

"Yes, of course. I'll do my best for them, but it's you they need."

"Trust me, doctor. You have no idea what you're saying." Weldon slipped William's fishing pole under his sling and grabbed his son's hand. "Come along, William." But the boy pulled away and shoved his hands in his pockets. Weldon's shoulders slumped, and father and son walked off unhappily.

***

Every morning Doctor Dudley made his tea in his large stoneware pot and went to his porch to reread his medical journals for the thousandth time until his tea ran out. He would then write one letter to a Sister of Mercy back east, make his bed, and go for a stroll before sick call. Dudley took his last swig of tea just as Crook's small party stopped in front of the Weldon place, with Weldon's dark horse already saddled. Dudley sighed.

Katherine followed Weldon on to the porch in her simple wrap made of the same gingham blue as the curtains. Dudley remembered her confessing when the fabric first arrived in the mail from the East that she hated to sew. But the dress from a distance in the soft light of sunrise suited the lieutenant's wife just fine, with her hair falling to the lowest part of her back in thick waves. He wanted to shout to Weldon, "Look at her, you fool!" but Weldon barely glanced at her after he climbed on his horse.

The doctor watched her stare after Weldon, but it was impossible to read what she was thinking. Her mouth was set and her eyes showed no emotion. After a while she turned and went inside.

The days weighed heavily on Frederick Dudley. He had given Weldon a promise he felt would be somehow dangerous to keep.

William came by often and helped the doctor organize and reorganize his "potions" before climbing up on his lap and falling asleep like he had done when he was still little with the old doctor. Dudley was at first uncomfortable with the boy's loneliness but had grown to see William as the younger brother he never had. Dudley didn't have the heart to tell Willy he was too old and too heavy, so he put aside his normal, albeit flexible and simple, schedule to give the boy the rest and care he was no longer getting at home.

"Willy, how is your mother?"

"Fine."

"And Eliza?"

"Fine."

Dudley made up his mind to visit when on the fourth day he noticed how ravenously William devoured the mescal an old squaw gave him. He worried now. Grabbing his case, he arrived on the Weldon's front porch with a strange mix of excitement and fear. Dudley knocked and waited and knocked again, debating whether to push the door open when Katherine finally answered it. "Doctor Dudley."

He searched her face for signs she was happy to see him, and followed her in, apprehensive and uncomfortable. She turned to him with tired eyes as if she had been crying for days, and he felt guilty for not coming sooner.

She poured him tea, knowing he preferred it to coffee, and he smiled. Eliza, white and exhausted, sat primly cross-stitching an alphabet sent by Sarah.

The two said nothing for a while as Dudley glanced around, noticing troubling things—the candles were low, the lanterns empty, the pots were dirty, and there was no smell of bread.

Katherine pinned her hair back into a knot, but it was too thick and fell to her waist again so she tucked it behind her ears. She wore simple little ear-bobs. Blue again. Maybe a gift from Weldon. "I thought you were avoiding me, Doctor Dudley."

"Pardon me, Mrs. Weldon. Why would I do that?"

She shrugged and shook her head. She trembled while drinking her foul-smelling ginger water. Dudley remembered making it at the orphanage for the men who worked in the fields.

"I've missed you, Frederick—we used to have such interesting talks."

"Mrs. Weldon, I loved our discussions too, but ..."

She rose from the table and took Eliza's work from her as the little girl drifted and tucked her in. "I realize you must side with the lieutenant."

"Mrs. Weldon, side in what way? I have the greatest respect and sympathy for you."

Her eyes were wide. "Oh, you pity me? I'm so pathetic!"

He went to her and impulsively took her hands in his. "Mrs. Weldon, I never said I pitied you. Lieutenant Weldon has always said that you're stronger than you realize, and I agree."

She sobbed and covered her face, sitting at the table. Dudley, in his best doctor fashion, put his arm around her shoulders. "There, there, Mrs. Weldon. Everything will be all right."

"No, it won't!" she said, lifting her head.

Her face flushed and from the angle Dudley stood at, he could see down the front of Katherine's dress to the curve of her belly.

"Oh, Frederick, I thought you'd left me too. I imagined I'd made a mistake in reading you and that maybe you were John's friend only, but you're here now."

"Mrs. Weldon, you were so wrong! I've always admired everything about you. You're like a ..." He couldn't say it—she was not like a sister to him.

"Oh, I'm so relieved! You don't know how fond I've grown of you," she said. "I feel the same ... you're like a brother."

But Dudley wasn't listening anymore. He grabbed her and kissed her, his hands in her hair now and on her neck. She didn't fight it. It felt nice for a moment to be loved, but it wasn't John. She pulled away. William sat on the bed with Eliza. The two of them stared. Katherine backed away, overturning a chair, and Dudley cursed himself—how depraved he must be to fall in love with a pregnant woman!

"Please, Mrs. Weldon, forgive me!"

She cried, and for a moment he fooled himself into believing that she shared his feelings.

"Doctor Dudley, why did you go and ruin everything? I hoped you were my friend ... a true friend ... the only friend I have out here."

"Mrs. Weldon, I am your friend, please ..."

"No. It's over. Oh and the children! What would John think if he knew?"

"Mrs. Weldon, who cares what the lieutenant thinks! He treats you horribly. I would treat you like royalty and Willy too, and I would care for you and your baby. We could leave here and go anywhere!"

"No!" she said, keeping a safe distance. "I trusted you! Oh, why did you have to do this? Now I'm completely alone. You've ruined it all, Frederick Dudley. You lovely, foolish man! Please leave!"

He grabbed his bag and ran to his quarters. He was breathless, out of shape, and as shaken as the first time he was rejected as a young man at Harvard. As an adult though, he understood the consequences of his rash actions. He would never be able to help the Weldon family again. Pacing the floor, he huffed and fumed over what he had done. He took out a cigarette, lit it, and held it between his lips tightly as he rummaged behind his medicine bottles for some brandy or whiskey—whatever he could find. Taking a swig of rotten whiskey from the bottle, he found a glass and filled it. He sat at his desk for a long time, listening to the wind blur the sounds of camp.

Dear Mrs. Weldon,

The way I behaved today was shameful and incredibly rude. Please believe me when I tell you that I never planned for it to happen. Lieutenant Weldon asked me to watch out for you and the children while he was away, and I have taken advantage of his trust. None of it is your fault; I am fully to blame. I would like to tell you that it was just loneliness or missing my girl in Boston, but that would be a lie. I didn't fully realize my feelings for you until recently—since you have kept to yourself. You are simply the kindest and prettiest woman that I have ever known, and intelligent too. I do not understand the lieutenant at all. I would never let you out of my sight, but it is not my place to say.

I am heartbroken that you feel our friendship must end. I was rash and forward today, but I can promise you that it would never happen again. I worry about you and the children caring for yourselves properly. Please do not push me away. I will behave like a gentleman from now on.

Sincerely,

Fred. Dudley

PS I will not pressure you. If you ignore me and this note I will understand and leave you be.

He carried the note himself, and like a smitten school boy slipped it under the Weldon door. Katherine was home, and he saw the shadow of her feet and hands as she took the note. Then he went home and waited. The Weldon quarters remained dark and quiet even as night set in, and he almost went to check on the family a few times. Willy did not come out for evening parade, and the men looked worried. Finally, Dudley could take it no longer and ran to Katherine's door. She answered but had obviously been asleep.

"Pardon me, Mrs. Weldon, I wanted to make sure that everything is all right."

"Right as rain," she said frostily.

When on the next day Katherine, on her way to the commissary, turned her face away under her broad planter's hat, Dudley knew he must leave her too.

The doctor had time off and would visit Prescott or Tucson. Nothing could be done for Eliza now anyway, and the family was perfectly safe with the other men. He hesitated though. Should he stay for Katherine in case she was alone when the child died?

He packed a few things and set them on his porch. He would go out with the teamsters, who were leaving for supplies. Spotting Katherine sweeping her porch, he packed a bag full of useless concoctions mostly but cough suppressant and morphine too, for the end, and resolutely made his way to the Weldon home.

"Mrs. Weldon, I'm sorry to intrude. It's all very awkward now, I know, but little Eliza ... I've grown quite attached to the children ... too. How is she?"

Katherine bit down hard on her lip and looked across the lonely camp. "You know, we picked a place for Elly by the stand of cottonwoods with the columbines all around. She loved to play there, but now I worry. It's silly, but I worry that somehow she'll feel all alone out here. I don't think I can stay." She glanced his way for a second.

"Mrs. Weldon, I have taken some time," he said, checking for her reaction. "I may go to Prescott, I don't know, but if you'd like me to stay—for Eliza, just in case ... I will."

She smiled. His face brightened too, but then she grew more serious again. "Doctor Dudley, you've done all you can do for Eliza and all of us. I wish it wasn't true, but it is. I can't keep you here. You're young and should be free as a lark instead of being cooped up on your little porch with all of those manuals." She took his hand. "Frederick Dudley, escape this misery for a while. You're a wonderful man, and you deserve every happiness. I'm sorry if I've hurt you in any way. It was never my intention."

"Mrs. Weldon, I know that you didn't mean to break my heart, but you have. I don't want to lose our friendship."

"No, doctor, we just need to have our own lives for a while. Maybe then we can have our old times again."

He gazed at her warmly. "I hope so. I've brought you supplies. They should last until ..."

"Thank you, Frederick—for everything. Now go and forget us for a while." She forced a smile. He kissed her hand and walked off.

Chapter Fifty-Six

Every part of Katherine ached. Even her swollen fingers seemed weighted. She struggled every second just to stay awake, to move from sleeping to sitting, from sitting to standing. Eliza rested on the blood-stained sofa, and by ten each morning began her upsetting and irritating chant for John, followed by fresh coughing and blood so bad Katherine thought every attack would be the last. She tried to calm Eliza, but she had had enough too, and since she couldn't fight the disease she fought her mother, pushing and kicking her away. "I want Papa! I want Papa!"

"He's not here! For heaven's sake, get it into your head! He's left us!"

"Papa loves me even if he doesn't care for you, Mommy!"

Katherine cried out and slapped her, slapped her sick little girl who didn't know what she was saying. William came between them then and hugged Eliza until she fell asleep. Katherine hated them both—and herself. She cooked the last of the griddle cakes, threw them on a plate at the table, and ordered William to eat but couldn't remember the last time she had eaten and secretly hoped to somehow starve out the baby she carried ... until she felt the first fluttering of it.

In the night when some small relief came from the heat of the desert, Eliza called for her mother.

Katherine had long since exhausted her soothing phrases. She sat on the edge of the sofa and sighed.

"Mommy, I'm scared it's dark in Heaven, and I don't think I'll get along with God much."

Katherine took her daughter's wrist and ran her fingers up and down along the inside where the skin was soft and smooth. Eliza giggled but then relaxed under the mesmerizing touch.

"Mommy?" Eliza needed her mother's voice. Katherine lifted her onto her lap. The girl couldn't get close enough and nuzzled her head against Katherine's neck, feeling the beat of her mother's heart.

"When I was a young girl like you, Grammy used to sit me on her lap just like this, and when I asked her about Heaven she said that there's so many delightful people there who are waiting for us even now and love us already that you'll forget about earth because the love will be so much better there."

"I don't want more than I've got—even the soldiers love me."

Katherine rocked her gently. "Grandma said that in Heaven everybody is healthy and strong again and can do as they please and time just speeds by. Soon enough every one you loved on earth is there too."

"How long? A week?" Eliza grabbed Katherine's loose hair and twirled it.

"I don't know."

"I think I can wait about a week," Eliza said bravely, but then sobbed and clung to her mother. "I'm afraid you'll get a new girl and love her better and forget about me!"

"Never!" Katherine cried. "You will always be my beautiful girl. I'll miss you until the end of time! No one will ever take your place. I don't know how I'll live without you!"

She kissed Eliza's hair, and they both wrapped themselves around each other until they fell asleep.

Chapter Fifty-Seven

The men of Camp Grant liked the order of things, the simple consistent behavior of their friends and enemies, the way the flag always flew and the dogs always scampered around the horses when their owners arrived back from a scout, and the way the Weldon family—Katherine, Willy, and Eliza—always ran out and enthusiastically greeted them. Mrs. Weldon pushed right in among the horses and pulled the lieutenant down for a kiss. The soldiers took some of this cheer as their own. Today the flag flew and the dogs still yelped at the kicks of the horses, but each man wondered and hoped that the worst had not occurred in their absence. Weldon's chest closed to air and his heart raced—where was Katherine?

The horses eagerly trotted toward their rest and food. Weldon braced himself for a telling sign as they rode past the barracks, but all was quiet. As they turned toward the corral, Willy swung a short stick at debris in the path. Everyone greeted him, but he ignored them. The men looked to Weldon, who jumped from his mount and handed the reins to a corporal. William was filthy, like a soldier just back from a long campaign.

"Willy, I'm home!" Weldon said, grabbing his son, who stood stiffly to his father's embrace. "Let's go to your mother."

William shook his head and refused to look at his father. Weldon pushed the door to their home open. The air was thick like rancid soup, and Weldon's eyes needed time to adjust to the darkness after hours in the sun.

Food, it was hard to tell from when, lay rotting at the table covered with an array of brightly hued insects. Strips of half-washed, bloodstained cloth hung over the backs of chairs and on a makeshift line near the stove. In the dark on the sofa lay Eliza, looking old and small, wrapped in one of his shirts—the last of the clean clothes. Her eyes shone. "Papa, I knew it," she whispered.

He wanted to turn away from this poor little thing he tried to ignore. He had hoped somehow that he would return and find his real and healthy girl.

Katherine sat next to Eliza dreamily, her boots unlaced but still on, her face grey and nearly as dirty as her son's by the door.

Weldon scooped up the damp rags and threw them in a pile on the floor. Noisily he gathered up the plates in disgust as the insects scattered and threw them into the washing tub full of cloudy water. Before he could settle down, the telltale rumbling in Eliza's chest began, and the little girl gurgled blood with the cough. Katherine swayed unsteadily, strangely, and pulled Eliza into sitting up against her. The girl coughed and cried in frustration, putting her hand to her mouth as new hemorrhag-

367

ing sent blood out between her fingers. Katherine spoke quietly to her. John detected a slur to Katherine's words and went over to them. Old stains on Katherine's dress where Eliza had rubbed her face repulsed him.

"This place is filthy," he said. "Katherine, have you been *drinking*?"

"So what if I have?"

"You're drunk!"

"What does it matter? Why do you care?"

"You stupid, stupid girl!" He grabbed her and shook her. "I *will not* take care of a *drunk ever* again! I can't and I won't! You were different, and I depended on you! Are you even listening, you stupid bitch? Tell me! How can you let this happen? I did everything to make things different and you—you drink? No, that's it for me. That's it!"

"I had only one drink!" Katherine cried. "Our children, you say? *My* children! You don't care about them. You go off and have your fun while I suffer here in this hovel you've given us for a home!"

"The way you clean and cook, you're not fit for a real home! You sit here drinking while Willy goes unfed and unwashed? What kind of mother are you?" Weldon yelled, pacing before her. "Kate, has anyone been to see you? Anyone?"

She shook her head and poured a drink. "No, not since Dudley left ..."

He hit her arm down. "You will *not* drink, Katherine! I need you to ..."

"What do you need? Do you need to desert me? Do you need me to wash your clothes?"

"Don't start it again!" he ranted. "Your job is to mother the children! You were supposed to take care of things!"

Eliza coughed again, unable to stop.

"For God's sake, stop that coughing!!" he shouted.

William came to his father's side. "Don't yell at her! It's not her fault. You never even try to help anymore, and I hate you!"

Weldon did not know that Katherine and William had been up the last three nights believing that Eliza would die before he returned. He did not realize that Eliza was so afraid now that she would not allow Katherine to leave the bed. He did not realize that his wife was too proud to ask for help from anyone. The stark loneliness, the darkened room, the neglected boy ... Weldon turned from them.

"Where are you going now?" Katherine asked timidly.

"Outside."

"Just like you to run. Everybody said it, and now I see they were right! You're worthless—nothing more than a coward!"

Weldon turned on her, grabbing her by the arm, "You make me sick! That's why I leave you!"

"You're a weak coward! Go on hit me! See if I care. I'm defenseless against you—just like the Indians you hunt down now like dogs!"

He threw her to the bed and ran out and around to the side of the house and was sick. Wiping his mouth on his sleeve, he walked off clear of mind, knowing what he had to do.

Oonagh's laundry hung out in the desert heat, dry like bone. The men, so accustomed to Weldon's strict adherence to military etiquette, were surprised when their crisp salutes were ignored. The girl must be gone, they thought.

Bent over her work and as strong as ever, Oonagh turned her face to the lieutenant's footfall and smiled. Her age and smoking habit showed on her teeth and in the deep lines around her eyes and mouth. Her brood of children tramped around in the distance playing with a mangy dog.

"Well, if it ain't Lieutenant Weldon come for a visit. Sure, it's been a while—a right bit longer than I'd expected."

"You know why I'm here," he said. "Have you got anything? You're still in business?"

"Course I am, sir. A soldier's pay ain't much ta live on, is it?"

Weldon wondered what she could want with money. The laundress hadn't elevated herself much since he last spoke to her.

"'Tis a shame about your wee daughter—and I hear yer wife's gone off a bit—real tragic."

"My family's fine."

"Sure they are, lieutenant. No concern of mine."

"Exactly. So what have you got?"

"Well, let's see. Doctor Dudley runs a tight vessel, but I've got a friendship with a teamster—can get me most anything from the Chinks."

"That doesn't help me right now."

She pushed her hair behind her and stood up, folding her arms. "Lieutenant, you've become a fine-lookin' man. Why do you want to go ruinin' yerself again?"

"What have you got?" he pressed.

"Well, sir, I've got somethin' I've been keepin' for my own occasional pleasure, but you'd appreciate its fine design. Have any tools?"

"No."

"Well then, it's a fine kit, just the size for keeping secret," she said in a mocking whisper. "Will you be wanting some laundry done, sir, or will that offend the missus?"

"Don't worry about my wife!" he said, remembering the things that needed cleaning. "I'll be back."

"Again and again, I'd say," Oonagh said to herself as she watched him jog off. Weldon reentered his home.

"John, I'm sorry over the state of things and ... what I said," Katherine whimpered.

William sat washing dishes on the floor, making more mess in the process.

"Willy, what are you doing?" Weldon complained as he raced around ignoring Katherine's words. Forgiving her would make it more difficult to escape, so he hardened his heart to her pleas, finding it pathetic that she would not get up from bed. He shoved everything into a sack.

"John, I haven't gotten the chance to clean those, I ..."

"I can see that ... and stop crying!"

"I don't understand why you hate me!" she sobbed. "What have I done? Why am I so hard to love?"

"Your children love you."

She flew from the bed at Weldon. "How could you? Why did you bring me here just to kill me with your words? I need you!"

"You're pitiful," he said. "Get off me. I can't take it anymore. You smother me!"

"Smother you? I love you!"

"Katherine, I don't love ... let me go," he said softly, trying to believe his words. He pushed her away.

Willy let the last of the dishes sink back into the dirty water and ran to his father. "Please don't leave us!"

"Clean up the mess you've made, William," he said, detaching himself from his son's grip. He threw the sack of laundry over his shoulder and walked double-time to the dark-eyed laundress awaiting his call.

Like a boy on parade, he carried his bag of bloody blankets with true military bearing. He dropped the sack before Oonagh in tribute, took out the last of his cash, put aside enough for a can of condensed milk for Willy, and received his new kit. It was silver and opened like a little matchbox, but inside a safely secured syringe sat in the middle with little vials all around it, each in their own safe spot. He checked it for damage.

"A nice size, ain't it? Progress is a brilliant thing, sir."

Weldon nodded, slipping it into his breast pocket. It felt like a family reunion and his chest pounded with excitement. He knew just where he would go—he had been planning at the back of his mind for weeks.

Oonagh Lyons watched him walk off, almost sad, but business was business, and it was a free country to do what you liked. If she didn't supply him he would steal from the doctor, and she wouldn't be able to keep her brood with such round and full bellies.

She sighed at the size of the bag. She separated the things smallest to largest and started with the easier rags, scrubbing the stains with her hands and fingernails when the soft brush wouldn't do. Oonagh, at best a half-hearted laundress, squatted before her lukewarm basin and put real effort into her job, spending a good few hours trying with no success to wash the stains out.

She hung the small and handmade things from back east on the line, but in a spontaneous act of frustration, she pulled them down again, walked off to the commissary, threw down her money—Weldon's money—and demanded any flannel, any soft fabric the army might have. She cut small cloths and finished the edges with bright darning thread. Washing was not her forte, but she was a good seamstress with nimble fingers that Katherine would envy. When she finished her final piece—an elegant red pinafore—simple enough and about an hour's work, she stacked everything in a neat pile, called for her eldest daughter, Bridget, and off they went to visit Katherine.

William slipped like a phantom around back when he spotted them coming. It was pitch dark, but Bridget held a candle. They heard a weak cough and pushed open the door without knocking.

"By Christ, this is the worst I've seen yet," Oonagh said. She took Eliza first and cleaned her face with water from a drinking cup. "Would you go back and get us a proper dress for the girl, Bridget?"

"The girl?"

"For God sake, Mrs. Weldon, and be quick about it!"

Oonagh darted around the room, making a clean spot in a large crate for Eliza to lounge in and bringing her near the open door for air. Taking the filthy dishwater around back, she discovered Willy looking like a stray pup. "Ay, young William is it? I hear you take good care of yer mum. Will ya help us ta set things straight? There'll be a nice reward in it."

He followed in silence. Bridget brought back flour, a few cans of beans, and some sausage. Oonagh smiled and set the girl to building a proper fire and starting food on the stove.

"Now, young man, I'd say yer old enough to clean yerself ain't you?"

The kettle boiled, and she mixed the water with cool water from the finished dishes. "Here, make yerself nice fer yer mum."

Oonagh swept the floor, helped William into a clean shirt, and was tempted to trim his gold hair, but the smell of biscuits, coffee, and real meat woke Katherine. William scrambled over to her looking bright-eyed. "Mother! Food!"

Katherine sat up and scanned the room from behind her blanket. Eliza sat primly against a stuffed bed of hay brought in from the stables. A pile of folded clothes or fabric lay neatly on the bookcase.

"Right so, let's set to makin' the bed," Oonagh said to her daughter.

Pulling the blanket around her to hide her dirty clothes, Katherine got up.

"No, we'll be needin' those, I'm afraid. Bridget, bring Mrs. Weldon the clothes."

"I don't understand. Did my husband send you?" Katherine asked.

Oonagh looked at Katherine with pity but said nothing and tried not to be sickened by the bedding over the sofa so long unchanged.

The laundress dragged it all from the house and pulled one of her own soft calico sheets, neatly pressed, over the old sofa and covered that with a colorful quilt. Bridget pulled Katherine's clothes from her roughly and helped her into a comfortable clean house wrap. Oonagh glanced at Katherine and shook her head. Katherine's belly was more pronounced. She stacked some army issue blankets at the head of the makeshift bed and led Katherine back into it.

Katherine wept at the cheerful calico as they brought her a fragrant meal as William looked on.

"You poor lad—didn't I tell ya ta take as much as ya liked?"

"Mommy!" a small voice cried from the corner. Katherine made to get up, but Oonagh stopped her and lifted the wasted child to the sofa.

"Oh, my!" Katherine exclaimed as she ran her hands over the soft little dress. "It's the most exquisite ..." she began, wiping her eyes. "I don't understand. I really don't, but thank you so much. I can never repay you, Mrs. Lyons." Katherine smiled and pet Eliza. "You look so beautiful in red, my little darling."

"Mommy, I need to say goodbye to Papa now."

Katherine went rigid and looked to Oonagh as if she sensed she might know where to find Weldon. Oonagh sighed and ran her hand along Katherine's arm, surprised by her grateful tears.

"Mommy, I'm scared to leave you. Can't you come too, and Papa and Willy?"

"No. We can't come until God calls us."

Eliza fidgeted and pulled at her curls. "Willy's lucky, Mommy. It's not fair."

Katherine kissed Eliza's forehead, and the girl put her arms around her mother's neck for a moment then dropped them to her sides. Unaware that the end had come, Katherine rocked Eliza into her final slumber until Oonagh stopped her. The laundress took the child and tucked her into bed and then took the mother in her arms.

Chapter Fifty-Eight

Oonagh Lyons had not provided him with as much as he would have liked. He hid in the hay barn. Weldon's jumbled mind played unceasing tricks—he visited his boyhood or hid in an abandoned farmhouse during the war. All thoughts were brighter and better for a while. But as the high tide wore off and the waves receded, the solid forms of Katherine, Willy, and Eliza took shape. He sat up, picking hay from his hair and wiping sleep from his eyes. He reached for his kit and hoped that somehow he had missed something—a little extra for what he knew would be hard work ahead.

He lit his pipe and walked out into the soft light of the early desert morning. The sky was always so damned beautiful no matter the weather of life below. No one was yet astir but for the buglers, their shadowy forms walking at a sleepy gait toward the parade ground.

As he climbed the stairs of his porch, their reveille began. He had always loved the buglers' calls—any time of day. The order of it all and how the specific tunes brought on specific feelings—the strange melancholy of a new day, the excitement of boots and saddles, and finally taps putting the sad world back to sleep.

The lieutenant put out his pipe and opened the door to find the laundress snoozing in a chair by the sofa. "What the hell are you doing here?"

Oonagh slowly got to her feet with a yawn. "The things you gave me to clean were too far gone, Lieutenant Weldon."

"Get the hell away from my family, you miserable ..."

"Your family?" Oonagh laughed. "Some fancy way you got of treatin' em!"

"And you'd be one to give me a lecture on that, would you?" he said. "Don't ever set foot near them. I want to protect them from the likes of you!"

"Well, you've got one less to protect this morning."

Katherine and William woke to the racket of the two as Oonagh gathered up her things.

"No, Oonagh, where are you going? Please don't!" Katherine pleaded as she rushed from the sofa. "Please!"

Katherine's clean dress and the way her freshly washed hair hung over her shoulders took Weldon's breath.

Katherine grabbed Oonagh but saw she was on her own now. "Mrs. Lyons, you're a saint. I'll always be grateful," she said and kissed her hand.

"I haven't a clue how you've made it this far, poor thing," Oonagh said, pushing her daughter out the door.

Only then did Weldon notice his little girl in the red dress who did not stir, did not cough or cry. He went to the bed and knelt beside it, choking up at the sight of the red dress against Eliza's black curls. Weldon thought to pick her up, to shake her back to life, but her body was cold and set. Katherine hung back with William's hand in hers.

"Katherine, I'm sorry ..." he said.

She turned away from him and rekindled the fire. William sat at the window with chin in hand.

"What shall we do now?" Weldon asked.

"What shall *we* do? No. You'll do the rest, John. You don't seem to mind burying things that are of no use to you anymore. I've done all I can."

Jones, accompanied by a few others, knocked at the door. "Lieutenant Weldon, we just heard the news, and we're sorry for you. How's Mrs. Weldon?" he asked, craning his neck to look within.

Weldon stepped forward and closed the door behind him.

"If there's anything, anything at all we can do ..."

"Thank you," Weldon replied. "I guess we'll have a service."

"Well, sir, there's no chaplain, but we can have someone say a prayer. Lieutenant, would you like to do that?"

"No." Weldon said.

While her daughter waited to be buried, Katherine tidied the table, clearing it for the first time in weeks, possibly months. Some internal evil caused her to feel almost celebratory, but it was temporary, a brief interlude. One of the beautiful dresses Sarah had made for Eliza had been overlooked by John and Oonagh, having fallen beneath the stove. Katherine spotted it as if her eyes had been suddenly cleared of a dull film. The white bib cried out to her, and she scooped it up. Without hesitation, she threw it into the fire. Something, a sense of perverse freedom, compelled her to seek it all out now, remove all the sickness. She flung open the chest that Oonagh had just organized and dug through it, pulling out underthings, stockings, worn shoes, and the extravagant baby things she had been saving as keepsakes. One by one at first, but then in bundles, she threw everything into the fire until John reentered.

"You've lost yourself, Kate!" he shouted, trying unsuccessfully to retrieve the last remnant of Eliza's life from the inferno and grabbing his wife.

She pulled away from him like a wild animal and would have scratched his eyes out if he had not set her free.

He tore at his hair. "What will she wear? What will Elly wear now? You dumb girl!"

"In her coffin? In her *coffin*? What does it matter?" Katherine asked as she made for the box with Weldon trailing her closely, not sure what she would do next. She grabbed the red dress. "*This* is what Eliza will wear. It'll be soft against her decaying body!"

"Shut up!" he shouted.

She swung her arm back and slapped his face harder than she'd ever come up against anything. "*No!* You have no authority over me! You care about what your daughter wears now? Where were you when Elly asked for you last night? Oonagh Lyons made this dress, and she was here at the most important time!"

"Oonagh made the dress?" he asked, collapsing onto the sofa. "I'm cursed!"

"You're what you let yourself be!" Katherine said. "Move from the sofa."

Weldon stood up hopelessly and caught Willy's eye. He held out his hand to his son who slipped beneath it and clung to his mother, looking back only once with blazing eyes.

Katherine took down the small bag she kept hanging from the peg over the mirror. Pouring the contents on the sofa, she let Willy pick which pretty trinkets should go with Eliza. She clipped curls from her daughter's hair and enclosed them in a folded piece of stationery. William took a charm bracelet that both children loved from Katherine's childhood and wrapped it around his sister's wrist, brushing away a fly.

Private Coulter delivered a coffin with a few men trailing him. The soldier was a splendid wood carver. Katherine gasped at the sight of the tiny coffin covered in carved desert blooms, which the men had been preparing for weeks. She ran to it and felt the smooth petals and wondered at the tung-oil finish before reading the small inscription: "*In memory of our sweetest pet and prettiest soldier girl ~ Elizabeth Weldon.*"

"We're so blest for friends!" Katherine cried, and without thinking hid her face against her husband. Weldon put his arm around her, equally moved by the beauty of the soldier's craftsmanship and the sentiment of the men, a few of them near tears themselves at the sight of their little friend in red. Katherine got a hold of herself and led the men to the table. They opened the box and within were fresh flowers of every color and description the men had gathered as soon as they heard the news.

"Land sakes, Mrs. Weldon, we're family in the army—you know that by now. We've all had a soft spot for you and the children right from the start." Jones patted her shoulder and left. The other men offered their help and condolences and left too after saluting Weldon.

She never imagined doing anything like this by herself with no guidance, but in the end it was the easiest thing to do. She lifted Eliza and lay her in the box, the flowers bringing life back to her cheeks. Katherine took down one of the clean towels Oonagh had left and tucked it around Eliza, with the decorative edging up against her face. Sarah's doll was tucked in last. Each of them said goodbye—Katherine, William, and then John.

She closed the world to her daughter and nailed the coffin shut herself.

Chapter Fifty-Nine

Frederick Dudley had a year left of his commission, but all the way back to Camp Grant he considered transferring or deserting. Of course he would do neither; Dudley was a man who stayed the course. He knew that Eliza had passed long before he spotted Katherine Weldon sitting alone in black on her porch.

He picked through his mail and opened a big package of spoiled meats and canned delicacies he didn't like from back east sent by his girl. The girl had her own tastes and paid no attention to his. He would never return to her. A large piece of cotton fabric lined the bottom of the box. It was presumably sent to make shirts with, but he had never mastered the skill and apparently neither had the girl—or maybe she just couldn't remember his size.

The doctor saw two men that afternoon both with fever and ague. The rest of the day was spent with his tea and correspondence. First a thank you note to the girl:

Dear Miss Lucena,

Having just received your thoughtful package, I wanted to thank you. Only a few of the meats were spoiled. I don't sew or wear plaid ever really. You might have noticed that over the many years you saw me at school and at the hospital. The truth is, I want a girl who notices little things about me and does not want to compete with me. You will make a competent doctor someday I suppose, but not a very good wife and I want that more than anything. I want a girl who wants lots of my children and cooks and cleans and likes me as I am plaids or no plaids. I don't know how many times you've tried to push them on me!

I don't blame you for sparking with Joseph Hale. He's a nice fellow with more of the social pretensions so lacking in me. After all, I am just an orphan boy as you used to joke. I've been faithful in body though not in mind. I wonder why you ask in your letter for permission to spend time with others. I was never under the illusion you were a chaste or loyal girl ...

"Doctor Dudley, you in?"

A sudden panic in the pit of Dudley's stomach caused him to hesitate before opening the door to let Weldon in. They stood together uncomfortably in the center of the room.

"Lieutenant Weldon, about Eliza ..."

Weldon scanned the room, searching for any place to rest his eyes. "Dudley ... I have a problem, a concern really ..."

"Yes?"

Weldon rolled up his sleeve.

"Lieutenant Weldon, what happened here?"

"Well, it's a burn, I think ..." Weldon said.

"You *think* it's a burn? You would know if it was. You would remember it, I'm sure. This is no burn."

"Well," Weldon stuttered, "I d-don't know ..."

"Lieutenant Weldon, this is badly inflamed. What have you been doing to yourself?"

Weldon scratched the sore skin behind his ear.

"Are you listening?" Dudley asked, thinking of Katherine and how she would feel if her husband died of blood poisoning.

"Yes, I'm listening ... it's not a burn. No, it's not a burn at all ... I've never told anyone. I don't know why I'm telling you ..."

Dudley looked him in the eye. "How long have you been doing this to yourself?"

"On and off ... I hoped you might know a cure. I trust you won't tell my wife ... my career, my family ...." He drifted a moment but came back. "I want to stop ... I tried."

"Well, good luck," Dudley said dismissively, trying to collect his thoughts while sifting aimlessly through stray papers.

"What? Is that all you have to say?" Weldon asked, the hopelessness in his voice reminding Dudley of his vocational duties.

Dudley reluctantly looked at the sore again and roughly let go of the arm. "There's been missing stores of morphine. I assume you've been stealing them."

"No! I haven't. A laundress gets ... I haven't taken anything from you, I swear it!"

"For Mrs. Weldon's sake, I won't seek charges against you. I can't believe you fooled me. I even felt some sympathy for you when you left."

"I've come to you for help. I'd never steal from you," Weldon said in a surprisingly indignant tone. "I figured you might have experience with other veterans."

Dudley sighed. "I can put a little carbolic acid on your arm. It might help prevent further inflammation." When his voice shook, he wondered at his inability to stay neutral and professional. "I'm so disappointed for you ... for Katherine ... there's no cure for what you have. I've heard of people like you who've freed themselves from it, but I've never met them. Most just got sent home to be taken care of by their families." He was cold in relating the facts. He had been taught how at school. "This is your life, lieutenant. Get used to it. Most don't live long—their teeth go bad, they lose their hair. And you're already using it through a syringe and probably not diluting it that much ... am I right?"

Weldon shook all over. He searched the doctor for some little hope or sympathy even but didn't expect it.

"Weldon, your wife should be prepared. Mrs. Weldon should be told so she can plan for the future. Soon enough you'll be too much a mess to care for yourself. You both should leave here before that happens."

"I—I can't leave the army! What would I do? There's *no* cure at all then?"

"No, lieutenant." Dudley looked for his carbolic acid, sprayed it onto the swollen, sore skin, and wrapped a bandage around it. "I've never seen someone stop the habit once they use the needles."

"I've tried to tell Katherine."

"Well, trying and doing are two different things. Listen, you wouldn't want to embarrass your wife. Mrs. Weldon isn't looking well. I see she'll have another child, and you're no help to her anymore. She should be with someone stronger," Dudley said, regretting his spitefulness.

Weldon nodded. He pulled his sleeve down and walked out into the bright twilight.

Katherine and William were in the riding ring. The soldiers had set up jumps for the children. She wore her old white dress. The black silk of mourning drew the heat and sunk into her like oil on sand. William jumped from the horse and ran to John.

Katherine turned away from them both and ordered Willy back on the horse. Her hair was bleached and straight in the heat, and her skirt moved slightly in the light breeze coming up.

"Papa! Look at me!" William shouted as he coaxed the Indian pony to trot straight up the middle of the ring and over a barrel jump.

"Bully for you, Willy!" Weldon said.

Katherine glanced over at him and back to her son. "William, your landing was off. You should get him back down into a nice trot more quickly. At the next bend ask him to canter."

William shortened up the reins and moved his outside leg back. Lunging forward with little grace, the pony took off.

"William, half-halt him there. You don't want him so fast. Keep your legs quiet and your heels away from his sides."

For a moment the pony appeared to slow and pay some attention to the boy's hands, but around the bend it took off again.

"Slow him down, Katherine," Weldon said.

"I think I know what to do, but thank you."

The pony raced at full gallop. William's loose hold of the reins and his legs drawn firmly into the animal's sides for balance pressed the animal forward dangerously fast especially in the corners.

"William! Take those reins and for heaven's sake keep your heels off the horse!" Katherine yelled. "Stop the horse, William!"

William tugged with all he had on the reins. The pony shook his mane and slowed to a trot long enough for William to regain his balance in the saddle. As William came past Katherine, he tried to tell her something and loosened the reins when the horse tugged, giving the horse the leverage to bolt again. This time its ears sat flat against its head, and its eyes were wild and reckless. Twice the pony lost balance in the corners, but righted itself with Willy hanging on. The boy lost his stirrups and control of the reins altogether and still the animal raced.

Weldon watched spellbound for what felt like hours until William's pitiful voice called out to him. Weldon ran into the ring, but the horse avoided him and threw its body more forcefully into its charge. The wind and the motion of the horse made it impossible for William to hear anything his parents might say to him. Finally, the horse stumbled and fell to its knees. William soared through the air like a feather and hit the ground with a thud, his head just missing a barrel jump.

Weldon met William almost before he hit the ground, sand splashing everywhere. The horse galloped off to the other side of the ring and halted to inspect a soldier who had just wandered up to watch the lesson. The boy sat up slowly, winded.

"Oh, God, Willy!" Weldon cried breathlessly.

"I ... I stayed with her quite a while, Papa, didn't I?"

Weldon laughed in relief. He pulled Willy up and patted him off. "That's enough riding now," he ordered, putting his arm around William. He turned, expecting Katherine to be at his side, but she was with the renegade horse.

She tugged the reins and scolded the animal with a hard hit on the nose when it tried to make up and nuzzle. She led the horse over.

"William, get back on," she ordered.

The boy looked to Weldon but warily went forward to remount.

"No, Katherine, Willy won't ride that animal again."

"William, how do you feel?" she asked.

"A little dizzy ... but I'm fine."

"Then you must show this animal who's boss."

As William put his foot in the stirrup Weldon rushed forward and grabbed him. "He is not riding today! How dare you defy me! And what sort of crazy and heartless notions run through your head, making our son get back on such a dangerous animal? My nerves can't stand to see him put in harm's way!"

"Willy can't be afraid to live. He can't run away."

"I don't care! Let him be afraid then! Do you want him dead too?"

"How can you say that?" she asked angrily.

"Look at you!" he shouted. "As if nothing's happened. You have a heart of stone, playing with Willy so soon after. Would it have killed you to stay in black long enough to show some respect for the dead?"

"You have no respect for the living!" she shouted. "How would you know anything about my heart? You ran off!"

Weldon dropped the boy down and shoved him toward his mother. "That's it. I can't be with you or Willy. You need to go home."

She grabbed his arm, and it throbbed. "But John, this is our home now, please ..."

"You don't understand. Seeing you is unbearable. I can't stand it anymore. Leave. Go back east! Anywhere but here!"

"But Papa, I don't want to!" Willy cried.

"Damn it, Willy! I don't care what you want!" Weldon shouted, but regretted it. He took William's small face in his hands. "Take care of your mother."

"John, don't send us away. I want to help you. I need you ..." Katherine begged.

"I don't want your help! You can't help me. This is more than I ever wanted," he said softly and walked off. His vision blurred, his nose ran. He was a mess. He didn't like that, didn't like feeling stripped down to nothing—not in front of his wife and his boy—not in front of anybody.

Chapter Sixty

Scott put another log on the fire and brought a throw from the sofa. "Sarah, you'll catch your death."

Sarah pulled him close over her knitting and kissed him. "Isn't this nice? And when you go into retiracy you can be here all day to take care of me."

"I'd venture a guess you'd get tired of me mighty fast," Scott said with a chuckle. He stoked the fire and sat beside her to read.

A small voice in the rain made them both jump from their seats.

"Willy! Katie! You're soaked to the bone! Come in, come in!" Sarah cried when she opened the door. "You were told to send word. Father would have come get you from the station."

The two stood dripping in clothes too light for the weather. William's shyness broke, and he threw himself at his grandmother.

Sarah hurried him in. Katherine stood like stone before her father.

"Seems like you always bring the weather, Katie."

"I can leave if you want me to."

Scott pulled Katherine to him and she cried. "Father, I understand if you hate me. I promise I won't stay long. I'll find work somehow ..."

"Please, what kind of man do you think I am? You can stay forever and I'm happy to have you."

"I never should have left," she said. "You were right."

He rubbed her wet back and brought her toward the kitchen. "I'm sorry to be right this time, but no matter. You're here with us now, and we'll help you build a new life for yourself."

Scott and Katherine joined Sarah and William in the kitchen where tea steeped, a small fire was growing with Sarah's help and William, with a blanket wrapped around him, sat eyeing the flames.

Sarah embraced Katherine. "Oh, Katie, you poor dear."

"That good-for-nothing husband sends you back in bad shape and left to care for yet another child on your own!" Scott said. "Thank the Lord, you're through with him."

"No, John just needs time," she said, wiping rain from the tip of her red nose. "In the spring things will be different. I'll find work ..."

"No daughter of mine is going to embarrass our family by setting off to work with child!" Scott said. "And what are you qualified to do? No. We'll care for Willy

383

and you and the new child. It's settled. But you won't go back to that derelict husband of yours. I've never liked divorce, but it's necessary in this case."

Sarah shook her head at Scott. "This is no time to talk about such things. Katie, you need sleep and rest, and we'll sort the future out later."

Chapter Sixty-One

"Kursteiner School is the best school for young men in the area, and how convenient. Willy can walk home in five minutes. Mr. Kursteiner even gives private lessons at piano for children," Sarah said. "We can have Willy play. William, you look so slicked up and dashing today in your new suit."

"It ain't fair. Mother won't let me stay home to care for her. Papa said to," William muttered, keeping his eyes on the floor.

Pulling up the still slight boy from his chair, Sarah roughed William up a little. "You're such a good boy to worry for your mother, but I can mind her for a few hours—to give you a little break. Your Papa would want you to learn new things and to play with the other boys."

"But Grammy, I feel awful streaked."

"Be brave, Willy."

"What if something bad happens when I'm gone?"

Katherine hurried in. "William, let's go. You can't be late on your first day. Say goodbye to Grammy," she said, pinning on a shabby hat she'd brought back from the West.

"I'll bring him," Sarah said. "There's no need for you to go out in the cold ... and in that hat."

"No, Mother. I'll bring him today. Come now, William," Katherine said sharply, ignoring Willy's shaky behavior. "Button up."

They shivered this frosty morning in silence past the new frame houses, still skeletons with the wind at home in them. The rain of the last week made a soup of the road, and the planks laid out for brave pedestrians were half-rotted and slick. William clung to his mother as Katherine dragged him over the pools of black, leafy muck. The new Gothic-styled school in blue sat upon a massive lawn planted with trim new trees in tinseled gold foliage. The mud gave way to a brand new road of cobble, choked with family carriages delivering exuberant and studious looking boys to school just in time for assembly. Katherine noted with dismay William's lack of polish. His hair, so lightened by the Arizona sun, gave him an all-over bronzed appearance like a ginger cat, but here in the East it was too long. Even his eyes, so like John's as a baby, had changed to the shade of weak tea. To Katherine he was a beautiful oddity, but easterners were not nearly as accepting of oddity as the rough people of the frontier army.

As the path grew more crowded with students, a wide-eyed William hung a few steps behind Katherine, looking small and helpless as strong-lunged boys ran past, already weeks into their studies. Suddenly William wrapped himself around Katherine's arm. "No, Mother, don't make me go! You can teach me, *please*! Papa told me to look after you. Don't make me go!"

She gripped his arms. "You will do as I say. I can't have you hanging on me like a baby anymore. You can't take care of me."

"But what if something happens?" His chin quivered as he squirmed to break free of her painful grip.

"Nothing will happen," she assured him through clenched teeth, aware of the scene he was creating.

"But Mother, what if you die while I'm at school?"

"I wouldn't be so lucky, William."

"But Eliza ..."

"Enough!" She shook him. "I can't talk any more about it! About *her*! She's dead! That's it. Don't bring her into everything."

He stared up at her like a wounded puppy.

"Stop crying and go to school!" Katherine shouted.

William walked off, rubbing his nose on his new coat. Katherine felt like a monster. She almost ran after him, but a familiar carriage stopped before her, and Margaret stepped down. Katherine had not responded to any of her friend's letters in months.

"Katie! Oh, my dear, how are you?" Margaret asked, giving her a stiff embrace. "Graham and I were so sorry to hear about ..."

Before Margaret could finish, her two boys jumped out looking even stronger and larger than they did last Christmas. Fred and Buck were unfriendly, almost surly, and Katherine hated them. "Run along boys!" Margaret said. They made no response and said no goodbyes. Margaret sighed. "Oh, boys ... I'm nearly driven to drink. Girls are so much easier."

Katherine peered into the carriage to see two girls daintily attired waiting for their mother and annoyed that Margaret was not watching the time.

"The girls are so grown up," Katherine said, not caring at all.

"Oh, yes, and another on the way and little Nathan at home! I bet you thought it was an overly rich diet I suffered from," Margaret laughed as she pointed to her expansive waistline. "One more little scalawag."

"Well, that's nice, Maggie."

Margaret looked Katherine over and in her old forward way pulled at Katherine's cloak. "Now, you're not much for sweets, so when are you expecting?"

Katherine blushed, trying not to think of the new life growing inside her. She had no feelings for it and wished it did not exist. "Not for a while," she finally answered.

"Well, I dare say you look more and more like your mother every time I see you." Margaret caught her friend's annoyed expression and tried to cover her blunder. "Your mother is quite an attractive woman. The little bit of extra weight does you good, but I suppose you'll melt away like you always do after the baby. Are you hoping for another girl ... or a boy?"

"I really must go," Katherine said as she backed away.

Taking her hand, Margaret pleaded, "Oh, Katie, I've missed our friendship. You think it was wrong of me to tell your mother about your letter, but I was frightened for you. Please let me ride you home ... or we could go for a drive like old times."

Katherine hesitated, but a flash of nostalgia caused her to accept her old friend's offer.

"Good then—we'll just drop the girls off first. Meg and Thankful, this is Mama's friend Mrs. Mc ... I mean Mrs. Weldon."

"Thankful is a lovely old-fashioned name," Katherine commented as she settled into her seat.

The two well-dressed girls glared at Katherine from behind black-lacquered ringlets of hair. They were handsome but had Doctor Crenshaw's sad eyes.

"Oh, I find the name Thankful appalling," Margaret said, "but it was in Graham's family forever and it fell upon us to keep the tradition alive. Graham so loves traditions."

After years of the desert, Englewood seemed puffed up and over-full of everything. The grey air of the oncoming eastern winter left Katherine with a permanent headache. Out west the constant complaint was against the heat, but this chill, dank day sapped any optimism. Katherine worried about William but tried to stay on track with Margaret's endless chatter. As the carriage bumped along the East Hill section of town, her stomach turned and her heart burned. "Please, Margaret—I'm sick. Stop the carriage. I need to be still."

"We are so close to my house now, dear. We'll stop there so you can rest."

Katherine said nothing. Not even in the smallest things did her desires matter. She gazed out in amazement at the furious work that had been done since the last time she had been up this way. Swiss chalets clung to the Palisades. Gothic and Second Empire mansions competed for the most picturesque impressions as they sat upon new lawns fading in the late autumn. Margaret's house had settled into its surroundings, looking more established and conservative than Katherine had remembered. Japanese maples and dogwoods displayed the last of their finery, and the lawn was a carpet of crimson and gold.

"The new poor-master, Katherine, has so much to do these days. Seems there's quite a few couples living in the third and fourth wards with no marriage certificates. To top things off, the unlucky soul is now responsible for unleashed dogs and goats in town that have become a real nuisance of late, biting children and tearing down laundry. The poor-master was ordered to shoot them if no one claimed them, and so he did. I heard he cried having to kill all those animals, but he's a veteran after all, and I bet he's seen worse— just a private he was."

Katherine soon found herself in front of a roaring fire and a fine china tea set. Mint tea usually sickened her, but she craved it now and was glad to have it. Everything about the place had changed. The still-life paintings remained and the substantial furniture, but years of human habitation had made it a messy, comfortable home. There were live things everywhere. Cats and small dogs lounged and yapped. Small boots were half tucked beneath sofas and children's sheet music—Christmas carols—littered the beat-up piano stuck dead center in the room like the star amusement at a fair.

"Maggie, do you still play?" Katherine asked, suddenly intrigued by her friend's life.

"Oh, the piano you mean? Yes, I do—when the children let me. Didn't your parents tell you music was an important charm for a woman to possess?" Margaret laughed and went to the keyboard.

"My parents expected me to learn things through whispers on the wind," Katherine stated. "Besides, they were never much interested in music." Katherine remembered how John sang and hummed all the time when he was happy.

Margaret patted the bench beside her and Katherine, feeling some of the old warmth she had for her friend, complied. They giggled, the two of them, shoved up against each other on this bench more suited to children with smaller frames. A cat hung over the edge of the piano top mildly interested in the fluttering pages being turned beneath him. Katherine had never been allowed a cat. Her mother feared them and had passed that fear onto her daughter, who shyly fingered the cat's pink nose.

Margaret set her fingers in motion not playing the music before her in the end, but something from memory. The notes spiraled together falling into an ethereal and familiar tune, bringing back to Katherine a flood of memories. Mozart's Serenade No. 10 adagio, on the clarinet. It lost some of its power on the slightly off-key piano, but Margaret played it with a sensitive hand, and Katherine's delight in the spirit of the piece made up for any lack.

They'd been married only a week when Scott gave them the tickets to the concert in town. John was reluctant and sneeringly dismissive of the crowd he expected to be there, but agreed to go for her sake. Laughing at his place by the fire, Simon made much of the joys of bachelorhood, watching John squirm as Sarah fixed his tie and brushed him off.

Once away from the house John brightened. He was the picture of health, looking dashing in uniform. They strolled on the cool autumn evening down into town. John adjusted his long stride so Katherine could keep up. Katherine giggled at John's grim determination to seem excited for a concert he imagined would bore him, moving in closer as he hummed "Tramp, Tramp, Tramp."

She gamely sang the words:

Tramp, tramp, tramp the boys are marching,

Cheer up comrades they will come,

And beneath the starry flag we shall breathe the air again,

Of the freedom in our own beloved home!

The small stretch of road in town glistened beneath the new oil lamps purchased by Sarah's Village Improvement Society. All was festive as the holidays approached, and she delighted in the greetings of people, proud of her new appendage and imagining they made a striking pair.

The music was lovely as in the dark of the theater her hand strayed up along the inner seam of John's trousers. John stiffened but was still determined to listen to the music. He ran his fingers along her inner arm, tickling her at its bend, knowing how it excited her. They sat quiet and breathless until the music—the same Margaret played—swept over him and something happened. When the clarinetist made his final ascent through the notes, he left. She followed after him, too bemused to be annoyed at his abrupt departure. She ran out the door and a familiar face, a young man from church, pointed out his direction. She found him smoking one of the Turkish cigarettes Simon had given him, but none too pleased with it.

"John, what's the matter?"

He stamped out the thin tobacco roll with his foot. Sometimes he looked very young. She kissed his chin, and he smiled.

"That music. I don't know what it was ..."

She fingered through her program.

"But it reminded me of things ... certain times I never think about ..." He looked at her and she smiled. "It was like my father was with me. I felt his forest all around me. I've only had that feeling once before … in the Wilderness." He lit a proper cigar. "That music was just too much for me, Kate."

It was the first time he called her Kate.

The music ended, and Margaret waited through Katherine's reverie. "That was the most beautiful playing, Maggie. Thank you," Katherine said with a lonesome sigh.

"Would you like me to teach you?" Margaret offered. "I would love for you to come by and play once or twice a week—what do you think?"

Katherine ran her fingers lightly over the keys. "Thank you, but I have no music in my soul."

Margaret took her in a warm embrace. "Poor thing, losing your daughter and your husband in one go. If you need anything …"

Katherine pulled away and stood in exasperated anger. "What do you know about the state of my marriage? Nothing!"

"Katie, I'm so sorry—I assumed since you're here again without him that things were over for good!"

"Did you bring me up here to learn the horrible details of my life?" Katherine shouted, gathering up her things. "My daughter died a slow, cruel death. Do you want more? Yes, John and I have fought—we're devastated."

"Katherine! Stop it!" Margaret tried to take hold of her friend, but Katherine pulled away with unexpected force.

"If you are so bored in your perfect little life, find another poor soul to amuse you! I don't need you to gloat over me!" Katherine dashed to the door.

"Please, will you wait?" Margaret shouted after her. "You can't walk all the way home. You're not thinking clearly. I'm trying to be a friend to you."

Katherine spit her words now. "I don't want your friendship! You have always delighted in pointing out John's flaws, and now you see a way to prove your point. This is not an empty game to me—it's my life."

Margaret stood to her full height in indignation. "Is it my fault you picked a nasty buffoon to marry? Did you expect to change him? John Weldon certainly has changed you. Or did you do it to embarrass your poor parents? I would not be the only one happy to see you leave that man."

"How dare you! You know nothing about me or my husband. Never have you asked why or how I could love him. All that mattered was that he didn't amuse you. We are not here for your amusement. I listened to everything about your trivial daily events, but you never once asked me about myself. John judged you correctly if he's done nothing else right."

Margaret opened the door with a flourish as she spoke. "You should go, Katherine McCullough or Weldon or whatever it is you call yourself. I don't care how you get home."

"I never imagined you did, Margaret."

The uneven stones of the street made a quick and graceful escape impossible, but Katherine gathered steam, hardly noticing the crisp wind at her back. It was better not to have women friends; men at least were honestly disinterested. Women pretended to care but were only interested in foraging for gossip. Katherine had never really been interested in Margaret's life either, so maybe they were even.

Katherine missed Simon and wished for the old days when he was here to help and cheer her, but she didn't deserve him now. She never kept a promise to him in her life. He asked for just two things—letters and forgiveness. Katherine had only grudgingly given him efforts at both.

As she plodded through town from Margaret's, she avoided the eyes of the men dressed in Wall Street suits and farmers' duds and the women all more fashionably attired than she was. These people were new to her, and there were so many! Englewood was too big for her now. Katherine hated everyone for going on with their lives. How did they have any more right than Eliza to live? She hated herself and her life-giving body. It repulsed her. This child could be no replacement for everything Katherine lost when her little girl died.

Rounding the corner of Demarest onto Tenafly Road, a small form with flailing arms ran toward her.

"*William*!" It was only midday. He ran coatless and breathless into her arms. "Willy, what's happened?! Why are you not at school?"

"Where were you?" he cried. "I looked everywhere for you, Mother! And you said you'd stay home!"

"I had no chance—oh, never mind! How did you get out of school?"

"I walked out. No one cared," he said, his nose dripping.

"Don't you ever do that again!" she scolded. "Do you want to grow up to be a stupid man?"

William stood thinking.

She was flushed and tired now. "Where's your coat?"

He stared until she shook him.

"I lost it."

"How could you lose the coat in two hours of school? That was my savings!" she yelled. She dragged him back toward school, only later remembering how cold his skin was against hers. "Don't come home without that coat!"

"But Mother ..."

They arrived at the school door, two students standing at the window and laughing. Katherine didn't even give Willy time to wipe his face. The director's secretary met them at the door, and Katherine shoved him in.

"I shouldn't be made to round up my son off the street!"

"Well, Mrs. Weldon, I hope your son doesn't present us with a discipline problem. This isn't a prison. We expect our students to stay of their own accord, not to go running to their mothers at the slightest turn of events! Good day, Mrs. Weldon!"

The door slammed unceremoniously, but through the last bit of open space she caught a glimpse of her spindle-armed child being shoved by another student. A blanket of dark sorrow blinded her to the nicely warming afternoon. Once home she plunged into the pantry and ate more than her fill of a vinegar pie, fuming over the missing new coat.

The afternoon turned to early evening. No William. No coat.

"Katie, I should go and see where Willy is," Sarah said as she ran her fingers over her lips in concern.

"No, Mother. He has to take responsibility for himself. I can't care for him forever!"

"That's a mother's duty!" Sarah cried.

"Mother," Katherine said, swallowing hard. "Willy needs to learn to care for what belongs to him, not just throw it off."

But even Katherine relented. It was 5 o'clock, dark and frosty again. Sarah and Katherine walked in silence toward the school. As the unlit building came into view Sarah shouted, "Willy!"

Katherine grumbled, but beneath her pretended anger she feared another loss when she did not find William sitting on the school steps, where she had imagined he would be.

Beneath an oak at the back, William sat hunched over on a bench. Sarah spotted him first.

"Land sakes, child, we worried you'd been taken by an old tramp! You're frozen solid." Sarah wrapped him in her shawl, giving Katherine a look that stopped her in her tracks. "Let's go home and get you warmed up."

"I didn't get my coat back."

"Of course not," Katherine said in anger. "You're an irresponsible child who only cares about himself."

"*Katherine!*" Sarah snapped. "Don't worry, Willy, Grammy will get you a new coat. It's only money."

"But it's all the money I had!" Katherine cried.

"And is that the child's fault?" Sarah asked aggressively.

Scott sat on the porch smoking and wondering where his supper was when the three arrived home. He built an extra fire while Sarah and William fought for possession of the shawl. They looked on in horror as Sarah took it at last, uncovering William's battle torn face. He held his chin out defiantly. William's arms and hands were purple with cold, and the dried blood and mucus on his mouth and nose gave a clear map of the fight from the loser's perspective.

Katherine ran to him, but he pulled away, burying his face in his grandmother's arms. Sarah sent a justified look of superiority Katherine's way. Scott wrapped the boy's shaking shoulders in the blanket from his chair. Sarah sat down and put the boy on her knee while Katherine warmed water and prepared to wash him up.

"I *hate* school. Grammy, don't let her send me!"

"Sweetie, did the boys who did this to your face take your coat?" Sarah smoothed his hair.

William nodded and let out a small burst of emotion. "I tried hard to get it back and gave one of them boys a real polt, but there were so many of them against me, and nobody likes me or wants to know me!"

"Son, you can't give up that easily," Scott said.

"I'm not your son, Grandpa."

"It's just an expression, but you had better watch your tone with me," Scott said.

"I *hate* that school, and I'm *not* going back to it!" William said through shivers and a black mouth of dried gore.

Katherine knelt in front of him and dabbed his cuts and scrapes. "You'll go to school, and I'll come too. I mean to retrieve that coat."

"*No*! You mustn't! You'll make them hate me more!"

Sarah nodded in agreement. "Let it rest, Katherine. William, you were upset this morning, and you had a terrible day, but Grandpa's right. You don't want to give up while you're beaten. Try school again for me. You can do that."

"But I don't have a coat."

"I can find something for you of Uncle Simon's just for tomorrow, and then I'll get you something in town. You know, Uncle Simon hated school at first. He thought the uniform looked too girlish."

William smiled.

"Once Simon came home and told me he'd thrown the teacher through the wall and crumbled it all down."

"Did he?"

"No, of course not, but he was angry and upset. The teacher thought little of Simon's Christopher Columbus drawings and said so in class, but your uncle stuck to his studies and proved them all wrong."

"He even graduated from West Point," William said in awe.

Sarah, Scott, and even Katherine smiled, knowing how close Simon came many times to not making it at the academy.

Katherine dried her son's face. "I won't embarrass you tomorrow. But you must try your best."

William sighed. "Today I was afraid you might die, but I guess it was me the devil was after."

Chapter Sixty-Two

Katherine spent the winter like a hibernating bear. Sarah taught her rug-hooking and suggested Katherine make a few to send to Simon and John. With no intention of doing so, she grimly hooked flat, lifeless motifs onto deadened backgrounds. At least it kept her out of the kitchen. Sarah was certain it was Katherine's sour expression that ruined her last cakes.

She waited all morning, sitting in the parlor window, watching through the snow for the post as her toes froze through her stockings and her face against the windowpane melted back just the smallest bit of frost to see through. Only one letter, one word from John, and she would pack her things and go. How could he not love her?

William grew surlier with each passing week and taller too, inching up past his mother at an alarming speed.

"Willy, how was school today?" Scott asked one evening.

"I don't like it when you call me Willy. It's William. I'm not a little child anymore."

"Don't you shout at me like that young man!" Scott scolded. "Have you turned completely savage?"

William jumped up from the table so violently the chair behind him tipped with a crash. "I'm not a savage! Did you tell them at school when you signed me up?"

Scott looked to Sarah. Katherine lifted the chair.

"William, dear, it was me," Sarah said, "but I mentioned it only to Mr. Kursteiner so he might be warned to protect you if the boys weren't nice."

"Well, why did you go and do that? That was stupid, Grandma—the boys hate me—the teacher too."

"Don't yell at your grandmother!" Scott shouted. "You look like a damned Indian! The boys would guess it on their own." Scott turned to Katherine. "This is what I warned you about, bringing mixed-blood children into the world—it's selfish and cruel. And another one on the way!"

"You're right, Father. It was a terrible, stupid thing to do. Maybe if we *all* had died you would have been happier. It would have saved a lot of trouble. Maybe you could have devoted your life to bringing up the freedmen and engineering their lives to your taste."

"William, you *are* part Indian even if your mother and father want to ignore it," Sarah tried to explain. "The boys at school are mean, and if it wasn't your different appearance then it would be something else. The boys do it because you let them."

"Willy, you're becoming a coward like your father, who can't take care of his own responsibilities," Scott mumbled as he rose from the table.

William ran at his sizable grandfather with fists flailing. "Papa is braver than you'll ever be. He killed Rebs and Indians too, and I hate you!"

"Your father can't even send money to keep you clothed and fed," Scott said as he swiped away his grandson like a nuisance of a cub. "Do soldiers not celebrate Christmas in the West? Where are your gifts?"

Katherine ran from the room.

Sarah pulled the angry child to her, but he hit and kicked until he was free of them and ran out the door to the porch and down to the barn.

"Oh, poor thing!" Sarah cried out, but Scott pulled her back.

"Let him go. He'll come back with his tail between his legs just like his father. And Katherine will do nothing about it. We're destined to see this repeated again and again, I'm afraid."

Katherine didn't want to raise William alone or another baby alone. She unbound her corset and felt the tight hammock of her abdomen cradling the new little child inside and hated it. Crawling under the quilts and blankets, she listened to William crying in the yard, talking to the stars. What would become of him? What examples had they set for him?

Before too long Katherine heard the light footsteps of William on the stairs. She listened as he stopped at her door and knocked only once and only lightly. She kept still, breathless, pretending to be asleep. It was true what her father said. William could never escape who he was, who she had made him to be. It would have been easier for Eliza. Even with her dark curls, Eliza looked like a McCullough and was brave. Katherine saw much of herself in William and it disappointed her. It was a long minute before William moved on, up to his tiny attic room, closing the door behind him with a forlorn creak. It occurred to Katherine that he had never had his own space until coming to live here and that maybe he didn't like it. She listened for the nightly prayers she had taught him and the suppressed sobs that usually followed since Eliza had gone, but tonight there was silence as he wrote a letter:

Dear Father,

I wont call you Papa again. I am almost grown and a real Papa wood not send his son away from him for no good reason maybe you liked my sister cause she didn't look like me and I bet she probably was a sight smarter then me who can barely read and write in school. I think you and mother lied to me and fooled me to thinking I was smart, but now my teacher don't think so

and you cant help me and mother wont. Now since everything got bad moth-
er hates me and cant ever walk me to school she is getting so big I guess she
might have another baby but no one wants it because no one says one thing
about it. And I bet you don't care anyway you probably just get to do all the
fun things we always did like ride horses and go on adventures. I bet you are
too busy to write me and I don't care. I wont wait by the window like moth-
er. Grandpa says waiting for you is like waiting for the world to end. I think
he is write but I hate him too.

William S. Weldon

***

Dear Katherine,

It seems William is doing poorly at school and what are you doing about it?
Is it possible for you to help anyone? You cannot even walk the poor child to
school? You give up too easily on people. You let them on their own too fast.
I know that nothing I ever did was good enough for you, but Willy is differ-
ent or should be. You should fight for him at least. I do not want William in
a school where his teachers look down on him. You should teach him. What
else do you do with your time? At the very least I want you to go to his school
and see what can be done for him.

Weldon forgot to sign the letter, but Katherine was glad of that. When the letter arrived in February, months after her return east, her heart thrilled in misguided expectation at the shaky script on the envelope. Surely he was calling her back. The letter came as a blow. For hours Katherine sat with the letter against her belly, rereading it for some small hope, wanting to believe the lack of a signature meant it was not really John's letter, his hostility ... and then William came in from school.

She ran at him. "How dare you interfere with your father and me? Do you hate me that much to undermine me to your father?" She went to slap him, but he dodged her. She grabbed his books from his hands and took him by the collar into the kitchen where the table remained a mess. With one swipe, cups and saucers, melted butter, and spoons flew into a heap and his books fell on top of the cleared but soggy table.

"I'll be hit for stains on the books!" he cried.

Katherine threw him into a chair. "You say I don't help you with school? That I'm useless? Now let me help you—what don't you understand, you stupid boy? *What?*"

He pulled his hair—his father's bad habit his own now, after much imitation. She slapped his hand. "I'm such a terrible mother, Willy. I want you to let me help you." She flipped through his primer and grumbled in frustration. "You know this, William. You learned it in Arizona. Why do you lie? Is this to humiliate me?"

"Mother ... it's a blur ..."

"Well, you better take your head out of the clouds and ..."

"No, it's not in the clouds, it's with Eliza."

She grabbed his face roughly in one hand. "You aren't with Eliza. She's gone forever—and so is your father—this work must be done."

William pulled away. "*No*! I *won't* do it!"

"Fine then," she said coolly as she picked up his Peter Parley book and threw it into the fire. "You win."

Sarah, just returning from a ladies' luncheon at the church, ran into the kitchen when she heard her grandson cry out. She grabbed William as he leapt toward the fire. "Man alive! Katherine, what are you doing to Willy?"

"He wrote John I was a useless mother. Willy said I was no help to him."

Sarah hesitated. William looked to her and shook his head. "No I didn't, exactly."

"Go to your room, William," Sarah said, running the back of her hand along his face.

Katherine cringed as William leaned into the tenderness like a needy dog.

"Katherine, I am raising two children again. These tantrums won't do. Did you expect him to lie about the way he feels or should he not be allowed to write John at all?"

"He needn't lie, Mother. I've always taken care of him. What has John done?"

Sarah raised her brows. "I only hope when this baby does come that you'll have recovered your senses."

"I have not lost my senses."

"I'm afraid a doctor would consider you quite hysterical, Katie. You're too hard on the boy."

Katherine grabbed the poker and tried in vain to retrieve Willy's book. "I just don't care anymore—about anyone."

"Well, that's a sad state of affairs, but you have no choice. You're responsible for William and the child on the way. You need to stay active, take walks ..." Sarah looked her daughter over before touching on another topic of concern, "and Katie dear, it's not helpful to get so fleshy on a small frame such as yours. It won't go away so easily after the baby, you'll see."

"Oh, Mother, it's not your funeral."

Chapter Sixty-Three

William was just about out the door next morning when Katherine caught him. "William, wait. I'll come with you today."

He rolled his eyes. "I can go alone. I don't need your help."

She gulped down her annoyance. "I'm sorry for yesterday. I want to let your teacher know that it was no fault of your own about the book, and I intend to pay for a new one."

"Why don't you give me the money?" William suggested with a strange glint in his eyes. "I can do it."

Katherine was suspicious and decided to carry out her visit no matter how much he protested.

He lagged behind her, dragging a branch over the frozen road.

Boys filed into the school bundled up to their noses. Katherine caught a few of them flashing looks of unmistakable dislike at William. In the distance she spotted Margaret's elegant carriage and hurried in past the other boys.

Mr. Kursteiner approached her. "Mrs. Weldon, the very person I wanted to see."

Katherine turned around seeking William, who slid past her behind other tall students.

"So you finally received our note?" Mr. Kursteiner asked.

"A note?"

Mr. Kursteiner gave a knowing glance toward his secretary as he led Katherine into his office. She kept her warm cloak on, having not dressed for a formal meeting, and defensively awaited Mr. Kursteiner's reason for delaying her with a resentful glance around the dark-paneled office. "Is it something serious?" she asked.

The musical school master tapped his fingers to the beat of Katherine's racing heart and frowned. "Well, Mrs. Weldon, you may or may not be aware that William has been having a difficult time of it here, and after careful consideration we feel he may not be suited for our school."

"My mother assured me that William's mixed background would be of no consequence here," Katherine said, her swollen cheeks flush with color.

"Mrs. McCullough is correct, although what boys get up to on the field I have no real control over. It is William's behavior and dismal academic performance that concern us. It has been brought to my attention that some of his classmates have had things taken from them, and while there is no proof, they all suspect your son." Mr. Kursteiner flashed a sickly smile.

"Willy would never steal. He's told us that the boys are cruel. It seems fair to assume they're lying."

"You may be right, but William is a distraction. Maybe if his work showed outstanding intelligence."

"Are you saying that my son is not intelligent?" Katherine's voice heightened.

Mr. Kursteiner gathered his thoughts with a sigh and tapped his fingers again, keeping pace with his speech. "No, Mrs. Weldon, I am not saying that exactly, but this school prides itself on excellence. It was on the recommendation of your father that William was given a place here. Something is preventing him from achieving the results we expect; whether it is a lack of intelligence or something else is not our concern. As I am sure you understand, all of our families want their children to be among students who are serious about their studies. When William actually attends class, he displays a lack of discipline and is disrespectful to his teacher. You may have wondered at the shape of your son's hands in the last weeks. I have already had a word with Mr. Finney, his teacher. The paddle does little good in cases such as William's."

She had noticed nothing about William's hands. Was she losing track of the reality around her?

"Would you like a glass of water or some tea?"

She shook her head. "I don't understand it. William has always followed the rules. He's a good boy."

Mr. Kursteiner cleared his throat. "Mrs. McCullough mentioned that you have suffered a loss ..."

Katherine filled her lungs with air and began. "William's sister ... his sister Eliza recently—she died and you know my husband, Mr. Weldon, is in the army." She sobbed despite her best efforts and rose to leave, but Mr. Kursteiner stopped her. "We are expecting another child," she went on, "but ... it's too soon after losing our little girl. William knows the work—all of it—we taught him out west." She gathered herself up, ashamed at her display of emotions.

The school master poured her a glass of water and asked her to sit again.

"I'm so sorry," she said more calmly now. "I'll take William home with me."

The headmaster sighed and contemplated the situation. He called out to his secretary. "Please get the boy, Mr. Baxter. Mrs. Weldon, I wouldn't feel right about sending William from the school without giving you both the opportunity to make one last effort, but his grades and behavior must show great improvement. Will Mr. Weldon be home soon?"

Katherine shook her head, her eyes welling up again.

"Well, it can't be helped, can it? I'll take the boy on as my personal project, but it is fair to say that William cannot be depended upon to make it to school alone each day. Please bring him yourself, and in that way we will be better able to communicate."

"Thank you, Mr. Kursteiner. I will make every effort."

William's crisp step hesitated at the door of the headmaster.

"Master Weldon, please come in."

The sunny complexion William had left the West with was gone and was as white as the headmaster's collar now.

"Young man, tuck in your shirt and take a seat," Mr. Kursteiner ordered.

"Yes, sir," William mumbled, sitting and tucking at the same time. He had forgotten his uniform sweater and looked cold.

Katherine wanted to tuck him under her cloak and take him away.

"Mrs. Weldon and I have been discussing your progress here, or lack of it, and have decided to give you one more chance to prove yourself. This is a great opportunity for someone like you, but you must behave and obey Mr. Finney."

At this William stiffened but said nothing.

"William, do you have anything to say for yourself?" the headmaster asked.

Katherine held her breath.

"No, sir," William answered through a thin, straight mouth.

"Mr. Kursteiner, it may be best for me to take William home today so I can have a proper talk with him. We can start fresh tomorrow," Katherine suggested, hoping William would stay quiet.

With little faith in a turnaround for the boy, Kursteiner agreed. Katherine left the money for the new book in the office and took her son out the door.

William burst from the school, jumping the stairs, stumbling to his knees, and running off again, clumsy with his new long legs. Soon he would need another coat. The one he wore hung off him as he trotted along unbuttoned. Katherine let him go in resignation. There was no need to shout at him over small things. The cold air at the back of her neck quickened her pace and did her spirits good. She had never fit in either—anywhere. This was not about being Indian. It was about being so like her. She remembered the loneliness of wanting to belong, but not belonging. William belonged to her, and she loved him. It was her job to make him believe that.

By the time Katherine entered the sunny kitchen, William had already tossed his shoes off and plunged into his grandfather's chair, dreamily staring into the fire. Sarah gave her daughter a perplexed look. Katherine waved her off as she hung her cloak and sat down at the table. The teapot was cold to the touch, so she rose again, but Sarah took charge moving the kettle to boil. Katherine picked at a breakfast cake.

"William, how would you like meat from last night's supper? An egg and some ham?" Sarah asked.

"Yes, Grammy, that sounds bully," William said. "Can we get a cat?"

"No, Willy," Sarah answered. "Now why on earth would you bring that up?"

"Well," he said with a smile, "I was just thinking that today might be lucky."

Katherine looked up from the paper on the table. "Lucky?"

"You took me from school, and you don't seem too huffed at me."

She laughed. Sarah brought them both steaming plates of food. William ate a little, but lost interest soon enough. Katherine finished what was left. "William, I should be upset with you."

Sarah understood that Katherine wanted time with her son alone, and after kissing them both she went about her work in the rest of the house.

"Mr. Kursteiner mentioned that your classmates are missing things."

"I didn't take them," he answered, staring into his hands on his lap.

She tapped his head—his hair was so smooth. He looked up, prepared to mount a defense.

"You mustn't think I hate you or that I'm not on your side. I don't believe you took anything from those boys."

"The boys hate me. That's it. Everybody does."

"But Willy ..."

"*William*!" he corrected with great annoyance.

"Why do they dislike you, do you think?"

He glanced at the door as if wanting to escape any more talk on the subject. But his mother waited.

"The boys say I'm ugly. They call me *ears*. I have big ears."

She almost laughed at the absurdity but knew it was quite a serious matter to her son. "William, your ears are a bit small!"

"I'm just so glad to be away for one day."

"But it seems you've taken several secret days off," she said, lifting his chin with her finger.

"I go down to the river and imagine us taking a boat to San Francisco to meet Papa and Eliza."

Katherine's color rose again. "I want to help you. You must believe me, but I cannot live in the past with you. You must face the truth. We must. There is no more

Eliza. I don't want to hear her name. And Papa, your father, is far away, and you must realize he cares very little."

He cried. "Mother, why do you have to get so mean and ruin everything? Father will get better and call us back, and we can go with the baby and be just the same as ever."

"Get better? William, Papa never gets better, only worse. He fools people for a while. He makes them think they're safe and then sends them off. It's always the same."

"Maybe you make him," the boy mumbled and moved from the table.

"Say that again!" she ordered, grabbing his arm.

"Maybe you make Papa send us away because you're mean! You burned up Eliza's things and my books too! You don't care about other people's things!"

"How dare you!"

Her intention was to drag him to his room. He looked as if he expected a blow but recovered himself and stood in unblinking challenge. Katherine wanted to strangle him, but something caused her to look down at his hands. She ran her hands over the bruised and broken-skinned palm of one and took his other. It looked just the same. William waited, mildly defiant even as she embraced him, but he could feel the baby up against him, rocking to the sobs of their mother.

"William, I can't help you. You're right. I'm mean and ugly!"

"Mother, I didn't mean it!" he cried, pulling himself closer to her. "I'll be good at school for you if I can."

"We only have each other, William. We must both try to be good."

Katherine rummaged through a pile of gardening tools in various stages of decay and dysfunction in the cramped mudroom and found Sarah's homemade hand balm. On Scott's big chair by the fire, the two spent the morning squeezed together as Katherine rubbed balm over William's hands delicately so as not to disturb the deep maize-and-violet-hued hemorrhages beneath the skin. He dozed against her, and for the first time in months the weight of her children felt not like a burden but a comfort, a door back into contentment and purposeful existence.

Chapter Sixty-Four

The sparrows chirped their endless cheer, building nests in the eaves of the McCullough home. It was sunny the day the baby was born. The icy blue sky highlighted the first pink buds of apple blossoms as they opened on the last hunched backs of scraggly orchard inhabitants. Englewood had once been a grand sea of apple, cherry, and peach orchards before the Joneses and the Van Brunts came upon the land to build their castles on the sandy soil of Bergen County. The founders had drained the soggy bottom land to rid the place of its malarial heritage, planned roads, diverted streams into ponds for ice around a brand new cemetery—Brookside. Soon enough people felt funny about the decomposing bodies around their ice supply, and the icehouses died too, looking like oversized and rotting coffins by the train tracks. An old mill fell into disuse and was burned to the ground, it was said, by a naughty boy or by a tattered old bummer, as a prank or an accident.

Spring arrived with William inches taller. Like his father before him William sprung up early, and throughout the painful winter of growing, his mother and grandparents watched in astonishment and scurried to keep him fed and dressed.

John knew nothing of this. He hardly knew the day or the month. His hands shook. When was the last time he had eaten? Things like that ... they were the things he could not keep track of. Where was he this morning? Who saw him? Weldon panicked and stayed put. Someone knocked at the door.

"Lieutenant Weldon, sir?"

Weldon recognized the voice and slipped to the door. "Yes?"

"Sir, I am sent to tell you that the captain wants you present at the concert tonight," the private said as he looked past the lieutenant into the dark room.

"What time ..."

"It is six now—the concert is at eight, sir."

"Yes, of course. Thank you." Weldon pushed the door shut before the private could salute and be off. He lit his pipe and sat on the edge of the bed. So it was still Wednesday. *I had coffee and something else this morning.* He remembered now. He had walked to the horses—in fact he had done all his duties. Came back and slept. He had done nothing wrong. *Good.* What would he do now till the concert? He couldn't bear the thought of a concert ...

Dear Willy,

Here I am unwell again, but I am fighting it. I want you to come back. I figure the baby must be almost ready to come. Tell Mother she looks lovely for me. I am sure she does. I am sorry to not have written sooner.

Only a few months of school left for you. I hope you will finish out the year. I have not received any letter from you since your first days of school. I hope you received my Christmas gift and Mother too. You must take care of Mother for me. When you come if you come, I will get you a yellow dog like I had when I was your age. Tell Mother I miss her and you too.

Your loving father,

John Weldon

He would send this letter if he remembered, and he would remember if he could just get through this day, and if he could get through this day then he could start again to try ...

He did remember, and William received his letter. The boy read it out on the porch, ripped it to pieces, and threw it under the lilac bush just bloomed. His life was here now with no hopes of the West.

He took a pile of books from Scott's library and stacked them on the table in his mother's room. William worried about the shadows lining her face.

"Mother, you look lovely today," he blurted.

Katherine looked at him in amused wonder. "How silly of you!"

He turned away but then in all seriousness looked back at her. "Mother, that's from Papa. He told me to tell you that in his last letter, but don't worry I won't tell him what you said."

"He wrote to you?" she asked, her eyes so like the abandoned fawn he had found in the woods.

He had begun secretly hunting with his friends whenever he could slip away.

Rest in peace kept knocking on his mind. He was unsure about childbirth and worried that the child might rip a hole through his mother's midsection and squirm out like his father's intestines had done in the war. He wondered did he leave such a scar on his mother's belly as he had seen on his father. He had seen a cow give birth down the road but could not bring himself to imagine the places of a woman's body that a baby might escape from.

"William, what shall we name her?"

"I don't know."

"Just in case," Katherine said, taking his hand. "I want you to give her a name now."

"You're scaring me. Stop it. You name him or her what you like."

"William, please. It will be a girl. I feel it. I don't want to scare you. I just want someone to share this with."

"Sarah then. Call her after Grammy."

Katherine smiled. "Yes, that's fine. Even your father will like it. William, you need to have your hair cut again. Ask Grandma soon."

He nodded and read the first pages of *Great Expectations* for the twentieth time—a favorite request. His voice droned on as Katherine closed her eyes and thought of her babies. William had come with fear, turbulence and excitement. John had been absent, but she knew he loved her then. Eliza was so easy. It was as if the baby had floated above her for nine months. John had been attentive from afar and then promoted. They made great plans and journeys while marveling over Eliza's raven hair with curls from nowhere that maybe she would have grown out of. There were Indians and officers and the heat of Arizona and the heat between husband and wife ...

There were no plans now, no future, just a dark walk along the edge of the Palisades. She had not one thing in mind for after. John had not written, money came sporadically, and she could not forgive herself for placing all her hopes in him.

Something different was happening in her body too, and she wondered if this little girl was meant to take her place in the world because she was well and truly tired of it. William was fine now. Having two Sarahs would be enough.

A few days later William sat waiting, sun shining through the window in the hall by the door—waiting for the angel of death. Every time the front door opened, he worried it had arrived on the April gusts that followed the doctors up to his mother's room. Doctor Banks, Doctor Currie, and a queer lady with bony face and big eyes loped in.

William heard about a sea of water and blood and a blue baby—it was a girl. And too much blood and not enough air and no cries or celebrations and a tiny coffin. He waited for a larger one breathlessly and thought about taking a boat on the river to the West around South America or through the jungles of Panama or walking straight across to find his father.

William was a ghost too. Disappeared. The living brushed past and felt his chill maybe. He didn't know how, but he had definitely gone invisible. Grammy had disappeared too. Only Grandfather remained—a guard at the door, too big to get by—but not for long.

"Let me see my mother," William shouted, but was invisible. Scott said nothing, just stood there. "I hate you, old man! You killed my mother. She's dead and you won't let me see her. I've always hated you. I hope you die and go to hell!"

He reappeared when his grandfather slapped him and sent him to his knees. He sat on the floor crying. No Sarah, no Mother. Nothing but not invisible, just alone.

An owl-eyed Sarah emerged from Katherine's room after the sun fell beneath the window sills and William had fallen asleep on the floor. Doctor Banks stepped over the boy and patted Sarah on the shoulder before descending the stairs with Scott. The creaking of the stairs under the heavy feet of the men woke the boy. Sarah pulled him to his feet and sat him on the crowded hall bench where linens toppled in disarray.

"My Willy," Sarah began, rocking him gently. He didn't fight it and leaned his head against her. The thoughts he held were too heavy for him.

"Mother knew she would die. She said so," William cried still somewhere between slumber and wakefulness.

Sarah squeezed him closer. "Your mother isn't dead. We must pray for her. She's very weak."

"Why wouldn't Grandpa let me see her? I want to see her!" he said as he ran to his mother's room before Sarah could stop him.

A dim circle of light still flickered in the room, but the usual scent of violets hid under the strange smells of medicinal spirits and the human smell of blood. It repulsed his senses. His throat convulsed and he was sick, but he swallowed and went to her. There was no movement from the bed but for the spreading out of small deep red and brown stains of blood through the thin coverings. He noted as he crept up on her the flattened pasty look of her face. Her body beneath the blanket was like a collapsed cream puff. He held his breath and made for the door.

"William," Katherine whispered through purple, dry lips.

William ran and fell upon her. "Mommy, don't leave me!"

Sarah pulled at her grandson, but Katherine would not let him go. Weak tears ran their course down the sides of her face. The serenity she thought she felt in the weeks leading up to this moment, the almost longing notion that death would be a fine reprieve, disappeared in the face of William's pleas. In this hour of weakened defenses she allowed, could not control, her emotions. She could not steel herself from loving her son. Even as her arms grew too weak to hold him and slipped to her sides, she begged God to allow her to see her son grow up.

William held her hand as tears continued and her lips quivered. Her body shook with the love she had held back from this boy since Eliza. She had wasted so much time.

The blood, still unchecked, poured like a knocked-over bottle of milk. She tried to close her legs to it, use her muscles, but the current was too strong.

Sarah saw the darkening sheets and sought to remove William from the horror of watching his mother bleed to death, but Katherine clung to him with her small strength in desperation. "Willy! Willy! Promise to stay with me! I'm afraid ... William, you're everything to me. Please, please stay!"

Sarah was frustrated in all efforts after that. Scott ventured in but fled at the sight of the reeking mess.

"William, this is not for you to see. If you must stay keep your eyes away from my work," Sarah warned, trying to hide her panic and despair as she mopped with rags and towels the sheets that were too hard to remove alone without upsetting her patient.

While Sarah emptied the room of blood-stained fabric, William climbed on the bed beside his mother. Katherine felt cold and William covered her better with blankets hanging over the chair—one an Indian blanket from Arizona. He got back in bed and curled up against her and was asleep before Sarah returned and cried. Her grandson's healthy, ruddy complexion made her daughter's milk-white features more ghastly to look upon.

Scott worked up the courage to peek in again. Sarah's grief brought him to her side. He sobbed at the sight of his little girl all grown up and far away from them now between the living and the dead. Scott could not console his wife, but he waited until her eyes blinked shut for the final time as she fell asleep on the side chair next to Katherine. He descended the stairs, poured himself a drink, and found his spectacles and some stationery.

Lieutenant Weldon,

I am writing to inform you that my daughter, the girl you at one time proclaimed to care for in sickness and in health before a body of men and women of the church and God, is now at death's door, and you are nowhere to be found. It might interest you to know that the child she carried for you is gone, living only 43 minutes. I assure you that Sarah Jane will receive a proper burial at no expense to you.

It is too bad that you are so "civilized." It would be nice if in somehow killing all of the Apache and Sioux, a soldier mistook you for the enemy. You seem to encompass the worst of all breeds. Even the great chiefs you have made contact with rarely desert their families. I do believe they fight for them, but perhaps you know better the ways of the savage.

I would not dream of asking you to come back for my daughter's funeral nor would I allow you to attend. William will continue to be well taken care of and will find his way amongst the more civilized nations of the world, unlike his father who prefers the wild frontier.

Scott J. McCullough III

***

Dear John,

You are needed here at home. Katherine gave us a great scare with such a loss of blood that only a soldier could be hardened to. We think with rest she will recover, but she has little strength and is despondent over the poor baby. She blames herself and although she does not say it, a mother knows, she is missing you.

I do not like to scold, but John, we are all truly disappointed in you for making no effort all these months to support Katherine and William. Imagine your Willy all alone if Katherine had died, which we all believed she would. William loves his grandparents, but you are his guiding light and Katherine's too. You are a man, and you must take on your responsibilities as such, not just in happy times, but all the time.

I am remembering in the beginning, Mr. Weldon, when you were courting Katherine. The last one hundred spring crocuses had been nestled in the earth and put to bed under a comfortable layer of straw. I tip-toed on up to my chair and planned to have myself a small nap on the side porch, but the busy sky made the world seem to race along and from the open window I could hear my daughter and her new soldier friend ramble on, tease and whisper. Your strange conversations amused and interested me especially since you were usually quiet to the point of exasperation. You were different when you were alone with my daughter.

I remember Katherine asked you a strange question. Had you ever been inspired? The two of you never thought to clear a space for yourselves at the table, and there was flour from my baking and bowls and things everywhere. I watched you with your shy smile push loose flour into neat little rows. "Inspired? I don't think so," you replied, but my Katherine did not believe you. "I bet you have at least once or else why would you smile like that?" She pulled your rows of flour into flying clouds that scattered again on the table.

You confessed then to being inspired by my garden and Katherine looked wide-eyed and amused. She was so young. She thought you were joking, but you said, "No, a garden takes lots of work. It's amazing to me that since I've met you so many flowers have fallen away only to be replaced by equally beautiful yet wholly different ones. Your mother has timed it perfectly." Katherine poured you both tea and said something like, "So, you're inspired by my mother's timing and orderly planting. That is very soldierly of you." You said, "Miss Katherine, I do enjoy order in life, obviously," as you pointed to the flour unconsciously pushed back into rows. "There's something more to it," you continued, "Your mother plans and plants things almost to perfection, but still there are stray seeds dropped by wandering birds and nine out of ten times the stray plant enhances the overall beauty of the place."

Dear John Weldon, I remember your optimism then, but you missed something about my garden. There were disasters too. Disease and horses run amuck through my vegetables, but I never give up. You were observant then, but naive too, and it was sweet to hear you go on about the different and interesting new insects and birds that would come to my garden when something different was planted, but you didn't see that each new gorgeous flower brought its own host of challenges and small heartaches.

You said something lovely that I will always remember, you said: "I thought when I first saw the garden that it was like a beautiful painting, but then after spending time in it I realized that your mother's labor had been rewarded, by God maybe, with a whole experience; the calls of the birds, strange butterflies, the scents." You thought there was a message in it all. Katherine believed you were the sweetest thing. "What's the message do you think?" she asked. You leaned back and brushed your boot against her shoe "And we know that all things work together for good to them that love God, to them who are called according to his purpose." You said that you thought maybe God rewarded those who worked with whatever little bit they had and blessed them with more than they could expect for themselves. You said that what inspired you about the garden was that you knew that at some point I realized that there was meaning in what I did. It celebrated God's gifts.

Katherine was a gift to you and when you were kind to her you improved her. You do not seem to realize the meaning of your own life, your own hard work. You were given a family, and they grew in your care. Eliza was lovely and fleeting. We do not know why some flowers last just a season. We just know we love them.

Katherine was like the stray seeds you spoke of. She flourished in the oddest desert environment and with the strangest of men. I remember her brushing flour from her pink dress that you liked so much. "I have never felt inspired and my life has been meaningless ... up till now," Katherine said. This hurt my feelings at the time, but it was true. She folded her hands on the table, and I could see you smiling at her dusty sleeves when she said that you inspired her. She said her happy duty was to listen to you and care for you. I almost cried watching you steal a kiss. I had had my doubts about you, but you told her a little story, you said "Let me tell you something foolish, Miss Katherine." You said that on the day that you met her on Palisades Avenue after the hop, you thought that she was the prettiest girl you had ever seen, but that you made up your mind you had no chance with her. You said you lied about having to visit friends. You saw an older couple at the train station arm in arm just in from the city maybe and happy. There was something about them that made you wonder, made you need to know how Katherine would turn out twenty years down the road. Well it's ten years now and disease and heartaches have taken their toll, but you must not give up!

You used to inspire me with the love and kindness you showed Katherine and the way you fought to be well and to marry her. Remember how you loved her, John? Now you have not only broken Katie's heart, but mine. Please come home.

Sincerely,

Sarah McCullough

Chapter Sixty-Five

Weldon volunteered in a moment of restlessness for the opposite of a plumb assignment at a small outpost, with a skeletal company of infantry, full strength just forty-five men, and half of them sick—partly due to the poor location of the place, but mostly due to the excesses allowed to continue under the captain, who in lonely insanity had slipped from the rocky desert cliffs to his death. A third of the men openly plotted desertion, and the rest were halfwits and malingerers. Weldon took the three-month assignment until a new commander of higher rank could be brought in from the east or the settlers could be persuaded that the garrison was no longer of much use to them except for the occasional pay the soldiers wasted in the already crumbling town on pastries, gambling, and the one known woman of low moral character.

There was little to be done with so few men but try to convince them to stay until the next visit from the paymaster. Weldon played at order for about a week. He did not even try to learn names, did not grumble at the ridiculous marches often consisting of no more than a line sergeant, a few privates, and the disreputable surgeon who still carried leech tins and bleeders. Weldon took over the medicinal supplies—a treasure trove of unopened treatments—and brightened as he considered the best way to remove his favorites without notice.

In a rare moment of sobriety, he glanced out from his porch thinking of Simon, who would have organized the place into one big card game in exchange for having the men declare him king of the desert. But thoughts of Simon led to thoughts of Katherine and the children. He retreated into his medical supplies. All his studies, first looking for God's will in the Bible and then to the military for precise strategy, had left him defenseless against the enemy he faced—and what was that enemy? Addiction? Death? Hunger? Love? It didn't matter.

How had he tricked himself into proposing to Katherine? He remembered convincing himself that since he knew how it would end, the ending would be easier. He'd be prepared for it. Like the military maps of the unexplored West, trails looked straightforward, but on the march one grew to love the surprises—the shades of color changing in the sand, the unfamiliar call of the desert owl, the small traces of water that trickled for only one month of the year, even the taste of the air. The path of his marriage was like the bold trail markings of the maps, but their life together was full of exploration and surprising landscapes and outcomes his internal map had never suggested. He missed the scent of his wife in the desert—perspiration mixed with the flowery hair oil—and the way Kate pushed her head under his arm when she came up behind him and kissed him at his jaw ... and the stories they told each other again and again ... and the children ... the map could not be folded and put back neatly in his pocket. His life had taken a three-dimensional form. It was fuller than he had expected it would ever be, and he loved it too much.

Weldon went on a scout, hunting. A few others came along. The purpose of the scout officially was to search for the bandits who annoyed the ranchers' stock. Unofficially the party wanted a more scenic place to lounge.

After a scramble up into a small cave, the men set to building a fire. They fought over five-cent bets and drank. Weldon slipped off, partook of his medicine, and stumbled back. The boys had sized him up from the start and were certain he'd fall into a canyon or be court-martialed for a past impropriety. It was three days of no food but hardtack, coins passed around, delirium tremens, sad paranoia, and then the quiet march back, parched and weary in the heat.

Weldon's room reeked of cigars and turned milk—someone had brought it to him ... maybe that little sergeant. It was after he had thrown his played-out body into bed, boots on, that he spotted the letters in their cream envelopes strewn across the floor where the wind swept them. He closed his eyes, too tired to read ... later ... but what if there was something from Willy? He groaned, sat up, and lit a cigar, half used and stale. With the cigar clenched between his teeth, he got to his feet and grabbed the letters. Two? He lit what was left of his candle. It had been a long time since he had wanted any light.

Katherine, William, Sarah, and even Scott exploded back into his life. The baby dead? Katherine nearly gone? The letters were a month in the past, redirected from Camp Grant. Weldon had missed it all. But Katherine! How could she die? He slid back into the world of Scott and Sarah with their comfortable home and the garden and the trees! He had almost convinced himself that he was no longer a part of that, that it meant nothing to him anymore, but even Scott's angry letter felt like home to Weldon—a home he had given up for caves with men who ... who were just like him. Scott's letter reminded him that at one time he had led a semi-respectable life where decent people expected things of him. Sarah's letter allowed him to imagine for just a minute that he would be welcome back in Englewood if only he would come.

Weldon kept a mirror. It was Katherine's from before. He surveyed his bearded face and was surprised how like his father he looked, but it was his drunken mother he had become.

He fumbled around for his pen and carefully uncorked his inkwell, but it made a mess anyway.

Dearest Katherine

I am writing this unsure of your well-being. I am a bankrupt man. Why did you ever care for me? I have always wondered that. It is easy to know the reasons I have loved you.

I am remembering the morning when you came out all in green on the side porch of your mother's house. You petrified me because I knew I would have to make a decision about you. You let me win that horse race, I think. I am not the rider you are. You were generous with me from the start. That night at the dance when you offered to teach me the waltz I will never forget because you were careful with my pride. No one had ever done that for me. You have been my only friend in this world. That night was the first time I thought of leaving you, but I could not. I was proud of that for a while, but it was selfish. I only thought of me needing you. I never thought how you really might grow to need me. When you asked for help over Eliza I deserted you and sent you off because I knew that I was going to fail.

Remember our wedding night in the small cabin? You were beautiful then, but not as beautiful as the last time I saw you leaving me. I was ashamed back then of the old scars, but you just smiled and waited to find out later the stories I could not tell you yet. I guess I thought you might wait for a long time to know everything. I guess for a while I wanted to fool myself into believing we had forever.

You have been a gift I never deserved. I was meant for a certain life, but you took me off my path and showed me a world I still have trouble believing ever existed. Somehow at certain times you have made me believe I deserved you. In the desert, sometimes you looked so proud of me I could feel it for myself. Those hot days I will think upon fondly forever. I think I made you happy for a while there.

I wish I had not learned to love so well from you. Losing Eliza ...

He folded the unfinished letter. What was the point? All these words were nothing like actions, the proper actions he should have taken. And if Kate was dead ...Weldon tucked the letter away, pulled out his little kit of medicine, and called it a night.

Chapter Sixty-Six

William earned the grudging respect of the other students attending the Kursteiner School. He punched and kicked his way through most of them, rarely being the clear winner but never backing down and always managing a sneer of superiority at fight's end. "Half-breed," which technically he was not, gave way to more satisfactory sobriquets.

William's essay, "Why and How We Should Kill the Indians," won him even greater acceptance among the boys who loved the gruesome and unforgiving depictions of half-imaginary soldiers and their foes brutalizing and outwitting each other. Mr. Finney was less impressed, having become active in the latest Indian welfare movement after the excitement of saving freed Negro souls had waned.

Students also enjoyed the strange debates between pupil and master over Indian policy. In the eyes of the ten-year-olds, William was a god. First because he wasted hours of valuable learning time and second because he had been with soldiers and knew things.

Mr. Finney with his spectacles, congested breathing, and monotonous lectures on the Constitution was at a great disadvantage from the start.

Finally, William won over his classmates with Handsome, the horse his father had bought for his mother, and the reckless way William rode him. The horse was lathered up in a thick froth every afternoon when the boys were not off hunting with a cache of stolen rifles and revolvers from one of the boy's family collections. It was in fact a fire set up by this troupe of hunters to cook or scorch their rabbits and squirrels that had put an end to the old mill.

Mr. Finney noted the change in the dynamics of the class. William stretched out long and lean now, casting a shadow over the boys who had once mocked him. Mr. Finney preferred the Willy of the fall who struggled and suffered. In May, William had become formidable, looking far older than his years.

"Master Weldon knows something of the Indians for he shares their noble blood," Finney said one day in irritation.

"Mr. Finney, not all Indians are noble," William said.

"You should not think so poorly of yourself, young man."

The classroom buzzed.

"I should say the same to you, sir. You're white, and I don't blame you for every slave or every death of an Indian. I bet you never had slaves or fought to free them."

"I fought in spirit, helped in any way I could," Finney said, taking off his spectacles to polish them with his bad breath and causing a sprinkling of suppressed laughter. He looked like a blind opossum without the gold frames, and a few boys took advantage by passing notes and continuing an earlier battle of flying bits of chalk.

"Indians are just like the Irish and the Germans and the plain old whites. If they're bad they should be killed," William continued.

One boy clapped in delight, just as Mr. Finney placed his spectacles upon the bridge of his nose. The boy received a ferocious stare.

Finney turned back to Weldon. "I am not at all surprised that you adhere to the justice of a soldier, young man, but that is why we have learned men in government, judges and the like ..."

"The government's what makes all the Indians mad, and they even give the Indians guns—not even just the scouts on our side! So the soldiers have to go off and kill them when the stupid ones shoot somebody when they're stealing things. One time there was a soldier who got caught by some Indians ..."

"Not another story, William."

The students sent up hoots of protest, convincing Finney their attention to studies could only be secured if he relented. "All right, go on."

"Well, the poor soldier was nearly at the small fort's door and safety, but a band of Indians, I forget which type, took the soldier—an officer—and made him dig a hole and get into it up to his neck, and they buried him in front of all the soldiers in the fort, but there wasn't enough soldiers to fight those Indians so they could just watch and hope for the best."

Mr. Finney rolled his eyes. "Pure propaganda."

"No, I don't think it was that tribe. I never heard of them."

Students snickered.

"Anyway, these Indians kept these stinging ants or maybe the ants were in a hill right there, but they scalped the officer and set the ants on him—on his head! And the officer cried like a baby with the soldiers looking on and wanting to help. I bet they really wanted to kill some Indians after that, or the time when the Indians came along wearing the scalps of two women settlers—the hair still in fancy clips and combs ..."

"William Weldon, that is quite enough!"

"Well, we beat them, and they should all do as they're told."

"You need to do as you are told and be quiet. The Indian problem is more complicated than a fight on the grounds of school with a winner and loser, but you are too immature to grasp ..."

"It's real easy, sir, if you ever have met Indians. It's like when you're getting licked outside of school. Even if your mother or auntie comes along and breaks it up and brings you home and washes your face—you're still licked through and through. It's done, and then when you come back the next day you have to accept you're never gonna be in charge, and you have to be careful."

"But your logic, young man, is faulty. You, for example were 'licked' as you say, many a time—I witnessed it from this very window—but you don't seem ready to give up the fight. You are no more careful or beaten."

"But Willy became like us," piped in a timid friend in the last row who was rarely heard from. "We don't have to fight him now that he's one of us."

"And, may I ask, for purely scientific reasons, how did he become like you? What changed?" Finney guiltily wished it would change back.

William gave him a smug, open look. "We have the same enemy now."

The boys all turned back to their compositions, heads down.

Finney was unprepared for such brazenness. The totality of the silence and the bowed heads upset the teacher's image of himself as tough and serious but liked well enough by the boys. Finney had his suspicions that William led a few students in the pranks and mishaps of class, but now he saw written on William's face that he had the backing of the entire class.

At first Finney pretended to ignore the statement, but it ate at him and would poison the rest of the day, the year even. "The only real enemy you have, William Weldon, is your mouth. Mr. Kursteiner took pity on you against my judgment because of your sister's death and the desertion of your father."

"My father didn't desert!"

"Really, William, we have heard quite enough fantastic half-truths about your life with your father. I assume he sent you away for showing the lack of respect you show me now."

"Don't talk about my father!"

"Yes, let's not talk about him. I think that is wise. Anyone else want to talk about their family?" Finney looked around confidently at the bowed heads.

By the end of the day, when the last of his students filed out the teacher realized that for the brief joy it had given him, hurting Weldon might bring more trouble than peace. Peering out the window, his face flushed with anger as he watched a group of his students and some younger ones standing around William Weldon being infected with his rebellion.

Two days later the school secretary had William by the collar on the McCullough front porch.

"What has William done now, and may I ask who you are?" Scott, on a rare day off, asked.

"I, sir, am Mr. Kursteiner's secretary. He will be along shortly to speak with William's mother personally before the afternoon is through. Are you the boy's father?"

"Land sakes, no. I'm his grandfather."

"Your grandson tried to poison his teacher this morning and nearly succeeded in killing him. We are still not altogether certain that Mr. Finney is out of the woods yet, as the boys—yours and another—have refused to tell us what exactly they added to their teacher's water jar."

Scott took William by the ear and held him high enough to make it difficult for the boy to keep his footing. "What did you put in the water? You had better damned well tell us!"

"It was just an old medicine bottle—blue pills, I think. We only thought it might make Mr. Finney queasy for the examination tomorrow."

"*Mercury*? My God—you could sicken the man for life or worse," Scott yelled. "What were you thinking?"

"I'm sorry to say there is more to the plot. We found Mr. Finney's grade book in with William's things."

"You're a thief now too?" Scott asked and then turned to the secretary. "When will Mr. Kursteiner come by? I will have my wife and daughter ready for his arrival."

Scott closed the door still gripping his grandson's ear. William tried to pull away "Do you have any idea how much trouble you have caused?"

William tried to scratch free like an animal in a trap. "I don't care! I hate Mr. Finney!"

"You hate everyone—do you plan to poison us all?" Scott dragged the boy through the hallway into the kitchen and toward the side door.

"You'd have done it too if he called you a liar and said things about your father!"

"No, I would not!"

"Then you're just a dumb old coot!" Willy said as he pulled and got free. Out the side door he went, but Scott surprised him and caught him as he flew off the steps, landing with a great thud.

"You've become as savage as a meat ax, and I will have to put a stop to it if you will continue living in my house."

"I don't want to live here anyway!"

"Believe me, young man, I'd love to send you away, but your father won't take you!" Scott continued, pulling his grandson toward Simon's willow. With his strong right arm he kept hold of William, who began to plead. Scott ripped a long branch, still in bloom, from the tree. Unfortunately for William his school trousers were of a shoddy, thin weave and every strike across his backside stung as if hitting his skin directly.

The women had made their way into the kitchen and out the door onto the porch after they heard William's voice beneath Simon's window but were too late to interfere with Scott's discipline. "Scott! Stop this now! You're humiliating him!" Sarah cried.

Scott stopped for a moment. "I'm to worry about his feelings after he has poisoned his own teacher?"

Katherine put her hands to her mouth. William was crying and submissive, so Scott stopped, throwing the switch as far away as he could. He pushed William off. The boy stumbled but did not fall and averted his eyes as he walked past the women.

"Go clean yourself up, William Weldon, and stay in your room," called Scott.

"Katherine, you've done a terrible job disciplining that boy. I've never seen the likes of it. I don't think he's a bit sorry for what he's done. And he'll surely be asked to leave the school."

"Willy was so good in Arizona ..." Katherine simpered.

"So you say, but the standards are more rigorous for a boy being raised in the East with something other than a military life to aim for. That boy is ruined, and I'm not even going to get into the embarrassment this brings upon the family. How will we face Mr. Kursteiner at church each week with him knowing we raised a heathen? It was on my reputation that William was accepted." Scott fought to get his breath back, still recovering himself after the beating.

Sarah spied the headmaster making his way up to the front porch and ushered them inside to meet him. Before opening the door she neatened the parlor, opening the windows and pulling the shades. As Mr. Kursteiner entered she smiled nervously. "Mr. Kursteiner, please take a seat, and I'll get you some tea and cakes."

"That won't be necessary, Mrs. McCullough. I wouldn't feel right eating when I know Mr. Finney suffers greatly from the poison," Kursteiner said as he turned to Katherine.

"Mr. Kursteiner, I'm sorry about all that's happened, but would you outline it clearly for me. There was no time for my father to explain."

"William not only stole the teacher's grade book but also poisoned his water with some old Blue Pills."

Scott jumped in. "That's mercury, Katherine!"

"Yes, Scott, it is—I don't know where the boys could have gotten the stuff," Kursteiner continued, "but it little matters. By the time one of the boys ran into my office, Mr. Finney was salivating profusely. Doctor Banks worries about the poor man's gums and teeth—he says he saw cases during the war where men with stomach complaints ended up dead or with a mouthful of painfully loose teeth and rotten gums."

Katherine ran from the room up to her son's without uttering a word. She dragged William back down the stairs and into the parlor. He stood motionless in front of the adults.

"I want William to understand what he has done, Mr. Kursteiner," she said through clenched teeth, digging her fingers into her son's boney shoulder.

"As I was saying, Mr. Finney could die or have his mouth deformed for life."

Scott turned to William. "Do you know what necrosis is?"

William shook his head.

"It's when the flesh is eaten away. Mercury in those Blue Pills does that—your teacher's teeth could fall out or his intestines could be eaten away—is that what you hoped for?"

"They dared me to do it. I didn't know what it was."

"We don't believe you!" Scott said.

"But I only wanted the book—I didn't mean to really poison him!"

Mr. Kursteiner took up the interrogation. "So stealing a teacher's book is not such a bad thing?"

"Well, they told me that Mr. Finney draws pictures of me!"

"Pictures?" Sarah asked.

"I got mad when someone told me that there were pictures—mean ones of me in his book. I didn't take the book at once, but everyone kept telling me, and then I thought he was looking at me to make more pictures."

Scott stuttered, "I-s-s Mr. Finney an artist of some sort?"

All eyes were on Kursteiner.

"Well, not that I know of, but it does not excuse the fact that William stole the grade book, which affects all the students."

Scott continued to question William. "What sort of pictures, boy?"

"Well, it was like he was having fun against me. There were stories—pictures in a row saying the things I say, but changed to make me look foolish, and sometimes the book was open, and a boy would see it—like he meant for them to see. But the fellows always told me."

"Mr. Kursteiner, I feel we have a right to see the book in question," Scott said.

"There is no point in it, Mr. McCullough. It might only aggravate the situation. As it stands, your grandson was involved in the poisoning of a respected teacher who should not be required to fear for his life each day at school. Once this gets out, your grandson ..."

"It won't get out, Mr. Kursteiner. I should like to retain our cordial relationship, sir. You may keep the book to yourself, but I suggest that after recording the necessary grades the book be destroyed, and I will continue to support the school financially."

"Of course your friendship is quite valuable to me and the school, but I am sure you will understand why William will not be allowed finish the year."

"Are you certain you won't have some tea?" Sarah asked.

"Thank you again, Mrs. McCullough, but I really must be on my way to see Mr. Finney." He brushed past Katherine rudely and walked out the door.

"He walked past me as if I didn't exist!" she cried when the door was shut.

"I'm sure in his eyes you don't exist," Scott said. "The boy has completely run amok, and you've done nothing to stop him—just the same as ever with all the boys and men in your life!"

Chapter Sixty-Seven

Weldon lingered outside the door to Crook's headquarters wondering why he had been summoned to Prescott and worrying that news of his feeble command experience may have reached his superior. Lieutenant Hadley, a close friend of Crook's, came up from behind. Weldon jumped at the sound of the man's voice. "Weldon, good to see you, old man. Waiting out here for a reason?"

"No," Weldon said, finally knocking at the door.

Hadley reached over and pushed the door open. "General, look what the cat dragged in."

Weldon stepped forward. "Good morning, sir."

Crook looked up from papers. "Glad to have you back in time. I hope you enjoyed your stay at Ehrenberg."

Weldon said nothing.

"The officers miss your way with words," Crook said.

"Sir, is there some reason why you sent for me?"

"Nothing like cutting to the chase, eh?" Crook commented. "I wanted to make sure you left with us for the Platte. It wouldn't feel like a proper campaign without my best young lieutenants."

"Thank you, sir."

"Bring back Mrs. Weldon if you like. Fort Laramie would be exciting for her and the children ... I mean, Willy."

"When should I be ready?"

"Oh, day after tomorrow. Come to the banquet at the Burnt Ranch tonight though."

"Sir, may I ask permission to stay in tonight? It's been a tiring journey to get here."

"Of course. You do look worn out. Wouldn't want you falling out on the way to Los Angeles." Crook pulled at his divided beard. "Are you sure you're strong enough for the campaigning? I don't recall the last time you've had leave. A few months away with Mrs. Weldon might do some good."

"I took leave for Christmas before Eliza ..."

"Yes, yes, but still that was ages ago."

"Sir, I'm tired of this heat and would be happy to follow you north. Besides, there's a friend of mine up there," Weldon said.

Hadley stood with a cup of tea, gawking at Weldon.

"Lieutenant Hadley, will you excuse us a moment?" Crook asked.

"Of course, sir."

"Lieutenant, please take a seat," Crook said, evaluating the lieutenant's appearance. "Weldon, the journey to Los Angeles is over five hundred miles and will take over ten days if we're lucky. It's rough terrain through the Soda Lake and Death Valley. I have to be quite honest here. I don't trust you'll make it."

"Sir ..."

"John, listen, this has been a bad time for you. It's hard to imagine the full extent of your grief. You've worn yourself down with work, and I hear of strange behavior from you these last months. I know things can be exaggerated when there is a clash of personalities, and you have always been an honest and steady soldier but ..."

"Sir, staying here away from all active duty will kill me. I beg you to let me go. If I don't hold up you can leave me in California, but I must have the chance to be out of here and busy again."

"All right, John."

"Thank you, sir."

"But Weldon, one more thing ... if you've been drinking intemperately maybe you should stop."

"Sir, I don't drink."

***

The journey was the hardest of Weldon's life. They passed through Indian territories and across the Colorado River and through lower Nevada and the horrid Soda Lake, where the dust and whiteness of the land and sun hurt their eyes and aggravated Weldon's nerves. He took just enough medicine to get by, and he stayed quiet. Crook had vowed to watch after him, but the general was busy with other things.

The men marveled at the quick and wonderful change of scenery once past San Bernardino. Fruit and flower of every kind greeted and brightened them. Kate would love the rolling land spotted with livestock. Weldon considered writing a quick note, but didn't. They rode by coach to Bakersfield and met the Southern Pacific to Nebraska and the Department of the Platte.

Weldon and a few others were sent at once to Fort Laramie with correspondence. It was expected that the little group might encounter unfriendly Sioux, Cheyenne, and Arapaho warriors, but they were lucky and things were quiet.

The sparse landscape fit the lieutenant's bleak outlook. He often thought about how Fred Dudley said life would end for him, and on this new journey he began to feel things give way. His old injuries conspired with crippling pain and stiffness, and his skin itched, dry and inflamed.

He asked after Simon as soon as he arrived at the bustling and sociable Fort Laramie. Soldiers crowded the place with grins and bets and gossip. He felt old and out of place, looking for his friend's temporary quarters.

"Weldon?!" Simon shouted, running up behind him.

John wheeled around, and Simon held out his hand with a jaunty grin, but much to his astonishment and discomfort Weldon captured him in a bear hug.

"Weldon, please! I've got my reputation ... that's quite enough," Simon joked stiffly.

Weldon stepped back and stood in awkward silence.

"John, are you all right? You look peaked. Come along, I'll find you a place to sit."

Simon directed him under his shady fly, but Weldon walked into the hot tent and sat on Simon's bunk. The place was a mess, and Weldon smiled a little. Simon looked at him pleasantly though a bit confused.

"What is it? Have you any news about Katherine?"

"Simon ... I-I've, well, I've hated you for such a long time ... it's been a poison ..."

"What?"

"I've *hated* you ... I still do ... I-I don't want to, and I've tried to f-fight it, but you ruined everything for me—that day in the W-Wilderness." Weldon caught himself with his hand in his hair. He stood to go but began to shake. "So there it is ... I hate you."

Simon shoved him back down onto the bed. "What the hell are you on about? You come all the way here to tell me this?"

"I've wanted to tell you for so long! I came to Englewood that first time to tell you what happened to my life because you always did just as you pleased! My life wouldn't have turned out this way.... I was on my way up in the war."

"You're joking, right? Everyone hated you! They thought you were a standoffish, self-righteous bastard! I got you every promotion you received!"

"I earned those promotions!"

"Is that what this is about?" Simon laughed bitterly.

"You never did as you were supposed to do! You were never where you were supposed to be, and we all depended on you!"

"Okay. I know you blame me for all that happened in the Wilderness. I was wrong to run off that night and do what I did, but ... I've thought about it over the years and realized that it's all bunk. If I had been with you that morning—with all of you—how would that have changed things?"

"You should have been with your men."

"But how would things be different? The only difference I can think of, Weldon, is that I would have been left for dead on the field too, and there would have been no one left to help you survive."

"And what a great life it's been since then."

"Well, why don't you just get it over with then?" Simon shouted. "Just end your terrible existence. Kill yourself!"

Weldon scratched his sore arm.

"You were able to see another day and marry and have children. What about the others who died? You think they're better off? What about Anthony, remember him? His old mother keeps him indoors she's so ashamed of the way he looks now. It's frightful. You sicken me sometimes. Katie has cared for you, and your children have too, and you act as if you deserve better than that!"

"That's not true!" Weldon shouted. "They deserved better than me!"

"Oh, get off it!"

"It's the morphine, Simon ... the morphine from the hospital ..."

"What?"

"I've kept it secret ... all these years ... from everyone, from Kate. You saved me Simon, but ... you killed me too. You're right—I still have a life of sorts, but ... once I met Katherine ... I couldn't tell ..." Men, mules, horses, and wagons made for a racket outside. Simon and John sat in quiet. "It was your responsibility that day once the captain went down to ..."

"You defy logic. It was you who knew all the rules and regulations. You read all the manuals, but you never saw that in real life sometimes the responsibility becomes yours. Not from some promotion in a staff office but among the men. I lied a little before. The men didn't hate you, they just didn't know you, but they did respect you."

"You weren't there that day to see it all."

"But I'd seen things like it a hundred times—so had you! Only this time you were seeing it with real responsibility. Why did you take the men headlong into the woods that way, I've always wondered?"

Weldon rubbed his nose. "I was scared I guess ... I tried to imagine what you might have done."

"That was your first mistake. You've always been blind to your own strengths. It amazes me. Those men got themselves slaughtered because they trusted your steady ways."

"You always do just as you please—you've never taken responsibility when it mattered! Whatever foolish thing you do, your reputation never suffers. Even if you fell flat, you have your parents and their money."

"Are you jealous of my grand fortune? It's not much really!"

"It would have been to me for Katherine and the children."

"Please, I know you better than that. You never would have accepted my father's money."

"You just don't realize how lucky you are. You're ungrateful."

"Coming from you? Don't make me laugh!" Simon lit a cigar. "I actually know that I'm lucky and that's why I'm happy. I think it's my attitude I'm most lucky to have. You're one for Bible quotes—I like to think of my motto as: 'It is well for a man to eat and drink and enjoy all the fruits of his labor under the sun during the limited days of his life which God gives him—this is his lot.' I tell this to Emily all the time."

Weldon smiled and returned, "'Sorrow is better than laughter because when the face is sad the heart grows wiser.'"

They sat pondering their lots in life. Simon chuckled and added, "I have one—'Yet, there is no man on earth so just as to do good and never sin.'"

"Well said," Weldon admitted, and then it struck him. "Did you say *Emily*?"

Simon waited for Weldon to put it all together while tightening the belt beneath his thickened middle.

"*Emily Watson?* Langellier's niece? No ... are you with?" Weldon looked at Simon incredulously. "But she's the temperance one and ..." He laughed at the idea of such a partnership.

"Don't laugh, bub, she knows what I'm like, and I've grown quite fond of her over the years. Emily will spend the rest of her days trying to reform me, but she finds me irresistible, I guess," Simon bragged, patting his once svelte physique. "Anyway, Weldon, we're too old now to keep abusing our bodies. I need a change. I'm willing to put up with her Bible-thumping as long as she lets me ease into semiretirement from my *sinful ways.*"

"When you make a decision things fall right into line for you. It's what I mean about you being lucky."

"Again you miss the point. I'm honest. I always have been. I ask for what I want. People never need worry that I have ulterior motives. They never have to guess. Emily has seen my major mistakes, but she also sees that there will be no guess work. Ask and you shall receive."

"You can stop with the Scripture truisms now—somehow it's troubling, coming from you."

Simon laughed, but took a long hard look at his friend. "Looks like you need a holiday. Won't Crook give you any time off?"

"He would, I guess, but ... what would I do with myself? I have nowhere ..."

"Come back east with us!"

"No, no I couldn't."

"You need to tell my sister the truth, or I may have to. It's unfair to leave her thinking she's done something wrong. You've been a coward, John, and now's the chance to change that. If you really think she's too good for you then you need to tell her about yourself and let the chips fall where they may. I know she still cares—although why you didn't go home right after Katherine's loss ..."

Weldon broke down, hands covering his face. Simon rolled his eyes. "Come on, bear up. This does no good." He fumbled in his jacket. "Here, have a smoke—come on now."

Weldon brushed it aside. "I'm so ashamed ... since Eliza ... I don't remember whole days. I've stolen from surgeons—opium pills—anything. I don't understand how I'm still in the army at all. I can't tell you when I've even made it a whole week to roll call. When the news came in about Katherine losing the baby, I wasn't around and not myself. I couldn't, I can't face her. I never should have sent them away from me, but I was afraid they would see me as you see me now."

Simon worked the cigar between his teeth. "You should have given Katie more credit. She was devoted to you. You never trust people and now ... well how can she trust you?"

"She can't. That's just it. I can't fight this anymore and recover and fight again—I've just wanted to escape. In the end I sold almost everything I owned to characters I would have sneered at only a few years back. I sold your father's ring. The one Katherine wouldn't wear. It was to stay in the family ... maybe Emily could have worn it."

"Listen, Weldon, you should come home—even if it's for the last time. Whatever your plans, your responsibilities are still with Katherine and William. At least let them know that you didn't desert them because you hated them—you just love something more." Simon couldn't help a small dig. "Are you still using the stuff now?"

"No ... well, I'm trying not to."

"Then come with us, for Willy's sake. That boy adores you."

"Maybe you're right." Weldon sighed. "I need to come clean with them and let them be free of me for once and for all."

There was a padded knock on the flap of the tent. "Is that room service?" Simon asked.

Emily poked her head in. She hadn't aged much since the last time Weldon saw her but something in her attitude had softened. Seeing that Simon was not alone she smiled shyly, but came forward to greet Weldon. "Good day to you, sir."

Simon laughed. "You don't remember this fellow, do you?"

"Oh, my! Mr. Weldon! It's been years and years it seems," she said. "You look terrible worn out!"

He stood. "It's nice to see you again although I am surprised at the company you keep."

"Well, it's only natural for a wife to accompany her husband."

"Simon, you're married?!"

"He didn't tell you first thing? What a scalawag!"

"So he is," Weldon agreed. "Does everyone at home know?"

"I keep things close to my vest," Simon said, beaming at Emily. "No, they don't know, and don't think of telegraphing Kate."

"We're going back to surprise them," Emily said.

"Congratulations. I'm sorry, Emily, but this is some shock. Simon did tell me that he was with you, but ..."

"Well, that doesn't sound too proper, Simon McCullough," she scolded.

"Oh, Weldon's making it all come out wrong. Some things never change," Simon replied. "I was working my way into telling when you arrived just in time. Sit with us a while."

"Lieutenant Weldon, have you any more interest in the temperance movement these days?" Emily asked in an uneasy way as she fidgeted with her gloves.

"God, no," he answered all too quickly. Simon signaled Emily to change the subject, but she stubbornly took it as a challenge.

"Captain McCullough thinks that my interests and faith are foolish things and embarrass him, but I think I can rely on the fact that a man as temperate as I remember you to be would at least support the banning of liquor in the Indian territories."

Simon shook his head. "Emily, must you?"

"Emily," Weldon began, "I mean, Mrs. McCullough, I think people who want to drink will do so whether you ban spirits or not. Drink is easy enough to make. You know the Apache made tizwin."

"But you, Lieutenant Weldon, you're a good Christian."

"Mrs. McCullough, you've confused me with a person I left behind some years ago. I prefer not to discuss God and all his wonderful fatherly traits. God is the last illusion you want to use to convince men to give up their vices."

"God is the only one to rely on for strength against vices. Society is lost without a moral compass."

"Where is this God?" he asked. "He always failed to show up when I needed strength."

"Simon has told me about your loss, and I fully understand why you might lose faith, but turning to alcohol or other earthly vices instead of to the Lord is where man falls."

"Mrs. McCullough ..."

"Oh, please call me Emily."

"Emily, while I'd like to believe that your heart is in the right place, I don't appreciate your implications. How you can pretend to know the first thing about me and my 'loss,' as you so delicately put the death of my daughter, is beyond me. It looks to me that you have a big enough project of your own sitting beside you. Kindly stick to that."

"Weldon, I apologize for my wife," Simon said. "Her mouth gets ahead of her funny little brain sometimes."

"Do accept my condolences. I didn't mean to make light of your struggles. It's just that my personal relationship with the Lord has brought me such comfort in my own trials." Emily glanced at Simon, and he smiled warmly at her. "I only want to share with others."

Simon took out his flask and gulped deeply.

"Simon!" Emily cried.

Weldon sat, legs stretched out and arms folded. "I am pleased for you—really I am—that the Lord has taken time from his busy schedule presiding over wars and famine to assist you in your personal dramas."

"Weldon, cut it out," Simon warned.

"You're very lucky, but God never deemed it important enough to send me signs or angels or voices whispered through the trees. He's left me to my own devices as far as I can tell, and good riddance to Him."

"I've married into a family of true heathens!" Emily said to Simon.

Simon chuckled. "Yes, but we're a good-looking bunch."

"I'll leave you boys alone. Lieutenant Weldon, I hope you find peace someday."

Weldon said nothing until the last of Emily's skirt was out of sight between the tent flaps. "Damn, Simon, what have you gotten yourself into?"

"I'm sure you didn't mean that the way it came out!"

Weldon grinned despite himself.

"Seriously, don't be too hard on her. She's a good sight younger than us and a bit naive. I like her though." Simon looked pleased. "She's turned into a real stunner and tough as nails, like a little bulldog. She never quits—she never quit with me. I thought our Kate was more like that, but it seems she was only playacting."

"Yes, she fooled me too. She let me get away with far too much—and I always took advantage of that."

"Yeah, you did take advantage of her trust. I guess she was a fool to believe she could rely on her husband."

Weldon had nothing to say.

"I'm taking a leave of absence," Simon said, tapping his fingers against the arm of his camp chair.

"Oh. Any special reason?"

"The obvious reason would be that I just got married. I want to bring Emily around to the family. Maybe have a baby—you know, work on that a bit," Simon said with a hint of worry. "Emily wants to try even with the danger."

"What danger?"

"Well, anyway, I need a break from this Indian stuff. The rough ones need to be subdued, but I find that I sort of like some of them, and it gets so complicated. I want a simple life now. I don't even know if I really want to ever come back. I'm tired of all the changing alliances and bad deals and roaming. I guess I'm getting old, and I don't want to leave here after I have no good feelings at all for mankind."

"So that's why you married 'Emily the Good'?"

"Weldon, has anyone ever told you how perceptive you are?" Simon asked. "Emily can be annoying at times, but she lives her life with dignity and standards. She's forgiven me for things I don't deserve to be forgiven for. She's the only person I've met since you that I trust. You used to be a lot like her."

"Only you could see similarities between Emily and me."

"Yes, well, I might not be visited by angels either, but I have my own powers of observation. I used to think it would always be the same in life—wherever you went you'd pick up new and equally good friends. You could be careless about the old ones. But I see that I was wrong on that count."

"Continue, oh great philosopher ..."

"Go to hell, you! I'm just saying that I appreciate my family and friends a lot more than I did when I took them for granted." Simon pushed his burnt-down cigar into the ground and stood to leave. "So, will you come home, and we can all be together for a while?"

Weldon leaned back on the bed thinking it over.

"Well," Simon went on, "let me know what you decide. I'm off on a few errands now."

Weldon watched his friend go, and for a moment it was exactly like old times. He sighed and lay flat on the bed, looking up at the ridgepole, reliving the quiet times of the war. His thoughts soon brought him back to the present.

He had just confessed to Simon McCullough, and still they were friends. He had half expected a duel or a few fists, but nothing had happened ... not anything he had imagined at least. This friend who, on some level, he had always seen as shallow was really not that at all. It was he, not Simon, who had seen it shallowly. When Simon threw out now and again that he considered Weldon a brother, he must mean it. It never occurred to Weldon that it was any more than Simon's natural friendliness. He had missed just how dependable and concrete a friend Simon had been to him and Katherine. All of those letters that Simon had written ... Weldon never imagined that he was anything more than an afterthought in them. It amazed him that Simon forgave him! Simon knew how he hurt Katherine, but still he wanted Weldon to come back to the family. This was beyond his comprehension, and he suddenly felt puffed up and elated. An intense desire to somehow repay Simon came over him. His heart pounded with gratitude ...

Just then the tent flap opened, and it was Emily. Weldon sat bolt upright.

Emily backed up as she spoke. "I'm terribly sorry, Lieutenant Weldon, I thought Simon was still here."

"Wait!" he called to her as he jumped from the cot.

They stood outside the tent for a moment saying nothing. Emily looked about nervously and tucked a wisp of her blond hair back under her bonnet. He stood with his hands in his pockets, looking past her at the bustle all around. "I just wanted to wish you well ... with Simon, I mean. I've known him even longer than you have, and there has never been a truer man in the world."

She stared up at him.

He wanted to say something more, something meaningful and inspired. She was patient.

"You know he saved my life during the war?"

Emily shook her head no, and the small, prim smile slipped from her face.

"Yes, he found me left for dead ... and he got me new boots—ones like I could never afford. I still have them ... at home." He adjusted his hat and sighed away the emotion in his voice. "I hope you'll be good to him. I'm happy for you both."

She took his hand. "I intend to take the best care of him. I know that's what you did for him and kept him out of at least some of the troubles he could have managed. I'm grateful to you for that. God brought the two of you together for a reason."

He patted her hand and smiled. "Mrs. McCullough, you will be loved by Simon's parents."

"Do you think so?" she asked with obvious reservations. "Simon has warned me that his father is rather tough on newcomers."

"No, he's just protective of his family. I haven't been much of a son-in-law."

She hesitated. "Lieutenant Weldon, years ago, when I first met your wife, we had an argument she may have told you about."

His eyes followed every word intensely, and his back was straight.

"It was about you. Your father-in-law may not have had much faith in you, but your wife certainly did. I'm sorry to even recall what I said because it was none of my business and rude and unfeeling. I insinuated that I had seen you—acting strangely—I assumed drunk ..."

He looked to the heavens and then back at her fiercely.

She continued, "I'm so sorry that I said it now. In fact I was sorry the moment I said it, but Katherine wouldn't forgive me then. She warned me never to speak to you again. She tried so hard to protect you."

"Why do you pretend to know anything about Katherine and me?"

"I know what you must think of me, but I feel that it is an act of divine providence that caused us to meet by chance again. Lieutenant, we're family now, and as such I must warn you that there have been rumors bubbling up from Arizona. Rumors that imply that the climate or the work has run you down. That your behavior has been ... unbecoming."

"Why do you tell me this? Do you enjoy this?"

"Please, don't misunderstand. I'm in no position to judge you."

"Yes, I'm sure you're involved in much devilment."

"Lieutenant Weldon, hate me all you like, but I tell you because, as of now, they are only rumors from a bad lot of men at a far-off post."

"Well, then they're only groundless rumors," he said.

Looking directly into his eyes, Emily spoke. "I've never even told Simon, but ... do you remember Oonagh Lyons?"

"Oh, hell," Weldon moaned.

"She told me about you before we went to Texas. She seemed to have a grudge against you and Katherine. I didn't really believe her, and to be honest I didn't think much about it till recently." She waited for some reaction, but was denied. "Men aren't good on their own. Simon finally realizes that. And you must too. God works through his people. Your wife is your helpmate whom God has given you. We're all put in each other's path for a reason."

"You're disgusting to me!" Weldon said. "You spy and prey on other people so you can give your useless advice and feel superior!"

"Lieutenant, you're so wrong!"

Weldon tried to walk off, but she would not allow it.

"What's wrong with you?" he asked in exasperation, aware of how all this appeared to men passing through. "Haven't you said enough, but you want to torture me further?"

"Please wait!" she said in tears. She placed herself in front of him, stubbornly entrapping him. "I do have an awful way of putting things. I only wanted to help you. We're all sinners. I wanted to warn you."

"Your sins written down would fill quite a short book, I'd bet."

"You might be surprised if I told you."

"I don't care to know."

Emily grabbed Weldon's arm and dragged him under the fly. "I—I have the disease too."

"What?"

"Like Simon."

"I don't understand."

She began to cry. "Seems like all the soldiers got something from the war," she sobbed. "And Simon passed it on to me ... before we were even married ... and my family ... they don't want to know me or Simon anymore."

"You're sick?" Weldon's voice softened. "I'm terribly sorry. I had thought he was cured ..."

"No, he wasn't. He didn't know when he ... gave it to me. I feel frightened all the time that someone will find out, but then I've always loved Simon McCullough and I'm the happiest girl in the world when I think he might really and truly love me back."

"I know he is pleased as punch to have you. He's better than I've ever seen him ... he ... he does love you, I think—a lot."

"Thank you for saying that." She sniffled. "I so make a mess of my words and land myself into all sorts of tight spots. Maybe Simon will tire of me."

Weldon laughed. "Simon said we are alike, but I didn't believe him."

"Excuse me?"

"Oh, nothing."

"Lieutenant Weldon, please believe me. I would never tell a soul about any rumors—even if they were true. I don't judge you. Everyone has things that they don't want other people to know, but you have to trust sometimes. I trust you with my secret—I don't know why, but I do. I hope we can be friends one day." Emily heaved a sad sigh as she walked out into the sun.

"Emily!" Weldon came after her. "Would you mind if I come along east with the two of you?"

Chapter Sixty-Eight

The hot parlor in June, still dim with winter drapery, smelled of unaired upholstery. The plum velvet over the windows, which looked so festive in December, had a funereal affect in June. Sarah had never gotten around to spring cleaning.

"Sit out on the porch, Katie. There's at least a faint bit of air," Sarah said tentatively. Yesterday they fought over the style and fabric for Katherine's new clothes, and William had already skirmished with his testy grandfather today over hunting in the woods.

The heat and torpid air combined against comfort, but Katherine did not think to open the windows as she set about finding, under all the half-started and nearly finished rugs, the one her mother hated—the only one Katherine had designed herself. A farm, one simple line across the burlap, curving down into a valley with a small house in the bottom left-hand corner. Although it was a fundamentally flawed layout, unbalanced and irritating to the eye, Katherine found it completely unchangeable. The fields lay barren, for there were no bits of fabric in her basket that struck her as healthy vegetation. Puffy trees of faded emerald from one of Simon's old sweaters looked cheerful and out of place no matter how she hooked them through, and after much effort at bringing life to the long strips of wool, she gave up, pulling each loop from its geometric station. She tried to convince a small farmer to course the landscape, but the correct shape and size of him eluded her, each attempt looking more and more frayed and loose until she pulled him from the burlap altogether. She only liked the fiery sky. On this she had taken a risk, shredding an old garibaldi jacket and short skirt, a favorite set from her late youth, into strips of gaudy gold and crimson floral with hints of blue throughout. The soft fabric passed over her fingers like silk, and she felt for once an excitement for her creation. The texture of a late summer evening from long ago emerged on the roughly woven canvas.

Happier days it seemed now, but at the time they all worried terribly for Simon. Nights spent on the porch after the latest of the young soldier's letters had been read and reread, nights when a small wisp of music playing in someone's open house would reach the McCullough family, and they'd cry because it was Simon's favorite song. On those nights when she was young and hidden in the shade of the porch and sitting on an ottoman dragged from the library right close up to her father, she felt she could touch everyone she loved. Scott absently twirled her hair around his fingers as he told Sarah about his day. Sarah's quiet whisperings tickled her ears and sometimes lulled her to sleep. In her memories she always held one of Simon's letters, for his stories of the campfires under the stars gave her the sky. The way the sky slid over yonder, over to wherever he was ...

Poor Simon ... where was he now? The great maple trees had grown up since the war, hiding the sky behind them.

Three quarters of the way across Katherine's lively sky, the skirt fabric ran out. She should have planned it better. Sarah found it abrasive to the eye anyway, and if Katherine could just pull it out and give her some of it, then Sarah could finally finish her staid floral that had been waiting for a bit of dash. The rest of the scraps from her childhood could be hooked to make the little farmstead.

Katherine let the landscape with the weather-less sky and barren plain fall over her round hips. Reaching into her basket of wool, she pondered the sky again. The basket was a sea of dull possibilities, and so it would have to be. She had nothing else to do but wait for William's return and another fruitless try by her to rein him in. Part of her wished he would never be tamed—one of them should be allowed to escape the heat of this house.

And so the morning went, each drop of perspiration gliding along the curves of her body, keeping time with the lazy notes of the clock winding down. A trapped fly fitfully buzzed at the window and crickets purred. The porch door in the kitchen squealed open and banged shut every time Sarah came in to retrieve a tool from the mudroom for work in her garden. A notion passed through her mind that planting some tomatoes from the conservatory might be a nice thing to do for her mother, but everything in that glass house reminded her of John. He loved Sarah's garden, and it spoiled it for Katherine to think she might recall him being jolly, discussing the merits of the ladybug or boyishly soaking Katherine with rainwater from the barrel sitting beneath the eaves of the greenhouse roof.

She listened to the world go by and force its way up the drive. A loud clopping of hooves and the sing-song call of a driver brought her to the window. She peeped like a clam from its shell around the edge of the shade and watched Margaret Crenshaw hop down from the carriage. Margaret spoke a few cheerful words to her husband, and Graham chuckled. Some last-minute thing Margaret said brought Graham down out of the carriage. Margaret came round to him and gazed up at him as he spoke with his hand tenderly holding her chin. He kissed her then, and she remained still, transfixed until he turned south onto Tenafly Road with the horses. They seemed terribly in love. Katherine tried to swallow her bitterness, but also wondered why Margaret had come at all.

"Oh, dear! I was just about to knock! You startled me, Katie!" Margaret said when Katherine opened the door. She let Margaret inside, all decked out for summer in a lavender linen walking suit with pinstripes and a simple straw cap with a single fresh lily dangling over the brim. "Did I wake you?" she asked, looking over her friend's worn and sloppy dress.

"Margaret, you're looking well."

"You look ... I can't bring myself to say it, Katie. You look like the wreck of the Hesperus. Please don't be huffed at my honesty!"

Katherine tried to hide her bare feet and folded her arms over her body as she led Margaret into the parlor.

"Certainly you don't sit in here all day? It's too terribly hot and unhealthful," Margaret gasped, opening every window as Katherine settled into her work again.

Margaret pulled a chair beside Katherine and said nothing for a long time, fingering the tassels on her bag.

"What brings you here?" Katherine asked.

"You do. Katie, I'd like to help you. Please, don't push me away. I am your only ... your friend. I can take you riding for air and ..."

"If a carriage ride could solve my problems I might have tried that already."

Margaret mopped her head of perspiration and exhaled. Katherine hid beneath her shoddy clothes and unkempt hair. Margaret leaned over and pulled a stray lock from Katherine's face. "You never knew what to do with your beautiful hair, Katie."

Something in the way Margaret said the words or maybe the way she touched her, awakened a part of Katherine that had been deep in slumber. Margaret's gesture reminded her that at one time she had a friend. This friend thought of her hair! Margaret looked at her and simply wanted to fix her hair and gossip and go on short rides ... but Margaret also might want to talk about children. Katherine could barely speak William's name for fear of cursing him somehow. She poisoned children—John had said as much. She stood suddenly, in terror—her son was lost somewhere. She must find him. Abruptly she ran for the door, with Margaret trotting close behind. "Merciful heavens, where are you off to?"

The sun and the heat stunned her.

Margaret grabbed her. "Katherine. What are you doing?"

She sank down on the stairs. Margaret looked around for snooping neighbors and, seeing none, sat alongside of her, taking her hand. Katherine's eyes were full and pale in the sun.

"Maggie, the consumption, the months of it," she sobbed, "the months! They were torture, and I failed at it all."

"I'm sure you did everything you could have."

"No, no! I was cruel and incompetent. My parents told me they would help me if I stayed, and they would have gotten the best doctors, but ... I chose John! And he needed something I couldn't give him. I don't even know what—but I've failed everyone!"

Margaret embraced her.

"I've never pleased anyone, Maggie. I've never made good decisions or protected myself and my family no matter how I love them and try my hardest! I've ruined Simon, John, Eliza, and now Willy!"

Margaret grabbed her by the shoulders and looked deeply into her eyes. "John Weldon came from nothing, from nowhere. If it wasn't for you he would have stayed a third-rate man. He needed you if he was to become anything."

"No, that's not true."

Margaret went on. "I don't doubt John Weldon has his strengths, but some men seem like children—always so afraid to show failure, afraid to risk letting people help them."

"Oh! And he's alone now!"

"But Katie, *he* sent you away. He loves you. That was always plain, but there's something the lieutenant won't tell you or hides from you. I'm sure of it."

"Do you think so? I've wondered if there's been someone else he's loved better."

"Here comes Graham—it's so awfully muddy for June isn't it? I came to ask you a favor, and I almost forgot. You may laugh at me, but the ladies' political club at church—mostly grey-haired abolitionists—have become quite concerned for the Indians and well ... will you come sometime to a meeting to give us your impressions?"

"No, I'm sorry, but I couldn't," Katherine replied, looking down at herself. "I've never been able to speak intelligently before a crowd and look at me!" She hated sounding so pathetic. "And I don't have a stitch of clothes for an eastern group of ladies."

"You're such a dear. If you would ever let anyone *know you*, they'd be mighty impressed by your smarts and how sweet you are—I am! They won't even recognize you from the little waif of years ago. Anyway, we can hem up one of my skirts and shorten the sleeves of a bodice, and of course I'll take care of your hair. It will be a fun project. We should begin tomorrow, say 10 o'clock. I'll come for you. The meeting is Thursday next so that gives us a little more than a week to prepare."

Katherine nodded, feeling frightened but alive for the first time in months.

***

Every morning Katherine woke early with the robins, rehearsing in her mind all she would say to the society women about Indians.

She dressed early on the day in anticipation, pulling her corset tighter to fit into the borrowed cranberry suit.

The sound of Margaret's carriage brought her to the landing where Willy sat reading a book. "Mother, you look so nice!"

She hugged him, feeling elegant and happy. Sarah let Margaret in through the kitchen, and they both came to the bottom of the stairs.

"Oh, my, Katie, you look like an overstuffed turkey in that suit!" Sarah burst out.

Margaret rushed up the stairs. "Don't listen to her! You look lovely! Your mother is being cruel and jealous—excuse me for saying so, Mrs. McCullough."

"You should have included me in your activities, girls," Sarah sniffed. "I would know how to dress Katie more appropriately."

"She's old enough to dress herself, Mrs. McCullough."

Katherine closed her ears to their squabbling. How had John been so unfeeling to throw her back to the wolves? Her eyes burned and her throat tightened.

"Katie, I brought this hat for you as a surprise," Margaret said as she pushed her friend back up the stairs so she could fix her hair.

"Oh, Maggie! I can't wear that! It's too ..." Katherine said glancing in humiliation at her mother eyeing them both smugly. "It's too much!"

"I know you're grateful, but please—it matches so well and I've added these feathers especially."

Sarah held her sides, laughing and gasping for air. The hat, looking like a world gone mad with ornamental flowers and fowl not to mention the added feathers, made a mockery of the McCullough women's sensibilities.

Margaret clapped delightedly at Katherine's bold new look and sat her before the mirror. "Katie, you're positively glowing. I've never seen you look so well."

"Thank you, but you're laying on the compliments too thick to trust."

"You're too influenced by your mother! She wishes she could be like you. The dress is tighter than you're used to, but it's the style. Only your mother would find fault. And when I get done plaiting your hair and setting the hat just so, you'll see I'm right about everything."

William slinked in to watch the elaborate proceedings from the corner of the bed. Katherine smiled when she caught his serious expression in the mirror, and he smiled back.

"Willy, what do you think of your mother?" Margaret asked, as she finished pinning the last strand of hair.

He grimaced at being called Willy but answered anyway. "She looks just like a queen."

"You have a smart son, Katie. Now take a proper look at yourself."

Katherine had become ordinary, not just older, but for the first time she saw herself as others must see her now—plain. She looked like any other matron on the street. When she was young there was a little something about her, but that something had slipped away. It was a relief somehow to be just like everybody else. Maybe now she would be left alone.

Margaret brought the carriage around, and Katherine climbed in.

"Katie, I've really enjoyed our time together," Margaret said jauntily.

"Me too," Katherine replied with a smile and breathed deeply. The scent of someone burning cattails brought up from the stream filled the air. Everyone sat lazily peering out from their porches or sitting on their steps to watch the passersby.

Katherine, like Sarah, had complained many times on the overactive curiosity of the average Englewood inhabitant, but after suffering under the unforgiving silence of the officers' wives at Camp Grant she welcomed the change. All along the wide avenue of Demarest, she had been hailed at first politely and by week's end more heartily as the neighborhood grew more accustomed to seeing her ride by at half past ten. And she found that, unlike her mother, she enjoyed the way her neighbors took an interest in her mundane daily activities. The smiling lady watering her new petunias had been the first to pull Katherine from her forward stare. After so much time in the West, she had forgotten how close Englewood people lived to each other and so it was impossible, when the old farmer led his milk goat across her path with a friendly greeting, not to notice him. It was less taxing to smile and greet the neighbors back than to ignore them.

"Mrs. Weldon, is there a new show at the Athenaeum?" the goat man asked from his comfortable spot.

"No, Mr. Drake, I'm off to a church meeting."

"Say a prayer, will you? The wife's not speaking to me again," he said, whittling a creature from a stray piece of lumber he'd picked up.

She laughed and promised she would, unable to remember the last time she said a prayer she actually believed in.

Her hands sweated inside her new gloves as Margaret tapped the reins to the right. There stood the church in darkness. Her heart raced. Maybe the meeting had been cancelled.

"The meeting is around back, Katherine, before you cheer," Margaret said, with a knowing grin. She settled back in her seat and asked her Friesian to stop. Katherine slid from her seat uncomfortably, afraid of tearing her skirt. They took care of the carriage and made their way through the new church gardens. A small plaque dedicated to Eliza lay in there somewhere, but Katherine did not care to see it.

Margaret led her into the church through a long and badly lit hallway toward the sounds of women chatting and china cups clinking against saucers. The reception area had the feel of an elegant country retreat with walls of stone and finely stained wood. A large masculine sofa sat near a Thomas Cole landscape hung above the fireplace. Tempering the manliness of the place were the ladies themselves in their finest attire and the extravagant elegance of the refreshment table trimmed with donations from someone's flower garden.

An elderly lady with pinched features greeted the two. "Dear Mrs. Crenshaw, so pleasant to see you again. Choral practice was a disaster, don't you agree? I won't name names, but some ladies will have to be asked to leave the group, or we shall be the laughingstock of all Englewood and the concert only weeks away!"

"Mrs. Humphreys, I'd like to introduce you to Mrs. Weldon of Tenafly Road—an old friend," Margaret said.

"You are the McCullough girl."

"Yes."

"Your son has crossed my path a few times—snooping around our horses."

Margaret took Katherine's arm in hers. "Mrs. Humphreys, I must introduce Mrs. Weldon to the others."

A rotund and red-headed lady dressed in mourning frock and gown rang a small servant's bell. "Please, ladies, kindly take your seats."

As the women settled themselves, she continued, "Margaret Crenshaw, the newest member of the *Humanitarians for the Friendship and Refinement of the Indian Society* has brought along an old resident of Englewood who has traveled extensively throughout Indian country and resided until recently with her husband, Lieutenant John Weldon of the Cavalry, in Arizona. As an aside, some of you may remember Mrs. Weldon's brother, Simon McCullough—most of us girls in the younger set had a soft spot for him, although I remember his troubles in town greatly annoyed the old settlers."

A polite and knowing bit of laughter followed from the ladies. Katherine cringed.

"We also have with us—yes, a full night indeed—I hope your husbands will not be waiting up! We have Reverend Clarke from the New York Missionary Society to speak with us about the wonderful work being done amongst the Indians, the freedmen, and the Chinese. Ladies, we might want to resolve the question tonight about shared subscriptions to the various journals we have discussed that will further our knowledge of the red man and what problems he faces."

Mrs. Humphreys cleared her voice to speak as all eyes rolled. "As you all know, my dears, I am greatly interested in the plight of all mistreated tribes and peoples, but especially women. To please my conscience, I again desire to remind you all that without the vote our opinions here have no meaning, no teeth as it were, and I wish to continue where we left off at the end of last week's extended meeting."

"Mrs. Humphreys, with all due respect, the purpose of our group is to discuss and find a solution to the Indian problem alone, and that is what the majority of us have joined to do," Mrs. Allen explained.

An elegantly dressed and, until now, silent member of the group added her voice to the discussion. "Mrs. Allen, we need to make clear to Mrs. Humphreys that we respect her right to share her opinion on the vote, but most of us, if not all of us, are against it. We have tried to be polite, but I must say with my full force that to give women the vote would destroy the family and our esteemed place within it. We all have some influence over our men—that is known. To sully our virtue by entering into the political fray is not something we desire. So for us, Mrs. Humphreys, we plead with you to keep up whatever misguided interest you have in the matter, but leave *this* time open for discussion of the Indian question and the Indian question only."

Mrs. Humphreys pulled back her head proudly. Katherine wondered how she kept it up on her thin neck. "Well, Mrs. Lamont, if that is how an older and more experienced member of this society is treated then I shall have to think twice before returning."

"Maybe it's time to move along to the true order of business," Mrs. Allen said as she turned to Katherine with a gentle smile. Katherine froze under the heavy gazes of the outspoken women. "First I might say, Mrs. Weldon, that you are wearing a gorgeous hat."

Katherine pulled it from her head, pins flying and stabbing her scalp in the process. "Oh, it belongs to Margaret—I mean Mrs. Crenshaw."

Margaret gazed at her with pained expression.

Mrs. Allen picked up one of the fallen hatpins and returned it to Katherine. "Yes, well, moving along, I wish you would tell us a little about your travels and your insights."

"I, I'm not sure that I can really speak insightfully on ..."

Margaret elbowed her with force, and Katherine started again. "When my husband was promoted to lieutenant, he was ordered to Arizona at Camp Grant, and I went out with him, and with our children."

"Margaret had mentioned that your husband is half-Indian himself—how has that affected his soldiering?" asked Mrs. Lamont. "Is he an Indian scout?"

"The lieutenant is a regular in the United States Army and has been for most of his adult life," Katherine replied shakily.

"So, he's been to West Point then?" Mrs. Lamont continued.

"No, he hasn't been to West Point, but pardon me for saying so—I was under the impression that I was brought here tonight to discuss Indians, not my husband."

"I meant no offense. You may recall that we attended school together briefly, Katherine. I only asked because your husband's blood is related to the Indian story," Mrs. Lamont replied sweetly.

"I don't remember you, Mrs. Lamont, I'm embarrassed to say. Forgive me. My husband is also of British descent."

"Trinidad?" Mrs. Lamont said with arched brows and a serene smile.

"No, England."

"Your curiosity and intelligence are great, Mrs. Lamont, but my friend should be allowed to speak unimpeded. I promised her a gentle crowd," Margaret stated firmly.

Mrs. Lamont smiled. "I'm sorry, Katherine, if I intimidated you in any way. I'm very interested in your remarks and remember you as the cleverest girl of our class before you gave it up."

"Don't listen to her," Margaret said. "The rest of us want to hear you."

Katherine swallowed and went ahead. "Arizona is unlike any place I could have imagined. It's more beautiful and captivating—its flowers and flocks of the tiniest shimmering hummingbirds ... and there's forests of pine in Prescott and pink canyons and at noon a white-hot sky. It's so arid and bleak, yet Lieutenant Weldon in a two-days' march reached snow-covered heights and peered out over the desert below. It's too harsh and rugged for most people, but like the plants and animals there, the Apache people seem well adapted to the climate."

"Are you saying the Apache people are animals?" Mrs. Humphreys asked.

"Well, no, not exactly. I mean it only in the sense that we're all animals suited ..."

"From what I hear the word animal would best describe the soldier," Mrs. Lamont added.

"The soldiers are asked to do all that we bid them to do but wouldn't have the courage to do ourselves!" Katherine replied.

"What about the reports that the Indians are starved as our government debates appropriations, and the military officers hoard the food for themselves?" Mrs. Lamont said as she stirred her tea.

"The government could be equally accused of starving out its soldiers," Katherine said.

"You don't look starved," Mrs. Lamont pointed out.

"I've been back a while." Self-hatred coursed through Katherine's veins.

"Our concern," Mrs. Allen said, "is with the brutality involved in the management of the Indians. I don't like to use the word against men who so valiantly fought to free the slaves, but some say the army is on an active mission to exterminate the Indian."

Katherine sighed, unsure that the subtle nuances of the army's work could be conveyed to a group of women who spent more time in Europe than anywhere else except the eastern seaboard.

"And how did Lieutenant Weldon feel about Indians?"

"John didn't like them but tried to treat them fairly. Their treatment of women is barbaric. When the Indians are no longer on the loose maybe we can show them the right ways ..."

"You use the phrase 'on the loose.' Do you really mean once they are no longer free?" Mrs. Humphreys asked.

"If by free you mean free to steal, intimidate, and murder on both sides of the border then, yes, that is their ancient way of life under their definition of freedom."

"But if they don't steal, they'll starve."

"That may be true, but it's been their way long before the army or the settlers came along. Plunder is looked upon as a means for attaining personal status. But I suppose many of the miners and contractors act the same way."

"And so do you think it's possible to educate the Indians to follow the Ten Commandments?" Mrs. Humphreys inquired.

"You can get them to agree on nothing or everything—it makes little difference," Katherine replied, warming to the memories. "They don't want to see that their time of power is over, and then, of course, the army is sent to make them see that it is."

"So do you say that the Apaches are fully responsible for their fate?"

"It's hard to tread lightly in this world. The Mexicans have always fought and traded with the tribes of the southwest. Guns and stolen stock are exchanged constantly, and good Indians are given our guns which are traded to bad Indians, and then there's the settlers who fear some Indians and build lasting friendships with others ... and then, too, there are the miners and hunters and agents and missionaries—all with their bits of good and evil. It's all breathtaking and vibrant and confusing and sad at the same time ... and I don't see how a group of pampered ladies with good intentions can really do much about it all."

The room turned cold. Mrs. Allen after moment directed her attention to Reverend Clarke, a bone-faced man of about forty-five years, clean shaven and wiry. "Reverend Clarke, would you care to add anything?"

"Certainly, if I may," the reverend began, pushing his spectacles up the bridge of his small, regular nose. He turned to Katherine. "Mrs. Weldon, is it? Yes, well Mrs. Weldon presents a bleak and I might add an understandably one-sided picture of the troubles, especially where the soldiers are concerned. Nothing is impossible with God. There is no need to depend on congressional appropriations or soldiers where God is concerned."

"But without the money to pay for more soldiers or at least to compensate the Indians for what they've lost, there won't be an end to the troubles," Katherine explained.

"Mrs. Weldon, I ask that you be patient as I was with you when you spoke. I too have visited the West, and while I didn't make it down to lonesome Camp Grant I can say that our army forts, if they can really be called that, are demoralizing and in many cases flagrantly unchristian places to be. It occurs to me now that the average soldier without the settling influence of a strong church community and women is probably in more grave danger of losing his soul than the Indian."

Mrs. Lamont glanced smugly at Katherine.

"We ask these rough men to round up the innocent, uneducated children of God and wonder that Indians don't always respond to civilization except in the forms of whiskey and weapons," the reverend continued.

"I think you're wrong, sir, to blame the soldiers for the Indians' bad habits!" Katherine responded.

"As Christians it is incumbent upon us to send the proper sorts of people into the field to educate the children. All children wait to be molded. Many of the adults have been too corrupted or are too set in their ways. It sadly is too late for them, but their children can be saved. The smart chiefs already see the future and gladly send their children to our schools. They will have to be educated anyway, if they are ever let survive, and unlike my new friend, Mrs. Weldon, I think nearly all the Indians through their children can be convinced of the superiority of civilization if led to it by believers."

"You put too heavy a burden on children," Katherine said. "How will their educations affect their relationships within the tribe?"

"The children will be little emissaries sent back after their time is served at a good boarding school," the reverend said.

"My children *love* boarding school," Mrs. Lamont said. "I don't believe in letting them run around like gypsies pilfering from other people's stables."

"Mrs. Weldon, truth be told, it is a woman like you, who sees the complexities of the situation and has a heart for children, who would be best suited to teach them. Have you ever considered missionary work?"

"No."

Mrs. Lamont laughed. "Katherine, what age were you when you left school?"

Margaret huffed and stomped her foot. "Katherine Weldon was tutored at home and has more knowledge and sensitivity in her little finger than you do in your entire body!"

"Now ladies, there's no need to snipe at one another," the reverend said. "I should say not an ounce of real work would get done in politics if it were run by women—always more concerned with personal politics!"

"Reverend Clarke, it is only because we have no outlet that we turn on ourselves like caged rodents," Mrs. Humphreys said. "You can be certain of one thing—women in politics would civilize the whole art. Women's natural nurturing qualities would be brought out on a grand scale and bring more peace and civility to the world."

"Pshaw, throughout the Bible there are stories—Leah and Rachel for instance—attesting to the natural inclination of women toward profitless competition. That is one state of affairs I have little hope of changing!"

"Reverend Clarke," Mrs. Allen joined in good-naturedly, "I respectfully disagree with you. Women may quarrel excessively, but it is men who start and maintain wars."

"Except of course for Helen of Troy," the reverend kidded. "But on a more serious note, I will say that men are capable of at least debating issues civilly. Women rarely get past dragging their perceived opponents into personal mud slings where every real issue is used purely to win pin money for their personal aggrandizement."

The women did not deny it.

Mrs. Allen waddled to the floor. "I suggest we refresh ourselves with the wonderful display of delicacies donated by Mrs. Humphreys."

Margaret leaned over to Katherine. "Now you will see why we keep old Mrs. Humphreys—come along."

"Margaret, I do appreciate all you have done for me, but I really would like to leave. I don't feel comfortable here," Katherine whispered.

"Let me tell you a secret. Sometimes the best things for you aren't the most comforting. You've done a fine job tonight and don't worry about Christina Lamont. Did I tell you that her husband is the most audacious philanderer in Bergen County and maybe New York even? And look how beautiful she is even with that puss on her face! It makes me sick."

Katherine followed Margaret like a stray, hoping to be taken home while Margaret chatted about her new neighbors and her travel plans to Cortland County in New York to see some of Graham's family. Katherine had no plans, no designs, nothing to add to the light conversation. Everything about her was heavy, deep, and unsophisticated. She took up a plate to calm her nervous hands but could not eat after being teased about her size. Holding an empty plate and an untouched cup of tea, she felt utterly ridiculous. Every normal motion of her body became excruciatingly embarrassing and oafish and unbearable. With utmost concentration, she set the china down and made for the door.

Out in the safety of the unlit churchyard she took a proper breath—her seams didn't burst as she imagined they would all night. So much worry. She sighed and gazed at the sky so full of worlds, sunny spots for distant strangers ... and John had his world and Simon his, and now Eliza somewhere had hers.

"Katie! There you are. I worried you would steal my carriage or walk home in the dark. The meeting is about to start up again."

"Maggie, you should stay, but I can't. I'm tired of trying to avoid the slings and arrows. I'm tired of not being pretty or smart. I feel like a bug."

Margaret laughed and threw her arm around Katherine's shoulder. "You are not a bug! But I'll tell you what you are—you're mean and cruel—to yourself. And you're getting worse staying in your parents' house. You let everyone treat you like you're a speck in their eyes—like you are some kind of annoyance. And Katie, let me tell you that the mean people in the world love to eat your sort up because you're so easily digestible. You're a willing victim."

"That's cruel," Katherine cried. "I didn't know you thought so little of me!"

"You may get as huffed as you like, Katie, because you know I'm right. But you've gotten right comfortable where you are. I'll tell you something else—it's a sin how you waste your brains and your experience sitting around feeling sorry for yourself all the time."

"Goodnight, Margaret." Katherine stormed away, walking off for home. Soon a light surrey came up beside her.

"Mrs. Weldon? Is that you in the dark?"

Katherine recognized the reverend's voice.

"Where are you off to? May I offer you a ride home?"

"No, thank you, Reverend Clarke, I'm fine."

"Well, could you do me the favor of accepting my offer—the streets are not as safe as they once were."

She felt no fear but had the feeling this reverend would not give up, so dutifully she climbed aboard, clasped her hands, and stared ahead, grinding her teeth.

"So, Mrs. Weldon, you're just visiting the East then?"

"No, actually I'm rather at loose ends."

"Will you be going back to your husband soon?"

She glanced out of the corner of her eye, trying to get a sense of the man's intentions. "No ... my husband ... is on assignment, but I thought I'd made it plain at the meeting that I didn't want to discuss Lieutenant Weldon."

"My apologies. I'll admit that I have ulterior motives for asking."

Katherine braced herself.

"You see, Mrs. Weldon, I'm always on the lookout for women of intelligence to recruit for our missionary teaching posts."

She sighed.

"It's only the beginning for us. We really want to prepare all the tribes for the civilization that beats down their door. Usually we're sent young innocents full of mawkish sentimentalism for the natives or the overly pious types who do more harm than good. You strike me as neither, although I don't pretend to agree with all of your impressions."

"Before you go any further, Reverend Clarke, I have no interest or talent for teaching. Besides, my son is here."

"Yes, I see, but you could bring your son if you wanted to. We pay fairly well, at least better than the army. Anyway, it's only summer now, and if you change your mind we could find you a place where you'd make a real difference. Here's my card—come visit us in the city any time."

"Oh, I never visit the city, so ..." she stammered.

"Well, I hope you turn a new leaf then."

Chapter Sixty-Nine

Katherine dreaded the appointment with Reverend Clarke of the Missionary Society in a few days as she pulled her wrap closer and began her walk home from the cliffs. The long, high whistle of her father's train blew as she rounded Engle Street onto Demarest. If she hurried she could catch her father and walk him home like old times.

The station bustled with commuters and carriages everywhere. The small new birch trees lining the tracks glistened in the breeze. A familiar shout caught her attention and her stomach dropped in excitement.

"Katie! Are you blind? Over here!" Simon called.

She whirled around to find her brother pushing through the crowd to greet her.

"What a happy coincidence!" he shouted. "We met Father on the train and nearly killed him with surprise!"

She took him in her arms. "Oh, Simon, I've missed you!"

"It's bully to be home, but there's more."

She glanced around. "Where's Father?"

"Oh, the old man's over on the other side of the station minding our things and getting acquainted with Emily."

"Emily? You haven't brought ..." Katherine gasped. "Not the colonel's niece?"

"Yes, I'm afraid so. I've finally gone and married. But I know you'll grow to love her, everybody does. Don't look so shocked. Did you never think I might settle down?" His smile faded. "Katherine, what's wrong?"

"Won't Mother be upset that you didn't tell her before now?"

"Well, I hinted in my letters."

"But why didn't you write to me? Did you think I wouldn't care if my brother found someone to marry?"

"Oh, no. Don't spoil things. Now here they come." He nervously wiped her tears away and turned her to meet her father, Emily, and John Weldon.

Katherine fell into silence.

"Forgive Katherine, Emily. We've put her into shock."

Katherine saw no one but Weldon.

Emily stepped forward in a drab and careworn gown looking like all army wives of the West. The sun had matched her hair to the exact shade of sandy blond as Simon's, and she wore it pulled into an elegant braided bun that sat on top of her head. Tanned and freckled, she had grown into an unusual beauty and stood almost at Simon's height. They could easily have passed for brother and sister. "Mrs. Weldon, it's

450

so lovely to see you again." When Katherine did not respond, Emily continued uneasily. "Lieutenant Weldon has been speaking of you and especially about your son, Willy. Is he at home? We've brought some things for him—toys from St. Louis."

Katherine only glanced at Emily. "He no longer plays with toys and likes to be called William now."

"*Katie* ..." Simon said with a hurt look.

When Weldon turned his gaze away Katherine gave Simon her full attention. "I'm surprised, Simon, but I am happy for you if you're happy," she choked out.

Weldon spoke up. "Katherine and I will go get the carriage from the house."

John took her by the arm, and only when they turned out of sight of the others did she break free. The evening settled in as they passed St. Cecilia's Church. Her insides churned. John, looking more careworn than Emily's dress, brushed his long arm against hers, but she refused to take hold and could scarcely see through her burning tears, but out of the corner of her eye she watched him light a cigar. His hands trembled.

"Kate, you're ...well ...the picture of health. I'm glad you've fattened up some," Weldon stammered. "You used to get too skinny ... I mean ... I was so worried about you."

"Were you? I find that difficult to imagine," she said. "Why did you come back?"

"Well, I was given time off and where else would I go? I mean ... I wanted to visit you and ..."

"I know! You wanted to see *especially Willy*! You and Emily will be so happy."

"No, I wasn't going to say that! Of c-course I want to see Willy, but that's not it. I wanted to tell you something."

"I'm tired of your voice, John Weldon. And you ride in on Simon's coattails too! I can't believe he's married that awful girl!"

He took off his hat and smoothed his hair. He kept it shorter now and she didn't like it. "Simon is happy, Kate. He couldn't wait to come share his news."

"I don't care!" Katherine snapped. "It was a big mistake for him! I'm so disappointed. She'll never take to his ways."

"I don't know. He seems ready for a change. Besides, Emily knows army life and is well suited for it."

"I guess she's altogether perfect then."

"Katherine, no one's perfect."

"Especially not me? Is that what you're trying to say?"

"I think the opposite, but everyone disappoints *you* ..."

"Especially you, John Weldon," she cried angrily. "Now please leave me be! Take the carriage yourself."

She dragged herself heavily up the kitchen stairs then followed John with her eyes as he walked to the barn. He seemed used up and sad too. The door opened before her, and the yellow haze of the oil lamp annoyed her eyes.

"Where's your father, dear?" Sarah asked, distractedly as she lit the outdoor lamp. "Is that him in the barn? Was the train delayed? I thought I heard the whistle."

"No, Mother. There's a surprise at the station. John is here getting the carriage to bring it to you."

"John Weldon is here?" Sarah craned her neck past her daughter and waved enthusiastically as John rode out. "Shall I wake Willy?"

"No, Mother, let him sleep."

"Sometimes, Katherine, you're too unfeeling."

"I warn you, Mother, you've said enough. You'll need some extra dessert for coffee tonight."

They moved around the kitchen, gathering up the dirty dishes and pots. Katherine grabbed her apron and set to work scrubbing away her son's half-eaten supper. Only the clinking of the dishes and the crackling fire being fed one last time for the evening broke the silence of the two for a long while. Sarah put away the last of the pots and leaned against the door, squinting out into the darkness. "A nice supper ruined. William waited forever for you, but I sent him to bed for picking at his meal and being saucy. The poor thing doesn't enjoy eating alone ... oh! Is that them now?" Sarah ran out onto the kitchen porch.

Scott was grinning like a cat when he pulled the carriage to a halt.

"My heavens! Simon's here with his lovely wife!" Sarah ran down the stairs, two at a time.

Simon jumped down first and once again was smothered in kisses. "My Simon, a married man, finally!" Sarah cried.

Simon helped Emily from the carriage next. Sarah laughed and gave the girl a hearty squeeze. "Simon wrote that you were a pretty girl, but he didn't give you enough credit. What a beauty. I must confess I've known for years that you were the one by the way Simon complained about you so in his letters!"

Emily blushed and turned to Simon who kissed her and laughed. "This is my wonderfully honest mother!"

"Come along, sweetheart, you must be terrible tired after such a journey," Sarah said.

"Oh, no, Mrs. McCullough. I'm just so excited to be here."

"Please call me, Sarah, sweetie. I feel I know you already from Simon's letters, and it was so sweet of you to send along a note of your own." Sarah moved them all inside where Katherine stood sullenly drying the last dish. "What pretty handwriting you have too! I do wish you would have married here though. Our church is just finished now, not like when Katherine and John were married in the tiny chapel."

Before long Scott came in with John, who had helped put away the tack and horses. Simon and Emily held hands.

Scott looked about the quiet room. "Have I missed something?"

"No, Father," Simon said gravely. "We're just bursting with surprises tonight. Emily will have a baby in the new year."

"Simon, you do beat all! This is glorious news isn't it, Scott?" Sarah called out as she ran off to find an appropriate drink for toasting.

Scott slapped Simon on the back and laughed. "I'm so overcome with surprise and pride."

The company looked to Katherine for something. Putting down the dish in her hand, she stepped deliberately toward Simon and Emily. "I'm just overwhelmed and shocked," she began, but Simon's expression pained her. "Simon, I'm happy for you." She hugged him, and with all the politeness she could muster, she took Emily's hand and kissed it.

Drinks were offered up for the new couple. As usual Weldon looked on soberly, not quite finding a comfortable spot for himself. Sarah came up beside him and put her arm through his. "John, dear, it's so good to have you home again," she confided quietly. "But my goodness, as much as we feed you, you come back to us skin and bones. Do you ever eat?"

"I do forget at times."

"You need your wife to cook for you."

"Yes, well," Weldon's smile vanished. "Excuse me, Mrs. McCullough."

Katherine watched her husband leave the crowded kitchen for the barn. She could see the smoldering tip of his cigar as he turned behind the building.

The party moved to Scott's library after Emily expressed an interest in his collection of medical books. Sarah pulled Katherine aside.

"John is in an awful state. I'm shocked at the look of him. Whatever your troubles, Katherine, it's your Christian duty to get to the bottom of it."

"Mother, you may recall it was John who sent *me* back east. He never wants any help."

"Dear, you need to remember that men are not as easy to read as we are."

"I think they're quite easy," Katherine said.

"Well, you're overconfident then. For the life of me I can't match up the unfeel-ing man you've made John out to be with the man here tonight."

"Of course you side with him!"

"Why must it be a battle with two sides? William needs you both."

Katherine threw off her apron and turned to leave the room. "I'm tired of every-thing being about William!"

"*You* are his *mother*," Sarah whispered, "as much as you want to avoid it in your childish selfishness! This is your job. That boy who you deprive of even seeing his father tonight—for the sake of sleep! I have tried to support you, but I've watched you neglect Willy's feelings so many times. When did you become so self-centered?" Sarah gathered up the small sandwiches on their tray noisily, shaking with feeling, and pushed through to the library.

Katherine stood squarely in the center of the kitchen, unable to move as she heard the crunching underfoot of leaves and gravel on the drive. Weldon entered the room, dismayed to find himself alone with his wife.

Katherine searched for traces of the man she had loved for so long. John's eyes, once so steady, seemed diabolical to her now and repulsed her. His cheeks were canyons. His clothes hung from him in layers—more layers than most people would wear this time of year. He reminded her of the pictures of the prisoners returning at the end of the war. She shuddered. If only he'd escaped the military after the war and taken a job in the city ... but she was being dishonest with herself now. She had fallen in love with John Weldon the soldier.

"Is there something wrong?" he asked, gingerly taking a seat by the fire.

"John, you look played out."

"No, no, Kate, I'm as fine as I ever was."

"There's something strange about you tonight." She sat on the ottoman. The whites of his eyes shone yellow in the firelight. "I'm ... my mother is worried about you."

"Sarah is a sweet woman ... the best. You're lucky," he replied unsteadily. He glanced at her. "Kate, I want to tell you—no—I mean I have to tell you something."

"John, stop."

"Please, I know that you hate me for sending you home, but ..."

"Don't do this, to yourself or me—it's humiliating. We're not any good at caring for each other. If we were you wouldn't look the way you do—I wouldn't have lost the baby. Don't say you love me."

"I wasn't going to!" he said. "How would that help anything?"

"It's all for the best then," she said. "You may meet with William in the morning, and then I see no reason for you to stay—unless there's something else you need from me?"

He laughed unnervingly. "No, Katherine, not anymore. I had hoped, but no. There's nothing I want from you."

***

Katherine found her mother and William playing chess and her father asleep in the armchair where he read *The New York Telegraph* each morning. It was Saturday. Katherine had forgotten that. Lukewarm coffee sat on the stove, and unwashed china waited on the counter.

She poured herself a cup and sat down at the table. A dog barked in the distance. "I'm sorry about last night, Mother."

"Never mind."

"I don't think I've ever seen you play chess before," she said. "I didn't know you liked it."

"Well, William likes it. We play sometimes when you're out," Sarah said flatly.

"Oh." The coffee was horrible, but she drank it anyway, not knowing how to exit the room with her pride. "Has John been up?"

"I don't believe he stayed here last night, Katherine. We haven't seen him."

William turned to her with red eyes. "And why didn't you tell me Papa was here last night?"

"You were sleeping, William. I thought you would see him today."

"Well, you should have let me see him! Now I might not get to!"

The kitchen was too hot. She got up and left them to their game. In the parlor she could breathe again but still she felt how mean she had become and lay on the sofa miserably. The door suddenly opened, and she sat up, pulling her wrap around her. Weldon strode in looking cleaned up and alert. He was mild, almost timid. The kitchen door slid open, and William slunk in surveying the room warily, but his face flushed with excitement. Weldon turned and was astonished. "Willy?! Land sakes! Is that you? You're almost as tall as me!"

William stared at him, exposed and mute.

"What was I thinking to let you go?" Weldon said quietly.

Willy raced up to embrace him. Weldon kissed his son's forehead tenderly.

Katherine watched a rare smile spread across William's face as he looked to his father adoringly. She wanted to cry. Weldon handed William a haversack full of

Sioux and Cheyenne artifacts. William sorted through them hungrily for clues into his father's life over the past year.

Katherine had convinced herself that John cared little for the lost babies, but she saw him sadly eyeing the dollhouse that had never been sent to Eliza from that happy Christmas morning only a few years back. Weldon ran his fingers along the steep rooftop and then through his hair in the old way that maddened Katherine now.

"Were you too busy to write this year?" she asked.

"I was in bad shape, I guess."

"I was in bad shape, I guess, too, not that you cared."

"Kate ... I sent you away because I knew you were already beginning to hate me, and I hoped maybe with time ..."

"*Time?* For what?"

William, wide-eyed and nervous, pretended not to listen to their talk.

"I never thought ... I never thought you would really marry me," Weldon tried to start from the beginning.

"So that explains it?" she asked. "It was all a lark for you?"

"No, no ... that's not the way it was ... it's coming out wrong."

"*Everything* about you comes out wrong! And do you know what? I never minded!" she cried. "I never minded till you threw us away! But it doesn't matter now."

Weldon stepped forward.

"Just stay away from me!"

He felt sick and panicked, like a drunken sailor only just realizing he was drowning. He went to her on the sofa and grabbed and kissed her. "Please, Kate, come back with me to stay," he pleaded. Yet, he felt, for a moment, relieved when she pulled away.

"No, it's too late. I've made plans for myself ... and for William. I've accepted a teaching position at a missionary school."

"But ... you're married ... you can't ..."

"John, you might not like to know this, but no one really considers me married anymore. The reverend seems quite anxious to have me."

"And Willy—what about him?"

"I've been investigating good boarding schools."

"B-but how will we pay for ..."

"My parents will pay as they have been, for all intents and purposes—the real parents to William since we returned."

"Mother, you're so unfair to Papa!" William shouted. "He always sent money when he could! I don't want to go to boarding school! I don't want to and I won't! You want to get rid of me just like you did Eliza and Papa and the baby!"

"William Weldon, don't you ever talk like that again!" John said.

"Please, Papa," William begged. "Please, I'm sorry, but let me come with you even if Mother won't! I hate it here! *Please*!"

"William," John began, "your mother will make arrangements, and I promise to write you."

William looked up at his father with brooding eyes. "You make promises you never keep. It's not fair. Please ... I'll run away if you don't take me."

"You're right ... maybe ..." Weldon's heart raced with the wild notion that he would be able to change for William. "Yes, for you, I'll do it."

Weldon glared at Katherine.

"William cannot go with you, John. You aren't capable of caring for anyone, not even yourself."

"You're one to talk. A child should never go to boarding school! And my son isn't happy here."

Katherine laughed. "And so a year later you come to his rescue?"

William moaned and covered his face.

Scott, standing at the door, could take no more. "John Weldon, you can't take our grandson from the only home he's ever known to go on your Indian hunts. A real father wouldn't want to turn his son into a savage!"

"Mr. McCullough, William wrote to me about the thrashing you gave him."

"He needed to be civilized!"

"I have no intention of leaving William here when your prejudice against me is so strong. He won't be treated like a mongrel any longer."

"How dare you, when I've taken care of your family for years!" Scott shouted. "I love the boy!"

"Well, I hate you!" William yelled and stepped right up to his grandfather, goading him to strike out.

John pulled the boy back.

"Please, Scott," Sarah said. "That's enough."

Weldon caught Katherine's sad eyes. "Kate, I'm sorry ..."

"I don't believe you anymore."

William slipped his hand in his father's.

"William, gather up your things as best you can," Weldon said. "Run to it."

"Katherine, certainly you will not allow this?" Scott asked.

"You're not happy with me, are you William?" Katherine asked.

William stared at her with guilty wide eyes. "No."

"Get your things then."

William bolted past his grandparents and clambered up to his tiny attic room.

"Thank you, Katherine," Weldon said. "I'll wait in the yard." He couldn't look at her. He picked up his one small bag and limped to the door. Katherine knew her son would forget his coat or stockings in his excitement. She ran up the stairs as her parents looked on in disbelief.

Weldon sat smoking on the porch, wishing he had never come back at all. Seeing Katherine tore at him, and he feared he would not be able to keep Willy from harm. It had all gone so differently from the way he had hoped and imagined.

William and Katherine came out now with a few small bags and the tattered haversack John had given him years ago. William hesitated for a moment and hung close to his mother, but Katherine pushed him along placing her hands on his shoulders. "Be a good boy for Papa, Willy."

Katherine and Weldon exchanged mild glances—the fight was out of them for now. Weldon stood and picked up William's things. "Goodbye, Kate," he said as calmly as he was able.

Katherine could not find any words. John was, even now, still handsome, and her son looked the same. She hugged William, and for once he did not protest.

"Mother, I'm sorry ... I just hate it here," William sobbed.

She tried to smile and nodded. "I understand."

Weldon slowly stepped off the porch, and William trotted to his side. They all waved. Katherine choked on her emotions and held herself tightly as she watched William cling to John, occasionally looking up at him in wonder. They marched from the yard onto Tenafly Road and out of view down to the station that would carry the two of them—her life—away.

She sat on the front step still in her robe and nightgown. She was numb for minutes or hours. A hand on her shoulder returned her to consciousness. "Come inside, dear. You look a sight."

"I don't care."

"Yes, well, your father does. At least wrap up. There's a chill today," Sarah said as she pulled at Katherine, directing her to sit out of view from the street.

Katherine pulled a blanket from the chair around her and sat on the small sofa. Sarah joined her and sighed. "Maybe this is all for the best," she suggested philosophically.

"For whom?" Katherine asked, bristling beneath the blanket.

"For all of us. Maybe Willy will breathe some life back into John, and the boy has been unhappy for some time now. Now you can try your hand at teaching with no worries."

Katherine stared out to the front gate waiting, hoping to see William return to her. "This is all such a shock! Yesterday all was quiet, but now William and John ... and Simon. Now things will be so different ..." Katherine's voice trailed off.

A carriage of smartly dressed young girls from town rode by. They waved to Sarah, and she smiled and waved back. Katherine shook her head at her mother's ability to mask her feelings when acquaintances were about.

"Will Simon and ... will they stay in town or here?" Katherine asked.

Sarah hesitated, clasping her hands on her lap. "Simon spoke of taking a leave from the army and staying here in Englewood. If you don't mind, Katie, I'll let them have your room while you're away—it has the big bed; it's more comfortable. And it will save me the trouble of moving my sewing projects from Simon's old room."

"Mother, I haven't gotten the final word on the Indian school!"

"Oh, I'm sure you'll do fine," Sarah assured her almost too eagerly.

Katherine's impulse was to fight for her one bit of territory, but she was in no mood to argue. "Mother, I will take William's room for the time being."

Sarah gave her daughter a squeeze. "Now that's the old Katherine I know and love."

"I do feel old," Katherine sobbed.

"Dear, William is not dead," Sarah began, regretting her words. "He is just going on an adventure with his father. I know you'll miss him. We all will, but you'll get the break you need. You have been closed up here too long. I'll worry about you all, but your father and I have had no escape from worry even with you here."

***

It surprised Katherine how little she owned. All her personal things fit into one medium-sized carpet bag. She had only a few dresses, now that her mother had given away the ones that didn't fit or were too old-fashioned. Her most precious things had been lost on that first journey into the desert, and she'd never had the heart or funds to replace them. A few old daguerreotypes sat upon the one shelf above the wash basin, but they rightfully belonged to Simon, who had never asked for any family things. Soon he would set up a home.

Katherine placed her bag just inside the attic room door and straightened things up. Under William's small iron bed were his secret things—playing cards, a pipe with tobacco, and a small stack of letters bound with string. She left everything where it was, dusted off the windowsill, and stared out like a big bird in a small house. Simon and Emily soon came walking up the drive with jolly faces. Emily wore a turquoise porkpie hat with dainty feathers and a smart brown suit trimmed with just a bit of lace at her throat. She gazed up at Simon, who showed off his mother's gardening. Simon brought her to the yellow willow tree for privacy but did not realize the perfect view from the highest window in the house. The couple spoke to each other there for a short while before Simon kissed his wife with passion. Simon was in love with Emily and hadn't settled or been pragmatic, and Katherine was glad for him as the couple wandered back into the house. She moved from the window and climbed into bed, wondering what it would be like to share the place with them.

She heard Simon's heavy boot steps on the stairs and more distantly in the kitchen, Mother and the tinkling laughter of Emily.

"Katherine, are you up here?"

Simon's voice filled her with shame. How could she have behaved so horribly to him yesterday even if she disliked Emily?

"Yes, come in."

Simon entered, bending his head beneath the low doorway and smiled. She remembered when they used to hide in the attic as children. The room seemed expansive then, but now they hardly fit.

"I wanted to thank you for the room. You didn't have to move your things immediately though. Emily and I will visit army friends in the city and Connecticut—a honeymoon of sorts."

"Oh, it doesn't matter. I needed to do something," she said, suddenly embarrassed sitting in a tiny room, useless and alone.

Simon seemed uncomfortable too—as if he worried bad fortune would rub off on him.

"I'm sorry I didn't warn you about Emily. I know you don't like her but ..."

"No, I behaved foolishly. We're not children anymore. I wanted to keep you to myself like old times, but that's silly and unfair. You deserve a happy life. I hope Emily gives that to you." She tried to sound upbeat.

Simon's eyes twinkled, and he smiled. "Emily makes me more than happy. We've grown up together, she and I. We laugh at the same things and know the same people. And Emily's pretty, isn't she?"

Katherine burst into unexpected tears. She and Simon would never be close again. So much had already slipped away.

"Now you've done it again, Katie. Come now, don't cry," Simon coaxed uselessly.

"I'm sorry, I want to be happy for you. I do, honestly, but everyone I love has been taken from me in the last two days."

Simon sat beside his distraught sister on the little bed. "Don't worry about me. I still love you like I always did."

"No, it's different now. For all these years your successes have been mine. You have always been so generous, but now it's only right for you to share your successes with Emily."

"And you have John, Katie."

She tried to laugh but cried again. "Didn't you hear? He's taken William."

"Yes. Why did you let him do it? I wish I'd been here," Simon said. "Weldon told me he wanted to settle things with you."

"Well, we have settled things in a way ... I love him still, but ... I guess it's over between us, and William begged ... he *begged* to leave here. What could I do?"

"You should have gone with Willy," he said, worrying for William and Weldon. "Did you get a proper chance to talk to each other?"

"Yes, we talked enough. There was nothing more to be said."

Simon hesitated. "I must ask you ... what did John say to you?"

She shrugged, not wanting to relive the past day.

"Katie, people are worried about Weldon, that he's not himself—that he hasn't been himself since Eliza."

She stood, clutching her neck nervously. "I know, I know, but ... he doesn't listen to me."

"Katie, he has had problems since the war," he began.

"*Yes, I know*!" she cried. "They're his problems to sort out. I make no difference to him."

"But Willy ..."

"Willy has burned all of his bridges here, and John has a way with him."

"But Weldon is a sick man. You can see that, can't you? And not easily cured ..." He tried to tell her flat out, but she begged him to stop.

"I've sympathized with all of John's struggles as no one else has, and he has torn me to pieces. Even William no longer wants me, and I can't keep forcing my love on them only to be hurt again and again. Simon, you must understand my position. Maybe Mother is right that this is best for all of us right now." She tried to convince herself and Simon.

"But ... Weldon is sick, really, Katie."

"Yes, I know. Since the war, for as long as I've known him. He's never been right. He was always trying to convince me of it, but I wouldn't listen."

Simon was satisfied that she understood and hated lecturing her over the decision to let William go. After all, the boy was almost old enough to care for himself, and the men, though poor substitutes for family, would take good care of him if Weldon did not.

"Maybe it is for the best," Simon said, but couldn't see his sister as a teacher. He'd never had much time for them himself.

Sarah called them to supper, but Scott did not attend. The pain he felt over Willy had sent him sick to bed.

***

It took only a few weeks for the newlyweds to settle in and dominate the tone of things on Tenafly Road. Everyone seemed refreshed and excited with Simon home. Finally, Simon was becoming what Scott had wished for. He was lively still but sober and even hinted one evening that the army life was growing stale and that Emily liked Englewood. Katherine tried to like Emily but could not. She didn't like the way Emily hovered over Sarah in the kitchen—though Sarah didn't mind her friendly enthusiasm at all—and Katherine hated that Emily would never let her alone with Simon. Sarah said Emily was jealous and insecure, but Katherine found Emily imperious, greedy, and manipulative. One morning Katherine convinced Simon to go out for a ride. They snuck out before the others were awake. Katherine saddled her horse and was out in the street warming up her mount, trotting and tightly cantering him, when she spotted Emily in her nightgown on the front porch and went to her thinking there was some trouble.

"Emily, you'll freeze. What's the matter?"

The girl's face was grim and her mild eyes were dark. "Where is Simon?" Emily asked.

"He's around back, Emily. Is Simon *allowed* to ride?"

Emily's chin quivered, and for a second Katherine considered apologizing.

"He always bragged about your riding, but that must have been long ago—you're not so impressive!" Emily cried.

Katherine rolled her eyes and trotted back to the street as Simon came out of the barn and was called to the porch by his wife.

Simon jumped from his horse without minding where the animal might get off to, and Katherine was forced to round him up while Simon ran to the porch.

She watched from a distance in high annoyance as Simon on bent knee tried to console Emily. Katherine drew closer impatiently and heard snippets of their conversation as the wind carried it.

"Of course I love you best, sweet pea. I'll take you riding after the baby comes. You know I will ..."

"But I'll never ride as well as her, and she'll always hate me!" Emily sniveled.

Simon chuckled and kissed her. "Katherine doesn't hate you, silly ..."

Katherine brought the horses right up to the porch now. "Simon, shall I put the animals away?"

He hardly noticed her. "Simon?"

"Oh, yes, I'm sorry, Katherine, would you? Emily is worried about the baby and not feeling well. I must take care of my poor wifey."

She yanked his horse and her own into the barn, unsaddled them, and spent the morning cleaning the place from top to bottom until Simon came looking for her. "Katie, Mother wants you."

"Well, she'll have to wait until I'm finished here," Katherine said. "I guess I'll be late for kitchen Bible study with little miss perfect."

"Kate." He sounded different. "What if something happens because of the thing I gave her? She had pains this morning and worries. She doesn't want Mother to know the truth."

Katherine turned to Simon and saw how anxious he was. "You must tell her that pains are perfectly normal."

"I don't say the right things. I don't know what is natural and what's not. It's all quite nerve shattering."

She smiled. "Emily is lucky to have such a doting husband."

"No, I'm the lucky one," he said with a small smile. "Emily imagines you don't like her—I hope she's wrong."

She sighed. "I suppose I've held a grudge against her for too long. She loves you, and that's all that matters."

He grinned. "I knew you couldn't be so mean, sis. It's not you." He squeezed her and a small weight lifted.

"I'll talk to her if she wants me to, and I was thinking ... maybe you could let her ride Handsome in the spring when she's ready. It might give her something nice to look forward to. He's such a gentle thing and neglected."

She had never seen her brother at a loss for words and watched in shock as he wiped his eyes. "You don't know ... how your kindness comes just when we need it. She worries you think less of her ... she knows you know about everything, and I worry too."

"You need never worry again. Please, you have my word!"

"Good. Good. Your friendship means the world!"

She took him by the arm, and they entered the kitchen together. Emily gazed into the hearth, her eyes red and her skin pale. Katherine figured she was missing her mother and sister and sat beside her by the fire. "Emily, I was thinking you might like to mind Handsome for me. He's gentle like you, and you would be doing me a great favor."

Emily looked wide-eyed up at Simon, who chewed on his cigar with a smile. "Are you certain? I don't want to take things that don't belong to me," she said.

Katherine laughed. "I have to learn to share a little better. And if you ever need my advice about babies ..."

Emily jumped up and hugged her. "You were so good with Willy as a little boy, I remember! My aunt said you spoiled him, but you were the perfect mother in those days, and that boy adored you. Thank you so much! God bless you."

Katherine sighed and pulled away gently. "I suppose I should gather the last of my things for tomorrow."

Emily looked stricken. "But you will write us won't you? Simon always gets such a thrill when you write him."

Simon grinned again and shrugged at Katherine.

"Yes, I promise for once I will write more regularly to all of you," Katherine said with resolve, yet petrified to be going all on her own to do a job she had never done before.

The time passed too quickly that day, pushing her forward. She had hoped she would hear some word from William before leaving, but it was not to be so she spent the last hours of daylight folding his things and packing them in storage. She listened to Simon and Emily in her old bedroom playing and laughing like children. It reminded her of childhood and made her lonely too for John, the John of their first days. Emily had been sent to bed but hadn't been left alone one minute. Through the walls and ceiling the demure laughter of Emily mixed with Scott's gruff though friendly inquiries and Sarah's lighthearted chatter.

Katherine could stand it no longer and plodded heavily down past the room so full of bustle and cheer. Out on the front porch the evening turned grey and chilly. The dry air gave everything in that final hour before darkness a gaunt and wanting appearance. The rubbing of a creaking carriage wheel against the hard earth passed along the road and the new bell mourned the six o'clock hour at St. Cecilia's. Everything passed into darkness so quickly. She pulled her shawl tighter and lit the porch lamp. A Jersey cow cried plaintively to be milked. A lonesome whistler slunk along with his head low and his shoulders thrust against the cool wind like a bull before a billowing cape. He glanced toward the flickering lamp on the porch and waved. Katherine waved, but the man's head was back into his walk.

The door flung open, almost hitting her chair. It was Scott. "Always leaving lights on," he complained. "Oh, Katherine. I didn't see you sitting there. It's a bit chilly isn't it?"

She said nothing. He turned to move back inside, but something stopped him. Instead he opened the door a crack to pull his overcoat from the rack and joined Katherine. He had not spoken a word to her since William sauntered down the stairs with John not even bothering to say goodbye to his grandparents.

He stared out at the road, tapping his fingers against the arm of his chair. He sighed and turned to her with an appraising eye. "Ah, well," he began as if in mid-conversation, "you know it's hard to believe looking at you now that you are the same little girl who used to sit out here on a summer evening with me reading my medical and financial journals."

"I always wanted to please you, Father," she said, hoping this would be the end of the silence between them.

"It's strange that you, not Simon, always had a better grasp of my work," he said. "Look what good it did you."

She straightened in her seat. "For a moment I hoped you might say something complimentary."

"You are a mystery," he said. "I look at Emily. She is the perfect little wife for Simon—not too bright or accomplished but a good girl. I don't know that you were ever suited to marriage. Maybe that's why you picked someone like Weldon. And you are not a very able mother—William is a disaster. I should have steered you toward a life in business. A useful spinsterhood would certainly have been better than what you've done with the last ten years."

"Father, when did you grow to hate me so?" she asked as waves of familiar self-hatred buffeted her weak defenses. "These are the worst things anyone has ever said to me!"

He waved her off, shaking his head as he spoke. "I've watched you sink further and further into contemptible self-pity and weakness. You are a great disappointment to us all—the way you put so little effort into yourself and life."

"How dare you! When all you've ever done is belittle my efforts!"

"What efforts?" he challenged.

"Tomorrow I will go off to teach!" she cried.

"Great educators lead by example. What examples have you ever set? You give up on your son, your marriage, and yourself!"

"You've never given me any credit!"

"Credit for what? For marrying a fool? I would have given you some credit if you had made something of Weldon and yourself. Should I give you credit for having offspring? A cow can do that, and a cow fights harder to keep her children than you did with John!"

"You never let me believe I could do anything right on my own," she began, but he interrupted.

"And I've been proven right! You've got no fight in you and like to paint yourself as blameless, but you're just weak. It disgusts me, and I wonder sometimes where you come from."

She stood and shoved her chair away from the door. "I'm glad William is away from this ... from you. You treat everyone as your inferior, but what kind of animal crushes all it loves? You treated William like a dog, just as you have always treated me. And it's true I've acted like a ridiculous obedient groveling dog all these years. I thought you loved William too much to let your hatred for John and me spill onto him." She wanted to slap the smug look from his face. "The best decision I ever made was sending Willy away from you. By letting you abuse him I gave up my right to be considered a good mother, but you are a great disappointment as my father!"

"My money was no disappointment!" he countered, visibly hurt by her words.

"You're right. I should never have used your money. I should have worked at something, but I never would have worked in finance or medicine. I only read and studied to impress you, and now that is the last thing I care about."

Sarah pushed open the screen door. "Land sakes! You'll have the neighbors' ears ringing," she whispered.

"Our talk is over, Mother," Katherine informed her as she pushed past into the house and back to the kitchen.

"Scott, must you torture her on her last night with us? The girl has enough to worry about."

He shifted in his seat uncomfortably. "She is a spoiled and bitter woman. Someone needs to be honest with her."

"Your honesty is always so cruel!" Sarah scolded and slammed the door before he could follow.

Katherine sat before the steeping tea pot when Sarah entered the room. "Katie, don't pay any attention to your father."

"I hate him! I really hate him."

Sarah pulled a chair over to her daughter. "No you don't, dear. You're both just so much alike."

Katherine stared at her mother resentfully. "I never want to be like him."

"Well, I'm afraid you are. Both of you sit and wait for others to bring you contentment instead of finding it for yourself, and both of you feel bitter disappointment when the people you love don't live their lives the way you want them to." Sarah poured them both some tea.

Katherine said nothing.

"Scott always tells me what he wants and needs, and I give him all I can. I know what I want and I have it, and if I didn't I would get it. You expected John to bring you everything, to do everything, but he is not like me."

Katherine dropped cube after cube of sugar into her tea. "I can handle most of Father's insults, but I'm most angry over his treatment of William. I should have stopped him."

Sarah nodded in agreement. "You let your father undermine your authority with the boy, but William needed a father. You don't remember how hard Father was on Simon, but your brother was a different kind of boy. Simon never put up a fight. William is more stubborn."

"John never should have sent Willy back here after ..."

"You never should have let John send you both back. That is where you should have fought him. He never wanted you to go. That was plain when the lieutenant was here. He's lost without you. You should have all stayed together. That is what family does, and that is what you should have taught John Weldon."

"No, you weren't there. I worked harder than ever to keep things together, but John ... he was always pushing us away."

"You're right. I wasn't there, and what's done is done. But just know this: Father and I love you even if we don't understand all that you do and don't do."

"Maybe when Father sees I can do a good job at the school, he won't be so disappointed," Katherine said as Sarah checked the dough rising in a massive bowl on the counter.

Wiping her hands on her apron, Sarah turned again to her daughter. "Your father thinks you already have a child that needs you. Charity starts at home, he says. You must not live life hoping for his approval. Do not go amongst the Indians if it is just to prove something to Father."

"I'm afraid of my judgment," Katherine confessed. "It's never served me well."

Sarah stood behind her and unbraided her hair as she spoke. "I don't believe we ever get to see all sides of things, dear. Your decisions may have brought you pain, but there is no escaping that in life. I'm proud of you. When you were young, very young, you were quite adventurous. It used to make me crazy with worry, but I was happy for you. Then, after the Undercliff boy ... well, you changed, and I was grateful if you worked up the courage to leave the front porch without Simon. It saddened me because I was afraid you'd turn out just like me—afraid to leave this mile of town without your father."

"You never seemed afraid," Katherine interrupted.

"Well, I made my peace with the adventurous dreams I once had for myself."

"I don't remember having any adventurous dreams."

"Well, I decided I could surprise myself right here in my own little world, and I've been mostly happy. It's enough adventure for me now to worry about my two traveling children," Sarah said with just the faintest touch of sadness. She pulled Katherine's long hair into a bun at her neck and let it drop. "I am proud of you. This is a big challenge you've set for yourself."

"But if I hadn't failed at marriage I would never want to go off teaching. I do it not for excitement but because I have nothing else."

Sarah put her arm around Katherine's shoulders. "It still takes spunk. Your father sees your marriage as a failure, but I'm not so sure there still isn't hope."

Katherine shook her head.

"I think you've done each other some good," Sarah said.

"Only you could find a silver lining in our marriage!"

"Well, maybe that is my small talent," Sarah said. "Despite what your father says, your marriage to John *has* strengthened you. You are not forced to strike out on your own, but you do it. First with the Missionary Society meeting and now teaching. Finally you exercise that mind of yours. John always bragged how smart you were."

"So, John has prepared me to be without him then."

"I'm not willing to say that, but poor John always believed you could do anything, even save him from himself if you wanted to, but you can't." Sarah smiled at her analysis. "And that is where you disappoint him."

Katherine grew defensive. "Disappoint *him*? What do you mean?"

"John told me once that he wished you were not so perfect ... he got his wish."

"Mother!"

"He still has to learn that he must save himself a little too. You've given him the chance to take responsibility with Willy. That will be a good thing for him."

Katherine wasn't so sure, but the next day she would be all alone traveling west. She felt a pang of guilt and sadness over leaving her mother, and wrapped her arms around her. "Oh, you are the maddest woman in the world, but I don't know what I'd do without you!" she said.

"Stop it now, Katie," Sarah said with a laugh. "Go get your father for supper."

"No, I will not. I'm not finished being angry with him yet."

"Never mind then. Set the table." Sarah hung her apron and marched out for her husband. Katherine finished the table and called for Simon and Emily with the chill of the open front door at her back.

"Katherine, for God's sake will you close the door?" Simon yelled as he waited with Emily at the top of the stairs, protecting her from the cold.

Katherine felt a knot in her stomach when she heard the soft rare cry of her mother and ran onto the porch. Scott sat dead in his chair.

"It's too late—nothing can be done. He's gone from me!" Sarah whimpered.

Simon dashed out. "What's happened?"

Katherine gripped Simon's hand as he sobbed with his mother.

Chapter Seventy

Katherine cursed the garish new suit as she pulled it from her bag. Why had she chosen orange? Ignoring Sarah who had spoken against it seemed heartless and foolish now.

Katherine, the new missionary teacher, sat petrified on her cot in a closet-sized room with just enough space for the cot and a table at its side holding a candle and a Bible on top. Four pegs hung above her bed for her clothes and a tiny shelf in the corner offered space for displaying personal artifacts—not that she had brought any. She regretted not bringing a likeness of the children but knew it would depress her. The only window hung high, small, and impossible to open.

She had never dreamed of independence—had never wanted it. Every creak in the floor and every fly at the window startled and amazed her. How had she never noticed her own breathing or the sturdy sound of her footfall? She relit the candle and relived the day that had just passed.

A week late after the funeral, she had arrived sore and bruised from the rough roads and careless driving. No one helped her with her bag so she dragged it, one awkward lurch at a time, toward the only building in view from the road. Timidly, she knocked at the door, breathless and grimy.

"Mrs. Weldon, is it? I'm Superintendent Hammond. You come highly recommended, but then so do all the ladies the minister sends our way. I dare say he sends the prettiest ones to keep them from tempting him." The superintendent closed the door behind him and looked her over in a way that made her skin crawl. "Usually they're young and far too attractive for the job. It's unsettling to the older boys, and by year's end they're married off to ruffians from town. It's good to see he's finally gotten sense." Hammond beckoned her to join him on the tour.

"You'll have the fourth class instead of the first like I wrote you. Things change quickly around here sometimes. We had to do a little reshuffling. Yours is a rough bunch, but you look the type to handle it. Some children haven't come in yet and some are far older than you would expect to see in the fourth year. These are not like white children, you know. But you'll understand everything tomorrow. This class has been out a teacher since last spring."

"But why, sir?" she asked.

He did not respond. A reedy looking man with blue fingers and mouth, his skin was like milk and his eyes were almost pretty but cold grey. Hammond walked stiffly, hardly bending a joint, and only his rusty, stubborn hair could not be kept in perfect order, so like a cat he licked his hand and smoothed it back now and again. She detected only the slightest accent on the man but couldn't place it—Kentucky or Tennessee. It didn't matter. She worried over why a teacher had never been found until her.

"Mrs. Weldon, here is your classroom. We're proud of our facilities. One day we hope to expand and become exclusively a boarding school for a whole range of tribes. No more day school. Minnesota ain't much in for having this agency here long. They want the Sioux across the way west as far as they can send them, and I don't blame them after the massacre and all."

Hammond opened the door to Katherine's schoolroom. A diminutive stove stood right in the middle, and a picture of President Grant hung just over the clean blackboard. The room smelled musty, but the bright sun of late afternoon in September stirred warm memories of the little school back east she had attended briefly. She smiled and felt a small thrill of excitement, imagining little coats on the pegs at the back of the room and students at the clean board doing figures. Maybe this would be great fun. Mr. Hammond brushed past her to open her closet.

"Come, Mrs. Weldon, let me show you the agency from this window. If you stand on this stepping stool here you can see it perfectly well."

She blushed when the superintendent took her hand and led her up the little steps. She craned her neck and saw the very tops of trees and that was all.

"Be careful now, dear. Can you see?"

"Yes," she lied and turned to walk down, but Mr. Hammond pulled her just enough to throw her off balance.

He grabbed for Katherine's waist but ended with his hands a little higher. "Mrs. Weldon, do be careful next time. I won't always be here to catch you."

"I have no intention of looking for the agency again, sir."

"Very good then, ma'am. I'll take you to the fifth-year teacher to make introductions."

Across the dark hallway, Mr. Hammond knocked and entered a quiet classroom and motioned her to follow.

"Miss Boyd, here is our new fourth-year teacher, Mrs. Katherine Weldon."

A woman with hawkish eyes and thick brows looked up from the note she was writing with a sedate expression. Miss Boyd had the smallest shadow over her red mouth. Katherine felt weak and frightened and wondered what children must think when first seeing her.

"Mrs. Weldon, nice to meet you," Miss Boyd said, rising from her creaking chair. "She's safe with me, Mr. Hammond. I'm just closing shop in a minute, and I'll take her to her room if you like."

Mr. Hammond smiled, tipped his hat, and was gone.

"Please have a seat, Mrs. Weldon, while I finish up here."

"Thank you, Mrs. Boyd."

"Is there something you want to ask me, or do you stare at everyone so rudely?"

"I'm sorry. I didn't mean at all to stare ... um ... I do have a question though. Why did the last teacher leave?"

"Some just ain't meant for teaching. Miss Weeks was young, and no one had ever disliked her in her life. She thought she might make friends with her students and bought them treats from town—let them run about like animals. So a new boy comes in, is dragged in by his father, with no English between them, and he's dumped in Miss Weeks' room. She pats the boy's head, sets him in his place, and sure enough he panics. One of them boys told me later the new one thought Miss Weeks was an evil spirit cause of her real blond hair—she looked almost albino. As soon as she turns to the board the boy jumps on her back and sends her to the ground while kicking her and screaming and wailing and pulling her blond hair out in clumps the likes you've never seen. A few students tried to stop him, but most just watched on in that dumb-faced way they have. There was no way of keeping her here after that. Her neck was scratched raw, and she was all but bald on one side of her head." Miss Boyd pushed her chair in to go. "The poor little boy was just an untamed animal, filled with fear. He's in your class still, but the other children have made him see there's nothing to be afraid of. Just keep that grim look and you'll be fine, Mrs. Weldon."

Katherine spent the night imagining wild beasts tearing her apart and remembering her own less than happy experiences at school as a child. After a sleepless night she dressed. Sarah was not there to pull her in as tightly as when she had bought her new suit so it was snug. She sat at the edge of her cot like a boulder squeezed into a fine silkworm's web, feeling pinched and lonely. Miss Boyd was who she would be in twenty years, Katherine imagined, suddenly not wanting to teach at all.

The pale light of dawn made its way through the tiny window of her room. A musty smell filled the place, but it was too hot to start a fire in the stove. She counted the minutes until breakfast, though she was too upset to eat. When the bell rang, she ran out into the long hallway and stood at her door smiling at the other sleepy women passing her, but her friendly gesture slid off the women like water over grease. She swallowed hard. A cool breeze rolled in when the front door opened, and her damp spirits rose as she stepped into the open air. Minnesota was beautiful with the leaves changing. Following the others to the dining hall, she hesitated and watched where there might be a friendly place to sit. More to herself she said, "What lovely tables for breakfast!" The pink room had two tables covered in starched white cloths with delicate vases filled to bursting with autumn wildflowers.

Miss Boyd came from the kitchen and noticed her admiring the settings. "We teach the girls how to set a proper table and to cook and clean with tremendous results."

"Oh, I should sign up for that class," Katherine joked.

The woman gave her a bemused look. "Whatever do you mean? You're already signed up. Cooking is taught to the fourth and fifth year in earnest. Before that they're too young. You'll be joining me in the kitchen tomorrow at 5 a.m. sharp. Our boys work out in the field and at gardening."

Katherine's heart pounded in panic.

Miss Boyd moved a chair out for Katherine, who gratefully accepted. "I'm afraid we cooks don't get much socializing over breakfast, but just this once we'll sit with the rest of the staff."

The women introduced themselves one by one, but Katherine didn't remember a single name as they all looked the same in plain country dresses. Once they had their coffee, everyone spoke and laughed at once and lost interest in the quiet new teacher. She breathed a sigh of relief. Girls in white aprons brought steaming bowls of cereal and plates of biscuits and fruit preserves and meat. They took the dishes and brought yet more coffee. One teacher scolded a girl for dirt under her nails.

"We stress cleanliness here, Mrs. Weldon," Miss Boyd said between bites of a biscuit. The smallest bit of butter clung to her lip until she wiped it with the cloth napkin on her lap. "There ain't nothing better we can teach these girls than basic hygiene. Disease and filth run rampant among them. Have you been with Indians before this, Mrs. Weldon?"

"Yes, Apache, but ..."

"Oh, so you're acquainted with their stubborn backwardness."

"I didn't find the Apache to be that much dirtier than the average settler in the desert, and although I didn't understand them I admired certain things. For instance I was given a darling cradle box for my daughter."

"We *don't* admire Indian ways here, ma'am," another teacher cut in. "Because of the way they live at home, we're forced to deal with consumption. Have you any dealings with that?"

"Yes, I ..."

"Well, then you know it's horrendous and I dare say caused by the filth they live in."

Miss Boyd went on. "We lose a few each year to consumption and sometimes we're blamed, if you can believe it! It's a simple fact that after every vacation is when most cases come in—not to mention head lice and scrofula!"

"Scrofula?"

"Why yes, look over there—Betsey Kibbe—she's a half-breed—and she has it. It's the swelled up sore on her neck. I still say she shouldn't be on kitchen duty," Miss Boyd said. "You have two in your class, twins. The only way to tell them apart is by their necks. One has it bad on the left and the other has it on the right. I don't know what we would do if they ever got cured."

Betsey poured Katherine coffee. Her neck oozed pus and shined with mercury ointment. Katherine felt she might be sick but tried to smile when the girl smiled wanly at her. "So the children are sent to school sick?"

"Well, most board here anyhow, but yes. They come to us in all states of disrepair. Their parents know they must learn."

"Mrs. Weldon, you're lucky in a way," the other teacher at the table said. "Though your class is bad, they do speak a little English."

"One teacher, a little off to begin with," Miss Boyd said, "insisted that the children speaking Lakota were plotting to kill him. He didn't last but three months. The bigger boys teased him so. He weren't very mannish and didn't stand his ground. When he bent to pick up a note someone had written, a chair mysteriously fell on his back, and he had to be carried to the infirmary. He never could believe that it wasn't done on purpose. Seems the boys were just horse playing, and they stumbled over him. And once it was found out he kept a pistol in his desk and brandished it at times to quiet the class, well, he was sent off."

"What class did he have?" Katherine asked shakily.

"Not the fourth year, Mrs. Weldon. Don't panic just yet. Your students aren't violent—they're just cruel and ignorant."

"Oh," Katherine responded, wringing her hands on her lap.

"I wish that someone would have told you that out here we dress plain. Vanity is looked down upon."

"Miss Boyd, I'm in no mood to be lectured on about my appearance. I would think much better of you if you tried to be supportive of a jittery new staff member instead of acting like an old humbug." She gasped at her own words.

"Well," the old lady huffed, "I guess you're one of us with a mouth like that. We're all free thinkers and outspoken here. That might explain the lack of men in our lives!" She laughed. "I'm sorry—have you lost your husband recently?"

"In a way," Katherine said and took a long unsteady sip of her coffee before setting the cup on its saucer.

"Oh, I see ... well I don't have much use for men myself. I had one of my own, and he was more trouble than he was worth. We're better off without them. You'll see once you're used to it. It's a nice thing to do as you please and support yourself. We go on lovely trips and hardly cook or clean all year."

"I didn't mind the cooking or the cleaning. It was only ... being invisible."

Miss Boyd smiled. "Well, you're hardly invisible now in that suit!"

Katherine thought about having her own money and time. Maybe it would be nice. She'd get paid for doing something productive. Father would finally be proud. She choked back a sudden swell of emotion, remembering how close they'd been before John had come and ruined everything. She took the last biscuit and tried not to cry. The little bell rang again and breakfast ended. The faculty filed out.

Mr. Hammond arrived to escort her to class. "Mrs. Weldon, you're looking smart this morning. I hope you had a comfortable sleep. Were you hot?"

"I see I am overdressed, sir," she said. "I will be better prepared tomorrow."

"Yes, well, tomorrow you'll begin in the kitchen, and you wouldn't want such a bold outfit ruined. It looks to have cost a pretty penny. We try hard to teach our girls and boys modesty and frugality."

"This dress was a gift, sir! And as a military wife I can be depended upon to be modest, frugal, and as grim as you, sir!"

Mr. Hammond ran his hand over her arm. "Mrs. Weldon, your attitude is unusual for someone just come to a new job and trying to make an impression."

"My looks may not be what you expected or hoped for, Mr. Hammond. I have just enough money to go home before the bad weather, and you can wait till spring for your fourth year to be taught. It's your choice, but I will not spend my days defending my appearance any longer!" Katherine sighed. "I'm sorry, Mr. Hammond. Maybe I overreacted. I'm very nervous."

Hammond smiled as they made their way down the little school hallway. "Oh, by the by, please remember to call the children by their Christian names."

"Sir?"

"It's really quite simple. We have discovered that it's just too ridiculous for teachers to pronounce and spell some of the students' names. Oftentimes, the translation of a student's name brings embarrassment to the child, making it harder for the student and teacher to bond. Imagine the humiliation of a young girl whose name translates as 'Fat Dog' or 'Ugly Smile.'"

"I imagine that would be quite awful, but who would name their children such names in any language?"

"Well, I don't know, they're just examples, you understand. But you see the dilemma." Hammond smoothed his hair and continued. "So ... the course of action taken here is that the teacher asks the new student for his father's name, say, 'Many Eagle Feathers,' we shorten it to 'Eagle' or 'Feather'—probably 'Eagle'—it sounds better. We take the name 'Eagle' and use it as the child's last name."

Katherine giggled but realized Hammond was serious. "It seems complicated ..."

"No," Mr. Hammond said, speaking slowly, "it is simple if you concentrate very hard. May I continue?" He flicked invisible dust from her dress at the collarbone.

She folded her arms and dug her fingers into the bones of her corset, trying to control her temper.

"Very well. The next step which you might find less taxing is to give the children their Christian names."

"Christian names?"

"Yes, Mrs. Weldon. You are a Christian, are you not?"

"Yes, Mr. Hammond, I am."

"It's up to you if you will allow the children to pick from a list of names or if you will assign them their new names. They will come to you with their last names. We wouldn't expect you to translate. At the end of the first day you will send us a list of the completed names. But not to worry, by fourth year most of the children already have their names. I think only two will come to you brand new."

"You mean to say I'm responsible for naming these children? How will they be made to understand that they're given new names?"

"That too is your responsibility to sort out, but some of the older students will help you along," Hammond assured her as he made his way to the door.

"It seems so strange a responsibility—the naming of school-age children. My son would certainly put up a fuss."

"But, I'm sure, Mrs. Weldon, that your son has a Christian name already."

She took a deep breath. "Well, thank you. It just hadn't occurred to me the problems a name could cause."

Hammond opened her door for her and followed her in to wait for the arrival of the children. She noticed today that a few of the desks had symbols and letters carved into them and worried about knives. She hoped she would name the students well. Into her head came her familiar names—Scott and Sarah, William and John, Simon and Eliza, but she erased them from her mind and opened the Bible at her desk. She fingered through the stories of floods, great trials, and transformations, looking for appropriate names, and turned to the board to write them in her thin, refined style.

"Excuse me, Mrs. Weldon, let me by you to open the windows," Mr. Hammond suggested, squeezing between Katherine and the board. His chest brushed against her bodice.

Katherine's face burned, but the superintendent acted as if he took no interest, and she wondered if she was imagining his rude behavior. She had only been west with the army, where men respected officers' wives. She took her seat safely behind her desk and wrote her own names, considering how each had changed her. Katherine Francis McCullough, Katie, Kate, Katherine Weldon. As a McCullough she was part of a tribe. Katherine Weldon was aligned with a man of no tribe who set her adrift. Would her new charges drift along as she did now, belonging to no one, with meaningless names to be called by strangers who would forget them as soon as they turned their backs?

The bell rang out front, and the chatter of children filled the hall. A group lined up noisily outside her door, and Mr. Hammond directed them in. She stood at her desk leaving no opportunity for a child to get up behind her and pull her hair out. The girls filed in first, standing straight and stiff in ill-fitting homespun dresses. The boys followed with closely shorn hair cropped by a malicious barber. They all stood gaping at her. Katherine didn't smile, and neither did they.

"Class, this is your new teacher."

They continued to stare at her without a blink. Mr. Hammond scanned the room impatiently. "Well, Mrs. Weldon, good luck. Good day, children."

Still, the children stared. Mr. Hammond briskly exited, licking his hand and slicking his hair back in place. The big boys in the back mimicked him. Katherine grabbed a yardstick from the wall and smacked the boys' desks. "That will not do. You must show Mr. Hammond proper respect."

The boys snickered as she rushed to the front of the room. When she turned to face the class again many of the girls were crying. One boy with fair skin and blue eyes raised his hand in front of him so no one else would see.

"Yes, young man?"

"The girls don't like loud noises or loud teachers."

Katherine took a breath and clasped her hands. "Girls, my apologies. This is not the way I planned for our year to begin." She glanced at the fair boy shaking his head. "Young man, what is your name?"

"Alfred Campbell, ma'am."

"Alfred, what's the matter?"

"They got no English, ma'am," he said. "There's only me, I think and one other—Edna White, but she ain't come in yet."

"I was told ..." she began, but the boys in the back laughed and pointed at her, speaking in their native tongue. She looked down at her dress and more of the boys snickered.

"Alfred, what do they say?"

The boy blushed and said nothing.

"Alfred Campbell!"

"They say, ma'am," he said with his head low, "they say you look like a squash, I think. Like a pumpkin, a round pumpkin, and they don't like pumpkins."

For a second her spirits sank. She looked at her class with the girls sniffling and the boys in all states of hilarity and glanced down at her plump body and laughed. It was true. She looked like a ripe pumpkin. She walked to the board and wrote her name first and then drew an enormous pumpkin. The classroom went silent. "I am Mrs. Weldon," she said as she pointed to her name and then to the pumpkin. She ran her hands over her orange skirt and repeated the words. The girls smiled, but the boys were disappointed.

Much noise and commotion filled the day. Feet thumping and braid pulling, threats and yelps of pain conspired to demoralize the new teacher. Katherine could get none of them to utter a word of English. The girls kept their slates up to block eye contact, and the boys stared Katherine down with looks of complete idiocy. She felt in her bones it was an act for most of them but held her temper as best she could. The day went from sentences, to words, to letters pronounced or mispronounced by a few of the students while the rest of the students stared blankly. Their writing was no better, and mathematics was worse.

One boy volunteered to do a problem at the board. He sauntered up, stopped to tie his boot and grinned at the girls who looked to be keen on him. He stood at the board for what seemed like hours calculating and recalculating with his fingers and erasing and starting again. Katherine boiled but said nothing, since the boy pretended not to understand her. The classroom was abuzz with slates being scratched and little Lakota whispers. The girls remained uncomfortably erect and prim or sat grooming each other, undoing and redoing their braids.

Finally the boy finished and, with a flashy grin, faced the class. His large body hid the work. Katherine motioned for him to sit, and he played at not understanding her until he got bored and shuffled back, knocking two girls' slates to the floor and cracking one. The writing on the board was too small to read even up close. Katherine erased it and sat at her desk. She had forgotten to even ask their names and didn't care to know them now as they easily communicated in their indecipherable language like normal young people. Gone were the dumb stares as the teacher gave control of the room over to the students.

"They don't like me," she thought and felt embarrassed for caring. The fair Alfred lifted his head from his book, and their eyes met.

Katherine had been instructed to march the class out into the yard in an orderly fashion at dismissal, but when the time came everyone including the smaller girls stampeded toward the door. She stood with her arm blocking their exit. The students shied away at first, but the biggest boy pushed to the front defiantly. He towered over her and glared at her menacingly. She glared up at him though her insides quaked. "There will be two lines. Alfred will you tell them?"

Alfred looked pained and quietly spoke to them. The big boys jeered at him and all at once pushed past Katherine with the rest of the class following like sheep.

"Sorry, ma'am," said Alfred.

"No, don't be. How on earth did you end up here?" she asked.

"My father works sometimes for the agency, ma'am."

She closed the door of her classroom and followed the boy out. "Alfred, I will teach you all I know and maybe you might teach me a few Lakota words?"

Alfred agreed politely but without enthusiasm. He waved and headed off over the hill to the agency.

***

Dear Mother,

I hope your health and spirits are holding up all right. I have just completed my first three weeks of school.

You might be amused to know that the children of my class have a name for me already, and it is a quite unflattering one. It started with the orange dress I insisted on having and the way I obviously look in it. On the second day of class and on most days since the boys and girls deliver to me pumpkins of all sizes and shapes for my desk and windowsill. I do not know if most of them understand a thing I say, but some try in their own way to be kind and obedient. One of the teachers suggested that we make pumpkin pies with the gifts, and they have been a great success in the kitchen and the dining hall.

I was frightened at the prospect of cooking for the school, but it is to be my duty for the first year at least with one other teacher, Miss Boyd, and a few of the older girls here at the school who have mastered English and plan to further their studies away from their tribe. It is a reward for them as they seem to enjoy the kitchen. I have found that although my regular meals are less than inspired, my desserts are always good. Any attempt at watching one's figure here is foiled. The other teachers have warned me that any of them who have worked with Miss Boyd in the kitchen have raised a dress size and so it is true. Today I went into town and bought a plain skirt and matching top and a few work dresses that are ugly, but they are comfortable, and I do not care. It is hard for me to explain the thrill I feel to be able to do just as I like. I can spend my salary and grow fat with no one who knows how I used to be or regrets what I did not become. I will never want another man, so why should I worry and fret over a small waistline and fashionable clothes? What did any of my worries do for me in the past? Some of the women don't wear corsets here and mine is getting terribly small so I'm not sure that I will buy another.

I do not believe that I am much of a teacher. I am better in the kitchen and the garden with the boys. Maybe it is true that the apple never falls far, Mother.

Maybe Father was right. Maybe I was better suited to spinsterhood and a career.

Your loving daughter,

Katherine Weldon

***

Dear Katherine,

We have just received your note and are glad to hear that you are safe. Simon has been at wit's end, what with Emily. He has never been one to handle responsibility well, but he tries his best.

It is a wonder that you compare yourself to me. I would never forget to ask after a sister-in-law who is set to have a child. Do you think we need to hear about your new work dresses when Emily is confined to her bed and Simon *is worried for his lovely wife? It is shameful really that you did not ask after her.*

I hope you have received a word from John and William that maybe you forget to mention to us who worry for the boy.

Katherine, as your mother, I would like to remind you that selfishness is a sin and will lead you down a sorry path. Do not pretend to me who knows you that freedom is the same as reckless self-destruction. I am glad to know that you will work in the garden. There you can do some good. Remember your pumpkin patch as a child? You always did have a green thumb once you put your mind to it.

With great affection your mother,

Sarah McCullough

Katherine finished the letter written on her mother's sky-blue and expensive stationary and tore it to pieces. She fretted about her expanding size, but felt full for once after all of those lean years with John. He had been all her appetite needed, but he was gone. For someone who had always been so light this soft armor was a strange thing. She was uncomfortable with fast walking, or leaping the steps, or climbing into a carriage now, but these were little things in comparison to the acceptance she gained among her peers. They loved her baking and sought out her quiet conversation. They asked for her opinions and invited her shopping. She put the scraps of the letter into her tiny stove and reached for the package with John's messy scrawl over it. She didn't want to know how they were doing.

Dear Katherine,

I am writing to thank you for allowing Willy to stay with me. He has done me a world of good. I miss having a family, but it is good to have a part of it. I understand why you could not come with me after the way I treated you when Eliza died, so I doubly appreciate your generosity with William.

Taking a teaching position is a noble thing to do. It is only fair that I offer you the chance for a divorce when you are ready, but until that day I will continue to send you my funds (except for as much as is needed to help William along here).

Enclosed is a small Derringer. A strange gift I am sure you think, but I would be much relieved to think that you keep it with you on your travels.

Love,

John Weldon

***

Dear John,

Thank you from the bottom of my heart for the weapon, which I may just use to put myself out of my misery! You have taken everything from me including my son and now you want to pay me for a divorce? I do not need a cent of your money. Please keep it!

You sign your letter with love? What a strong word you use to hurt me! I am homeless except for a cot, childless and utterly alone. I am a horrible teacher so I do no better taking care of children than I did you, although with you I tried with all of my heart and soul! Maybe you can wait for a divorce until I settle into my work or you can hope I put a bullet through my head.

Your wife for the time being,

Katherine

Chapter Seventy-One

On her way to breakfast across the yard one blustery morning, Katherine jumped at the sound of her name.

Alfred Campbell and his parents stood beside the only large tree for miles.

"Alfred, good morning to you," she said, trying to convey confidence and command as she strode up. "Good morning," she said to the adults.

The adults greeted her politely but with no friendliness. Alfred's father had rough good looks and blond hair but made no eye contact and seemed ill at ease, pained even. The boy's mother was Indian and unusually sophisticated. Katherine felt clumsy and grotesque beside them as Alfred's mother extended her hand and spoke. "Mrs. Weldon, I am Rachel Campbell and this is my husband Stephen Campbell."

"I'm pleased to meet you both. Alfred is a lovely boy."

"Yes, he is ... but we want more for Alfred than condescension and false promises from his teacher," Rachel said.

"I beg your pardon?"

Mr. Campbell cleared his throat. "Our boy tells us there's no learnin' being done in your class and that you promised it to him in particular."

"Mr. and Mrs. Campbell, I'm ashamed to say your son is right about everything."

"Well, of course he is," Mrs. Campbell said. "We've brought Alfie up to have good Christian values."

"It's what makes this country sound," her husband added.

Katherine almost allowed herself to use Eliza's death as a tool to gain sympathy but cursed herself for even thinking it. "Mr. and Mrs. Campbell, I'm afraid I've been distracted at my work and have made promises to your son which I've unfairly failed to keep. There's no excuse. This is the first time I've been on my own and in class most of the children have no English so ..."

"Well, that's no reason to penalize Alfred."

"I know. It's just been a little overwhelming."

"Have you ever taught before?"

"No."

"Have you any children?"

"Yes, two ... I mean only one now."

"Whatever gave you the idea you could teach then?" asked Mrs. Campbell, flashing her husband a frustrated glance.

"I don't know. I suppose I wanted to be of some help."

"Mrs. Weldon, I'm a graduate of the Cherokee Female Seminary, and I can tell you that letting your class cling to the old ways and behave like savages is no help, and you should go home now if that's your plan."

"I don't mean to be rude, and I take full responsibility for my faults, but may I ask why you don't teach your son at home?"

The couple looked at each other and laughed.

"Mrs. Campbell has enough trouble keeping me and our seven other children happy."

"It's no trouble at all," Mrs. Campbell said to her husband. "But it is time consuming, and I prepare them as best I can for learning, but Alfred is a shy boy and needs to get used to being with others."

Katherine had hardly noted how the other boys ostracized Alfred. She realized that it was more than being half-breed. Alfred was Cherokee. Now Katherine understood why he shied away from teaching her Lakota.

"We don't believe in violence, Mrs. Weldon," Mr. Campbell said.

"I've never struck your child or any other for that matter," Katherine said.

"Alfie, tell your teacher ... go on."

The boy kept his eyes and his voice low and shrunk with each word. "Over the hill the boys throttle me, ma'am."

"Which ones?" she asked. "It's all right. I won't tell anyone you told me."

"It's Joe Fox and Dan Wolf."

"But they're so quiet and little."

Alfred's face went red with shame.

"They have it in for our son, ma'am, and we want something done about it."

"Alfred, you'll have to stand up to these boys," Katherine counseled.

"We don't believe in violence," Mr. Campbell said again. "We want you to talk to these boys and explain that what they're doing is wrong."

"But ... well, they have no English," Katherine said, knowing that a talk from her would make it worse for Alfred.

"Some of them are tricking you," Mrs. Campbell said. "They have English enough. They seem to know enough words at the agency to get what they want. And they know how to get out of work. This is why they dislike Alfie. He tries and makes their lazy, backward ways look bad."

Mr. Campbell laughed uncomfortably. "You see, I married a thoroughly modern Indian girl."

"Only a fool wouldn't want their children to be prepared for the real world," Mrs. Campbell said, folding her arms with an imperious air. "It's all well and good to make children feel nice about their culture if that's what you like, but in the end you must choose to take on life or sit in the poverty of your memories most of which are only half truths anyway."

"Mr. and Mrs. Campbell, I will fully understand if you make a complaint against me to Mr. Hammond, but I hope you'll give me one more chance to do the right thing for my son ... I mean your son."

Mrs. Campbell smiled primly. Mr. Campbell nodded

"Thank you both for coming," Katherine said. "I needed a jolt of reality, and you have given it to me. I promise you won't be disappointed. I will do all I can for Alfred."

Alfred followed his parents to the top of the hill and waved them off after his elegant mother kissed him. The boy pulled a book from his bag and sat beneath the tree as the sun lit the cold day, and Katherine rushed off to kitchen duties.

***

She opened her classroom door, surprised to find Mr. Hammond already there. He gave the class a severe look and ushered her into the hallway. "Mrs. Weldon, good morning. There's been an incident in the boys' dormitory. I'll be with your class today for about the next hour. You'll be sent for when I'm through. Miss Boyd mentioned that you would like to get a sense of her teaching methods—you may sit in with her."

Katherine looked past him at the boys teasing the girls. "Was anyone hurt?"

"No, not really," Hammond said with a resigned laugh. "I'll explain later, but boys will be boys."

She turned to go.

"Mrs. Weldon," the superintendent said, moving to take hold of her arm, but brushing his fingers lightly over her bodice. "I've been meaning to ask you. Is there a reason for these pumpkins? We don't want to attract rodents."

Her face went hot. "Sir, I'm embarrassed to say ... it's a name they've given me. I suppose keeping me so well fed here hasn't helped matters."

Mr. Hammond smiled and took off his spectacles to wipe a smudge. "Mrs. Weldon, some men admire a girl with your figure. I didn't notice at first, but you're pretty when you smile."

"Mr. Hammond, I ..."

"You had better get to Miss Boyd's class. That's what we pay you for."

Katherine turned again to go but not before Mr. Hammond's hand ran down her back. She almost forgot where she was and had to backtrack to Miss Boyd's room. She smoothed her hair and walked in without knocking. Miss Boyd stopped mid-sentence, and Katherine at the last second knocked, red-faced and flustered. "Mr. Hammond sent me."

"Yes, he said he would," Miss Boyd answered in her severe classroom voice. "Please class, you are to stand and greet all adult visitors."

"Good morning, Mrs. Weldon, and God bless you."

She scanned the room for a place to sit and spotted space on the last bench in the room next to the older boys. She walked back with all eyes on her and sat quietly with her hands clasped. There were whispers. "Pumpkin lady ... the fat little pumpkin—squash!"

Miss Boyd pounded a wooden mallet against her desk. Katherine sat straight up in surprise. An unopened Bible and a small empty vase adorned the desk. Not once for the entire morning until the bell rang for lunch did Miss Boyd move from her seat. All morning the students hardly listened. Miss Boyd didn't seem to care. With acute shame, Katherine figured this was probably how Alfred saw her class. At least Miss Boyd went through the motions of teaching.

"Open your geography primers, class." Miss Boyd held one of the books up over her head. A few students opened their books, but no two were on the same page. A girl flipped through hers dutifully but seemed confused. She turned to Katherine with a proud expression and waved as if it were highly commendable to have opened the correct book. The other girls stared out the window.

From her seat, Miss Boyd stretched to write page 131 on the board. A few children opened to that page. Some others took their cues from the quicker ones when Miss Boyd wasn't watching. A few of the serious students were constantly tormented by the others who teased or threatened them in Lakota.

"Now, Adam, please read for the class," Miss Boyd ordered.

All eyes turned to a gangly boy with red sore eyes and a sunken face scarred with an old case of smallpox. Adam stood but obviously did not want to.

"Start with being remote ... What does remote mean, class?"

No one responded.

"Begin, Adam."

"Be-eing re—mote ..."

"Louder, Adam, please."

"Be-eing re—mote ..."

"Okay, that's enough. Take your seat."

Adam sat and put his head down.

"Miss Sheila, please stand. Turn the page, dear ...*You are on the wrong page ...*"

"Oh." Sheila looked back embarrassed, but Katherine smiled in encouragement.

"Being re—mote ..."

Miss Boyd sighed and tapped her pencil.

"... remote from the sea, Tennessee is not exposed to sudden changes of temperature. The winters are mild, and it has been observed that the season of vegetation lasts three months longer here than in Maine. The climate of East Tennessee is considered one of the most desirable in North America. The mountains of Tennessee contain a great number of caverns. But few of them have been explored and little more is known of them. Among the Enchanted Mountains ..."

"Sheila tell us what enchanted means."

"Um ... spirits ... magic ..."

"No, Sheila. There is only one spirit. The Holy Spirit. All others are humbug, and it's a sin to worship any but the one true God. Magic is evil, and you will burn forever in the pits of Hell if you take part ..."

"Miss Boyd, what's a humbug? Do they live in Tennessee in caves?"

"Are they magic?"

A girl wailed. "I saw magic once! I don't want to burn forever!"

The boys laughed and Miss Boyd scolded her. "God will understand that it's not your fault, but your tribe's, that you have taken part in bad ceremonies. Just don't do it again."

The girl stared longingly out the window toward home.

"*Sheila*, please continue ..."

"Among the Enchanted Mountains, a name given to several spurs of the Cumberland ridge, are some very singular footprints marked in the solid limestone rock. These are tracks of men, horses, and other animals as fresh as if made yesterday. On the shore of the Mississippi is a similar impression of two human feet in a mass of solid limestone. The tracks of human beings have uniformly six toes on each foot. Walls of faced stone and even walled wells have been found in many places undoubtedly the work of a remote generation. The description of the curiosities of Tennessee would fill a large volume."

"Class, how many toes do we have?"

Another girl excitedly raised her hand.

"Yes, Dora?"

"Six toes! We've got six!"

The class laughed, and as she sat down the girls around her poked and punched her, once again teasing in Lakota. In English they sang, "Dora's got six toes!"

"No, Dora, we have five toes on each foot. That's what makes Tennessee so interesting," Miss Boyd explained.

She ordered the books shut, and the students took their slates out for figuring math problems she dictated. When a student finished the problem he held up his slate and Miss Boyd indicated whether the answer was correct or not, but nothing more. She finally stood.

"Now, let's bow our heads, like this ... in prayer ... *Dora,* bow your head."

The class waited.

Miss Boyd sighed and looked to heaven or the ceiling and then lowered her head heavily. "Dear Almighty Father in heaven, thank you for providing us with this lovely school. Help our children to understand that while they may not be good at much, you love them. Teach them to work hard and not complain and to have clean thoughts and to never lie or steal or join in magic. Thank you for our daily bread ... Amen."

The children lined up in silence before Miss Boyd's stern face. Katherine tried to walk out too.

"Mrs. Weldon, wait for me. I'll walk with you to dinner."

"Oh, Miss Boyd, it's such a fine day I thought I might walk about and skip dinner."

"It's ghastly out and cold. Are you ill, my dear?"

"No, it's just being stuck indoors all morning."

"So I gather you were none too impressed with my class."

"I don't know what to say." Katherine stalled for time. It was snowing in the yard.

"Oh, I know. I was shocked at first by their stupidity, but now I'm used to it, and really they make me laugh at times."

"Do you really think the likes of Dora and Sheila are inherently stupid? I mean, English *is* their second language, and they speak it fairly well."

"Yes, they're nice little girls, and they'll make fine domestics someday. Their accents and their looks, though, might keep them closer to home."

"It seems such a shame for them to go untaught."

Miss Boyd stopped in her tracks. "Mrs. Weldon, I hope you ain't saying that I don't try my hardest to teach them!"

"No, I only mean that we might underestimate their abilities," Katherine suggested as they walked across the yard.

"My dear, I think you're naive. You don't see the pull of the old ways."

"Alfred, Adam, Sheila ... they don't seem one bit uncivilized ... I bet ..." Katherine began.

"We don't go in for betting ... and Adam? What about him?" Miss Boyd asked.

"The boy is terribly shy, but I noticed he worked hard at his seat and got all the math right—and fast too."

"The boy's as ugly as a rat."

"*So?*"

"*So*, he won't go far, looking as he does, and besides he's too awkward. Adam's best suited to an industrial or farming job."

"Well, I think if he's smart he should be encouraged."

"I'd like to see how different you are with your class!" Miss Boyd said. "Mark my words. Them children won't fit in anywhere one day. That Sheila brags she's forgotten Lakota. How will she ever speak with her mother if she goes off teaching somewhere?"

"But it's for the best if she knows English and does the civilized things," Katherine said.

"Do you think it would be best for you to never communicate with your family again?"

"Sometimes," Katherine said with a wry smile.

"Don't be silly. *My* goals are simple—get them some English, a little math, and make them ready to be employed out. If it takes all year I won't leave even one child behind."

"But ..." Katherine hesitated, "What about the bright ones? It seems a shame for them."

"There's none that bright. You see how dumb they are at simple geography—they have no idea of the world."

"I had difficulty following that lesson."

Miss Boyd glared at her. "Well, maybe you shouldn't be teaching then."

"Miss Boyd, I didn't mean ..." Just then she spotted Mr. Hammond hurrying toward them. "Merciful heavens!" She tried to hide behind her friend.

The old lady pulled herself free in bewildered aggravation.

"Ladies, good afternoon."

Miss Boyd greeted the superintendent, but Katherine stood aloof.

"Mrs. Weldon? Mrs. Weldon, you might like to know why I took your class. Mrs. Weldon ..."

"I'm sorry ... I ..."

"By jinx, I forgot to give you these from my last trip into town. Letters from secret admirers, I suppose."

She took the two letters and slipped them into her pocket.

Miss Boyd was curious. "So why did you take the fourth class?"

"Well, it's funny in a way. I decided last night, because, as you know, the third-year boys like their three-day weekends and try to escape every Thursday night, that I would lock them in for once with a new lock I purchased in town. I had the best sleep, let me tell you, with dreams—the women here were in one—but that's all I'll say."

Miss Boyd giggled.

"Well, it was that luckless fourth-year boy—Alfred Campbell that started it all. He was slinking about early this morning, and I sent him with the key to let out the little ruffians. Seems they took out all their frustration on him. A good lot of the fourth graders joined in the commotion when they heard the ruckus. Yes, it seems that in my enthusiasm for the new lock I forgot to provide bed pans, and I guess something in the supper you prepared last evening didn't sit well with them—though I ate a second helping myself, Mrs. Weldon, and feel fit as a fiddle. Anyway, the boys, well, they did what they could out the window, but the rest, the solids, if you understand ..."

"*We understand*!" Miss Boyd said, pretending to be shocked and disgusted, but Katherine saw she enjoyed the story.

Mr. Hammond laughed. "Do you not find the story amusing, Kate?"

"No, I don't, Mr. Hammond. Even if it was an accident on your part, it's still horrible. I would understand their anger."

"Yes, but they took out their anger on Campbell. Because I sent him to do my bidding, they mistakenly thought it was yet another 'half-breed conspiracy.' Alfred was outnumbered badly, and his parents *do not believe in violence*. Before some of the more civilized older boys could stop them, he was covered in excrement and crying like a baby."

"Where is he now?!" she asked.

"Oh, I sent him over the hill and told him not to worry. It would all be forgotten by Monday."

"It won't be though," she said with emotion.

"Well, maybe not," Mr. Hammond said, "and it would be a shame to lose a student, but Alfred's not suited for here. His parents thought he'd fit in better with Indians than the whites he went to school with last. He's just too soft."

"How could you lock those boys in? And I promised Mr. and Mrs. Campbell that I would look after their son!"

Mr. Hammond looked at her in surprise. "When did you meet with the parents?"

"This morning, sir. They came to me with valid concerns."

Hammond looked at his watch and snapped it shut. "Hmmm. Well I have an errand in town that has to be seen to, but I would like to speak with you privately later today, say 5 p.m., about a few things."

"Sir, can we not finish our discussion now?"

"No, I really must run—5 p.m."

The women watched Hammond turn toward the wind and guard against losing his hat.

"Now what shall I do?" Katherine cried.

"Whatever do you mean? He only wants to know the details of your meeting, I suppose."

"Oh! I can't meet with him alone—will you come?"

Miss Boyd brushed her off. "Come now, don't be such a child. Who do you expect will be stuck doing supper alone but me?"

"Well, I won't go. I can't."

"Katherine Weldon, what's the problem?"

"I'm a married woman."

"Yes?"

"This morning, in the hallway, Mr. Hammond ... well, he was very forward and not for the first time, and he touched me!"

Miss Boyd laughed. "Oh that! He does that with all of us. Don't take it personally. It's just his way."

"He does it to you?"

"Don't act so surprised. It's insulting. There's no harm in it. I find it's nice to have a man that's close but not too close."

"Well, I don't like it a bit."

"Oh, don't be such a stick-in-the-mud. Enjoy it—it's not too often women like us get a second glance."

And then she saw them—Mrs. Campbell and Alfred riding up in a fine carriage. "This is turning into a true Jonah day!" she moaned.

"Well, I won't miss my lunch over it. Good luck. Just tell them Mr. Hammond is out and come join us."

"Mrs. Weldon!" Mrs. Campbell called as she stopped her frisky horse and jumped down athletically just as Katherine used to do. "Mrs. Weldon, here is my son for afternoon class."

"I'm surprised you brought him back after the morning he had."

"We're no quitters in our family, ma'am. I'm infuriated at you for sending him home so filthy all by himself to get laughed at by the agency hags!"

"I just found out about the whole thing a few minutes ago. Mr. Hammond took my class this morning. I was appalled and never would have sent him that way," she said with feeling. "I would have kept him home the weekend."

"Our boy is to get a proper education somehow!"

"Oh, Mrs. Campbell, I promise to keep him under my wing this afternoon. If he wants I can walk him home this evening."

Rachel gave her an odd look. "Would you do that? I don't like leaving my brood by themselves much ... it is ration day though ..."

"That's fine. I was with the Apache before this."

"The Apache?"

"Yes, my husband is in the army," she said.

"So was mine! Yes, he only gave it up three years ago—decided to see if farming would suit him, and it seems to. We're hoping to give Alfie more choices. We don't want him mixed up in the military."

"Funny enough, but I miss it now and then," Katherine mused. "I'm still proud of the men who serve ... most of them anyway."

"Of course. I was always impressed with my husband—the Major—but he's had a conversion of sorts and has renounced his old occupation. A preacher came through when we were stationed in the South and said the right things, I guess. I always thought he was a near saint, but he's a happier man now and that's all that matters. Alfie has it rough though. He tries to turn the other cheek, but it's hard for a mixed blood to find his place."

"I think my husband, Lieutenant Weldon, suffered in that way too. It's never completely left him even though he's done well for himself."

"Well, you're more interesting that I imagined, Mrs. Weldon," Mrs. Campbell said. "So you will keep your husband in mind when you see what my boy goes through and protect him."

"I promise to do better," Katherine assured her.

Rachel smiled. "Alfred, come down from the carriage."

The boy hopped down, clean but uncomfortable in what appeared to be last year's clothes. The trousers were snug and short, and his shirt was faded, patched, and well above the wrists at the sleeves. His coat hung open in the cold.

"Alfred, Mrs. Weldon will walk you home this evening."

He looked stricken.

"Alfie, don't be rude. It's for your own safety." Rachel grabbed his hand and bent to his level. "Remember, Daddy and I care for you a great deal, and we're so proud of your bravery." She gave him a quick squeeze and jumped back up into her carriage.

Alfred followed his mother with his eyes until she vanished over the hill. His hair was still wet from the quick bath he had taken.

"Come along, Alfred. You'll catch cold. We'll have some tea before class begins."

"It's okay if you don't walk me today."

"I'll walk ten paces behind you and pretend that I'm on a private errand."

He sighed in relief and followed her into the school.

Back in the classroom, Katherine stoked the fire and poured tea into banged-up tin cups.

"This weekend I'm going into town," she said. "I'll bring back the newspapers so next week we can discuss things going on away from here."

The boy nodded dutifully and sipped the tea. His nose was red.

"I'm afraid I've made terrible mistakes so far, Alfred. I had to leave school when I was young and it greatly disappointed me, but I guess coming back as a teacher I've been a little scared I might fail. You impress me. I never would have returned after what happened this morning."

Alfred stared out the window.

"My husband ... he had an Indian mother too, but not nearly as lovely as yours."

He smiled.

She put more wood into the fire. "Yes, Mr. Weldon is a lieutenant in the army."

A few whispering girls entered the room. Katherine took Alfred's cup and turned to write the date on her board. The rest of the class burst in. The boys, before arriving at their seats, knocked over most of the girls' things, pulled their braids, and made them shriek and giggle. Katherine wrote assignments on the board, and the few children who took the time to pay attention and could read English began their work. She refused to sit at her desk with the image of Miss Boyd still fresh in her mind. Walking around the four children at work, she helped only when they asked, but she passed them candy from her pocket when their work was good. They smiled and lowered their heads further into their studies. Now and then a boy or girl moved closer or peeked over a worker's shoulder until half the class scribbled roughly on their slates or sat trying to read the Bible verse of the day.

One of the big boys noticed what was happening. He tried to distract the others, but they ignored him. Katherine smiled too gleefully his way, and he found some English. "Hey you! Pumpkin!"

She ignored him, but the girls looked worried and closed their books.

"Hey pumpkin! You not teach me! Fat pumpkin!" The boy slammed his hand against the bench. "Squash!"

The boy was large but not so big that she felt truly threatened so she ignored him some more. Alfred could not. The Campbell boy's knuckles were white as he clenched his fists, but before Katherine could calm him the big boy spoke again. "Dumb white bitch only help the half-breeds!"

"Shut up!" Alfred cried and stood to face the full-blood.

"Why you smell like shit?" the boy asked.

Alfred hurled himself over the benches as the students made way. Katherine ran to them, but the fight was too out of control, and Alfred was making the most of it. She mustered a "Please stop it!"—secretly enjoying Alfred's success. Suddenly he pulled a knife from his pocket and flipped it open. The girls and boys groaned in horror and delight at the spectacle of their teacher throwing herself into the mix long enough to grab the knife. She took it by the blade and within seconds the three had a fair amount of blood on them.

She struggled to her feet out of breath. The girls raced to get a scarf hanging on its peg and wrapped their teacher's hand in bright purple wool. Alfred stayed on the floor contemplating the trouble he was in, but the big boy came right up to his teacher's side with a cup of water and a look of regret. The cut looked worse than it was, but she let the children be useful.

"Children, please, take your seats now," she said, trying with one hand to fix her hair. A usually timid girl scurried up and helped pin Katherine's braid into a loose, messy bun and then primly and proudly marched back to her seat. The class waited for Katherine to say or do something, but for a few long minutes she had no idea how to handle what had just happened and was not sure who would understand anything she might say. She scanned the class. Even the big boys were quiet and waiting.

"Well. I think we should start fresh. I don't believe that anyone would like for Mr. Hammond to find out about my hand. I take some of the blame. As a teacher I'm supposed to guide and teach you, and I haven't done that. But you also must be responsible for yourselves and your learning. Some of you can read English and

speak it. It's up to you to help those who can't. You'll need the new things to succeed in this new world. I don't care if you speak Lakota amongst yourselves, but I
expect you to read aloud in English every day, and I will *not* permit the teasing of
your classmates! If you aren't prepared to try and only work to drag your classmates
down then I'll have you removed from my class. Any mistakes made so far will be
forgiven, but from now on we'll work and support each other's efforts."

Katherine formed the students into small groups led by the best English speak-
ers and had the students practice their recitation. She pretended not to listen, dust-
ing off the windowsills and adjusting the shades. At first the students slipped back
into Lakota, but every once in a while the groups haltingly tried their English. She
furtively glanced at them and saw that it was with painful shyness they ventured into imitating the white man's words, but they were not as bad at it as they imagined
themselves to be.

Alfred had refused to sit in the group he was assigned to and kept his distance
at the far end of the bench staring at his Bible verse. Katherine came and sat beside
him. He gazed more intently into his book, but she calmly pulled it away from him.
He looked at her despairingly. "I didn't mean for you to get hurt, Mrs. Weldon."

"I should have paid more attention to how they picked on you, Alfred."

"Will you tell my folks then?"

"No, we'll keep it between us. But you must realize you had already won the
fight fair and square without the knife. I suspect you could whip most boys
here—but don't say I said so."

"So you won't tell my folks about me thrashing him?" Alfred asked with a glimmer of pride in his eyes.

"Not a word. Sometimes, no matter how you try, things can't be solved with
words."

"I know."

Classes were let out early on issue day at the agency. The boys, after working for
a while, drifted. They stared dreamily out the windows and the girls followed suit.
Katherine was curious to visit the agency "over the hill" for the first time. She waited for Alfred to finish washing the board for her and then bundled up for the cold
walk. Outside, she tried to keep ten steps behind her charge, but he kept slowing up
and waiting for her, finally letting her catch right up to him. He laughed. "I think I'd
rather walk next to you than have you following me."

She sighed.

"Mrs. Weldon ..."

"Yes."

"I want to join the army."

"Oh, well, it seems your parents are dead set against it."

"I know."

"You're still young and bright too—what about a doctor or a lawyer?"

"Nope."

Katherine thought of Willy. She wondered what he wanted to do with his life. Since Eliza's death, she never much listened to what Willy said, and now he was gone. She ran her fingers over the letter in her pocket and was glad to have something to look forward to.

The blustery morning had given way to a sunny and still afternoon, and once over the hill and as they descended into the shallow valley the air grew warmer. She had not realized how close the river was to the school. A different world existed over the small swell of land between the school and the Indian agency. As they approached the small network of buildings, she was unsettled by the lack of strong military presence she had become accustomed to in Arizona. She grabbed Alfred's hand. His family homestead lay another half mile out, but it was impossible not to be drawn in by the commotion at the agency. Throngs of Indians in a mix of modern and ancient regalia stood in groups. Children raced and screamed through and around the men and women waiting for their "presents," laughing and smoking. Two white ladies stood apart from the crowd sneeringly. Three girls still in their school dresses played crack-the-whip with loosened hair and moccasin feet. Many boys still had their thick, long hair, while others had school hair and stood aloof.

Alfred pulled her through the crowd with new confidence and brought her up against a fence where soon enough the show began. Dogs scampered everywhere, adding to Katherine's nervous excitement. A few women were stunning but looked overrun with pests. She pulled herself in as close as possible, afraid of catching something.

Suddenly a great surge from the crowd pushed Katherine up against the fence. Everyone cheered as two mounted Sioux galloped into the ring. A giant steer came rumbling out of nowhere and was immediately pounced upon by the "hunters" with arrows. The crowd roared and celebrated as two more beef steers, confused and angry, nearly trampled each other to escape, but they too were shot through. Blood spluttered everywhere as the animals struggled to keep their footing, but it was no use. The animals fell with their eyes staring out and their mouths licking the last of the air. They moved and moaned on the ground for a few moments. The people laughed and sang and frightened her, trapped among them. Women came out then into the ring and began the butchering just as they might have done on a real hunt, and the children hovered wide-eyed. The fifth quarters of the beasts were yanked from within and fought over by the children, who pulled apart the intestines and smoking hot livers.

Alfred poked her. "Look, it's Sheila!"

Katherine gasped and covered her mouth in horror. Sheila, sitting in rags, tore animal intestines open with her teeth. Blood slid over her wrists and into her sleeves as she devoured the delicacy. Katherine stared in disgust as Alfred called out to Sheila. The girl heard her school name and stopped feasting instantly. Sheila spotted Katherine and Alfred and ran off. Katherine pushed her way out of the crowd, dragging the boy behind her.

"Mrs. Weldon, are you all right?"

"No, Alfred. I've never been so revolted. Let me take you home."

They walked silently for a while.

"Mrs. Weldon, are you angry at her?"

She thought a minute. "No. I'm not exactly angry ... I'm not sure what I feel. Disappointment maybe."

"Yeah, I think we ruined her fun," he said. "There's my father up the field! Thank you, Mrs. Weldon."

She waved him off and waved to Mr. Campbell behind his team, plowing the snow into the soft earth. She remembered her letters and read William's as she made for home.

Dear Mother

Its near Christmas here and I no what I want from you. For you to never write anymore. You may hate Papa but I don't and cause of your letters you make things worse. Papa wrote you a lovely letter for Christmas but you won't never see it. Your so mean to Papa and your last letter made him awful down. After a while he took me for a walk with U.S. He's the dog Papa got me like you never wood. who he gets on with real well and he told me he never got sick of me or my sister who YOU NEVER even REMBER to talk about. We talk about her all the time how sassy she was when she did funny bad things like fill up Papa's boots with your bad soup you made. Papa likes to remember things with me. So we sometimes just sit under the stars and talk to her up there. Papa says if I want to stay I can stay forever and U.S. too. He even lets U.S. sleep at the bottom of his bed. I guess you are wrong about everything. You think school is so good. I don't even want to go to col-

lege. Papa is smart and he never tells me I have bad grammer even if I no I do.

William S. Weldon

For a moment she allowed herself a memory of the four of them, cots and cradle pulled out of their quarters with the other soldiers, hoping for some small relief from the heat of the desert. Eliza's dark curls clung to her face like hairy worms as she bounced on John's lap. William ran along with a boy visiting camp from a distant city. Her son came up breathless and parched. Willy hung over her shoulder with his wet head against hers. At the time she was irritated and almost shrugged him off but hadn't. Something told her not to. A voice seemed to let her in on the secret that this would be a moment she would recall happily down the years. The heat from William changed from an irritation to a serum, a warm flow of love between them, and she pulled him onto her lap and kissed his moist cheeks. He bent down and pulled a rag from the bowl of cool water and mopped his face, dipped the rag again and ran it along his mother's neck and stretched to reach her forehead with a smile. She squeezed him and noticed John with a look on his face, in the glorious glow of the desert sunset, so like the first happy look he had given her.

John sang a song for his Eliza:

Sittin' by the roadside on a summer's day,
Chattin' with my messmates wastin' time away ...
Goodness how delicious eatin' goober peas!"

And Eliza sang too. It was her favorite song when she was three. They laughed and finally fell off to a perfect sleep ...

What had she done to make them all go away? Snow flurried, and it was almost dark when she stepped up to Mr. Hammond's office door and knocked. She glanced over to the well-lit teachers' dormitory, thinking she might find solace in her tiny closet of a room sleeping the weekend away. Katherine was about to knock again, but Mr. Hammond appeared, fixing his collar, and she stepped in.

"Mrs. Weldon, you're late." The superintendent guided her into the musty room and showed her to a seat by the fire.

"I was down at the agency and lost track of time, sir."

"We prefer our teachers to stay where they're safe."

"My apologies. I didn't realize there was a rule."

He looked her over and sat across from her, but the chairs were close and his knees touched hers. She tried to stand. "Mr. Hammond, I'm afraid Miss Boyd waits for me in the kitchen."

He grabbed her arm almost roughly. "Miss Boyd will manage without your great talents tonight. I wanted to talk to you about this morning's breakfast. It was a great success with the children."

"I'm happy to hear it."

"Well, I'd prefer that you stick to the prescribed meals in future. Indian food is to be avoided."

"But French toast is hardly Indian food, sir."

"It's too close to that fry bread they eat. A few teachers complained—it confuses them."

"The teachers or the students?"

Mr. Hammond eyed her. "Mrs. Weldon, I like a woman with spunk."

"Is that all, Mr. Hammond?"

"May I ask you a personal question? Where is your husband, and why are you not with him?"

"My husband is ... I don't see why you need to know my personal life, Mr. Hammond," she replied and stood to go.

He shadowed her, and at the door he put his fingers to her lower back. She would never have a man's touch again and would be just like Miss Boyd.

"Mrs. Weldon, please sit back down. We must discuss the Campbell boy."

"No, I don't want to talk about him. Why do you have your hand on my backside?"

He pulled his roving hand away. "I meant nothing by it, I assure you!"

"I've heard that you like to touch all the women here at the school. Do you like to embarrass them or is it because you're unable to do anything more? You enjoy groping women, but you must be afraid of them too!" Her heart pounded. No one cared what she did, and suddenly she craved physical pleasure.

Hammond stared at her with bright eyes, his mouth open like a dog. "M-Mrs. Weldon, I don't know what you mean."

"You know exactly what I mean," she said, annoyed but excited in a way totally unlike herself. Sarah's moralizing letters were so far away. "Do you want to do more than just sneak a touch? How about a better look?" She imagined that the sight of her, the rolls of flesh hanging over her long lost ribs, her thick arms and legs, and the smooth skin stretched over her expansive middle would send him off and stop him forever from annoying and manipulating weak women with his compliments and touches.

"Mrs. Weldon ... I ..."

"Well, I guess I should go then," she said, reaching for the door.

"No, please don't! Forgive me, Mrs. Weldon ... you've just surprised me is all ...ummm ..." He looked around, ran to the window and pulled the drapery shut, then raced back to the door and locked it.

When he turned to her, she had her bodice undone and was about to unbutton her skirt.

"Oh, let me!"

She watched him with bemused indifference as he fumbled with her petticoat. It fell to the floor. She stood there in just her chemise. Hammond caught his breath. She had expected embarrassment or repulsion to eventually set in for him, but it did not. Instead the superintendent grinned like he had just discovered gold. He looked so idiotic she laughed. He kissed her. It felt nothing like John's kiss, and she was glad. This was meant to be different. She had never been so big before, and she was curious, as he seemed to be, about how this body would work. Hammond explored her and admired her for the heavy monument she had become.

Taking her down to the rug on the floor, he buried his face in her belly, kissing it. She was lost somewhere inside of this weight, but this new body gave her distance. Her last bit of tightness and control had vanished. She spread out and let the superintendent do what he wanted and watched her big thighs around him—and for a second remembered the skin-and-bones sex she had with John when they were right up against each other and their insides were so close to the surface. She could have that no longer, but this soft sex, this faraway sex, had its merits. She could not, would not get hurt. She ran her hands over her own body, not Hammond's, as he pushed inside of her. He didn't have to do much—she had never felt so good so fast.

After, the superintendent put on his spectacles. He was scrawny, and she wished he would dress. She reached for her chemise.

"Mrs. Weldon, are you cold?"

"No."

"Well, do you mind just staying as you are for a while? Ever since the day you first stopped wearing a corset—well, I've been thinking about what you were like under your clothes."

He put his trousers on and his prim little shoes. "Mrs. Weldon, I'll steal out and get us some vittles. There's wine in that closet. Help yourself."

She didn't answer him; she didn't care to say a word to him. He left with a skip in his stride, and she went for the wine. Mr. Hammond had a few of her favorite books on a shelf and a picture on his immaculate desk of a severe, gaunt-faced woman and a cross-eyed child with a large head. She put down the frame guiltily.

The superintendent came back with provisions enough for a scouting trip of four men. Katherine told herself she must stop thinking in army terms.

"Now, Mrs. Weldon, I want you to make yourself perfectly at home—do you like to read? Take a seat on the sofa, and I'll turn up the fire and make you a nice meal."

Mr. Hammond fried steak from the butchered meat sent over the hill, with potatoes. A tray of pickled vegetables and two pies—one vinegar, one pumpkin—taken from the school kitchen rounded out the feast.

She ate everything put before her, and although she wasn't the least bit hungry she swallowed piece after piece of pumpkin pie until she could scarcely move. Hammond never made comment or stopped her. Only after did she notice that he had set his small meal into little piles that were hardly eaten. She dared him to say something when she took the last slice of pie.

"You are some woman," he said with a slow shake of his head and moved around the table to kiss her neck before dragging her to the floor.

She was slow and dumb and faraway and excited, and there wasn't an hour of that weekend that didn't end the same way.

The superintendent fell asleep Sunday night after he came back from services, and Katherine finally dressed. She would have to move the button to make her skirt fit again.

Monday morning came. She pulled her biggest work dress from its hook and noticed with dismay that it was getting tight. Quickly she wrapped an apron around her, accentuating her belly, and ran out the door all the way to the kitchen huffing and puffing. As she opened the door the girls and Miss Boyd were finishing their breakfast dishes. Sheila turned away.

"Oh, I'm terribly sorry! I overslept."

Miss Boyd glared at her. "And how are you feeling?"

"Fine, just fine. I don't know what was wrong with me this weekend, but I've never been sicker."

"Yes, I came to check on you, but you didn't answer your door," the old woman said. "Do you remember that you promised to do the girls' hair for the dance? Poor Sheila and Dora came all the way back from the agency in the snow, mind you, but I guess you weren't answering the door then either. Dora tells me Sheila was really broken up about it."

"I was so ill after going to the agency," Katherine stammered. "Is she that upset over the hair?"

Sheila burst into tears. Katherine went to her. "Sheila, I'm so sorry, but we can do it next time."

The girl hid her face and shook her head. Dora came to console her, giving Katherine the evil eye. "Sheila thinks you hate her, Mrs. Weldon, for what you saw."

"What do you mean?" she began, but then remembered the agency. "Oh, no, Sheila, please don't think that. I could never hate you! I was shocked, I admit it, but I have great affection for you. You know that!" She took the girl's miserable face between her palms. "I have the highest of hopes for you and will help you in any way I can. Don't be sad."

Sheila still wouldn't look at her, and both she and Dora didn't seem to believe her.

Miss Boyd came over, wiping her doughy hands on her white apron. "We didn't see much of Mr. Hammond this weekend either. Maybe he was *under the weather* too."

Katherine poured her coffee shakily. "I don't know about him, but I was sick."

"We did see the superintendent this morning, and he seemed better than fine, right girls? Mr. Hammond told us of your desire to work as his secretary instead of helping us here."

"What? We never discussed any such thing!"

"Well, what did you *discuss* this weekend—I mean Friday?" Miss Boyd asked.

"Oh ...well ..." She was truly sick now. "We discussed fry bread."

The girls and Miss Boyd stared at her.

"Yes, Mr. Hammond was angry at me for changing breakfast and, well, that's it really."

"Katherine Weldon, that makes no sense and you know it!"

"I don't pretend to understand the man, and I intend to sort things out about the kitchen. I've grown to love this part of my day and working with all of you."

She grabbed her cloak and left them to finish their dishes. It was grey and looked like snow again, but she was hot in her clothes. Across the yard, Alfred, unbuttoned as usual in the cold, waved to her. Her stomach sank—she had promised him papers from town. She turned and made for Mr. Hammond's office. "Sir, I need to borrow two of your books this week—and the paper."

Hammond smiled. "Of course, my little dumpling."

Katherine cringed and walked in as he patted her backside.

She grabbed the books and the newspaper and turned to him. "Mr. Hammond, about the kitchen ... I enjoy my work there."

"Anyone can see that," he said.

"I'd like to stay there if I may."

"No, I think not. I don't much trust that Miss Boyd with secrets, and I'd rather you kept your distance from her." He looked her over and moved close, running his hands under her cloak. "I've given you a new job and thought you'd be pleased. It's no work at all, and we can have our fun and frolic after classes."

Katherine hadn't considered coming back to him.

"Mrs. Weldon, you enjoyed yourself, I assume."

"I think it best we don't speak of whatever this is between us. I had no intention of telling Miss Boyd a thing about us, but she's already suspicious, and I'm having misgivings about this weekend myself."

"Why? We hurt no one."

"It's me ... this isn't me."

"That's probably why you enjoy it," he said as he hiked up her skirt and thrust himself into her while she stood against the door.

She passed the day in a fog, forcing herself not to think of what she had done. But it hung like a storm cloud. She did manage her class better, and Alfred was grateful for the newspaper and the help she gave him and the others on their more difficult math. The big boys were subdued and did what was asked of them as best they could. For most of the day she let them alone in small groups and smiled as their shyness faded when they thought their teacher was occupied elsewhere. At the end of the day she read to them a book on Greek mythology, which interested them greatly, it seemed, for they kept their eyes on her and their feet still. The idea of yet another worldview delighted some and perplexed others, and still others had no idea what their teacher was saying but liked the smooth, soft voice she used. The bell rang and off the class ran out the door. She must work on that still—tomorrow. She wrapped her scarf around her neck and head and debated whether she should go back to her room or report to Mr. Hammond. During the day she him and hated everything about him, but now in the dull light of a winter evening she wanted what he could give her—that sleepy, satisfied sensation.

And so Katherine went to the superintendent night after night throughout the winter. The holidays came and went without a word from Englewood or from William ...or John. Mr. Hammond bought her a gift. She opened it, swollen and sick from the last of the pumpkin pies. A new red dress with white lace trim fell from the brown paper. It was of fine linen but not anything Katherine would have picked for herself. "Thank you, Mr. Hammond, but I'm afraid it will be too big."

"Not for long the way you eat those pies. How do you find room?"

She never listened to what the superintendent said. She didn't care for his opinions, and she would throw him away sometime soon. When a month later she struggled into the Christmas dress she despaired, imagining what her mother would say.

Miss Boyd was hurt that Katherine kept her distance now and worried over her
heavy and tired looks.

"I've never been better, Miss Boyd," Katherine lied. She was nursing a sore ankle
after slipping on the icy path and to her own great embarrassment spent her classroom hours seated behind her desk. A student rushed in from the third year. "Mrs.
Weldon, mail come through. Box for you and letters."

"Thank you, Matthew. Please take it to my room ..." she said, but the top letter
slipped. It was from John. "Go ahead. I'll keep this one. Thank you."

"Yes, ma'am."

While the students practiced their cursive writing, she fingered the envelope.
She didn't want word from John Weldon anymore, but if there was news of William
...

Dear Katherine,

*You are the only woman I have ever wanted, but no matter my intentions
I always hurt you and see that you must have your own life now. I always
knew this day would come and it's best for us to be honest.*

*We are not meant to be no matter how I wish it. I know that you will be
a wonderful teacher. Remember how you taught Willy to read on those hot
days in Arizona? I can still see you in that beautiful white dress that you always complained about, sitting in the shade with our son. I was almost jealous of him. He had such a wonderful mother. I know those days were hard
for you, but they were the very best of my life. I was so proud of my skinny
little wife and family.*

*And now we are worlds apart and it is my fault that we can never be together
again. I could never be as good and strong as you have always been so I need
to let you go though I look at your likenesses every night, but they do not compare to the real you.*

Sincere regards,

John Weldon

She folded the letter and dismissed her surprised class early. She did not rise or say goodbye. Instead she stared at her hands and her finger with her wedding ring wrapped tightly around it for a long time until there was a knock at her door. Mrs. Campbell and Alfred stepped in.

"Oh, you must be here to ask why I let them go early," Katherine said.

Mrs. Campbell carried a few books Katherine had lent to Alfred and placed them on the edge of her desk. At first she said nothing and Katherine did not look up. "Mrs. Weldon?"

"Well ... they were working hard and ..."

"Mrs. Weldon, I came to ask you for supper this weekend," Mrs. Campbell began, "but you don't seem yourself."

"I haven't been for some time," Katherine replied, and their eyes met.

"Please come for the weekend," Mrs. Campbell said. "Alfred is a changed boy ever since that afternoon you took him home. It's a miracle the way he carries himself."

"Another time, Mrs. Campbell. Thank you—it's sweet of you, but unnecessary."

"They surely give you time off, Mrs. Weldon."

"Yes but ..."

"Oh, please come," Alfred begged.

"I'll try ... but I don't want you to go to any trouble."

Mrs. Campbell leaned over and slapped Katherine's hand. "I do just hate it when people say that! Of course we'll go to trouble for you. You're special to our son and so to us."

Katherine burst into tears. "I'm sorry ..."

Mrs. Campbell sent Alfred to the sleigh and moved behind the desk. She tried to make Katherine come with her, but Katherine pulled away. "Please, I'd rather you didn't ..."

"Mrs. Weldon, why don't you come home with us tonight?" Mrs. Campbell took her hand and pulled her to her feet. "Have a nice rest away from here tonight, and we won't have time to do anything special for you so you'll have your wish."

Katherine laughed and wiped her nose. "Would it really be okay?"

"Of course! You can walk back with Alfie in the morning." Mrs. Campbell put her arm through Katherine's. "It looks like you need a break—mind you, we do have the seven other children."

They rode out to the trim little house on the Minnesota prairie in silence. The wind and the cold made it impossible to carry on conversation. Steady smoke rose from the chimney, and golden welcoming light shone from the windows. Coats and wraps lay in a pile inside the door.

"Those little ruffians are tall enough now to hang their things," Mrs. Campbell said more to herself than to Katherine as she scooped up the pile and let her guest into the warm room.

Katherine sighed at the coziness of the place filled with too much furniture, dried prairie flowers, and children's things. Mrs. Campbell pushed her in as four little girls ran up with big news of small kittens getting into a scrap. They all spoke at once and dragged her to a box at the side of the stove, where a pile of kittens with their mother slept. One girl grabbed a kitten and handed it to her.

"Oh, I don't much like cats," Katherine explained, holding the little thing at a distance.

"Well, it ain't a cat, ma'am. Only a kitten," the girl pointed out and ran off.

Mrs. Campbell was already busy with potatoes to be peeled.

"Mrs. Campbell, I can help with supper ..."

"Please, call me Rachel, and I prefer you to relax."

Katherine was in the way no matter where she stood. The crowded room served as the main eating and living area for the family. A large table with endless chairs dominated the place. "Rachel, how about dessert then ..."

"No, no—we don't go in for sweets. I want the children to have good teeth. I always had real problems with mine."

"Oh." She wondered what this tall, elegant woman must think of her. She wished she could go back to her room and sleep the rest of her days away, but then Mr. Hammond would come for her as he had lately done on the few nights she wanted to be alone.

"Mrs. Weldon, please, you look so ill at ease. Take a seat."

Katherine sighed and sat near the fire, absently petting the sleeping kitten in her arms. Soon there was a commotion at the door and the boys barreled in. They all looked the same but in various sizes. Alfred came in first, after putting the sleigh and horse away, and was the only quiet one. Mr. Campbell carried the smallest child in his arms, and the little boy sang out and hit the floor at a run to check on the kittens. The next in size tackled him, and they wrestled over an unresolved grievance from the barn. The parents ignored the two. Mr. Campbell gave his wife a peck on the cheek and turned to Katherine. "Mrs. Weldon, good to see you again. Oh, don't get up. Alfie told how you slipped on the ice. Lucky not to break anything, I'd say."

One of the small girls sat beside her. Alfred sat at the table near them and read to himself with a satisfied smile, so proud was he to have his teacher over for supper and staying the night. The little girl stared up at her. "May I sit on your lap?"

Katherine laughed. "Sure you may."

The girl took the kitten and climbed up. "How come you hate cats? They ain't scary, and they battle the mice good."

"My mother didn't like them—I guess I learned to be scared from her."

The girl patted her belly. "Are you going to make a baby?"

Rachel turned around with a pained look.

But Katherine smiled. "No, not at all."

"Then why are you so fat?"

Alfred jumped up, hissing at his sister, "Elizabeth, you're mean, and I hate you!"

"*Alfred*! Please, she's only a little thing. Go back to your book. It's all right," Katherine assured him. "Elizabeth, I eat too much."

"Oh."

"I had a little girl once too with the name Elizabeth, but we called her Eliza."

The girl gave her a strange look. "Yes, I know," she said matter-of-factly as she slid off Katherine and put the kitten in its box. Katherine stared after her with her heart racing.

"Where is Eliza now, Mrs. Weldon?" Alfred asked.

"Eliza is in heaven, I guess. She's dead."

Mr. and Mrs. Campbell stopped supper preparations. "Mrs. Weldon, I'm sorry for being so rude. Would you like some tea?" Rachel asked.

"I'm sorry about your daughter," Alfred said. "I bet that's why you always look so sad."

She leaned over and patted his hand. "You're such a kind boy. You remind me of my son, Willy."

"Is he dead too?"

"No, he's not. He prefers to be with his father." She wiped her eyes.

"Alfred, please get more wood and check on the pigs," Mr. Campbell said.

"But I already checked ..."

"Check again, sweetheart," Rachel ordered as she brought a huge pot of hot tea over and poured some out. "Forgive the children. They always say such surprising things."

Katherine wiped her face. "No, I'm just so humiliated to break down in front of strangers."

"There, there, don't be silly. I'm glad I came to school today. I hate to think of you so sad and lonely. Alfie kept taking apples and things to cheer you, so I guessed something was wrong."

"I'm afraid everything's wrong. If you only understood how bad I've become you wouldn't have me here as a guest."

Stephen Campbell turned from the fire he was stoking. "We're all sinners, Mrs. Weldon."

"With all due respect, Mr. Campbell, my sins are larger than you know, and I've never met a person who doesn't judge."

"But Mrs. Weldon, it's never too late to get back on track with God," Stephen said, taking a seat at the table.

"Oh mercy, please tell me I wasn't invited here to be converted!"

Rachel laughed and stood behind her husband with her hands on his shoulders. "No, this is how he always is."

She did not want to be drawn into this conversation, but something about the two of them compelled her. "Even as my Eliza was dying, even then, I had faith. Sometimes she said things—things she couldn't have come up with on her own. And the men ... the men in camp, they prayed for us, and I felt ... that God was taking care of me and people were too, but ..."

"Maybe God wanted you to walk alone here for a while and learn to care for yourself."

"Yes, God's deserted me and how wonderful I've done! I used to be so little," she sobbed.

"Maybe you were never as little as you imagined. Maybe God wants you to see that," Mr. Campbell said. "Why did you come out here all on your own?"

"Someone suggested it."

"But it took bravery ..."

"No, it was the easiest thing in the world. Everything was lost," she cried. "I was good—I tried very hard. I believed, and it seems so childish now, that if I tried and was very good then I could keep John forever. He was the only thing I ever wanted."

"You were more dependent on him than God."

"*Yes*! And I don't mind saying it! John made me feel ... loved, but then ... he hated me! I still don't understand! And where is God in that?"

Rachel shooed away the children gaping at their brother's teacher crying.

Mr. Campbell said, "We don't know God's plan."

"Oh! I'm so sick and tired of hearing that! I want certainty. I want someone I can love who will love me back! I don't think I'm asking too much!"

Alfred wrapped his final scarf around his neck to go out to the pigs. "Mrs. Weldon, *I* love you."

Katherine laughed and cried. "You're the only thing good to come out of this work—you and your kind family."

Rachel kissed her son and sent him off.

"You see, maybe you already have what you want," Stephen pointed out.

"It's not the same and you know it," she said. "It would be hard, I'm sure, for you two who seem so suited to understand my situation. It seems so unfair that God, if He exists, lets the two of you have everything and I have ..."

"You have decisions, Mrs. Weldon. There's power in that and God's guidance if you only ask. You can't control who on Earth will love you, but rest assured you're loved. You have children at the school—those girls in the fifth year. I've heard them on the school grounds," said Rachel.

"But I've disappointed them."

"They care for you anyway because you're honest and decent and you treat them like little girls not just Indians. Mr. Hammond says you've worked wonders with the fourth year."

"He spoke of me?"

"Yes. He said that you're passionate about your work," Rachel added.

"He's a filthy and disgusting man!" Katherine cried. "I can't stay here. I'm sorry, but I don't belong here." She raced to the door and out into the night, but Rachel followed her. The full moon lit lacy clouds as they drifted by.

Rachel pulled Katherine's cloak around her. "Mrs. Weldon, you can trust me. What are you so upset about? Maybe I can help."

"Rachel ... I'm a terrible person! No little white lies for me! I've fallen so low so quickly. I never knew that it could be possible. I used to be good, but now ..." She wiped at her eyes with the back of her hand.

Rachel took her hand firmly in her own.

"This dress, this hideous dress I'm wearing," Katherine confessed. "He bought it for me—Mr. Hammond. It's so horrible what I've become. Just a few years ago I was a normal mother and wife, and that was all I ever wanted."

Rachel sat her down on the porch bench.

"I don't know why I'm telling you this." Katherine smoothed her hair, but the wind did what it liked. "My parents always blamed me for something that happened when I was a girl. I'm not angry at them any longer, but they were wrong. I was *good*. And then I met John, and he was the only one who saw me that way, and we were happy. Once he realized I wasn't perfect he hated me. And now I'm worse than any-thing they all could have imagined."

"And now you're lying with Mr. Hammond?"

"*Yes*! And it's disgusting! I wanted to make the superintendent suffer. I wanted to embarrass him, but of course I was crazy. I thought I'd do it once, but it felt good to just give up. It felt like freedom."

"Well, this is certainly a night of surprises!" Rachel said. "Katherine, you can't rid yourself of faith and expect nothing to take its place. It's fine to try to be good on your own, but there's no strength in it. Look at the clouds. They're lovely tonight. You know Stephen has taken to quoting Scripture," she said, giving her an amused look.

Katherine smiled.

"This is one of my favorites," Rachel said. "'I have blotted out, as a thick cloud, thy transgressions, and as a cloud, thy sins: Return onto me; for I have redeemed thee.'

"We all wonder at the clouds, their changing shapes and fleeting existence, but never once has man been able to rid the sky of them. We can look and worry over them and what they mean, but only God can push them away.

"Katherine, you're forgiven already if only you ask God. You know what you must do. If the only reason you were called to come here was to say a few kind words to my son, then that is a big enough thing to me. I liked you the moment you told us that you were not doing a good job with your class. I was ready to see to it that you were fired until I met you and saw how honest you were. And you're naturally kind. I see that with the children. I'm glad I followed the voice in my head that said to give you a chance—you've changed Alfred's life. I'll help you in any way I can, but this is your life to figure out. Just remember that you're not alone up over that hill."

"That was lovely," Katherine said, sniffling. "I'll keep it in mind. I can't believe I have such a sweet person only a few miles away from me."

"I can't believe you let that greasy superintendent poke you!" Rachel whispered with a sly giggle.

Chapter Seventy-Two

Katherine listened to the soft, comforting sounds that poured through the room on a cot in the crowded kitchen by the stove. For a while the place flurried with activity until the children lost their fight with sleep. She listened to the light breathing of the eight so snugly packed into their room.

The wind rattled the modest windows, but it was a lovely thing to hear as the fire died down. She listened to Rachel and Stephen talk in low, hushed voices and muffle their laughter before joining their children in slumber. Only the smallest golden light from the fire flickered. It made the room shine like magic. She wrapped a blanket around her and sat beside the box of kittens on the floor, feeling rich and lucky to have this night so like a childhood Christmas.

When morning came she made a plain healthy breakfast and good strong coffee, proud that she could do something nice, however small, for the family. After morning chores and before they sat down to eat, Mr. Campbell read from the Bible: "'I will greatly rejoice in the Lord, my soul shall be joyful in my God; for He hath clothed me with garments of salvation, He hath covered me with the robe of righteousness.'

"Now, children, remember as we go out in this great big world that God is with us, and He gives us chances to do right—mind me, Sam—even helping in the barn instead of teasing the animals is for to teach you things He wants you to know."

One of the boys shook his head, not happy to be singled out.

"God gives us everything we need, children, and that we must be grateful for," Rachel added and passed the food.

"Excuse me all, but I need to hurry back to school this morning. I have a few things to set in order," Katherine said.

Rachel gave her a knowing and supportive glance. "You'll come back for the weekend?"

"I'll try," Katherine said, avoiding promises.

With new resolve she raced over the hill in the bracing cold. Above the low clouds she heard the crows complaining. Soon there would be more snow.

Shivering in her frigid room, she changed her underthings and put on her flannel petticoats, wool underwear, and Mr. Hammond's dress again. She sat for a second and said a tremulous little prayer. "Help me, Lord."

The girls turned from the last of the dishes when she arrived at the kitchen. "Mrs. Weldon!" Sheila came over and hugged her. "Have you come back to work with us again?"

Katherine glanced over at Miss Boyd. "I'd love to. I plan to fight for my job. I've been a fool, Miss Boyd, and I've hurt your feelings, I know."

Miss Boyd gave the girls a sickly smile. "Sheila and Dora, go bring Mr. Hammond and his wife their breakfast."

Katherine froze. The girls hesitated.

"Go, girls!" Miss Boyd shouted and turned to Katherine with a look of complete disgust. "Mrs. Weldon, you must think that I'm a blamed fool! The fact that you breeze in here so confident of getting your job back proves that my suspicions about you are true. I didn't want to believe it at first, but the dress and the never being in your room convince me you're nothing more than a common floozy. It's revolting, and to think I defended you against the early rumors. I didn't expect you'd be bought so easy ... a few meals and a dress! Look at you! This is a well-regarded place of learning, and we have a puffed-up whore in an adulterous affair! I don't want you anywhere near me, and it will be over my dead body that you'll set foot in here again."

Katherine held back her tears, but only just.

"I see you don't deny a thing. And don't cry. You embarrass yourself with this fake meek-and-mild routine. The superintendent bragged about your entertaining ways to a field hand—stupid man."

Katherine turned to leave, but the door opened and in walked Mr. and Mrs. Hammond.

"Ladies," Mrs. Hammond said. Just a little taller than Katherine, but years older and slightly hunched, Mrs. Hammond's mouth stretched across the width of her face in a straight, stiff, colorless line, sunken in where her lower teeth leaned inward. Her hair looked painted on, and her neck, the part showing over her high collar, was a mass of stringy tendons. Holding her hands in front of her like an upright squirrel, she marched in, looking around the place aggressively. Mr. Hammond dragged along a child who struggled under several physical afflictions. His eyes strayed and his mouth hung and drooled. His back curved in like a question mark and his head was far too large.

"Mr. Hammond and me, we wasn't too pleased with our food. Jay, which one of 'em is in charge?"

"I am, Mrs. Hammond," Miss Boyd said, giving Katherine a hateful look. "We've lost some kitchen help lately. Please accept my apologies."

"It don't take no kitchen help to send coffee and some hardtack. That's all we need." Mrs. Hammond was the skinniest woman they had ever seen and when she took off her cloak Katherine wanted to turn away. "Most foods is dirty. I don't care what folks reckon. If Jesus lived on bread so can we."

No one said a word.

Mrs. Hammond looked the two women over and laughed a horrible little whistling laugh as if using her last bit of lung. "Back home we all chipped in years of our money to make my cousin here something. We was told Jay was awful smart, but he always was chasin' them girls in town. I 'magine he gets injun tail out here most nights, but no matter. He never did want to go and marry me, but our daddies was preachers and they know'd it was meant to be. Jay weren't this skinny and scrawrny back home. You girls look like you make sure to get moren' your fair share—t'aint right."

The clock ticked. The boy begged through grunts and groans to be held. One eye seemed to hold the key to his soul. Katherine had a difficult time looking at him. Mr. Hammond picked up the boy with tenderness, and the boy settled down.

"Will ye wipe him up? The boy's droolin' like a dog," Mrs. Hammond said to her husband. "The boy ain't right. I felt it in my interior parts. Come out all silent like. I thought he was surprised, but he's just backward. Takes after some of them cousins—the low-down ones—right, Jay?"

"So it's hardtack you want?" Miss Boyd said. "We can get some from the agency. We don't much like that sort of thing here."

"Excuse me!" Katherine said as she pushed past them and trotted heavily down the stairs out into the open air.

"Mrs. Weldon!" Mr. Hammond called when she was halfway to the dormitory.

She quickened her step, but he soon caught up, his eyes wild with pain and passion. "Where were you last night? I have mail for you ... from town. Come with me, and I'll get it for you."

"No, Mr. Hammond, have a student bring it to me later. I have to get to class."

Recklessly the superintendent dragged her to a shed for gardening tools and pushed her inside. He pulled her braid at the nape of her neck and yanked it. "Where *were* you?"

"I-I was only at the Campbell's! What business is it of yours?"

Hammond pinched her arm hard.

"You think pinching will hurt me?" she said. "I'm done being your kept woman!"

"Kept woman?" Mr. Hammond asked with a derisive laugh. "You came along freely—I didn't have to threaten anything to get you to spread your legs!"

She made to hit him, but he took both of her arms and held her with surprising strength. "Kate ..."

"*Don't* you ever call me that!" she cried.

"Mrs. Weldon, you can't leave me! I don't want you out and about. I never want to miss a night with you. See, feel how hard ... just thinking of the way you suck the grease from your fingers. You're one big mess, and I enjoy it immensely."

"You disgust me!" she said. "I disgust myself! You have a wife and child. I used you, and I'm sorry!"

"You don't mean it!" he said as he pulled at her skirt. They toppled over, set off balance by the loose tools. She banged her head on a shovel and he Hammond cursed. "Not many men would go for a used up body like yours. Remember that. I'm different. You should be grateful!"

Her head spun. She grabbed a trowel and surprised him with the sharp blade against his cheek. "Get off of me now! I have a gun in my room, and I'll come and find you and kill you if you don't get off me!"

Hammond tried again to enter her, but she slashed him before he could grab hold of the tool, and it suddenly occurred to her that she had the weight and the strength to throw him off. It wasn't feminine or graceful, but it worked.

The superintendent rolled on to the floor in surprise. She struggled to her feet. "Mr. Hammond, if you fire me or tell a soul I'll write to your home missionary society and all others I can find to tell the world how you are. I have nothing important to lose but this job. I've lost my family and reputation already, and I've lost my self-respect."

She ran from the building and all the way to her classroom through the thickening snow. The hall was dark, and her room was unusually quiet. Maybe school had been cancelled, but she had nowhere else to go so she opened the door and was met with polite applause and Rachel Campbell. Alfred took her hand and brought her to her desk. On a teacup saucer was a tiny dainty cake and a small candle.

"Happy birthday, Mrs. Weldon," Alfred said. The class smiled and Rachel made them clap again.

Katherine stared at Rachel. "But, it's not my ..."

Rachel whispered to her, "It might be if you've done what I think you have."

Katherine nodded and embraced her. "Rachel, I don't know what will happen now."

***

"And so a noun is any person, place, or thing," Katherine explained, her soft, bored voice flowing over most of the students' heads like water over stone. She sighed. Grammar had been so easy for her as a child, but she had been reading English at four years of age and hearing it since birth. Still, she began to hate nouns, verbs, and especially adverbs. "Sam, give us an example of a noun, please."

A small boy with heavy eyelids and thick bangs stood to answer. "*Me*," he pointed to himself proudly, "am a noun."

She smiled. Close enough. "Very good."

The superintendent opened the door and strode in, silently scanning the children.

"Good morning, Superintendent Hammond. God bless you," the students said in singsong style.

The superintendent still wore a small scar on his face from the trowel she had used to fight him off with in the shed. They never spoke directly to each other again, and something changed in him after his wife went home.

"Children, you may be seated," Hammond said with his fingertips touching as he rolled one thumb over the other. This mesmerized the children. "I have a big surprise for Mrs. Weldon."

Katherine's stomach dropped. She hoped the new primers had come in, but instead she received her brother. Simon stood by the door grinning. She screamed and ran to him, laughing and crying. Some of the students stood and eventually dragged the others up. They were proud of their greeting.

"Good morning ..." They turned to each other discussing how they might address this noun before them and came upon a quick solution. "Good morning, *man*, and God bless you!"

Simon laughed. "And to you! Oh! And God bless you all." He tipped his hat.

Katherine pulled him across the floor. "Children, meet my brother, Captain Mc-Cullough."

Alfred's eyes lit in awe of the soldier, and some of the girls whispered and smiled back at him. Alfred raised his hand. "Captain McCullough, I'd like to be a soldier one day."

There was a hush then and a tension amongst the students.

"Mrs. Weldon, please take the time you need to spend with your brother. The captain tells me this is to be a short visit," Mr. Hammond said.

"But the children ..."

"Don't worry. Now run along."

Katherine waved to her students, grabbed her coat, and dragged Simon from the room, down the hallway, and out into the cool prairie spring.

"So, Katherine, what's new?"

She laughed and squeezed him again. "It's so good of you to come see me! I can always depend on you for showing up just when I need cheering!"

Simon looked her over more seriously than she liked. "Katie, you look really well. The superintendent says that you're doing a fine job. I guess they feed you enough."

She blushed. She was much closer to herself now than she had been in December, but still a bit stout. "I don't make much difference here ... but who cares now anyway? I want to hear all about you and Emily and the baby!"

Simon's face lit with pride. "I'm sorry to have not written you but ..."

"Oh, you're easily forgiven! Mother has written me plenty, but I'm so happy to be able to see you face to face. Please tell me that your health is holding up."

"Katherine, don't panic," he said, taking her hand and steering her to a bench near a small stand of cottonwoods. "We're as well as can be expected."

The siblings sat shoulder to shoulder.

"As well as can be expected sounds not as good as I've hoped. You've been receiving my letters?" she asked, wanting credit for her efforts after so many years of neglect.

"Yes, and it's meant a lot to receive them. The superintendent seems ... different to what I imagined," he said.

She covered her ears. "I don't want to think about him anymore! Please, Simon!"

He hugged her shoulders. "Your secret is safe," he assured her with a funny grin. He stared out over the prairie and laughed a little.

"*Stop it*! You're so bad!"

"Now we're both bad, I guess." He kissed his sister's forehead and sighed.

"And you—you've never changed and I thank God for that."

"Don't be so silly!" He shoved up against her shoulder playfully.

"No, it's not silly. Maybe you just can't see yourself, but you ... all of your large and small gestures ... there are even too many to recall, but all the beauty and adventure I've had in my life you've been responsible for. You saved me from that awful boy in the snow, and you never pushed me away."

"Katie, stop it."

"You brought me John."

"And that's turned out to be a great thing?" he asked, taking in the dreary grounds.

"I'm no longer angry at him, Simon. For whatever reason he couldn't love me, but I know sometimes he did, and I'm lucky for that. As you probably realize with Emily—the good times are worth everything else."

"Kate, you still understand so little about him, don't you?"

She worked a button free from her jacket and lied. "It doesn't matter now. He's mentioned divorce, and I'm leaning toward it myself."

Simon lit a cigar. "Sakes alive, it's bleak here."

"Anyway, what I wanted to say is that I'm so thankful to have such a kind brother, a true friend. No matter the mistakes you've made, I'll always love you."

"How can you do that, Katie? I've always wondered. How can you put me on a pedestal the way you do and keep yourself so mired in the mud? You're the good one. What have you done in life that convinces you that you deserve so little?"

"Nothing. I've done nothing."

"That's not an answer."

"What have I ever done—of any real value?"

He sat back and pulled on his cigar. "Well, I don't know where to begin .... Look, you're here all by yourself, and you're giving these children a chance to help their people adjust to their new lives. I wasn't sure you'd stick it out on your own, but you have. And contrary to what you may think, you're a wonderful mother. Willy's been through a lot, but he adores you, and the way you were with your little girl .... But Katie, it's more than that. Those things are the kinds of things forced on you in a way. It's the other things that are lovely about you. Remember, during the war, those Christmas packages? Your notes were funny and sweet and had half the officers wanting to be your beau. Remember the one I asked you to send Weldon?"

She shook her head.

"That Christmas one I asked for? Well, you sent a special little card on green that you made with little sketches of trees and things—don't you remember?"

She cried.

"Well, he got the package, the only one he ever got during the war. He was tickled by it—never said a word about it, but I saw it in his eyes. We became friends after that, and you know the only thing he saved was that card? I found it in his jacket. He had no other personal belongings when we brought him to the hospital. I wonder now, did he come to the house to meet you? I don't know." He smiled. "Remember the boots I asked for? They came to me and I traveled to the hospital on leave for a short visit. I wasn't sure he was still alive, but he was. He had a whole troupe of nurses in love with him there for some foolish reason. He acted so odd—now I realize it was the morphine. But I came with the unopened box, and we opened it. As usual Mother had stuffed the package with onions and all sorts of interesting truck, but you packed a book and made a marker for it and put dried flowers inside from the garden. It's funny, I had completely forgotten, but it's clear now. He was so overwhelmed, Weldon was, by the hand-sewn bookmark. Couldn't believe someone would go through the trouble—and, Kate, you know how bad your sewing is! I wouldn't be surprised if he still had that rag somewhere."

"But those are such little things in a long life! Things anyone would do."

"No, Katie, no one had done those things *for him*. That's the point. They were sweet and thoughtful things, and sometimes that's all someone needs. I don't understand why you treat yourself so badly. You don't see anything."

"I try to protect myself, Simon, I really do, but it's hard when every happiness is always stolen from me! Everybody has always loved *you*. You don't know how it feels to always be in your shadow!"

"My shadow doesn't stretch across a continent," he said.

"I think that even with John, maybe his friendship with you is what kept him in our marriage for so long."

He put his finger to her mouth. "Katherine, I care for you and I know you do for me ... but there is something ... I had hoped Weldon told you ... and I should have done it, but I thought it wasn't my place. Your marriage is my fault."

She grinned. "We've already established that."

"No, that's not what I mean. I did things during the war, and Weldon covered for me. It became a habit between us."

"Of course he covered for you. The men were devoted to you. John has said so himself."

"Well, they were stupid, and I was arrogant, but so few of them lived to tell, so I guess it doesn't matter." He adjusted his hat against the wind.

"What do you mean?"

"John Weldon is sick today because of my behavior in the Wilderness."

"Sick today?"

"Yes, he struggles with it," Simon said. "As strange as it may seem, I enjoyed a good part of the war. It was exciting and there were so many new characters to talk to and problems to solve. I even liked the food. I loved to wander into a new town and flirt with the girls and steal a chicken or two. It was a good lark for a time.

"The problem with it though was that it weakened me when I didn't realize it. Suddenly I was falling asleep at the oddest of times or running off at the mouth with no brakes on whatsoever. But the thing that weakened me the most was when I started to notice that some fellows never seemed to die off. They stayed with me for months and then years, and I thought nothing of it, just as I thought very little about those who fell away. But then two years become three and four and now you're family in a way. I began to hate all of the new ones—the reluctant draftees, the bounty jumpers, the real young ones too, even as they tried so hard to make a place for themselves. I tried not to care. At first it was easy—but then, like Weldon, for instance. It took months before he'd even sit and laugh with us. You start to see who you can rely on—Weldon and a few others. He always kept his eye out for me even when I was an ass.

"Anyway, little by little toward the end, some of the men I'd known for years started dropping off—captured, dead, who knows where, and it started bothering me. When would this ever end? It bothered me a lot then. It was almost that way, that way it is when you've been drinking and you feel sort of a click in your head. Something shifts, and you're suddenly far gone, over-the-top drunk when just two minutes ago you thought you were nearly sober. But the clicking in my head kept happening. Weldon kept warning me, but it didn't matter. At any little thing I'd go after a man. I wanted to fight them all—my own men—over nothing, minor infractions that even Weldon had learned to overlook. But it was like I was watching the world from behind my eyes. I can't explain exactly, but it was like a mask that trapped my thoughts and made them too noisy to take anymore.

"I hoped breaking winter camp that spring and being back in the field might set me straight, but the Wilderness happened, Katie. They were the most beautiful few days I'd ever seen strung together. The weather was like a dream, with the sky so blue and a gentle haze over the land like a painting. Life looked better than it was as we marched back toward Chancellorsville. Everyone was singing—thousands of men marching and singing with colorful battle flags fluttering and glittering musket barrels swaying to the beat of the shoulders they leaned upon all in columns. Drums and bugles rang out as the men entered the woods. We heard that friends in the artillery had been crushed under their gun carriage when their horses stampeded, but that was the only hint of bad news that shaped our morning. Yet I was a wreck over it and sullen as can be. That night the stars showered around midnight, and we raked the ground digging up the remains of men from last year's fighting and laughed at the dead and scared the new men a little.

"Weldon made us laugh, giving a new young fellow, a real Jonah, a hard time for knocking over his coffee. I remember later seeing Weldon giving the same poor private useful last advice about keeping his canteen full or some such thing. The young ones always hung about Weldon—feeling safe, I guess.

"Next day we marched out again along Catharpin Road, wondering where and when we might again meet Lee. I just wanted to move away from the woods. The forest was so thick with scrub oak and pine and cedar. No one wanted to dawdle near it. We were to march out to Todd's Tavern, but at some point in the day we were sent back again to link with Getty and fight Hill. It struck me then that the brass, as usual, were confused and useless and keeping us in a dangerous wasteland. In the distance, but getting closer, I heard the big guns and saw the smoke and heard the occasional pop of a musket. It really aggravated me to have to fight there.

"We got to the Brock Road and helped in building earthworks, cutting trees as fast as we could, but within the hour we were ordered over them and into the deep woods. Everything got confused. We all began to get lost and Mud Walker's Rebs were filling us with shot. We could only see the Vermont men we had somehow got behind of, and then they ran off, leaving us lying behind them like sitting ducks. Weldon and I did our best to keep our men from falling back, but it was such a blind muddle, and the firing was severe. A lot of our men were nearing the end of their three-year enlistments. We were trounced, which burned me more, and we left good men there to suffer and die. There was a bunch of small fires always threatening and sometimes the poor wounded were killed if the fire got to their cartridge boxes. The explosions made an awful mess of the men. So we were all broken up and shattered and needing to get reorganized, but it was coming on night. I was cursing Grant and Meade and the new recruits and the bounty jumpers. There were only a few of us, and our captain was missing. Weldon was always one to eat for the future—he was the one man I knew to grow heavier in the war."

"John?" Katherine asked.

Simon nodded as if barely hearing her and continued. "So Weldon had a fire and coffee and the men threw what they had together, but for a few shirkers who I'd seen rushing back for the earthworks almost as soon as we were ordered forward. There were three of them—foreigners and nasty beats. I knew they'd run at the first chance. And now I spied them viciously eating their own rations and plunder they picked up somehow. It boiled my blood. They had a look about them like they might leave this night, and I said as much to Weldon. I said I'd hunt them like dogs.

"He laughed, but realized I was dead serious. He didn't want me to go. For the first time he seemed skittish, but I didn't care. There'd be no fighting till morning.

"I knew he would cover for me. He always did. I checked my Colt and put it back on my belt. I pulled out my flask and got a little tight and was almost asleep on the ground when a private Dan—we couldn't pronounce his last name—Polish or Russian or something—woke me to say the three shirkers had indeed slipped off and who should he report it to.

"I don't know what made me so bloodthirsty for these men in particular. One of them had hunched shoulders, and he always rubbed his hands together to keep warm, and I just felt like killing him for having so little gumption that he wouldn't start a damned fire.

"It was near pitch dark. The moon was gone, and I stumbled along thinking every moment I was lost. No one dared use lanterns. The rebels were so close I could hear their jokes and complaints. Occasionally a shot rang out and then a blistering volley and then nothing again, but the rustlings and moans of the men from both sides who could not be rescued. I stepped on them and kicked them accidentally. I thought Private Dan must have played me for a fool. I never expected to find my prey in this thin spot between the two armies, but I plodded on, keeping low as I could, and there came a sort of works. Soldiers had stacked bodies along with trees and other truck for defense, and I heard them—the shirkers. Their accents gave them away, and so I snuck up to take a look as quiet as a mouse. They were just after stripping a Federal of his belongings and arguing over the booty. Another few men, blue and grey, were dead and dying and being roughly treated by the scoundrels. So I shot at them. Their rifles were resting alone. The one with the forever cold hands I shot in the face, and the other stood cowering and begging me in German to spare him. And there was this click in my head, and he sickened me. I took my pistol and knocked him with it to the ground. By now nervous pickets for both sides were blazing away, and the man kept talking that German and I kept thinking why the hell did this fool come here anyway? I kicked him and was gonna just leave him, but saw then that his idiotic words were because I had smashed his brains. The third bounty jumper made a run for it, and I moved to go, but one of the near dead Federals begged me to pull him from the pile of bodies so he could rest in peace. His jaw was half gone, but he motioned for my canteen. I explained it wasn't water, but he took it anyway, and the alcohol burned him. He cried out pitifully, and I just left him like that and followed my last man.

"Katie, the ground moved with men, some begging, some past hope altogether. There was no way to avoid them, and I was of half a mind to just stay with them, but up ahead in a small clearing I saw a man run off, and I burst ahead like forty with the brush tearing my duds to shreds. By the time I caught up, as he foundered in muck, I saw as he did that we had stumbled back into Union lines. A sergeant of the guard almost shot us, but we ducked, and I made myself known. The guard gingerly came forward and was convinced finally that I was no Reb. I grabbed the shirker by the collar. He turned in resignation and shrugged. 'You got me,' he said like it was a game of tag.

"'Yes, you bastard!' I said, 'and I hope they burn you at the stake for your $300 bounty!'

"The sergeant took him off my hands but not before I shaved half his head of hair with my pocket knife. I grubbed brandy from a captain who had lifted it from a surgeon and then I wandered off. I didn't know where I was going. I just kept walking until I came upon the idea to visit these girls I met the year previous on a forage. We had taken most everything they had, but they were pretty and their mother was long since dead, so we let them keep their horse and a cow (it was a starveling anyway), and they were grateful.

"I went off looking for this farm and the girls way up the road. I don't know how, but I found it in pitch dark and all, and I rapped my revolver against the broken down door. Finally I had to pry it open with my knife. Of course I scared them. The whole time I was waving my revolver, and I was fairly drunk ... and they let me use them, Katie. I don't know why, unless my forced entry and dangling weapons convinced them it was the prudent thing to do. They didn't put up a bit of a fight, and I did it to both of them. And ... you know, I wasn't even cured then though I thought I was ... but to two sisters ..." His voice trailed off.

"But Simon ..." Katherine began, stiffly patting his hand.

"I like to think I'd just gone temporarily mad to do such low things, but ..." He wiped his face. "Well, when I woke up the next day they were gone and my gun too. They could have killed me in my sleep. Maybe they tried to. My head roared like my brain wanted to exit my skull, and after a little investigating I fingered the place on my head where they clobbered me."

"So that's how you got that scar?" she asked. He had always made the war seem almost a party in his letters.

He took a long pull from his cigar and pointed to a young Sioux girl with a billowing pink bow tied at the back of her head as she tiptoed over to some of the older boys, who were set to cultivate the school vegetable garden. She kept her hands behind her with a note—the one good reason to learn the alphabet. The braves pushed one of their own to the front, and he faced the girl with a look of bashful disdain but took the note. The girl turned and ran as her teacher emerged from the school, pretending anger and ushering her back inside.

"It's a mighty job you've set for yourself, Katie. I wouldn't have minded the childhood of one of these Indians. I guess this will be the last generation to remember what it was like before *school*."

"I don't understand what happens to men when they go to war, but we all act in unpredictable ways. As long as the girls didn't seem to mind ... how old were they?"

"I don't know. I guess about my age at the time—22 or 23—spinsters maybe. Sometimes I wonder though ... did those girls have a brother?"

"It was different—what happened to me—I was a little girl."

He nodded. "I just hope that if those sisters had put up a fight I would have done the right thing," he said, shivering in the cold. "You know, back in Englewood everybody thought I was trouble."

"Not bad trouble."

"No, maybe not, but troublesome all the same. For some reason, I didn't believe them. I had faith in my own goodness. But now I don't seem to know which side is right anymore. Katie, I've resigned from the army."

"Mercy!" she cried as if her dreams had been shattered. She could see Simon as nothing but a soldier. "But what will you do?"

"I thought maybe I'd try farming too, like the Indians are being told to do. Don't look so sad. I still love the army, but I'm tired of trying to separate bad from good. I just want a normal family life."

"You have every right to that."

The wind picked up to remind them that winter had not quite finished in this part of the world. The sun shone just over the next ripple of scrubland, but where they sat fell under the cool shade of a passing cloud.

"The weather changes so darn fast out here. I've never gotten used to it," Simon said, buttoning his jacket at the collar. "So, I'm thinking of moving ... of farming out in Washington Territory. Emily's been there and says the weather's just mild all year. An old army friend is selling off his land. I'm on my way to see it."

She took his hand. He was freezing and hadn't dressed properly. "Well, that's wonderful. Maybe I can visit you in the summers."

He laughed and wiped his nose.

"Simon, what's wrong? Emily must be excited ..."

They sat silently for a few minutes. The blackbirds cawed, and the sun sank from view.

"Katherine, there's been a complication with baby Lucy."

She pulled a handkerchief from her coat and gave it to him.

He looked broken and lost and his nose ran. "Well, it's her eyes ..."

"Trachoma?"

"No. It's a complication from the ... disease. Her eyes may never work right. Her eyes get inflamed, and it goes away, but then comes back."

She embraced him. "It will be all right. You'll see."

"I've brought such disgrace to Mother and Emily. Mother seems not to want to get too close to me anymore. She dotes on the baby and Emily, and I'm glad for that, but ... well, it's just been very difficult."

"How is Emily?"

He took another deep breath and shoved his hands in his pockets. "Em is wonderful. I know she can be too self-righteous at times, but she's got some call to be. I've never gone to church willingly before, but now I find it's hard to deny the message of God when I see how she has forgiven me the way she has. When she took me back after that last visit home after Christmas, I was more of a mess than ever."

She cringed, remembering how hard she had been on Simon when he stood in her room before leaving Tenafly Road. Emily had outshone her.

"I very nearly wanted to die. I thought at first she took me back because she felt I had ruined her for anybody else, and I was prepared to live with that."

"She was already in love with you by the time I first came west!" Katherine said. "Now it seems such a romantic thing that she tried to convince me to get you to attend one of those temperance meetings."

"I was never that nice to her. She was like a child to me then. Her preaching and her sister annoyed me greatly, but over time ... we spent so much time together, and she was terribly pretty, and in the end I just couldn't do without her—and her conscience. And then I had to go and bring her over to my selfish way of doing things. Honestly, Katie, I thought I was cured! But anyway, she forgave me. When I came back to Texas after Christmas, that very first day as I walked back to my quarters her skirt rustled behind me. She never looked so lovely, so perfect and she said to me. 'Simon McCullough, I can forgive you if you promise to love me forever.'

"And we never spoke of the disease again. Even now I wait for her to blame me for Lucy, but she never says a thing, and I begin to believe she is one of those people who really knows how to forgive. And I am awed by my luck. Katherine, Weldon deserves the same chance that I've had."

"I'm happy that Emily is teaching you something about forgiveness and religion, but you and John are no longer a working team."

"You should try to forgive him."

"Don't do this to me. I have forgiven him, but I can't depend on him anymore, and I don't see why you defend him."

"Because I'm responsible for him—that's why!" Simon cried. "You didn't know him before! Maybe I should have let him die—I don't know—but he struggles under the decision I made for him. I took away what he valued most! You should know that!"

"I don't understand. The war is long since over. He makes his own decisions now. You can't be responsible for his actions. Only he can. You make him out to be a pathetic victim. He does as he pleases."

"No, that's not true! He tries, but ..."

The students were let from school now, and two raced by feigning a contest but really wanting a glimpse of the teacher's brother. Katherine ignored them all. "Well, trying is not good enough anymore."

"I had hoped ..." Simon began but was distracted by the students circling them and pretending not to.

"Simon, I don't want to fight with you. I know that you want all of us to live happily ever after and maybe we will, but John and I won't be together. Why do you want to spoil the visit with this?"

"Please, just listen. I know it might be hard to imagine now when Weldon is so changed, but he was a hero to me. We were so different, and never once did I aspire to be like him, but I did admire him greatly. He was brave in battle but careful with his men. He put himself out on a limb for me many times, and I would have done the same for him if he ever let me, but he had a good bit of pride in his self-sufficiency and sobriety. You know how I don't go in much for that sort of thing, and I enjoyed watching him fight against having any fun with the group at first. I thought he was independent and dignified, but I began to see over time that he just wasn't much good at making friends. I made it easy for him, and I guess he was grateful. And although I counted him my only real friend in the army, I used him. He'd never break a rule, but he'd help me get around them all the time. It became harder and harder for him to conceal his enjoyment, but ... I used him plain and simple. He was reprimanded at least twice for fixing the books to explain away my absences. Things like that done on a regular basis, and with his awkward personality it kept him from promotion a number of times. The captain didn't like how he had mixed loyalties—they had served together before the war. Weldon said he didn't give a hoot about rank, but I shouldn't have kept putting him in bad positions. And I did it to him again at the Wilderness when I ran off and left him to fight alone. It never occurred to me that he had grown dependent on me in any way. Not for one second did I think he'd go off and do anything stupid, but he did."

"What did he do?"

"He sacrificed himself! The fool! And got shot to pieces!" Simon cried angrily. "I rushed back to find them all, but with my head pounding and pandemonium everywhere—it was rough going. I'd missed the early battle on the sixth. The woods everywhere were scattered with fresh dead and mixed-up troops. The underbrush was ablaze again too, and there were no medical people anywhere that I could see.

"I took a gun and cartridges from a dead man and moved along till I came upon men from the 26th Pennsylvania, who told me the Jersey men hadn't made a good showing when they were surprised along a railroad ravine and had collapsed like dominoes when Sorrel attacked. Everyone was making their way toward the earthworks at Brock Road through the densest thickets and brush. Branches and whole saplings smacked our faces and tripped our feet. It was the worst place to fight or maneuver, and I'll never forgive Meade and Grant for getting us stuck there! All the day long I searched for my regiment, my company, and got caught up in fights and wandered some more till near evening when the private Weldon had helped, the cowering unlucky new recruit, Wilson, spotted me and told me what had happened. McAllister's men were surprised and ran mostly, but small groups hung on. Finally, after much of the army had skedaddled, they were ordered to retreat, but Weldon wouldn't go. He took up the colors and charged ahead like a mad man right into the enemy. And some men followed him and some just stopped to watch, but most fell there and the rest ran off after Weldon went down. Private Wilson was captured but escaped. He tried to get Weldon, but the firing was too close, and he couldn't gain any sense of direction in the smoky woods. So he rushed down to the earthworks and fought the day out.

"There were men—thousands of them screaming. The men suffered so fearfully in the thickets. The woods scared us all. And Weldon was out there. He had told me once that as a young boy in the big woods with his father he had wandered off and been paralyzed with fear, but couldn't scream out, and I thought of him now and had to find him. I jumped the barricades on Brock Road and ran as the men watched and cursed me and cheered. A young fellow was hollering for help and our eyes met in the gloom so I helped him while the bullets flew by, chopping flowery branches from the trees. I dragged him to the works and our men huzzahed. And then there was another and another until Private Wilson came out on hands and knees. He took me to where the men had fallen.

"We crawled off, and it was that in-between time before dark sets in. We hadn't brought any ammunition. I hadn't even brought my gun, and I don't know how we weren't shot or taken as we skirted blue and grey pockets of men all back up toward the railroad ravine. We heard someone say that Longstreet had been shot and killed by his own men. We pressed on until I thought the private was lost, but like a good hound Wilson grew excited remembering a rise here and a gully there and then we found Weldon. The side of his face was a mess of blood and his guts, Katherine ..."

"No! I don't want to hear any of this!" she wailed, "It's too much!"

Simon pulled her hands from her ears. "Listen to me! Sometimes life is too much! If Weldon would have died then ... if I would have let him die ... he would have been a hero! He took up the colors in a daring act of bravery. By dragging him off the field that night I stole his dignity, and he's been angry about it ever since."

"You saved him! Who wants to die? You saved him for me."

"No. I saved him for myself. I had let down my men. I let him down. I had to make it up to him. But someone had gotten to him first and gave him opium to make him comfortable." Simon hesitated. "Katherine, how is Willy doing?"

She stiffened. "Never better, I guess. I so rarely hear from him. He blames me for everything, and John can be a good father at times."

"Your husband is *very sick*. I'm sure he's trying to care for Willy, but ..."

"You keep saying sick ... what do you mean?"

"Katie, I tried to tell you before! It's the morphine. They gave it to him at the hospital."

She stared over the land teeming with wild children. "The hospital? What hospital? You mean during the war?!" A door opened in her mind. "No, it can't be true. I would have known all these years."

Simon looked at her steadily. "I didn't understand either. I should have realized when I got the strange letter from Washington ... and then there was that Lyons girl ..."

"*Oonagh?*" she cried, "No, I don't believe it! Oonagh helped me! You're just making more excuses for him."

"Weldon told me himself, before we came back east."

She pulled away from him. "And you didn't tell me?"

Two little Indian girls whispered anxiously over their teacher's distress.

Simon shooed them away. "Katie, I thought *he* would tell you. He came home to tell you."

She shook with anger. "And you let me send Willy off with him! How could you?"

"I don't know. By the time Em and I came back that evening they were already gone. I thought maybe, I don't know, that Willy could save him."

"So because of your crazy guilt about something you did to John during the war you were willing to sacrifice my son?"

"As far as we know William is having a grand time," he said, "and Weldon can be a good father—you said so yourself."

"Maybe it's the sore on his side. It never healed properly, and it gives him pain at times ... yes, that makes sense then ... for those times when the pain is too much ... and his arm ..."

Simon stared at her soberly. "I didn't get that impression when he spoke about it." He shoved his hand into his pocket and pulled out his watch, his face lined grimly. "I have to go."

She pulled at his jacket sleeve. "No, can't you stay the night?"

"Katie, forgive me, but I can't," he said and hugged her tightly. She was still so small, and he felt that if he didn't leave now he could never go. Childhood was over, and he was glad she had a gun.

Chapter Seventy-Three

Weldon waited until he heard Willy's quiet breathing turn regular and deep. William insisted that he sleep only on Indian blankets and hay and let the real soldier keep the bunk. After some time fighting it, Weldon gave in.

Upon seeing John Weldon arrive with his son at headquarters, General Crook would not allow his overworked and undernourished lieutenant to join him in the big fighting this season. It was coming on late fall, and frost had already hinted at the unpredictable and harsh storms of the plains. Crook wanted Weldon for spring, but the lieutenant took the news of transfer none too well, and young William was embarrassed for his father. Crook insisted, with a worried glance at William, that it was best for the army and for Weldon to have the winter to rest up.

The two traveled to a quiet post to start fresh with new men and, for Weldon, no real power. This mortified the lieutenant at first, but the traveling, though wearing, gave him time to reacquaint himself with his son. It also kept Weldon from medical supplies and the growing habit of stealing from them.

Weldon bought William a proper gun—a nice old Spencer carbine from the war—the kind William always wished for. As the weather turned cold, the two sat at their fire and cleaned and polished their weapons while chatting about their most recent hunt for jackrabbits and the like. He coached his son meticulously in the use of his new gun but found William a surprisingly good shot for a beginner. William was lucky from the first time out. "Willy, you've been shooting back east. Why didn't you tell me?" he asked, throwing his arm over his son's shoulder.

William just shrugged with a proud grin. When they had been together last, he seemed such a little boy, often happiest when pleasing his mother and standing at her side, but things were decidedly different now. The quiet post gave the two real time together.

It had taken Weldon time to get used to this lanky boy traipsing after him everywhere and begging to be of service, but he enjoyed it tremendously. Food and clothing took on new importance, and he laughed to himself on evenings he spent mending his son's things as Katherine used to do. He planned a big garden for the spring, for deep down he sensed he would not be asked to join the fighting with Crook whenever it came. In the meantime he dug up the last of the wild onions outside his quarters and spent what money he had on winter vegetables and canned goods from town.

He almost allowed himself to imagine he was doing a fair job of raising the boy. His responsibilities kept him almost completely on the straight and narrow.

William was great company for him, except in the evenings. When William shifted in his blankets with the candle down low, Weldon worried for Katherine at school, and he missed her. No matter how he filled his days, the nights still came on the same. So he waited for his son's breathing to change. He waited for the candle to sink into oblivion. Routine made him less vigilant, and the moon was out and full. After waiting for what seemed like hours, Weldon, in bed with his back against the rough wall, reached behind the mattress, filled the syringe and ...

"Father!" William was suddenly over him.

The warmth from the needle already began passing into him. "Damn it, Willy!" Weldon shouted as he pulled the needle from his leg. Shit, shit, shit. He sat up.

William, wide eyed, stood with his Indian blanket around him. His hair was a matted carpet of gold against the moonlight, his mouth slightly ajar. "Papa, are you ill?"

"No, William, now go to sleep, please."

But still William stood and watched him shove his kit behind the bed, behind the likenesses of Katherine. William watched his father turn toward him awkwardly, finding the floor with his feet. "I need something to help me sleep sometimes, Willy."

"Mother often gives me milk or chocolate ... I could go find some, I think. Couldn't I? For you?" William asked and attempted to reach for the kit, but his father pulled his arm away. "Does it hurt?"

The look on Weldon's face scared the boy.

"Papa, will you die?"

Weldon glanced at his son with a beaten, humiliated sigh. "I was about to lie to you, but I can't. I'm sorry about what I'm going to tell you. Just remember that you've been the world to me ... you and your mother."

"Papa, please don't say you're dying!"

"Let me tell you the truth. No one knows about dying or when it happens. I don't think I'm dying yet ... but it's worse. I was going to lie to you and tell you I take morphine and opium to sleep but ..."

"Morphine?"

"During the war ... my injuries ... I didn't know it would happen, but once they gave it to me I ... I just never really managed to stop completely."

"Since the war?" William mulled it over. "That's a long time. But doesn't it hurt?"

"It sort of hurts if I don't do it."

The two stared at the silver-fringed world outside their window.

"Is it bad for you then?" William asked.

"Yes, of course it's bad!" Weldon shouted. "I can't stop it! I have no control over it!"

"Why don't you just stop?" William asked, his voice apprehensive in the face of his father's frustration.

"You know what a drunk is? Of course you do. Can you see how that's bad? We both like Private Potter, but do you see how bad his life is?"

William thought about it. "Well, he has to wear shoddy clothes, I guess."

"He sold his clothes to get drink. He has no family ... he has nothing."

"Did you ever sell stuff to get morphine?"

"Yes! I've done things, William ... I've stolen, I've begged ..." Weldon pulled at his hair. "I need to send you back home. I'll ruin you. You don't realize the enormity of my problem. And you shouldn't have to." His voice trembled. "I've been selfish. I wanted to raise you, but I shouldn't have let you see this. There's something wrong with me."

"But Papa, you're not like Private Potter. You have a family and clothes ... why can't we help you?"

Weldon almost laughed at the boy's naiveté.

"Papa, I'll never leave you if you're sick. Every boy would like a father like you."

Weldon tried to remain focused.

"You always take me on adventures and hunting and you taught me reading and you don't care if I get scared. You treat me like I'm a real person," Willy said and threw his arms around his father.

Weldon ran his fingers through his son's hair. "My beautiful boy ... I love you ..."

William looked up. "Then why did you send me and Mother away? I thought you were mad at me, and Mother thought it too—you didn't come when Mother was dying."

"I was so stupid ... so stupid. I wanted to protect you. No, that's not fair—I'm not that noble. I wanted to escape. You and your mother were in the way of my escape. I wanted to pretend that Eliza didn't die. I didn't want to remember, so I fell back into the morphine."

"Mother wouldn't talk about Eliza either. She used to sit by the window all day. She hoped you would come home. Didn't you want to help her? I had to do it."

Weldon sank back into his pillows, not wanting to hear any of it. "How can you want to stay with me when I left you like that?"

William worked up his courage. "I poisoned my teacher at school. I didn't know it was that bad ... the stuff we used, but ... but Mother forgave me. I got kicked out of school and everything, but Mother still loves me. And we fought all the time too." William slipped his hand into his father's like he used to do in Arizona. "I'm glad you didn't send us away because you hated us."

"I was so afraid you'd grow to hate me—your mother has." Weldon choked up. "I've been sent such good people, but all I do is hurt them."

"But I love you, Papa. I'm not mad at you anymore. Mother helps people she doesn't even know. She would help you too if you asked her."

"No! Willy, you can't tell her. Please, I'm not ready for that yet."

"When I promise, it's for keeps, Papa. I won't tell anything, but you can't send me away. It's only fair."

"Willy, please forgive me. I've made so many mistakes ..."

"You're my best friend forever, Papa. You and Mother!" William buried his face in John's collar, missing his mother for the first time since leaving her.

"I'm so proud of you, William."

"But I did get thrown out of school."

Weldon laughed, wiping his nose and his eyes. "Who gives a damn, Willy? You've got a heart of gold. That school was no good for you."

They sat for a while until Willy began to nod. Weldon placed him on the bed and sat beside him, studying his boy's sleeping face, tracing his fingers over his cheekbone and brow. What a gift.

***

Seeing his father that night had changed everything for William. It set the boy to thinking about and watching every move of his father's. He noted Weldon's mood shifts now as symptoms, as regularly arriving as mess call. On Christmas he celebrated the day watching his father sleep and trying to make a dinner that even the dog turned his nose against. This sickness of his father's was nothing more than weakness, and all the pride he felt for the lieutenant, with the accompanying hero worship, melted away as spring came in.

He admitted to himself in the lonely hours right before dawn that Mother was right to leave Papa alone and almost wished he'd stayed back east now as he watched his father, instead of fighting, allowing himself to slip further into addiction. He cringed at the mishaps on parade or at drill time and got angry when hunting and gardening fell by the wayside. The lieutenant still went through the motions of waiting until William was out or asleep to dose himself, but William knew the truth when their eyes met.

William acted as buffer in camp. All the men held theories and suspicions about Weldon. Something had changed with Lieutenant Weldon, was not right, since Christmas ... and why had he been sent there anyway? The soldiers did not know the man before and only saw that he was now often late for dress parade, ambivalent about his appearance, and just recently neglectful of the boy. But because of this boy, for the boy's sake, they said nothing.

William was finishing sweeping out the quarters when Weldon woke up, reveille long since passed. "William, I'm sending you away from here."

William kept sweeping.

"For God's sake, did you hear me? I'm sending you away."

"I heard you, Papa, but I'm not going anywhere!"

William leaned the broom against the wall and reached for Weldon's ragged shirt hanging over a chair. It needed mending, but Mother had always done his father's shirts. He helped Weldon bring the shirt around to his sore arm, but Weldon snatched it from him. There were still some things he could do himself. Weldon saw his son's hurt eyes and cursed. William was tall, thin, and strong like Weldon had been but more refined because of Katherine. Weldon almost hated William for the slim hopes his son still might have if he got away. But Weldon loved him too and needed to save him. "I'm sending you back east—to school. Your grandmother will find a way."

"I don't want to go back there! I won't go! I don't belong in school." William's hair hung so long and dirty now. Weldon hated to see him so wild.

"You don't belong here, Willy."

"I belong with you, Papa," William cried. "Till you're well ..."

"I don't want you here any longer. You're too much trouble for me now. I can't be ..."

"*Selfish*! That's what you are, Papa! You want to do just as you like! You send us off and take us back whenever you want! You say you love us and then you don't!"

"You're right. I don't play fair. I can't honestly say I love you enough. There's no reason to believe me. I won't promise you anything anymore. So you *will* go to school and have a normal life."

"*No*! I'll never do it, and you can't make me!" William sobbed, embracing Weldon. "I don't care that you won't stop! I'm not leaving you!"

"God damn it! Don't you realize that when I see you trying to make me something I'm not, I'm seeing my childhood repeated? If you stay you'll turn out like me!"

"Never! I will never ever be like you! I won't throw people away like garbage!"

Weldon sank back into bed with a moan. "Everything you say is as I said it years ago! I tried to be different!" He pulled the covers up over himself, and William timidly sat beside him, placing his hand on his father's shoulder. It was like fire to Weldon. The humiliation of it all and the weakness ... to have a child at his bedside like this. He struggled out of bed, pushing the surprised and nervous boy aside. Grabbing his son's rucksack, he shoved anything he spotted of the boy's into the bag as William stared. "You must escape this, Willy, before I hate you as much as I hate myself."

William pulled at his father tenderly. "You won't hate me really."

Weldon stopped his feverish packing and gazed at his son. William had such a wise old look to him, having seen too much already. It stabbed him in the gut to see such a serious child.

"I stayed with my mother until the end. That was a mistake I won't let you repeat while I have some sense. If you stay I *will* grow to hate you. I'll hate your stupidity and sentiment. I used you—and your mother to try and save myself. I have nothing to give anymore."

"I don't care that you used me!" William cried. "But ... I can't have you hate me so I'll go!" William took the bag, finished his small bit of packing, and dragged himself outside wiping his nose on his sleeve as he went. Once in the open bracing air of the prairie, he realized he had nowhere to go and sat down on the steps crying bitterly, his dog, U.S., at his side.

Weldon washed up as best he could with water from the basin that had sat there for days. The cool weather made his leg stiff and his arm sore. He kept a cane—a gift from a soldier who spotted his troubles. The lieutenant pushed U.S. with his foot after opening the door and ordering the dog to move, but there was no bright spark of intelligence with the wolfhound. Weldon jabbed the dog with his cane, and the dog yelped. William pulled the dog to him and buried his face in its matted fur until Weldon passed and lifted his head to watch his father limp like an old man to the lieutenant colonel's quarters.

The adjutant sat at a worn desk napping. He opened one eye and then the other when Weldon walked in. "Fancy seeing you here this early in the day, Lieutenant Weldon."

"What?"

"Nothing, lieutenant. Is there something you need ... a discharge maybe?"

"I need a schedule of the trains running to St. Louis and the nearest place to get the coach. Also I need to hire someone to escort my son back east."

"If you quit the army you could escort him yourself, but that would take energy, old soldier."

The colonel breezed in then, the essence of vitality. "Lieutenant Weldon, just the man I wanted to see. Come inside my office. We'll have a small chat."

Weldon limped in.

"At ease, Lieutenant Weldon. Take a seat," the colonel ordered with a sigh. He looked Weldon over. "How old are you now, Weldon? Forty-five or so?"

"Thirty-six years, sir."

"Is that all? Well the army sure does take its toll, doesn't it?"

"I don't know, sir, I suppose for some ..."

"Lieutenant, I'm sure at one time you were a fine soldier. You come highly recommended from General Crook, but I have no confidence in your present ability to lead. Because of the boy (who is a fine little fellow—you must be proud—real soldier material) I've said nothing. But the medical department, such as it is, complains of incomplete orders and the books at the commissary are fitfully done at best. There's grumbling in the ranks too, and we have a fine young sergeant, just out, whom the boys have really taken to. This is difficult for me. You have a long history of service, but ...well, it seems your better days are behind you."

"Am I being brought up on charges?"

"Is there a reason you should be brought up on charges, lieutenant?"

"No, sir, I just don't feel ready to retire. My son's been a distraction, it's true, but I'm sending him back east to school."

The colonel jotted down some notes. "I'm afraid it's too late. I've given your duties to Sergeant Wise for the present. I advise you to at least take the time you are owed to give yourself a break. We can see what's what in a few months."

When Weldon returned to their little home, William was gone and Weldon panicked. The boy had no money and no directions, but then he spotted the dog with its head on his son's things. U.S. had pulled the bag apart for a more comfortable pillow.

It was only midday. Usually, lately, Weldon was just getting out of bed at noon and now—now—there was absolutely no reason at all to be up. He sat at the table and found his son's sloppily scrawled note. Willy went for a hunt with some of the boys ... the very men who had probably complained to the colonel about him.

The morphine itch was worse than the army itch they had all suffered during the war—the scabies—little bugs that laid their eggs beneath a person's skin. Weldon scratched his arms until they bled again and rolled down his sleeves in repulsion. Thirty-six years old ...

He finished Willy's sweeping and dumped the dirty water from the dish basin and the washing basin out by the door. U.S. ran out and licked it up—they hadn't thought to put water down for the poor creature. Weldon found his brush. It depressed him to use it now. It had been a gift from Kate and was matted with his brittle hair. Calling the dog in, he sat by the new fire in the stove, heating clean water for dishes and tea. There was no coffee. Weldon had forgotten to order it—that, more than anything else, angered the men.

Maybe it was a good thing ... this break from duty. Weldon could set things in order here—clean the mattress, make food for the boy like he had done in the beginning, and then take Willy back east himself. He'd like to visit Sarah again. But that was ridiculous. Sarah would not want to see him anymore, of course. At least Weldon would be able to make sure William made it home. Englewood was home, but not for him any longer, and the army ... he was no longer fit for it. What would he do now?

Weldon took a deep breath and pulled himself up with the help of the table. He needed *not to panic*.

All the cups were dirty. Old rags, remnants of the blue gingham Kate loved and faded with use, hung on pegs. He pulled them down and threw them into a pile on the floor. Beneath one of them hung Katherine's teacup—the only survivor from their journeys in Arizona. William must have found it among the things Weldon had not bothered to unpack after Katherine had gone. He heard it as it hit the floor. With his cane he pushed the gingham out of the way and saw now what it was. It hadn't broken. The rags saved it.

Slowly and with effort, he picked it up with his bad hand. Some movement and feeling had come back to it, but everything he held in it seemed somehow far away. He remembered the whole set. "Kate, remember?" he began, turning to where she might be if she were still with him. It was strange how many times he'd do that. Weldon forgot about his tea and took the cup to the desk at the window, setting the delicate piece of history before him.

Dear Katherine,

Remember the china tea set from Englewood? I remember surprising you in late September with my promotion. Everybody knew about it but you. I came in, and it was a bright day and still warm. Your mother was packing the tea set in the dining room. Her eyes were red from crying, but she smiled when she saw me. She was so like a mother to me. You came in and jumped at me. I remember you smelled of your mother's laundry water—lilacs. Sarah introduced me as Lieutenant Weldon, and you knew right away what that meant and why your mother had been packing all of your pretty things. I was surprised because somehow, Kate, having our little Eliza changed you and made you more womanly than ever. How could I have been so lucky?

You, Katherine, gave me the only clear, real years of my life. This teacup before me reminds me that it was not a dream. It was a short, but sweet taste of life. This cup is an excavated treasure. William found it. Our boy deserves better than what I've given him. I will take care to get him back to his real home on Tenafly Road.

Kindest regards,

John Weldon

Weldon finished the letter just as William opened the door, sending his father a withering look.

"Willy, look what I've found," Weldon said, showing him the cup. It held no real memories for the boy. William had only hung it up after using it when everything else was dirty.

"So what?"

"It was your mother's ..."

"So I guess that's the only nice thing Mother had that you didn't break."

The hunting trip had not gone well.

William tried hard to stop them, but tears escaped and streamed down the sides of his dirty face. His teeth had grown in a little crooked and his breath whistled through the space between the front two.

Weldon lit his pipe. "How was the hunt? I'd like to go again sometime—maybe."

"That ain't never goin' to happen and you know it!" William shot back, throwing a slab of wrapped meat on the table.

"Speak properly, William."

"I'll speak as I like! Did you steal from the medical supplies?"

"What?"

"You heard me!"

"No! I didn't steal ... I need it. I was going to replace it when my pay came in. I ..."

William covered his ears. He looked so like Katherine. "Oh, Papa, how could you shame me like this? They all know! Now I *have* to leave!"

"I haven't had anything since yesterday. I'm going to bring you back myself ... back to Englewood."

"No! I don't want you to! I can't stand the sight of you anymore. How could you lie and steal?!"

Weldon grabbed him. He shook as he spoke. "*Shut up*! You don't know anything about me! You don't know all I've been through! I'm still your father, and you'll do as I say!"

William pushed free of him. Weldon fell back into his chair.

"You haven't acted like my father in a long time. I hate you!" William yelled and ran out into the cold air and down to the horses. One was special. He thought he'd ride it and then the idea of escape came to him. He needed his mother.

The private on guard was a friend and let the boy take his ride on an old, nearly useless Indian pony William loved because no one else did. He rode around until darkness hid him and snuck back home taking the pony out back. A dim light escaped through the window. He intended to stay calm and pretend to accept his father's plan, but he need not have prepared for talk. Weldon had floated away to his medicine already and stared out from the bed.

William shoved his stuff back into the bag, cursing the dog. He looked around and saw the china cup. He took it to spite his father and was about to leave when he spotted the letter to his mother. Something made him open and read it. His father tried to be good. William couldn't stay mad at him, but he was curious. He took his father's knapsack that hung from a peg on the wall—the one so full and always carried by the lieutenant. The boy lit a candle for better light and sifted through the notes and letters, all to his mother. A few were so old they crumbled in his hands as he unfolded them, but why had Papa never sent them? Pictures of them both—Mother and Papa—slipped from a side pocket of the bag. His parents were young and happy, his father dashing and his mother so elegant and in love. William wiped his eyes on his sleeve and took the cup from his bag, placing it next to his father on the little box that served as a bed stand, and left, but not before kissing his father good night.

***

William could pass for twelve easily now, but his sense of the world and his place in it remained the murky imaginings of a dreamy boy. Minnesota and his mother lay somewhere north—or east. William had not taken his time with geography. He had not taken his time with much at all except Sunday lessons. Bible stories were mysterious and frightening, with violence and love entwined in something called redemption. As a young child he had preferred the Greek and the Roman gods each jealously guarding their virtues and flaws, but now William saw, through his father, that someone like a god to him could be aloof and frightening and gentle as a lamb all in one.

William, even with his gun and knife, drifted on the endless sea of grass in a constant state of terror. He was dead afraid of Indians. At the agency once, two sun-bleached white children who had been kidnapped by some tribe were returned. They didn't have a word of English and stood like exotic totems of evil, their pale eyes blank like lifeless buttons. He would fight them hard—those Indians—if anything like that ever happened to him, but he prayed to God, who confused him greatly, to guard him against Indians and wolves.

Fearing being spotted by Blackfoot or Sioux or Cheyenne—he didn't know into whose territory he had wandered—he spent shivering nights without fire, keeping guard over his pony. Indian stories used to excite him when he was with the soldiers, but no longer. After only a few days with the wind whipping his face, he ached to go back and try again with his father, but the undulating prairie hills had taken him in, and he was lost. Even the pony seemed to miss the dependably monotonous life of the army. The boy despaired at getting anywhere and fell asleep in the saddle.

The horse found a lonely outpost—a mining town already at death's door. A small ribbon of silver had been picked at and carted away. A few degraded souls, who had left behind families or their troubles, lingered on in the town, finishing the last of the liquor in the tiny, windowless saloon.

William woke to the lapping sound of his mount's tongue deep into a green and moldy trough outside the Wise Moon Saloon. Two men leered at him.

"He don't look drunk ... but hey, there. It's an army hos. See U.S. tattooed on his rump there ..."

Panic roused William as he righted himself in his saddle. He couldn't tell if it was dusk or dawn, but his gun was gone and so was everything else not wrapped securely around his body.

"Git off the hos, son."

William obliged.

"You ridin' stolen goods ain't you, boy?"

William considered the wrathful God looking down at him, and it was a mighty big sky here. "Yes."

The man not doing the talking was big and dumb looking. His eyes flamed red where the whites should have been.

"You little bastard, stealin' from the government! Are you injun?"

"I'm American ... I don't know what I am!"

The men laughed and the dumb one took the boy to the little never-been-used jail. It was clean and warm out of the wind, and they locked him there. As William fell asleep again the men snickered as they led his pony away, and when he woke up next it was true light and the air was drenched with a strong and sickening perfume.

William was afraid to open his eyes when a hand reached in and shook his shoulder. It was a girl. "Hey, little boy, what you doin' in jail?"

He quickly gathered up the few things around him and got to his feet. "I ain't little. I'm bigger than you!" He shoved his hands into his pockets with a sudden shyness.

The girl smiled a mouthful of crooked teeth, which she covered quickly with her hands.

"Sophie, what you up to, girl?" a harsh-voiced woman called, blocking the light at the door for a moment as she made her way in.

William noticed the stain of tobacco on her fingers and teeth. The soldiers sometimes talked about loose women, and William knew by the looks of her that the woman was one of them as she leaned forward a little to get a better look at him. It amazed him how much of herself the woman showed to him, and he worried she might fall out of her dress if she stared at him much longer. He knew that men kissed loose women and did like dogs do, but he couldn't understand why a soldier would ... the stains and her skin ruined by smallpox!

"You find yerself a pet, girl?" the woman asked, straightening up. She questioned William. "What you doin' here? You lost?"

"I guess so, ma'am."

"How'd you get stuck in here?"

"I stole a horse and was caught at it."

A wizened look came over her face. "So that's where them bastards got the pony and run off without payin.'"

"They weren't the law, ma'am?" he asked.

"Land sakes, no! The law!" the woman spurted, slapping her knees. "You a funny boy. Sophie, you let him out and bring him on home."

The woman walked back into the sun and met two other women on the half-finished plank boardwalk. The wind roared and whistled. Through it William heard the whore say, "Girls, we got us a little man in there—sweet thing."

With a bit of effort he could have gotten himself out. The builders seemed to have lost interest in the place before making it secure. Sophie unlatched the door and set him free.

Out in the open he saw that the town was bigger than he thought. There was a feed store with no feed in it, a hardware store all closed and boarded, and the Wise Moon. A house with great big rockers on the narrow porch and craven-looking women sitting in them was where they were headed. He glanced up at the heavens and slunk along with Sophie.

"What's a boy like you doin' here? You an orphan or somethin'? I ain't never had no daddy so don't feel so bad." Sophie looked him over and gazed into his caramel-colored eyes. "You injun? I'm half."

William had always felt it was a secret thing and was surprised at the girl for asking. "Well, my Pa—my father—I think he's half too."

"Oh, then we just the same, nearly," Sophie said, smiling. Her teeth weren't so bad, just out of place a bit, and she put her arm through his just like a grown lady as they marched to the house. Soon he stood on the porch between two low ladies all wrinkled up. He couldn't look at them. He didn't want to follow Sophie into the dark interior, and he couldn't stop thinking about what dogs did on the parade ground. He stepped back and stumbled down the small set of stairs. The old ladies laughed and shook their heads at the clumsy boy, but Sophie lured him back with bread. She patted the step beside her, and he joined her in eating. The sun warmed his lap and his spirits until the bread was gone.

Sophie put her hand on his knee. "How old you?"

"Thirteen," he lied.

"Me too. We still jus' the same. Do you think I'm pretty?"

"Yes."

Sophie leaned over and kissed him hard, digging her hands into his knees. His stomach churned in confusion, but something felt nice too, and he let Sophie keep at it. He hoped God noticed that he kept his hands to himself until the hand of God pushed them apart, using the tobacco woman's boot.

"Enough of that now. Sophie, you go wash up."

Sophie gave his legs one last squeeze and left with a groan and a roll of her eyes as the tobacco woman slapped her backside. The woman pulled him up to his feet and smiled a secret sort of smile that frightened him. "You like that, boy?" she asked with a laugh. The two hags laughed too.

"I have to find my horse," William said.

"You funny. That hos is gone now. You got money?"

"No." His voice quivered.

"You stay here. You want more bread? If you work hard we pay and feed you till we go."

"Go where?"

The tobacco woman stretched her bare arm out. The skin hung from it. Loose women, he thought.

"This place no good no more. We gonna set up in the Black Hills soon."

William looked about him. In all directions was endless prairie.

Chapter Seventy-Four

The ax was chopping. Weldon's head was splintered. Where was he? Ah, yes ... his father was chopping wood. Before they could grow corn for whiskey and hogs Father had to chop the wood. The thud and the crack of the perfect hits, when the timber sliced like bread, soothed him to sleep in his mother's arms. Her black hair tickled his face, and she sang strange songs ...

No. It was Simon's ax. He loved a contest, and he'd chop against anyone—win or lose. Simon mostly won and shared out the wood but saved the best pieces for their little winter shack. It was always warm there and full of people playing cards, arguing and joking, while Weldon smoked and read, eventually falling asleep to the tune of it all.

No. This thudding was knocking. It was an incessant knocking with a voice to it. There was someone at the door, and when Weldon opened it the air came in cold. It was Corporal Sloane in a handmade and strange fur cap. He saluted Weldon half-heartedly.

"Sir, your boy took a horse last night. Do you know anything about it?"

Weldon shivered and let the man in. Grabbing a blanket from the bed and wrapping it around himself, he tried to recall the previous night. Sloane built a fire for him.

"William!" John called as he walked through the tiny rooms. All the boy's things were missing. "He's gone ..."

Sloane slammed the stove shut. "You let him go off on his own, sir?"

"No! Of course not." Weldon sat on the bed again and put his hand through his hair. "He must have gone without me knowing ... I ..."

"For God's sake, lieutenant, he's just ten years old! He could be lost for good! And just like him to take the worst horse in the lot. We can't depend on that animal holding out at all ... and the Indians! My God, sir, but you've really made a mess of things here!"

"Oh, Katherine, what have I let happen now?" Weldon muttered to himself.

"Sir, is Katherine your wife? You must alert her. Would he be going to her?" Sloane watched the lieutenant lie back down. "*Sir*!! I don't know what's happened to you over the last months, but this is your son! You have chosen to destroy a solid career for some reason that's none of my business, but the boy ..." He went to pull the lieutenant up, but Weldon shoved him away.

"What would you have me do, corporal? My son despises me already and with good reason. He's better off roaming the prairie."

"That's a romantic notion, sir, but the reality is that he's *ten*! The prairie is just as dangerous as the desert. I don't know much about you, but I'll risk saying that when you get out of this funk you're in you won't be able to live with yourself."

"Have you got family, corporal? Have you ever lost a child to illness? Have you ever been beaten and starved by your mother? You don't know a damn thing about me!"

"I've met people like you before, sir. We all got our own problems. Hell, most of the men you were supposed to lead are only in the army cause they got nothin' else. You think you're so different. And you know, maybe you are. There's not a man in this company that would let a little boy like Willy out into the world on his own because his momma years ago didn't do right by him!"

Weldon stood up too quickly and swayed. "Get the hell out of my home."

"Yes, sir." Sloane stopped right before leaving and turned to Weldon. "When you and your son first arrived most of us were jealous of you. You seemed a good father then. When you got him that dog and when you used to hunt and grow things around the place ... that kid worshipped you. It's a shame it wasn't enough for you." He slammed the door shut and marched off to tell the others all about the lieutenant's abysmal failure as a parent.

Weldon couldn't get warm though his skin glistened with perspiration. He kicked the dog off his coat then found a hat and the pair of wool mittens in tatters given to him by Sarah years back. He took the old carbine he owned and the army's ammunition down to the stables.

Two privates were finishing up grooming the animals.

"At ease, men. Please get the Morgan ready," Weldon ordered.

The men stared at him.

Impatiently he pointed to the sable horse in the last stall. "That one is the Morgan."

"Off for a nice little ride on this fine day, sir?"

Weldon's dark eyes narrowed. "I think you know that my son has gone off with the weak little pony. I'm going to try and find it ... and the boy."

There was a time not so long ago when mounting a horse, though not in the most graceful manner, came easily to the lieutenant, but he was lopsided now with his right limbs weak and tender. He led Bright around to a quiet spot where a pile of boxes stood for him to clamber up on the horse's back. U.S. lumbered down behind them and would not stay alone at the fort. He nipped at Bright's hind leg and was kicked good and hard.

"For God's sake, dog!" Weldon cursed as U.S. got up and continued to follow, favoring its side, but still determined to make a nuisance of itself.

The colonel stood in his high boots, his trousers up, but his suspenders down. A clean, red flannel shirt hugged his middle, and he drank tea. "Lieutenant Weldon."

"Sir!" Weldon saluted and struggled from the horse.

The colonel stopped him. "As you were, soldier."

"I'm off to find my son, sir," Weldon said, but the wind carried his voice away.

"I know, lieutenant, I know," the colonel said, waving his hand irritably.

"Sir, I have no horse of my own ... may I take her?" Weldon asked, running his fingers over the patches of hair behind his ear. He had nothing. "I will make sure she is well cared for."

"I have no worries there. You've been good with the animals. I hope you're taking that nasty cur too. I think his fucking all the bitches on parade is responsible for this impossible increase in dogs here. Good luck, Weldon. Don't hurry back. Just find William."

***

They called him Bill or Billy, never William. That suited William fine. The women lounged mostly and smoked some but seemed particularly fond of chewing tobacco. William enjoyed his pipe now that he had no need to hide it.

Sophie hugged and kissed him like a doll and dragged him from place to place even in front of the others. He tried to walk away several times, but the sun hadn't shown itself for days and the prairie howled. He knew that the sun rose in the east and set in the west, but that was all. He didn't know how the pony had come into this town while he slept, and Sophie kept pulling him back.

And sometimes it was nice to have a girl to be with instead of being alone, but other times were troubling to him. Sophie had never read a single book and thought William was near genius when he read from the Bible his mother had given him to feel like a real Christian soldier. It had been Simon's during the war, and it was his parents' joke that it had never seen the light of day until he took it.

Sophie loved the stories of Joseph and his brothers and the story of a woman washing the feet of Jesus. It gave her ideas. The two played hopscotch and tag, but when Sophie suggested he play Jesus he declined. One day she took him to the feed store and behind the bare counter.

"Come here, silly Billy. I want to show you something."

William rounded the counter, mildly curious. Sophie was pulling her stockings off and William assumed she would show a good scar or something, but she asked, "You like my legs?"

"I guess they're okay. They work, don't they? Let's go ..."

Sophie giggled. "No." She pulled him down to his knees. "I got somethin' for you that I ain't never given for free ... a peek." She lifted her skirts. There were no pantaloons. She opened her legs with a broad and generous smile. "Go on, you can touch it. It don't bite unless you want it to."

William rushed to his feet. He didn't want anything biting him but took one last look and was about to bolt when he noticed Sophie crying. He stood there looking at his shoes, hands in his pockets.

"Billy, don't you like me no more?" she asked, pulling her stockings back on.

"Course I like you, Sophie."

"Men pay money to see that and like it—not you. Don't you like girls?"

"I think so, but it ain't right to gawk at their privates. That's mighty bad and you might go to hell, Sophie, if you keep doin' it, so I wouldn't."

She threw a piece of lumber his way. "You think you so special readin' all those big words like you come from a king, but your momma and papa did naughty stuff to get you—I bet more than gawk at their privates!" She softened her approach then while he stood thinking about his mother and father. "Want me to make you feel big and strong? I know how. C'mon, it don't hurt and then you do me after."

He hesitated. He didn't want to hurt her feelings, and he was interested.

She plunged her hand into his trousers and worked on him for a while. He knew they should stop, but it felt good when he kissed her a little. She grabbed his hand with her free one and led him back down to the floor. She showed him what to do to her, and they played all afternoon like that until the men came through.

The familiar sound of teamsters chirruping their four-in-hand wagons made his heart skip. He buttoned his trousers and ran to the window, sure the army and his father had come to get him, but the men were roughs and miners. Sophie sidled up to him while braiding her long, yellow hair. The two looked alike in a way, maybe because they were both so alone.

"Sophie! Billy! Come out where ever you are!" called one of the women from the brothel. Anna Tucker was a Scandinavian blonde with tiny eyes and only a few phrases of English. William had read about the Vikings and liked her. Anna never acted too friendly like the rest did with him.

He stepped out first, and she smiled. She kissed her hand and wiped it on Willy's forehead and messed his hair. The men had brought a bag of bright hard candy, and Anna gave them each a piece. With the sugar rolling around their mouths, they walked until the boardwalk gave way to dirt and prairie grass.

The little avenue had come alive with men. The saloon doors stayed open, and the quiet talk of women was replaced with the more boisterous laughter of men excited by the prospects of drink and sex.

William enjoyed the noise and the movements of the men and horses. It reminded him of home and the real world outside this town. He stood on the grey and shabby porch alone. The two old guards on rockers were taken into some dark cavity of the hotel as bad for business. The tobacco woman opened the door and pulled William inside. "Help Sophie finish rooms upstairs. Fill basins. You make real money today—no bread—real money." She smiled and kissed William's cheek before sending him off. This group of men had been here before. The tobacco woman knew their ways and inclinations and readied herself for them knowing that when the last of the Wise Moon's bottles were emptied they would come.

William followed Sophie around, dutifully filling basins as she smoothed the ragged bedcovers. William peered out of each window down toward the street, wondering what sort of money he'd make. When they were done, Sophie walked to her door but wouldn't let him follow. She looked unhappy. "You be—no you are my best boy, Billy," she said, playing with his collar.

William walked down the back set of stairs into the kitchen where the old souls were now knitting like perfectly respectable ladies, though one had a cigar between her teeth. The tobacco woman came in red-cheeked and dark-eyed like a nightmare. William was about to take a slice of grease-sodden fry bread from the table, but she slapped it from him gently. "Not now, boy—you hungry, you eat later. Man out front. You bring to Miss Sophia ... wait." She pulled William back, found a bottle of perfumed oil, and poured it into her hands. She combed William's hair down with her fingers. The smell overpowered him. "There, much better ... a little gentleman. Now go."

An unexceptional man of medium build sat in the hall smoking a Turkish cigarette. William almost laughed. Only a sissy would smoke them, and not out here in the West.

The man's hair hung long with a dark wave and his face was clean-shaven, but for a repulsive tuft of hair just beneath his lower lip. He didn't much look like a teamster or a miner. The man gave William an impatient stare.

"Sir, you're to follow me, sir, to Sophie's, I mean Miss Sophia's room," William announced nervously. He wanted to do everything right so the tobacco woman would pay him.

The man followed him but hesitated on the landing. He suddenly seemed out of sorts and dependent on the boy for guidance.

"Sir, her room is all the way at the end."

The man took off his hat, exposing a dome-like white head above his long hair. Rolling his hat in his hands like he was thinking something over, the man asked, "Are you new here?"

"Yes."

"Hmm, well you know that I'm a writer?"

William turned friendly. "My Papa writes for the newspaper sometimes ..." He stopped himself. William tried not to think of his father, and the man seemed disturbed by his words. "Her room, sir ..." William said again and pointed.

The man stood still. "What's that in your hair?"

"I don't know ... it's nothing ... grease I guess."

"Like I was saying, I am writing about the West and such. I'd like to talk to you later."

"Sir, I'm mighty sorry, but I'm working for wages to leave here." William looked downstairs. "She might get mad."

"Oh. Well, of course I'll pay you. The madam will understand. This is her business." The man whispered then, getting so close to William's ear that it tickled and smelled of licorice. "I'll pay you better than any of the others, and you'll be in my book."

William stepped back. "Maybe you can just hurry and talk to me now ... and pay me."

The man chuckled. "I like you, young sir. We'll talk later." He winked.

William guided the man to Sophie's room. The man opened the door, and William peeked in to find "his girl" as he was beginning to think of Sophie, stark naked and painted like her mother.

The rest of the evening was filled with men. They smoked and drank on the porch, and the spittoons were awful to contemplate, but the tobacco woman kept William busy in the kitchen, helping with drinks and feeding him the occasional glass, which he sipped cautiously. His thoughts grew fuzzy, but still he worried about getting paid.

"You somethin', Bill. Fit in real nice here. Knew you would," the tobacco woman said. She pulled at his cheeks. "Mr. Weaver want you now."

"But you don't need me here?"

"Everythin' good. A good deal. Now go, but it's a secret. Wait till no one in hall up there."

"Okay." He walked invisibly by the men who were drunk or cuddling the women on the settees in the parlor. The hallway was empty and dimly lit by one dying candle on a shelf of unread books. He knocked lightly on the door, Sophie's door, but the man answered. He was fully dressed and ushered the boy in. Sophie had gone. William stood in the middle of the room with his arms folded. The man sat at Sophie's small table and opened his notebook. "Your name is Billy. How old are you?"

"Ten—I mean twelve years old."

"You're a beautiful boy—almost pretty as a girl."

"I ain't no girl!"

The man smiled and wrote.

"Hey, what are you writing?" William asked.

"Come here, and I'll show you. Come on now—I won't bite."

The man reached into his pocket, took out a few coins, and put them on the table. "For you, Willy. Is it all right if I call you that?"

William came over and scooped up the money.

The man grabbed his wrist. "Now, you don't get that money or any more of it for free. What are you going to do for me, young sir?"

"Do you want a drink or something?" William asked.

"No ... it's not a drink I want. Look, what do you think of my drawings?" The man flipped through the pages of his notebook.

William looked at the detailed, rough sketches of Sophie and others. They were ugly and disturbing. The ones of his Sophie were sad.

His heart beat in panic. "Where's Sophie?"

"Why, I don't know—I guess knocking about with someone else by now," the man answered. He pulled Willy close and kissed his neck.

The boy pulled away. "*Hey!*"

But the writer jumped him fast and pushed him to the bed. "You want to play rough, Willy? I like that too sometimes!" He unbuttoned his trousers while strad-dling the boy and slapping his face when William tried to wriggle free. "You like this?"

"*No!*" He tried to kick, but it was no use. When the man put his hand out, William bit it hard.

"What the hell!" the man cried and punched the boy in the eye but also let down his guard. William broke free. The man fumbled with his buttons while William ran for the door, but not before spotting an old leather wallet. He grabbed it and flew into the hall and down the stairs. The quick steps of the man followed him in hot pursuit. "Catch that little ruffian! He's got my money!"

No one cared but the tobacco woman and Sophie. They had trusted William not to make any trouble and ran out from the kitchen, following the writer onto the porch. William jumped on a horse and galloped off into the dark street. The writer cursed. "That little bastard has all my money!" He ran across the black street and found a horse too, jumped on its back and raced after his fortune.

William was never any good at picking a horse, and this time was no exception. The animal was mean and tired and resented being ridden. The wind blew in his ears. He could not hear the calls of the writer behind him. He kicked and kicked the animal beneath him and swore and cursed, but the horse was stubborn and here came the writer! In desperation William took the reins, turned, and with everything in him slashed the ends across the horse's backside and middle. The animal jumped and bucked, but William held tight to his mane. In the starlight the boy saw the horse's ears pinned back and waited for the angry animal to bolt. He didn't have to wait long. Snorting and galloping, the horse carried its rider far ahead of his pursuer but for a high price. William had been thrown too many times to count, but this time was different. He didn't get up.

***

Weldon rode for days through settlements and over open prairie aimlessly. Each step felt like walking on glass, always afraid of what he might find, afraid to finally be cut from the last person who had stuck with him.

Though late spring, the days stretched out long and grey. The towns, when he found them, held lonely people, suspicious and silent with the soldier. He had not guessed correctly at his son's direction anyhow. He'd guessed Willy would have struck out toward Minnesota, toward his mother.

The wind went right through his threadbare jacket, chilling his arm. Mounting and dismounting Bright served as the big challenges of each day. Withdrawals were not so bad this time because this time he had no illusions about quitting it ever again. When he suffered on those first days, the horse took over and led them.

Riding out alone had a certain appeal. He had never been without orders from others, without people around him, judging him and expecting things of him. His own low expectations led him now—a relief and a barren wilderness.

And then it rained. The leaden sky, so low for days, fell even closer to the blue-grass that now bent beneath it, like riding under sodden bed sheets. A steady stream of wet fell, and the muck wore on Bright's step so they stopped on this spot of earth exactly like the spots on every side of them.

Weldon slid down and took his rubber poncho to make a little tent that would keep just enough water off him to light a cigar—one Simon had sent him a while back that he had saved for a special occasion. Only his head and shoulders fit beneath the poncho held up by his carbine. He lay on his belly in the mud, long since soaked through, and could feel the water trickle around in his boots right along his toes. Weldon laughed. If anyone saw his setup!

Always he ended up in the wilderness, yet, he had this cigar ... a simple gift from a faraway friend who had thought of him. The cigar was supremely good in this smoky shelter from the storm, and he suddenly noticed that leaning on his elbows no longer hurt his arm. The weather usually made it worse. He thought of Katherine. She was like this little shelter—too small to keep him completely from the rain, but just big enough to allow him to enjoy all the simple pleasures of life. He had been the luckiest man all along but had only noticed the rain.

He turned on his back and pulled the poncho down over him like a blanket. U.S. trotted over wagging his tail, but ran off with a few barks. Weldon pulled the poncho over his head and took his gun from the ground, digging mud and grass from its barrel. Still he felt no real pain in his arm. He leaned against Bright, and for the first time since the war hospital and without aid of medication he recited a small prayer of thanks—he didn't know why.

Still U.S. barked. Weldon could not see him under the clouds and the rises of the land all around. It took a few minutes of strenuous hopping and pulling to get back on Bright. He whistled to the dog and followed the barking because one direction felt as good as another. The rain had turned to sleet.

The dog, unusually energetic and noisy, ran off after showing himself again momentarily. Weldon thought that maybe up ahead there was someone or something he did not want to meet and then a shot rang out.

Bright stumbled in fright to the side, but Weldon took her back under control with a firm and confident hold of the reins and his soft, steady talk. He hoped that his gun would work in this weather and held it over his saddle pressing forward but worried that he would find more than just a dead dog.

As Weldon reached a rise in the prairie the next dip became clearer and in a moment U.S. ran up, shaken but lively. In the distance though (and it wasn't as far as it seemed), Weldon spotted a horse and two men. They were obviously the shooters, and he thought it best to avoid them. He directed the horse with his leg, but suddenly Bright stood stock still, her nostrils flaring and her ears moving in concert with fast thoughts. Before Weldon could realize what was happening, Bright bolted toward the men. Weldon held on, but the wet reins leapt from his hands and he grabbed Bright's mane and his saddle. His gun hung down on its strap, no use to him now if they shot.

But they didn't. They jumped at the sudden company and darted to get out of the way of this dark force galloping at them. The little horse they had with them grew wild now too and broke free of his line. Weldon lifted his head slightly just in time to see the other animal rushing at him. Bright slowed a bit, and Weldon grabbed the reins back with a quick lunge and a forced breath. The Indian pony trotted up with a friendly whinny. The two animals had had a little romance in the army and remembered each other's scent. Weldon just stared at them.

But he remembered himself fast enough, jumped, and fell from Bright. He scurried up and wiped his gun, but it was all too wet now. The men came up then. "Well, I reckon it's love at first sight in this darn weatherin' all. Goddamned animals got some senses don't they? We didn't hear nor see a soul but yer dog."

"I heard the shot," Weldon informed them, flashing his gun.

"The bastard was botherin' our hos. That ain't right," the talker scolded.

Weldon spotted William's gun and his heart jumped. "Where's my boy?!"

The two looked at each other between the sleet and raindrops falling from their hats. "What boy?" The men had a ragged tent set up for themselves and smoke still came up from a fire put out by the downpour.

Weldon limped and ran to the tent, opening its flap of blankets. The men came after him. "Hey! Whatcha doin' goin' through our truck?"

"*Where's my son*?!" Weldon shouted wildly. He grabbed the closest man by the throat.

"We ain't done nothin' to no boy, sir," he gasped, noticing Weldon's government-issue shirt. The man was a deserter as was the silent one and realized the pickle he was in over the horse, the boy, and the desertion if there were more soldiers nearby.

"That's his gun! Where is he, you bastard? Tell me before I kill you!" Weldon shook him.

The big man stepped up and drew his pistol. The talker's eyes widened, and he warned his friend. "Fer God's sake, Frank, put the gun down. We have no issue with this *soldier*." He looked at Weldon, who still had him by the neck. "We ain't got the boy—'tis true we took his hos and gun, but we didn't hurt the boy—not a bit."

Weldon threw him to the ground and landed on top of him. "You stupid bastard! The boy! *My son* is all alone with not a soul to defend him—no gun even! You piece of shit!" Weldon lifted the butt of his gun overhead. "Where did you leave him? Tell me before I crack your skull!"

The talker began, "The Wise Moon—north of ..."

But the big man had had enough. He pulled Weldon's gun away and batted him unconscious.

Chapter Seventy-Five

Friday. The lessons dragged on in the sweltering classroom. The children picked at their bare toes, complaining that their shoes had grown too small and too hot in this freakish heat wave of spring. Two boys flicked dead flies from the windowsills even after Katherine ordered them to their seats. The girls passed descriptive, barely literate notes that she no longer bothered to read.

She pulled her watch from its pocket—only two. A fly flew by and she swatted it.

The door opened. Mr. Hammond walked in. "Mrs. Weldon, you are needed in the office."

The superintendent gave her an oddly tender look.

"What is it, sir?"

Once in the hallway, she heard the students' giggles and whispering.

"Mrs. Weldon, there seems to have been an accident."

"With John?"

He gave her a strange look. "No, it's your son I believe—Billy."

"No. No one calls him that. It's a mistake ..." she declared and turned back to her classroom. The superintendent took her hand, and she burst into tears.

"Mrs. Weldon ... Katherine ... please ... there's someone to see you in my office."

The writer in a shabby, black suit and pointed boots gave her a woeful look. Katherine hated him instantly. He stood up and extended his hand, but she kept her hands at her sides.

"Pleased to make your acquaintance, ma'am. Pardon me for interrupting your work here at this fine establishment," he said, his eyes flitting round the room.

"Where's my son?!"

"Ma'am, he's a few miles from here. We found a doctor, and we thought it best he stay put a while."

"What's happened, and who the devil are you?"

"Ma'am, you see it's like this ... the boy was in a bit of trouble and stole my money and a horse. He had a tragic fall."

"He's fallen many times," she said, "but he's always been just fine. He's a good rider."

The writer looked at Mr. Hammond, who with a solemn nod urged him on. "You see, we haven't been able to wake him. He breathes but he won't wake. The doctor said that we shouldn't have moved him so far—clear across the country it feels like—but we couldn't care for him. In fact this trip has really put me out for cash."

"Mr. Weaver, not now," Hammond said. "Mrs. Weldon, go with this man. Don't worry about classes. We'll pray for you and your son."

Katherine raced to her room and grabbed a shawl and her pistol. The man had a surrey big enough for just two tightly squeezed in. He smelled of oriental spice and was a terrible driver.

"Give me the reins, sir!"

"What was that?"

"Give me the damned reins!" she exploded, shakily pointing her little gun at him.

The writer gave her the reins.

She said nothing else, and the man only ventured to speak when there was need for directions. The horse arched its neck gratefully on the comfortable lead and raced along at a nice canter all the way to the doctor's door. She sprang from the surrey and for a second noticed the cobalt blue sunset over the distant northern forests and thought nothing really bad could happen on such a beautiful night as this. She knocked at the door and called to the doctor. A grim old lady answered. The tobacco woman and a crying Sophie sat on a small bench. Katherine brushed past them to find the doctor. He emerged from a darkened back room.

"I've come for my son. I was told that he's here." Still she believed there must be a mistake. She glanced back at the "fallen women" staring rudely at her then turned to the doctor impatiently.

The man did not appear to be in the best of health himself. His nose was red and thick and his office cluttered with papers and empty bottles. "You're the mother?"

"I don't know—until I see him." She wanted to push him aside, but he frightened her a little and so did the dark room with someone's boy in it.

"There ain't much hope, if he is your son."

"Let me see him!"

"Certainly."

Katherine pulled back the curtain and crept through the darkness. The doctor brought a dim candle behind her. The injured boy lay still. "Oh! Willy! What's happened?" she cried. Below the bandages wrapped round his head, two blackened eyes, closed in a slumber, stood out starkly against his white cheeks. The doctor had arranged his damaged leg in a useless splint.

"It ain't good, mother. His brain is swelled and his neck's broke, I reckon. The leg could be fixed better, but there's no point in it. I don't know how they got him this far—those whores out there. The girl said your son used to talk of the injun school a lot. She's a smart little girl—a shame she's a whore."

"Can he hear me at all?" Katherine cried.

"I reckon not, but talk if it makes you feel better. I'll be outside."

"William, for God's sake, *wake up*!" she shouted, slapping his hand in hers. His nails were dirty and long like they always were, and she sobbed.

Sophie heard the yelling and burst in. "Don't you dare go and yell at my boy!"

The tobacco woman came to retrieve her daughter. "Sorry, ma'am!"

"Just get her away from my son, you horrible ...!" Katherine ran at them. The writer pushed through and got between the women as the doctor looked on with a cup of coffee in hand.

"And where were you, I ask?" the writer inquired, "letting a twelve year old on his own?"

"Twelve? He's ten. Willy was to go back east with an escort ... my husband wrote ..." She shook and dropped her shawl. The writer reached down to grab it, but she stepped on his hand. "Don't touch it, sir! I warn you!"

"So this is the payment we get for being good Samaritans."

She turned back to William and climbed into bed with him. If he was to die like Eliza, she wanted him not to feel alone. The others left them and the doctor checked on them only once. "Ma'am, there's a telegraph line a mile away if you'd like to send for the father."

Katherine buried her face in her son's long, scented hair and wrapped her arms around him. William looked so perfect and handsome in the light cast from the blue moon. She sang in her small voice the songs John used to sing to them in the desert when they were frightened by the cries of the wildcats prowling the sandy nights. Even now it was his words and songs that came to mind. She had never had a single hope or song of her own that didn't involve John Weldon, but he had cast her off like a played-out melody.

***

The colonel, who cared mostly about horses, cursed as he peered from his window when Weldon led the Morgan and the pony back across the parade ground without William. The men in the stables watched him but did not salute. Weldon wandered back to his pathetic little room emptied of all William's and Katherine's things.

Katherine, only a faded paper girl now, floated on winds somewhere to the north. Weldon filled his syringe and realized he could no longer frame his wife's face in his mind. She was lost to him—out somewhere changing Indians, saving them. But he knew that nothing would change. She had not changed him. His chest tightened. He had trusted her to change him, erase him, and start him over like a new letter clearly written. But the alphabet in his head, the words and definitions of his early years, stubbornly persisted and resisted restructure.

"Lieutenant Weldon!" It was Corporal Sloane at the door. "Weldon open up this minute." The door was pushed before Weldon got to it.

"Yes?" he answered irritably but saw now that Sloane stood with the colonel and a group of William's hunting companions. Only the colonel and the corporal came in and closed the door behind them.

"Sir?" Weldon stepped forward timidly and saluted.

There was a long uncomfortable silence as Corporal Sloane pulled Weldon's medical supplies from beneath his bed. The colonel looked him over gravely. He hadn't even had time to clean himself up. The colonel held out a terse telegram from Katherine:

To: Lieutenant Weldon;

You are dead to me ... William is here ... I am caring for him ... if he lives he will never walk ... I always believed in you ... I thought you loved us ... never contact us again.

Katherine McCullough

"He's alive at least," Weldon mumbled.

The corporal and the colonel exchanged disgusted glances. "Weldon, you have been a great disappointment to us all here," the colonel said. "In fact, the men outside this door would have me kick you off our land this minute for losing your son. Not a single soul has warmed up to you here, and for stealing the morphine alone you should be cashiered. But somehow you have friends elsewhere who want you saved. Weldon, you're the luckiest man for friends. In the past month, since I sent my formal complaints to General Crook, I have been pestered by letters and telegrams ... Lieutenant Bourke, Retired Colonel Langellier, and Captain McCullough, a doctor too—Dudley, who wrote of the pain you suffer due to injuries received in the service ... and of course from General Crook himself. You must have been a different man. They all seem set on giving you one last chance."

"Sir, I'm not sure I want another chance ... I'm tired."

"Well, lieutenant, you have no choice. I won't have you stay here. I don't want to have you about. The transfer papers are in. You are to report in California. They'll be expecting you."

"The Pacific?"

"Yes. Another one of your many friends is here to escort you. As I said, in some ways you're quite lucky." The colonel stared at the strange emotionless form before him. "The men have a few things for William and hope you will go see him before

California. Sloane, take that box back to the infirmary. Weldon, as I suggested before, you should retire. Whatever your reasons for taking the medicines, there are no good reasons for the army to keep you. You can apply for a pension before any more trouble."

"I'd rather die than leave the military, sir."

"As you wish ... pack your things, lieutenant."

Chapter Seventy-Six

For the first time in her life, Katherine had a place of her own—above a saloon. It was small and broken down like she was, and Willy too.

The new room, quiet in the daytime, came alive at night. She didn't mind. She rarely slept. Every time William closed his eyes she waited breathlessly until he opened them again. He turned his head slightly, and once, although it felt like it may have been a dream, he closed his fingers around hers. And now if she forced him, he would open his mouth to drink. She begged him to know her and to speak, but he would not.

The place smelled of dirty laundry. She wondered how many times in the past she yelled at him to stay quiet when something more important was going on. She massaged his feet, rubbed his scalp gently, and smoothed cream over his bedsores. Still, he stared out, his slow breathing keeping time.

The door slammed below and boots hit the stairs up to their room at a pace too quick for townsfolk. It was a soldier. Her heart jumped.

"Mrs. Weldon, are you at home?"

"Oh, please, do come in, sir!"

The man took off his hat. "Mrs. Weldon, my, I'd hardly recognize you! But then you were just a girl. Oh, and Willy ..." The soldier went to the boy's bed. "I'm sorry for him ..." He turned to her again with kind eyes. "He's no better?"

She shook her head. The soldier looked strong and sported a thick, tidy beard. Katherine couldn't place him until he gave her a smile. "Private Higgins!"

"It's sergeant now, ma'am."

"Yes, the stripes! But I remember you hating the army. I can't believe it's you!"

"I'm a dog robber no more. I suppose the army grew on me in the end, and I haven't been able to shake it."

"It's so wonderful to see someone from the old times," she cried, her eyes welling with tears.

Higgins patted her arm. "None of this now."

"But why are you here? Is something wrong with my husband?"

Higgins gave her an odd look. "Well, ma'am, as you know he ain't been himself for a while, but when I heard he was havin' some trouble I called in all my favors to be his escort west. You know he was my best teacher—like a father. It's terrible sad how it's all turned for him."

"Sergeant Higgins, I don't understand ... he's gone west?"

"Why, no, not yet anyhow. He's waitin' down in the tavern. Lieutenant Weldon insisted on visiting you—I mean your son."

"Thank you, sergeant, for everything," she said with feeling. "For taking care of him ..." She swallowed hard. "Oh, you must make some nice girl such a happy wife!"

"'Fraid not, Mrs. Weldon. Lieutenant Weldon always told me how hard it was on you—and on him—being separated and bounced around. I wouldn't have the heart for it. Shall I fetch the lieutenant?" Higgins hesitated. "He said you might not want to see him, but the lieutenant would like to see his son."

"I'm not the monster he must make me out to be!"

"I'll just go fetch him and say it's all right," Higgins said with a mournful last glance at William.

Katherine sat in her corner chair pretending to read. Again after a short while there came noise on the staircase. With mixed emotions she listened to her husband's slow, uneven footfall. "There you are, lieutenant—call me when you need me." She heard Higgins say.

The knock came after a tentative pause.

"Come in then," she called impatiently.

Weldon shook a little. His bad leg was having a bad day. He leaned heavily on his battered stick as he turned to close the door behind him.

Katherine rose from her seat to help.

"No, Kate, I'm fine," he said like he always did. He refused to look at her, but she kept her eyes on him. He wore a scruffy beard, and his hair was thinner. It took him too long to get to his son. "William, I looked and looked for you ..." he choked out as he inched forward, "and I kept slipping from that damned Morgan ... it was your little pony who found us ... but you ... you were gone! I promise, Willy, to get the best doctors I can."

"Please, John, no false promises," Katherine said.

He didn't respond as he sat beside his son on the bed with a creak, running his hand again and again over William's head until Katherine felt she would go mad. Weldon turned to her. "I have some things he might like when he's well."

"He's as well as he'll ever be."

"No, I won't accept that."

He limped to the door like a sorry old man and grabbed his unwieldy bag with the butt of a rifle sticking out of it.

"William, I got your gun back from those bastards." He opened his son's hands and ran them over the muzzle, the trigger, and the worn wooden butt. "Remember our hunts? We didn't go out enough, I know."

William smiled. Weldon went on unaware that up until now he hadn't expressed emotion. Katherine inched over to him silently as Weldon continued to speak. "Some of the boys, Corporal Sloane too, sent you presents. Here's his nice Bowie knife. They wanted me to ask if you were still hiding tobacco from your parents. I told them you would never do such a thing, but I guess I wouldn't have known really ..." His voice trailed and a new voice rose up in laughter.

William laughed—first weakly, but then stronger, and Katherine pounced upon him.

"Katherine, is he all right?"

"I don't know ..."

Weldon and Kate watched until Willy wore himself out, not daring to touch him or interrupt. William sighed and smiled. "Papa."

Weldon fell in a heap at his side. "Forgive me, forgive me, Willy!"

"Papa! Mother! I dreamt this ... I told God if he made me come back that we would have to be together again, and I would be very good."

"William, you are very good!" Katherine cried.

"And I saw Eliza like I knew I would. This is just how I dreamt it ... I think ... where's U.S.?" William tried to move, but his arms refused. This startled him. "Where's my dog?"

"I'll send for him," Weldon said uneasily before admitting the truth. "I gave him to Sloane. I couldn't care for him ... but ..."

"You don't care for anyone, Papa! You've ruined everything! This ain't like the dream at all. You didn't have a nasty beard either and my legs ... they worked and all. I've been tricked!" William turned to Katherine. "Mother, you were prettier in the ..." He looked horrified. "Oh, no, you don't love Papa anymore do you?"

"No! *No*! I don't love your father anymore!" she cried. "He's done this to you!"

"It's not the same! I didn't want to come back! Papa, where are you going? Please don't leave! And where are your spectacles?"

Weldon gave him a strange look. "I don't wear spectacles, Willy. Mother will take you home and make you well if you let her, and I'll visit when I can."

"You're lying, Papa! I know I won't ever see you again! You're too sick. Mother, make him stay!"

William slid down into his bed in bitter silence. He watched his father limp to the door. Like a flood William remembered the horse he stole and the writer and the cologne and the grease of the fry bread. His stomach turned, and he was sick over himself but could not escape it because his legs didn't go and his arms remained still. He couldn't escape his crying mother either. She changed his shirt. He had no words for her, but when she wrapped her soft arms around him and pulled him close, he could smell her familiar flower water, and he forgot about God's promises and cried in gratitude. He was not a soldier or a bawdy houseboy, but his mother's child. He kissed her red cheek, and she rocked him and cried as they listened to Higgins helping the man of their shattered dreams stumble down the stairs.

***

As the train pulled in to Englewood, Katherine sighed with resolve. Everything would be for Willy now, and in a way that was comforting. She had made the mistake of expecting certain things out of life, but now there was absolutely nothing to expect at all—except maybe a cup of tea from Sarah when they walked through the door. Sarah had probably been packed for weeks. She and Simon had planned to visit the Centennial Fair in Philadelphia with Emily, who was already there visiting a friend before the three of them headed to the Pacific coast, but news of William had delayed them.

She hopped from the train, ignoring the railway man's hand. She looked and felt wretched and severe. Glancing along the depot walk, she noticed that the tree she had often brought the horses under when waiting for her father was gone and more sidewalk put in. With the last of her money she had bought a wheelchair for William. Gently the rail men carried him down and set him on the platform. She avoided the stares of so many strangers as William gazed out in quiet, still getting used to the bustle of the east after being so long away from it.

William had headaches now and pains in his neck too. A gentleman doctor along the way had suggested that the boy's hair was too much a weight on his disabled frame, and Katherine had a man come and cut it all off. William protested, and she hated the result—he looked like a sadly shorn sheep and his eyes stood out encircled in deep violet rings. The headaches persisted. It was as if William had been feeble his entire life. A boy passed that Katherine thought she recognized. William slouched forward hiding his crippled frame until his old schoolmate passed.

Englewood teemed with buggies and surreys and wagons "We'll walk, sir, if you'll just deliver our things ..." Katherine told a driver.

"It'll cost you the same, ma'am. Time is money."

"Fine," she replied testily.

"Mother, I think it will feel so good to be home again," William said. "I'm tired of travel and being pushed here and there. I won't ever leave my room again."

"William, you'll stay on the first floor for a while, in the parlor maybe. We need to make things easy on ourselves."

"Until I can get about on my own, you mean," he suggested, for the first time showing a spark of optimism.

She smiled. "Of course."

She rounded the heavy chair onto Tenafly Road and gasped at the sight of the house. Sarah had completely given up the garden, and the summer's growth of weeds had strangled off so many of her delicate plantings. Scott had always made sure to have the house painted regularly, but such things were of no concern to Sarah and it showed. Just around back, her conservatory lay barren. Katherine wanted to turn around and leave.

William stared at the closed green shutters and the empty barn with its open door. Scott had never allowed such things, and William began to cry. "Grandfather is dead! I hadn't remembered!"

She bent down next to him. "Yes, my sweet, but he loved you and would be happy that you finally came back to his house to keep it for him."

As upsetting as it all was, she was glad when William retrieved bits of his past. When his mood hadn't been too foul on the train, she tried to tell him as many family stories as she could think of. So many of them he didn't recall. He pretended sometimes to know things to keep the frightened look from his mother's face. "Your Uncle Simon ..."

"I think I was fond of him," William said cautiously, wondering if she just made some of these people up to test him. Sometimes he worried that this mother wasn't even really his, but then a memory would flood in of her hanging laundry in the desert and smiling a certain way, and he would cling to her. He upset her once on the train. "I know that you are real and mine, but I'm afraid when I forget you—I don't like this forgetting all the time. I get lost in my head and can't find you, Mother!"

She whispered softly to him, "You must *never* forget that I will be here always!"

The shadows stretched long over the front porch and the wind blew the vines on the old trellises. A blue jay barked orders overhead, and the sparrows conversed happily everywhere. The side door, the kitchen door, swung open and then slammed. Simon jumped two steps and trotted up the drive, returning from some errand. He stopped in his tracks at the sight of them.

"*Mother*! They're home!" he called to Sarah and ran to them. "Katie, you look so lonesome. Come here and give me a hug."

Sarah, with more white hair and a bit heavier, bounded out the front door with her apron still on. "I was just baking bread and a pie too! Poor Simon has had to keep up with my cooking!"

Simon patted his belly. "It has been no effort, I assure you, Mother."

Sarah pulled Katherine close and wouldn't let go. "Oh, Katie! What a mess your life is! I will stay with you if only you ask!"

Katherine glanced at Simon who looked pained.

"Mother, you have cared for me long enough—it's time that you baby Simon!" Katherine laughed.

Simon grinned and kissed her head.

They turned to William as if he were a museum curiosity. He was still teary-eyed over Scott's death, but when Sarah came close he nearly fell from his seat to get to her. "Grandma!"

She burst into tears. "You never should have gone away from us, you poor dear! I should stay with you, and we can make cookies like we used to."

"You're not staying?" William cried.

"Willy! I told you so on the train," Katherine reminded him gently.

"No, you didn't! You're a liar!" he wailed.

Simon stepped up. "Now we won't allow you to talk to your mother that way, Willy!"

"And who are you?" William asked with a sneer.

Simon glanced at Katherine then crouched down beside the boy. "It's me, Simon."

William knew that he should recognize him and grew agitated.

"We had bully times ..." Simon began halfheartedly, but William's eyes brightened when Simon took his hat off.

"Uncle Simon! Bully ... you always said bully, and you took my hat!"

Simon turned to his sister.

"Yes! The hat at Christmas that year, Simon. You kept knocking it off going to church!" Katherine said.

They all laughed at the memory, and William went on, "You came and gave me candy—just me—when Eliza was dying."

Simon softly ran his hand over William's head and stood up again. "Shall we get you inside?" He looked around for their bags.

"Oh, don't worry. The driver will bring them eventually if he wants his fare," Katherine said.

Simon carried William into the kitchen and placed him in his grandfather's old chair by the hearth. They all watched him grin happily as he took in the entire kitchen, remembering things. The place looked worn out and a little shabby somehow compared to Katherine's memories of only a year ago.

Simon brought in some books and placed them next to William. "Remember these, Willy?"

William looked mortified. "I don't like to read."

Simon saw by Katherine's expression that the boy couldn't somehow. "Well, that's okay, little man. I don't like to either!"

William smiled gratefully at Simon and pulled him to sit on the chair's arm. Simon felt honored and almost didn't want to leave for his own family now.

When Katherine returned from paying the driver at the front door, Simon and Willy chatted happily about horse racing, and Sarah busied herself making a supper for them all. As usual she wanted no help. Katherine watched. The cabinets were no longer polished, and there were no tiny plants lining the windows. The floor was swept, but not really clean. She had imagined coming home to the place being just the same as ever. Even Sarah, now that Katherine watched her, seemed different, and it was not just the hair and extra weight. She bent and started the fire, but with great effort, and when she did her swollen ankles showed through threadbare stockings she would never have allowed herself to be seen in when Scott was alive. Watching the way her mother struggled in her body, huffing and puffing, she never wanted to be that way again. It was better to realize that nothing could fill the void left when you lost people you loved. Sarah caught her sad stare and after stirring the pot sat down with her at the table. "What is it, Katie?"

"Mother ... please *do* take care of yourself better."

Sarah smiled. "I should say the same to you, but I won't."

Katherine moaned with a chuckle.

Sarah whispered, "You know what's done me in is that I was never meant to be alone. I got used to cooking for a family and expected them to stay around—maybe move down the road—and then Scott left me. Well, I can't seem to cook for less than the family I had when it was the four of us!" She laughed and cried. "And I guess I don't like to upset your father with wasted food! But you know I'm glad to be going, really. I think I can be of help to poor Simon. Lucy is sweet, but it really troubles Emily that her baby isn't just so! Simon needs my support even if he did bring on all this trouble himself."

"Mother, we all do make mistakes sometimes," Katherine said.

Sarah with surprising smugness didn't seem so sure. "I suppose we made our mistakes too, Scott and me, but our children were kept safe from things."

Katherine held her tongue. William fell asleep before supper, and she was happy for time alone with Simon and Sarah.

Morning came before they had time to go to bed. A few of Scott's old bottles had made their way to the table, and the three were all talked out when the last of the bottles were drained. Katherine heard her mother's footfall above as Sarah wandered through the rooms of her house, reliving happy memories one last time. Sarah would never smell Simon's cigars in his bedroom full of toy guns and weird specimens from the woods. Katherine's room needed new paper on the walls. Sarah tore a wrinkled piece off from the corner and placed it carefully inside her pocket Bible, remembering how excited she had been to make a fresh start in her new house on Tenafly Road. Katherine had been a wide-eyed dreamer back then and only really spoke when the lights were low and she padded down the stairs in the night to watch Sarah knit and sew. Katherine had whispered to her mother that she wanted walls the color of the lamp light, and the next day they ordered just that, sprinkled with tiny flowers. There was not a thing that Sarah didn't do for her daughter, and still things had turned out so messy. And now they hardly talked, and there would be no midnight meetings again when Katherine would whisper that she loved her. Everyone had grown up and grown old. Sarah sat on Katherine's bed and cried.

Katherine climbed the stairs and sat beside her. "Mother, it's all right. I'll take good care of the place."

Sarah dabbed her face with a clean and pressed handkerchief. "Oh, Katie, it's not that ... you know your father did everything for the two of you, and you were his pet. It bothers me that you never thanked him!" Sarah scolded.

"Mother, are you all packed and ready?" Katherine asked, standing up again. "Oh, you look so nice now in that suit. Powder blue will always remind me of you."

Sarah looked up and laughed. "Land sakes, Katie, I'm not dead yet, and you will come to visit when we are settled. It's so easy by train now."

Katherine smiled. Nothing was as easy as it seemed. "Yes, someday, I guess."

Simon swayed in. His eyes were bleary and his hair a mess. Sarah clicked her tongue. "Shame on you! You look a wreck. Now I'll have to be in charge of things today. Go clean yourself up, and I'll make us a breakfast."

The cab came soon after they sat one last time on the front porch together in silence. William remained grim. The horses snorted as they came up to stop under oak trees.

"Look, William, white Friesians! Aren't they lovely?" Katherine cried.

William wouldn't look at her or the horses. Simon jumped up and began loading their bags into the coach. Sarah got up more slowly. "I don't think any house Simon might get out west could be as comfortable and perfect as this! Katie, I do believe there are carpenter ants at work on the porch and you must see to it that any damage gets fixed."

Katherine nodded, afraid to speak. She didn't want her mother to go.

Sarah turned to William. "Sweetheart, there are tintypes and other things in a box next to your new little bed in the parlor. They're my memories. You must care for them till you come visit."

He stared past her angrily in his chair. Tears ran down his cheeks. Sarah wiped them and gave him a big hug before tearing herself away with a heaving chest. She stopped on the bottom step and reached down into the weeds. Pulling at them and pointing, she said, "Look, Katie—one of John Weldon's silly little desert blooms. It never did all that well out here."

Katherine gave her mother one last hug and with Simon helped her into the coach. "Dear, please write me for a change," Sarah begged.

Simon laughed, but it wasn't funny. "Mother, don't you know by now that Katherine isn't much of a writer? I guess she's always too busy." He came along side of his sister. "Take care, sis. Why don't you surprise us and write. We'd all be grateful."

Katherine kissed him and waved as the horses ran off.

She sat with William for a while in quiet on the porch. Without Sarah and Scott the place sounded hollow. She didn't even want to step back inside, but William looked blue and cold so she wheeled him in, banging up against the narrow hallway and into the parlor. She hadn't noticed yesterday that Simon and Sarah had transformed the place into a perfect boy's bedroom with new tartan plaid bedcovers and curtains with gold trim. Simon's big clock sat beside the bed, and a map of the United States hung on the wall. A jar full of powder-white cookies sat on the old knitting table. They both looked around speechless for a while.

"Mother, please put me to bed. I'm cold and I want to look in the box."

She tucked her son under the flannel blankets, then closed the windows and set a small fire in the hearth though it was only August. By the time she came back with tea for the cookies, William had set out all the old tintypes and even older daguerreotypes. News clippings and a ribbon of Katherine's from when she won an art contest at school were scattered on the bed. He came upon a likeness and held it out to her. "Mother, this is you?"

She smiled at the awkward young girl. "Yes, I'm afraid so. I smiled when I shouldn't have and look awful foolish."

"You looked pretty ... and happy," he said. "You look sort of like Eliza with your hair like that." He cried again.

"What is it now?" she asked, trying not to sound too impatient.

"Mother, please tell me the truth. Papa is dead isn't he?"

"Willy! *No*! Your father is very much alive! You saw him—in our room. Don't you remember?" She tried to assure him but felt panicked now too. "You must remember ..."

"No. What room?" he asked pathetically. "I know he's bad, and you hate him, but ... I think he's dead, and you won't tell."

"William Weldon, you're wrong! And you are never to say such things again. I would tell you if anything happened. I would know!" She gathered up some of the mementos, shoving them into the box.

"No! Leave me the likeness of him!" Willy ordered and took a picture of John and Simon from the war. "You sent him off when he was sick."

"Stop it!" she begged. "I have one invalid—I didn't need two! Your father made his bed!"

William leaned back on his pillow. His head throbbed. Katherine could tell by the deepening circles around his eyes. She sat beside him. "Willy, let's not talk about your father for a while. You need rest."

"But he talked about you all the time. I saw him use a needle in his leg, but he said it hurt more not to use it. I remember he bought you a pistol once, traded it for a handsome suit Grandma made him. I remember he said you were too pretty and someone would come and steal you."

She ran her hands over his head until he closed his eyes. She poured tea and took a cookie. It was too sweet. She put the scattered memories away on a high shelf. Maybe her son would forget them too.

Church bells rang out the midday hour—already—and William slept. Quietly as she could, she rose and left for the kitchen, closing the parlor doors gently behind her. All but a few of Sarah's things stayed behind where they had always been, and she wondered how her mother would feel without them—her delicate wedding china and crystal dessert dishes, her well-seasoned pots and pans. The place was too cluttered and overwhelming without Sarah to distract from the mess. Katherine, who had gotten so used to living simply, could not imagine living with full and toppling china cabinets, linens shoved and stuffed in drawers, and sticky countertops. Today she would begin the work of clearing things away to the attic. Like Rachel Campbell, she had had her fill of desserts, so the pretty little dishes were the first things to go. Scott's medical journals continued to arrive for months after his death and were stacked sloppily beside his old chair, dangerously close to the fire. Simon had complained that Sarah would not let them be disposed of. Katherine built a fire but could not burn them and moved them instead to the already overstuffed library. Sarah's delightful little kitchen desk, usually perfectly organized and oftentimes decorated with peonies and roses from the garden set in vases, had become the depository for the mail she did not want to deal with and Simon hadn't gotten around to. Katherine sifted through condolence cards that hadn't even been opened and subscription notices. She found a stray note from Scott to Sarah reminding her that he would be out late at a meeting and not to wait up, signed "Your adoring husband." Slipping it into her pocket Katherine would save it for Sarah and send it when she felt her mother was ready for it.

As clumsy as ever, Katherine tripped on her shoelace but did not fall. She smiled to herself and knelt to tie her shoe. Beneath a massive pile of dirty aprons and linen set aside for the laundress (who came irregularly since Sarah's grieving process included abusing the girl's shoddy work), she noticed a wrapped package with familiar handwriting. On hands and knees she pulled it out. It was from the Indian school. She wondered what she could have left behind and was curious if Mr. Hammond had sent her some unnecessary or inappropriate item—a dress maybe. She read the note:

> *Dear Mrs. Weldon,*
>
> *We received this strange package from a Sophie or Sophia. The address and name were smudged and sloppy. From what I could decipher from the letter the bag belongs to your son whom I hope is making great strides in recovery. You are lucky to have some hope.*
>
> *You never mentioned where your husband was stationed in the military, but I hope he was not with Custer's men this summer. Half of our teachers have resigned their positions. The Sioux are too savage they say. I do believe if things were different you would have stayed and become a very good teacher.*
>
> *Some of the children ask for you at the agency and wish to write you. I gave them your address. I hope that is all right.*
>
> *Jay Hammond*

Katherine tore the brown paper from the soft canvas haversack. It wasn't William's but John's—the bag he never went anywhere without. Her hands shook. How had someone else gotten his bag? She imagined Weldon finally killed by Indians and for a moment didn't want to unbutton the flap to look inside. What if there was horrible news within?

William called then, nervously. She could hear in his voice that he had forgotten where he was. Still clutching the bag she went to him.

"William, I'm here. We are at Grandma's—we're home ..." She bowed and kissed his forehead.

William sighed in relief. "Okay, it's okay," he said to himself. He caught sight of the haversack then. "Mother, Papa's bag! Where did you find it?"

"I don't know," she stammered. She didn't want to frighten him. "It was sent here."

"I took it, Mother. I don't remember why now, but I thought I lost it."

"When?! Who is Sophie?" Her heart raced.

His eyes lit for a moment, but he said guardedly, "She was just a girl."

"A girl?"

William thought about what he did with this girl and blurted out by way of confession, "She was a low girl ... but Mother, she was nice."

Katherine remembered now the crying girl at the doctor's. "Did your father bring you to her? Was he there with you?"

He gave her an odd look. "I never saw him there—I ran away."

She breathed deeply. So John was not dead somewhere, and he hadn't been with the low women. She opened the bag now, filled to bursting not with vain indecipherable attempts at short notes like the ones he had tried to write when his arm didn't work, but full and completed letters—most sealed and some even addressed, but all for her.

William laughed a little. "The letters ... yes, I found them."

She opened one and then another and read and read. William drifted again, and she read some more, stunned by all the little things John chose to write about—her cooking and her nose; her stories and how much he enjoyed her compliments; birthdays celebrated and then those that were forgotten and as the letters went on—he had kept them in chronological order. The forgetting and the struggling and the sadness crept in more and more, between the lines at first then boldly splashed across every page. Years of struggle and secrecy and all the strange times came to her differently, for the first time making real sense. Day turned to evening and the clock wound down. She read until the bag was emptied.

Dear Katherine,

You once told me to write more. Like so many things you have asked of me I have failed.

I am a coward. I have written this letter and so many like it without sending a one. I fooled myself into thinking if I was only dishonest about one thing I could be honest about everything else; but the one lie has poisoned everything between us. Kate, I tell you now that all of the maddening things I have done over the years were to protect this lie.

I first imagined I would tell you before we married. And then I thought I would rid myself of all need to tell you, but alas here I am so many years later still afraid.

I sent you away because I was scared. I was angry at myself too because I needed you to be with me when Eliza was sick when she should have been with eastern doctors. I wanted you to myself and allowed that desire to cloud my judgment. I let Oonagh Lyons get me what I needed. I could not bear the thought of you discovering what a pathetic failure I was. Over and over in my head I imagined the day when you would see how corrupted I was, and so I tried to delay it as long as I could.

I see that you are right, that Willy is not safe with me. I wish I could confess to you, my closest friend, that I am a morphine eater. I have always been since you have known me. Though I stopped for months and years at a time, I never stopped thinking about morphine and opium and laudanum; whatever I could get my hands on. I tried to make everything perfect between us, but I could never find the strength to quit for good although I tried over and over again.

I have wasted years of your life. I have missed important times in our children's lives. But I hate most that I deceived you. By the time you get this William will be gone back to Englewood.

It is not fair that I have played this game with you and William. Someone else could have given you the life you deserved. I was so greedy for my own comfort. I thought so much about my secret I am ashamed to admit that at times I almost hated you for not seeing what I really was. You are so perfect and good.

John Weldon

Chapter Seventy-Seven

Weldon carried a likeness of William in his pocket and took it out as he sat in a train full of wide-eyed new settlers. The lieutenant no longer held claim on William and Katherine. Like some of the homesteaders, Weldon had failed to prosper with all that had been given to him and lost it all.

He couldn't remember the last time since ditching Higgins days ago that he had spoken to anyone. When would this ride end? Weldon couldn't wait to get off the train as it pulled into the station.

"Weldon!" a husky voice called to him on the platform as brightly colored families and shady-looking men brushed by.

At first he did not answer, so deep in his own thoughts and looking for a discreet corner to dose himself in, but the voice insisted.

"Weldon? Is that you?" A spectacled man of small stature, wearing a polished uniform displaying the rank of major, ran up. He scanned Weldon for signs of rank, but found none. "I almost didn't recognize you, sir. It's been a long time, ain't it? By gosh, I'd hardly recognize you, sir."

Weldon feared this was one of the men he had hunted with after Eliza's death, but ...

"By gosh, you don't remember me, do you? Aw that's all right. T'was long ago, and I was just a raw pup when yer whipped me into shape—changed me, sir. If it weren't fer you I'd have long since left the good old army. I'm Private Wilson, sir."

Wilson had carried Weldon to the field hospital in the Wilderness with Simon and accompanied him to the hospital in the city by Simon's special arrangement.

"Private Wilson, of course! But ..." Weldon said, noticing the major's insignia, "you outrank me now, sir."

"No! It can't be true, no siree—what rank are ya?"

"Just a lieutenant, Wilson."

"Well, you know, I've had some lucky breaks along the way," Wilson said in an apologetic tone. He looked Weldon over again from his battered boots to his lazily half-buttoned shirt. "Lieutenant, you didn't get caught up in the drink, I hope."

"No, not that."

"And you're stationed here now?"

For a disconcerting moment, Weldon could not remember where he was. His hands sweated in his pockets. He pulled them out and ran them through his disheveled hair. "Oh, yes, I'm here. I'm stationed here at Point San Jose."

"Well, if that ain't a case of happenstance. That's the very place I'm stationed. I'm just waiting for my wifey and little ones (though they ain't so little anymore). They're just coming back from a trip to Missouri to see Louisa's folks. You got family now?"

Weldon fumbled for words and a cigar. The cigar fell, and Weldon bent to retrieve it. "No family, no."

"Always the individualist."

Just then there was a burst of activity from the end of the train as children and a blond, dowdy woman with healthy skin and a broad smile rushed toward the major. They smothered him with kisses and stories of their journey, only belatedly realizing Weldon's awkward presence. He stood off smoking and avoiding eye contact but felt he couldn't leave them without saying something to his superior officer.

The wife noticed first and looked aghast at his rough clothing and weathered features.

"Oh, Louisa, this is Sergeant Weldon—well, he's a lieutenant now—the man I told you all about—who set me on the right track."

The family looked on in disbelief.

"Major, sir, I have a few errands before reporting, sir ..."

"Of course, Weldon, I'll see you again! It will be good to have someone around to share memories. You know, of course, that Simon McCullough left the service but lives out in the Wallowa Valley now—real troubles there of late, but I'm sure the two of you have kept in touch. You were as thick as thieves."

"Yes, sort of," Weldon said, tipping his hat and stalking off.

How would he be able to stand seeing that private looking at him the way he did every day—so smugly happy with himself?

He arrived for duty at his new post a few hours later in a driving rain. Like a drenched scarecrow, he stood unsteadily before a young sergeant.

"You're drunk. This is no way to make a first impression," the man lectured. "Let me have your name so I can report you."

"I outrank you. Shut your mouth and show me to my quarters," Weldon ordered.

"Well, I would, *sir*, if you gave me your name!"

"Weldon, Lieutenant John Weldon."

A clerk looked up from his mounds of paperwork. "Lieutenant Weldon, there's been a number of telegrams for you. Let me see where I've put them."

Papers flew while the perfectly attired sergeant stared contemptuously at the beat before him.

"Yes, here they are, Lieutenant Weldon."

"Thank you," Weldon said and had a mind to read them later in private—but Simon's name caught his eye, and he stopped to read the first one:

"Lieutenant Weldon... come quick ... Simon McCullough ... family attacked."

***

The Wallowa Valley, lush, green and nestled between bold, blue mountains, illustrated to Simon why both Indians and whites wanted it for their own. Simon wanted it—a part of it at least—and paid his army acquaintance good money for it when the man's wife decided to wait in San Francisco until the Indians were disposed of.

A bracing wind swept up against the grey and soggy little home as Simon took in the early Sunday sky clearing after a storm in the night and wondered how Weldon could ever hate the Far West. Simon might sneak in a bit of gardening or finish painting his window boxes, having easily gotten used to being his own boss—no orders and curfews. Things could be done just as he wanted. He turned back into his home with a long, contented sigh.

The sun weakly made its way through the windows, and the cat they brought along greedily stretched out on the warming wooden planks to sun itself. Simon looked forward to the winter, all stuck together in cramped quarters with a toddler to play with.

The inside of their two-room house was rosy with firelight against the sable stained wood of the walls. The damp weather thickened Emily's pale mane. She tucked it behind her ears as she read her scriptures by the fire. Looking up, she smiled mildly at her husband.

"Emmy, let's go for a drive," Simon proposed. "It's such a fine day. The sun's coming out, and you look so beautiful in the sun." He pulled her up with a grin. The side of her face felt warm from the fire and he kissed her. "Come on, let's go. Mother and Lucy will be back from San Francisco before you know it, and then we'll have no time together."

"I don't know ..."

He squeezed her hard, and she laughed. "I can't resist you, Simon, no matter how I try."

He smiled and took out a cigar.

"Outside with that!" she warned and pushed at him playfully.

"I'm going, I'm going—just be quick about it, or I'll leave without you and hunt up a finer escort!"

Emily tilted her head with hand on hip. "No one would have you, captain. You're stuck with me."

"You're not nice!" he replied with a sly smile. "I'll meet you at the barn."

Emily hummed a hymn as she wrapped a shawl around her. After covering the warmed bread, she left for the barn. The wind pushed the clouds through the sky like a retreating army. It was a perfect day to be out. A great surge of birds came from the trees down by the barn. A flock of wild geese erupted and flew off further down the valley. Emily splashed through an unnoticed puddle and felt annoyed. Why did Simon take so long in the barn? He always dilly-dallied over the animals. She had wanted to spend the afternoon inside reading the scriptures, but he always distracted her. Each week she tried in vain to regain some of her religious discipline. She said a quick prayer for patience now and another in thanks as she smiled, thinking of how she would scold Simon but then convince him to take her up to the hayloft before their ride.

The barn door swayed. Just as she was about to pull at it, Simon pushed through.

"Simon! What's the matter?"

He whispered, "Go back."

"Go back?" she repeated. Maybe he had been kicked by that horrible mule they had procured.

He shoved her with a frantic look. "*Go*! *Go* and *hide*!"

"Simon?" she cried, but then she saw them—the ends of arrows—their heads lost in Simon's back.

When she pulled at him, he slapped his bloody hand over her mouth. "Hide yourself! I'll be all right! *Go*!" He shoved her hard, nearly knocking her to the ground, and finally she obeyed him and ran for the house. "Please God, save us—save Simon! Please!" She turned back for a second, but Simon, the person she had waited her whole life to be with, was gone. She heard two shots from the barn. "Please! Please! Please! *Save him*!"

Running up the steps, she thought only about getting the gun hanging over the door. Was it loaded? She raced through to the front room, and a young Indian shot her through and stepped over her. She couldn't move her legs, but she could hear Simon. "Thank God!" she cried out as he called to her. But she realized the man who shot her was hiding, waiting to ambush her husband. She called to Simon but knew he wouldn't hear her. He stumbled toward the house and climbed the three steps into the back room. The door opened with a quick, blunt thud, and the washbasin and pitcher crashed to the floor as someone was brought down. Long moments passed before she heard Simon sob or something like it. She called to him in a whisper he could not hear. Finally he finished using his ax on the intruder and came careening into the room. "Shit! Oh, shit! Emmy what have they done to you?" Simon stumbled down to her almost falling on his face. "Emily, talk to me, damn it!"

Emily couldn't feel the puddle of blood spreading around her middle. Tears streaked her face. "Oh, thank God, I can see you this last time to say goodbye. My dear, sweet Simon! Be good when I'm gone. I waited so long for you to love me."

He kissed her and stretched his arm over her as best he could. "I do love you, Emily McCullough! You can't leave me here!"

But she was gone.

The neighbor discovered them. Simon had foolishly pulled at the arrows. When the man arrived he felt the smallest pulse in Simon and trimmed the arrows as best he could. He did not attempt a complete extraction. The arrows were probably helping to keep things together. The bullets were lost and doing their damage, but the soldier hung on. The captain woke briefly when they moved him and asked for Weldon to be sent for. He had hacked the young brave apart into dark bloody chunks splattered over the plaids and cheerful calicos.

***

Weldon pounded on the door. An old settler opened it slightly and peered out, looking over the ratty, bearded man in uniform.

"Sir, I've just come up on the train. I was told a friend of mine ..." Weldon stammered. "It took longer than I wanted ...is he ...?"

"Are you family? Weldon, is it?"

"Yes."

The man spoke to him a little before bringing Weldon into a small comfortable room where a lithe old woman with a gentle look took his hand in hers. She whispered, "Simon's alert, dear ... has been the whole while since we took him in ...waiting for you. We prayed you would get here in time."

In time ...

Weldon stood in place until she pulled him over to the curtain Simon waited behind. He hesitated just before entering, but Simon called out weakly, and Weldon plunged forward. "Captain!"

"Finally, you've come," Simon said. "Are you all right? You look God awful."

Weldon knelt down beside his friend and cried. The woman dragged in a chair and pulled Weldon into it. The lieutenant tried to regain his composure. Simon looked so like himself—surely he would live. But in the silence between them Weldon heard the breathing and noticed Simon's dying color.

His voice was weak like the whistle of a faraway train. "It feels like years since I've seen you ... you're still at the morphine, aren't you, old friend?"

"Simon, I ..." Weldon started, "I'm so sorry about Emily and ..."

"My mother doesn't know. She went to see a doctor for Lucy in San Francisco. You must tell her," Simon wheezed.

"No, Simon, I won't. Let me take you from here. You'll see it will be all right."

"Weldon, listen to me ... I don't think I'll make it ... they haven't said so, but ... I think I know it."

"But ... you're strong and ... Lucy needs you."

Simon gazed at his friend for a few moments as if building courage. "Weldon, would you do me a favor? It's my back. Will you take a look and see what you think? Please ... Weldon, make sure everybody knows—they were hiding in the barn. I didn't even see them. I-I didn't run."

"I know ... everybody knows," Weldon assured him and sighed, not wanting to carry out Simon's request. Weldon stood over Simon and helped him sit up. Simon's lips were white with pain as Weldon moved him away from the pillow, and it became plain that the captain could not live. His back was shorn apart, his insides exposed and already rotting. The old settler had told Weldon that Simon's lung had been punctured and that although he had no real back, to lay him on his chest would suffocate him.

"We must get you something for the pain, captain," Weldon said as he gingerly lowered Simon against his pillows.

Simon looked glassy-eyed. "I will die, won't I, Weldon?"

Weldon nodded, unable to speak.

"I want to keep my wits about me, John Weldon." Simon labored over each breath. "Lucy ... you and Katie ..."

Weldon shook his head.

"No, Weldon. You can't let me go without knowing that Lucy's taken care of. And Katherine ..." He choked back tears.

"Simon! You can't leave us!" Weldon said. "I can't care for anyone. You know that! I don't want to!"

"You're a great disappointment to me then, Weldon."

"I know."

"And that's it? Don't you care? You've been my closest friend all these years ...you only think about yourself ... your mistakes, your weaknesses. All this time you never trusted me, you never forgave me, but I need to trust you."

"I have forgiven you! I can't forgive myself. You're right ... I never trusted that you or your sister could really care for me. I thought it was a game, and now you leave me here when I've never repaid you for all of your kindness."

"Take care of my family, Weldon—our family—you know you must. We're all weak and stupid in life, but we can rise above it sometimes. Be brave enough to trust my sister with everything ..."

"It's too late, Simon. Kate already knows about the morphine, and I wasn't the one to tell her. I don't blame her for not wanting me."

"When I first met you ... you'd let nothing stop you ... my sister ..."

"Your sister deserved better."

"No ... she wanted only you. When will you realize that people can and do care for you just the way you are? When we took you from the battlefield you wanted to live—you fought to live. Sometimes you have to fight."

"I'm sick of fighting."

"Well then, can you take my place?"

"I wish I could!"

Simon's eyes were full of pain. "No, you don't. I wanted to have my own little children around me, and I envied you and Kate for so long. It's a cruel joke to be taken out this way, but Emmy's gone now. I know I wouldn't find another like her. I was lucky to have her at least for a while." He faltered. "But ... I'll miss you and Kate and my mother ... and Lucy too, poor Lucy!"

"Simon, I'll do everything I can for your mother and Lucy, but ... but Kate won't have me and Willy ... I can't face them."

"If you care anything about them, and there is any bit of the man I knew left in you, then you will try harder—I expect that of you!" Simon grew agitated and suppressed a cough.

"Your expectations are too high," Weldon said.

"No, I see people as they really are. You don't. Give us a cigar."

"No, you shouldn't," Weldon said.

"It doesn't matter now. It feels so queer to sit here with you and know we'll never meet again," Simon choked out as Weldon lit his cigar. "I've missed you so many times ... I never thought of it ending for good." He looked off into the middle distance. "You know, I hope I can't see you all ... after. It would be too sad for me then. I want to be taken back to Englewood—that's my real home—Emmy will be buried with her folks."

Weldon took the cigar from his friend. Simon wasn't smoking it and was dangerously close to setting the blankets ablaze.

"Weldon, remember the hospital? I thought I had given you a second chance. I wanted to make things right. I took advantage of you ..."

"I was stupid to blame you. I didn't want to admit my own weakness. I didn't want to fail again. The only strength I've had these last years came from the knowledge that I had a friend out in the world somewhere. I don't know what I'll do without you now!"

"Promise me, Weldon, please ..." Simon begged—his eyes dark with exertion. "Take care of them and let them know how I thought of them in the end."

"Simon, they already know it. You are the glue—we all loved you."

"I've never heard such emotion, Weldon—you make me laugh ... but ... if I can see you after, I hope I'm able to watch your back."

"You didn't do a very good job of watching your own, captain."

"Oh! Weldon tries one last attempt at humor! You're a good man."

The lady of the house stepped in. "Captain McCullough, your dressings should be changed now."

"Martha, my friend's told me the truth. There's no need to fix things that can't be fixed, but thank you ... for everything." He reached out to her, and she sobbed.

"Poor dear! Those infernal savages!" She turned to Weldon. "Your friend is such a sweet man. And not a cry from him and in awful pain—the doc says so." She brushed the hair away from her patient's brow and kissed him. "I'll get some water," she said shakily as she left.

"I've still got it! Imagine that, Weldon!" Simon laughed but winced in pain and coughed again. Weldon handed him the last bit of water, but he pushed it away. He pulled a rag from under his blankets. Weldon looked despairingly at the blood and covered his face.

"Weldon." Simon's lips were rosy now with his own blood and his face was pale and old. "Weldon, I'm sorry for the Wilderness. I should never have left. You warned me not to and ..."

"I don't care a fig about the Wilderness! Now stop it. It was just chance—what happened. I wish I could bring you your mother and Kate."

"No, this is the right way. They'd never let me go in peace, and I'm too tired now for any hullabaloo."

Weldon smiled.

"Mother never forgave me about the disease."

"Your mother loves you. I always envied it. The way she looked after you and was proud of every little thing."

Simon wiped tears away. "She was wonderful, wasn't she? Just tell her I'm sorry. Isn't it lucky that you came in time? I've always been pretty lucky."

"How can you say that, captain, when things have gone so sour?" Weldon timidly wiped a little blood from the corner of Simon's mouth.

"Well, I won't say I'm not surprised to have this happen to me, and I wish I could have saved Emmy, but ... well, I hope it's true that I'll be with her soon. You will take care of Lucy?"

"Yes, Simon, don't worry."

"I'm a little aggravated that I waited so long for a family—I think I was a good father."

"You were a father to me at times."

Simon tried to laugh. "Please, can you bring me outside? I want to see the sky one last time."

"No, you can't be moved. It'll kill you."

"I'm already dead, Weldon. You won't deny me this last request will you?"

Weldon stood up, pulling his hair through his fingers and trying to think how it could be done easiest. "Ma'am, will you set up some blankets for my friend on your porch—on that swing I saw?"

She peeked in, about to complain that it should not be done, but a change had come over Simon, and she went for the blankets. Weldon tried to sit Simon up, but his back was so in pieces he was afraid that his friend would lose his insides on the bed. Pulling a sheet from a chair nearby, Weldon quickly wrapped Simon's middle and back as tightly as Simon would allow. Simon cried quietly, "John, I love this life too much. I don't want to leave it."

Weldon nodded and realized that moving him would be torture. Simon's lips were bloodless as he bit them and his hands gripped the blankets at his side. "Weldon, please ..."

Weldon pulled his kit from his pocket—hadn't thought of it until now. Simon looked on like a curious child. "All these years you've been a slave to that tiny thing ..."

Weldon prepared his syringe and looked to Simon who said, "Well, I suppose I won't get addicted—go ahead."

Simon's features softened as the drug coursed through his veins, and he grinned. The color came back to his face, and he seemed, briefly, almost his old self again. "We can do this now, Weldon. Bring me outside."

The old settler had been listening from the other side of the curtain. "Son," he said to Simon, "I'll help you outside—it's the least I can do."

They carefully placed Simon on the swing and kept it as best they could from moving.

"Weldon, give us some nice words, won't you?"

"Simon?"

"You know what I mean. I never had the memory for Scripture like you have ..."

"Oh no," Weldon said shying away. "I don't remember it anymore—none of it."

"Please, you must. I need that sort of thing now. You understand."

"It's all humbug."

"I don't know if it's humbug or not ... I don't think so ..." Simon said dreamily.

Weldon scratched his arms nervously. Everything was far away, a blur. Simon stared at him the way Willy used to—with confidence. He cleared his throat and tried hard ... "Oh Lord hear my prayer, and let my cry come to you. Hide not your face from me in the day of my distress. Incline your ear to me; in the day that I call answer me speedily. For my days...vanish like smoke, and my bones burn like fire. Withered and dried up like grass is my heart; I forget to eat my bread. Because of my insistent sighing I am reduced to skin and bone. I am like a desert owl; I have become an owl among the ruins. I am sleepless and I moan; I am like a sparrow alone on the housetop. All the day my enemies revile me...for I eat ashes like bread and mingle my drink with tears because of your fury and wrath; for you lifted me up only to cast me down. My days are like lengthening shadow ...'"

Simon looked on wide-eyed and disappointed. Weldon racked his cobweb mind for something more uplifting. Simon helped. He knew what he wanted. "Do the one from the hospital—remember? You said it over and over back then. I used to tease you about it. Emily taught me it—that's funny isn't it? Just the other day it was. It reminded me of you."

"Hmm." Weldon smiled at Simon and took his hand. "'I kept silent, my bones wasted away; I groaned all the day. For day and night your hand was heavy upon me; my strength withered as in a dry summer heat.'"

Simon smiled. "But you always stopped there—you left off the good stuff. Say the rest. Go on—for me."

Like a torrent it all came back to Weldon—the verses. "'Then I declared my sin to you; my guilt I did not hide. I said, "I confess my faults to the LORD," and you took away the guilt of my sin.'" Weldon cried, wiping his face on his sleeve. "But there is no reason to believe any of it, I don't deserve ..."

"Emily says no one deserves it, that's why it's a gift. I think I believe her," Simon said. "She told me just the other day—for you, I think now."

"Simon, I think maybe the morphine is making you ..."

"You know what you must do, friend." Simon sighed and looked out at the sky with shining eyes. "Three years and out, Weldon?" A joke from the war between them. "Sergeant Weldon, do you suppose we'll move out in the morning? I'm not tired yet. Will you come down by the fire for once—come join the frolic?"

Weldon smiled with a broken heart. "Of course, Captain McCullough. I'd follow you to the ends of the earth."

"Good, but it's a lot quicker to the fire," Simon chuckled, but suddenly realized he had drifted and grew serious. "We used to play a game, Katie and I—look at the stars, Weldon—Katie's looking too."

And Simon was gone as John looked up seeing only lights that stared back, promising nothing.

Chapter Seventy-Eight

It was the last of the Indian summer days in Englewood, and the Palisades glowed with maple color. The robins had departed south, but the birds that remained sang lively songs and the squirrels busied themselves for winter, bursting from behind trees and stumps in frenzied last-minute preparations. The sun was low but warm after the morning frost, and Sarah's old fall crocuses still bloomed stubbornly between the dying weeds.

Simon's funeral procession lurched past the new church and headed for the Brookside Cemetery, where the little wedding chapel had been moved. Many old friends filled the road. The smiles and good fun Simon had brought them, just fond memories now. William struggled but was making progress. His leg hadn't set right, and his headaches were often too intense to handle once out of bed. The news of Simon's death set him back. Today he adamantly refused to attend the ceremony. He was ashamed of his crippled body and who might see it. The new washerwoman offered to mind him and Lucy for a few hours.

Lucy had arrived with John and Sarah at the station a few days before. Margaret delivered them home to Tenafly Road. Simon's body had been carried up to the house in a wagon provided by the Village Protection Society and set in the parlor where flowers and cards abounded.

Simon was buried under wild azalea bushes. Uncle Phil attended the funeral with his big wife, and they helped Sarah from the carriage with her fall mums. She had cut every last one of them from her garden and brought them to the cemetery for her son in buckets and vases of all description. Graham and Margaret Crenshaw shadowed Katherine, keeping quiet watch over her, and she was glad of it. They had been such a help to her with William, and she felt the need to solidify her relations with her people. They were to be her family now that Simon was no longer ... Katherine quietly sobbed. Poor Simon.

A light wind blew colorful leaves under foot and through the air, their rustling the only noise there was but for the muffled cries of girls—women now—who at one time hoped for just a dance with Simon McCullough. The reverend (a new one Katherine hardly knew) spoke of a Simon that did not exist, patched together from short stories he dutifully gathered from family and townsfolk. He didn't get the essence of Simon right. Simon's good nature, generosity, his love of family slipped away like the last of the summer foliage, but Katherine and many others had their hearts to remind them.

Sarah waited until the crowd dispersed and got on hands and knees to decorate the bare earth. When Sarah's hands were good and dirty and the mums were all set out like a white blanket over Simon, Uncle Phil guided her away.

Katherine had not bothered to read the tombstone until this moment, still not quite believing that Simon was here and not out making mischief. She ran her fingers along the crest of the stone and smiled at the inscription: "*It is well for a man to eat, drink and enjoy all the fruits of his labor under the sun during the limited days of the life which God gives him.*"

"Kate ..."

She jumped and whirled around to see John standing stiffly before her. She almost didn't know him and had no words.

"Kate, I'm sorry for your loss ..." he said and began to cry.

She touched his arm lightly. "John, it's all right. I know."

Weldon wiped his face. "Yes, well ... my job is done. Simon wanted me to make sure you were all taken care of. Your mother said you were fine for money." He walked past her and patted Simon's stone awkwardly. "Bye, old friend." He sighed then and made to go, but Katherine wouldn't let him.

"John, it's a lovely headstone ... you chose it didn't you? And the verse too ..."

"Yes, Simon insisted ... certain things ... w-well," he began, falling back into his old stammer. "I should be off now. Take care." He wore spectacles now and his eyes looked big and glassy. His hair was streaked with silver like webs of a spider. "The dog should arrive any day now—for Willy."

"The dog?!"

"Yes, U.S."

Katherine smiled and then laughed, imagining Sarah's reaction to the wolfhound. "John, why won't you come see Willy? I'll never understand you. He's waited all week and given up hope."

"I-I thought you wouldn't like it if I came."

"He's your son, and he loves you."

Weldon looked at her with searching eyes.

"Your writing, John, all those letters ... why didn't you send them?" She took a seat on a bench nearby.

He seemed lost and sat beside her. "Letters?"

"*Your letters*! William brought them to me or at least tried to, and they were sent by a girl ... oh, it doesn't matter how I got them. William wanted me to see them ... thought it would make a difference ..."

"I'm a coward." Weldon pretended to laugh. "I was afraid you'd hate me ..."

"But the letters were beautiful! Didn't you mean any of them?"

"No, Katherine, those letters ... I meant every word, but the promises in them I could never keep ... it doesn't matter now."

"You look so old in those spectacles," she said as she reached for them, but he pulled away embarrassed and took them off.

"My eyes are going ... I think ... I think the medicine takes its toll."

She couldn't help herself and cried. "And why would you never let me help you from the beginning? After all those notes and letters I see how hard you struggled on your own. It hurts me more than anything else that you didn't let me help you when that's all I ever wanted."

"I wanted one person in the world, Kate, to think I was good and to find something about me that was special." He ran his hands over his head. "Oh, I've always been so pathetic ... I lied and lied to you ... you thought the James' were the lowest of the low while I was just the same."

"But you were never the same to me. The letters ... and the wonderful days we had ..."

He shook his head, and his eyes were full. "I was a liar and cruel. Nothing ever goes the way I expect it, and the more I tried to protect you, the more I seemed to hurt everyone! I loved you so much ... I was so afraid ... Eliza and the medicine ..."

"I know. I understand everything now. But I would have forgiven you then if only you told me."

"But now?"

"I don't know, John. I've never stopped loving you. I never will." She gasped. She hadn't wanted to say that. "I always used to be afraid to be alone, but there were times with you when it was worse than being alone. Being out west taught me how much I love the East. I'm tired of adventures and crises, and that seems to be the only way we are together. You don't trust me ... and you're too wild for me."

"Kate, I quit the army."

She stared at him.

"I need to learn how to take responsibility better," he said.

"Well, I guess that's good for you,"

He pulled some things from his pockets and placed them on the bench between them—syringes, a pipe, a few tiny glass vials. "Katherine, these are the things I use, and these are the places," he said as he pulled his sleeve up to show an old abscess on his skin, dry and scaled. He glanced up at her for a second and then back down at his treasure. "I've s-s-stopped since Simon. I promised him I'd take care of everything and be clean too, but it's so hard."

Their eyes met, and she pulled him close, holding him for a few moments. She could feel his thin body through his light jacket and held him tighter until he regained his composure. He sat back and sighed, running his fingers over his syringe. "These are the instruments I've allowed destroy all that is good," he cried.

She gave him one of her handkerchiefs.

"It smells like roses. I always loved that about you," he said, and instead of using it put it in his pocket as if to remember her by.

She took his weak hand in hers. "John Weldon, I've always loved everything about you."

"But how? It makes me angry to think how long you put up with me! I never thought you'd marry me, but you did and then you stayed with me out west till I sent you off ... and I never thought you'd speak to me again once you knew."

She rubbed his cold hands. "You were angry at people who couldn't hate you as much as you hated yourself. I thought you just didn't love me anymore until I read those letters that our wonderful son preserved for me. I realize that I was just meant to love you. I can't help myself even now, and I don't know why, and it doesn't matter. I tried when I was teaching to figure out what I was meant for if it wasn't for you. What talents did I possess? I couldn't think of a one but loving you.

"My father and Margaret expected more from me. Maybe I did too. But ... I'm best at loving you. It's what my heart's for. I don't understand why you ever doubted me. I don't know if we can ever be together because I need to feel that the person I'm with can put his confidence in me, and you can't do that. It's too tiring trying to convince you, but you will always be the one I loved most." She cupped his face in her hands tenderly.

Weldon pulled her hands into his own. He was trembling. The wind had picked up, and it was chilly now like their wedding day. "I don't want you to be tired anymore," he said. He looked over at Simon's grave and felt a calm he had never felt. He had nothing to lose. "You know I used to read the scriptures a lot. All the time when I was a child." He swallowed before continuing. "I never did understand grace. I didn't believe in it. I thought it was given to only some people ... I don't know. But you and Simon ... I understand now. What happened to me ... during the war, at the end ... when I found that I couldn't control the morphine ... I lost my faith. I tried to have faith in you, but ... but it was something Dudley said. When he said that God shows His grace through chance meetings, he saw something that I didn't. It was chance that I volunteered in New Jersey and chance that your brother and I both left the cavalry for the infantry and chance that he took me under his wing ... and grace that I met you ..." He wanted to say everything right for once. "I blamed Simon for things, but Simon ... he was it. He led me on a journey. I wanted it to be perfect with no mistakes, but he just kept on dragging me along, leading me right up until the end." He paused for moment. "Right to you."

Now he rummaged through his pocket again. Katherine wondered what secret thing he would pull out next. It was a frayed piece of card. "Do you remember this?" he asked and handed it over. "I didn't like to get my hopes up, didn't want to think that you were right about God's plan for us in case you were wrong. But I knew when I got that Christmas package, my very first from anyone, that I wanted to meet the girl who made that little card. I'd never gotten anything like it. You're the same girl to me, now all these years later." He stopped and cried.

Katherine kissed the card and threw her arms around her husband. "Oh, promise me, John, that you will never leave me again. Come home and never leave!"

John Weldon kissed her wet face. "Let me be your shadow till the very end."

Adrienne Morris is the author of *The Tenafly Road Series*, a family saga following the Weldon and Crenshaw families of Gilded Age Englewood, New Jersey. Her first novel, *The House on Tenafly Road* was selected as an *Editors' Choice Book* and *Notable Book of the Year* by *The Historical Novel Society*.

Authors rely on word-of-mouth! If you enjoyed *The House on Tenafly Road*[1] please leave an online review—even a short one! It makes a big difference and is greatly appreciated.

OWN THE SERIES!

THE TENAFLY ROAD SERIES[2]

The House on Tenafly Road[3] *(1)*

Weary of Running[4] *(2)*

The Dew That Goes Early Away[5] *(3)*

Forget Me Not[6] *(4)*

The One My Heart Loves *(5)*

The Grand Union *(6)*

ADRIENNE'S OFFICIAL NEWSLETTER[7]

CONTACT ADRIENNE:

AdrienneMorris.com[8]

Nothing Gilded, Nothing Gained[9]

INSTAGRAM[10]

BOOK COVER DESIGN by SAMANTHA HENNESSY

---

1. *https://amzn.to/2y7VZUh*

2. *https://amzn.to/2LaIjdK*

3. *https://amzn.to/2y7VZUh*

4. *https://amzn.to/2K2gwuJ*

5. *https://amzn.to/2KzvicF*

6. *https://amzn.to/2INoWZZ*

7. *http://eepurl.com/cnCwBP*

8. https://www.adriennemorris.com/

9. https://middlemaybooks.com/

10. https://www.instagram.com/middlemay_farm/